United States: Office of the Comptroller of the Currency

Annual Report of the Comptroller of the Currency

Second Session of the fiftieth Congress Volume 1

United States: Office of the Comptroller of the Currency

Annual Report of the Comptroller of the Currency
Second Session of the fiftieth Congress Volume 1

ISBN/EAN: 9783741190452

Manufactured in Europe, USA, Canada, Australia, Japa

Cover: Foto ©Andreas Hilbeck / pixelio.de

Manufactured and distributed by brebook publishing software
(www.brebook.com)

United States: Office of the Comptroller of the Currency

Annual Report of the Comptroller of the Currency

ANNUAL REPORT

OF THE

COMPTROLLER OF THE CURRENCY

TO THE

SECOND SESSION OF THE FIFTIETH CONGRESS

With the Compliments of

Comptroller of the Currency.

DECEMBER 1, 1888.

IN TWO VOLUMES.

VOLUME I.

WASHINGTON:
GOVERNMENT PRINTING OFFICE.
1888.

ANNUAL REPORT

OF THE

COMPTROLLER OF THE CURRENCY

TO THE

SECOND SESSION OF THE FIFTIETH CONGRESS

OF

THE UNITED STATES.

DECEMBER 1, 1888.

IN TWO VOLUMES.

VOLUME I.

WASHINGTON:
GOVERNMENT PRINTING OFFICE.
1888.

Treasury Department,
Document No. 1160, 3d ed.
Comptroller of the Currency.

TABLE OF CONTENTS.

REPORT.

APPENDIX.

REPORT

OF

THE COMPTROLLER OF THE CURRENCY.

TREASURY DEPARTMENT,
OFFICE OF COMPTROLLER OF THE CURRENCY,
Washington, December 1, 1888.

SIR: In obedience to law, I have the honor to submit a report for the year ending October 31, 1888, exhibiting—

First. A summary of the state and condition of every association from which reports have been received the preceding year, at the several dates to which such reports refer, with an abstract of the whole amount of banking capital returned by them, of the whole amount of their debts and liabilities, the amount of circulating notes outstanding, and the total amount of means and resources, specifying the amount of lawful money held by them at the times of their several returns.

Second. A statement of the associations whose business has been closed during the year, with the amount of their circulation redeemed and the amount outstanding.

Third. Suggestions as to amendments to the laws relative to banking, by which it is thought the system may be improved.

Fourth. A statement exhibiting, under appropriate heads, the resources and liabilities and condition of the banks, banking companies, and savings banks organized under the laws of the several States and Territories, such information being obtained by the Comptroller from the reports made by such banks, banking companies, and savings banks to the legislatures or officers of the different States and Territories, and where such reports could not be obtained the deficiency has been supplied from such other authentic sources as were available.

Fifth. The names and compensation of the clerks employed in the office of the Comptroller of the Currency, and the whole amount of the expenses of the banking department during the year.

This is the twenty-sixth annual report of the Comptroller of the Currency.

11028—CUR 88——1

FIRST.

SUMMARY OF THE STATE AND CONDITION OF EVERY NATIONAL BANK REPORTING DURING THE YEAR ENDING OCTOBER 31, 1888.

	December 7.	February 14.	April 30.	June 30.	October 4.
	3, 070 banks.	3, 077 banks.	3, 098 banks.	3, 120 banks.	3, 140 banks.
RESOURCES.					
Loans and discounts.	$1,574,702,436.38	$1,576,380,276.39	$1,590,273,484.28	$1,619,999,200.68	$1,674,886,285.20
Overdrafts	9, 179, 018. 58	7, 784, 094. 12	7, 124, 439. 67	8, 125, 364. 15	9, 294, 338. 98
U. S. bonds to secure circulation	186, 431, 900. 00	181, 845, 450. 00	181, 042, 950. 00	177, 543, 900. 00	171, 867, 200. 00
U. S. bonds to secure deposits	42, 203, 000. 00	56, 803, 000. 00	56, 043, 000. 00	55, 788, 000. 00	54, 208, 000. 00
U. S. bonds on hand	6, 988, 550. 00	6, 450, 500. 00	7, 639, 350. 00	7, 830, 150. 00	6, 507, 050. 00
Other stocks, bonds, and mortgages	90, 775, 413. 31	94, 153, 088. 97	95, 206, 917. 07	96, 265, 812. 31	99, 752, 403. 73
Due from approved reserve agents	132, 959, 765. 34	155, 341, 240. 86	146, 477, 902. 83	158, 133, 598. 31	170, 458, 593. 83
Due from other national banks	98, 227, 065, 30	92, 980, 682. 48	95, 519, 102. 26	101, 689, 774. 90	99, 821, 000. 57
Due from State banks and bankers	21, 095, 356. 41	21, 880, 069. 00	22, 709, 703. 01	22, 714, 258. 27	23, 707, 260. 53
Real estate, furniture, and fixtures	58, 825, 168. 16	59, 366, 247. 85	60, 111, 356. 86	61, 101, 833. 19	62, 634, 791. 74
Current expenses and taxes paid	10, 600, 817. 35	6, 531, 237. 71	9, 843, 637. 81	5, 685, 313. 21	8, 498, 758. 28
Premiums paid	18, 707, 205. 79	19, 779, 498. 56	19, 501, 461. 06	18, 903, 434. 54	17, 615, 898. 02
Checks and other cash items	13, 336, 455. 77	12, 255, 978. 69	14, 644, 675. 77	16, 855, 801. 15	15, 071, 024. 30
Exchanges for clearing-house	85, 097, 380. 41	73, 418, 037. 20	117, 270, 706. 86	74, 229, 763. 69	102, 430, 751. 67
Bills of other banks.	23, 447, 294. 00	23, 145, 206. 00	24, 434, 212. 00	21, 343, 405. 00	21, 600, 818. 00
Fractional currency.	554, 906. 55	683, 148. 93	662, 722. 27	632, 002. 42	684, 268. 41
Trade-dollars	328. 09	437. 59	351. 15	371. 76	419. 05
*Specie, viz:					
Gold coin	73, 677, 376. 76	74, 317, 628. 26	74, 921, 739. 83	74, 825, 782. 84	70, 222, 886. 95
Gold Treasury certificates	44, 341, 120. 00	55, 230, 029. 00	54, 604, 280. 00	68, 761, 930. 00	79, 883, 810. 00
Gold clearing-house certificates	25, 485, 000. 00	26, 246, 000. 00	24, 050, 000. 00	20, 884, 000. 00	10, 385, 000. 00
Silver coin, dollars	7, 724, 334. 00	7, 835, 028. 00	7, 569, 827. 00	6, 906, 432. 00	7, 051, 931. 00
Silver coin, fractional	2, 963, 267. 72	3, 256, 654. 36	3, 114, 507. 36	2, 819, 277. 92	3, 255, 891. 69
Silver Treasury certificates	5, 029, 545. 00	6, 945, 275. 00	7, 813, 657. 00	7, 094, 854. 00	7, 298, 298. 00
Legal-tender notes	75, 361, 975. 00	82, 317, 670. 00	83, 574, 210. 00	81, 995, 643. 00	81, 009, 461. 00
U. S. certificates of deposit for legal-tender notes	6, 165, 000. 00	10, 120, 000. 00	9, 330, 000. 00	12, 315, 000. 00	8, 935, 000. 00
Five per cent. redemption fund with Treasurer	8, 168, 503. 20	7, 993, 189. 22	7, 887, 950. 36	7, 765, 837. 16	7, 555, 401. 72
Due from Treasurer other than redemption fund	1, 068, 117. 43	1, 240, 035. 56	1, 361, 033. 74	1, 236, 675. 66	935, 799. 31
Aggregates	2, 624, 186, 330. 55	2, 664, 366, 304. 44	2, 732, 423, 198. 19	2, 731, 448, 016. 16	2, 815, 751, 341. 07
*Total specie	159, 240, 643. 48	173, 830, 614. 62	172, 074, 011. 19	181, 292, 276. 76	178, 097, 816. 64
LIABILITIES.					
Capital stock paid in	$580, 733, 094. 42	$582, 194, 263. 75	$585, 449, 487. 75	$588, 384, 018. 25	$592, 621, 656. 04
Surplus fund	175, 246, 408. 26	179, 533, 475. 38	180, 053, 507. 27	183, 106, 435. 70	185, 520, 564. 68
Other undivided profits	70, 899, 218. 06	66, 606, 930. 87	78, 196, 768. 91	70, 296, 173. 67	77, 434, 426. 23
National-bank circulation outstanding	164, 904, 094. 00	159, 750, 193. 50	158, 897, 572. 00	155, 313, 353. 50	151, 702, 809. 50
State-bank notes outstanding	98, 676. 50	98, 652. 50	94, 878. 50	82, 372. 50	82, 354. 50
Dividends unpaid	1, 343, 963. 08	1, 534, 314. 51	1, 766, 496. 11	7, 381, 894. 42	2, 378, 275. 70
Individual deposits.	1, 235, 757, 041. 59	1, 251, 957, 844. 42	1, 300, 731, 015. 16	1, 292, 342, 471. 28	1, 350, 320, 861. 11
U. S. deposits	38, 416, 276. 87	55, 193, 890. 19	54, 691, 454. 69	54, 679, 643. 93	52, 140, 562. 97
Deposits of U. S. disbursing officers	4, 515, 024. 05	4, 255, 362. 02	4, 789, 093. 63	3, 690, 652. 65	3, 993, 900. 51
Due to other national banks	223, 088, 927. 85	211, 038, 499. 93	237, 056, 940. 91	248, 248, 440. 03	260, 697, 968. 66
Due to State banks and bankers	98, 809, 344. 66	105, 539, 405. 53	104, 502, 668. 21	109, 871, 372. 41	114, 936, 397. 15
Notes and bills rediscounted	16, 268, 247. 74	12, 866, 722. 85	12, 724, 238. 71	13, 006, 119. 55	17, 305, 750. 61
Bills payable	5, 105, 112. 57	3, 796, 730. 99	4, 469, [illegible]	4, 935, 068. 27	6, 615, 813. 47
Aggregates	2, 624, 186, 330. 55	2, 664, 366, 304. 44	2, 732, 423, 198. 19	2, 731, 448, 016. 16	2, 815, 751, 341. 07

SECOND.

STATEMENT OF NATIONAL BANKS CLOSED DURING THE YEAR.

Name and location of bank.	Date of authority to commence business.	Date of closing.	Capital stock.	Circulation.		
				Issued.	Redeemed.	Outstanding.
First National Bank, Tecumseh, Nebr	May 19, 1883	Nov. 3, 1887	$50,000	$11,700	$4,380	$7,320
Third National Bank, Saint Paul, Minn	Aug. 5, 1884	Nov. 4, 1887	500,000	45,000	13,470	31,530
Fifth National Bank, Saint Louis, Mo	Dec. 12, 1882	Nov. 7, 1887	300,000	44,430	......	44,430
First National Bank, Marshall, Mo	Feb. 14, 1883	Dec. 6, 1887	100,000	22,500	7,600	14,900
First National Bank, Greene, Iowa	Nov. 2, 1883	Dec. 15, 1887	50,000	10,750	3,000	7,750
Fulton National Bank, New York, N. Y	July 31, 1865	Dec. 20, 1887	300,000	....	......	....
Fayetteville National Bank, Fayetteville, N. C	Dec. 21, 1870	Dec. 31, 1887	200,000	39,580	13,749	25,831
National Bank of Somerset, Ky	Dec. 8, 1870	Dec. 31, 1887	50,000	45,000	10,790	34,210
First National Bank, Richburgh, N. Y	Aug. 11, 1881	Jan. 10, 1888	50,000	25,905	9,770	16,135
Scituate National Bank, North Scituate, R. I	Sept. 7, 1865	Jan. 11, 1888	56,000	35,018	10,230	24,788
First National Bank, Auburn, N. Y	Feb. 4, 1864	Jan. 23, 1888	150,000	44,400	18,100	26,300
National Bank of Franklin, Ind	Aug. 29, 1882	Jan. 31, 1888	50,000	11,250	3,635	7,615
First National Bank, Hampton, Iowa	Oct. 13, 1881	Feb. 1, 1888	50,000	11,250	3,440	7,810
Metropolitan National Bank, Cincinnati, Ohio	July 12, 1881	Feb. 6, 1888	1,000,000	277,745	68,490	209,255
Greene County National Bank, Springfield, Mo	Feb. 17, 1868	Feb. 8, 1888	100,000	22,500	5,247	17,253
First National Bank, Greensburgh, Kans	Apr. 5, 1887	Feb. 10, 1888	50,000	11,240	1,960	9,280
First National Bank, Central City, Nebr	Feb. 2, 1883	Feb. 11, 1888	50,000	10,710	3,310	7,400
Duluth National Bank, Duluth, Minn	Aug. 26, 1882	Feb. 20, 1888	300,000	45,000	9,140	35,860
Union Stock Yards National Bank, Chicago, Ill	Mar. 12, 1868	Feb. 29, 1888	500,000	45,000	9,765	35,235
Bismarck National Bank, Bismarck, Dak	May 3, 1882	Mar. 1, 1888	50,000	11,250	3,160	8,090
First National Bank, Ashton, Dak	Jan. 19, 1886	Mar. 6, 1888	50,000	11,250	2,420	8,830
Commercial National Bank, Dubuque, Iowa	Mar. 11, 1871	Mar. 20, 1888	100,000	62,170	16,849	45,321
State National Bank, Raleigh, N. C	June 17, 1868	Mar. 26, 1888	100,000	22,500	....	22,500
Citizens' National Bank, Sioux Falls, Dak	Nov. 8, 1886	Apr. 24, 1888	50,000	11,250	1,730	9,520
First National Bank Stanton, Mich	Apr. 5, 1883	Apr. 30, 1888	50,000	11,250	2,460	8,790
First National Bank, Fairmont, Nebr	July 26, 1884	May 1, 1888	50,000	11,250	2,550	8,700
Second National Bank, Xenia, Ohio	Feb. 24, 1864	May 3, 1888	150,000	48,470	8,325	40,145
First National Bank, Greenleaf, Kans	Oct. 7, 1886	May 9, 1888	50,000	11,250	1,340	9,910
National Bank of Genesee, Batavia, N. Y	Apr. 28, 1865	May 21, 1888	75,000	44,434	7,090	37,344
Strong City National Bank, Strong City, Kans	July 13, 1883	May 26, 1888	50,000	11,250	1,900	9,350
Citizens' National Bank, Saginaw, Mich	Sept. 24, 1880	June 1, 1888	100,000	45,000	5,960	39,040
Madison National Bank, Madison, Dak	Dec. 7, 1886	June 13, 1888	50,000	11,250	....	11,250
Saugerties National Bank, Saugerties, N. Y	June 2, 1865	June 16, 1888	125,000	93,310	9,420	83,890
Hyde National Bank, Titusville, Pa	Mar. 16, 1880	June 21, 1888	300,000	74,730	18,990	55,740
State National Bank, Omaha, Nebr	Dec. 15, 1886	July 18, 1888	100,000	22,500	2,800	19,700
Cincinnati National Bank, Cincinnati, Ohio	Apr. 12, 1883	Aug. 1, 1888	280,000	52,510	3,010	40,500
First National Bank, Worthington, Minn	Aug. 19, 1886	Sept. 5, 1888	75,000	16,875	2,400	14,475
South Framingham National Bank, South Framingham, Mass	June 28, 1880	Sept. 8, 1888	100,000	21,720	1,350	20,370

STATEMENT OF NATIONAL BANKS CLOSED DURING THE YEAR—Continued.

Name and location of bank.	Date of authority to commence business.	Date of closing.	Capital stock.	Circulation.		
				Issued.	Redeemed.	Outstanding.
Lowell National Bank, Lowell, Mich	June 14, 1865	Sept. 11, 1888	$50,000	$24,870	$2,230	$22,040
First National Bank, Grass Valley, Cal	Mar. 16, 1887	Sept. 18, 1888	50,000	11,250	....	11,250
Merchants' National Bank of West Virginia, Morgantown, W. Va	Aug. 3, 1865	Oct. 4, 1888	110,000	81,480	1,070	80,410
First National Bank, Cawker City, Kans	Mar. 1, 1882	Oct. 9, 1888	50,000	11,250	....	11,250
Total	....	....	6,071,000	1,482,053	291,130	1,190,923

Of the above banks thirty-four went into voluntary liquidation and eight failed.

THIRD.

SUGGESTIONS AS TO AMENDMENTS TO THE LAWS RELATING TO BANKING BY WHICH THE SYSTEM MAY BE IMPROVED AND THE SECURITY OF THE HOLDERS OF ITS NOTES AND OTHER CREDITORS MAY BE INCREASED.

I have the honor to renew the recommendations made in the Report of 1887 and to ask for them attention at this session. After carefully considering all the suggestions that have been made from time to time toward providing an adequate and acceptable basis for national-bank circulation to take the place of the bonds now become too scarce and too dear for the purpose, I feel it my duty to submit for the consideration of Congress the following view of the whole subject of national-bank circulation:

Continued contraction in the volume of circulation has been the most prominent feature in the history of the national banks during the last ten years.

The statements in this report, under the proper head, exhibit the persistency of the influences heretofore operative to reduce the volume of national-bank circulation; they also indicate the advent of new influences which are accelerating this reduction, not only by curtailing the circulation of banks already in existence, but by repressing the normal increase of circulation incident to the formation of new banks.

Year by year the Comptroller's reports have called attention to the rising scale of reduction of circulation among existing banks and to the declining ratio in which new banks take out circulation in excess of the amount issued upon the minimum requirement of bond deposits; during the past year there has been practically no such excess, and the effect of the bond situation has extended beyond circulation. It is now checking the formation of new banks, which is like arresting a stream at its source.

During the past year only $2,375,550 was added to circulation by the new banks and banks increasing capital, while during the previous year $4,592,000 was added in the same way.

Besides the falling off in the formation of new banks this year, as compared with the two years preceding it, and with the average of the five years from 1883 to 1887, inclusive, 127 national banks have during the past twelve months reduced their bond holdings to the minimum, and this alone caused the withdrawal of bonds to the amount of $14,014,400, reducing circulation by $12,600,000.

On October 31, there were only 1,180 banks that held bonds in excess of the minimum. The amount of bonds so held was $77,255,863, and the circulation secured by these bonds amounted to $69,953,277. At the present rate of reduction the excess may disappear in two years, and is sure to do so when the 4½ per cent. bonds mature in October, 1891.

On page 60 is a table showing the net decrease of circulation during each of the last five years. The exceptionally large decrease during 1885 and 1886 is attributable to the redemption of the 3 per cent. bonds.

The limit of $3,000,000 a month imposed by section 9, act July 12, 1882, upon reduction of national-bank circulation does not apply to such reduction when it is a result of the payment of matured bonds; hence banks holding the 3 per cent. bonds in excess of the minimum requirement generally surrendered the circulation secured by those bonds as fast as these were called for payment, a conclusive proof that circulation was no longer profitable.

During the recent purchases of bonds by the Treasury the restriction of the above section has repeatedly operated to retard and in some cases to prevent sales of bonds held by the Treasurer as security for national-bank circulation; hence the reduction of circulation has not been as large this year as it would have been had there been no hindrance in the law.

The limit of $3,000,000 a month which restricts the voluntary reduction of circulation to $36,000,000 a year does not apply to the circulation of banks that fail or of those that go into voluntary liquidation, hence whatever addition to circulation may result from the formation of new banks, and from the smaller banks increasing their capital, is liable to be offset by the retirement of notes of failed and liquidating banks, so that the net decrease may amount to fully $36,000,000 in a year, and may even exceed that amount if the forces now repressing the growth of the system should reach an intensity sufficient to drive banks out of it.

Whether there is or is not at present any danger of the national-bank system being actually forced into a decline in consequence of the growing scarcity and high prices of United States bonds, there is enough warning in the facts of its recent history and present condition to demand prompt and effectual relief.

Our national banks are too valuable, too deeply rooted in the confidence of the public, too intimately interlaced with the industrial interests and employments of our people, to be left to the risks of neglect or even of inattention.

Apart from whatever danger to the system there may be in neglecting at an early day to provide adequate relief against the influences now operating adversely to its growth, the national-bank circulation taken by itself, merits earnest consideration and will be found well worthy of preservation.

For many years after the inception of the national-bank system the circulation was its most important feature; important to the banks, still more important to the public; for, besides performing a service of incalculable value in the promotion of internal trade through the regulation of domestic exchanges, it constituted up to 1879 an important check upon the gold premium, and thus assisted in the preservation and extension of our valuable foreign commerce on a secure basis.

Resumption would hardly have been attempted in 1879 unless the composition of the currency had been such as to engage the banks to co-operate in the movement, and without such co-operation resumption could not have been accomplished. On November 1, 1878, the outstanding legal tenders were estimated at $346,681,016; fractional currency at $16,000,000; the national-bank circulation outstanding against bonds was $319,652,121, and against lawful money deposited in the Treasury, about $2,500,000 more, making in all $685,000,000 of paper against which the Treasury held only $126,000,000 in gold coin and bullion and the banks less than $31,000,000.

Grave apprehensions were entertained as to the prudence of undertaking resumption with only $157,000,000 of gold to meet possible demands amounting to $685,000,000. There was a vast amount of discussion through the medium of the press and in Congress, while the records of Congressional inquiry on this subject, as late as December, 1878, make quite a volume and show with what misgivings the project was regarded.

The real strength of the situation, however, consisted in the fact that the national banks were holding in legal-tender notes and certificates $97,000,000, which, with the $15,000,000 in the 5 per cent. redemption fund, represented $112,000,000 of demands upon the Treasury that would not be presented for redemption, and thus the Government was set free to use its $126,000,000 of coin in preserving the convertibility of only $234,000,000 legal tenders, scattered all over the country.

The banks had the physical power, of course, to demand coin for their $112,000,000 on January 1, 1879, but to have exercised that power would have been to ruin themselves, because a run upon the Treasury would have induced a run upon the banks, and they owed the public $319,000,000 on their circulating notes and $620,000,000 in deposits, while their entire holdings of lawful money on October 1, 1878, were only $143,000,000, consisting of—specie, $30,686,866, legal-tender notes, $64,428,000, United States certificates of deposit, $32,690,000, five per cent. redemption fund, $15,205,541.

It is evident, therefore, that the resumption of specie payments by the Treasury on January 1, 1879, was made possible only by the relations which the law established between the national banks and the Government, because it was the coercion of the law in respect to reserve that accumulated in the banks so large a percentage of the legal-tender notes and thus brought them into hands where the highest conception of public obligation, as well as the most intelligent appreciation of self-interest, came into play to assist in the success of the Treasury policy.

The national banks, therefore, which had at the supreme crisis of 1863 saved the finances of the Government, rendered in 1879, a service only second in importance to that, in enabling the reunited industrial interests of the country to regain the firm footing of definite and stable values.

As soon as resumption was effected, however, the national-bank circulation came under the influences which have since been steadily reducing its volume. The maximum of circulation had been reached in December, 1873, when 1,976 banks, with an aggregate capital of $490,000,000, had outstanding $341,000,000 in circulating notes. The long depression following the panic of 1873 arrested the growth of the system so that in June, 1877, 2,078 banks had an aggregate capital of $477,000,000 and $299,000,000 circulation.

During three and a half years, therefore, the number of banks increased only 102, while there was a shrinkage in capital of $13,000,000, and in circulation of $42,000,000.

At that point of time the refunding operations of the Treasury and the preparations for resumption began to exercise upon the banks influences tending to reduce their number and capital, but even then their circulation increased slightly. In April, 1879, there were only 2,048 banks in existence, 30 less than in June, 1877, and in October, 1879, there were 2,052 banks, which had barely $454,500,000 capital, a falling off of $22,500,000 in two years and four months, while the total circulation had risen to $322,000,000 from $299,000,000, thus making up for the reduction of capital.

After this date new influences arose, the banks began to increase in number and to enlarge their capital, while the rapid increase of deposits, due undoubtedly to the confidence inspired by the success of resumption, enabled them to expand their accommodations to the public.

Individual deposits in national banks amounted in October, 1865, to $500,000,000, but in April, 1879, they were less than $600,000,000, although the banks had increased in number from 1,513 to 2,048; their capital, surplus, and undivided profits had gone up from $464,000,000 to $610,000,000, and their circulation had grown from $171,000,000 to $304,000,000.

During the thirteen and a half years between these dates the average amount of individual deposits, as shown by all the reports of condition, was a trifle under $600,000,000, while the maximum was only $683,000,000, but immediately after resumption was recognized as a fact established, deposits began to increase; in December, 1880, the aggregate exceeded $1,000,000,000; it rose in 1881 above $1,100,000,000, and has steadily increased since; the average of 1888 is $1,301,088,048, and the highest point was reached on October 4, 1888, when the amount was $1,350,320,861.

Year by year, with increasing capital and deposits, loans and discounts expanded. In December, 1873, they were less than $857,000,000, and in April, 1879, they were only $835,000,000, but in 1888 they have averaged $1,617,636,312, and have been as high as $1,674,886,285.

According to all natural laws the circulation of these banks should have kept pace with augmenting resources and with increasing deposits and expanding business, but it has not been so.

Since December, 1879, the national banks have increased in number from 2,052 to 3,151, which is over 53 per cent. Their capital, surplus, and undivided profits were then $617,501,367.68; they are now (October 4, 1888), $855,576,646.95, an increase of 38.55 per cent. Loans and discounts have gone up from $933,000,000 to $1,674,886,285.29, an increase of 79½ per cent.; but the circulation has declined from $322,000,000 to $151,702,809, a decrease of nearly 53 per cent.

If we deduct from circulation at each of these periods the amount represented by the obligatory deposits of bonds, the remainders will represent the circulation voluntarily maintained. In December, 1879, this voluntary circulation was $233,179,965; on October 31, 1888, it was only $68,956,627, a reduction of 70½ per cent.

The constant shrinkage of national-bank circulation is attributable largely to the growing scarcity and rising price of United States bonds, but there is also another influence at work of which the importance is not generally recognized, namely, the displacement of national-bank notes by other forms of money.

At the end of 1878 the paper money of the country amounted, as has been stated, to $685,000,000, which supplied all the needs of Treasury disbursements and of currency circulation, except those arising out of transactions in foreign exchange, the payment of gold interest, and the collection of duties on imports.

These latter needs were supplied by a stock of coin and of coin certificates held in the principal Eastern sea-ports, estimated at $35,000,000, which, with $40,000,000 coin said to have been in circulation in Texas and on the Pacific slope, and the $685,000,000 of paper, made the total circulation at the end of 1878 about $760,000,000. The Treasury held in United States and national-bank notes $82,600,000, against which there were outstanding certificates of deposit to the amount of $39,000,000, leaving the balance, viz, $43,000,000, to be deducted from the total of $760,000,000 in order to ascertain the amount of currency actually employed. Upon this computation it would appear that the effective circulation just before resumption was less than $720,000,000.

The resumption of specie payments went into effect on January 1, 1879, and as soon as the public became satisfied that it was permanent, the heretofore hoarded specie began to enter into general circulation. The effect, of course, was an expansion of the currency; not suddenly, because the habit of hoarding is never suddenly discontinued, but gradually, as confidence in the situation made its way among the people.

The amount thus added to the circulating medium has been estimated at $140,000,000, which includes subsidiary and minor silver coin, $70,000,000.

Another influence under which the volume of the circulating medium has constantly been expanded is that of the silver-dollar coinage law of 1878. Under that law the number of standard silver dollars coined up to October 31, 1888, is $309,780,790, and every month hereafter, as long as the law exists, at least $2,000,000 more must be coined and sent to the Treasury to be put into circulation.

The standard silver dollars, as coins, have never entered into circulation in numbers at all proportioned to the number coined, nor did the silver certificates issued under the act of February 28, 1878, fare any better, but the silver certificates authorized by the act of August 4, 1886, have been very largely absorbed by the public, not apparently because any attention is paid to the basis of their issue, but because they constitute the only supply of notes of small denominations.

As a result of all the influences that have come into play since 1879, the total volume of money in the United States has so increased that it is now estimated to amount to $1,700,000,000, against less than $1,040,000,000 on January 1, 1879, an increase of $660,000,000 in total volume, while the national-bank circulation in the same time has decreased by nearly $83,500,000.

The fact that for a long time past large sums have been accumulated in the Treasury without disturbance to business affords very strong grounds for believing that the volume of currency is excessive, and this inference is strengthened by two facts of recent occurrence—first, the fact that when the Treasury accumulations rose, as they did, during September, 1887, from $259,546,540 to $275,307,883.25, the effect upon business was immediate and serious, and, secondly, the fact that the transfer from the Treasury to depository banks of about $40,000,000 between October, 1887, and January, 1888, relieved the stringency, although a large part of this sum was offset by excessive revenues during that period, and although also the Treasury still contained a great deal of idle money.

While this is being written another fact of still greater significance is added to those already cited, namely, the export of gold. To any one who considers the component elements of our currency it must be obvious that gold is the only one that can be both increased and diminished in volume in response to the changing volume of the need or more properly of the use, for currency; and its export, except when assignable to other causes, is a sure indication that the total volume of currency is for the moment in excess of the amount that can be profitably employed.

The silver element is by statute constantly augmenting in volume, but the export of our silver coins is prevented because they have, in the United States, a value as compared with the same weight and fineness of silver uncoined as 100 is to 73, while everywhere else they have only their bullion value. For a like reason silver coins are not used in the arts as gold coins are; because to workers in silver, bars are far cheaper than dollars. Hence the silver coinage is an element constantly increasing in volume.

The legal tenders are fixed by statute at $346,681,016, so that their volume is subject to neither increase nor decrease.

The national-bank notes are theoretically subject to increase and decrease of volume, but apart from the influences which have for a long time produced a steady decrease, the law itself interposes an obstacle to flexibility. Section 9, act July 12, 1882, limits the voluntary decrease of national-bank circulation to $3,000,000 a month and forbids any increase of circulation to be issued to a bank within six months after it has made a deposit of lawful money for the purpose of reducing circulation.

The gold element of the currency is alone and peculiar in this, that its volume and distribution are determined not by statute, but by the natural laws of finance.

During the years subsequent to 1878, when business, restored to the solid basis of gold values, was constantly expanding and therefore constantly needing increased supplies of circulating medium, we not only retained for home use our large annual production of gold, but whatever additional amounts our business required flowed into the country from foreign nations, and that in spite of some very distinct efforts on their part to prevent it.

On the other hand, when from time to time there occurred a subsidence in the tide of national prosperity or a depression in any of our greater industries, so that for the moment the amount of money in circulation exceeded the use for it, gold exports relieved the situation.

Of late years, however, the gold movement across the Atlantic has become much more sluggish because something has been found to take its place, and, to some extent at least, to serve the purpose of regulating exchanges and transferring capital. Certain securities on the New York stock-list have come to be largely and constantly dealt in at the European monetary centers, and as, by means of cable communication and through the close competition of dealers, their values are generally nearly at a level in all markets, they supply a cheaper medium of settlement than gold and a more convenient basis for exchange operations.

This "arbitrage" business, as it is called, has already exercised an important influence upon the preservation and distribution of our stock of gold, and has probably contributed to crowding national-bank notes out of circulation by impeding the export of gold at times and under conditions which would at former periods have produced an outflow. To explain: Before this new business came in the dealers in foreign exchange, being dependent wholly upon gold to settle their balances, or to serve as a basis for drafts or credit whenever the supply of commercial bills proved insufficient, were compelled to carry a stock of coin or bullion, and this constituted a fund apart from the general monetary stock of the country; its transfer back or forth across the Atlantic followed the fluctuations in foreign-exchange premium, and only when it became exhausted, or threatened to become exhausted, was there any drain upon the general stock of gold currency. The publicity attending gold shipments enabled the whole business world to perceive the drift of the metal one way or the other, and bankers and merchants alike could prepare in advance for the moment when the stock of current coin should be drawn upon to supply the foreign demand.

It is not so with the securities in question; they have become the stock in trade of dealers in foreign exchange; they are shipped back and forth according as exchange quotations fluctuate; indeed, in many cases they are not even shipped; the ownership of them is transferred by a cablegram, and this transfer supplies a basis for bills or credits. Whether they are shipped or otherwise dealt with, however, the transactions in these securities, or in respect to them, are completely cloaked from public observation, and, therefore, neither bankers nor merchants can now obtain any warning of the approach of a state of foreign exchanges which may necessitate the export of gold, nor can they by any means perceive, nor by the exercise of any sagacity securely estimate, the extent to which such shipments may be made or the length of time they may continue.

The old computations as to what was called "the balance of trade" supplied some sort of basis for an estimate of probable gold movements, but now the utility of such computations has been destroyed because the values transferred through the medium of securities are very great and are utterly beyond determination.

Another feature of the present foreign exchange business should not be overlooked in tracing the relations between that business and our monetary system, namely, the existence of banking houses with partners or agents on both sides of the Atlantic, and employing a great money capital.

Formerly capital was seldom transferred from one country to another for long periods of time without either a change in its ownership or a change of domicile on the part of its owner, whereas now there are masses of capital that really belong to no particular country, but are always "on the road" in the form of bills of exchange. This capital, supplemented by the almost unlimited credit of the bankers who direct its employment, substantially controls the course of international exchanges, but its movements are as noiseless as those of the electric current by which they are guided, and as secret as the cipher language in which alone they are recorded.

It is impossible that there should be no danger in all this to a monetary system like ours. While the arbitrage business has set free some gold for other employment, it creates by that very effect a danger of considerable importance, namely, the danger of a general disturbance of industry whenever the balances to be settled or the movements of capital exceed the available supply of securities, and resort must again be had to gold shipments, producing not only a contraction of the currency, which, under existing circumstances, is no great matter, but also, what is far more disturbing, causing a visible depletion of reserves at the main center of our entire monetary system.

It must be remembered that gold has only been relegated to the second place in our foreign exchange dealings; it is not banished nor disqualified. It has not, like silver, become *functus officio* in international trade; it is still the measurer of commercial values, still the only medium of liquidation that is equally effective everywhere, and the danger now is that, instead of moving in small amounts promptly in sensitive response, as formerly, to fluctuations in exchange, it may some day slide away from us in masses under some sudden escape of influences heretofore concealed from observation, and also perhaps held in check, by the arbitrage system. If we are really exposed to such a danger, we can not begin too soon to prepare for it, and prudence counsels that the first step should be to protect the Treasury against any possible embarrassment.

The $346,000,000 of greenbacks are the weak point in our currency system. The gold coins and certificates stand first, the national-bank notes next, the silver coins and certificates third, and the greenbacks last in the order of assured value, and it would be a great benefit to the whole mass of the currency if this, its frailest element, could be eliminated from it.

The present state of things seems favorable to the substitution of national-bank notes for greenbacks, and to that end I venture to submit for the consideration of Congress the following measures:

1. Funding in bonds the greenback debt of $346,681,016, or so much of it as may be presented at the Treasury within a limited period of time, say three years.

2. The bonds to be issued only to national banks presenting greenbacks for that purpose; to bear a low rate of interest, not exceeding 2½ per cent., and to mature only upon the failure of the bank or upon its dissolution, whether voluntary or upon expiration of its corporate existence.

3. The bonds so issued to be available only as a deposit to secure national-bank circulation and to entitle the banks depositing them to receive circulating notes to the amount of their face.

4. Existing banks to be required, for a time at least, to retain on deposit the bonds they now have to the minimum amount required by existing laws and to use the new bonds only for procuring additional circulation, or in substitution for whatever bonds they may now have on deposit in excess of the minimum, but the new bonds to be available for all purposes by banks organized after the passage of the act.

5. The National Bank Redemption Agency at Washington to be transferred to New York, and a sub agency to be established at each central reserve city, the notes of all banks wherever situated to be redeemed at whichever agency they may be presented.

In support of these measures it may be said—

1st. That they provide for the retirement of the greenback circulation without even a temporary contraction of the currency, because arrangements can and should be made to issue the national-bank notes immediately upon the presentation of the greenbacks for the purpose of being funded.

2d. That upon the retirement of these obligations the $100,000,000 of gold held in the Treasury as a special fund for their redemption will become an available asset and may be paid out, adding just that much to the active circulation.

3d. With the greenbacks taken out of the category of demand obligations of the Government, the Treasury will be in a better position than now to maintain the silver coinage at par with gold; and, on the other hand, specie and specie certificates will be held much more largely by the banks than they are now, and this will tend to relieve the strain upon the Treasury.

4th. As the greenbacks will not be extinguished, but held in a state of suspended monetary vitality until the failure or liquidation of a bank requires their use in the redemption of its notes, they will constitute a reserve fund lying in the Treasury ready for use, at any moment of emergency, in the redemption of any portion of the national-bank currency that may become discredited.

5th. Assuming that $300,000,000 of greenbacks will be eventually funded in this way; assuming that the bonds bear interest at the rate of 2½ per cent. per annum, payable semi-annually, and assuming that the present tax on circulation is maintained at the rate of one-half per cent. every six months, the annual charge to the Government will be about $4,500,000, and against this it gets the use of $100,000,000 for paying off that much bonded debt bearing 4½ per cent. per annum interest, and escapes the expense of redeeming and renewing the legal-tender notes.

6th. Even if the entire $4,500,000 per annum should be added to the permanent expenses of the Government it would be but a small price to pay for the service which the banks will render both to the Government and to the public through the instrumentality of such a circulation as theirs will then be.

7th. The moderate profit of 1½ per cent. per annum will be materially reduced by the expenses of redemption and supervision, including loss of interest on the redemption fund, so that the banks will not realize quite as much as the Government pays, but still it will probably constitute a sufficient incentive to banks to fund all the greenbacks they can, and when the whole issue is funded whatever amounts are from time to time paid out in redemption of the notes of failed banks will probably be collected and presented afresh in order that circulation may be obtained for them.

8th. The public will be benefited by having a bank-note circulation amply secured and of which every note is redeemable in coin or in a certificate representing coin actually on deposit in the Treasury, and redeemable, too, not only at the bank which issued it, but at any central reserve city; a circulation large enough in volume to admit of easy and prompt adjustment to the varying needs of different localities, its flexibility secured by the constant pressure of the Government tax on the one side and the constant inducement of the bond interest on the other, while the numerous points of issue and their wide distribution over the country afford ample protection against combinations or other devices for artificially expanding and contracting the circulation.

9th. With such a resource at hand we may view with indifference the transfer abroad of a large part of our burdensome and unprofitable stock of gold, where it will be more useful to us in expanding the markets for our exports of agricultural products than it can be here locked in the Treasury.

10th. The national-bank system will be restored to healthy activity and stimulated to fresh growth especially in those parts of the country where such banks are most needed and are now found in least numbers.

LAWS REGULATING INTERSTATE COMMERCE.

Occasion was taken last year to call attention to the divergent, and even contradictory, character of the laws prevailing and of the decisions which have been rendered, in different States in respect to substantially the same points of general commercial practice. A more extended observation of interstate commercial relations, particularly in connection with so much of the business of the national banks as consists of operations in exchange arising out of transactions between citizens of different States, confirms the views intimated in the Report of 1887 as to the importance of national legislation for removing the confusion and friction caused by the differences of local laws and judicial construction.

The establishment and extension of the national banking system and the regulation by Congress of interstate transportation constitute successive steps in the direction of that regulation of trade between the States which the Constitution authorizes if it does not enjoin upon Congress.

The next step to these, in logical sequence, would appear to be the enactment of a commercial code applicable to transactions between citizens of different States, and as such a code would naturally tend to the extension of the benefits now derived by the public from the national banking system, it seems proper to include this subject among those which the Comptroller of the Currency is privileged to bring to the attention of Congress.

The proposition to establish an interstate commercial code rests, of course, upon the assumption that constitutional authority to do so is included in the power to regulate commerce between the States.

Without venturing to discuss the constitutional question, it may be said in support of the assumption, that the complete regulation of commerce would seem necessarily to involve the enactment, or at least the sanction, of some body of laws defining the obligations and securing the rights of persons engaged in such commerce. The identity in origin of our State systems of law and jurisprudence, and the similarity of the local conditions affecting their development, preserved among them for a long time sufficient uniformity to make them practically a common law, but of late years there has arisen more and more divergence, especially in court decisions, and now the commercial dealings between citizens of different States have become materially embarrassed by the variety and even the contrariety of law and practice prevailing in different parts of the Union with respect to negotiable instruments, partnership accounts, and contracts.

While the banks seem to have the chief interest in this matter, because the laws and decisions in question affect directly that in which they deal, yet this interest is representative only, because behind each check, draft, bill of lading, or promissory note held by a bank there is dependent upon the paper a commercial transaction in which the bank has no part and from which it can derive no profit.

The purchase and sale of merchandise is only the initial point of a commercial transaction; to render it complete the goods must be delivered by the seller and they must also be paid for by the buyer.

From the initial bargain to the final settlement each step is taken only upon the assurance that all the others will follow in due succession; hence an obstruction at any point, either to the delivery of commodities or to payment for them, arrests the whole current of dealings running toward consummation at that point, producing stagnation at the sources of its supply and the paralysis of every organ through which the demand should be transmitted.

Practical experience of the importance of preventing obstruction in the channels of transportation, produced and sustains the law regulating interstate commerce by railroad and river, and now the public is beginning to realize the importance also of preventing obstruction in the channels through which instruments of exchange must pass *pari passu* with the parallel passage of the goods they represent.

The free movement of interstate exchanges is as essential to the marketing of crops and to the distribution of industrial products as are railroads and steamboats. The latter never move a ton of anything until the exchange drawn against it is negotiated, and assurance is thus secured that the article shipped will be paid for. Producers have suffered a loss of markets from financial disorder much more frequently than from transportation derangement; hence, in facilitating financial transactions and relations between citizens of different States, Congress will promote the great industrial interests of the country quite as effectually as by facilitating the physical transportation of the products of those industries.

Without attempting to cite specific instances or to designate the States concerned, it is sufficient to say that in respect to commercial paper the conflict of law in different States extends to every branch of the subject; and it is not confined to cases of rare occurrence, or to those in which the circumstances are unusual or peculiar, but exists in respect to many matters which are elementary and fundamental, as, for example, the legal force of such instruments as bills of lading, promissory notes, bills of exchange, etc., the obligations of the parties thereto, the steps necessary to charge the different parties with liability, and the extent to which the instruments constitute a charge or lien upon the property in respect to which they are made. In many instances the force of the instruments has to be determined by the laws of a State in which the statutes or the leading decisions differ from those prevailing at the place of negotiation; and as bank officers can not be familiar with the laws of every State and Territory, and also with all the decisions throughout the country, they must often be thrown into perplexity about what might be a very simple business, except for this conflict of laws. In all such cases increased expense affords the only practicable solution, and such increase falls upon the producer in the form of premium or discount.

The laws of the various States differ most widely in respect to bills of lading. In some States a bill of lading is by statute a negotiable instrument, while in other States it retains its common-law characteristics. Even the statutes making it negotiable are much broader in some States than in others. For example, the statutes of Pennsylvania and Missouri prescribe simply the *manner* of negotiation, *i. e.*, by indorsement and delivery; but do not define the effect of such negotiation, nor place such instruments on the footing of instruments which are the representatives of money, so as to charge them with all the consequences which usually attend or follow the negotiation of bills and notes (Shaw *v.* Railroad Company 101, U. S., 557); whereas, on the other hand, the Maryland statute expressly declares them to be negotiable instruments in the *same sense* as bills of exchange and promissory notes (Tiedman *v.* Knox, 53 Md., 612).

Again, the laws vary in the different States as to the liability of the carrier for the representations made in the instrument. In New York, for instance, it is the rule that the carrier is bound by the representations of its agent that the goods were received, and though, in fact there were no goods received, it is estopped to set up such defense (Armour *v.* Mich. Cent. R.R. Co., 65 N. Y., 111); but in the Supreme Court of the United States, and in other jurisdictions, the English rule prevails, that the carrier is not liable if its agent issued the bill of lading without any actual receipt of the goods (Vinton *v.* Pollard, 105 U. S., 7). By the laws of some States, therefore, the banker need not look beyond the bill of lading, whereas by the laws of other States he must make further inquiries, if he would be sure of the security. To ascertain, then, how far he may rely upon the bill of lading, he must refer to the laws of the State by which the instrument is governed, which will often be a State different from his own. Nor can he always determine with certainty what laws apply to it; for it is frequently a very nice and difficult question to decide whether these are the laws prevailing at the place of shipment or those obtaining at the place of delivery.

As to the rules which may govern a draft, or bill of exchange, the conflict is equally great. In the first place, provisions which, by the laws of some States, may be properly inserted, would, by the laws of other States, destroy the negotiable qualities of the instrument, as might likewise the omission of certain provisions; and while the instrument might be negotiable according to the laws of the State where drawn, it might not be such according to the laws of the State in which it is made payable. Again, the rules as to the time of payment are different in the different States, and the banker (with whom it is often important to know the precise time he may expect payment of his bills receivable) may frequently be at a loss to know with respect to an important collection, whether it is payable immediately or is entitled to days of grace. Still again, the contracts of the indorsers may, by some decisions, be governed by laws different from those by which the contract of the drawer is determined. Numerous other questions of this kind will suggest themselves as likely to arise in respect both to the bill of lading and the draft; but it is needless to multiply illustrations.

It has been suggested that uniformity of laws on this subject might be secured by appropriate legislation by the various States. But such uniformity has as yet been unattainable in respect to other matters for which it has been desired. The subject of a uniform system of legal procedure has been agitated for many years, and some very strong efforts have been made in that direction, but as yet little has been accomplished. But were it possible to procure similar legislation by any considerable number of States, or even by all, we should be merely back again where we were under the common law, and as the different provisions of the statutory law would have to be construed by the various State courts, it is not unlikely that these courts would often reach dissimilar conclusions as to the meaning and force of the same provision in the different statutes, just as they have diverged in their application of identical common-law principles. We have an additional illustration of this tendency in the diversity of exposition given to the same or similar provisions in the various codes of procedure, and in the dissimilitude of the decisions in the different States as to the extent to which these provisions change or modify the old rules of pleading and practice. It is true that a system of commercial law adopted by Congress would likewise be subject to judicial construction, but being a statute of the United States, the duty of construing it would properly belong to the Federal courts, and the rules of interpreting it prescribed by the United States Supreme Court would be binding upon every other court; so that, in the main, and certainly in process of time, it would receive the same construction in all courts and in all parts of the country.

The objection to putting general rules of law into the form ot statutes would have no application to a code of the kind proposed, for the purpose is not to change the form of expressing the law, by substituting statutory rules for judicial precedents, but to render certain and uniform those rules of commercial law which are now uncertain or different in different localities, a purpose which can not be accomplished by any number of judicial determinations, since the decisions in one State are not binding as precedents in any other States, nor are the Federal courts bound by the adjudications of State courts, or the State courts by Federal decisions.

FOURTH.

STATE, SAVINGS, AND PRIVATE BANKS, AND LOAN AND TRUST COMPANIES.

In order to comply with the fourth requirement of section 333 of the Revised Statutes of the United States, the Comptroller has obtained, through the courtesy of the authorities of twenty-four States which exact returns of this nature, all the information received by them. This information, transmitted sometimes in detail and sometimes compiled by the State officers, embraces the affairs of 2,008 incorporated institutions and 212 private banking concerns, making 2,220 in all.

The returns of the 2,008 corporations obtained from the State authorities comprise statements of condition of 1,209 banks operated under State charters, aggregate capital, $130,288,327, surplus and undivided profits, $51,575,928, deposits, $387,017,523, of 56 loan and trust companies, capital, $26,913,200, surplus and undivided profits, $23.411,982, deposits, $208,739,626; and of 743 savings banks, of which 598 report no capital, and 145 report capital aggregating $13,122,434. The aggregate surplus and undivided profits of the 743 savings banks is $123,352,662, and their aggregate deposits amount to $1,248,072,843. Two hundred and twelve private banks report capital to the amount of $6,712.636, surplus and undivided profits of $2,212,158, and deposits of $20,353,852.

Even among the States which exact returns from banks there are but few that provide adequately for the scrutiny and compilation of the returns by any State officer, and of course no such provision exists where returns are not required. Without some such provision, however, there can be no certainty that there are not errors and omissions in the reports. In one State, in response to the request for a summary of reports of banks reporting, the chief of the department in charge of the returns wrote: "We have no printed report of the condition of banking institutions in this State. We can have an abstract if you wish it. It will cost you $25, as we will have to get some outside party to come in and make it." In reply that officer was advised that "while Congress requires the Comptroller to get that information (that is, all available information relative to the condition of banks other than national), no appropriation has ever been made to meet any expense attending it, nor are there funds available for defraying the cost of summarizing the reports filed in your office. In a number of States the condition is the same as exists in yours, but without an exception the reports have been intrusted to this office, a copy of the abstract being returned with the reports." The communication concluded with the request that the reports be forwarded at the expense of this office, and with the offer to return, with the papers, a copy of the abstract. Neither the papers nor a reply was received. In another State, banks report only such items as are required to enable the tax department to make the assessment.

In order to obviate error, and as far as possible to obtain complete information, the names and addresses of over 5,700 banks and bankers were secured, and to each was mailed a circular letter, inclosing a blank form, requesting a report of condition of date, June 30, 1888. The request was complied with by over 2,000 banking associations and bankers. Later in the season about one-third of the banks so responding were found to be included in those reported officially by State officers, so that the number, from which returns are classified as unofficial, is 1,307, namely, private banks 991, and incorporated institutions 316.

These 1,307 concerns are in States and Territories in which reports are not required to be made to local authorities, and they consist of 194 State banks having an aggregate capital of $18,643,541, surplus and undivided profits of $5,309,160, and deposits of $23,030,319; 64 loan and trust companies, with capital of $26,330,310, surplus and undivided profits of $12,539,705, and deposits of $49,138,488; 58 savings banks, of which 28 report capital amounting to $3,227,887. The aggregate surplus and undivided profits of the 58 savings banks is $9,343,620, and their aggregate deposits amount to $116,123,707. Nine hundred and ninety-one private banks report capital to the amount of $34,129,438, surplus and undivided profits of $12,665,828, and deposits of $74,524,990.

A comparison of these returns with those of last year will show an increase of 418 institutions reporting officially, a decrease of 47 reporting unofficially, a net increase of 371.

The returns indicate an increase in number of institutions of about 10 per cent., and of assets of about 9 per cent. Banks to the number of 341 have organized since the last report, the capital of which slightly exceeds $16,000,000.

As much interest attaches to the operations of the savings banks of the country, a special effort has been made to collect and tabulate all obtainable information relative thereto. The abstract shows returns, official and unofficial, from mutual and stock savings banks, separated and aggregated, and the average amount due each depositor in each class by States, the average of all by classes, and the average of all banks combined.

In 1887 reports were received from 684 savings banks, of which 600 were mutual institutions; this year 801 reported, of which 628 are mutual. Of the latter number all but 22 are located in the New England States and in New York, New Jersey, Pennsylvania, Delaware, and Maryland; in all of which, except the three latter States, statistics are at hand giving the average dividends paid; in one the rate is 2¾ per cent., in three over 3½ per cent. and less than 4 per cent., and in three over 4 per cent. and less than 4½ per cent.

It would be interesting to compare the earnings of the mutual savings banks with those of savings banks having capital stock, but it has been impossible to ascertain the earnings of the latter, owing to the fact that none but the California institutions report dividends and interest allowed depositors.

In California 23 such banks reported to the commissioners on January 1, 1888, of which 18 paid dividends on capital stock of from 4 to 13 per cent., making an average of 7.2 per cent., nearly; 21, namely, the 18 above mentioned and three others (two of the three having a reserve fund but no capital) paid interest to depositors to the aggregate amount of $2,551,043.31, the rate varying from 3 to 6 per cent., while two report the payment of neither dividends nor interest. As eleven of the 21 banks pay interest at two or more rates, the amounts on which each rate is paid not being given, it is impossible to show the average, though it appears to be about 4½ per cent. This would indicate that so far as the returns to depositors are concerned, the public benefit of the two classes of savings banks—the stock and the purely mutual—is nearly identical.

All stock savings banks in California are stated by the California bank commissioners, in their report for 1888, to be "business enterprises of private individuals with incidental benefit to the public, in nowise differing in this regard from commercial banks."

Such institutions are regarded on the Pacific coast as an improvement on the purely mutual system. The funds of the stockholders are a guaranty for the safety of those of the depositors, the stockholders being liable for all obligations of the institution to an amount equal to the value of their stock. In addition, the directors or trustees are jointly and severally liable to the creditors and stockholders for all moneys embezzled or misappropriated by the officers.

With a view of throwing some light upon the distribution of the circulating medium of the country, every effort was made to obtain from State banks, Private banks, and Savings institutions the details of their cash holdings. The result will be found on page 24.

In the appendix tables will be found showing by States and Territories the condition of these banks as obtained from official sources and from banks direct (classified as unofficial returns); aggregate resources and liabilities of each class and from both sources; comparative statements of condition of State banks, 1872–'88; loan and trust companies, 1883–'84 to 1887–'88; savings banks, 1883–'84 to 1887–'88; growth of savings banks as shown by deposits, by States, 1830, 1840, and 1850 to 1888; and deposits in savings banks, number of depositors, and average amount due each, by States, in 1886–'87 and 1887–'88.

The following tables present summaries of this information:

AGGREGATE RESOURCES, LIABILITIES, AND CONDITION OF STATE BANKS, LOAN AND TRUST COMPANIES, AND SAVINGS AND PRIVATE BANKS, ORGANIZED UNDER STATE AND TERRITORIAL LAWS. (FROM OFFICIAL SOURCES.)

	State banks.	Loan and trust companies.	Savings banks.	Private banks.	Total.
	1,200 banks.	56 banks.	743 banks.	212 banks.	2,220 banks.
RESOURCES.					
Loans on real estate	$21,404,692	$21,719,668	$479,369,744	$2,433,700	$524,927,804
Loans on personal and collateral security	125,881,958	133,078,950	141,598,935	12,266,824	412,826,667
Loans and discounts	253,163,012	28,634,649	66,333,458	5,822,935	353,954,054
Overdrafts	1,808,140	4,741	147,049	465,767	2,425,697
United States bonds	2,030,634	22,443,398	163,843,109	326,307	188,643,448
States, county, and municipal bonds	144,801	1,981,329	280,625,187	1,731	282,753,048
Railroad bonds and stocks	29,500	8,513,428	70,865,515	....	79,408,443
Bank stocks	86,004	437,988	40,741,610	....	41,265,602
Other stocks, bonds, and mortgages	28,122,372	21,441,353	40,006,319	737,680	90,307,724
Due from other banks and bankers	54,272,878	13,756,139	52,450,672	3,682,698	124,162,387
Real estate, furniture, and fixtures	18,113,980	7,647,122	26,431,082	1,678,696	53,870,880
Current expenses and taxes paid	1,454,014	139,117	221,181	41,764	1,856,076
Cash and cash items	101,054,228	11,662,751	17,414,793	3,090,773	133,222,545
All other resources	10,241,395	4,404,623	10,426,713	295,094	25,367,825
Total	617,807,608	275,265,256	1,390,475,367	31,443,969	2,314,992,200
LIABILITIES.					
Capital stock	136,288,327	26,913,200	13,122,434	6,712,636	183,036,597
Surplus fund	37,928,240	15,454,606	102,985,283	1,002,948	157,371,077
Other undivided profits	13,647,688	7,957,376	20,367,379	1,209,210	43,181,653
State-bank notes outstanding	121,244	a 5,066,708	....	....	b 5,187,952
Dividends unpaid	816,347	22,464	23,438	....	862,249
Individual deposits	387,017,523	208,739,626	1,248,072,843	20,353,852	1,864,183,844
State, county, and municipal deposits	721	26,309	....	....	27,030
Deposits of State, county, and municipal disbursing officers	261,086	....	....	11,732	272,818
Due to other banks and bankers	32,891,639	317,154	895,452	1,404,969	35,509,214
Other liabilities	8,834,793	10,767,813	5,008,538	748,622	25,359,766
Total	617,807,608	275,265,256	1,390,475,367	31,443,969	2,314,992,200

a Debenture bonds. b Debenture bonds, $5,066,708; State-bank notes, $121,244.

AGGREGATE RESOURCES, LIABILITIES, AND CONDITION OF STATE BANKS, LOAN AND TRUST COMPANIES, AND SAVINGS AND PRIVATE BANKS, ORGANIZED UNDER STATE AND TERRITORIAL LAWS. (FROM UNOFFICIAL SOURCES.)

	State banks.	Loan and trust companies.	Savings banks.	Private banks.	Total.
	194 banks.	64 banks.	58 banks.	991 banks.	1,307 banks.
RESOURCES.					
Loans on real estate	$2, 087, 884	$24, 886, 722	$21, 697, 345	$7, 140, 369	$55, 812, 320
Loans on personal and collateral security	13, 512, 317	41, 954, 043	23, 578, 691	54, 340, 185	133, 386, 136
Loans and discounts	15, 952, 800	425, 716	10, 576, 042	20, 972, 444	47, 927, 002
Overdrafts	193, 641	19, 570	11, 152	1, 606, 619	1, 830, 982
United States bonds	67, 000	456, 368	19, 684, 166	1, 302, 415	21, 509, 949
States, county, and municipal bonds	372, 320	25, 150	6, 823, 938	760, 673	7, 982, 081
Railroad bonds and stocks	3, 938, 380	7, 189, 002	18, 849, 843	1, 168, 584	31, 145, 809
Bank stocks	133, 049	222, 480	454, 556	695, 492	1, 505, 577
Other stocks, bonds, and mortgages	1, 960, 611	9, 868, 417	14, 655, 317	3, 680, 009	30, 164, 354
Due from other banks and bankers	4, 505, 328	6, 035, 783	4, 652, 485	17, 218, 193	32, 411, 789
Real estate, furniture, and fixtures	2. 132, 674	6, 304, 609	2, 558, 291	8, 431, 614	19, 427, 218
Current expenses and taxes paid	314, 144	466, 056	254, 226	866, 808	1, 901, 234
Cash and cash items	4, 260, 719	8, 725, 547	4, 150, 524	11, 136, 398	28, 273, 188
All other resources	4, 468, 842	1, 807, 798	1, 514, 136	2, 859, 484	10, 650, 260
Total	53, 899, 700	108, 388, 221	129, 460, 682	132, 269, 287	424, 017, 890
LIABILITIES.					
Capital stock	18, 043, 541	26, 330, 310	3, 227, 887	34, 129, 438	82, 331, 176
Surplus fund	3, 446, 228	8, 650, 765	6, 651, 657	8, 585, 290	27, 333, 940
Other undivided profits	1, 862, 932	3, 888, 940	2, 691, 963	4, 080, 538	12, 524, 373
State-bank notes outstanding	27, 190	a 9, 353, 829	....	21, 000	b 9, 402, 019
Dividends unpaid	229, 112	175, 855	14, 050	84, 658	503, 675
Individual deposits	23, 030, 319	49, 138, 488	116, 123, 707	74, 524, 990	262, 817, 504
State, county, and municipal deposits	114, 531	....	....	2, 419, 440	2, 533, 971
Deposits of State, county, and municipal disbursing officers	74, 618	....	10, 680	1, 052, 307	1, 137, 605
Due to other banks and bankers	1, 647, 303	1, 729, 811	159, 358	3, 496, 479	7, 032, 951
Other liabilities	4, 823, 935	9, 120, 223	581, 380	3, 875, 147	18, 400, 685
Total	53, 899, 700	108, 388, 221	129, 460, 682	132, 269, 287	424, 017, 890

a Debenture bonds. b Debenture bonds, $9,353,829; State-bank notes, $48,190.

AGGREGATE RESOURCES, LIABILITIES, AND CONDITION OF ALL STATE BANKS, LOAN AND TRUST COMPANIES, AND SAVINGS AND PRIVATE BANKS, ORGANIZED UNDER STATE AND TERRITORIAL LAWS.

	Official.	Unofficial.	Total.
	2,220 banks.	1,307 banks.	3,527 banks.
RESOURCES.			
Loans on real estate	$524, 927, 804	$55, 812, 320	$580, 740, 124
Loans on personal and collateral security	412, 826, 667	133, 386, 136	546, 212, 803
Loans and discounts	353, 954, 054	47, 927, 002	401, 881, 056
Overdrafts	2, 425, 697	1, 830, 982	4, 256, 679
United States bonds	188, 643, 448	21, 599, 049	210, 243, 307
State, county, and municipal bonds	282, 753, 048	7, 982, 081	290, 735, 129
Railroad bonds and stocks	79, 408, 443	31, 145, 809	110, 554, 252
Bank stocks	41, 265, 602	1, 505, 577	42, 771, 179
Other stocks, bonds, and mortgages	90, 307, 724	30, 164, 354	120, 472, 078
Due from other banks and bankers	124, 162, 387	32, 411, 789	156, 574, 176
Real estate, furniture, and fixtures	53, 870, 880	19, 427, 218	73, 298, 098
Current expenses and taxes paid	1, 856, 076	1, 901, 234	3, 757, 310
Cash and cash items	133, 222, 545	28, 273, 188	161, 495, 733
All other resources	25, 367, 825	10, 650, 260	36, 018, 085
Total	2, 314, 992, 200	424, 017, 899	2, 739, 010, 099
LIABILITIES.			
Capital stock	183, 036, 597	82, 331, 176	265, 367, 773
Surplus fund	157, 371, 077	27, 333, 940	184, 705, 017
Other undivided profits	43, 181, 653	12, 524, 373	55, 706, 026
State-bank notes outstanding	a 5, 187, 952	b 9, 402, 019	c 14, 589, 971
Dividends unpaid	862, 249	503, 675	1, 365, 924
Individual deposits	1, 864, 183, 844	262, 817, 504	2, 127, 001, 348
State, county, and municipal deposits	27, 030	2, 533, 971	2, 561, 001
Deposits of State, county, and municipal disbursing officers	272, 818	1, 137, 605	1, 410, 423
Due to other banks and bankers	35, 509, 214	7, 032, 951	42, 542, 165
Other liabilities	25, 359, 766	18, 400, 685	43, 760, 451
Total	2, 314, 992, 200	424, 017, 899	2, 739, 010, 099

a Debenture bonds, $5,066,708; State-bank notes, $121,244.
b Debenture bonds, $9,353,829; State-bank notes, $48,190.
c Debenture bonds, $14,420,537; State-bank notes, $169,434.

NUMBER, CAPITAL STOCK, SURPLUS AND UNDIVIDED PROFITS, AND DEPOSITS OF STATE BANKS, 1887-'88.

OFFICIAL.

States, etc.	No.	Capital.	Surplus and undivided profits.	Deposits.
New Hampshire	1	$50, 000	$14, 549	$40, 257
Rhode Island	10	1, 766, 685	173, 853	1, 267, 567
Connecticut	8	2, 390, 000	438, 533	3, 985, 603
New York	122	24, 920, 700	16, 374, 623	140, 043, 155
New Jersey	8	1, 085, 000	341, 654	3, 128, 522
Pennsylvania	77	7, 852, 589	2, 892, 777	30, 412, 607
Virginia	64	3, 468, 739	1, 167, 989	10, 653, 801
North Carolina	16	1, 095, 170	340, 648	1, 181, 422
Louisiana	6	2, 117, 259	567, 308	5, 819, 899
Kentucky	83	12, 597, 937	3, 357, 941	19, 919, 044
Ohio	25	1, 504, 100	319, 079	3, 837, 018
Indiana	32	1, 742, 500	259, 136	3, 304, 201
Michigan	31	2, 071, 200	549, 013	6, 539, 253
Wisconsin	64	3, 821, 100	1, 301, 602	22, 429, 490
Iowa	74	4, 028, 743	930, 462	7, 167, 008
Minnesota	61	5, 733, 000	1, 544, 270	14, 702, 727
Missouri	238	13, 430, 003	7, 667, 806	54, 058, 807
Kansas	177	6, 569, 090	985, 129	9, 887, 858
California	110	39, 893, 903	12, 341, 586	48, 309, 118
Montana	2	150, 000	8, 570	330, 675
Total	1, 209	136, 288, 327	51, 575, 928	387, 017, 523

NUMBER, CAPITAL STOCK, SURPLUS AND UNDIVIDED PROFITS, AND DEPOSITS OF STATE BANKS, 1887-'88—Continued.

UNOFFICIAL.

States, etc.	No.	Capital.	Surplus and undivided profits.	Deposits.
Delaware	2	$420,000	$71,419	$455,175
Maryland	9	2,484,480	536,279	3,861,217
West Virginia	10	453,744	241,900	1,471,307
South Carolina	8	420,000	110,700	436,720
Georgia	19	7,661,477	2,680,518	5,328,861
Alabama	7	705,625	216,660	716,333
Mississippi	14	1,079,000	368,210	2,245,511
Arkansas	5	288,000	46,811	618,174
Tennessee	28	2,336,600	578,580	4,033,526
Nebraska	69	2,201,100	370,500	3,314,267
Dakota	23	590,425	87,535	549,228
Total	194	18,643,511	5,309,160	23,130,319

NUMBER, CAPITAL STOCK, SURPLUS AND UNDIVIDED PROFITS, AND DEPOSITS OF LOAN AND TRUST COMPANIES, 1887-'88.

OFFICIAL.

States, etc.	No.	Capital.	Surplus and undivided profits.	Deposits.
Maine	5	$435,000	$44,223	$725,300
New Hampshire	3	400,000	41,173	297,520
Massachusetts	11	5,050,000	2,715,395	41,230,824
Rhode Island	2	1,500,000	159,804	8,180,236
Connecticut	8	1,036,600	299,007	2,985,733
New York	21	16,596,100	19,942,211	154,601,138
Minnesota	6	1,895,500	209,569	718,876
Total	56	26,913,200	23,411,982	208,739,626

UNOFFICIAL.

States, etc.	No.	Capital.	Surplus and undivided profits.	Deposits.
Pennsylvania	16	$14,106,610	$9,050,674	$38,580,403
Illinois	6	2,479,000	1,230,054	7,364,824
Iowa	6	1,415,000	173,917	343,190
Missouri	6	2,176,700	827,405	888,063
Kansas	17	3,838,600	801,577	1,649,194
Nebraska	6	1,390,000	310,821	258,219
Dakota	7	924,400	145,256	45,575
Total	64	26,330,310	12,539,705	49,138,488

NUMBER, CAPITAL STOCK, SURPLUS AND UNDIVIDED PROFITS, AND DEPOSITS OF SAVINGS BANKS (MUTUAL AND STOCK ASSOCIATIONS), 1887-'88.

MUTUAL, OFFICIAL.

States, etc.	No.	Capital.	Surplus and undivided profits.	Deposits.
Maine	56	....	$2,403,008	$38,819,643
New Hampshire	69	....	5,115,995	63,030,079
Vermont	19	....	772,025	13,009,847
Massachusetts	173	....	13,833,916	302,948,024
Rhode Island	37	....	2,096,982	55,363,283
Connecticut	85	....	3,514,772	102,180,934
New York	118	....	85,249,647	505,017,751
New Jersey	24	....	2,482,129	29,000,189
District of Columbia	1	....	21,006	923,958
Ohio	4	....	1,441,514	16,444,306
Indiana	6	....	183,203	2,045,067
Minnesota	7	....	183,208	3,780,366
Total	598	....	118,198,005	1,124,148,947

STOCK, OFFICIAL.

States, etc.	No.	Capital.	Surplus and undivided profits.	Deposits.
Vermont	10	$475,450	$129,347	$3,592,210
North Carolina	4	88,975	8,638	127,180
Louisiana	1	100,000	49,149	664,098
Ohio	22	1,712,400	339,028	7,009,074
Michigan	43	3,703,762	1,034,244	22,943,806
Iowa	42	2,037,400	540,120	11,268,079
California	23	4,404,447	3,053,527	77,718,534
Total	145	13,122,434	5,154,657	123,923,896

MUTUAL, UNOFFICIAL.

States, etc.	No.	Capital.	Surplus and undivided profits.	Deposits.
Pennsylvania	7	....	$5,110,704	$55,469,516
Delaware	2	....	284,410	3,187,886
Maryland	17	....	1,201,448	32,044,508
Illinois	4	....	198,330	1,249,614
Total	30	....	6,800,970	91,951,524

STOCK, UNOFFICIAL.

States, etc.	No.	Capital.	Surplus and undivided profits.	Deposits.
Maryland	5	$184,656	$35,492	$368,579
South Carolina	6	330,540	350,180	3,243,811
Georgia	5	308,600	85,022	1,761,282
Ohio	6	1,379,091	815,251	7,748,204
Illinois	5	975,000	1,234,231	10,581,240
Utah	1	50,000	22,465	469,067
Total	28	3,227,887	2,542,650	24,172,183

NUMBER, CAPITAL, SURPLUS AND UNDIVIDED PROFITS, AND DEPOSITS OF PRIVATE BANKS, 1888.

OFFICIAL.

States, etc.	No.	Capital.	Surplus and undivided profits.	Deposits.
North Carolina	10	$247, 000	$73, 267	$404, 026
Wisconsin	72	972, 978	554, 281	5, 742, 445
Missouri	91	1, 370, 241	892, 447	7, 014, 669
California	30	3, 793, 092	596, 838	6, 477, 331
Wyoming	9	329, 325	95, 325	715, 381
Total	212	6, 712, 636	2, 212, 158	20, 358, 852

UNOFFICIAL.

States, etc.	No.	Capital.	Surplus and undivided profits.	Deposits.
Maine	2	$60, 000	$6, 597	$146, 626
Massachusetts	5	420, 000	217, 210	620, 414
Connecticut	3	56, 285	2, 997	268, 804
New York	30	903, 738	364, 921	2, 259, 153
New Jersey	6	346, 214	206, 396	1, 470, 396
Pennsylvania	39	1, 286, 843	1, 116, 847	8, 932, 477
Maryland	3	133, 408	1, 465	63, 192
Virginia	3	110, 000	42, 726	386, 325
South Carolina	3	161, 353	5, 567	48, 513
Georgia	8	600, 898	34, 638	171, 672
Florida	7	129, 164	25, 772	374, 885
Alabama	6	278, 500	1, 228, 175	1, 315, 669
Mississippi	2	52, 000	18, 728	73, 161
Louisiana	2	167, 000	26, 125	82, 642
Texas	26	2, 833, 569	323, 067	2, 590, 754
Arkansas	7	219, 500	26, 030	437, 820
Kentucky	12	536, 180	60, 729	1, 010, 819
Ohio	69	2, 492, 534	984, 821	8, 637, 624
Indiana	39	2, 204, 609	354, 895	4, 893, 064
Illinois	120	5, 067, 412	2, 829, 321	15, 335, 137
Michigan	53	1, 087, 687	209, 922	2, 278, 518
Wisconsin	3	12, 000	6, 207	107, 349
Iowa	134	4, 174, 133	1, 010, 102	6, 388, 870
Minnesota	39	919, 652	293, 206	1, 796, 211
Missouri	5	200, 000	35, 834	447, 335
Kansas	122	3, 834, 127	734, 341	4, 084, 959
Nebraska	125	2, 402, 292	677, 848	3, 447, 089
Colorado	16	474, 897	135, 978	1, 259, 495
Nevada	2	168, 700	34, 834	102, 272
California	3	99, 573	7, 878	81, 930
Oregon	7	187, 900	18, 950	185, 612
Arizona	4	160, 000	60, 291	288, 407
Dakota	63	1, 130, 824	250, 886	874, 716
Idaho	1	50, 000	145, 008	12, 000
Montana	2	119, 320	80, 159	1, 365, 804
New Mexico	3	105, 800	8, 954	154, 345
Utah	6	279, 811	1, 025, 459	894, 021
Washington	9	488, 515	53, 368	1, 619, 370
Wyoming	2	30, 000	4, 524	16, 540
Total	991	34, 129, 438	12, 665, 828	74, 524, 990

NUMBER, CAPITAL STOCK, SURPLUS AND UNDIVIDED PROFITS, AND DEPOSITS OF ALL STATE BANKS, LOAN AND TRUST COMPANIES, AND SAVINGS (MUTUAL AND STOCK) AND PRIVATE BANKS, 1887-'88.

OFFICIAL.

Classes.	No.	Capital.	Surplus and undivided profits.	Deposits.
State banks	1, 209	$136, 288, 327	$51, 575, 928	$387, 017, 523
Loan and trust companies	56	26, 913, 200	23, 411, 982	208, 739, 026
Savings banks (mutual)	508	....	118, 198, 005	1, 124, 148, 947
Savings banks (stock)	145	13, 122, 434	5, 154, 657	123, 923, 896
Private banks	212	6, 712, 636	2, 212, 158	20, 353, 852
Total	2, 220	183, 036, 597	200, 552, 730	1, 804, 183, 844

UNOFFICIAL.

Classes.	No.	Capital.	Surplus and undivided profits.	Deposits.
State banks	194	$18, 643, 541	$5, 309, 160	$23, 030, 319
Loan and trust companies	64	26, 330, 310	12, 539, 705	49, 138, 488
Savings banks (mutual)	30	....	6, 800, 970	91, 951, 524
Savings banks (stock)	28	3, 227, 887	2, 542, 650	24, 172, 183
Private banks	991	34, 129, 438	12, 665, 828	74, 524, 990
Total	1, 307	82, 331, 176	39, 858, 313	262, 817, 504

A table in the appendix, page 139, shows, by States and Territories, the estimated population of each on June 1, 1888, and the aggregate capital, surplus, undivided profits, and individual deposits of national and State banks, loan and trust companies, and savings and private banks in the United States on June 30, 1888; the average of these per capita of population, and the per-capita averages of such resources in each class of banks, from which it appears that the estimated population of the United States is 61,394,000; total banking funds amount to $4,766,909,263, which is an average of $77.64. The per-capita averages of such resources in each class of banks are: National banks, $34.76; State banks, $10.13; loan and trust companies, $5.65; savings banks, $24.64, and private banks, $2.46.

The total "cash in bank" held by the 3,527 institutions reporting officially and unofficially is $161,495,733, of which $44,288,254 is taken as gold (that amount includes $5,587,144 in coin, $591,385 in gold certificates, $18,445,351 specie, and $19,664,374, the amount in the California banks), $1,358,513 silver coin, $553,507 silver certificates, $28,954,575 legal tenders and national-bank notes, and $86,340,884 not classified.

For purposes of comparison, the following table is appended:

STATEMENT SHOWING THE AMOUNT OF GOLD, SILVER, ETC., HELD BY NATIONAL BANKS AND OTHER BANKING ASSOCIATIONS, JUNE 30, 1888.

Classification.	National banks.	Other (3,527) banking associations.	Total.
Gold coins	$74, 825, 783	$25, 251, 518	$100, 077, 301
Gold certificates	68, 761, 930	591, 385	69, 353, 315
Gold certificates (clearing-house)	20. 884, 000	....	20, 884, 000
Silver, dollars	6, 906, 432	1, 358, 513	11, 084, 223
Silver, fractional	2, 819, 278		
Silver certificates	7, 094, 854	553, 507	7, 648, 361
National-bank notes	21, 343, 405	28, 954, 575	132, 293, 623
Legal-tender notes	81, 995, 643		
Specie, not classified	....	18, 445, 351	18, 445, 351
Cash, not classified	....	86, 340, 884	86, 340, 884
Total	284, 631, 325	161, 495, 733	446, 127, 058

FIFTH.

NAMES AND COMPENSATION OF OFFICERS AND CLERKS IN THE OFFICE OF THE COMPTROLLER OF THE CURRENCY, OCTOBER 31, 1888.

Names.	Grade.	Salary.
William L. Trenholm	Comptroller	$5,000
Jesse D. Abrahams	Deputy comptroller	2,800
George M. Coffin	Chief of division	2,200
John J. Crawford	do	2,200
Alonzo B. Dickerson	do	2,200
Thomas McGrain	do	2,200
George B. Faxon	Superintendent	2,000
David L. Perkins	Teller	2,000
Theodore O. Ebaugh	Book-keeper	2,000
Charles J. Stoddard	Assistant book-keeper	2,000
Charles E. Brayton	Fourth-class clerk	1,800
Edward A. Demaray	do	1,800
Watson W. Eldridge	do	1,800
John A. Hebrew	do	1,800
George T. May	do	1,800
Edmund E. Schreiner	do	1,800
Walter Taylor	do	1,800
Charles McC. Taylor	do	1,800
Thomas P. Kane	Stenographer	1,600
Harriet M. Black	Third-class clerk	1,600
Sarah F. Fitzgerald	do	1,600
Willis J. Fowler	do	1,600
William H. Heald	do	1,600
Edward S. May	do	1,600
Washington K. McCoy	do	1,600
Isaac C. Miller	do	1,600
Joseph K. Miller	do	1,600
William D. Swan*	do	1,600
Ephraim S. Wilcox	do	1,600
George H. Wood	do	1,600
William F. Colladay	Second-class clerk	1,400
Julia R. Donoho	do	1,400
R. LeRoy Livingston	do	1,400
Mary L. McCormick	do	1,400
Morris M. Ogden	do	1,400
Frank E. Patterson	do	1,400
Margaretta L. Simpson	do	1,400
Arthur M. Wheeler	do	1,400
Eveline C. Bates	First-class clerk	1,200
Willard E. Snell	do	1,200
Eliza R. Hyde	do	1,200
Carrie L. Pennock	do	1,200
Charles A. Stewart	do	1,200
Therese E. Tilley	do	1,200
Anna M. Whiteside	do	1,200
Frederick Widdows	do	1,200
Eliza M. Barker	Clerk	1,000
Alice M. Kennedy	do	1,000
Lafayette J. Garner	Engineer	1,000
Thomas H. Austin	Clerk	900
Margaret L. Browne	do	900
Philo L. Bush	do	900
Louisa Campbell	do	900
Sarah M. Cartwright	do	900
Virginia H. Clarke	Clerk	900
Sarah G. Clemens	do	900
Geraldine Clifford	do	900
Mary L. Conrad	do	900
William S. Davenport	do	900
Amanda W. Doty	do	900
Rossa F. Downing	do	900
Elizabeth E. Ege	do	900
Henry S. Goodall	do	900
Margaret E. Gooding	do	900
Mary B. Harvell	do	900
Lucretia W. Knowlton	do	900
Emma Lafayette	do	900
Loren H. Milliken	do	900
Franklin L. Mitchell	do	900
Mary E. Oliver	do	900
William W. Poultney	do	900
Carrie B. Pumphrey	do	900
Marie Richardson	do	900
Francis M. Richardson	do	900
Hannah Sanderson	do	900

*Additional as bond clerk, $200.

NAMES AND COMPENSATION OF OFFICERS AND CLERKS IN THE OFFICE OF THE COMPTROLLER OF THE CURRENCY, OCTOBER 31, 1888—Continued.

Names.	Grade.	Salary.
Eliza A. Saunders	Clerk	$900
Fayette C. Snead	......do	900
Mathilda C. Stoffregen	......do	900
Warren E. Sullivan	......do	900
Elise K. Taylor	......do	900
Sarah A. W. Tiffey	......do	900
Julia C. Townsend	......do	900
Caius E. Triplet	......do	900
Morris A. Moore	Messenger	840
Harry C. Derby	Assistant messenger	720
William Griffiths	......do	720
Silas Holmes	......do	720
John F. Robertson	......do	720
Langston W. Allen	Watchman	720
W. Frank Robey	......do	720
Samuel M. Freeman	Fireman	720
Bessie P. Cowell	Laborer	660
James F. Govern	......do	660
Herman Stiebeling	......do	660

EXPENSES OF THE OFFICE OF THE COMPTROLLER OF THE CURRENCY FOR THE YEAR ENDING JUNE 30, 1888.

For special dies, plates, printing, etc	$57,113.26
For salaries	101,878.04
For salaries, reimbursable by national banks	16,550.39

The contingent expenses of the office are not paid by the Comptroller, but from the general appropriation for contingent expenses of the Treasury Department; no separate account of them is kept.

ORGANIZATION AND EXPENSES OF THE BUREAU OF THE CURRENCY.

It is unnecessary to reiterate what was said in the last Annual Report upon this subject, and what will be found on one point or another in every Report of the Comptroller of the Currency since 1876, as to the inadequacy of the clerical force or means at the disposal of the Comptroller.

I respectfully repeat, however, the specific recommendations submitted last year, as, "in order that the present work of the Bureau may be properly performed, the following changes are essential:

"1. The Deputy Comptroller should have a salary of $3,500. No less sum can be depended upon to secure or to permanently retain any one entirely qualified for the position.

"2. There should be provided for the Bureau a responsible legal adviser, with such clerks and books as may be necessary to the proper examination of the questions that are daily presented in almost every branch of commercial law.

"3. There should be added to the four divisions now existing a division of archives and statistics.

"Provision should be made by appropriation for an annual conference in Washington of all examiners of national banks, for the employment of supervising examiners, as recommended elsewhere, for such traveling expenses as may be incurred by the Comptroller or Deputy Comptroller in visiting different sections of the country in connection with the banks and banking interests there, and for the accumulation of a library of standard books of reference on subjects relating to banking and financial legislation and administration."

INFORMATION.

Section 333 of the Revised Statutes of the United States, in prescribing the scope of the annual report to be made by the Comptroller of the Currency, imposes upon that officer the further duty of submitting to Congress such other information in relation to the banks as in his judgment may be useful. The following information is accordingly submitted.

THE ORGANIZATION OF NATIONAL BANKS.

During the year under review there has been no change in the laws governing the organization of national banking associations, nor in those which provide for the conversion into such an association of any banking corporation having a State or Territorial charter; hence what was said on this subject in the last Report still applies.

The four following tables give for each State and Territory the number, aggregate capital, bonds, and circulation of national banks existing October 31, 1887, and of banks organized during the year ending October 31, 1888, and show the net increase or decrease in capital, bonds, and circulation for each class of banks during the past year, including failed and liquidating banks.

It will be observed that in the first table the figures showing circulation do not bear in all cases to the figures showing the amount of bonds the relative proportion to be expected from the provision of law which is intended to keep the circulation at 90 per cent. of the par value of bonds. Where discrepancies exist they are attributable to two causes: (1) The occasional surrender of circulation prior to the actual withdrawal of the bonds. (2) The redemption of the notes of failed banks for which deposits have been made with the Treasurer out of collections by receivers in cases where the state of the trust allowed of the retention of bonds for the sake of the interest accruing upon them which would otherwise have been lost if the redemption fund had been provided for by their sale.

Banks newly organized are required to pay in the subscribed capital as follows: At date of authority to commence business, 50 per cent., each month thereafter 10 per cent.; bonds may be deposited in proportion to capital paid in; circulation is issued only upon bonds actually deposited.

States and Territories.	Banks existing October 31, 1887.				Banks organized during year ending October 31, 1888.			
	No.	Capital.	Bonds.	Circulation.	No.	Capital.	Bonds.	Circulation.
Maine	73	$10,490,700	$5,406,000	$5,004,545	2	$100,000	$25,000	$22,500
New Hampshire	49	6,205,000	4,019,500	2,622,402	.....	.....	.....	.....
Vermont	49	7,566,000	3,891,000	2,999,054	.....	.....	.....	.....
Massachusetts	252	95,710,500	33,596,750	30,504,347	2	300,000	62,500	56,250
Rhode Island	61	20,340,050	5,183,900	4,686,584	.....	.....	.....	.....
Connecticut	83	24,405,410	9,716,100	9,516,540	1	50,000	12,500	11,250
Division No. 1	567	164,747,660	61,993,250	55,333,562	5	450,000	100,000	90,000
New York	324	85,724,260	30,140,050	27,181,183	8	250,000	62,500	56,250
New Jersey	81	13,024,220	6,862,100	5,981,337	5	300,000	75,000	67,500
Pennsylvania	303	66,389,140	19,701,800	17,609,492	11	1,014,000	203,500	180,000
Division No. 2	708	165,137,620	56,712,950	50,772,012	19	1,564,000	341,000	306,000
Delaware	17	2,083,985	1,596,700	1,348,070	1	50,000	12,500	11,250
Maryland	48	14,509,960	3,417,000	3,290,409	1	60,000	15,000	13,500
District of Columbia	8	1,827,000	930,000	744,388	.....	.....	.....	.....
Virginia	25	3,796,300	1,352,500	1,171,366	1	50,000	12,500	11,250
West Virginia	20	1,961,000	761,250	707,392	.....	.....	.....	.....
Division No. 3	118	24,178,245	8,057,450	7,261,715	3	160,000	40,000	36,000
North Carolina	18	2,412,280	928,500	867,940	2	150,000	37,500	33,750
South Carolina	15	1,698,000	624,750	553,215	1	50,000	12,500	11,250
Georgia	21	3,050,520	988,500	888,151	4	250,000	62,500	56,250
Florida	10	600,000	217,500	141,108	3	250,000	62,500	56,250
Alabama	20	3,485,100	909,500	831,937	2	100,000	25,000	22,500
Mississippi	12	1,055,000	320,000	258,590	.....	.....	.....	.....
Louisiana	13	3,425,000	1,500,000	1,442,262	.....	.....	.....	.....
Texas	91	9,919,750	2,415,300	2,167,628	9	1,395,000	237,500	213,750
Arkansas	7	1,000,000	422,500	335,764	.....	.....	.....	.....
Kentucky	68	13,310,400	4,105,000	3,783,381	2	164,000	41,000	36,900
Tennessee	40	7,460,000	1,483,750	1,126,410	2	150,000	37,500	33,750
Division No. 4	315	47,416,050	13,906,300	12,396,276	25	2,509,000	516,000	464,400
Ohio	216	39,696,020	14,329,650	12,809,832	6	960,000	177,500	159,750
Indiana	93	11,894,500	4,848,800	4,477,806	4	420,000	105,000	94,500
Illinois	178	29,391,500	5,809,000	5,168,390	5	1,150,000	150,000	135,000
Michigan	108	14,558,140	3,387,750	3,150,395	5	350,000	87,500	78,750
Wisconsin	56	5,092,000	1,673,000	1,478,779	3	250,000	62,500	56,250
Division No. 5	651	100,832,160	30,048,200	27,085,202	23	3,130,000	582,500	524,250
Iowa	129	10,230,000	3,080,500	2,789,063	4	260,000	65,000	58,500
Minnesota	58	13,740,000	1,868,550	1,758,225	1	50,000	12,500	11,250
Missouri	50	11,757,280	2,053,300	1,857,068	3	650,000	125,000	112,500
Kansas	142	10,780,800	2,817,000	2,474,115	28	1,610,000	402,500	362,250
Nebraska	104	8,456,100	1,876,500	1,652,338	6	310,000	77,500	69,750
Division No. 6	483	54,064,180	11,696,850	10,526,700	37	2,880,000	682,500	614,250
Colorado	31	2,751,850	989,000	869,835	3	200,000	50,000	45,000
Nevada	2	150,000	37,500	15,444	.....	.....	.....	.....
California	33	6,870,000	1,838,750	1,549,135	6	650,000	162,500	146,250
Oregon	23	1,705,000	614,800	617,100	4	200,000	50,000	45,000
Arizona	1	100,000	25,000	21,870	.....	.....	.....	.....
Division No. 7	90	11,666,850	3,535,050	3,073,384	13	1,050,000	262,500	236,250
Dakota	62	3,720,000	993,500	866,207	1	100,000	25,000	22,500
Idaho	6	350,000	92,800	72,266	1	100,000	25,000	22,500
Montana	17	1,975,000	480,600	440,745	.....	.....	.....	.....
New Mexico	9	850,000	240,000	198,248	.....	.....	.....	.....
Utah	7	850,000	390,000	363,116	.....	.....	.....	.....
Washington	20	1,580,000	480,000	522,140	4	210,000	52,500	47,250
Wyoming	8	1,075,000	223,750	170,455	1	50,000	12,500	11,250
Division No. 8	129	10,400,000	2,869,650	2,610,262	7	460,000	115,000	103,500
United States	3,061	579,342,765	188,723,700	169,080,122	132	12,203,000	2,639,500	2,375,550

States and Territories.	Increase among banks existing October 31, 1887, and number of banks concerned in such increase.				Total increase, and number of banks concerned in such increase.			
	No.	Capital.	Bonds.	Circulation.	No.	Capital.	Bonds.	Circulation.
Maine	1	$100,000	$12,500	$22,490	3	$200,000	$37,500	$44,990
New Hampshire	1	....	....	11,250	1	....	....	11,250
Vermont	1	....	....	10	1	....	....	10
Massachusetts	2	500,000	....	....	4	800,000	62,500	56,250
Rhode Island	.....	....	....	....	.....	....	....	....
Connecticut	.....	....	....	....	1	50,000	12,500	11,250
Division No. 1	5	600,000	12,500	33,750	10	1,050,000	112,500	123,750
New York	6	820,000	121,250	182,095	9	1,070,000	183,750	238,345
New Jersey	1	....	....	11,250	6	300,000	75,000	78,750
Pennsylvania	3	314,000	525,000	378,350	13	1,328,000	725,000	561,500
Division No. 2	10	1,134,000	646,250	571,695	28	2,698,000	987,250	878,595
Delaware	1	....	....	10	2	50,000	12,500	11,260
Maryland	.....	....	....	....	1	60,000	15,000	13,500
District of Columbia	.....	....	....	....	.....	....	....	....
Virginia	.....	....	....	....	1	50,000	12,500	11,250
West Virginia	1	5,000	1,250	1,130	1	5,000	1,250	1,130
Division No. 3	2	5,000	1,250	1,140	5	165,000	41,250	37,140
North Carolina	.....	....	....	....	2	150,000	37,500	33,750
South Carolina	1	25,000	6,250	5,625	2	75,000	18,750	16,875
Georgia	2	75,000	18,500	50,380	6	325,000	81,000	106,630
Florida	1	50,000	....	31,370	4	300,000	62,500	87,620
Alabama	1	....	....	11,250	3	100,000	25,000	33,750
Mississippi	1	50,000	12,500	11,260	1	50,000	12,500	11,260
Louisiana	1	....	....	10	1	....	....	10
Texas	7	445,700	61,200	55,200	16	1,840,700	208,700	268,950
Arkansas	1	....	....	10,000	1	....	....	10,000
Kentucky	3	330,000	....	....	5	494,000	41,000	36,900
Tennessee	4	115,000	17,750	15,985	6	265,000	55,250	49,735
Division No. 4	22	1,090,700	116,200	191,080	47	3,599,700	632,200	655,480
Ohio	6	725,000	88,500	34,630	12	1,685,000	266,000	194,380
Indiana	2	70,000	30,000	81,070	6	490,000	135,000	175,570
Illinois	1	150,000	....	....	5	1,300,000	150,000	135,000
Michigan	2	135,000	8,750	8,310	7	485,000	96,250	87,060
Wisconsin	1	200,000	6,000	5,415	4	450,000	68,500	61,065
Division No. 5	12	1,280,000	133,250	129,425	34	4,410,000	715,750	653,675
Iowa	1	50,000	62,500	9,010	5	310,000	127,500	67,510
Minnesota	6	755,000	77,500	24,750	8	805,000	90,000	36,000
Missouri	2	000,000	350	300	4	1,150,000	125,350	112,860
Kansas	6	350,000	56,250	113,005	20	1,900,000	458,750	475,255
Nebraska	6	870,000	31,250	22,530	12	1,180,000	108,750	92,280
Division No. 6	21	2,025,000	227,850	169,655	58	5,105,000	910,350	783,905
Colorado	5	480,000	32,500	29,240	8	680,000	82,500	74,240
Nevada	2	132,000	33,000	29,700	2	132,000	33,000	29,700
California	7	650,000	62,500	56,280	13	1,300,000	225,000	202,530
Oregon	3	375,000	25,000	22,510	7	575,000	75,000	67,510
Arizona	.....	....	....	....	.....	....	....	....
Division No. 7	17	1,637,000	153,000	137,730	30	2,687,000	415,500	373,980
Dakota	1	100,000	25,000	50	2	200,000	50,000	22,550
Idaho	1	....	....	24,750	2	100,000	25,000	47,250
Montana	1	....	....	7,520	1	....	....	7,520
New Mexico	1	50,000	37,500	33,750	1	50,000	37,500	33,750
Utah	1	50,000	....	....	1	50,000	....	....
Washington	3	75,000	16,250	33,360	7	283,000	68,750	80,610
Wyoming	1	50,000	12,500	11,240	2	100,000	25,000	22,490
Division No. 8	9	325,000	91,250	110,670	16	783,000	206,250	214,170
United States	98	8,096,700	1,381,505	1,345,145	230	20,897,700	4,021,050	3,720,695

Total.	Decrease in capital, bonds, and circulation, with number of banks concerned in such decrease.							
States and Territories.	Failed and liquidating banks.				Banks existing October 31, 1887.			
	No.	Capital.	Bonds.	Circulation	No.	Capital.	Bonds.	Circulation
Maine	.....	.....	.....	.....	12	.....	$572,500	$515,250
New Hampshire	.....	.....	.....	.....	5	.....	355,000	319,500
Vermont	.....	.....	.....	.....	5	.....	377,000	339,300
Massachusetts	1	$100,000	$25,000	$21,720	39	.....	5,985,650	5,386,380
Rhode Island	1	56,000	15,000	13,500	3	.....	550,000	495,000
Connecticut	.....	.....	.....	.....	16	$300,000	954,000	857,000
Division No. 1	2	156,000	40,000	35,220	80	300,000	8,764,150	7,913,030
New York	5	700,000	254,500	102,450	35	162,000	3,488,200	3,139,350
New Jersey	.....	.....	.....	.....	8	20,000	383,350	345,015
Pennsylvania	1	300,000	50,000	45,000	26	125,000	1,508,000	1,357,200
Division No. 2	6	1,000,000	304,500	147,450	69	307,000	5,379,550	4,841,565
Delaware	.....	.....	.....	.....	.....	.....	.....	.....
Maryland	.....	.....	.....	.....	7	.....	1,268,500	1,141,650
Dist. of Columbia	.....	.....	.....	.....	1	.....	100,000	90,000
Virginia	.....	.....	.....	.....	1	.....	210,000	189,000
West Virginia	1	110,000	50,000	10,700	1	.....	37,500	33,750
Division No. 3	1	110,000	50,000	10,700	10	.....	1,616,000	1,454,400
North Carolina	2	300,000	75,000	62,080	3	.....	175,000	157,500
South Carolina	.....	.....	.....	.....	3	.....	175,000	157,500
Georgia	.....	.....	.....	.....	1	.....	75,000	67,500
Florida	.....	.....	.....	.....	.....	.....	.....	.....
Alabama	.....	.....	.....	.....	.....	.....	50,000	45,000
Mississippi	.....	.....	.....	.....	.....	.....	.....	.....
Louisiana	.....	.....	.....	.....	.....	.....	.....	.....
Texas	.....	.....	.....	.....	3	72,900	80,000	72,000
Arkansas	.....	.....	.....	.....	.....	.....	.....	.....
Kentucky	1	50,000	50,000	45,000	6	20,000	684,000	615,000
Tennessee	.....	.....	.....	.....	5	.....	97,500	87,750
Division No. 4	3	350,000	125,000	107,080	21	92,900	1,336,500	1,202,850
Ohio	3	1,430,000	167,500	165,470	19	100,000	2,298,850	2,068,965
Indiana	1	50,000	12,500	11,250	7	125,000	330,000	297,000
Illinois	1	500,000	50,000	45,000	10	27,500	274,500	247,050
Michigan	3	200,000	75,000	81,120	5	.....	212,500	191,250
Wisconsin	.....	.....	.....	.....	1	.....	50,000	45,000
Division No. 5	8	2,180,000	305,000	302,840	42	252,500	3,165,850	2,849,265
Iowa	3	200,000	50,000	84,170	3	100,000	38,000	34,200
Minnesota	3	875,000	118,750	106,875	.....	.....	.....	.....
Missouri	3	500,000	100,000	89,430	4	.....	508,400	511,560
Kansas	4	200,000	50,000	44,900	2	25,000	50,000	45,000
Nebraska	4	250,000	63,000	56,100	1	.....	12,500	11,250
Division No. 6	17	2,025,000	381,750	381,625	10	125,000	608,900	602,010
Colorado	.....	.....	.....	.....	.....	.....	.....	.....
Nevada	.....	.....	.....	.....	.....	.....	.....	.....
California	1	50,000	12,500	11,250	2	.....	125,000	112,500
Oregon	.....	.....	.....	.....	1	.....	200,000	180,000
Arizona	.....	.....	.....	.....	.....	.....	.....	.....
Division No. 7	1	50,000	12,500	11,250	3	.....	325,000	292,500
Dakota	4	200,000	50,000	45,000	.....	.....	.....	.....
Idaho	.....	.....	.....	.....	.....	.....	.....	.....
Montana	.....	.....	.....	.....	1	25,000	.....	.....
New Mexico	.....	.....	.....	.....	.....	.....	.....	.....
Utah	.....	.....	.....	.....	.....	.....	.....	.....
Washington	.....	.....	.....	.....	2	.....	77,500	69,750
Wyoming	.....	.....	.....	.....	.....	.....	.....	.....
Division No. 8	4	200,000	50,000	45,000	3	25,000	77,500	69,750
United States	42	6,071,000	1,268,750	1,011,165	238	1,102,400	21,363,450	19,225,370

States and Territories.	Net increase and decrease during the year ending October 31, 1888.					
	Net increase.			Net decrease.		
	Capital.	Bonds.	Circulation.	Capital.	Bonds.	Circulation.
Maine	$200,000				$535,000	$470,260
New Hampshire					355,000	308,250
Vermont					377,000	339,200
Massachusetts	700,000				5,738,150	5,102,850
Rhode Island				$56,000	565,000	508,500
Connecticut				250,000	941,500	846,350
Division No. 1	594,000				8,511,650	7,635,500
New York	208,000				3,546,450	2,992,205
New Jersey	280,000				308,350	266,265
Pennsylvania	903,000				790,000	805,150
Division No. 2	1,391,000				4,644,800	4,063,620
Delaware	50,000	$12,500	$11,260			
Maryland	60,000				1,253,500	1,128,150
District of Columbia					100,000	90,000
Virginia	50,000				137,500	123,750
West Virginia				105,000	86,250	43,320
Division No. 3	55,000				1,564,750	1,373,060
North Carolina				150,000	212,500	185,830
South Carolina	75,000				156,250	140,625
Georgia	325,000	6,000	39,130			
Florida	300,000	62,500	87,020			
Alabama	100,000	25,000	33,750			
Mississippi	50,000	12,500	11,260			
Louisiana			10			
Texas	1,767,800	218,700	196,950			
Arkansas			10,000			
Kentucky	424,000				693,000	623,700
Tennessee	265,000				42,250	38,015
Division No. 4	3,156,800				779,300	609,450
Ohio	155,000				2,200,350	2,040,055
Indiana	315,000				207,500	132,680
Illinois	772,500				174,500	157,050
Michigan	285,000				191,250	185,310
Wisconsin	450,000	18,500	16,665			
Division No. 5	1,977,500				2,755,100	2,408,430
Iowa	10,000	30,500				50,860
Minnesota				70,000	28,750	70,875
Missouri	750,000				543,050	488,130
Kansas	1,735,000	358,750	385,265			
Nebraska	930,000	33,250	24,870			
Division No. 6	3,355,000				140,300	190,730
Colorado	680,000	82,500	74,240			
Nevada	132,000	33,000	29,700			
California	1,250,000	87,500	78,780			
Oregon	575,000				125,000	112,400
Arizona						
Division No. 7	2,637,000	78,000	70,230			
Dakota						22,450
Idaho	100,000	25,000	47,250			
Montana			7,520	25,000		
New Mexico	50,000	37,500	33,750			
Utah	50,000					
Washington	285,000		10,800		8,750	
Wyoming	100,000	25,000	22,400			
Division No. 8	560,000	78,750	99,420			
United States	13,720,300				18,239,150	16,545,740

With a net increase during the year of 90 in the number of banks, and of $13,726,300 in national-bank capital, there has been a net decrease in circulation of $16,545,740.

By reference to the table on page 61, showing the details of bond deposits by banks organized within the year, it will be seen that these banks deposited only the minimum required by law, and the same is true of banks increasing their capital.

The table on page 28, exhibiting the elements of increase and decrease during the year, shows that of the $3,720,695 added to national-bank circulation since November 1, 1887, $2,375,550 has been issued upon bonds deposited, not for the sake of circulation, but to secure the other advantages afforded by the national-bank system; while on the other hand, with the exception of $1,041,165 in notes of failed and liquidating banks, the whole reduction in national-bank currency represents the voluntary surrender of circulation by banks which have heretofore held bonds in excess of the minimum requirement.

The circulation surrendered by such banks is $19,225,370, which is about 20 per cent. of the circulation outstanding a year ago on the bonds representing the excess above the minimum required by law and which may be called the voluntary circulation.

Two new influences have come into play during the past thirteen months, accelerating the retirement of national-bank circulation, viz, (1) the transfer to national-bank depositaries of a part of the redundant revenues of the Government, and (2) the large purchases of bonds by the Treasury Department.

National Bank Depositaries.

In October, 1887, with a view to averting a threatened monetary stringency arising from the abnormal accumulation of cash in the Treasury, the Secretary resolved to increase the amounts in national bank depositaries under section 5153, Revised Statutes. The depositaries have always been required to give United States bonds as security for the public moneys intrusted to them, but owing to the high price, of the bonds and the requirement of section 5191, Revised Statutes as to the reserve to be held against all deposits, the banks were unwilling to receive additional amounts at the old rate of 90 per cent. on 4½ per cent. bonds and par on the 4 per cent., so that it was determined that banks depositing $1,000,000 in 4½ per cent. bonds might carry not exceeding $1,000,000 of public moneys, and those depositing $1,000,000 in 4 per cent. bonds might carry $1,100,000. Subsequently banks were allowed to deposit less than $1,000,000 in bonds and to carry balances in the above proportions. Since the bonds of both classes held as security for circulation entitled the banks to only 90 per cent. of their face in circulating notes, against which beside they had to keep up a redemption fund of 5 per cent., the opportunity of obtaining Government deposits on the above terms operated as an inducement to the surrender of voluntary circulation, in order that the bonds thereby released might be transferred to the Secretary to be held as security for public moneys.

The precise extent to which this influence was effective in reducing circulation can not be shown because the transfers were not always made directly. In some cases banks intending to withdraw 4½ per cent. bonds and to surrender the circulation outstanding against them, deposited lawful money to effect the withdrawal and afterward sent on 4 per cent.

bonds as security for the public moneys, and in other cases the deposit of 4 per cent. bonds was made first and the withdrawal of 4½ percents effected afterward, but in both cases it was the terms on which Government funds could be obtained that operated to reduce national-bank circulation.

The subjoined table, showing the transfers directly made from circulation account to public moneys account in each month for the past two years, exhibits in a striking manner the effect of this influence.

STATEMENT BY MONTHS, SHOWING THE AMOUNT OF UNITED STATES BONDS TRANSFERRED FROM THE SECURITIES HELD IN TRUST BY THE TREASURER OF THE UNITED STATES FOR NATIONAL-BANK CIRCULATION TO THE SECURITIES SO HELD FOR PUBLIC DEPOSITS DURING THE TWO YEARS ENDING OCTOBER 31, 1887-'88, AND THE METHODS BY WHICH SUCH TRANSFER WAS MADE.

Date.	Total.	Exchanged.	Substituted.	Transferred by retirement of circulation.
1886.				
November	$70,000	....	....	$70,000
December	200,000	$100,000	....	100,000
1887.				
January	530,000	....	....	530,000
February	220,000	....	....	220,000
March	145,000	....	....	145,000
April	40,000	....	....	40,000
May	155,000	....	....	155,000
June	60,000	....	....	60,000
July	130,000	....	$50,000	80,000
August	30,000	30,000	....	....
September	202,500	140,000	....	62,500
Total for eleven months	1,782,500	270,000	50,000	1,462,500
October	715,000	115,000	100,000	500,000
November	2,018,000	50,000	250,000	1,718,000
December	2,804,000	....	300,000	2,504,000
1888.				
January	2,470,000	100,000	870,000	1,500,000
Total for four months	8,016,000	265,000	1,520,000	6,231,000
February	75,000	....	....	75,000
August	200,000	....	....	200,000
September	1,000,000	1,000,000	....	....
Total for nine months	1,275,000	1,000,000	....	275,000
Total for twenty-four months	11,073,500	1,535,000	1,570,000	7,968,500

The total transfers during eleven months ending September 30, 1887, amounted to $1,782,500, an average of $171,127 per month, while during the next four months the transfers amounted to $8,016,000, an average of over $2,000,000 a month, which four months embrace the period in which the Government funds in national-bank depositaries were being increased, for no new depositaries were designated and no increase of deposits was made after January. During the nine months since January last the transfers amount to only $1,275,000, of which a million dollars represents merely an exchange or cross transfer between the two accounts, and should not, therefore, be considered at all in this connection.

The effect upon circulation is shown by the fourth column of the table, *i. e.*, during the first eleven months of the period the amount of bonds withdrawn from circulation account without being replaced was $1,462,500; during the next four months this amount was $6,231,000, while during the remaining nine months it was only $275,000, viz: $75,000 in February and $200,000 in August, 1888.

BOND PURCHASES BY THE TREASURY.

As has been shown, there was almost a cessation in bond withdrawals from security for circulation as soon as the designation of new depositaries was discontinued.

On April 17 a circular was issued inviting proposals for the sale of bonds to the Government, which resulted in purchases as follows:

Month.	4 per cent. bonds.	4½ per cent. bonds.	Total.
April	$1,075,000	$2,490,000	$3,565,000
May	12,112,200	5,027,450	17,139,650
June	5,094,900	820,100	5,915,000
July	444,550	564,700	1,009,250
August	4,373,050	1,628,000	6,001,050
September	15,800,250	7,674,350	23,474,600
October	11,502,700	15,038,000	26,540,700
Total	50,402,650	33,242,000	83,645,250

The subjoined table shows the bond withdrawals from circulation account during the year ending October 31, 1888, divided into two periods of six months each, namely, from November 1, 1887, to April 30, 1888, and from the latter date to October 31, 1888.

STATEMENT SHOWING TOTAL WITHDRAWAL OF BONDS HELD AS SECURITY FOR NATIONAL-BANK CIRCULATION BETWEEN OCTOBER 31, 1887, AND OCTOBER 31, 1888, IN PERIODS OF SIX MONTHS EACH, AND THE REDUCTION OF CIRCULATION CONSEQUENT THEREON.

Period.	Bonds withdrawn.	Circulation reduced.
From October 31, 1887, to April 30, 1888	$8,672,500	$7,805,250
From April 30, 1888, to October 31, 1888	13,470,372	12,123,335
Total	22,142,872	19,928,585

During the first period the withdrawals amounted to $8,672,500, from which should be deducted the withdrawals for transfer directly to public moneys security account, as shown in a previous table, viz, $5,731,000, which leaves a balance of $2,941,500 withdrawn otherwise.

During the second period the total withdrawals were $13,470,372, and of this amount, the bonds withdrawn for delivery directly to the Secretary for purchase amounted to $5,066,950, as is shown by the following statement:

BONDS WITHDRAWN FROM DEPOSIT AGAINST CIRCULATION AND TRANSFERRED TO THE SECRETARY OF THE TREASURY FOR PURCHASE UNDER TREASURY CIRCULAR OF APRIL 17, 1888, SHOWING AMOUNTS OF EACH CLASS OF BONDS AND THE EFFECT OF SUCH WITHDRAWALS UPON CIRCULATION.

Date.	Withdrawn.			Substituted.				Total withdrawn upon deposit of lawful money.
	4 per cent.	4½ per cent.	Total.	4 per cent.	4½ per cent.	P. R. R. 6 per cent.	Total.	
1888.								
May	$637, 500	$196, 000	$833, 500	$16, 000	....	....	$16, 000	$817, 500
June	180, 000	210, 000	390, 000	....	$20, 000	....	20, 000	370, 000
July	209, 500	171, 000	470, 500	....	....	....	....	470, 500
August	90, 000	75, 000	165, 000	....	....	....	....	165, 000
September	992, 500	65, 000	1, 057, 500	....	....	$50, 000	50, 000	1, 007, 500
October	1, 877, 650	748, 800	2, 626, 450	390, 000	....	....	390, 000	2, 236, 450
Total	4, 077, 150	1, 465, 800	5, 542, 950	406, 000	20, 000	50, 000	476, 000	5, 066, 950

NOTE.—Total of bonds withdrawn, $5,542,950; total of bonds deposited in substitution, $476,000; net withdrawal of bonds, $5,066,950; which is made up of reductions in bonds deposited as follows: 4 percents, $3,671,150; 4½ percents, $1,445,800, and an increase of 6 per cent. bonds of $50,000.

It is not as easy to trace bonds withdrawn for sale as to follow those transferred from one account to another in the Treasury, hence the records of this office do not show the displacement of circulation by bond-purchases quite as fully as they show the displacement by Government deposits, but there can be little doubt that the absorption of so large an amount of bonds in so short a time must have produced a strong influence tending to the reduction of the voluntary circulation of banks, and in the absence of any other known influence of the same tendency this must be considered as accounting for the pressure to withdraw bonds which has for three months in succession carried the deposits of lawful money up to the limit of $3,000,000 imposed by section 9, act July 12, 1882.

In some cases banks have withdrawn their bonds and sold them on the general market, but in time these bonds, or others which they replaced, have come into the Treasury purchases.

The influence of high prices for bonds in reducing voluntary circulation is more a matter of inference than of demonstration, but the following table of prices of bonds during the year will be of interest in this connection:

OPENING, HIGHEST, AND LOWEST PRICES OF UNITED STATES REGISTERED 4 PER CENT. AND 4½ PER CENT. BONDS IN NEW YORK FOR EACH WEEK FROM NOVEMBER 4, 1887, TO NOVEMBER 2, 1888

[Compiled from the Commercial and Financial Chronicle.]

Week ending—	4 per cent. bonds.			4½ per cent. bonds.		
	Opening.	Highest.	Lowest.	Opening.	Highest	Lowest.
Nov. 4, 1887	126¾	126¾	126¾	108¾	108¾	107⅝
Nov. 11, 1887	126⅞	127	126⅞	107⅝	107¾	107⅝
Nov. 18, 1887	127	127	126⅜	107¾	107¾	107½
Nov. 25, 1887	126⅝	126⅝	126⅜	107½	107½	107⅜
Dec. 2, 1887	126⅜	126⅜	124½	107½	107½	107⅛
Dec. 9, 1887	124½	124½	123½	107⅜	107⅜	107
Dec. 16, 1887	124	125	124	107½	107½	107½
Dec. 23, 1887	125	125⅝	125	107⅝	108⅛	107⅝
Dec. 30, 1887	126	126	125½	108¼	108⅜	108
Jan. 6, 1888	125½	126	125½	107½	107¾	107¼
Jan. 13, 1888	125½	126½	125½	107½	108½	107¼
Jan. 20, 1888	126¼	126½	126¼	108	108	108
Jan. 27, 1888	126¼	126¼	125½	108	108	107½
Feb. 3, 1888	126	126⅜	125¾	108	108	106¾
Feb. 10, 1888	126⅛	126½	125¾	106¾	106¾	106¾
Feb. 17, 1888	125¾	125⅞	125½	106¾	106¾	106½
Feb. 24, 1888	125⅝	125⅞	125⅜	106½	106⅝	106½
Mar. 2, 1888	125½	125½	124½	106½	106½	106
Mar. 9, 1888	124½	124⅝	124½	106⅛	106⅜	106⅛
Mar. 16, 1888	124½	124½	124⅜	106⅜	106¾	106⅜
Mar. 23, 1888	124¾	124½	124⅝	106½	106¾	106⅛
Mar. 30, 1888	124⅝	124¾	124¼	106½	106½	106⅛
Apr. 6, 1888	124	124	123½	106½	106½	106⅛
Apr. 13, 1888	124	124½	123⅛	106⅛	106⅛	106⅛
Apr. 20, 1888	123½	124¾	123½	106½	107½	106½
Apr. 27, 1888	124¾	126⅝	124¾	107⅝	107¾	107½
May 4, 1888	126½	126½	126¼	107⅜	107⅝	106½
May 11, 1888	126⅝	126⅞	126⅝	106⅝	106¾	106⅝
May 18, 1888	126¾	127½	126¾	106⅝	107	106⅝
May 25, 1888	127⅛	127¾	127⅛	106⅞	107⅛	106⅞
June 1, 1888	127⅝	127⅝	126⅝	107	107	107
June 8, 1888	126⅝	126⅝	126½	107	107	107
June 15, 1888	126½	126¾	126½	107⅛	107⅛	107
June 22, 1888	126¾	127	126⅛	107	107⅞	107
June 29, 1888	127	127⅛	127	107⅛	107¼	107⅛
July 6, 1888	127⅛	127¼	127⅛	107¼	107¼	107¼
July 13, 1888	127¼	127⅜	127¼	107¼	107⅜	107¼
July 20, 1888	127¼	127¼	127¼	107⅜	107⅜	107⅜
July 27, 1888	127¼	127⅜	127¼	107⅜	107⅜	107⅜
Aug. 3, 1888	127⅜	127½	127⅜	107⅜	107⅜	106
Aug. 10, 1888	127⅞	127⅞	127⅜	106⅞	106⅞	106⅞
Aug. 17, 1888	127⅞	127⅞	127½	106⅞	106⅞	106⅞
Aug. 24, 1888	127⅞	128½	127⅞	106⅛	106⅝	106⅛
Aug. 31, 1888	128½	128½	127½	106⅝	106⅝	106⅝
Sept. 7, 1888	127½	128	127½	106⅝	106¾	106⅝
Sept. 14, 1888	128	128½	128	106¾	106¾	106¾
Sept. 21, 1888	128⅝	128⅞	128⅝	106⅞	107⅛	106⅞
Sept. 28, 1888	129	129	128⅞	107⅛	107⅜	107⅛
Oct. 5, 1888	129	129	129	107⅝	108⅛	107⅝
Oct. 12, 1888	129	129	127¾	108⅛	108¼	108⅛
Oct. 19, 1888	127¾	127¾	126⅞	108¼	108¼	108¼
Oct. 26, 1888	127⅛	127⅝	127⅛	108¼	108⅜	108¼
Nov. 2, 1888	127½	127½	127⅛	108⅜	108⅝	107¾

The quotations given in the above table are not higher than some quotations in previous years, but as the bonds approach maturity their investment-value declines, and this is to be considered in comparing present prices with those prevailing at past periods of time.

The following table will serve to illustrate this:

COMPARATIVE INVESTMENT-VALUE OF UNITED STATES BONDS, AS DETERMINED BY MONTHLY AVERAGES TAKEN AT INTERVALS OF THREE MONTHS DURING THE YEARS 1885, 1886, 1887, AND 1888.

[Compiled from the records of the office of the Actuary of the Treasury.]

Date.	4½ per cent. bonds.		4 per cent. bonds.	
	Average price flat.	Rate of interest realized by investors.	Average price flat.	Rate of interest realized by investors.
1885:	*Per cent.*	*Per cent.*	*Per cent.*	*Per cent.*
January	112.7788	2.655	121.9080	2.720
April	112.4850	2.488	121.8028	2.721
July	112.7525	2.365	122.0462	2.668
October	112.9421	2.250	123.4004	2.610
1886:				
January	112.7000	2.208	123.4325	2.607
April	112.4750	2.150	126.2980	2.444
July	111.8156	2.149	126.4975	2.420
October	111.9855	2.003	128.6650	2.289
1887:				
January	110.2775	2.200	127.8325	2.320
April	110.1047	2.019	129.2451	2.227
July	109.1475	2.340	127.8425	2.284
October	108.5553	2.330	125.7885	2.390
1888:				
January	108.2375	2.289	126.1275	2.341
April	107.1025	2.478	124.0400	2.409
July	107.5175	2.195	127.4825	2.230
October	108.4213	1.698	128.1204	2.178

INCREASE AND REDUCTION OF CAPITAL BY NATIONAL BANKS.

The laws relating to changes in the capital stock of national banks have undergone several modifications, and still need amendment in important particulars as pointed out in Annual Report for 1887. The changes recommended are embodied in the draught of a national-bank code submitted with that report. The latest enactment on the subject is the act of May 1, 1886, and the tables which follow are designed to show the changes which have occurred since that date.

TABLE SHOWING NUMBER OF BANKS INCREASING CAPITAL UNDER THE ACT OF MAY 1, 1886, SHOWING CHANGES IN EACH STATE DURING EACH YEAR SINCE THE PASSAGE OF THE ACT, AMOUNT OF INCREASE AND PERCENTAGE OF INCREASE IN PROPORTION TO CAPITAL.

States and Territories.	1886.			1887.			1888.		
	No.	Amount of increase.	Percentage on former capital.	No.	Amount of increase.	Percentage on former capital.	No.	Amount of increase.	Percentage on former capital.
Maine							1	$100,000	.950
New Hampshire				1	$50,000	.800			
Vermont				1	50,000	.606			
Massachusetts							2	500,000	.518
Rhode Island									
Connecticut									
New York				1	50,000	.005	6	820,000	.945
New Jersey									
Pennsylvania	3	$350,000	.540	1	100,000	.010	3	314,000	.467
Delaware									
Maryland									
District of Columbia									
Virginia									
West Virginia	1	25,000	1.107	1	50,000	2.040	1	5,000	.240
North Carolina									
South Carolina							1	25,000	1.040
Georgia	1	50,000	1.802				2	75,000	2.161
Florida							1	50,000	.557
Alabama									
Mississippi				2	80,000	7.508	1	50,000	.452
Louisiana									
Texas	4	265,000	3.040	7	235,000	2.322	7	445,700	3.764
Arkansas	2	125,000	16.050	2	95,000	10.000			
Kentucky				1	50,000	.379	3	330,000	2.420
Tennessee	1	50,000	.810	4	775	10.354	4	115,000	1.490
Missouri							2	600,000	4.359
Ohio	2	135,000	.305	3	700,000	1.702	6	725,000	1.765
Indiana							2	70,000	.582
Illinois	1	100,000	.305	1	200,000	.682	1	150,000	.501
Michigan	1	50,000	.305	2	105,000	.718	2	135,000	.902
Wisconsin				2	35,000	.066	1	200,000	3.510
Iowa				2	70,000	.688	1	50,000	.489
Minnesota	4	675,000	5.031				6	755,000	5.415
Kansas	5	248,000	3.051	6	460,000	.407	7	350,000	2.680
Nebraska	4	375,000	5.004	4	350,000	4.147	6	870,000	9.280
Nevada							2	132,000	4.080
Oregon				2	170,000	9.030	3	375,000	15.849
Colorado	1	50,000	2.050				5	480,000	13.900
Utah							1	50,000	5.555
Idaho									
Montana				2	57,500	2.071			
Wyoming							1	50,000	4.255
New Mexico	1	50,000	5.080				1	50,000	5.555
Dakota	2	50,000	1.050	2	85,000	2.020	1	100,000	2.615
Washington				4	200,000	10.206	3	75,000	4.021
Arizona									
California	1	200,000	3.053	8	575,000	8.030	7	650,000	7.914
United States	34	2,798,000		59	4,542,500		90	8,696,700	

Total increase in three years, $16,037,200.

TABLE OF BANKS DECREASING CAPITAL UNDER THE ACT OF MAY 1, 1886, SHOWING CHANGES IN EACH STATE DURING EACH YEAR SINCE THE PASSAGE OF THE ACT.

States and Territories.	1886.			1887.			1888.		
	No.	Amount of decrease.	Percentage on former capital.	No.	Amount of decrease.	Percentage on former capital.	No.	Amount of decrease.	Percentage on former capital.
Maine									
New Hampshire									
Vermont				3	$175,000	2.312			
Massachusetts				5	550,000	.560			
Rhode Island									
Connecticut				2	125,000	.516	3	$300,000	1.239
New York				4	240,000	.277	2	162,000	.186
New Jersey							1	20,000	.149
Pennsylvania	1	$75,000	.115	1	100,000	.149	3	125,000	.185
Delaware									
Maryland				1	50,000	.343			
District of Columbia									
Virginia									
West Virginia									
North Carolina									
South Carolina									
Georgia									
Florida									
Alabama				1	50,000	1.404			
Mississippi									
Louisiana	1	100,000	2.919	1	500,000	14.059			
Texas	1	125,000	1.631	1	20,000	.197	1	72,900	.615
Arkansas									
Kentucky				1	50,000	.378			
Tennessee							1	20,000	.258
Missouri									
Ohio	3	200,000	.519	1	75,000	.182	1	100,000	.244
Indiana				1	50,000	.412	1	125,000	1.030
Illinois				2	125,000	.426	2	27,500	.910
Michigan									
Wisconsin									
Iowa	1	10,000	.097	4	100,000	1.573	1	100,000	.918
Minnesota									
Kansas							1	25,000	.191
Nebraska									
Nevada									
Oregon									
Colorado									
Utah									
Idaho									
Montana							1	25,000	1.205
Wyoming									
New Mexico									
Dakota				1	10,000	.204			
Washington									
Arizona									
California									
United States	7	510,000		29	2,280,000		18	1,102,400	

Total decrease in three years, $3,892,400.

CONVERTED AND ORIGINAL BANKS.

National banks are of two classes, viz, institutions already organized under State laws, converted to national banks under section 5154, Revised Statutes of the United States, and national banking associations primarily organized as such under various acts of Congress.

The following tables show the history of these two classes:

WHOLE NUMBER OF STATE BANKS CONVERTED TO NATIONAL BANKING ASSOCIATIONS, THEIR CAPITAL AT DATE OF CONVERSION, PRESENT CAPITAL AND SURPLUS, SPECIFYING SUCH AS HAVE SINCE GONE INTO VOLUNTARY LIQUIDATION, AND SUCH AS HAVE BECOME INSOLVENT.

Years.	Whole number converted.	Existing.				Voluntary liquidation.				Insolvent.		
		Number.	Capital at date of conversion.	Present capital.	Surplus.	Number.	Capital at date of conversion.	Capital at date of liquidation.	Surplus at date of liquidation.	Number.	Capital at date of conversion.	Capital at date of failure.
1863	12	12	$6,110,000	$9,610,000	$3,048,000							
1864	150	145	66,589,500	71,965,200	27,214,100	2	$260,000	$250,000	$38,900	3	$417,000	$367,000
1865	284	220	58,395,000	57,135,700	28,354,800	50	12,496,200	10,582,200	1,996,400	14	4,401,100	4,371,100
1866	6	3	860,300	250,000	43,000	2	275,000	250,000	52,200	1	3,410,300	2,500,000
1867	1					1	50,000	100,000	11,100			
1868	3	1	250,000	50,000	10,000	2	200,000	200,000	29,700			
1869												
1870	1	1	1,000,000	1,500,000	300,000							
1871	5	2	1,378,000	925,000	164,000	3	278,000	300,000	35,000			
1872	5	3	1,110,000	1,030,000	211,000	2	150,000	150,000	13,500			
1873	4	4	855,000	605,000	221,000							
1874	11	9	2,244,000	2,410,000	540,100	2	250,000	250,000	15,500			
1875	7	5	850,000	675,000	229,500	2	200,000	130,000	12,000			
1876	2	2	161,000	141,000	29,500							
1877	5	3	680,000	830,000	320,030	1	50,000	50,000	4,500	1	130,000	130,000
1878	7	7	710,000	769,000	244,000							
1879	10	10	1,285,000	1,435,000	470,560							
1880	6	6	1,147,000	1,340,000	354,700							
1881	11	11	1,445,700	1,863,200	479,400							
1882	13	12	990,300	1,630,300	331,900					1	200,000	300,000
1883	16	11	925,000	1,075,000	158,400	5	305,000	300,000	11,200			
1884	1	1	50,000	100,000	600,000							
1885	5	5	850,000	850,000	170,500							
1886*	10	8	2,100,000	2,610,000	503,100	1	50,000	50,000	500	1	50,000	50,000
1887†	11	11	1,350,000	1,500,000	227,600							
1888‡	7	7	350,000	300,000	13,300							
Totals	593	499	151,685,800	160,769,400	64,238,400	73	14,504,000	12,602,200	2,220,500	21	8,608,400	7,718,100

* To November 1. † From November 1, 1886, to November 1, 1887. ‡ From November 1, 1887, to November 1, 1888.

Percentage of capital of national banks, organized as such, that went into voluntary liquidation . 14.5
Percentage of capital of national banks, organized as such, that went into insolvency . 2.6
Percentage of capital of national banks, organized as such, that are in existence . 82.9

Percentage of capital of converted banks that went into voluntary liquidation . 7
Percentage of capital of converted banks that went into insolvency . 4.3
Percentage of capital of converted banks that are still in existence . 88.7

Percentage of increase of capital of national banks organized as such . 18.6
Percentage of increase of capital of converted banks . 6

WHOLE NUMBER OF NATIONAL BANKS OF PRIMARY ORGANIZATION UNDER THE NATIONAL-BANK LAWS, CAPITAL AT DATE OF ORGANIZATION, AND PRESENT CAPITAL AND SURPLUS, SPECIFYING SUCH AS HAVE SINCE GONE INTO VOLUNTARY LIQUIDATION, AND SUCH AS HAVE BECOME INSOLVENT.

Year.	Whole number organized.	Existing.				Voluntary liquidation.				Insolvent.		
		Number.	Capital at date of organization.	Present capital.	Surplus.	Number.	Capital at date of organization.	Capital at date of liquidation.	Surplus at date of liquidation.	Number.	Capital at date of organization.	Capital at date of failure.
1863	474	294	$40,428,900	$61,842,450	$25,557,200	147	$14,984,200	$25,424,600	$7,839,300	33	$3,620,000	$5,569,500
1864	104	69	11,848,100	19,523,450	9,641,300	31	4,310,000	6,166,000	1,558,900	4	450,000	500,000
1865	603	437	107,503,000	111,198,875	37,068,911	146	19,816,700	18,675,000	4,934,400	20	2,525,000	3,610,000
1866	33	23	2,730,000	5,035,000	2,230,200	8	800,000	775,300	176,200	2	100,000	150,000
1867	9	7	850,000	1,800,000	654,000	2	150,000	150,000	14,300			
1868	10	5	410,000	450,000	141,000	4	400,000	800,000	127,500	1	100,000	100,000
1869	8	4	850,000	650,000	215,000	2	260,000	310,000	48,500	2	350,000	350,000
1870	62	38	4,188,000	4,998,000	1,534,400	22	2,511,000	3,130,000	475,300	2	300,000	350,000
1871	148	108	11,568,000	14,363,900	5,168,900	34	3,040,000	3,000,000	656,000	6	1,100,000	1,400,000
1872	156	97	9,074,700	12,951,100	4,042,800	48	4,255,000	3,843,100	585,100	11	1,450,000	1,485,000
1873	53	38	4,655,000	4,611,000	1,283,100	13	925,000	1,125,000	116,700	2	370,000	350,000
1874	72	46	3,726,500	4,483,000	1,443,600	22	1,350,000	1,320,000	86,900	4	350,000	350,000
1875	94	79	10,012,000	11,224,000	2,964,200	14	1,000,000	1,010,000	75,800	1	50,000	50,000
1876	27	23	2,020,800	2,377,800	743,200	4	250,000	250,000	11,400			
1877	26	21	1,864,000	2,749,000	1,368,000	3	150,000	150,000	21,000	2	300,000	1,011,300
1878	23	18	1,625,000	1,760,000	417,300	5	250,000	250,000	21,400			
1879	30	25	2,550,000	3,595,000	691,200	4	200,000	200,000	13,200	1	60,000	60,000
1880	47	40	4,522,100	5,797,100	1,395,400	6	950,000	750,000	86,800	1	50,000	50,000
1881	97	84	7,735,000	9,531,000	2,731,700	11	1,820,000	1,870,000	95,100	2	555,000	1,050,000
1882	230	208	28,068,000	34,977,000	9,334,300	18	1,630,000	1,830,000	157,200	4	225,000	225,000
1883	236	208	22,182,000	26,234,000	4,465,900	22	2,935,000	2,715,000	109,000	6	550,000	350,000
1884	179	169	16,719,000	20,106,800	3,090,800	9	1,009,000	1,000,000	21,000	1	50,000	50,000
1885	142	139	13,593,000	14,478,000	2,216,300	3	200,000	200,000	5,500			
1886*	142	135	15,128,000	16,855,000	1,545,200	6	425,000	425,000	11,000	1	1,000,000	1,000,000
1887†	214	212	29,096,000	30,331,000	1,250,100	2	100,000	100,000	3,500			
1888‡	125	125	11,603,000	10,309,741	72,600							
Total	3,344	2,652	361,550,100	432,242,216	121,266,611	586	63,711,900	75,469,000	17,251,000	106	13,555,000	18,060,800

* To November 1. †From November 1, 1886, to November 1, 1887. ‡From November 1, 1887, to November 1, 1888.

SUMMARY OF NATIONAL BANKS ORGANIZED AND DISSOLVED SINCE FEBRUARY 25, 1863, AND THE NUMBER EXISTING NOVEMBER 1, 1888.

Banks organized.	Number.	Dissolved.					Now existing.		Remarks.
		In liquidation, voluntary or by expiration.		Failed.		Total number dissolved.	Number.	Per cent.	The difference ($15,553) in the aggregate amount of surplus, as shown by this and the preceding table, when compared with the table on page ——, is accounted for by the fact that in estimating the surplus for this table all amounts under $50 were rejected.
		Number.	Per cent.	Number.	Per cent.				
Converted from State system	593	73	12	21	3	94	499	85	Of 659 banks which have gone into voluntary liquidation 503 took that step for the purpose of winding up their affairs, 79 for the purpose of reorganization, and 77 went into liquidation by reason of expiration of charter, 38 of them having since been reorganized.
Other banks	3,344	586	17	106	3	692	2,652	80	
Total	3,937	659	17	127	3	786	3,151	80	

EXTENSION OF THE CORPORATE EXISTENCE OF NATIONAL BANKS.

During the past year seven associations have availed themselves of the provision made by the act of July 12, 1882, for the extension of the corporate existence of national banks. Annexed is a table brought down to October 31, 1888, showing the capital of these extended banks and their geographical distribution.

TABLE SHOWING, BY STATES, THE NUMBER AND CAPITAL OF NATIONAL BANKS, THE CORPORATE EXISTENCE OF WHICH WAS EXTENDED PRIOR TO NOVEMBER 1, 1888.

States and Territories.	No. of banks.	Capital.	States and Territories.	No. of banks.	Capital.
Alabama	2	$350,000	Montana	1	$500,000
Arkansas	1	250,000	Nebraska	3	750,000
Colorado	3	400,000	New Hampshire	36	4,655,000
Connecticut	73	22,450,820	New Jersey	48	9,783,350
Delaware	11	1,503,185	New York	222	72,672,460
District of Columbia	2	500,000	North Carolina	3	650,000
Georgia	6	1,450,000	South Carolina	3	850,000
Illinois	48	6,240,000	Ohio	82	14,854,000
Indiana	32	4,157,000	Oregon	1	250,000
Iowa	25	2,695,000	Pennsylvania	107	44,704,390
Idaho	1	100,000	Rhode Island	59	19,959,800
Kansas	3	300,000	Tennessee	6	1,750,000
Kentucky	11	3,150,000	Texas	4	625,000
Louisiana	2	1,300,000	Vermont	20	5,256,000
Maine	53	8,630,000	Virginia	10	2,016,000
Maryland	29	12,069,000	West Virginia	11	1,341,000
Massachusetts	200	85,962,500	Wisconsin	19	1,685,000
Michigan	19	1,575,000			
Minnesota	8	2,225,000	Total	1,241	340,819,505
Missouri	8	3,150,000			

TOTAL NUMBER OF BANKS ORGANIZED UNDER THE NATIONAL CURRENCY ACT OF FEBRUARY 25, 1863, AND THE NATIONAL-BANK ACT OF JUNE 3, 1864, THE NUMBER EXTENDED UNDER THE ACT OF JULY 12, 1882, AND STILL IN OPERATION UNDER THEIR ORIGINAL CERTIFICATES OF ORGANIZATION, AND THE TOTAL NUMBER IN OPERATION OCTOBER 31, 1888.

	Banks organized.						
	Totals.	Under act February 25, 1863.		Under act June 3, 1864.			
				Before 1882.		Since 1882.	
Originally organized	2,766	......	488	......	2,278		
Out of existence July 12, 1882	493	......	146	......	347		
In operation July 12, 1882	2,273	......	342	......	1,931		
Organized since July 12, 1882	......	......	......	......	......	......	1,171
Since passed into voluntary liquidation to wind up affairs	173	7	......	111	......	55	
Since in voluntary liquidation by expiration of corporate existence	77	20	......	57			
Placed in hands of receivers	35	1	......	*23	......	11	
			28		191		66
Extended under act of July 12, 1882	1,241	......	314	927			
Passed out of the system since extension	......	......	......	26			
Still in existence	......	......	......	901			
To reach the term of corporate existence	......	......	......	839			
Passed into voluntary liquidation since extension	......	3					
Placed in hands of receivers since extension	......	5					
			8				
Still in operation under original organization certificate	2,046	......	306	1,740			
Total number in operation October 31, 1888	3,151	......	306	......	1,740	......	1,10

* Twenty-four banks were in this category, but one was restored to solvency and resumed business.

From the foregoing table it will be found that all of the banks organized under the national currency act of 1863 have either ceased to exist or have had their corporate existence extended, while of those organized prior to July 12, 1882, under the national-bank act of 1864, 1,740 are still in operation under their original certificates of organization.

The following table shows how many of these banks will reach the expiration of their corporate existence during each year from 1889 to 1902, inclusive, with their capital and circulation:

Years.	No. of banks.	Capital.	Circulation.	Years.	No. of banks.	Capital.	Circulation.
1889	3	$600,000	$184,500	1897	24	$3,410,000	$1,171,205
1890	61	9,580,500	364,000	1898	25	2,670,000	1,198,350
1891	97	12,358,900	4,040,685	1899	30	4,995,000	2,270,700
1892	100	13,815,100	4,562,760	1900	50	7,807,100	2,153,330
1893	38	4,701,000	1,982,925	1901	108	14,660,150	3,702,350
1894	63	7,628,000	2,812,720	1902	132	21,177,300	5,352,350
1895	76	11,259,000	4,431,610				
1896	23	2,173,800	980,650	Total	830	116,842,850	35,214,225

The number, capital, and circulation of the national banks of which the periods of succession terminated between October 31, 1887, and October 31, 1888, are shown by the following table, which also indicates the number of which the corporate existence has been extended:

Date.	No. of banks that have expired.	Capital.	Circulation.	No. of banks that have extended.	Capital.	Circulation.
1887.						
November	1	$250,000	$45,000	1	$250,000	$45,000
1888.						
January	1	100,000	22,500	1	100,000	22,500
February	2	200,000	67,500	Liquidation		
March	1	100,000	22,500	1	100,000	22,500
May	1	75,000	18,000	1	75,000	18,000
June	1	100,000	22,500	Failed		
August	1	125,000	28,800	1	125,000	28,800
September	1	50,000	45,000	1	50,000	45,000
October	1	50,000	11,250	1	50,000	11,250
Total	10	1,050,000	283,050	7	750,000	193,050

The corporate existence of one national bank, with a capital of $50,000, will expire in November of this year, and that of three national banks, with an aggregate capital of $600,000, will expire during the year 1889, as shown in the following table:

NATIONAL BANKS OF WHICH THE CORPORATE EXISTENCE WILL EXPIRE DURING THE YEAR 1889, WITH THE DATE OF THE EXPIRATION, THE AMOUNT OF CAPITAL STOCK OF EACH BANK, THE UNITED STATES BONDS ON DEPOSIT WITH THE TREASURER, AND THE AMOUNT OF CIRCULATION ISSUED THEREON.

Charter number.	Title of bank.	State.	Expiration of corporate existence.	Capital stock.	U. S. bonds.	Circulation.
1689	The Ohio National Bank of Cleveland	Ohio	Jan. 1, 1889	$400,000	$56,000	$50,400
1692	The First National Bank of Murfreesborough	Tennessee.	Feb. 27, 1889	100,000	100,000	90,000
1694	The National Bank of Lebanon	Kentucky.	April 7, 1889	100,000	50,000	45,000

SHAREHOLDERS IN BANKS.

The table subjoined hereto exhibits the distribution of national-bank stock as reported by the banks on the first Monday in July, 1888.

DISTRIBUTION, BY STATES, ETC., NUMBER, AND PAR VALUE AT $100 EACH, OF SHARES

	State, etc.	No. of banks.	Number of shares held by—		Same, in detail, held by—				
			State residents.	Non-State residents.	Natural persons.	Religious, charitable, and educational institutions.	Municipal corporations.	Savings banks, loan and trust and insurance companies.	All other corporations.
1	Maine	75	100, 557	6, 043	80, 469	3, 707	116	22, 230	78
2	New Hampshire	49	56, 439	5, 611	49, 036	496	....	12, 378	140
3	Vermont	49	65, 533	10, 127	71, 851	194	272	3, 179	164
4	Massachusetts	198	412, 096	35, 309	363, 635	7, 303	139	75, 488	780
5	Boston	54	473, 013	37, 587	283, 075	14, 798	107	212, 003	917
6	Rhode Island	60	188, 653	14, 188	163, 780	6, 733	705	30, 477	1, 137
7	Connecticut	83	218, 818	22, 625	156, 509	10, 394	277	73, 395	778
	Division No. 1	568	1, 516, 009	131, 490	1, 109, 054	43, 085	1, 616	429, 150	3, 994
8	New York	270	335, 150	16, 769	350, 491	659	....	647	131
9	New York City	46	319, 998	171, 002	458, 813	4, 084	24	31, 968	511
10	Albany	6	16, 463	1, 037	16, 691	220	....	589	....
11	New Jersey	84	118, 376	14, 207	130, 009	632	3	1, 871	68
12	Pennsylvania	245	315, 605	21, 398	334, 240	1, 066	5	1, 176	516
13	Philadelphia	43	216, 550	13, 530	226, 460	839	10	2, 574	197
14	Pittsburgh	24	100, 873	3, 427	100, 668	719	....	2, 877	36
	Division No. 2	718	1, 423, 024	241, 370	1, 612, 372	8, 819	42	41, 702	1, 459
15	Delaware	18	17, 709	3, 546	20, 771	270	....	243	61
16	Maryland	31	26, 957	1, 210	26, 958	454	....	263	492
17	Baltimore	17	110, 268	6, 865	98, 562	7, 179	1, 151	9, 669	572
19	Washington	1	2, 050	461	2, 410	....	....	110	....
18	District of Columbia	7	12, 044	3, 706	15, 607	....	....	143	....
20	Virginia	25	30, 480	7, 483	36, 358	448	....	342	815
21	West Virginia	19	15, 790	2, 720	17, 300	900	10	....	300
	Division No. 3	118	215, 397	25, 901	217, 966	9, 251	1, 161	10, 770	2, 240
22	North Carolina	18	19, 845	2, 915	22, 701	....	....	29	30
23	South Carolina	16	16, 434	1, 296	17, 000	80	....	530	60
24	Georgia	23	22, 573	10, 037	31, 153	14	....	1, 429	14
25	Florida	13	7, 171	1, 829	9, 000	....	....	....	....
26	Alabama	21	31, 420	4, 020	35, 209	....	....	211	20
27	Mississippi	12	7, 689	2, 861	10, 545	....	....	5	....
28	Louisiana	5	4, 855	145	4, 960	9	....	....	31
29	New Orleans	8	20, 914	8, 306	28, 278	4	....	968	....
30	Texas	98	90, 757	23, 900	114, 475	30	....	152	....
31	Arkansas	7	8, 227	1, 273	9, 500	....	....	....	....
32	Kentucky	60	95, 419	5, 610	100, 118	446	....	465	....
33	Louisville	9	31, 360	4, 155	35, 119	225	....	121	50
34	Tennessee	41	69, 827	7, 473	76, 845	55	....	400	....
	Division No. 4	331	426, 521	73, 820	494, 963	863	....	4, 310	205
35	Ohio	197	228, 849	15, 141	241, 400	219	....	2, 371	....
36	Cincinnati	14	79, 982	11, 818	88, 630	380	100	2, 476	214
37	Cleveland	9	63, 882	2, 618	66, 500	....	....	....	....
38	Indiana	94	108, 502	10, 893	119, 154	24	....	130	87
39	Illinois	162	135, 901	10, 489	146, 033	33	....	305	19
40	Chicago	19	132, 256	20, 244	151, 725	....	....	775	....
41	Michigan	100	98, 080	10, 666	108, 675	34	....	20	17
42	Detroit	8	37, 851	2, 149	39, 960	40	....	....	....
43	Wisconsin	56	43, 226	3, 774	46, 975	10	....	15	....
44	Milwaukee	3	5, 263	3, 237	8, 500	....	....	....	....
	Division No. 5	662	933, 792	91, 029	1, 017, 552	740	100	6, 092	337
45	Iowa	129	82, 719	18, 881	101, 114	....	....	486	....
46	Minnesota	55	97, 076	42, 124	137, 039	87	....	1, 935	139
47	Missouri	34	21, 549	2, 761	21, 270	....	....	40	....
48	Saint Louis	4	25, 155	6, 845	31, 504	201	....	295	....
49	Kansas City	10	25, 092	39, 908	60, 389	73	....	4, 538	....
50	Saint Joseph	2	2, 357	643	3, 000	....	....	....	....
51	Kansas	157	86, 534	38, 957	122, 278	85	....	2, 738	390
52	Nebraska	96	49, 302	12, 538	61, 703	....	....	137	....
53	Omaha	7	16, 968	7, 032	24, 000	....	....	....	....
	Division No. 6	494	406, 722	169, 779	565, 447	446	....	10, 079	529

OF STOCK OF NATIONAL BANKS ON THE FIRST MONDAY OF JULY, 1888.

Total shares issued.	Number of shareholders.					Number of shareholders owning specific amounts.				
Number reduced to par value of $100 each.	Natural persons.	Corporations.	Resident.	Non-resident.	Total.	Owning shares to the par value of $1,000 and less.	Over $1,000 and less than $5,000.	Over $5,000 and less than $30,000.	Over $30,000.	
106,600	6,925	708	7,014	619	7,633	5,396	1,828	397	12	1
62,050	3,690	191	3,400	481	3,881	2,668	995	203	15	2
75,000	3,864	60	3,471	453	3,924	2,495	1,118	293	18	3
447,405	30,269	1,449	28,630	3,088	31,718	22,189	7,802	1,569	68	4
511,500	16,819	3,467	17,875	2,411	20,286	11,209	6,289	2,663	125	5
202,841	12,224	632	11,353	1,503	12,856	8,105	3,877	839	35	6
241,443	12,987	1,247	12,426	1,808	14,234	9,706	3,587	806	85	7
1,647,409	86,778	7,754	84,169	10,363	94,532	61,768	25,586	6,820	358	
351,928	15,183	57	14,140	1,160	15,240	8,516	5,154	1,488	82	8
491,000	14,862	507	8,813	6,556	15,369	6,804	5,880	2,504	181	9
17,500	609	9	562	56	618	292	228	94	4	10
132,583	9,243	74	8,255	1,062	9,317	6,410	2,397	490	14	11
337,003	21,909	177	21,230	946	22,176	14,906	5,759	1,446	65	12
230,080	10,739	133	10,009	863	10,872	6,363	3,345	1,126	38	13
104,300	3,931	69	3,818	182	4,000	2,010	1,433	530	27	14
1,664,394	76,566	1,026	66,827	10,765	77,592	45,307	24,196	7,678	411	
21,345	1,742	23	1,416	349	1,765	1,072	573	118	2	15
28,167	1,938	43	1,888	93	1,981	1,335	547	96	3	16
117,133	5,224	264	5,068	420	5,488	3,192	1,782	487	27	17
2,520	157	1	119	39	158	83	66	9	....	19
15,750	608	2	513	97	610	345	199	62	4	18
37,903	1,518	16	1,260	274	1,534	925	399	201	9	20
18,510	900	4	759	145	904	533	294	72	5	21
241,388	12,087	353	11,023	1,417	12,440	7,485	3,860	1,045	50	
22,760	865	2	726	141	867	449	301	110	7	22
17,730	1,075	32	1,040	67	1,107	759	279	66	3	23
32,610	1,056	24	868	212	1,080	621	267	178	14	24
9,000	308	....	216	92	308	186	83	36	3	25
35,440	849	6	698	157	855	369	277	195	14	26
10,550	355	1	274	82	356	185	106	64	1	27
5,000	99	2	97	4	101	42	29	26	4	28
29,250	701	5	550	156	706	320	228	144	14	29
114,657	2,564	9	1,870	703	2,573	1,185	738	593	57	30
9,500	242	....	201	41	242	112	84	43	3	31
101,029	3,850	40	3,668	222	3,890	1,952	1,393	528	17	32
35,515	1,279	11	1,168	122	1,290	699	405	179	7	33
77,300	2,422	7	2,205	224	2,429	1,065	916	427	21	34
500,341	15,665	139	13,581	2,223	15,804	7,854	5,196	2,589	165	
243,990	7,997	53	7,497	553	8,050	3,826	2,876	1,286	62	35
91,800	1,504	36	1,396	144	1,540	428	536	531	45	36
66,500	865	....	801	64	865	169	270	390	36	37
119,395	2,410	6	2,128	288	2,416	868	857	630	61	38
146,300	4,432	10	4,063	379	4,442	2,226	1,405	760	51	39
152,500	1,614	4	1,351	267	1,618	354	485	688	91	40
108,746	3,312	4	2,964	352	3,316	1,455	1,107	666	28	41
40,000	627	1	579	49	628	142	214	246	26	42
47,000	1,303	2	1,143	162	1,305	613	302	287	13	43
8,500	144	....	40	104	144	52	67	19	6	44
1,024,821	24,208	116	21,962	2,362	24,324	10,133	8,269	5,503	419	
101,600	3,317	10	2,430	897	3,327	1,682	1,081	520	35	45
139,200	3,004	24	2,095	933	3,028	1,164	1,009	796	59	46
24,310	826	1	691	136	827	423	265	133	6	47
32,000	704	7	454	257	711	282	251	163	15	48
65,000	1,593	51	366	1,278	1,644	748	494	379	23	49
3,000	48	....	28	20	48	20	13	13	2	50
125,491	4,157	64	2,598	1,623	4,221	2,381	1,126	677	37	51
61,900	1,534	5	1,130	409	1,539	682	458	374	25	52
24,000	133	....	101	32	133	21	17	70	25	53
576,501	15,316	162	9,803	5,585	15,478	7,403	4,714	3,134	227	

DISTRIBUTION, BY STATES, ETC., NUMBER, AND PAR VALUE AT $100 EACH, OF SHARES

	State, etc.	No. of banks.	Number of shares held by—		Same, in detail, held by—				
			State residents.	Non-State residents.	Natural persons.	Religious, charitable, and educational institutions.	Municipal corporations.	Savings banks, loan and trust and insurance companies.	All other corporations.
54	Colorado	33	26,752	4,008	30,825	....	....	25	....
55	Nevada	2	1,817	683	2,500	....	....	....	....
56	California	35	46,980	4,270	50,978	72	....	200	....
57	San Francisco	3	25,842	1,158	26,068	....	....	932	....
58	Oregon	25	10,967	2,933	22,815	....	....	85	....
	Division No. 7	98	121,358	13,142	133,186	72	....	1,242	....
59	Dakota	58	18,950	16,800	35,401	....	7	332	10
60	Idaho	7	3,650	850	4,500	....	....	....	....
61	Montana	17	14,438	5,062	19,500	....	....	....	....
62	New Mexico	9	6,257	2,243	8,440	....	....	35	25
63	Utah	7	7,610	890	8,500	....	....	....	....
64	Washington	24	11,443	7,207	18,559	....	....	91	....
65	Wyoming	8	5,722	5,028	10,670	....	....	....	80
66	Arizona	1	515	485	1,000	....	....	....	....
	Division No. 8	131	68,585	38,565	106,570	....	7	458	115
	United States	3,120	5,111,408	785,186	5,317,110	63,876	2,926	503,803	8,870

OF STOCK OF NATIONAL BANKS ON THE FIRST MONDAY OF JULY, 1888—Continued.

Total shares issued.	Number of shareholders.					Number of shareholders owning specific amounts.				
Number reduced to par value of $100 each.	Natural persons.	Corporations.	Resident.	Non-resident.	Total.	Owning shares to the par value of $1,000 and less.	Over $1,000 and less than $5,000.	Over $5,000 and less than $30,000.	Over $30,000.	
30,850	568	1	470	99	569	235	162	160	12	54
2,500	38	....	31	7	38	4	15	18	1	55
51,250	893	4	801	96	897	284	319	265	29	56
27,000	141	3	133	11	144	17	40	66	21	57
22,900	325	1	293	33	326	94	86	136	10	58
134,500	1,965	9	1,728	246	1,974	634	622	645	73	
35,750	1,040	8	596	452	1,048	537	312	195	4	59
4,500	83	....	67	16	83	33	23	26	1	60
19,500	261	....	187	74	261	111	68	68	14	61
8,500	203	3	120	86	206	86	75	41	4	62
8,500	253	....	238	15	253	137	76	37	3	63
18,650	377	2	249	130	379	162	93	119	5	64
10,750	142	1	59	84	143	30	42	64	7	65
1,000	6	....	4	2	6	3	....	1	2	66
107,150	2,365	14	1,520	859	2,379	1,099	689	551	40	
5,896,594	234,950	9,573	210,703	33,820	244,523	141,683	73,132	27,965	1,743	

NOTE.—The difference in the amount of capital stock, as shown by this table and by the reports of condition on October 4, is accounted for by the fact that twenty-two banks were organized during the three months just preceding that date, and other banks increased their capital stock.

DISSOLUTION.

The total number of national banks organized since February 25, 1863, is 3,937, of which there are now in operation, as shown elsewhere, 3,151; passed out of the system 786, accounted for thus:

Passed into voluntary liquidation to wind up their affairs	512
Less number afterward placed in hands of receivers	9
	503
Passed into liquidation for purpose of reorganization	79
Passed into liquidation upon expiration of corporate existence	*77
Placed in hands of receivers	128
	787
Less restored to solvency and resumed business	1
Total passed out of system	786

* Thirty-eight of these have been reorganized.

The corporate existence of ten national banks expired during the year ending October 31, 1888; of these, seven obtained an extension in accordance with the provisions of the act of July 12, 1882, two suffered dissolution, and one failed.

FAILED BANKS.

Eight national banks, with an aggregate capital of $1,900,000, failed and were placed in the hands of receivers during the year, as is shown in the following tabulated statement, to which is appended an account of the chief cause of failure in each case. In one case the creditors have been paid in full, principal and interest; in two others they have received 80 per cent., and in the remaining cases 40, 25, and 20 per cent., respectively, on account of the claims proved:

STATEMENT OF FAILED BANKS, THEIR CAPITAL, SURPLUS, AND LIABILITIES ACCORDING TO LAST REPORT OF CONDITION.

Name and location of bank.	Date of authority to commence business.	Date of failure.	Receiver appointed.	As shown at date of last report of condition in each case.			
				Capital.	Surplus and undivided profits.	Other liabilities.*	Date of last report of condition.
Fifth National Bank, Saint Louis, Mo	Dec. 12, 1882	1887. Nov. 7	1887. Nov. 15	$300,000	$59,456	$1,305,883	1887. Oct. 5
First National Bank, Auburn, N. Y.†	Feb. 4, 1864	1888. Jan. 23	1888. Feb. 10	150,000	42,379	611,703	Dec. 7
Metropolitan National Bank, Cincinnati, Ohio	July 12, 1881	Feb. 6	Feb. 20	1,000,000	221,810	1,585,840	Dec. 7
Commercial National Bank, Dubuque, Iowa	Mar. 11, 1871	Mar. 20	Apr. 2	100,000	26,410	736,771	1888. Feb. 14
State National Bank, Raleigh, N. C	June 17, 1868	Mar. 27	Mar. 31	100,000	27,561	351,155	Feb. 14
Second National Bank, Xenia, Ohio†	Feb. 24, 1864	May 2	May 9	150,000	20,020	364,872	Feb. 14
Madison National Bank, Madison, Dak	Dec. 7, 1886	June 13	June 23	50,000	6,166	86,738	Apr. 3
Lowell National Bank, Lowell, Mich.†	June 14, 1865	Sept. 11	Sept. 19	50,000	17,768	126,023	June 30
Total				1,900,000	421,570	5,168,985	

* Total, as per report, except capital, surplus, circulation, undivided profits, and unpaid dividends.
† Extended.

The Fifth National Bank of Saint Louis, Mo., closed its doors November 7, 1887, and on November 9 its cashier was arrested on a warrant charging fraud and falsification of entries, and placed under bond. The case has not yet been reached in the courts, and the cashier is still at large.

The failure may be traced to the fact that the bank, originally a savings institution, was carrying, when it became a national bank, a considerable amount of doubtful and worthless paper, which was allowed to remain among the assets. Then the officers and some of the directors of the new organization were interested in various businesses carried on with the funds of the bank, and dependent wholly upon that support. The general administration was weak and in some respects vicious. Overdrafts were permitted in large amounts, and bad accounts were disguised by passing fictitious drafts through the bank. The statutes were violated with respect to overloans, false entries were made upon the books to deceive the national-bank examiner and the Comptroller, and these were concealed by the use of notes in several names for money borrowed by one and the same party.

The directors claimed to be unaware of these transactions, and sought to excuse themselves by saying that the bank was managed wholly by the president and cashier to whom alone the facts were known, and on whose statement the directors relied.

In December, 1886, at a meeting of the shareholders it had been resolved to increase the capital stock from $300,000 to $500,000, and subsequent publication was made in the Saint Louis newspapers that the stock of the bank was $500,000.

After the failure it transpired that the payment on account of the new shares amounted to only a little over $126,000, and the subscribers to the increased capital now insist upon being treated as depositors to the extent of the amount paid in on the subscriptions. The receiver claims that these subscriptions are binding, and the question is now pending in the courts.

As preliminary to an action against the directors of the bank to establish their individual liability under the provisions of section 5239, Revised Statutes, proceedings were taken by the Comptroller for the forfeiture of all the rights, privileges, and franchises of the association, and in April last the United States circuit court adjudged the forfeiture.

A dividend of 50 per cent. was paid to the creditors about three months after date of failure, and, as will be seen elsewhere, 30 per cent. more has been paid since, making 80 per cent. within the first twelve months of the receivership.

The First National Bank of Auburn, N. Y., closed its doors on the morning of January 23, the cashier and one of the book-keepers having previously absconded to Canada, taking with them a considerable amount of money belonging to the bank. The association was found to be hopelessly insolvent; past-due paper in large amounts had been accumulating for some years, and leaves which had been cut out of the ledgers and hidden, showed when discovered, that overdrafts had been carried to an amount greatly exceeding the capital stock of the bank. The records had been negligently kept, and in many cases entries were altered and false entries were made, so that the ascertainment of the condition of the association has been slow and difficult, while transactions to considerable amounts are still involved in obscurity. In one case, however, funds of the bank have been traced into a local "bucket shop." The bank was sustaining outside business firms with large loans and overdrafts, having little or no security.

The case of this bank furnishes still another instance of an officer enjoying unlimited confidence, mismanaging its affairs, squandering its resources, and finally stealing its cash under the eyes of directors and stockholders. It also adds another to the numerous illustrations of the temptation to dishonesty which is the direct effect of the facility of escape to Canada and the immunity from extradition enjoyed by such fugitives.

A dividend of 25 per cent. has been paid during the year, but there seems little doubt that the loss to depositors will be heavy.

The Metropolitan National Bank of Cincinnati was reported by the national-bank examiner, in January, as being in a perilously weak condition. The officers and directors were large borrowers, and the management of the bank was found to be inefficient and unbusinesslike. Irregular means had been resorted to in order to cover up large loans, and evidences of the publication of false reports and of violations of the provisions of section 5209 of the Revised Statutes were discovered.

The examination showed, however, that the assets were undoubtedly sufficient to pay creditors in full, and the examiner united with the directors in an effort to tide over the exigency. Considerable collections were made from the directors and large stockholders who were debtors to the bank, and from those who were unable to pay, the examiner succeeded in obtaining available securities to a considerable amount. The directors on their part fortified their cash resources by obtaining loans from other banks, and for a time there seemed to be a fair prospect that the bank could be saved from suspension. It proved impracticable, however, to make headway against the growing distrust among depositors, and the board of directors resolved, on February 6, to close the doors. A receiver was appointed, and the president and vice-president are now under indictment.

Every effort was made by the receiver to expedite the liquidation, and there was no litigation of any consequence, so that within six weeks from the date of failure the creditors were paid in full, principal and interest, and assets to the nominal value of upward of $1,300,000 were turned over to the agent of the stockholders in accordance with the provisions of the act approved June 30, 1876.

The Commercial National Bank of Dubuque, Iowa, failed March 20. The bank was wrecked by the diversion of funds to sustain outside business interests of the president and those of his immediate family connections. An amount not less than four times the capital stock of the bank was borrowed by members of the family and persons connected with them in support of enterprises which depended upon the bank for their existence, and the immediate cause of failure was the inability of these borrowers to liquidate their indebtedness.

The violation of the statute, which the excessive and illegal loans involved, was concealed by making use of the names of irresponsible persons, and the security upon which the directors affected to rely has proved to be insufficient or worthless.

Dividends amounting to 40 per cent. have been paid, and an assessment to the full extent authorized by law has been levied upon the stockholders.

The State National Bank of Raleigh, N. C., closed its doors March 27, the president and cashier having absconded to Canada, taking with them about $25,000. An examination disclosed the fact that the bank had been completely wrecked, and that preparations for defalcation had been in progress for a long time.

The rogues in this instance had resorted even to forgery, and thereby became amenable to extradition. So swift was the pursuit and arrest that most of the stolen money was found still concealed in the clothing of the prisoners and in the original packages.

The offense being one against the State statutes, subsequent proceedings are beyond the official cognizance of the Comptroller of the Currency.

The history of this association is instructive.

A private banker in Raleigh organized the bank, took shares for the assets he turned over to it, and upon the credit thus created he obtained deposits enough to carry on business. His assets, taken as capital, were really worth very little, if anything. His management of the bank was no better than that of his private business. He went on making bad debts and unprofitable investments, and when he died, in 1883, his successors continued to do likewise. His estate and family owned most of the stock, and were also debtors to nearly the par value of their shares. His wife assumed the presidency of the bank, and her brother, the cashier, succeeded to the actual management. Always weak he rapidly became dishonest, and finally ended his career by entering into collusion with the new president, a son-in-law of the deceased founder of the bank, to seize all the plunder they could and decamp.

A dividend of 20 per cent. was declared and distributed June 8.

The Second National Bank of Xenia, Ohio, closed its doors May 2, having been reduced to insolvency by the negligence of the directors and the incompetency of its officers. The cashier was utterly unfit for his position, and nobody else looked after matters. Bad debts and large overdrafts were allowed to accumulate, and the bank's funds were locked up in all sorts of investments that should never have been even entertained.

The directors, active business men, supposed to be in good financial condition, were large borrowers, and allowed their over-due obligations to lie unpaid.

The receiver has collected about $190,000 from the assets, and the directors have contributed $42,000 more in order to facilitate a speedy liquidation. There has been but little litigation attending the administration of this trust.

Dividends amounting to 80 per cent. have been paid since the failure.

The Madison National Bank of Madison, Dak., was organized in December, 1886, having been converted from a State bank. The officers, directors, and stockholders were composed of the president, cashier, their wives, and one other person, the first two holding 470 of the 500 shares into which the capital stock was divided. From the first the management of the bank was so conducted as to call for repeated notices from the Comptroller to the directors to correct irregularities, such as shortage in reserve, dealings with a mortgage and investment company, of which the president and cashier were trustees, excessive loans, overdue paper, etc. Plausible explanations were made by the directors, who alleged inexperience in national-bank methods and misunderstanding of the law. They professed both the intention and the desire to do right, and repeatedly made statements which appeared to show amendment of administration. In May last, however, transactions were discovered which were not only in violation of the national-bank law, but which also involved criminal misconduct of the officers.

The case was so obviously one of premeditated plunder that the examiner was directed to act in concert with the district attorney; and accordingly on a day agreed upon these officers met at Madison, the examiner took charge of the bank, and the president and cashier were arrested.

A receiver was duly appointed, and every effort has been made by attachment and otherwise to save something for the creditors, but these efforts have not received the local support necessary to their success. The accused officers readily obtained bail, and seem to have access to sufficient means to thwart and embarrass the receiver.

After the alleged capital of the bank had been withdrawn in loans to the officers, and its deposits had been absorbed by these officers through the transfer of worthless paper, they set about selling their stock, offering it generally at distant points, and succeeded in making considerable sales, mostly in New England.

The Lowell National Bank of Lowell, Mich., failed September 11, principally on account of the bad management of its president, who seemed to have been uncontrolled by the directors.

Among the nominal assets the receiver has found a large amount of worthless paper, most of it connected with a manufacturing company which was obviously insolvent during the whole time that it was absorbing the resources of the bank. The methods resorted to by the officers of this company with the connivance of the bank were simply scandalous.

Besides the losses incurred in this way the bank's valid resources had become gradually locked up in unproductive real estate and in other inconvertible investments.

As stated in the last Report indictments were found against several persons connected with the Fidelity National Bank of Cincinnati, Ohio, and suits were brought against the directors implicated in violations of law. These suits have not yet been decided.

Upon trial, the vice-president and assistant cashier were found guilty, and sentenced to serve a term in the penitentiary, the former for ten years. The cashier died before the trials came up.

A table, appendix, p. 172, has been prepared with great care and minute particularity, showing under appropriate heads all collections made from the assets of each of the 128 national banks which have become insolvent, how and for what purpose disbursements were made, and accounting for all moneys and every asset of whatever description which passed through the hands of the receiver or the Comptroller. The labor involved in the preparation of this table has been very great, but as the accounts of receivers are now kept upon the principle applied in the table, and their quarterly reports conform to the same arrangement, there will be no difficulty hereafter in carrying forward the results from year to year.

DIVIDENDS, THIRTY-FOUR IN NUMBER, PAID TO CREDITORS OF INSOLVENT NATIONAL BANKS DURING THE PAST YEAR, WITH TOTAL DIVIDENDS IN EACH CASE, UP TO NOVEMBER 1, 1888.

Name and location of bank.	Date of appointment of receiver.	Dividends paid during the past year.			Total dividends paid depositors (per cent.).	Proportion of interest paid depositors (per cent.).
		Date.	Total amount.	Per cent.		
First National Bank of Angelica, N. Y.	Apr. 10, 1886	Jan. 20, 1888	$13,400.01	15	100	100
First National Bank of Auburn, N. Y.	Feb. 20, 1888	July 21, 1888	100,612.75	25	25	....
Pacific National Bank of Boston, Mass	May 22, 1882	May 31, 1888	147,367.80	5	53	....
First National Bank of Buffalo, N. Y.	Apr. 22, 1882	Jan. 4, 1888	44,736.58	5	43	....
Farmers' National Bank of Bushnell, Ill	Dec. 17, 1884	Jan. 24, 1888	51,750.75	60	100	100
Metropolitan National Bank of Cincinnati, Ohio	Feb. 10, 1888	Mar. 16, 1888	400,997.59	100	100	100
First National Bank of Corry, Pa.	Oct. 11, 1887	Jan. 21, 1888	85,992.86	50	50	....
Commercial National Bank of Dubuque, Iowa	Apr. 2, 1888	July 20, 1888	118,732.73	30	30	....
Do	....do	Oct. 26, 1888	39,577.62	10	40	....
Henrietta National Bank of Henrietta, Tex	Aug. 17, 1887	Mar. 1, 1888	20,572.27	25	75	....
Do	....do	Oct. 16, 1888	12,323.31	15	90	....
Middletown National Bank of Middletown, N. Y.	Nov. 29, 1884	Oct. 31, 1888	65,431.92	10	80	....
Marine National Bank of the city of New York, N. Y.	May 13, 1884	Dec. 6, 1887	223,713.28	5	55	....
Do	....do	Apr. 17, 1888	222,852.07	5	60	....
Exchange National Bank of Norfolk, Va.	Apr. 9, 1885	May 21, 1888	144,704.01	5	45	....
Do	....do	Oct. 24, 1888	144,508.93	5	50	....
First National Bank of Pine Bluff, Ark	Nov. 20, 1886	Apr. 19, 1888	20,677.72	20	45	....
State National Bank of Raleigh, N. C	Mar. 31, 1866	June 8, 1888	61,427.93	20	20	....
Richmond National Bank of Richmond, Ind	July 23, 1884	May 1, 1888	18,294.17	5	61	....
Do	....do	Oct. 20, 1888	36,586.10	10	71	....
Vermont National Bank of Saint Albans, Vt.	Aug. 9, 1883	Oct. 31, 1888	90,425.94	25	67.50	....
Fifth National Bank of Saint Louis, Mo	Nov. 15, 1887	Feb. 1, 1888	479,805.70	50	50	....
Do	....do	Apr. 9, 1888	143,929.74	15	65	....
Do	....do	Oct. 20, 1888	143,907.93	15	80	....
Stafford National Bank of Stafford Springs, Conn.	Oct. 17, 1887	Jan. 27, 1888	123,718.14	50	50	....
Do	....do	Mar. 15, 1888	61,859.07	25	75	....
Do	....do	Oct. 20, 1888	60,918.24	25	100	100
National Bank of Sumter, S. C.	Aug. 24, 1887	Dec. 21, 1887	37,402.30	50	50	....
Do	....do	May 17, 1888	9,248.04	12	62	....
Do	....do	Oct. 27, 1888	13,501.07	18	80	....
First National Bank of Wahpeton, Dak.	Apr. 8, 1886	Aug. 2, 1888	27,677.19	25	35	....
Do	....do	Oct. 23, 1888	11,065.87	10	45	....
Second National Bank of Xenia, Ohio	May 9, 1888	July 21, 1888	119,020.55	40	40	....
Do	....do	Oct. 20, 1888	119,020.55	40	80	....
Total	....	....	*3,523,055.82	....	....	....

* The number of dividend checks involved in the payment of this amount to creditors was 17,850.

The following table shows the number, capital, and liabilities of national banks, organized and failed, up to the end of each official year from 1864 to 1888, inclusive, and the percentages in each case:

Year.	Number.			Capital, surplus, and undivided profits.			Other liabilities.		
	Organized.	Failed.	Percentage.	Aggregate of banks organized.*	Aggregate of banks failed.	Percentage of capital, surplus, etc.	Aggregate of banks organized.*	Aggregate of banks failed.	Percentage of liabilities.
1864	561	......	......	$94,775,480	......	......	$202,332,715	......	......
1865	1,601	1	.062	464,270,865	$50,000	.011	895,713,298	$160,089	.019
1866	1,665	3	.180	501,975,133	550,000	.109	1,027,072,808	1,535,133	.150
1867	1,673	10	.597	522,537,865	2,017,417	.386	984,770,208	5,821,596	.591
1868	1,685	13	.771	536,983,183	2,257,027	.420	1,031,167,125	6,271,508	.608
1869	1,694	15	.885	555,815,793	2,564,007	.461	959,660,912	6,686,094	.703
1870	1,729	15	.867	565,633,365	2,564,007	.453	954,329,973	6,686,094	.700
1871	1,894	15	.792	604,130,906	2,564,007	.424	1,135,875,911	6,686,094	.589
1872	2,061	21	1.019	641,134,136	4,623,661	.721	1,129,979,707	10,633,084	.941
1873	2,129	32	1.503	674,076,245	8,773,998	1.300	1,184,811,768	20,086,170	1.695
1874	2,200	35	1.591	683,265,502	9,057,837	1.326	1,223,665,826	20,692,549	1.691
1875	2,307	40	1.734	702,350,609	10,199,810	1.452	1,213,587,296	23,528,788	1.939
1876	2,449	49	2.001	689,795,508	11,345,779	1.645	1,174,104,032	25,288,394	2.154
1877	2,372	59	2.487	661,958,797	15,137,227	2.287	1,158,816,770	29,548,677	2.561
1878	2,400	73	3.042	642,294,048	18,312,619	2.851	1,176,717,660	33,419,956	2.840
1879	2,438	81	3.322	629,711,325	19,556,491	3.106	1,298,512,595	34,880,000	2.696
1880	2,494	84	3.368	644,468,749	20,256,491	3.142	1,517,682,833	36,108,466	2.371
1881	2,581	84	3.254	668,597,284	20,256,491	3.030	1,746,155,064	36,108,466	2.068
1882	2,808	87	3.098	698,331,568	22,069,594	3.163	1,766,769,875	43,198,173	2.445
1883	3,070	89	2.899	735,571,822	22,319,594	3.034	1,703,296,794	43,892,658	2.577
1884	3,261	100	3.067	758,167,132	23,606,512	3.113	1,595,385,736	50,452,476	3.162
1885	3,406	104	3.053	757,714,293	24,229,722	3.198	1,753,992,684	54,564,253	3.054
1886	3,580	112	3.128	796,921,031	24,927,616	3.128	1,797,645,019	53,783,683	3.103
1887	3,805	120	3.154	850,314,980	26,487,616	3.115	1,856,731,276	60,365,174	3.251
1888	3,937	128	3.251	883,964,263	28,387,616	3.212	2,024,120,015	63,945,321	3.159
Averages, 25 years				638,614,112	12,884,605	2.018	1,299,759,916	27,053,960	2.081

* Exclusive of banks in voluntary liquidation.

Out of 3,937 national banks organized since February, 1863, only 128, or about 3¼ per cent., have been placed in the hands of receivers; this includes 9 which had been previously placed in liquidation by their stockholders, but upon their failing to pay their depositors the Comptroller appointed receivers to wind up their affairs. Out of the above total of 128 failed banks, 45 have paid their creditors in full, while 33 have besides paid interest, 27 in full and 6 in part. The affairs of 90 banks of the 128 have been finally closed, leaving 38 in process of settlement, of which, as has been seen, 8 are virtually closed, with the exception of pending litigation, leaving 30 receiverships only in active operation.

The total amount so far paid to creditors of insolvent national banks has been $33,027,451 upon proved claims amounting to $51,924,977. The amount paid during the year has been $3,523,955.82, besides $68,510 paid for dividends declared prior to November 1, 1887, on claims proved since that date. Assessments amounting to $12,555,350 have been made upon stockholders of insolvent national banks under section 5151 of the Revised Statutes of the United States. From this source the gross collections amount to $5,346,171, of which there has been received during the past year $308,591. Suits are pending in some cases.

Each year's experience confirms the opinion that it would be wise to so amend the laws as to allow banks to commute the liability of their shareholders into a special reserve fund, as recommended in the Reports of 1886 and 1887.

Upon a general view of the data relating to insolvent national banks, it appears that while the number of failed banks is about 3¼ per cent. of the total number of banks organized, the percentages of their capital and other liabilities, taken at time of failure, are less.

To make the comparison complete, however, there should be added to the capital, surplus, and undivided profits, as given for the year 1888, viz, $883,964,263, the capital, surplus, and undivided profits of all banks that have gone into voluntary liquidation, and of all that have been wound up at the end of their corporate existence, because in these cases shareholders have recovered all they put in and kept in. The amount is $125,894,506, and with the aggregate in the table makes $1,009,858,769, for which the system has been accountable to its proprietors. Against this vast sum should then be set the capital, surplus, and undivided profits of failed banks, viz, $28,387,616, increased by amounts collected by assessment from shareholders, $5,346,171, diminished by the amount, as nearly as can be ascertained, repaid to shareholders out of assets, viz, $3,535,545. The net loss will then be seen to be only $30,198,242, which is not quite 3 per cent. of total investments. Against this loss a superabundant offset is afforded by the dividends paid out of profits amounting in many cases to very large percentages.

Again, from the total "other liabilities" of failed banks, viz, $63,945,321, should be deducted, amount of circulation $15,432,360, and total dividends paid to creditors $33,027,451, aggregate $48,459,811, net loss $15,485,510, which is 0.83 per cent. upon the $1,872,417,724 of such liabilities resting upon the system at large.

The affairs of five failed banks have been closed during the past year, and final dividends have been paid to their creditors. These banks, with the total dividends paid in each case, are given below:

Name and location of bank.	Date of appointment of receiver.	Total dividends on principal.	Proportion of interest paid.
		Per cent.	*Per cent.*
First National Bank, Angelica, N. Y	Apr. 19, 1880	100	100
Farmers' National Bank, Bushnell, Ill	Dec. 17, 1884	100	100
Metropolitan National Bank, Cincinnati, Ohio	Feb. 10, 1888	100	100
Stafford National Bank, Stafford Springs, Conn	Oct. 17, 1887	100	100
National Bank of the State of Missouri, Saint Louis, Mo	June 23, 1877	100	100

INACTIVE RECEIVERSHIPS.

These were fully described in the last Annual Report.

The following table shows the receiverships that are now in this condition:

Name and location of bank.	Date of appointment of receiver.	Dividends paid.
		Per cent.
First National Bank, Albion, N. Y	Aug. 26, 1884	....
First National Bank, Anderson, Ind	Nov. 23, 1873	39
Third National Bank, Chicago, Ill	Nov. 24, 1877	*100
Central National Bank, Chicago, Ill	Dec. 1, 1877	60
People's National Bank, Helena, Mont	Sept. 13, 1878	40
Hot Springs National Bank, Hot Springs, Ark	June 2, 1884	100
First National Bank of Union Mills, Union City, Pa	Mar. 24, 1883	65
German-American National Bank, Washington, D. C	Nov. 1, 1878	50

*And interest.

During the past year the following trusts have passed into this category, viz, the First National Bank of Albion, N. Y., and the Hot Springs National Bank of Hot Springs, Ark.

By reference to the Report of 1887 it will be seen that the National Bank of the State of Missouri, Saint Louis, has disappeared from the inactive receiverships. At the date of that report the receivership had not terminated because of the failure of the agent elected by the shareholders in June, 1887, to qualify by giving the bond required by law. During the present year the receivership was closed, and cash assets were turned over to the agent amounting to $26,720, and nominal assets amounting to $36,957. Among the nominal assets was real property which has enormously increased in value, and it is not unlikely that enough may be realized by the agent to reimburse the shareholders for the amount paid under assessment upon stock.

The First National Bank of Albion, N. Y., which was wrecked by its president, who squandered the funds of the bank in speculation, has been placed on the inactive list. The assets of the bank were almost entirely worthless, and a sufficient sum has not been realized to pay a dividend.

An assessment of 100 per cent. was levied upon the stock, nearly all of which was owned by an estate, and a judgment obtained by the receiver, but the demand of the trust was met by counter claims of the estate, which have not yet been judicially determined.

The receiver brought suit against the brokers through whom the president carried on his speculations, and, as will be seen by reference to page 89, obtained judgment for a considerable sum, but the defendants have appealed.

CIRCULATING NOTES.

Under present laws the minimum deposit of bonds required to be made by the 3,140 national banks in operation in the United States on October 4, 1888, amounts to $91,988,805.

A table in the appendix, p. 149, shows by States and geographical divisions the national banks in operation on October 4, 1888, separated into two classes, namely, banks of which the capital does not exceed $150,000 and banks of which the capital exceeds $150,000. The first class contains 2,229 banks, with an aggregate capital of $185,551,921;

the second, 911 banks, with an aggregate capital of $407,069,735. The minimum of bonds required to be kept on deposit by the entire body of banks in the first class is $46,387,980; the minimum for the 911 banks of the second class is $45,550,000. If all banks held only the minimum of bonds, the total national-bank circulation could not exceed $82,744,025, while the possible maximum of circulation, namely, 90 per cent. of the aggregate of the national-bank capital, would be $533,359,491.

The actual circulation on October 4, 1888, was $151,700,809, which is exclusive of $88,521,813 still outstanding, but which, having been surrendered by the banks that issued it, is no longer represented by bonds, but by that amount of lawful money deposited with the Treasurer of the United States to redeem the notes as they are presented.

The $151,700,809 of circulation for which the banks are responsible consists of $68,410,823 secured by the bonds deposited by the 2,229 banks having $150,000 capital and less, and $83,289,986, secured by the bonds belonging to the 911 banks of which the capital exceeds $150,000. The first class of banks have, therefore, $26,661,641 more than their minimum, and $98,585,906 less than their possible maximum circulation, while the larger banks have $42,294,986 more than their minimum and $283,072,776 less than their maximum.

The following table shows the number of banks organized from July 1, 1882, to July 1, 1888, their capital stock, amount of bonds deposited, and the circulation issued thereon:

Year.	No.	Capital.	Minimum bonds required.	Bonds actually deposited.	Per cent. of excess.	Circulation issued.
July 1, 1882, to July 1, 1883........	251	$26, 552, 300	$5, 155, 500	$7, 116, 400	28	$6, 404, 760
July 1, 1883, to July 1, 1884........	218	19, 944, 000	4, 016, 000	4, 676, 100	14	4, 208, 490
July 1, 1884, to July 1, 1885........	142	15, 205, 000	3, 061, 250	3, 332, 800	8	2, 999, 520
July 1, 1885, to July 1, 1886........	163	17, 553, 000	3, 404, 500	3, 715, 500	8	3, 343, 950
July 1, 1886, to July 1, 1887........	217	31, 414, 000	4, 986, 000	5, 051, 300	1	4, 546, 170
July 1, 1887, to July 1, 1888........	164	16, 734, 000	3, 308, 500	3, 324, 750	0. 5	2, 992, 275

From the foregoing table it appears that 1,155 banks have been organized between the dates given, with a capital of $127,432,300; that they have received circulation to the amount of $24,495,165 on bonds deposited to the amount of $27,216,850, and that the minimum deposit of bonds required by law for these banks is $23,931,750.

The actual deposit of bonds during the whole period exceeds the minimum by about 12 per cent. only, and taken year by year the percentage of excess has decreased from 28 per cent. in 1882–'83 to one-half of 1 per cent. in 1887–'88.

Of the 164 national banks organized during the past fiscal year, 93 have a capital of $50,000 each, amounting to $4,650,000; 55 have a capital of over $50,000 and not exceeding $150,000, amounting to $5,384,000; and 16 have a capital of $6,700,000. The 16 largest banks deposited the exact amount of bonds required by law, with one exception, and out of 148 banks, of which the capital does not exceed $150,000, only 4 have deposited bonds in excess of the requirement.

Tables will be found in the appendix, p. 147, etc., showing for the national banks in each State, Territory, and reserve city the minimum amount of bonds required by law, the bonds actually held, and the circulation thereon outstanding October 4, 1888; also all other information deemed useful as to circulation.

INTEREST-BEARING FUNDED DEBT OF THE UNITED STATES, AND THE AMOUNT HELD BY NATIONAL BANKS.

The connection between the banks and the distribution of the funded debt of the United States renders the following statement appropriate:

The public debt at its maximum, on August 31, 1865, amounted to $2,844,649,626, of which obligations not bearing interest amounted to $461,616,311, leaving interest-bearing debt $2,383,033,315. On October 31, 1888, the interest-bearing debt amounted to $958,123,282.

The following table shows the class of bonds, authorizing act, date of maturity, rate of interest, and intermediate changes:

BONDED DEBT AT DATES NAMED.

Date.	6 per cent.	5 per cent.	4½ per cent.*	4 per cent.†	6 per cent.‡	Total.
Aug. 31, 1865....	$908, 518, 091	$199, 792, 100	....	....	$1, 258, 000	$1, 109, 568, 191
June 30, 1866....	1, 008, 388, 469	198, 528, 435	....	....	6, 042, 000	1, 212, 958, 904
June 30, 1867....	1, 421, 110, 719	198, 533, 435	....	....	14, 762, 000	1, 634, 406, 154
June 30, 1868....	1, 841, 521, 800	221, 588, 400	....	....	29, 089, 000	2, 092, 199, 200
June 30, 1869....	1, 886, 341, 300	221, 589, 300	....	....	58, 638, 320	2, 166, 568, 920
June 30, 1870....	1, 764, 932, 300	221, 589, 300	....	....	64, 457, 320	2, 050, 978, 920
June 30, 1871....	1, 613, 897, 300	274, 236, 450	....	....	64, 618, 832	1, 952, 752, 582
June 30, 1872....	1, 374, 883, 800	414, 567, 300	....	....	64, 623, 512	1, 845, 074, 612
June 30, 1873....	1, 281, 238, 650	414, 567, 300	....	....	64, 623, 512	1, 760, 429, 462
June 30, 1874....	1, 213, 624, 700	510, 628, 050	....	....	64, 623, 512	1, 788, 876, 262
June 30, 1875....	1, 100, 865, 550	607, 132, 750	....	....	64, 623, 512	1, 772, 621, 812
June 30, 1876....	984, 999, 650	711, 685, 800	....	....	64, 623, 512	1, 761, 308, 962
June 30, 1877....	854, 621, 850	703, 266, 650	$140, 000, 000	....	64, 623, 512	1, 761, 512, 012
June 30, 1878....	738, 619, 000	703, 266, 650	240, 000, 000	$98, 850, 000	64, 623, 512	1, 845, 359, 162
June 30, 1879 ..	310, 932, 500	646, 905, 500	250, 000, 000	679, 878, 110	64, 623, 512	1, 952, 339, 622
June 30, 1880....	235, 780, 400	484, 864, 900	250, 000, 000	739, 347, 800	64, 623, 512	1, 774, 616, 612
June 30, 1881....	196, 378, 600	439, 841, 350	250, 000, 000	739, 347, 800	64, 623, 512	1, 690, 191, 262
June 30, 1882....	Continued at 3½ per cent. 58, 957, 150	Continued at 3½ per cent. 401, 593, 900	250, 000, 000	739, 349, 350	64, 623, 512	1, 514, 483, 912
June 30, 1883....	....	32, 082, 600 Funded into 3 per cents, act July 12, 1882. 304, 204, 350	250, 000, 000	737, 942, 200	64, 623, 512	1, 388, 852, 662
June 30, 1884....	....	224, 612, 150	250, 000, 000	737, 661, 700	64, 623, 512	1, 276, 897, 362
June 30, 1885....	....	194, 190, 500	250, 000, 000	737, 719, 850	64, 623, 512	1, 246, 533, 862
June 30, 1886....	....	144, 046, 600	250, 000, 000	737, 759, 700	64, 623, 512	1, 196, 429, 812
June 30, 1887....	....	19, 716, 500	250, 000, 000	737, 800, 600	64, 623, 512	1, 072, 140, 612
June 30, 1888....	....	....	222, 207, 050	714, 177, 400	64, 623, 512	1, 001, 007, 962
Oct. 31, 1888....	....	....	197, 302, 000	682, 068, 150	64, 623, 512	943, 993, 662

* Funded loan 1891; authorizing act, July 14, 1870, and January 20, 1871; date of maturity, 1891.
† Funded loan 1907; authorizing act, July 14, 1870, and January 20, 1871; date of maturity, 1907.
‡ Pacific railroad bonds; authorizing act, July 1, 1862, and July 2, 1864; date of maturity, 1895 to 1899.
The Navy pension fund, amounting to $14,000,000 in 3 percents, the interest upon which is applied to the payment of naval pensions exclusively, and $120,620 of refunding certificates are not included in the table.

During the year ending October 31, 1888, $50,412,650 of 4 percents and $33,242,600 of 4½ percents were purchased for sinking-fund purposes, making a total of $83,655,250. Of this amount $4,077,150 of 4 percents and $1,465,800 of 4½ percents were withdrawn by the national banks from deposit to secure circulation, making total withdrawals from this cause $5,542,950, while the replacement by deposits of 4 percents amounted to only $406,000.

Changes in the debt have induced corresponding changes in the bonds held by the national banks. In January, 1866, 1,582 banks, with capital, surplus, and undivided profits of $475,330,204, held $440,380,350 of United States bonds. On October 4, 1888, 3,140 banks, with capital, surplus, and undivided profits of $855,576,646, held only $232,582,250 of bonds. The total bank circulation on January 1, 1866, was $213,239,530, and on October 4, 1888, that which was secured by bonds was $151,702,809.

The amount and classes of United States bonds owned by the banks, including those pledged as security for circulation and for public deposits, on June 30 in each year since 1865 are exhibited in the following table:

Years.	United States bonds held as security for circulation.					United States bonds held for other purposes at nearest date.	Grand total.
	6 per cent. bonds.	5 per cent. bonds.	4½ per cent. bonds.	4 per cent. bonds.	Total.		
1865 ..	$170,382,500	$65,576,600	....	....	$235,959,100	$155,785,750	$391,744,850
1866 ..	241,083,500	86,226,850	....	....	327,310,350	121,152,950	448,463,300
1867 ..	251,430,400	89,177,100	....	....	340,607,500	84,002,650	424,610,150
1868 ..	250,726,950	90,768,950	....	....	341,495,900	80,922,500	422,418,400
1869 ..	255,190,350	87,661,250	....	....	342,851,600	55,102,000	397,953,600
1870 ..	247,355,350	94,923,200	....	....	342,278,550	43,980,600	386,259,150
1871 ..	220,497,750	139,387,800	....	....	359,885,550	39,450,800	399,336,350
1872 ..	173,251,450	207,189,250	....	....	380,440,700	31,868,200	412,308,900
1873 ..	160,923,500	229,487,050	....	....	390,410,550	25,724,400	416,134,150
1874 ..	154,370,700	236,800,500	....	....	391,171,200	25,347,100	416,518,300
1875 ..	136,955,100	239,359,400	....	....	376,314,500	26,900,200	403,214,700
1876 ..	109,313,450	232,081,300	....	....	341,394,750	45,170,300	386,565,050
1877 ..	87,690,300	206,651,050	$44,372,250	....	338,713,600	47,315,050	386,028,650
1878 ..	82,421,200	199,514,550	48,448,650	$19,162,000	349,546,400	68,850,900	418,397,300
1879 ..	56,042,800	144,616,300	35,056,550	118,538,950	354,254,600	76,603,520	430,858,120
1880 ..	58,056,150	139,758,650	37,760,950	126,076,300	361,652,050	42,831,300	404,483,350
1881 ..	61,901,800	172,348,350	32,600,500	93,637,700	360,488,400	63,849,950	424,338,350
	Continued at 3½ per cent.:	Continued at 3½ per cent.:					
1882 ..	25,142,600	202,487,650	32,752,650	97,429,800	357,812,700	43,122,550	400,935,250
1883 ..	385,700	7,402,800 3 per cents: 200,877,850	39,408,500	104,954,650	353,029,500	34,094,150	387,123,650
1884 ..	....	172,412,550	46,546,400	111,690,900	330,649,850	31,203,000	361,852,850
	Pacifics.						
1885 ..	3,520,000	142,240,850	48,483,050	117,901,300	312,145,200	32,195,800	344,341,000
1886 ..	3,505,000	107,782,100	50,484,200	114,143,500	275,974,800	31,345,550	307,320,350
1887 ..	3,175,000	5,205,950	67,743,100	115,842,650	191,966,700	33,147,750	224,814,450
1888 ..	3,181,000	37,500	69,670,300	105,423,850	178,312,650	63,618,150	241,930,800

SECURITY FOR CIRCULATING NOTES.

The following table shows the amount of bonds held by the Treasurer as security for the circulating notes of the national banks on October 31 of each year from 1882 to 1888, inclusive, the amount held by the banks for all other purposes, and the total of these two:

Year.	Number of banks.	United States bonds held as security for circulation.					United States bonds held for other purposes at nearest date.	Total.
		4½ per cent. bonds.	4 per cent. bonds.	3 per cent. bonds.	Pacific 6 per cent. bonds.	Total.		
1882.......	2,301	$38,754,650	$104,927,500	$40,621,950 179,675,550	$3,526,000	$362,505,650	$37,563,750	$400,069,400
1883.......	2,522	41,319,700	106,164,850	*602,000 201,327,750	3,463,000	352,877,300	30,674,050	383,551,350
1884.......	2,671	49,537,450	116,705,450	155,604,400	3,469,000	325,316,300	30,419,600	355,735,900
1885.......	2,727	49,547,250	116,391,650	138,920,650	3,505,000	308,364,550	31,780,100	340,144,650
1886.......	2,868	57,436,850	115,383,150	69,088,050	3,586,000	245,444,050	32,431,400	277,875,450
1887.......	3,061	69,696,100	115,731,400	144,500	3,256,000	188,828,000	34,671,350	223,499,350
1888.......	3,151	66,121,750	100,413,600	None.	3,468,000	170,003,350	60,715,050	230,718,400

* Three and one-half per cent.

The foregoing tables show how the banks have shifted their investments from one class of bonds to another, and the following table exhibits especially the steady decrease in the amount of bonds held for circulation.

It is worthy of note in this connection that the recent increase in bonds held otherwise than as security for circulation is directly attributable to the requirement of these as security for deposits of public money. It is matter of general knowledge that a considerable percentage of bonds deposited as security for public moneys are not owned by the banks making the deposit, but that they have been borrowed for the purpose.

TABLE SHOWING THE DECREASE OF NATIONAL-BANK CIRCULATION DURING EACH OF THE YEARS ENDING OCTOBER 31, FROM 1884 TO 1888, INCLUSIVE, AND THE AMOUNT OF LAWFUL MONEY ON DEPOSIT AT THE END OF EACH YEAR.

National-bank notes outstanding October 31, 1883, including notes of national gold banks	$352,013,787	
Less lawful money on deposit at same date, including deposits of national gold banks	35,993,461	
		$316,020,326
National-bank notes outstanding October 31, 1884, including notes of national gold banks	333,559,813	
Less lawful money on deposit at same date, including deposits of national gold banks	41,710,163	
		291,849,650
Net decrease of circulation		24,170,676
Net outstanding as above, October 31, 1884		291,849,650
National-bank notes outstanding October 31, 1885, including notes of national gold banks	315,847,168	
Less lawful money on deposit at same date, including deposits of national gold banks	39,542,979	
		276,304,189
Net decrease of circulation		15,545,461
Net outstanding as above, October 31, 1885		276,304,189
National-bank notes outstanding October 31, 1886, including notes of national gold banks	301,529,889	
Less lawful money on deposit at same date, including deposits of national gold banks	81,819,233	
		219,710,656
Net decrease of circulation		56,593,533
Net outstanding as above, October 31, 1886		219,710,656
National-bank notes outstanding October 31, 1887, including notes of national gold banks	272,041,203	
Less lawful money on deposit at same date, including deposits of national gold banks	102,826,136	
		169,215,067
Net decrease of circulation		50,495,589
Net outstanding as above, October 31, 1887		169,215,067
National-bank notes outstanding October 31, 1888, including notes of national gold banks	239,385,237	
Less lawful money on deposit at same date, including deposits of national gold banks	87,018,909	
		152,366,328
Net decrease of circulation		16,848,739

The following table extended from the last Report shows the diminishing scale on which banks organized during each of the past six years have availed themselves of the privilege of issuing circulation upon bonds in excess of the minimum which the law obliges them to keep on hand.

For the sake of conciseness in the table the circulation is omitted, but as every bank has received circulation to the amount of 90 per cent. of the bonds deposited, the proportions of the table reflect faithfully the features of the circulation.

NUMBER AND CAPITAL OF NATIONAL BANKS ORGANIZED IN EACH GEOGRAPHICAL DIVISION OF THE UNITED STATES FROM OCTOBER 31, 1882, TO OCTOBER 31, 1888, SHOWING THE AMOUNT OF BONDS DEPOSITED TO SECURE THEIR CIRCULATION, THE MINIMUM AMOUNT OF BONDS REQUIRED BY THE ACT OF JULY 12, 1882, AND THE EXCESS DEPOSITED OVER REQUIREMENTS BOTH IN AMOUNT AND PERCENTAGE.

Divisions.*	Number of banks.	Capital.	United States bonds.			
			Deposited.	Minimum.	Excess.	Excess over minimum.
1883.						*Per ct.*
First	7	$1,275,000	$995,000	$312,500	$682,500	218.40
Second	38	2,975,200	1,854,500	743,800	1,110,700	149.32
Third	5	295,000	155,500	73,700	81,800	110.99
Fourth	43	3,643,650	1,238,100	748,400	489,700	65.43
Fifth	61	11,210,000	2,578,000	1,765,000	813,000	46.06
Sixth	71	7,085,500	1,729,250	1,246,400	482,850	38.73
Seventh	11	620,000	268,400	155,000	113,400	73.16
Eighth	26	1,550,000	556,800	375,000	181,800	48.48
Total	262	28,654,350	9,375,550	5,419,800	3,955,750	72.99
1884.						
First	10	810,000	313,000	190,000	123,000	64.73
Second	22	1,662,250	718,000	340,500	377,500	110.86
Third	6	280,000	166,500	70,000	96,500	137.85
Fourth	27	2,861,100	693,600	627,700	65,900	10.49
Fifth	34	3,413,100	927,000	570,700	356,300	62.43
Sixth	68	5,492,780	1,239,750	1,135,600	104,150	9.17
Seventh	5	380,000	120,000	95,000	25,000	26.31
Eighth	19	1,143,000	309,250	285,700	23,550	8.24
Total	191	16,042,230	4,487,100	3,315,200	1,171,900	35.35
1885.						
First	4	400,000	100,500	100,000	500	.50
Second	18	2,635,000	1,037,500	543,700	493,800	90.82
Third	3	660,000	112,500	112,500	....	....
Fourth	20	2,025,000	561,500	506,100	55,400	10.95
Fifth	35	7,123,000	1,963,500	1,218,200	745,300	61.17
Sixth	41	2,350,000	759,800	587,500	172,300	29.33
Seventh	8	725,000	169,000	168,700	300	.18
Eighth	16	1,020,000	255,000	255,000	....	....
Total	145	16,938,000	4,959,300	3,491,700	1,467,600	42.03
1886.						
First	5	500,000	125,000	125,000	....	....
Second	15	4,000,000	525,000	525,000	....	....
Third	4	450,000	112,500	112,500	....	....
Fourth	23	1,638,000	404,750	402,000	2,750	.68
Fifth	27	5,465,000	843,000	743,750	99,250	13.34
Sixth	58	5,830,000	982,500	982,500	....	....
Seventh	18	2,100,000	367,500	360,000	7,500	2.08
Eighth	24	1,355,000	353,250	313,750	39,500	12.59
Total	174	21,338,000	3,713,500	3,564,500	149,000	4.18
1887.						
First	5	400,000	100,000	100,000	....	....
Second	27	7,025,000	771,550	743,750	27,800	3.74
Third	6	500,000	115,000	112,500	2,500	2.22
Fourth	50	6,190,000	1,202,500	1,202,250	250	.02
Fifth	37	5,010,000	959,500	952,500	7,000	.74
Sixth	70	9,002,000	1,400,500	1,400,500	....	....
Seventh	17	1,510,000	377,500	377,500	....	....
Eighth	13	900,000	225,000	225,000	....	....
Total	225	30,546,000	5,211,550	5,174,000	37,550	.72
1888.						
First	5	450,000	100,000	100,000	....	....
Second	19	1,414,000	341,000	341,000	....	....
Third	3	160,000	40,000	40,000	....	....
Fourth	25	2,509,000	516,000	514,750	1,250	....
Fifth	23	3,130,000	582,500	582,500	....	....
Sixth	37	2,880,000	682,500	682,500	....	....
Seventh	13	1,030,000	262,500	262,500	....	....
Eighth	7	460,000	115,000	115,000	....	....
Total	132	12,053,000	2,639,500	2,638,250	1,250	....

*See page 147.

The following table exhibits in detail the changes which have occurred during the past year in the amount of national-bank circulation, so arranged as to illustrate the process by which the circulation steadily decreases concurrently with the accession of new banks and an increase in the aggregate national-bank capital:

CAPITAL AND CIRCULATION.

	Paid-in capital.	Circulation represented by bonds.
Increase by banks existing November 1, 1887	$8,696,700	$1,345,145
Increase caused by formation of new banks	11,789,000	2,372,400
Increase by banks organized during year	414,000	3,150
Total increase	20,899,700	3,720,695
Decrease of banks still in operation November 1, 1888	1,102,400	19,225,370
Decrease by banks going into voluntary liquidation and failed	6,071,000	1,041,065
	7,173,400	20,266,435
Net increase of capital	13,726,300	
Net decrease of circulation		16,545,740

BANKS WITHOUT CIRCULATION.

As reported last year, some national banks have not availed themselves of the privilege of taking out circulating notes, and others have surrendered their entire circulation. The following is a complete list of such banks, with capital and bonds:

Title of bank.	Capital.	Bonds.
Chemical National Bank, New York, N. Y	$300,000	$50,000
National City Bank, New York, N. Y	1,000,000	50,000
American Exchange National Bank, New York, N. Y	5,000,000	50,000
National Bank of Washington, D. C	200,000	50,000
Chestertown National Bank, Chestertown, Md	50,000	12,500
First National Bank, Houston, Tex	100,000	25,000
Mechanics' National Bank, New York, N. Y	2,000,000	50,000
Metropolitan National Bank, Washington, D. C	300,000	50,000
Total	8,950,000	337,500

ISSUES AND REDEMPTIONS.

The following table exhibits the number and amount of national-bank notes of each denomination which have been issued and redeemed since the organization of the system, and the number and amount outstanding on October 31, 1888:

Denominations.	Number of notes—			Amount—		
	Issued.	Redeemed.	Outstanding.	Issued.	Redeemed.	Outstanding.
Ones	23,167,677	22,783,281	384,396	$23,167,677	$22,783,281	$384,396
Twos	7,747,519	7,649,436	98,083	15,495,038	15,298,872	196,166
Fives	104,109,700	90,617,308	13,492,392	520,548,500	453,086,540	67,461,960
Tens	44,219,831	36,443,660	7,776,171	442,198,310	364,436,600	77,761,710
Twenties	13,786,873	10,940,346	2,846,527	275,737,460	218,806,920	56,930,540
Fifties	1,897,847	1,624,608	273,239	94,892,350	81,230,400	13,661,950
One hundreds	1,422,156	1,198,720	223,436	142,215,600	119,872,000	22,343,600
Five hundreds	23,924	23,413	511	11,962,000	11,706,500	255,500
One thousands	7,369	7,329	40	7,369,000	7,329,000	40,000
Fractions outstanding						24,408
Total	196,382,806	171,288,002	25,094,804	1,533,585,935	1,294,541,113	239,060,230

Notes of gold banks are not included in this table.

Distinct accounts are kept for the incomplete currency issued to banks in replacement of notes redeemed and destroyed under the provisions of the act of June 20, 1874, to banks taking out new circulation upon an extension of their corporate existence under the act of July 12, 1882, and to old and new banks increasing the volume of their circulation by adding to the amount of bonds deposited.

TABLE SHOWING BY STATES THE AMOUNT OF "ADDITIONAL CIRCULATION" ISSUED AND RETIRED DURING THE YEAR ENDING OCTOBER 31, 1888, AND TOTAL AMOUNT ISSUED AND RETIRED SINCE JUNE 20, 1874.

States and Territories.	Circulation issued under act of July 12, 1882.	Additional circulation issued.	Total issued.	Circulation retired.		Total retired.
				Under act of June 20, 1874.	Insolvent and liquidating banks.	
Maine	$591,080	$44,990	$636,070	$771,015	$570,037	$1,341,052
New Hampshire	586,750	11,250	598,000	448,894	347,749	796,643
Vermont	531,090	10	531,100	672,176	455,901	1,128,077
Massachusetts	3,218,085	56,250	3,274,335	7,361,043	4,986,483	12,347,526
Rhode Island	961,305		961,305	1,335,223	1,435,692	2,770,915
Connecticut	1,373,000	11,240	1,384,240	1,752,806	1,502,145	3,254,951
New York	4,406,200	238,345	4,644,545	2,962,185	3,533,870	6,496,055
New Jersey	1,133,550	78,750	1,212,300	537,439	664,769	1,202,208
Pennsylvania	1,585,945	558,350	2,144,295	4,405,535	3,496,982	7,902,517
Delaware	299,325	11,260	310,585	22,560	79,660	102,220
Maryland	300,335		300,335	920,380	744,047	1,664,436
District of Columbia	63,150		63,150	47,110	16,368	63,478
Virginia	98,240	11,250	109,490	206,280	182,525	388,805
West Virginia	152,170	1,130	153,300	86,730	142,555	229,285
North Carolina	30,800	33,750	64,550	110,855	35,879	146,734
South Carolina		16,875	16,875	197,941	26,147	224,088
Georgia	34,150	50,380	84,530	181,320	94,214	275,534
Florida		87,020	87,020		7,650	7,650
Alabama	17,750	11,250	29,000	122,920	36,526	159,446
Mississippi		11,200	11,200	600	40	640
Louisiana	12,400	10	12,410	118,237	128,862	247,099
Texas	38,770	268,950	307,720	102,245	20,448	122,693
Arkansas		10,000	10,000	3,781	13,685	17,466
Kentucky	125,350	36,900	162,250	1,423,695	308,887	1,732,582
Tennessee	66,400	49,735	116,135	278,260	95,679	373,939
Missouri	92,470	112,860	205,330	216,579	164,686	381,265
Ohio	689,821	194,380	884,201	2,890,840	1,460,726	4,351,566
Indiana	438,320	81,070	519,390	826,248	592,257	1,418,505
Illinois	270,725	135,000	405,725	759,401	507,246	1,266,647
Michigan	88,480	87,060	175,540	450,909	287,448	738,357
Wisconsin	147,100	61,665	208,765	227,434	185,234	412,668
Iowa	169,290	67,510	236,800	439,885	223,302	663,187
Minnesota	53,630	36,000	89,630	140,944	123,058	264,002
Kansas		458,380	458,380	111,254	32,202	143,456
Nebraska		92,280	92,280	165,763	61,226	226,989
Nevada		29,700	29,700		40	40
Oregon		67,510	67,510	51,550	8,650	60,200
Colorado		74,240	74,240	46,103	79,063	125,166
Utah				29,260	416	29,676
Idaho		36,000	36,000	14,550		14,550
Montana		7,520	7,520	8,945	3,770	12,715
Wyoming		22,400	22,400			
New Mexico		33,750	33,750	81,151	3,800	84,951
Dakota		22,550	22,550	38,720	24,860	63,580
Washington		80,010	80,010	32,550	6,891	39,441
California		202,530	202,530	140,390	7,350	147,740
Arizona					7,010	7,010
Total	17,635,681	3,502,660	21,138,341	30,831,715	22,706,035	53,537,750
Surrendered to this office and retired						189,830
From June 20, 1874, to October 31, 1887			207,878,247	193,732,779	76,713,746	270,446,525
Surrendered and retired same dates						15,537,733
Grand total October 31, 1888			229,016,588	224,564,494	99,419,781	339,711,838

Notes of gold banks are not included in the above table.

Of the above $3,502,660 there were issued to banks organized during the year, $2,356,235, and to already existing banks increasing their circulation, $1,146,425.

ISSUES.

The total issues of incomplete currency during the year are shown by the vault account, as follows:

National-bank currency in vaults, October 31, 1887		$50,210,250
Amount received from Bureau of Engraving and Printing during the year ending October 31, 1888		44,488,880
Total		94,699,130
Amount issued to banks during the year	$49,668,460	
Amount canceled during the year, not having been issued	861,500	
		50,529,960
Balance in vaults		44,169,170

REDEMPTION.

The provisions of law relating to the redemption of the circulating notes of national banks were fully described in the Report of 1887, and need not be here repeated. Two principles have been adhered to in all legislation on this subject.

These are, first, that every bank must redeem on demand at its place of business any of its circulating notes presented there for redemption during business hours; and, second, that the medium of redemption must be "lawful money of the United States."

The act of June 3, 1864, established redemption cities, but the act of June 20, 1874, establishing the National-Bank Redemption Agency of the Treasury at Washington, repealed all requirements as to redemption agents elsewhere, and obliged every bank to keep up a redemption fund in the hands of the Treasurer of the United States equal to 5 per cent. of its outstanding circulation.

The following table, compiled from the Treasurer's reports, shows the practical working of the law as to the 5 per cent. redemption fund:

TABLE SHOWING MODE OF REIMBURSEMENT OF FIVE PER CENT. REDEMPTION FUND BY NATIONAL BANKS, BY FISCAL YEARS, FROM 1875 TO 1888, INCLUSIVE.

Years.	Deposits of lawful money with assistant treasurers, United States.	Deposits with Treasurer United States.			Total.
		Deposits received at counter.	Remittances of lawful money by express.	Proceeds of national-bank notes redeemed.	
1875	$88,834,053.12	$989,040.63	$32,308,100.78	$18,742,163.00	$140,874,503.53
1876	105,134,528.37	664,980.45	19,042,491.62	52,643,065.00	177,485,074.44
1877	116,044,751.34	(*)	7,678,759.57	91,856,760.92	215,580,271.83
1878	100,819,824.59	(*)	5,035,806.80	98,552,739.98	205,308,371.37
1879	101,194,291.04	(*)	4,894,393.06	50,581,484.09	156,670,138.19
1880	46,960,242.06	(*)	2,627,861.16	6,924,097.88	56,512,201.10
1881	41,411,430.87	(*)	3,106,187.40	4,313,702.36	48,831,320.63
1882	50,531,496.68	(*)	2,975,682.27	4,534,598.69	58,041,777.64
1883	113,726,801.90	(*)	2,039,882.01	5,248,120.14	121,014,804.05
1884	89,338,255.34	(*)	3,801,957.46	5,727,786.37	98,867,999.17
1885	106,264,901.13	(*)	4,503,141.79	6,376,897.26	117,144,940.18
1886	92,363,184.15	1,787,241.84	3,433,468.78	5,775,498.84	103,359,393.61
1887	46,254,700.76	2,077,837.82	2,000,214.04	2,189,546.65	52,522,359.27
1888	38,499,139.68	1,832,545.34	1,574,222.07	1,384,316.03	43,290,223.72
Total	1,137,378,236.04	7,352,201.08	96,822,100.50	354,850,786.21	1,596,403,444.73
Average	72.05	5.09	5.95	21.36	100.00

* No record.

The following tables, compiled from the Treasurer's reports, show, for the fiscal years 1874–'75 to 1887–'88:

1. The amounts of national-bank currency received annually at the Redemption Agency, and the disposition made of it.
2. The points from which this currency was forwarded and the percentage of the whole received from each point.
3. The total amount of notes redeemed, and the mode of redemption.
4. The cost of redemption.

TABLE SHOWING RECEIPTS AND DELIVERIES OF MONEYS BY THE NATIONAL-BANK REDEMPTION AGENCY (UNITED STATES TREASURER'S OFFICE) FOR EACH FISCAL YEAR FROM 1875 TO 1888, INCLUSIVE.

Year ending June 30—	Cash balance on hand at close of previous year.	To national-bank notes received for redemption.	To "overs" reported in national-bank notes received for redemption.	Aggregates.	By national-bank notes fit for circulation, deposited in the Treasury, and forwarded to national banks by express.	By national-bank notes, unfit for circulation, delivered to the Comptroller of the Currency.	By notes of failed and liquidating national banks, deposited in United States Treasury.
1875	....	$155,520,880.48	$24,644.85	$155,545,525.33	$26,166,291.09	$115,109,445.00	$6,579,217.00
1876	$6,031,022.32	209,038,854.94	16,491.42	215,086,368.68	102,478,700.00	78,643,155.00	24,927,900.00
1877	7,942,539.00	242,885,375.14	24,996.58	250,852,910.72	151,079,300.00	62,518,600.00	24,439,700.00
1878	11,505,312.52	213,151,458.56	37,619.20	224,694,420.28	152,437,300.00	51,585,400.00	11,852,100.00
1879	8,410,848.33	157,656,644.96	22,146.42	166,089,641.71	112,411,800.00	40,204,700.00	8,354,250.00
1880	3,785,389.29	61,585,675.68	6,461.30	65,377,526.27	24,080,500.00	25,861,700.00	6,671,700.00
1881	3,097,983.77	59,650,259.43	13,231.38	62,761,474.58	6,763,600.00	40,080,700.00	12,435,400.00
1882	2,844,107.37	76,089,327.48	11,222.13	78,944,656.98	3,801,500.00	53,838,500.00	16,953,730.00
1883	2,630,989.32	102,699,676.73	8,092.09	106,338,758.14	15,572,100.00	78,664,758.00	4,667,060.00
1884	6,672,963.85	126,152,572.34	6,066.30	132,838,602.49	26,255,500.00	95,616,064.00	3,507,950.00
1885	6,910,452.03	150,209,129.01	17,060.07	157,136,641.11	45,634,800.00	98,598,170.00	5,591,730.00
1886	6,791,087.93	130,296,606.82	25,528.97	137,113,223.72	46,701,100.00	82,256,713.50	3,910,573.00
1887	3,840,402.05	87,689,687.15	16,404.07	91,546,493.27	20,786,640.00	66,841,550.60	1,133,215.50
1888	2,165,539.41	99,152,364.34	14,749.28	101,332,653.03	17,453,780.00	75,912,756.45	92,672.00
Total	73,628,637.19	1,871,778,513.06	244,746.06	1,945,658,896.31	752,513,911.00	969,732,211.95	131,117,797.50

Year ending June 30—	By United States notes deposited in the Treasury of the United States.	By packages referred and moneys returned.	By express charges deducted.	By counterfeit notes rejected and returned.	By national-bank notes—less than three-fifths, lacking signatures, and stolen—rejected and returned, and discount on United States currency.	By "shorts" reported in national-bank notes received for redemption.	Cash on hand at close of year.
1875	....	$1,620,557.39	....	$3,741.00	$15,028.12	$20,223.50	$6,031,022.32
1876	....	1,065,602.20	....	5,188.00	7,709.22	16,175.26	7,942,539.00
1877	....	1,278,903.86	....	5,634.00	4,756.91	29,704.43	11,505,312.52
1878	....	384,372.22	....	4,008.00	3,997.13	16,394.60	8,410,848.33
1879	$959,132.00	329,323.34	$25,842.15	3,016.00	6,282.58	9,996.35	3,785,389.29
1880	428,686.00	305,432.14	9,938.41	3,846.75	7,870.23	9,868.97	3,097,983.77
1881	30,645.00	509,971.06	3,345.03	4,324.50	22,763.37	6,618.25	2,844,107.37
1882	24,970.00	672,427.09	1,152.09	4,151.00	3,832.35	13,405.13	2,630,989.32
1883	7,267.00	727,282.98	725.84	4,559.50	4,337.62	10,103.35	6,672,963.85
1884	81,858.00	455,333.05	523.54	3,770.50	3,365.77	3,785.60	6,910,452.03
1885	177,350.00	329,249.19	612.25	3,560.00	3,636.49	6,445.25	6,791,087.93
1886	111,924.50	277,194.78	526.96	2,720.00	3,822.28	8,246.65	3,840,402.05
1887	126,727.10	464,413.45	573.58	2,924.00	2,554.23	22,356.00	2,165,539.41
1888	182,678.30	806,396.48	716.62	2,722.00	1,979.40	2,741.70	6,876,210.08
Total	2,131,237.90	9,285,859.23	43,956.47	54,165.25	91,934.70	175,975.04	80,501,817.27

TABLE SHOWING, BY FISCAL YEARS, FROM 1875 TO 1888, THE AMOUNTS OF NATIONAL-BANK NOTES RECEIVED AT THE UNITED STATES TREASURY FOR REDEMPTION FROM THE PRINCIPAL CITIES AND OTHER PLACES, AND THE PROPORTION OF EACH AMOUNT TO THE WHOLE.

Year.	New York.		Boston.		Philadelphia.		Chicago.		Cincinnati.		Saint Louis.	
	Amounts.	Per cent.	Amounts.	Per cent.	Amounts.	Per cent.	Amounts.	Per cent.	Amounts.	Per cent.	Amounts.	Per cent.
1875	$80,925,000	52.07	$17,598,000	11.32	$9,096,000	5.85	$6,814,000	4.39	$3,676,000	2.37	$1,384,000	.89
1876	78,389,000	38.37	55,878,000	27.35	9,778,000	4.79	10,106,000	4.89	3,085,000	1.51	1,019,000	.50
1877	76,693,000	32.47	75,212,000	31.84	20,968,000	8.89	4,162,000	1.76	2,781,000	1.18	1,292,000	.55
1878	66,273,000	31.48	80,527,000	38.26	10,836,000	5.15	3,194,000	1.52	2,268,000	1.08	999,000	.47
1879	54,170,000	35.00	59,375,000	38.36	7,052,000	4.56	1,719,000	1.11	1,219,000	.79	1,487,000	.96
1880	26,460,000	42.96	11,701,000	19.00	3,358,000	5.45	1,673,000	2.72	819,000	1.33	392,000	.64
1881	23,319,000	39.09	5,565,000	9.33	4,919,000	8.25	2,655,000	4.45	996,000	1.67	673,000	2.13
1882	28,012,000	36.82	7,370,000	9.69	5,939,000	7.81	3,545,000	4.66	1,188,000	1.56	1,061,000	1.39
1883	36,042,000	35.10	16,631,000	16.19	7,333,000	7.14	6,146,000	5.98	1,774,000	1.73	1,372,000	1.34
1884	54,327,000	43.07	19,971,000	15.83	6,830,000	5.41	5,794,000	4.59	1,822,000	1.45	1,155,000	.92
1885	75,409,000	50.20	27,473,000	18.29	7,220,000	4.81	4,558,000	3.03	1,910,000	1.27	977,000	.65
1886	49,487,000	37.98	30,031,000	23.05	7,323,000	5.62	5,493,000	4.22	2,263,000	1.74	3,422,000	2.63
1887	31,314,583	35.71	13,219,209	15.08	6,972,856	7.95	5,315,319	6.06	2,244,310	2.56	3,421,698	3.90
1888	43,411,196	43.78	13,062,289	13.17	6,400,953	6.46	5,508,460	5.56	2,725,689	2.75	3,033,908	3.06

Year.	Baltimore.		New Orleans.		Providence.		Pittsburgh.		Other places.		Total.	
	Amounts.	Per cent.	Amounts.	Per cent.	Amounts.	Per cent.	Amounts.	Per cent.	Amounts.	Per cent.	Amounts.	Per cent.
1875	$1,902,000	1.22			$1,388,000	.89	$1,449,000	.93	$31,189,000	20.07	$155,421,000	100.00
1876	3,265,000	1.60			3,247,000	1.59	1,425,000	.70	38,108,000	18.70	204,300,000	100.00
1877	1,821,000	.77			5,653,000	2.39	1,322,000	.56	46,286,000	19.59	236,210,000	100.00
1878	1,085,000	.52			4,989,000	2.37	1,141,000	.54	39,179,000	18.61	210,491,000	100.00
1879	693,000	.45			3,772,000	2.44	635,000	.41	24,647,000	15.92	154,769,000	100.00
1880	415,000	.67			1,454,000	2.36	547,000	.89	14,767,000	23.98	61,586,000	100.00
1881	673,000	1.13			1,419,000	2.38	606,000	1.01	18,825,000	31.56	59,650,000	100.00
1882	947,000	1.24			1,426,000	1.87	880,000	1.16	25,721,000	33.80	76,089,000	100.00
1883	1,626,000	1.58			1,666,000	1.62	917,000	.89	29,193,000	28.43	102,700,000	100.00
1884	2,853,000	2.26			1,820,000	1.44	819,000	.65	30,761,000	24.38	126,152,000	100.00
1885	3,705,000	2.47	$2,063,000	1.37	2,293,000	1.53	683,000	.46	23,918,000	15.92	150,209,000	100.00
1886	3,546,000	2.72	1,423,000	1.09	1,731,000	1.32	526,000	.40	25,051,000	19.23	130,296,600	100.00
1887	3,102,500	3.54	1,316,036	1.50	1,015,131	1.16	527,800	.60	19,240,185	21.94	87,689,657	100.00
1888	2,927,000	2.95	1,327,699	1.34	874,700	.88	647,089	.65	19,233,381	19.40	99,152,364	100.00

TABLE SHOWING TOTAL AMOUNT AND MODE OF PAYMENT FOR NATIONAL-BANK NOTES REDEEMED, BY FISCAL YEARS, COMMENCING WITH YEAR ENDING JUNE 30, 1875.

Fiscal year.	Transfer checks.	United States notes.	Fractional silver coin.	Standard silver dollars.	Redeemed at counter.	Credits to assistant treasurers and U. S. depositaries in general account.	Credit in redemption accounts.	Total.
1875	$58,825,756.00	$50,858,842.00			$100,000.00	$24,066,844.00	$19,040,413.00	$152,891,855.00
1876	92,374,801.00	40,120,338.00			4,738,979.00	19,078,209.00	52,643,065.00	208,955,392.00
1877	95,212,743.45	34,588,129.15	$468,971.00		6,675,000.00	12,789,757.00	91,856,769.92	241,591,373.52
1878	75,361,427.23	23,046,418.44	549,645.40		2,661,021.00	12,669,083.76	98,552,739.98	212,780,335.81
1879	51,718,253.06	14,617,619.41	52,178.90	$96,683.32	5,089,222.80	35,148,181.33	50,581,484.69	157,303,622.96
1880	10,852,505.53	21,174,826.66	28,230.59	174,831.85	3,883,417.60	18,218,070.37	6,924,097.88	61,255,580.48
1881	22,415,972.28	19,567,744.21	85,164.56	215,045.27	3,522,607.00	8,936,232.92	4,313,702.36	59,056,468.60
1882	32,992,144.72	23,222,831.83	246,447.42	269,918.44	4,033,402.40	10,106,238.45	4,534,598.69	75,405,581.95
1883	56,018,447.71	23,668,064.66	296,257.79	242,518.37	3,941,638.00	12,428,692.86	5,248,120.14	101,843,739.53
1884	77,991,916.83	24,080,304.62	158,127.60	1,015,519.10	3,826,293.00	12,960,221.66	5,727,726.37	125,760,163.18
1885	105,840,234.80	19,236,730.27	135,773.22	482,500.35	3,848,090.50	13,944,370.50	6,443,697.26	149,931,396.90
1886	74,149,555.26	9,204,752.76	103,843.62	451,194.22	8,385,485.00	31,007,087.20	6,727,706.96	130,029,625.12
1887	39,996,984.07	15,657,298.62	97,670.41	248,970.92	4,200,651.50	24,768,344.79	2,243,346.65	87,213,269.96
1888	53,463,333.36	19,280,725.65	90,684.97	202,537.79	3,229,772.00	20,149,324.00	1,830,349.65	98,246,727.42
Total	847,214,075.30	338,324,626.28	2,312,998.48	3,399,719.63	58,125,582.80	256,210,657.99	356,667,877.95	1,862,265,538.43

TABLE SHOWING, BY FISCAL YEARS FROM 1875 TO 1888, EXPENSES INCURRED IN THE REDEMPTION OF NATIONAL-BANK NOTES AT THE UNITED STATES TREASURY.

Year.	Charges for transportation.	Costs for assorting notes.						
		Salaries.	Printing and binding.	Stationery.	Postage.	Contingent and other expenses.	Furniture.	Total.
1875	$88,098.31	$158,227.39		*$12,290.72	$3,298.80	$16,131.47	$12,918.68	$290,965.37
1876	159,142.84	188,018.94		*9,174.68	3,391.00	1,993.01	3,472.84	365,193.31
1877	189,362.05	150,695.68	$6,604.30	3,818.10	3,716.66	2,869.31		357,066.10
1878	173,420.00	136,560.63	2,060.32	3,090.00		2,193.93		317,942.48
1879	98,296.75	133,956.27	2,894.60	2,597.22		3,203.11		240,949.95
1880	34,764.24	104,350.08	2,632.69	1,034.29		947.09		143,728.39
1881	33,843.86	89,564.72	1,220.60	1,051.27		531.67		126,212.12
1882	39,203.31	87,593.56	1,535.42	806.51		390.58		129,529.38
1883	57,190.86	86,213.35	2,401.54	890.41		896.11		147,592.27
1884	68,684.11	88,426.79	1,935.91	1,133.84		716.00		160,896.65
1885	85,255.48	93,371.82	1,670.77	1,114.19		444.90		161,857.16
1886	74,490.52	89,065.18	3,190.89	1,163.65		333.11		168,243.35
1887	48,020.53	87,450.54	1,430.93	1,053.39		1,011.61		138,967.60
1888	51,529.76	86,232.40	2,580.78	687.44		111.10		141,141.48

*In 1875 and 1876 "Printing and binding" was included with item "Stationery."

REDEMPTION OF CIRCULATION OF BANKS IN THE HANDS OF RECEIVERS, OF THOSE IN VOLUNTARY LIQUIDATION, AND OF THOSE REDUCING CIRCULATION UNDER THE ACT OF JUNE 20, 1874.

The redemption of circulating notes of failed banks at the United States Treasury was provided for originally as it is now, by giving the Comptroller power to cancel or to sell the bonds of the banks, and in case of deficiency in the proceeds to make it good out of the assets of the corporation; but before the act of 1874 went into effect the notes of such banks were called in by public advertisement, whereas now they are left in circulation until they are brought by the ordinary currents of redemption into the office of the Treasurer or of one of the assistant treasurers, or into the hands of a designated depositary of public moneys, or one of the national-bank depositaries.

Section 8 of the act of June 20, 1874, requires the Treasurer, assistant treasurers, designated depositaries, and national-bank depositaries to assort and return to the Treasurer for redemption the notes of such national banks as have failed, or have gone into voluntary liquidation, and of all such as shall thereafter fail or go into such liquidation.

The following table, compiled from the records of the Bureau of the Currency, shows the course of redemption of the notes of failed banks. Total circulation of all failed banks, $15,432,360; amount redeemed, $13,911,335; balance outstanding or lost, $1,521,025.

TABLE SHOWING, BY YEARS, FROM OCTOBER 1, 1865, TO NOVEMBER 1, 1888, THE TOTAL CIRCULATION OF BANKS FAILED, THE AMOUNT REDEEMED, AND THE BALANCE OUTSTANDING AT CLOSE OF EACH YEAR. (COMPILED FROM REPORTS OF COMPTROLLER OF THE CURRENCY.)

Year ending—	Total circulation outstanding at end of previous year.	Total circulation of banks failed during the year.	Aggregate of two previous columns.	Amount of circulation of failed banks redeemed during year.	Balance of circulation of failed banks outstanding at close of year.
October 1, 1865	....	$44,000	$44,000.00	None.	$44,000.00
October 1, 1866	$44,000.00	265,000	309,000.00	$5,320.00	303,680.00
October 1, 1867	303,680.00	748,900	1,052,580.00	163,288.00	889,292.00
October 1, 1868	889,292.00	321,800	1,211,092.00	648,533.00	562,559.00
October 1, 1869	562,559.00	45,000	607,559.00	274,820.55	332,738.45
October 1, 1870	332,738.45	129,700	462,438.45	143,602.60	318,835.85
October 1, 1871	318,835.85	None.	318,835.85	110,284.25	208,551.60
November 1, 1872	208,551.60	1,388,393	1,596,944.60	1,095,581.60	501,363.00
November 1, 1873	501,363.00	2,522,100	3,023,463.00	720,915.00	2,302,548.00
November 1, 1874	2,302,548.00	230,000	2,532,548.00	494,910.00	2,037,638.00
November 1, 1875	2,037,638.00	638,676	2,676,314.00	1,279,346.50	1,396,967.50
November 1, 1876	1,396,967.50	540,609	1,937,576.50	961,279.80	976,296.70
November 1, 1877	976,296.70	2,349,114	3,325,410.70	2,299,785.25	1,025,625.45
November 1, 1878	1,025,625.45	1,385,068	2,410,693.45	858,239.45	1,551,454.00
November 1, 1879	1,551,454.00	516,825	2,068,279.00	919,600.00	1,148,679.00
November 1, 1880	1,148,679.00	506,143	1,654,822.00	322,546.00	1,332,276.00
November 1, 1881	1,332,276.00	None.	1,332,276.00	382,534.00	949,742.00
November 1, 1882	949,742.00	999,500	1,949,242.00	547,610.00	1,401,632.00
November 1, 1883	1,401,632.00	108,200	1,509,832.00	648,704.00	861,128.00
November 1, 1884	861,128.00	850,120	1,711,248.00	612,960.00	1,098,288.00
November 1, 1885	1,098,288.00	486,550	1,584,838.00	451,424.00	1,133,414.00
November 1, 1886	1,133,414.00	434,810	1,568,254.00	110,228.00	1,458,026.00
November 1, 1887	1,458,026.00	307,738	1,765,764.00	339,799.00	1,425,965.00
November 1, 1888	1,425,965.00	614,084	2,010,049.00	519,024.00	1,521,025.00
Total	....	15,432,360	....	13,911,335.00	....

Before the act of June 20, 1874, banks reducing their circulation could withdraw their bonds from the Treasury only upon surrendering there, for cancellation, an amount of their circulating notes proportioned to the amount of bonds to be withdrawn, and up to July 14, 1870, banks for one year after going into voluntary liquidation had to resort to the same means in order to withdraw their bonds; but after the expiration of the year such banks might deposit lawful money for the difference between the whole amount of circulation issued to them and the amount surrendered, and thereupon get back the rest of their bonds. The amount of such deposits and the time at which they should be made were left to the choice of the bank. The act of July 14, 1870, made the deposit of lawful money obligatory upon liquidating banks, and the act of June 20, 1874, fixed six months after notice of liquidation as the limit of time allowed for making such deposits.

The act of June 20, 1874, provided also that any national banking association might withdraw its circulating notes upon the deposit of lawful money with the Treasurer of the United States in sums of not less than $9,000. Under this act, and on account of liquidating and insolvent banks, and under section 6 of the act of July 12, 1882, which provides for a deposit of lawful money to retire the old circulation of national banks whose corporate existence has been extended, $409,664,244 of lawful money has been deposited with the Treasurer. This includes $2,663,720 for redemption of the notes of national gold banks and $96,958,887 for the redemption of national-bank notes under section 6 of the act of July 12, 1882.

During the year ending October 31, 1888, lawful money to the amount of $37,781,464 was deposited with the Treasurer to retire circulation, of which $2,107,978 was deposited by banks in liquidation, $14,520,956 by banks reducing circulation under the act of June 20, 1874, and $21,152,530 by banks retiring old circulation under the act of July 12, 1882. The amount previously deposited under the acts of June 20, 1874, and July 12, 1882, was $320,681,226, by banks in liquidation, $65,446,364, making a total of $423,909,054. Deducting from the total the amount of circulating notes redeemed and destroyed without re-issue, which was $336,890,145, there remained in the hands of the Treasurer on October 31, 1888, $87,018,909 of lawful money for the redemption and retirement of national-bank circulation, including $188,987 for the redemption of the circulating notes of national gold banks.

Prior to June 20, 1874, there were redeemed and destroyed $10,431,135, and since that date $326,459,009 of bank notes have been redeemed, destroyed, and retired. This latter amount includes $2,474,733 of the notes of national gold banks, and $50,226,314 of the notes of national banks whose corporate existence has been extended under the act of July 12, 1882.

There are at present no national gold banks in existence. Of those which have been organized, three went into voluntary liquidation and the others became currency banks, under the provisions of the act approved February 14, 1880.

Under all the laws now in operation the Treasurer has received for redemption up to November 1, 1888, national-bank notes aggregating in amount $1,899,039,275.

During the past year the receipts at the Treasury amounted to $103,945,471, of which amount $46,849,990, or 45 per cent., was received from the banks in the city of New York, and $14,327,098, or 14 per cent., from banks in the city of Boston. The amount received from Philadelphia was $6,259,673; from Chicago, $5,694,050; from Cincinnati, $2,337,754; from Saint Louis, $2,501,100; from Baltimore, $3,086,055; from New Orleans, $1,444,067; from Providence, $902,677, and from Pittsburgh, $666,786.

The following table exhibits the amount of national-bank notes received monthly for redemption by the Comptroller of the Currency during the year ending October 31, 1888, and the amount received during the same period at the Redemption Agency of the Treasury, together with the total amount received since the passage of the act of June 20, 1874:

Months.	Received by the Comptroller of the Currency—					Received at United States Treasury Redemption Agency.
	From national banks in connection with reduction of circulation and replacement with new notes.	From the Redemption Agency—			Total.	
		For replacement with new notes.	For reduction of circulation under act June 20, 1874.	Insolvent and liquidating national banks.		
1887.						
November	$92,930	$1,555,575	$2,321,042	$1,005,938	$5,975,485	$5,709,075
December	42,340	1,820,780	2,043,736	1,464,735	5,371,591	8,228,278
1888.						
January	7,950	2,384,230	3,071,765	1,956,642	7,420,587	12,232,503
February	2,250	2,853,080	3,411,525	2,206,185	8,473,040	9,176,389
March	20	2,615,800	2,778,293	1,918,341	7,312,454	7,916,274
April	2,780	2,572,775	2,698,282	2,102,422	7,376,259	9,642,000
May	5,325	3,054,700	3,234,179	2,421,301	8,715,653	12,302,623
June	1,560	2,834,220	3,104,570	2,380,175	8,829,525	11,387,583
July	....	2,268,735	2,179,307	1,637,574	6,085,616	9,224,900
August	1,250	1,873,305	1,900,938	1,519,240	5,294,823	6,984,802
September	....	1,975,540	1,932,047	1,537,671	5,445,258	5,205,273
October	1,805	2,790,610	2,103,501	1,546,751	6,442,727	5,845,727
	158,270	28,599,530	30,779,165	22,706,035	82,243,020	103,915,472
Received from June 20, 1874, to October 31, 1888	16,345,425	765,708,615	193,727,009	76,588,755	1,052,369,804	1,795,093,803
Grand total	16,503,695	794,308,145	224,506,194	99,294,790	1,134,612,824	1,899,039,275

Notes of gold banks are not included in the above table.

The following table, compiled from the books of the Comptroller of the Currency, exhibits the amount of national-bank notes received at this office and destroyed yearly since the establishment of the system:

Prior to November 1, 1865	$175,490	During year ended October 31—	
During year ended October 31—		1879	$41,101,830
1866	1,050,382	1880	35,539,660
1867	3,401,423	1881	54,941,130
1868	4,602,825	1882	74,917,611
1869	8,603,729	1883	82,913,766
1870	14,305,689	1884	93,178,418
1871	24,344,047	1885	91,048,723
1872	30,211,720	1886	59,989,810
1873	36,433,171	1887	47,729,083
1874	49,939,741	1888	59,568,525
1875	137,697,696	Additional amount of insolvent and liquidating national banks	109,850,919
1876	98,672,716		
1877	76,918,963		
1878	57,381,249	Total	1,294,515,314

Notes of gold banks are not included in the above table.

There was in the vault of the redemption division of this office, awaiting destruction, at the close of business October 31, 1887	$136,310
Received during the year ended October 31, 1888	82,293,962
Total	82,430,272
Withdrawn and destroyed during the year	82,325,502
Balance in vault October 31, 1888	104,770

SUPERVISION.

Supervision over the national banks is maintained through a corps of examiners, but it embraces also the scrutiny of the five reports of condition required of every bank each year, and of the reports of earnings and dividends which are made twice a year by all banks, and oftener by those by which dividends are oftener declared.

The Comptroller may call upon any bank, at his discretion, for such special reports as he thinks proper, and an extensive correspondence is kept up with officers and directors in regard to matters contained in the examiners' reports and in the various reports received directly from the banks.

Since directors are responsible in their individual capacity for all violations of law which they knowingly commit or permit (sec. 5239 R. S.), the rule has been adopted of addressing to the board of directors of each bank such correspondence with it as relates to violations of law, and when the matter is serious a separate note is sent to each director informing him of the letter addressed to the board.

Letters relating to the internal administration of the bank are addressed to its president, all others to the cashier.

From a review of the correspondence, as thus classified, it appears that the matters requiring most frequent attention are as follows:

VIOLATIONS OF LAW.

1. EXCESSIVE LOANS.

Section 5200, Revised Statutes, forbids loans to any person, firm, company, or corporation exceeding 10 per cent. upon the capital of the bank.

This restriction is too general in its terms, and is necessarily exceeded by banks in large cities, where the magnitude of deposits and of transactions make conformity with the law impracticable. On the other hand, it is a most salutary restraint upon banks in small communities, preventing the accommodation they afford from being monopolized by a few favored individuals, usually the directors and their friends or relations.

The enforcement of the law in these latter cases is, however, seriously impeded by the notorious disregard of it in the former, and I therefore earnestly repeat the recommendation made last year for new legislation on this subject.

2. LOANS UPON THE SECURITY OF REAL ESTATE.

Section 5137, Revised Statutes, prohibits national banks from holding real estate by title or under mortgage, except in certain specified cases, and the courts have construed this as forbidding, also, loans upon the security of real estate.

The language of the statute is not explicit, and it has been variously construed by different courts, nor has the restriction that popular support which is almost necessary to the official enforcement of any law. On the contrary, there is a widespread feeling that the national bank law discriminates against real estate unjustly, and in agricultural communities this feeling is so strong that in many cases it is resentful, and is made the ground of popular opposition to the whole national-bank system. Even among experienced and conservative bankers in certain sections there appears to be a feeling that the restraint in this respect is unreasonable.

Among the amendments to the national-bank law which were submitted with my last Annual Report will be found certain modifications of the provisions bearing upon real-estate security, and I respectfully repeat the recommendation for their speedy enactment.

3. INVESTMENTS IN BONDS, STOCKS, AND OTHER SECURITIES.

The Supreme Court (*First National Bank* v. *National Exchange Bank*, 92 *U. S.*, 122) has pronounced the dictum that a national banking association can not deal in stocks. Two State courts (Pennsylvania and Maryland) have decided that such associations are not authorized to act as brokers or agents in the purchase and sale of such securities.

Like other restrictions upon the national banks, this one, which in the main is wholesome and in most cases necessary, in view of the public uses to which the capital and resources of national banks are dedicated, has been found in some peculiar cases to be inconvenient. In some sections, especially in New England, the number of banks and the amount of floating capital are in excess of the business needs of the locality. The more active and enterprising among these banks secure the commercial paper, and the others have either to lend out their money at distant points, or invest it in securities. The latter is undoubtedly the safer, and therefore the better course, and the officers and directors who resort to it are naturally disposed to dispute any interpretation of the law which is adverse to such investments.

The more I learn about the banking business of the country, however, and in this position the opportunities for learning are incessant and excellent, the more satisfied I am that banks of deposit should never invest in anything but bills of exchange or short-date commercial paper. If capitalists desire to combine for the purpose of holding securities, or dealing in stocks and bonds, they have abundant facilities for doing so outside of the national-bank system. There can be no question of the right of all citizens to invest their own means as they please, but the national banks, under the operation of the laws made for their government, have become the principal depositaries of the floating capital of the country, hence the managers of these banks are bound by duty to their depositors to regard strictly the limitations upon investments imposed by the law, and this obligation becomes strengthened when, as in this case, the law is in harmony with sound banking principles.

Those who are charged with the enforcement of the national-banking law can not be too persistent in keeping the system as clear as possible of every variety of what may be called incrustations of capital.

4. DEFICIENT RESERVE.

There has been a marked improvement all over the country during the last few years in the observance of the law as to reserves and in the conscientiousness and accuracy with which reports are made.

The modifications suggested in the law would be very acceptable to the banks, and would tend to the improvement of the system.

5. EXCESSIVE AND UNLAWFUL DIVIDENDS.

The provisions of law relating to dividends are substantially as follows:

1. The authority to declare dividends and to pay them is vested in the board of directors.

2. A dividend may be declared only when the net profits actually realized and on hand equal or exceed the total amount to be paid to stockholders.

3. Net profits are to be ascertained by deducting from gross earnings and profits: first, all expenses and losses incurred up to the date on which the books are closed; and second, all bad debts, which are thus defined:

All debts due to any associations, on which interest is past due and unpaid for a period of six months, unless the same are well secured, and in process of collection, shall be considered bad debts within the meaning of this section.

4. Until the surplus fund amounts to twenty per cent. of the capital, ten per cent. of net profits must be added to that fund every time a dividend is declared, so that in such cases the fund available for dividend is only ninety per cent. of net profits.

6. Improper reduction of surplus.

In many cases banks have passed to surplus account more than 10 per cent. of net profits, and subsequently before the surplus was full some of these have claimed that such excess might be withdrawn in dividends. Such a claim does not appear to be consistent either with the language of the law or with its manifest purpose. In construing the language of the law, it is to be observed that the act of 1863 required and that of 1864 authorized dividends every six months out of individual net profits actually on hand, while the latter act prescribed that every six month each bank should make to the Comptroller a report of its profits, expenses, and losses, whether or not any dividend should be then declared. The provision for a tithe to the surplus was from the first implicated with the regulations as to dividends and the charging off of losses, expenses, and bad debts, hence it seems clear that according to the sum already carried to surplus is no longer a part of the undivided profits. The surplus account is by the statute co-ordinated with shareholders as a beneficiary in the dividend fund, and if an amount in excess of the obligatory tithe is once added to the surplus, that amount ceases to be a part of the undivided profits out of which alone dividends may be declared.

As long as the surplus is below 20 per cent. of capital, it can not be reduced except by losses in excess of undivided profits.

The intention of the law in providing for a surplus fund seems to be to afford to shareholders a protection against assessments. Such protection is valuable to all shareholders who are not capitalists, and who, therefore, presumably are not prepared to respond to assessments upon their shares, but it is of vital importance to small investors and to the beneficiaries of trust and estate funds invested in national bank stock. The surplus fund stands between such shareholders and their wealthy partners as a safe guard against the process commonly known as "freezing out." Without this protection improvident or designing directors would be constantly exposing their shareholders to assessments, and on every such occasion the weak and helpless would be sacrificed, while their stock would pass into the hands of the designing or the grasping.

REPORTS.

During the past year 15,505 reports of condition, about 6,137 reports of dividends and earnings, and 3,166 reports from examiners have been received at the office of the Comptroller of the Currency, and fully 17,000 letters and circulars have been sent out in connection with them. The reports received are all carefully examined, compared with one another, and abstracts are made from them.

From these various reports, after examination and verification, the subjoined tables have been compiled, and other tables compiled from the same sources will be found in the Appendix, pp. 180 to 215, showing the condition of the reserve of national banks, their loans and discounts, abstract of reports of dividends and earnings, ratios to capital and to capital and surplus, and other valuable information as to the condition of the national banks on the date of the last report.

A large table on folded sheet, appended hereto, exhibits for October, 1888, in aggregate, every detail embraced in the tabulated reports required of the banks. Similar tables are made up for the information of the Comptroller from the reports gathered from all banks five times each year. The amounts are given separately for each State, reserve city, and Territory.

DIAGRAM.

With the Report of 1886 a diagram was submitted grouping graphically the main features of the national banking system, and showing by continuous lines the variations occurring between January 1, 1866, and October 7, 1886. It has not been considered necessary to reproduce this diagram, because any one interested in the subject can extend the lines by means of the figures contained in the summary of the condition of the banks, given on page 2 of this Report.

The following table groups in a compendious form the most important facts shown in the diagram, extended to October 4, 1888. The exact figures in each case are given in the table; in the diagram they had to be abridged into round millions.

	Jan. 1, 1866.	Oct. 4, 1888.	Highest point touched.		Lowest point touched.	
			Amount.	Date.	Amount.	Date.
Capital	$403, 357, 346	$592, 621, 656	$592, 621, 656	Oct. 4, 1888	$403, 357, 346	Jan. 1, 1866
Capital, surplus, and undivided profits	475, 330, 204	855, 576, 646	855, 576, 647	....do	475, 330, 204	....do ....
Circulation	213, 239, 530	151, 702, 809	341, 320, 256	Dec. 26, 1873	151, 702, 809	Oct. 4, 1888
Total investments in United States bonds	440, 380, 350	232, 582, 250	712, 437, 900	Apr. 4, 1879	223, 242, 050	Aug. 1, 1887
Deposits	520, 212, 174	1, 350, 320, 861	1, 350, 320, 861	Oct. 4, 1888	504, 407, 586	Oct. 8, 1870
Loans and discounts	500, 650, 109	1, 674, 886, 285	1, 674, 886, 285	....do	500, 650, 109	Jan. 1, 1866
Cash:						
National-bank notes	20, 406, 442	21, 600, 818	28, 809, 699	Dec. 31, 1883	11, 841, 104	Oct. 7, 1867
Legal-tender notes	187, 846, 548	81, 099, 461	205, 793, 579	Oct. 1, 1866	52, 156, 439	Mar. 11, 1881
Specie	16, 909, 363	178, 097, 816	181, 292, 276	June 30, 1888	8, 050, 330	Oct. 1, 1875

An examination of this table shows that the aggregate capital, surplus, undivided profits, circulation, and deposits have increased from $1,208,781,908 in January, 1866, to $2,357,600,316 in October, 1888, which is less than double, while the loans and discounts have gone up from $500,650,109 to $1,674,886,285, which is more than treble, showing how much more widely the banks are now identified with the general business of the country than they were twenty-three years ago.

The investments in bonds have taken an opposite course. Amounting to $440,380,350 in 1866, increasing to $712,437,900 in April, 1879.

they amounted on October 4 last to $232,582,250. Of this amount $60,458,450 were held by the banks for public deposits and other purposes than circulation.

The specie, which at the beginning of the period was but $16,909,363, had got down in October, 1875, to $8,050,330, is now $178,097,816, and on June 30, 1888, was $181,292,276, the highest point yet reached. In October, 1887, the specie amounted to $165,085,454.

It is interesting to see how these changes appear when reduced to percentages.

The capital, surplus, undivided profits, circulation, and deposits constitute together the fund upon which a bank does its business.

Loans and discounts, United States bonds, specie, etc., are different forms in which this fund is invested. Taking the fund at $1,208,781,908 in 1866, at $2,240,587,843 in 1887, and at $2,357,600,316 in 1888, these investments represent the following proportions of those amounts, viz:

	1866.	1887.	1888.
	Per ct.	*Per ct.*	*Per ct.*
Loans and discounts	41.32	70.52	71.04
United States bonds	36.36	9.98	9.87
Specie	1.57	7.37	11.90
Total	79.25	87.87	92.81

Another striking fact is that in 1866 the circulation was $213,239,530, and on October 4, 1888, it is only $151,702,809. At the former period, therefore, the circulation was nearly 45 per cent. of the capital, surplus, and undivided profits, while now it is only about 18 per cent.

LOANS.

The following table gives a classification of the loans of the national banks in each of the central reserve cities of New York, Chicago, and Saint Louis, in other reserve cities classified in groups of four each, and in the rest of the country at nearly the same dates in each of the last three years:

OCTOBER 7, 1886.

	No. of banks.	On United States bonds on demand.	On other stocks, bonds, etc., on demand.	On single name paper without other security.	All other loans.	Total.
New York	45	$2,002,551	$91,636,791	$24,646,007	$135,447,027	$253,732,376
Chicago	15	85,900	10,663,006	12,593,921	32,058,515	55,401,342
Saint Louis	5	....	1,028,430	355,373	8,291,968	9,675,771
Group No. 1, 4 cities*	123	258,210	36,017,888	33,409,662	168,072,545	238,448,305
Group No. 2, 4 cities*	40	69,005	7,440,098	6,239,954	35,235,704	48,984,761
Group No. 3, 4 cities*	32	325,330	7,715,715	7,958,224	38,967,756	54,967,034
Group No. 4, San Francisco*	2	10,000	304,787	2,157,837	886,241	3,358,835
Country†	2,590	563,717	41,008,812	110,677,534	626,849,753	779,099,816
Total	2,852	3,314,721	196,415,477	198,128,533	1,045,809,509	1,443,668,240

OCTOBER 5, 1887.

	No. of banks.	On United States bonds on demand.	On other stocks, bonds, etc., on demand.	On single name paper without other security.	All other loans.	Total.
New York	47	$1,445,000	$95,075,844	$17,585,400	$143,906,941	$258,014,181
Chicago	18	500	10,821,735	15,498,986	34,754,972	61,076,193
Saint Louis	5	....	1,182,214	279,603	8,920,936	10,382,753
Group No. 1, 4 cities*	126	56,805	37,717,725	32,464,759	177,884,888	248,124,177
Group No. 2, 4 cities*	41	60,430	7,710,369	6,111,182	35,568,827	49,450,807
Group No. 3, 4 cities*	35	48,400	8,087,222	7,887,689	43,232,749	59,256,060
Group No. 4, 4 cities*	21	7,500	1,117,443	8,213,092	20,827,885	30,166,020
Country	2,750	1,413,918	44,335,803	124,035,463	693,790,281	863,575,555
Total	3,049	3,033,453	206,048,445	212,076,270	1,158,887,479	1,580,045,647

OCTOBER 4, 1888.

	No. of banks.	On United States bonds on demand.	On other stocks, bonds, etc., on demand.	On single name paper without other security.	All other loans.	Total.
New York	46	$2,132,159	$108,406,001	$28,026,205	$153,271,020	$292,405,481
Chicago	19	359,290	9,631,825	14,155,001	41,129,615	65,275,737
Saint Louis	4	....	921,854	300,450	6,988,242	8,210,546
Group No. 1, 4 cities*	128	148,770	44,271,104	41,430,120	182,567,297	268,417,291
Group No. 2, 4 cities*	41	10,765	7,806,794	7,162,779	37,435,637	52,435,975
Group No. 3, 4 cities*	33	75,000	6,570,938	7,260,665	42,188,407	56,095,010
Group No. 4, 4 cities*	22	1,200	1,205,506	8,501,966	21,303,327	31,012,089
Country	2,847	577,484	42,586,172	136,067,639	721,806,861	900,038,156
Total	3,140	3,304,674	221,400,344	243,430,915	1,206,690,352	1,674,886,285

* Group No. 1, Boston, Albany, Philadelphia, and Pittsburgh. Group No. 2, Baltimore, Washington, New Orleans, and Louisville. Group No. 3, Cincinnati, Cleveland, Detroit, and Milwaukee. Group No. 4, Kansas City, Saint Joseph, Omaha, and San Francisco.

† Kansas City, Saint Joseph, and Omaha were not reserve cities in 1886.

In the table below is given a full classification of the loans in New York City alone for the last five years:

Loans and discounts.	Sept. 30, 1884.	Oct. 1, 1885.	Oct. 7, 1886.	Oct. 5, 1887.	Oct. 4, 1888.
	44 banks.	44 banks.	45 banks.	47 banks.	46 banks.
On indorsed paper	$116,010,002	$114,013,775	$121,381,380	$115,310,625	$117,707,044
On single name paper	82,550,443	25,331,820	24,010,008	17,585,400	28,026,205
On U. S. bonds on demand	2,033,785	3,280,124	2,002,550	1,445,000	2,132,159
On other stocks, etc., on demand	69,805,215	80,687,265	91,636,701	95,075,844	108,406,001
On real-estate security	163,307	215,885	211,482	146,885	113,494
All other loans	3,881,375	13,289,229	13,854,215	28,443,431	35,450,488
Total	205,353,277	236,823,508	253,732,370	258,014,181	292,405,481

The subjoined tables bring forward to the latest date the usual summary of information as to the course of deposits and reserves since the act of June 20, 1874, went into effect. They show the amount of deposits and the state of the reserve at about October 1 of each year, in each central reserve city, in all the reserve cities, and in the States and Territories, and conclude with a general summary embracing all banks.

NEW YORK CITY.

Date.	No. of banks.	Net deposits.	Reserve required (25 per cent.).*	Reserve held.		Classification of reserve.			
				Amount.	Ratio to deposits.	Specie.	Other lawful money.	Due from agents.	Redemption fund.
		Millions.	*Millions.*	*Millions.*	*Per cent.*	*Millions.*	*Millions.*	*Millions.*	*Millions.*
Oct. 2, 1874	48	204.6	51.2	68.3	33.4	14.4	52.4	....	1.5
Oct. 1, 1875	48	202.3	50.7	60.5	29.9	5.0	54.4	....	1.1
Oct. 2, 1876	47	197.9	49.5	60.7	30.7	14.6	45.3	....	0.8
Oct. 1, 1877	47	174.9	43.7	48.1	27.5	13.0	34.3	....	0.8
Oct. 1, 1878	47	189.8	47.4	50.9	26.8	13.3	36.5	....	1.1
Oct. 2, 1879	47	210.2	52.6	53.1	25.3	19.4	32.6	....	1.1
Oct. 1, 1880	47	268.1	67.0	70.6	26.4	58.7	11.0	....	0.9
Oct. 1, 1881	48	268.8	67.2	62.5	23.3	50.6	10.9	....	1.0
Oct. 3, 1882	50	254.0	63.5	64.4	25.4	44.5	18.9	....	1.0
Oct. 2, 1883	48	266.9	66.7	70.8	26.5	50.3	19.7	....	0.9
Sept. 30, 1884	44	255.0	63.7	90.8	35.6	63.1	27.0	....	0.7
Oct. 1, 1885	44	312.9	78.2	115.7	37.0	91.5	23.7	....	0.5
Oct. 7, 1886	45	282.8	70.7	77.0	27.2	64.1	12.5	....	0.4
Oct. 5, 1887	47	284.3	71.1	80.1	28.2	63.6	16.1	....	0.4
Oct. 4, 1888	46	342.2	85.5	96.4	28.2	73.9	22.1	....	0.3
Average for 15 years...	47	247.6	61.9	71.3	28.8	42.7	27.8	....	0.8

CHICAGO.

Oct. 5, 1887	18	64.6	16.2	19.7	30.5	12.9	6.7	....	0.05
Oct. 4, 1888	19	69.3	17.3	21.0	30.2	13.1	7.8	....	0.05

SAINT LOUIS.

Oct. 5, 1887	5	10.3	2.6	2.7	26.4	1.3	1.3	....	0.03
Oct. 4, 1888	4	7.9	2.0	2.1	27.0	1.0	1.1	....	0.02

*All in cash.

RESERVE CITIES.*†

Date.	No. of banks	Net deposits.	Reserve required (25 per cent.).	Reserve held.		Classification of reserve.			
				Amount.	Ratio to deposits.	Specie.	Other lawful money.	Due from agents.	Redemption fund.
		Millions.	*Millions.*	*Millions.*	*Per cent.*	*Millions.*	*Millions.*	*Millions.*	*Millions.*
Oct. 2, 1874	182	221.4	55.3	76.0	34.3	4.5	36.7	31.1	3.7
Oct. 1, 1875	188	223.9	56.0	74.5	33.3	1.5	37.1	32.3	3.6
Oct. 2, 1876	189	217.0	54.2	76.1	35.1	4.0	37.1	32.0	3.0
Oct. 1, 1877	188	204.1	51.0	67.3	33.0	5.6	34.3	24.4	3.0
Oct. 1, 1878	184	199.9	50.0	71.1	35.6	9.4	29.4	29.1	3.2
Oct. 2, 1879	181	228.8	57.2	83.5	36.5	11.3	33.0	35.7	3.5
Oct. 1, 1880	184	289.4	72.4	105.2	36.2	28.3	25.0	48.2	3.7
Oct. 1, 1881	189	335.4	83.9	100.8	30.0	34.6	21.9	40.6	3.7
Oct. 3, 1882	193	318.8	79.7	89.1	28.0	28.3	24.1	33.2	3.5
Oct. 2, 1883	200	323.9	81.0	100.6	31.1	26.3	30.1	40.8	3.4
Sept. 30, 1884	203	307.9	77.0	99.0	32.2	30.3	33.3	32.3	3.1
Oct. 1, 1885	203	364.5	91.1	122.2	33.5	42.0	34.9	42.4	2.9
Oct. 7, 1886	217	381.5	95.4	114.0	29.9	44.5	26.0	41.3	2.2
Oct. 5, 1887	223	338.5	84.6	100.7	29.7	36.3	23.2	40.0	1.2
Oct. 4, 1888	224	384.9	96.2	116.9	30.4	40.0	24.5	51.5	0.9

* Reserve 25 per cent., one-half in cash.
† Includes Chicago and Saint Louis up to October 5, 1887.

STATES AND TERRITORIES.*

Date.	No. of banks.	Net deposits.	Reserve required (15 per cent.)*	Reserve held.		Classification of reserve.			
				Amount.	Ratio to deposits.	Specie.	Other lawful money.	Due from agents.	Redemption fund.
		Millions.	*Millions.*	*Millions.*	*Per cent.*	*Millions.*	*Millions.*	*Millions.*	*Millions.*
Oct. 2, 1874	1,774	293.4	44.0	100.6	34.3	2.4	33.7	52.7	11.9
Oct. 1, 1875	1,851	307.9	46.3	100.1	32.5	1.6	33.7	53.3	11.6
Oct. 2, 1876	1,853	291.7	43.8	99.9	34.3	2.7	31.0	55.4	10.8
Oct. 1, 1877	1,845	290.1	43.6	95.4	32.9	4.2	31.6	48.9	10.7
Oct. 1, 1878	1,822	289.1	43.4	106.1	36.7	8.0	31.1	56.0	11.0
Oct. 2, 1879	1,820	329.9	49.5	124.3	37.7	11.5	30.8	71.3	11.2
Oct. 1, 1880	1,859	410.5	61.6	147.2	35.8	21.2	28.3	86.4	11.3
Oct. 1, 1881	1,893	507.2	76.1	158.3	31.2	27.5	27.1	92.4	11.4
Oct. 3, 1882	2,026	545.8	81.9	150.4	27.5	30.0	30.0	80.1	11.3
Oct. 2, 1883	2,258	577.9	86.7	157.5	27.2	31.2	30.8	84.1	11.3
Sept. 30, 1884	2,417	585.8	80.4	156.3	29.2	35.2	30.0	79.7	10.5
Oct. 1, 1885	2,407	570.8	85.6	177.5	31.1	41.5	29.9	95.9	10.2
Oct. 7, 1886	2,590	637.6	95.6	186.2	29.2	47.8	30.1	99.5	8.7
Oct. 5, 1887	2,756	690.6	103.6	190.9	27.6	50.8	32.6	100.9	6.6
Oct. 4, 1888	2,847	739.2	110.9	209.8	28.4	50.2	34.5	110.0	6.2

SUMMARY.

Date.	No. of banks.	Net deposits.	Reserve required.	Amount.	Ratio to deposits.	Specie.	Other lawful money.	Due from agents.	Redemption fund.
Oct. 2, 1874	2,004	710.5	150.1	244.9	34.0	21.3	122.8	83.8	17.1
Oct. 1, 1875	2,087	734.1	152.2	235.1	32.0	8.1	125.2	85.6	16.3
Oct. 2, 1876	2,089	706.6	147.5	236.7	33.5	21.3	113.4	87.4	14.6
Oct. 1, 1877	2,080	669.1	138.3	210.8	31.5	22.8	100.2	73.3	14.5
Oct. 1, 1878	2,053	678.8	140.8	228.1	33.6	30.7	97.0	85.1	15.3
Oct. 2, 1879	2,048	768.9	150.8	260.9	33.9	42.2	95.9	107.0	15.8
Oct. 1, 1880	2,090	968.0	201.0	323.0	33.4	108.2	64.3	134.6	15.9
Oct. 1, 1881	2,132	1,111.6	227.2	321.6	28.9	112.7	59.0	133.0	16.1
Oct. 3, 1882	2,269	1,118.6	225.1	308.9	27.2	102.8	72.0	118.3	15.8
Oct. 2, 1883	2,501	1,168.7	234.4	328.9	28.1	107.8	80.6	124.9	15.6
Sept. 30, 1884	2,664	1,098.7	221.1	346.1	31.6	128.6	91.2	112.0	14.3
Oct. 1, 1885	2,714	1,248.2	254.9	415.4	33.3	175.0	88.5	138.3	13.6
Oct. 7, 1886	2,852	1,301.8	261.7	377.2	29.0	156.4	68.7	140.8	11.4
Oct. 5, 1887	3,049	1,388.4	278.0	394.2	28.4	165.1	79.0	140.9	8.3
Oct. 4, 1888	3,140	1,543.6	311.9	446.2	28.9	178.1	90.1	170.5	7.6

*Reserve 15 per cent., two-fifths in cash in bank.

In the above tables the specie held represents the aggregate of the gold and silver coin and Treasurer's certificates and clearing-house gold certificates. In the appendix, page 198, will be found a table giving the amount of each kind of coin and certificate held by the banks in each one of the States and reserve cities in October, 1887, and October, 1888, conveniently arranged for purposes of comparison.

TRANSACTIONS OF THE NEW YORK CLEARING-HOUSE.

The New York Clearing-House Association is composed of 64 members, of which 44 are national banks, 19 are State banks, and the other member is the assistant treasurer of the United States at New York. Two national banks and 23 State banks in the city do not belong to the association, but clear through associate members. Mr. W. A. Camp, the manager of the Clearing-House, has kindly supplied the data for the following tables, showing the transactions during the year ending October 1, 1888:

COMPARATIVE STATEMENT FOR TWO YEARS OF THE TRANSACTIONS OF THE NEW YORK CLEARING-HOUSE, SHOWING AGGREGATE AMOUNT OF CLEARINGS, AGGREGATE BALANCES, AND THE KINDS AND AMOUNTS OF MONEY PASSING IN SETTLEMENT OF THESE BALANCES.

Year ending—	Aggregate clearings.	Aggregate balances.	Kinds of money and amount of each kind.				Percentages.	
			U. S. gold certificates.	Bank of America gold certificates.*	Treasury certificates for legal tenders, sec. 5193, U. S. Revised Statutes.	Legal tenders and minor coin.	Gold certificates.	Legal tenders.
	Dollars.	*Dollars.*	*Dollars.*	*Dollars.*	*Dollars.*	*Dollars.*		
Oct. 1, 1887	34, 872, 848, 785	1, 569, 626, 324	812, 231, 000	748, 400, 000	1, 410, 000	7, 576, 325	99+	1—
Oct. 1, 1888	30, 863, 686, 609	1, 570, 198, 527	889, 197, 000	655, 033, 000	18, 195, 000	7, 773, 527	83. 19—	16. 81+
Decrease...	4, 009, 162, 176	....	....	93, 376, 000	....	....		
Increase ...	....	572, 203	76, 966, 000	....	16, 785, 000	197, 202		

* When the Government ceased issuing gold certificates December 1, 1878, the New York banks agreed to have a common depositary for their gold coin. The Bank of America performed this function. None of its certificates are now outstanding, the last having been canceled in July of the present year.

Following is a comparative statement of transactions of the New York Clearing-House for thirty-five years, showing for each year the number of banks, aggregate capital, clearings, and balances, average of the daily clearings and balances, and the percentage of balances and clearings:

Years.	No. of banks.	Capital.*	Clearings.	Balances paid in money.	Average daily clearings.	Average daily balances paid in money.	Ratios.
							Per ct.
1854	50	$47, 044, 000	$5, 750, 455, 987	$297, 411, 494	$19, 104, 505	$988, 078	5. 2
1855	48	48, 884, 180	5, 362, 912, 098	289, 694, 137	17, 412, 052	940, 565	5. 4
1856	50	52, 883, 700	6, 906, 213, 328	334, 714, 489	22, 278, 108	1, 079, 724	4. 8
1857	50	64, 420, 200	8, 333, 226, 718	365, 313, 902	26, 968, 371	1, 182, 246	4. 4
1858	46	67, 146, 018	4, 756, 664, 386	314, 238, 911	15, 393, 736	1, 016, 954	6. 6
1859	47	67, 921, 714	6, 448, 005, 956	363, 984, 683	20, 867, 333	1, 177, 944	5. 6
1860	50	69, 907, 435	7, 231, 143, 057	380, 693, 438	23, 401, 757	1, 232, 018	5. 3
1861	50	68, 900, 605	5, 915, 742, 758	353, 383, 944	19, 269, 520	1, 151, 088	6. 0
1862	50	68, 375, 820	6, 871, 443, 591	415, 530, 331	22, 237, 682	1, 344, 758	6. 0
1863	50	68, 972, 508	14, 867, 597, 849	677, 626, 483	48, 428, 657	2, 207, 252	4. 6
1864	49	68, 586, 763	24, 097, 196, 656	885, 719, 205	77, 984, 455	2, 866, 405	3. 7
1865	55	80, 363, 013	26, 032, 384, 342	1, 035, 765, 108	84, 796, 040	3, 373, 828	4. 0
1866	58	82, 370, 200	28, 717, 146, 914	1, 066, 135, 106	93, 541, 195	3, 472, 753	3. 7
1867	58	81, 770, 200	28, 675, 159, 472	1, 144, 963, 451	93, 101, 167	3, 717, 414	4. 0
1868	59	82, 270, 200	28, 484, 288, 637	1, 125, 455, 237	92, 182, 164	3, 642, 250	4. 0
1869	59	82, 720, 200	37, 407, 028, 987	1, 120, 318, 308	121, 451, 393	3, 637, 397	3. 0
1870	61	83, 620, 200	27, 804, 539, 406	1, 036, 484, 822	90, 274, 479	3, 365, 210	3. 7
1871	62	84, 420, 200	29, 300, 986, 682	1, 209, 721, 029	95, 133, 074	3, 927, 666	4. 1
1872	61	84, 420, 200	33, 844, 369, 568	1, 428, 582, 707	109, 884, 317	4, 636, 632	4. 2
1873	59	83, 370, 200	35, 461, 052, 826	1, 474, 508, 025	115, 885, 794	4, 818, 654	4. 2
1874	59	81, 635, 200	22, 855, 927, 636	1, 286, 753, 176	74, 692, 574	4, 205, 076	5. 7
1875	59	80, 435, 200	25, 061, 237, 902	1, 408, 608, 777	81, 899, 470	4, 603, 297	5. 6
1876	59	81, 731, 200	21, 597, 274, 247	1, 295, 042, 029	70, 349, 428	4, 218, 378	5. 9
1877	58	71, 085, 200	23, 289, 243, 701	1, 373, 996, 302	76, 358, 176	4, 504, 906	5. 9
1878	57	63, 611, 500	22, 508, 438, 442	1, 307, 843, 857	73, 555, 988	4, 274, 000	5. 8
1879	59	60, 800, 200	25, 178, 770, 691	1, 400, 111, 063	82, 015, 540	4, 560, 622	5. 6
1880	57	60, 475, 200	37, 182, 128, 621	1, 516, 538, 631	121, 510, 224	4, 956, 009	4. 1
1881	60	61, 162, 700	48, 565, 818, 212	1, 776, 018, 162	159, 232, 191	5, 823, 010	3. 5
1882	61	60, 962, 700	46, 552, 846, 161	1, 595, 000, 245	151, 637, 935	5, 195, 440	3. 4
1883	63	61, 162, 700	40, 293, 165, 258	1, 568, 983, 196	132, 543, 307	5, 161, 129	3. 9
1884	61	60, 412, 700	34, 092, 037, 338	1, 524, 930, 994	111, 048, 982	4, 967, 202	4. 5
1885	64	58, 612, 700	25, 250, 791, 440	1, 295, 355, 252	82, 789, 480	4, 247, 069	5. 1
1886	63	59, 312, 700	33, 374, 682, 216	1, 519, 565, 385	109, 067, 589	4, 965, 900	4. 5
1887	64	60, 862, 700	34, 872, 848, 786	1, 569, 626, 325	114, 337, 209	5, 146, 816	4. 5
1888	63	60, 762, 700	30, 863, 686, 609	1, 570, 198, 528	101, 192, 415	5, 148, 192	5. 1
		†69, 182, 078	‡843, 806, 456, 479	‡37, 328, 810, 732	†78, 623, 608	†3, 478, 725	4. 4

* The capital is for various dates, the amounts at a uniform date in each year not being obtainable.
† Yearly averages for thirty-five years. ‡ Totals for thirty-five years.

The clearing-house transactions of the assistant treasurer of the United States at New York for the year ending October 1, 1888, were as follows:

Exchanges received from clearing-house	$353,718,586.60
Exchanges delivered to clearing-house	103,560,040.74
Balances paid to clearing-house	250,541,227.49
Balances received from clearing-house	382,681.63
Showing that the amount paid by the assistant treasurer to the clearing-house was in excess of the amount received by him	$250,158,545.86

The debit balances were paid to the clearing-house as follows:

United States gold certificates	250,387,000.00
Legal tenders and change	154,227.49
	250,541,227.49

COMPARATIVE STATEMENT OF THE EXCHANGES OF THE CLEARING-HOUSES OF THE UNITED STATES FOR OCTOBER, 1888, AND OCTOBER, 1887.

Clearing-house at—	Exchanges for October, 1888.	Exchanges for October, 1887.	Comparisons.	
			Increase.	Decrease.
New York	$3,194,301,364	$2,978,940,406	$215,360,958	....
Boston	472,338,749	387,775,488	84,563,261	....
Philadelphia	307,553,909	272,500,752	35,053,157	....
Chicago	323,057,170	267,556,325	55,500,845	....
Saint Louis	83,430,317	74,855,029	8,575,288	....
San Francisco	87,702,944	74,355,337	13,347,607	....
New Orleans	42,257,636	42,603,842	....	$346,206
Baltimore	61,987,682	56,795,652	5,192,030	....
Pittsburgh	56,777,983	46,775,066	10,002,917	....
Cincinnati	47,535,350	47,782,200	....	246,850
Kansas City	41,228,195	29,792,991	11,435,204	....
Louisville	24,812,647	23,210,780	1,601,867	....
Providence	23,748,800	23,837,500	....	88,700
Detroit	24,075,034	18,374,899	5,700,135	....
Milwaukee	24,265,352	20,123,277	4,142,075	....
Saint Paul	19,262,066	18,376,835	885,231	....
Minneapolis	27,377,185	22,826,010	4,551,175	....
Omaha	16,763,220	12,759,306	4,003,914	....
Cleveland	16,044,333	14,340,059	1,704,274	....
Columbus	10,121,511	10,616,739	....	495,228
Denver	12,608,062	10,812,462	1,795,600	....
Memphis	11,783,630	10,725,296	1,058,334	....
Indianapolis	8,564,210	8,777,909	....	213,699
Hartford	8,603,088	7,630,017	973,071	....
New Haven	5,576,345	5,360,758	215,587	....
Peoria	6,899,276	5,429,418	1,469,858	....
Springfield	5,604,758	5,653,280	....	48,522
Saint Joseph	6,217,191	6,659,426	....	442,235
Worcester	5,074,835	4,722,433	352,402	....
Duluth	11,521,332	13,050,016	....	1,528,684
Portland	5,013,220	4,607,692	405,528	....
Norfolk	5,780,841	5,818,627	....	37,786
Galveston	10,252,789	8,865,282	1,387,507	....
Los Angeles	4,062,667	5,160,513	....	1,097,846
Grand Rapids	2,161,752	2,725,819	....	564,067
Lowell	3,366,071	3,161,806	204,265	....
Syracuse	3,392,184	3,199,441	192,743	....
Wichita	2,426,217	2,844,044	....	417,827
Total	5,023,549,915	4,559,402,732	469,674,833	5,527,650
	4,559,402,732	....	5,527,650	....
Increase	464,147,183	....	464,147,183	....

COMPARATIVE STATEMENT OF THE EXCHANGES OF THE CLEARING-HOUSES OF THE UNITED STATES FOR WEEKS ENDING OCTOBER 27, 1888, AND OCTOBER 29, 1887.

Clearing-house at—	Exchanges for week ending October 27, 1888.	Exchanges for week ending October 29, 1887.	Comparisons.	
			Increase.	Decrease.
New York	$683,132,609	$647,590,729	$35,541,880	....
Boston	102,015,751	83,700,976	18,314,775	....
Philadelphia	69,077,942	58,729,071	10,348,871	....
Chicago	61,960,300	58,407,116	3,553,184	....
Saint Louis	17,079,627	16,057,751	1,021,876	....
San Francisco	15,500,311	17,405,345	....	$1,905,034
New Orleans	10,283,492	9,863,406	420,086	....
Baltimore	12,378,141	12,618,840	....	240,699
Pittsburgh	13,170,190	11,708,842	1,461,348	....
Cincinnati	9,938,900	9,749,950	188,950	....
Kansas City	8,953,105	7,407,620	1,545,485	....
Louisville	4,742,440	4,800,855	....	58,415
Providence	5,955,700	5,937,900	17,800	....
Detroit	4,563,739	4,079,159	484,580	....
Milwaukee	5,087,632	4,702,794	384,838	....
Saint Paul	3,811,615	4,108,446	....	296,831
Minneapolis	4,982,574	4,806,272	176,302	....
Omaha	3,550,527	2,812,343	738,184	....
Cleveland	3,599,380	3,263,297	336,083	....
Columbus	2,168,420	2,285,210	....	116,790
Denver	2,394,498	2,800,391	....	405,893
Memphis	2,796,774	2,532,120	264,654	....
Indianapolis	1,891,482	2,130,383	....	238,901
Hartford	1,654,034	1,482,341	171,693	....
New Haven	1,074,393	1,101,904	....	27,511
Peoria	1,456,481	1,177,341	279,140	....
Springfield	1,137,703	1,007,778	129,925	....
Saint Joseph	1,203,313	1,702,006	....	438,693
Worcester	1,079,739	969,381	110,358	....
Duluth	2,226,700	3,224,805	....	998,105
Portland	1,021,693	1,049,033	....	17,340
Norfolk	1,326,554	1,469,657	....	143,103
Galveston	1,904,297	2,103,758	....	199,461
Los Angeles	681,380	1,133,462	....	452,082
Grand Rapids	540,444	583,679	6,765	....
Lowell	802,151	650,419	151,732	....
Syracuse	688,518	623,200	65,318	....
Wichita	506,630	602,161	....	95,531
Total	1,066,579,239 996,499,801	996,499,801	75,713,827 5,634,389	5,634,389
Increase	70,079,438	....	70,079,438	....

The following tables exhibit the transactions of the clearing-houses located in thirty-eight cities for the year ending September 30, 1888, from official returns received from the manager of the New York Clearing-House, comparisons being made with the year ending September 30, 1887, the increase or decrease in the exchanges and balances being indicated:

COMPARATIVE STATEMENT OF THE EXCHANGES OF THE CLEARING-HOUSES OF THE UNITED STATES FOR YEARS ENDING SEPTEMBER 30, 1888, AND SEPTEMBER 30, 1887.

Clearing-house at—	No. of banks.	Exchanges for year ending September 30, 1888.	Exchanges for year ending September 30, 1887.	Comparisons.	
				Increase.	Decrease.
New York	64	$30, 863, 686, 609	$34, 872, 848, 786	....	$4, 009, 162, 177
Boston	54	4, 288, 878, 016	4, 408, 269, 992	....	119, 391, 977
Philadelphia	40	3, 155, 190, 287	3, 186, 188, 935	....	30, 998, 658
Chicago	21	3, 089, 288, 194	2, 887, 276, 059	$202, 012, 135	....
Saint Louis	17	886, 812, 201	879, 272, 738	7, 539, 463	....
San Francisco	17	823, 436, 263	800, 092, 859	23, 343, 404	....
New Orleans	14	450, 792, 807	412, 231, 400	38, 561, 407	....
Baltimore	23	614, 399, 374	665, 676, 756	....	51, 277, 382
Pittsburgh	10	566, 135, 994	490, 319, 705	75, 816, 289	....
Cincinnati	17	518, 620, 450	564, 377, 200	....	45, 756, 750
Kansas City	13	382, 284, 073	380, 407, 069	1, 877, 004	....
Louisville	21	295, 711, 094	269, 786, 547	25, 924, 547	....
Providence	34	248, 135, 800	240, 838, 100	7, 297, 700	....
Detroit	16	218, 695, 351	188, 629, 384	30, 065, 967	....
Milwaukee	11	222, 609, 808	240, 127, 909	....	17, 518, 101
Saint Paul	14	194, 026, 801	200, 364, 307	....	6, 337, 506
Minneapolis	16	204, 040, 477	184, 700, 022	19, 340, 455	....
Omaha	7	166, 007, 003	137, 220, 535	28, 786, 468	....
Cleveland	11	160, 430, 904	160, 010, 840	420, 064	....
Columbus	....	113, 647, 539	53, 311, 425	60, 336, 114	....
Denver	7	127, 570, 797	110, 240, 167	17, 330, 630	....
Memphis	8	105, 908, 056	94, 241, 496	11, 666, 560	....
Indianapolis	6	99, 576, 811	87, 149, 510	12, 427, 301	....
Hartford	15	88, 625, 991	89, 871, 078	....	1, 245, 087
New Haven	10	60, 704, 610	63, 931, 325	....	3, 226, 715
Peoria	9	67, 296, 258	55, 006, 344	12, 289, 914	....
Springfield	10	56, 383, 130	50, 593, 291	5, 789, 839	....
Saint Joseph	7	69, 449, 822	67, 239, 133	2, 210, 689	....
Worcester	8	51, 286, 739	47, 197, 687	4, 089, 052	....
Duluth	6	113, 280, 043	(New.)	113, 280, 043	....
Portland	6	50, 156, 342	49, 588, 652	567, 690	....
Norfolk	6	44, 877, 181	40, 016, 323	4, 860, 858	....
Galveston	7	57, 165, 444	63, 182, 557	....	6, 017, 113
Los Angeles	8	63, 050, 081	(New.)	63, 050, 081	....
Grand Rapids	7	31, 025, 179	26, 229, 598	4, 795, 581	....
Lowell	7	32, 086, 992	31, 070, 050	1, 316, 942	....
Syracuse	8	33, 845, 318	28, 596, 708	5, 248, 610	....
Wichita	....	35, 628, 078	(New.)	35, 628, 078	....
Total	....	48, 651, 654, 957	52, 126, 704, 488 48, 651, 651, 957	815, 982, 875	4, 290, 032, 406 815, 882, 875
Decrease	....	....	3, 475, 049, 531	....	3, 475, 049, 531

COMPARATIVE STATEMENT OF THE BALANCES OF THE CLEARING-HOUSES OF THE UNITED STATES FOR YEARS ENDING SEPTEMBER 30, 1888, AND SEPTEMBER 30, 1887.

Clearing-house at—	No. of banks.	Balances for year ending September 30, 1888.	Balances for year ending September 30, 1887.	Comparisons. Increase.	Comparisons. Decrease.
New York	64	$1, 570, 198, 528	$1, 569, 626, 325	$572, 203	....
Boston	54	502, 980, 813	510, 625, 457	....	$7, 644, 644
Philadelphia	40	305, 238, 423	298, 701, 297	6, 537, 126	....
Chicago	21	301, 387, 886	301, 574, 676	....	186, 790
Saint Louis	17	141, 142, 096	142, 259, 972	....	1, 117, 876
San Francisco	17	121, 091, 092	124, 200, 215	....	3, 109, 123
New Orleans	14	53, 726, 186	47, 805, 607	5, 920, 579	....
Baltimore	23	89, 604, 272	89, 504, 281	99, 991	....
Pittsburgh	19	99, 552, 128	81, 520, 388	18, 031, 740	....
Cincinnati	17	70, 969, 900	96, 204, 200	....	25, 234, 300
Kansas City	13	No record	No record	....	....
Louisville	21	67, 619, 594	63, 564, 157	4, 055, 437	....
Providence	34	17, 741, 600	No record	17, 741, 600	....
Detroit	16	36, 422, 898	31, 729, 276	4, 693, 622	....
Milwaukee	11	34, 537, 980	40, 817, 909	....	6, 279, 929
Saint Paul	14	34, 053, 304	33, 193, 845	859, 459	....
Minneapolis	16	32, 514, 595	30, 465, 326	2, 049, 269	....
Omaha	7	No record	No record	....	....
Cleveland	11	No record	No record	....	....
Columbus	....	No record	8, 378, 319	....	8, 378, 319
Denver	7	15, 640, 765	15, 866, 791	....	226, 026
Memphis	8	24, 012, 189	24, 020, 213	....	8, 024
Indianapolis	6	25, 096, 548	18, 660, 734	6, 435, 814	....
Hartford	15	24, 930, 316	25, 689, 768	....	759, 452
New Haven	10	13, 788, 891	15, 176, 902	....	1, 388, 011
Peoria	9	18, 060, 330	13, 974, 158	4, 086, 172	....
Springfield	10	17, 026, 378	14, 929, 388	2, 096, 990	....
Saint Joseph	7	19, 096, 231	17, 667, 401	1, 428, 830	....
Worcester	8	13, 813, 833	13, 466, 230	347, 603	....
Duluth	6	26, 087, 462	New	26, 087, 462	....
Portland	6	10, 145, 041	9, 495, 080	649, 961	....
Norfolk	6	6, 932, 332	6, 453, 157	479, 175	....
Galveston	....	No record	No record	....	....
Los Angeles	8	10, 572, 388	New	10, 572, 388	....
Grand Rapids	7	6, 411, 338	5, 670, 883	740, 455	....
Lowell	7	10, 079, 280	10, 168, 362	....	89, 082
Syracuse	8	7, 707, 597	6, 358, 243	1, 439, 354	....
Wichita	....	No record	New	....	....
Total	....	3, 729, 772, 214 3, 667, 768, 563	3, 667, 768, 563	116, 425, 227 54, 421, 576	54, 421, 576
Increase	....	62, 003, 651	....	62, 003, 651	

From the foregoing tables it will be seen that the exchanges in New York City during the past year amounted to 63.4 per cent. of the whole sum, and the balances in that city were 42.1 per cent. of the total balances.

The following table, compiled from returns made to the Clearing-House by the national banks in New York City, exhibits the movement of their reserve, weekly, during October, for the last twelve years:

Week ending—	Specie.	Legal tenders.	Total.	Ratio of reserve to— Circulation and deposits.	Deposits.
				Per cent.	*Per cent.*
October 6, 1877	$14,665,600	$36,168,300	$50,833,900	27.0	29.5
October 13, 1877	14,726,500	35,178,900	49,905,400	26.7	29.2
October 20, 1877	14,087,400	35,101,700	49,189,100	26.5	29.0
October 27, 1877	15,209,000	34,367,800	49,576,800	26.8	29.4
October 5, 1878	14,995,800	38,304,900	53,300,700	25.7	28.4
October 12, 1878	12,184,600	37,685,100	49,869,700	24.4	27.0
October 19, 1878	13,531,400	36,576,000	50,107,400	24.7	27.3
October 26, 1878	17,384,200	35,690,500	53,074,700	25.8	28.5
October 4, 1879	18,979,600	34,368,000	53,347,600	23.3	25.8
October 11, 1879	20,901,800	32,820,300	53,722,100	23.4	25.9
October 18, 1879	24,686,500	29,305,200	53,991,700	23.5	26.1
October 25, 1879	25,636,000	26,713,900	52,349,900	23.0	25.5
October 2, 1880	59,823,700	11,129,100	70,952,800	25.4	26.4
October 9, 1880	62,521,300	10,785,000	73,306,300	25.4	27.2
October 16, 1880	62,760,600	10,939,200	73,699,800	25.5	27.1
October 23, 1880	60,888,200	10,988,200	71,876,400	24.8	26.6
October 30, 1880	61,471,600	10,925,000	72,396,600	25.0	26.7
October 1, 1881	54,954,600	12,150,400	67,105,000	23.1	24.8
October 8, 1881	53,287,900	12,153,800	65,441,700	23.1	24.9
October 15, 1881	51,008,300	12,452,700	63,461,000	23.2	25.0
October 22, 1881	54,016,200	12,496,500	66,512,700	24.6	26.6
October 29, 1881	55,961,200	12,947,900	68,909,100	25.6	27.4
October 7, 1882	47,016,000	18,384,500	65,400,500	24.0	26.3
October 14, 1882	48,281,000	18,002,700	66,283,700	24.7	26.6
October 21, 1882	49,518,200	17,023,900	66,542,100	25.0	26.8
October 28, 1882	48,374,200	17,204,700	65,578,900	24.8	26.5
October 6, 1883	51,586,700	20,122,500	71,709,200	25.5	27.0
October 13, 1883	50,894,000	21,145,800	72,039,800	25.4	26.8
October 20, 1883	47,262,900	20,719,700	67,982,600	24.5	25.9
October 27, 1883	46,372,800	20,617,600	66,990,400	24.5	25.9
October 4, 1884	67,470,600	25,817,300	93,287,900	34.5	36.3
October 11, 1884	68,922,500	27,654,100	96,576,600	35.2	36.9
October 18, 1884	67,579,400	27,875,500	95,454,900	34.8	36.5
October 25, 1884	67,638,000	27,354,200	94,992,200	34.6	36.3
October 3, 1885	92,351,600	24,516,600	116,868,200	36.0	37.1
October 10, 1885	93,642,500	23,002,000	116,644,500	35.8	37.0
October 17, 1885	91,945,300	22,221,100	114,166,400	34.9	36.0
October 24, 1885	87,309,100	21,059,800	108,368,900	33.5	34.5
October 30, 1885	84,954,600	21,874,900	106,829,500	33.0	34.1
October 2, 1886	64,111,700	14,607,700	78,719,400	27.1	27.9
October 9, 1886	65,723,800	13,209,100	78,932,900	27.0	27.7
October 16, 1886	65,228,600	13,133,100	78,361,700	26.7	27.4
October 23, 1886	65,668,400	12,803,800	78,472,200	26.9	27.7
October 30, 1886	66,195,100	13,177,200	79,372,300	27.1	27.9
October 1, 1887	64,619,200	15,767,500	80,386,700	27.7	28.5
October 8, 1887	64,317,500	16,229,700	80,587,200	27.4	28.2
October 15, 1887	64,663,100	16,885,400	81,548,500	27.3	28.1
October 22, 1887	64,918,700	16,735,500	81,654,500	27.4	28.2
October 29, 1887	66,005,800	17,542,600	82,848,400	27.8	28.6
October 6, 1888	74,411,300	23,204,300	97,615,600	27.4	27.9
October 13, 1888	73,901,500	22,017,800	95,919,300	27.8	28.4
October 20, 1888	81,457,700	21,386,800	102,844,500	29.3	29.9
October 27, 1888	81,212,600	21,329,800	102,542,400	29.3	29.8

DUTIES, ASSESSMENTS, AND REDEMPTION CHARGES.

National banks are subjected to a semi-annual duty of one-half of 1 per cent. upon the average amount of their notes in circulation during the preceding six months. They are also required by the act of June 20, 1874, to pay the cost of the redemption of their notes at the office of the Treasurer of the United States at Washington and the cost of the plates from which their notes are printed. Banks extending their corporate existence have to pay for new plates. Previously to the act of June 20, 1874, the expense of the plates had been paid out of the tax on the banks, which at that time attached to capital and deposits as well as to circulation.

The banks are further required to pay the fees of the examiners employed to ascertain their condition, under section 5240, Revised Statutes of the United States.

The taxes and assessments collected during the past year are as follows:

Semi-annual duty on circulation	$1,616,127.53
Cost of redemption of notes by United States Treasurer	141,141.48
Assessment for cost of plates, new banks	14,100.00
Assessment for cost of plates, extended banks	3,900.00
Assessment for examiners' fees, sec. 5240, R. S	121,777.86
Total	1,897,046.87

The following table is a comparative statement ot taxes assessed as semi-annual duty on circulation, cost of redemption of notes, cost of plates, and examiners' fees for the past six years:

Years.	Semi-annual duty on circulation.	Cost of redemption of notes by United States Treasurer.	Assessments for cost of plates, new banks.	Assessment for cost of plates, extended banks.	Assessment for examiners' fees (sec. 5240 R. S.).	Total.
1883	$3,132,006.73	$147,592.27	$25,980.00	$34,120.00	$94,606.16	$3,434,305.16
1884	3,024,668.24	160,896.65	18,845.00	1,950.00	99,642.05	3,306,001.94
1885	2,794,584.01	181,857.16	13,150.00	97,800.00	107,781.73	3,195,172.90
1886	2,592,021.33	168,243.35	14,810.00	24,825.00	107,272.83	2,907,172.51
1887	2,044,922.75	138,967.00	18,850.00	1,750.00	110,219.88	2,314,709.63
1888	1,616,127.53	141,141.48	14,100.00	3,900.00	121,777.86	1,897,046.87
Total	15,204,330.59	938,697.91	105,735.00	164,345.00	641,300.51	17,054,409.01

The total tax collected on circulation up to July 1, 1888, amounted to $67,457,848.83.

LEGAL DECISIONS.

CONSTRUCTION OF STATUTES RELATING TO NATIONAL BANKS.

The "Digest of National-Bank Cases" presented in the Report of 1887 is reproduced in the appendix, page 101, enlarged by the incorporation of decisions announced during the last twelve months. The most important of these new decisions are as follows:

(1) An opinion rendered by the Supreme Court of the United States, February 20, 1888, in what is commonly called "The Pacific National-Bank Cases," holding that attachment of assets of national banks, whether insolvent or not, is invalid and that United States statute takes away the power of the courts to issue injunctions against national banks.

The opinion is as follows:

All of these cases involve the same general question, and they may properly be considered and decided together. From the records it appears that the Pacific National Bank of Boston was an association for carrying on the business of banking, organized under the national-bank act. On the 20th of November, 1881, it became embarrassed, and was placed in charge of a bank examiner, in whose control it remained until March 18, 1882, when its doors were opened for business with the consent of the Comptroller of the Currency.

By statute, in Massachusetts, civil actions are begun by original writ, which "may be framed either to attach the goods or estate of the defendant, and, for want thereof, to take his body; or it may be by original summons, with or without an order to attach the goods or estate." (Pub. Stat. of Mass., 1882, chap. 161, secs. 13, 14.) "All real and personal estate liable to be taken on execution * * * may be attached upon the original writ in any action in which debt or damages are recoverable, and may be held as security to satisfy such judgment as the plaintiff may recover." (Sec. 38.) "A person or corporation whose goods or estate are attached on mesne process in a civil action may, at any time before final judgment, dissolve such attachment by giving bond with sufficient sureties, * * * with condition to pay to the plaintiff the amount, if any, that he may recover within thirty days after the final judgment in such action." (Sec. 122.)

At the time the bank resumed business it was indebted to George Mixter in the sum of $15,000; to Henry M. Whitney also in the sum of $15,000; to Daniel L. Demmon in the sum of $25,000; and to Calvin B. Prescott in the sum of $5,000.

On the 24th of March, 1881, Mixter and Prescott each began a suit against the bank in the circuit court of the United States for the district of Massachusetts, by writ directing an attachment, to recover the amounts due them respectively. Demmon also began a suit in the same court and in the same way on the 28th of March, to recover the amount due him, and Whitney another on the 28th of April, upon the claim in his favor. At the time these suits were begun the bank had money on deposit to its credit in the Maverick National Bank and in the Howard National Bank, and the necessary steps were taken to subject these deposits to the attachments which were issued in the several suits.

The bank arranged with Lewis Coleman and John Shepard to become its sureties upon bonds to dissolve attachments in any actions that might be brought against it, and placed in their hands a certificate of deposit in the Maverick National Bank for $100,000, to be held as their protection against all liabilities which should be thus incurred. This certificate was afterwards exchanged for $121,000 of the bonds of the Nantasket Company, $20,000 of the bonds of the Toledo, Delphos and Burlington Railroad Company, and $15,000 of the bonds of the Lebanon Springs Railroad Company.

Immediately after each of the attachments in the above actions had been made, the bank executed a bond to the plaintiff in a penal sum suited to the amount of the claim, with Coleman and Shepard as its sureties, reciting the attachment, and that the bank "desires to dissolve said attachment according to law," and conditioned to be void "if the Pacific National Bank of Boston shall, within thirty days after the final judgment in the aforesaid action, pay to the plaintiff therein named the amount, if any, which he shall recover in such action." Upon the execution of the bond in each case, the attachment was dissolved.

After this the bank closed its doors a second time, and on the 22d of May, 1882, a receiver was appointed by the Comptroller of the Currency in accordance with the provisions of section 5234 of the Revised Statutes, and at once took possession of its assets and proceeded to wind up its affairs.

When the receiver was appointed he found the several suits which had been commenced still pending. In the cases of Mixter, Whitney, and Demmon he appeared, answered for the bank, filed motions to discharge the attachments, and motions to dismiss the suits. His motions were all overruled, and, his defenses not being sustained, judgments were rendered against the bank in each of the cases for the amounts found to be due the several plaintiffs, respectively. For the review of the action of the court in these cases the writs of error which are now under consideration were brought.

The suit of Prescott still remains undisposed of in the circuit court.

Failing in his motions and in his defenses at law, the receiver filed a bill in equity in the circuit court against the several attaching creditors and the sureties on the bonds given to dissolve the attachments, the object of which was to reduce to his possession the securities which were held by the sureties for their protection against liability, and to restrain the several attaching creditors from enforcing the attachment bonds on the ground, among others, "that the attachments made in said actions were unauthorized, illegal, and void." This bill was dismissed by the circuit court (22 Fed. Rep., 694), and from that decree the appeal, which is now one of the subjects of consideration, was taken.

In the view we take of the case, the most important question to be considered is whether an attachment can issue against a national bank before judgment in a suit begun in the circuit court of the United States. Section 5242 of the Revised Statutes of the United States contains this provision: "No attachment, injunction, or execution shall be issued against such association or its property before final judgment in any suit, action, or proceeding, in any State, county, or municipal court." The original national-bank act contained nothing of this kind, but the prohibition first appeared in the act of March 3, 1873 (chap. 269, sec. 2, 17 Stat., 603), as a new proviso added to section 57 of the act of June 3, 1864 (chap. 106, Sec. 2, 13 Stat., 116). That section was originally as follows:

"That suits, actions, and proceedings against any association under this act may be had in any circuit, district, or Territorial court of the United States held within the district in which such association may be established, or in any State, county, or municipal court in the county or city in which said association is located, having jurisdiction in similar cases: *Provided, however*, That all proceedings to enjoin the Comptroller under this act shall be had in a circuit, district, or territorial court of the United States, held in the district in which the association is located."

The amending act was as follows:

"That section fifty-seven * * * be amended by adding thereto the following: '*And provided further*, That no attachment, injunction, or execution shall be issued against such association, or its property, before final judgment in any such suit, action, or proceeding in any State, county, or municipal court.'"

Section 52 of the original national-bank act was as follows:

"That all transfers of the notes, bonds, bills of exchange, and other evidences of debt owing to any association, or of any deposits to its credit; all assignments of mortgages, sureties on real estate, or of judgments or decrees in its favor; all deposits of money, bullion, or other valuable thing for its use, or for the use of any of its shareholders or creditors; and all payments of money to either, made after the commission of an act of insolvency, or in contemplation thereof, with a view to prevent the application of its assets in the manner prescribed by this act, or with a view to the preference of one creditor to another, except the payment of its circulating notes, shall be null and void." (13 Stat., 115.)

This was evidently intended to preserve to the United States that "first and paramount lien upon all the assets of such association" which was given by section 47 as security for the repayment of any amount expended by them to redeem the circulating notes, over and above the proceeds of the bonds pledged for that purpose, and to place all the other creditors on that equality in the distribution of the assets of an insolvent bank which was clearly provided for in section 50, where the Comptroller of the Currency is required to make ratable dividends of the proceeds of the assets of the association realized by the receiver "on all such claims as may have been proved to his satisfaction, or adjudicated in a court of competent jurisdiction." (National Bank *vs.* Colby, 21 Wall., 609, 613.)

In the revision of the statutes, section 52 of the original act, and the amendment of section 57 adopted in 1873, relating to attachments and injunctions in State courts, were re-enacted as section 5242, the amendment of section 57 being put in the revision at the end of what had been the original section 52. As the Revised Statutes were first adopted, the proviso of section 57, which related specially to proceedings to enjoin the Comptroller, was re-enacted as section 736, but all the rest of the original section was left out. That omission was, however, supplied by the act of February 18, 1875 (chap. 80, 18 Stat., 316, 320), which re-enacted it as part of section 5198, putting it at the end of that section as it originally stood in the revision.

The fact that the amendment of 1873 in relation to attachments and injunctions in State courts was made a part of section 5242 shows the opinion of the revisers and of Congress that it was germane to the other provision incorporated in that section, and was intended as an aid to the enforcement of the principle of equality among the creditors of an insolvent bank. But, however that may be, it is clear to our minds that, as it stood originally as part of section 52 after 1873, and as it stands now in the Revised Statutes, it operates as a prohibition upon all attachments against national banks under the authority of the State courts. That was evidently its purpose when first enacted, for then it was part of a section which, while providing for suits in the courts of the United States or of the State, as the plaintiff might elect, declared in express terms that if the suit was begun in a State court no attachment should issue until after judgment. The form of its re-enactment in the Revised Statutes does not change its meaning in this particular. It stands now, as it did originally, as the paramount law of the land that attachments shall not issue from State courts against national banks, and writes into all State attachment laws an exception in favor of national banks. Since the act of 1873 all the attachment laws of the State must be read as if they contained a provision in express terms that they were not to apply to suits against a national bank.

The prohibition does not in express terms refer to attachments in suits begun in the circuit courts of the United States, but as by section 915 of the Revised Statutes those courts are not authorized to issue attachments in common-law causes against the property of a defendant, except as "provided by the laws of the State in which such court is held for the courts thereof," it follows that, as by the amendatory act of 1873, now part of section 5242 of the Revised Statutes, all power of issuing attachments against national banks before judgment has been eliminated from State statutes, there can not be any laws of the State providing for such a remedy on which the circuit courts may act. The law in this respect stands precisely as it would if there were no State law providing for such a remedy in any case. It was suggested in argument that the prohibition extended only to the use of the remedy by State courts, and that the remedy itself still remained to be resorted to in the courts of the United States. But we do not so understand the law. In our opinion the effect of the act of Congress is to deny the State remedy altogether so far as suits against national banks are concerned, and in this way it operates as well on the courts of the United States as on those of the States. Although the provision was evidently made to secure equality among the general creditors in the division of the proceeds of the property of an insolvent bank, its operation is by no means confined to cases of actual or contemplated insolvency. The remedy is taken away altogether and can not be used under any circumstances.

It was further said that if the power of issuing attachments has been taken away from the State courts, so also is the power of issuing injunctions. That is true. While the law as it stood previous to the act of July 12, 1882 (chap. 290, sec. 4, 22 Stat., 163), gave the proper State and Federal courts concurrent jurisdiction in all ordinary suits against national banks, it was careful to provide that the jurisdiction of the Federal courts should be exclusive when relief by attachment or injunction before judgment was sought. Until the act of 1882 the Federal courts had ample authority to grant injunctions in proper cases, and all a person need do to invoke that authority was to bring his suit in one of those courts. Whether since the act of 1882 this remains so is a question for the consideration of Congress. Some amendment to existing legislation may be necessary, but this does not shed any light on the interpretation of the old law. The difficulty arises from the change that has been made, not from the law as it stood originally.

We are, therefore, of opinion that the attachments in all the suits were illegal and void, because issued without any authority of law. But it is insisted that notwithstanding this the bonds are valid and may be enforced.

It is undoubtedly true that the sureties on a bond of this kind are estopped from setting up, as a defense to an action for a breach of its condition, any irregularities in the form of proceeding to obtain an attachment authorized by law which would warrant its discharge upon a proper application made therefor. As the purpose of the bond is to dissolve an attachment, its due execution implies a waiver both by the defendant and his sureties of all mere irregularities. So, too, it is no defense that the property attached did not belong to the defendant, or that it was exempt, or that the defendant has become bankrupt or is dead. In all such cases, where there was lawful authority for the attachment, the simple question is, whether the condition of the bond has been broken; that is to say, whether there has been a judgment in the action against the defendant for the payment of money which he has neglected for thirty days afterwards to make.

In the present case, however, the question is whether the bond creates a liability when the attachment on which it is predicated was actually prohibited by law. In other words, whether an illegal and therefore a void attachment is sufficient to lay the foundation for a valid bond to secure its formal dissolution. The bond is a substitute for the attachment, although not affected by all the contingencies which might have discharged the attachment itself. (Carpenter *vs.* Turrell, 100 Mass., 450, 452; Tapley *vs.* Goodsell, 122 Mass., 176, 182.) Such being the case, it necessarily follows that if there was no authority in law for the attachment, there could be none for taking the bond. If the attachment itself is illegal and therefore void, so also must be the bond which takes its place. Objections can be made to an attachment issued on proper legal authority, which can not be used as a defense to a bond taken under the statute for its dissolution; but if there can be no lawful attachment, there can be no valid bond for its dissolution. The case is to be considered as though there was no law whatever for the seizure of property by attachment before judgment in any case. As the taking of the property under such circumstances would be unlawful, so also would be the act of the magistrate in accepting the bond.

Neither is the bond binding as a common-law bond. If the attachment had been valid, and the bond taken had not been in all respects such as the statute had required, it could nevertheless have been enforced as a common-law bond, because it was executed for a good consideration, and the object for which it was given had been accomplished. But here the difficulty is that there was no lawful attachment, and therefore no lawful authority for taking any bond whatever. The bond is consequently neither good under the statute nor at common law, because there is no sufficient foundation to support it.

Objection is made to the relief which is sought in equity, because if the attachment bonds are void there is an adequate remedy at law in the suits that may be brought for their enforcement. If the suit in equity had been brought by the sureties to get rid of their obligation, this objection might be good; but such is not its character. The sureties have in their hands assets of the bank which the receiver seeks to reduce to his possession, and which they claim the right to hold until they have been fully indemnified against or discharged from liability on the bonds. The receiver says there is no liability, because the bonds are invalid; and to have that question settled once for all he has brought the persons interested, creditors as well as sureties, before the court in order that it may be conclusively adjudicated between them. Such a suit is clearly cognizable in equity. The sureties are in a sense stake-holders.

They do not claim the securities unless they are liable on the bonds, and the suit, although not brought by them, is in the nature of an interpleader to save them "from the vexation of two proceedings on a matter which may be settled in a single suit." The decree will bind all alike, and if the sureties are held not to be liable it will conclude the creditors from all further proceedings against them on the bonds, and leave them free to surrender the securities to the receiver. This will not affect the judgments that the creditors have recovered any further than to limit their operation, so far as the receiver and the sureties on the attachment bonds are concerned, to the adjudication of the debts as claims entitled to dividends from the proceeds of the assets of the bank. To that extent, certainly, the court had jurisdiction in each of the suits after the insolvency; but as the attachments were void the judgments are inoperative as a basis of recovery upon the bonds.

The judgment in each of the suits at law is affirmed, but the decree in the suit in equity is reversed, and the cause remanded with instructions to enter a decree setting aside and annulling the bonds which were given to dissolve the attachments, and enjoining each and all of the creditors, and those claiming under them, from proceeding in any manner to enforce the same against the sureties, and directing the sureties to surrender to the receiver the securities they hold for their indemnity.

(2) An opinion rendered by the United States circuit court, southern district of New York, in an action of trover to recover moneys of a national bank (afterward insolvent) alleged to have been wrongfully appropriated by certain brokers and used in stock speculations.

The opinion is as follows:

This action is in substance one of trover to recover moneys of the First National Bank of Albion, alleged to have been wrongfully appropriated by the defendants during the years 1880 and 1881. The case was tried with a jury, and the jury found a verdict for the plaintiff for $103,000 principal, with $44,759 interest. The case is now here upon a motion by the defendants for a new trial.

It appeared by the evidence that in 1880 one Warner was the cashier of the Albion bank, and for some time had been intrusted with the almost exclusive management of its affairs. In November, 1881, he became its president. In August, 1884, the bank failed, Warner absconded, and the plaintiff, who was appointed its receiver, took possession of the assets. An examination of its affairs showed that Warner had misappropriated moneys and securities of the bank to the amount of over $300,000 and was otherwise indebted to the bank in a considerable sum. It was further shown that Warner had been carrying on stock speculations through the agency of the defendants, who were stock brokers and bankers of New York city; that he opened a customer's account with them May 11, 1880, and continued to buy and sell stocks and securities upon margins through them, and to deposit with and draw upon them as bankers, during that year and the next; and that from time to time the defendants received large sums of money from him by checks of the Albion bank, payable to their order, drawn by Warner, as cashier, upon the Third National Bank of New York city. The defendants collected these checks, and placed the proceeds to Warner's credit in his account with them.

It was also proved that for many years the Albion bank had kept a banking account with the Third National Bank of New York, and had been accustomed to draw upon it at sight, and send it collections and remittances; that after Warner became the cashier of the Albion bank he took personal charge of the correspondence between that bank and the New York bank, and intercepted the letters of advice and monthly statements sent by the New York bank to the Albion bank, and adopted other methods to conceal from the other persons associated with him in conducting the Albion bank the true state of the account between the two banks; that from time to time he deposited with the New York bank, in the name of the Albion bank, funds in his possession, and from time to time drew checks and drafts in the name of the Albion bank, as cashier, upon the New York bank, for his own transactions and speculations; and that the checks and drafts thus drawn by Warner for his own use were not credited to the New York bank on the books of the Albion bank, nor were the deposits made in the name of the Albion bank by Warner personally charged to the New York bank on the books of the Albion bank, although they were credited to the Albion bank by the New York bank; and neither the checks nor drafts, nor the credit items appeared in any way upon the books of the Albion bank.

The evidence was sufficient to justify the jury in finding that Warner used the account of the Albion bank with the New York bank as the means of appropriating, without the knowledge of the directors or other officers of the Albion bank, and clandestinely, the funds and credit of that bank for his own benefit. It appeared by the books of the two banks that the checks and drafts upon the New York bank and charged to the Albion bank, but not credited by the Albion bank to the New York bank, during the period of Warner's defalcations amounted to $267,000, and the deposits credited by the New York bank to the Albion bank, but not charged by the Albion bank to the New York bank, during the same period amounted to $281,000.

The checks received by the defendants between May 11, 1880, and August 26, 1881, and including those dates, aggregated the amount of $103,000. During the same period they received from Warner from other sources $107,703. The defendants bought and sold stock for Warner on a margin of 10 per cent., and many of the checks in question were received by them pursuant to their request to remit for margins. The first and last checks were for $10,000 each; one was for $15,000. In January, 1881, they received checks for margins aggregating the sum of $50,000. Testimony was given for the plaintiff tending to show that Warner was rated, where he resided, as worth from $15,000 to $20,000; and testimony was given for the defendants tending to show that they supposed that other persons were interested with Warner in his stock transactions, and did not suspect that he was using the funds of the bank illegitimately. It also appeared that from time to time Warner drew on the defendants, and that during the period covered by the checks in controversy they paid on his drafts, into the Third National Bank, to the credit of the Albion bank, at various times, sums aggregating $89,202, and that this amount was credited to the Albion bank on the books of the New York bank, and $25,850 thereof was charged on the books of the Albion bank to the New York bank, but the rest did not appear in the books of the Albion bank.

Upon the trial, the court excluded the testimony offered by the defendants to show that it was customary with bankers and brokers of New York City to receive cashiers' checks and drafts drawn in favor of their own banks upon New York banks as cash, upon transactions with the cashier individually. At the close of the testimony, the defendants requested the court to instruct the jury to find a verdict for the defendants. Defendants also requested the court to instruct the jury that the defendants were not liable for any sum in excess of the difference between the sums received by them from Warner upon the checks of the Albion bank and the sums paid by them on Warner's drafts to the New York bank to the credit of the Albion bank. The court refused such instructions. The court instructed the jury, in substance, that it was incumbent upon the plaintiff to establish that the moneys represented by the checks received by the defendants were moneys of the bank which had been misappropriated by Warner; and that, when the defendants received the checks, they took them with guilty knowledge that Warner in using them was misappropriating the funds of the bank; and that, unless they found both these propositions established by the evidence, their verdict should be for the defendants. They were further instructed that they might find upon the evidence that Warner was permitted by the directors of the bank to draw such checks for his own use, or to use the money of the bank for his own purposes, or they might find that the directors of the bank were in collusion with Warner and cognizant of his transactions; that if they found that those who represented the stockholders of the bank as its directors or managers permitted Warner to draw such checks or use the moneys of the bank for his own purposes, not as co-conspirators or collusively, but trusting in his integrity or believing that the bank would not be injured, or through loose management on their part, the plaintiff could not recover; but if they did this collusively their consent could not shelter the defendants, because they had no power by virtue of their position to consent to a fraud upon the stockholders. The jury were further instructed that upon the issue whether the defendants received the checks with guilty knowledge, the question was not whether they were negligent in receiving them or in allowing Warner to deal with them as they did, but the question was whether they were guilty of bad faith; that defendants were bound to know that a cashier has no authority as such to loan the money of the bank or use its checks for his personal use; that the jury were to infer that the defendants knew this when they received the checks, and therefore the question was whether the defendants believed that by some special arrangement or confidence Warner was permitted by those who were associated with him in the management of the bank to use its checks and moneys as he did; and if the jury found that the defendants so believed, the defendants were not guilty of *mala fides*. The defendants insist upon this motion that the court erred in excluding the testimony of custom, in refusing to instruct the jury as requested, in the instructions given to the jury, and urge other grounds for a new trial.

In some aspects this is a hard case for the defendants. If the verdict stands, they are made responsible to pay over a very large sum of money which came to their hands to be invested and handled for another person in consideration of a small commission to be received by them, and which they have paid back to the person from whom they received it; and there is no reason to suppose that they had any active or defined purpose when they received the money, or at any time, of assisting the person from whom they received it to defraud others, or to injure others in any way. It is altogether likely that they could have shown, if they had been permitted to do so, by the testimony of any number of respectable bankers and brokers, that it is every-day practice in Wall street, for those in their line of business to buy and sell stocks for bank presidents and cashiers who are speculating there, and to accept drafts and negotiable paper of the corporations of these officers, made by them officially, in payment of the margins or purchase-money, and that such transactions are so frequent and common in Wall street that they do not attract special notice, and do not usually excite a passing suspicion that they are irregular or improper.

But no usage, however common and well recognized, can be invoked to justify a banker, or any one else, in taking money or negotiable paper in payment of an agent's debt, known to belong to his principal, or known to belong to a trust-estate, to satisfy the trustee's personal debt, or to shield the banker from accountability who wilfully closes his eyes and stops his ears to facts and circumstances which import notice that the agent or trustee is misappropriating the money or property intrusted to him. Therefore, if there is any significance in the fact that a bank president or cashier offers negotiable paper of his corporation, made by him in his official character, in payment of his personal debt, or to raise money for his personal use, it matters not that bankers generally do not appreciate it. If they regard the transaction as equivalent to one in which the individual comes with money in hand, they ignore its real character, because in that case he comes with what purports to be his own, having the possession which implies title and ownership, and the right to use it as he sees fit. When he comes with the money-obligation of a corporation, which is the contract of a corporation only because he has made it, and which is not its contract if he has made it without authority, the transaction is a very different one. Every person who takes such an obligation must ascertain at his peril that the agent who has made it was authorized to do so; and the moment that it appears that the contract has been made for the agent's own use and benefit, that moment his authority is impugned and impeached.

No principle of the law of agency is better settled than that no person can act as the agent for another in making a contract for himself. Therefore it is that a bank president or cashier has no implied authority to bind his corporation to negotiable paper made for his own use; and if it appears upon the face of the paper that it is payable to the individual who has made it in an official capacity, the obligation is nugatory, and no purchaser can enforce it.

Upon this principle it was held in Claflin *v.* The Farmers and Citizens' Bank (25 N. Y., 293) that a general authority to the president of a bank to certify checks drawn upon it does not extend to checks drawn by himself; and if the face of the check shows the president's attempt to use his official character for his private benefit, every one to whom it comes is put upon inquiry, and if the certificate is false no one can recover against the bank as a *bona fide* holder. So, too, it was held in West Saint Louis Savings Bank *v.* Shawnee County Bank (95 U. S., 557), where a bank cashier made his individual note payable to the order of his bank, and indorsed it officially, that a purchaser of the note was charged with notice that the indorsement was not within the implied authority of the cashier, and must prove actual authority in order to recover of the bank as indorser.

It can make no difference whether the agent or officer appears to be the party to whom the paper is payable upon the face of the instrument, or whether it appears by extrinsic facts that he is the real party for whose benefit it was made; consequently, whenever he offers the instrument under circumstances which show that he has made it officially for his private use, the party dealing with him must take notice of his want of authority, and can not treat it as the obligation of the principal, unless he can prove the existence of some special and extraordinary authority on the part of the agent. For these reasons the testimony offered by the defendants to show that cashiers' checks, when used in the private transactions of bank cashiers, are by usage regarded as cash, was properly excluded. If the tendency of the testimony was to establish a usage to the effect that such payments are regarded by bankers as ordinary payments of cash made by individuals for their own account, the usage would contravene well-settled legal principles. In any other aspect the testimony was immaterial.

The views thus expressed are pertinent in considering whether the instructions given to the jury were correct respecting the title acquired by the defendants to the checks and moneys the checks represented. If the instructions did not accurately present to the jury the legal principles by which, upon the evidence, the rights of the parties were to be determined, they certainly did no injustice to the defendants. The case was put to the jury upon the theory that the defendants, in taking the checks, occupied the position of purchasers of commercial paper, and as though their liability was to be tested by the rule applicable to actions for the wrongful conversion of such paper. If they acquired title to the checks as against the bank, of course they acquired title to the proceeds, and, if they were *bona fide* purchasers, their title was perfect; otherwise they became liable for the proceeds as for a conversion. (Comstock *v.* Hier, 73 N. Y., 269). The defendants were given the full benefit of the distinction between negligence and *mala fides* in the purchase of negotiable paper, and the jury were instructed that mere suspicion on the part of the defendants was not sufficient to charge them with notice that Warner was using the checks without authority. The doctrine of Goodman v. Simonds (20 How., 343) was adopted as applicable to the facts.

The facts in evidence certainly justified the submission of the question to the jury whether the defendants did not have notice that Warner was availing himself of fiduciary powers to use the funds of the corporation for unauthorized purposes. As the checks were made payable to the order of the defendants for Warner's individual use, in legal effect they were made payable to Warner's own order. The defendants knew that he was not acting within the scope of any ordinary agency when he made checks officially for use in his private transactions. The authority of a cashier to represent the bank does not extend to a contract involving the payment of money not loaned by the bank in the ordinary way. (United States Bank v. Dunn, 6 Pet., 51; United States v. City Bank of Columbus, 21 How., 356; Merchants' Bank v. State Bank, 10 Wall., 604.) As the executive officer of the bank, he transacts its business under the orders and supervision of the board of directors. Authority to use its credit, or transfer its funds for his private use, can not be implied from the fact that his official position puts it within his power to act dishonestly in this behalf.

Although the defendants were bound to know when they took the checks that the paper could not be treated as the paper of the bank unless the managers of the bank had loaned him the money represented by it, there was evidence which, unexplained, tended to show that such a loan had been in fact made. The evidence consisted in the circumstances that the checks were drawn upon the regular correspondent of the bank, were drawn frequently, were for large amounts, and the transactions extended over a considerable period of time. These circumstances indicated the improbability that the cashier was acting clandestinely or criminally, and suggested that he was acting with the acquiescence of the directors or that the directors were grossly inattentive to their duties. If the circumstances were sufficiently notorious and peremptory to preclude any other theory than that the directors were aware of what was being done, and were not such as to imply that the directors were willfully ignoring their duties, and acting collusively with Warner, they would afford sufficient evidence of Warner's authority to use the funds of the bank as he did, and would have justified the defendants in relying upon the ostensible authority evinced by the acquiescence and recognition of the directors. As was said by the court in Martin v. Webb (110 U. S., 14., 3 Sup. Ct. Rep., 428):

"It is clear that a banking corporation may be represented by its cashier—at least where its charter does not otherwise provide—in transactions outside of his ordinary duties without his authority to do so being in writing, or appearing upon the record of the proceedings of the directors. His authority may be by parol and collected from circumstances. It may be inferred from the general manner in which, for a period sufficiently long to establish a settled course of business, he has been allowed without interference to conduct the affairs of the bank. It may be implied from the conduct or acquiescence of the corporation, as represented by the board of directors. When, during a series of years, or in numerous business transactions, he has been permitted, without objection, and in his official capacity, to pursue a particular course of conduct, it may be presumed, as between the bank and those who in good faith deal with it upon the basis of his authority to represent the corporation, that he has acted in conformity with instructions received from those who have the right to control its operations. Directors can not, in justice to those who deal with the bank, shut their eyes to what is going on around them. It is their duty to use ordinary diligence in ascertaining the condition of its business, and to exercise reasonable control and supervision of its officers. * * * That which they ought by proper diligence to have known as to the general course of business in the bank, they may be presumed to have known in any contest between the corporation and those who are justified by circumstances in dealing with its officers upon the basis of that course of business."

The defendants could rightfully assume that the directors of the Albion bank did use reasonable diligence in acquainting themselves with the state of its account with its principal agent, the New York bank, and did exercise proper control and supervision generally in the management of its affairs; and the fact that Warner was nevertheless able to use the funds of the bank in such large amounts, for so long a period of time, and through the medium of the regular correspondent of the bank, was inexplicable, except upon the theory of the acquiescence of the directors, or of their guilty complicity with him, or of the existence of an extraordinary laxity on their part in the conduct of the affairs of the bank. The defendants, however, chose to rely upon appearances, instead of seeking authentic information. They were not certain, and could not be from the nature of the case, whether, notwithstanding appearances, the directors were not being deceived by Warner, and were not in fact ignorant that he had ever made any of the checks in question. It was incumbent upon the defendants to show that the directors knew and acquiesced in what was being done by Warner, before they could rely upon his official signature. The evidence raised a presumption of such knowledge and acquiescence on the part of the directors, but did not show it conclusively; it presented a question of fact for the consideration of the jury; and the jury found, as the evidence fully warranted them in doing, that the directors were ignorant of Warner's acts.

As is stated in Wharton on Agency (sec. 139): "The pretension by an agent to extraordinary or peculiar powers is by itself sufficient to arouse suspicion." When the transaction is such as should arouse suspicion of the agent's authority to represent his principal, it is the duty of those who deal with him in a representative character to apply to his principal for information. The defendants did not choose to take the safer course; they preferred to rely upon the evidence of Warner's authority evinced by the facts and circumstances which tended to show that the directors must have known of and consented to his use of the funds of the bank. The jury found not only that the directors did not know this, but also found that the defendants did not believe, when they took the checks, that Warner was authorized to make them by his co managers of the bank. The doctrine that a purchaser of negotiable paper acquires a good title if he acquires it for value, and honestly, notwithstanding he may have been grossly negligent in failing to make proper inquiries, has no application to a case like the present. A purchaser of commercial paper, made by an agent, can not acquire any title to it as against the principal, unless he is able to show that it is the paper of the principal, made by the agent, by due authorization. When he has information that the agent who has made the paper has made it in the name of the principal, for his own use, he must be prepared to show that special authority in that behalf has been delegated by the principal, and can not rely upon the implied authority of the agent to make such paper in the ordinary business of the principal. In accordance with these views, the defendants were not entitled to the instruction that they were only liable if the jury found they took the checks with guilty knowledge that Warner had no authority to use them; and it would have been proper to instruct the jury that the plaintiff was entitled to a verdict if they found that Warner had no authority, actual or ostensible, to use them.

It is insisted for the defendants that, inasmuch as the checks were paid by the New York bank out of funds in part contributed by Warner himself, the Albion bank was not a loser of the face amount of the checks and the plaintiff ought not to recover beyond the extent that the checks were paid out of the moneys of the Albion bank. The evidence did not indicate that the New York bank had any notice that the checks were not put out by Warner in the course of the ordinary business of the bank; consequently, when they were presented to and collected of the New York bank, the latter became a *bona fide* holder for value, and the Albion bank became liable to it for the face amount of the checks. Several of the adjudications which decide that the maker of commercial paper can maintain an action for conversion against the person who, with notice that it has been put fraudulently into circulation, negotiates it to a *bona fide* holder for value, also decide that he can recover the amount of the paper without averring or proving that he has paid it to the holder, and that it is enough, *prima facie* that he has become liable to pay it, to entitle him to recover the face amount (Decker *v.* Mathews, 12 N. Y., 313; Evans *v.* Kymer. 1 Barn. & Adol. 528; Payne *v.* Pritchard, 2 Car. & P., 558). It has been held that the defendant may prove the insolvency of the maker, and thereby lessen the damages; but, in the absence of evidence of any want of ability of the maker to pay, the presumption is that he is able to pay the paper, and will be obliged to do so (Potter *v.* Merchants' Bank, 28 N. Y., 641). It is enough for him to show that he has incurred a liability to pay the amount by the wrongful act of the defendant; but, if the facts are such that this liability will not result in actual loss, he will only be entitled to recover nominal damages. The law presumes that loss will follow liability; consequently, it is for the defendant to overcome the presumption by evidence which will take the case out of the ordinary category.

A check is not only a bill of exchange upon which an action can be maintained against the drawer by the drawee who has paid it, but is a bill which is presumed to be drawn on actual funds, and appropriates the funds to the drawee upon payment. Undoubtedly, in an action for the wrongful conversion of such paper, if the defendant proves that payment of the check was refused by the drawee, that it has never reached the hands of a *bona fide* holder, and that he is ready to surrender it to the maker upon the trial, these facts would go in mitigation of damages, and the recovery of the plaintiff would be limited to his actual loss. If, in the present case, the action was merely for the conversion of the checks, the plaintiff would be entitled to recover their face upon proof that they were paid by the New York bank, without more; but the action is for the money of the Albion bank, obtained upon its checks "paid by the New York bank out of and from the moneys and accounts of the Albion bank." If the evidence established that the checks were not paid by the New York bank out of the moneys or funds of the Albion bank, but were paid out of moneys provided for that purpose by Warner the jury should have been instructed that their verdict could be only for nominal damages. But the payment of the checks by the New York bank was none the less a payment by the Albion bank, or a payment out of its funds, because the latter was put in funds without the knowledge of its officers, and its correspondent paid the checks without their knowledge. If Warner had made deposits in his own name with the New York bank, and that bank, pursuant to his instructions, had charged the checks, when it paid them, against his account, the defendants might well insist that the checks were not paid by the Albion bank, or out of its funds. Under such circumstances, the plaintiff would certainly be required to prove that the deposits made by Warner were funds of the Albion bank. But when Warner caused deposits to be made with the New York bank in the name of the Albion bank, the title to the fund created by the deposits vested in the latter as against Warner. When the New York bank credited the Albion bank with these deposits it assumed the relation of a debtor, not to Warner, but to the Albion bank for the amount; and when it paid checks drawn against the fund and charged them to the Albion bank, it paid them out of the funds of the Albion bank as between itself and the Albion bank and as between the latter and Warner. It may be that third persons, whose moneys were misappropriated by Warner and deposited with the New York bank to the credit of the Albion bank, can reclaim the amount of the Albion bank; but Warner himself could not, because he relinquished his title by his own act. Whether the deposits made by him are to be regarded as the property of the Albion bank because made by a fiduciary who has willfully commingled his own funds with the trust funds in such a manner that the line of distinction between them can not be traced, or as voluntary payments which he can not reclaim because they were voluntary, need not be considered. He doubtless made them to conceal his use of the funds of the bank, knowing that he could not overdraw the account of his bank with the New York bank without risk of detection.

The defendants have no interest in the question whether the Albion bank paid the checks out of the moneys for which it is accountable to third persons, or even out of the money for which it may be accountable to Warner. It suffices that the checks were paid out of funds to which it had the legal title. Nor is it material that the defendants paid to Warner various sums of money which were ultimately received by the Bank of Albion. It was open to the defendants to show upon the trial that the Albion bank did not eventually sustain any loss by Warner's misappropriations of its checks or moneys, and thus reduce the plaintiff's recovery to nominal damages. This they did not attempt otherwise than by showing that Warner deposited various sums of money to the credit of the Albion bank, which were not charged by that bank to the New York bank. The presumption is as cogent that these deposits secretly made by Warner represented the moneys which he knew belonged to the Albion bank as that they were his own money. The case for the plaintiff was complete when it appeared that the checks which were wrongfully received and collected by the defendants had been paid by the New York bank out of funds standing to the credit of the Albion bank. He was then entitled to recover the full amount. It was unnecessary for him to assume the affirmative, and show that the deposits made by Warner in the New York bank were not the funds of Warner, but consisted of misapplied funds of the bank, or the proceeds of securities belonging to it, or for which it was responsible to others; but it was for the defendants to prove that, notwithstanding their wrongful participation with Warner in misappropriating the funds of the bank, the bank did not suffer loss. If they had shown that all his misappropriations had been made good by the return of what he had misapplied, it is not entirely clear that they would have been liable only for nominal damages. (Hanmer *v.* Wilsey, 17 Wend.. 91; Otis *v.* Jones, 21 Wend., 394; The People *v.* Bank of North America, 75 N. Y., 547.) These cases hold that the defendant in an action for conversion of property can only claim a mitigation of damages because of a return of the property, where the owner has accepted its return, or has resumed dominion over it as owner; and that it is not enough that the property, without his consent, has been applied to the satisfaction of his debts. It is not necessary to consider whether this doctrine should be applied to a case for the conversion of money which has been returned to the owner, and used by him without knowledge of the conversion or restitution. Here all the money returned by Warner was insufficient to replace his defalcations by an amount much larger than the sum sought to be recovered of the defendants, and the bank had no knowledge that he had returned anything to replace what he had misapplied until he had again misappropriated it. It is not unjust or unreasonable to compel the defendants to restore such of the funds of the bank as they received when they are unable to prove that the bank was not directly or ultimately a loser in consequence of their acts. It may be that Warner would have misappropriated the money of the bank in other ways, if they had refused to receive the checks, but certainly one temptation would not have been in his path if he had found that he could not use the paper of the bank for his speculations with the same facility as though it were his own money.

Several points discussed upon the motion for a new trial, among them the point that the jury should have been instructed not to include interest in their verdict accruing before the commencement of the suit, do not seem to merit consideration. The views expressed cover all the controlling questions in the case, and lead to a denial of the motion.

(3) An opinion rendered by the Supreme Court of the United States November 12, 1888, with respect to the liability of a married woman holding stock of an insolvent national bank to an assessment upon such stock levied by the Comptroller of the Currency where the assets of the bank were not sufficient to pay creditors in full.

On the 4th of February, 1885, Martin L. Bundy, receiver of the Hot Springs National Bank, of Hot Springs, in the State of Arkansas, filed his bill of complaint in the circuit court of the United States for the district of Kentucky against William M. Cocke and Amanda M. Cocke, his wife, and James Flanagan and Sue Flanagan, his wife, all of the defendants being alleged in the bill to be citizens of Kentucky.

The bill alleges that, on the 1st of March, 1884, the bank was a corporation created and organized under the national banking statutes, with a capital stock of $50,000, divided into 500 shares of $100 each at their par value; that it had its office of discount and deposit in the city of Hot Springs, in the State of Arkansas; that it suspended the business of banking on the 27th of May, 1884; that the plaintiff was duly appointed receiver of the bank on the 2d of June, 1884; and that, on the 25th of July, 1884, the Comptroller of the Currency determined that it was necessary to enforce the individual liability of the shareholders in the bank, to the amount of 50 per centum of the par value of its capital stock, "and did make an order and requisition on the stockholders and each and every one of them, equally and ratably, as the shares were held and owned by them respectively at the time said bank suspended and ceased to do business," and directed the plaintiff "as such receiver" to take the necessary legal proceedings to enforce such assessment against the shareholders in said bank, and each and every one of them.

The bill then contains the following allegation:

"And your orator would further state that, on the 27th day of May, A. D. 1884, when said bank suspended and ceased to do business, Amanda M. Cocke, wife of William M. Cocke (both of whom are made defendants hereto), was the owner of one hundred shares of the capital stock thereof, of the par value of ten thousand dollars, and the same still stands in her name on the books of the said association, on which the equal and ratable assessment and requisition made by the Comptroller as aforesaid is five thousand dollars, with interest thereon from the said 25th day of July, 1884; that said defendant Amanda is possessed of property in her own right amply sufficient to pay said assessment, but utterly refuses to do so."

Then follows a like allegation as to Mrs. Flanagan, as the owner of twelve shares of the stock.

The prayer of the bill is, that an account be taken of the shares of stock held by each of the married women defendants, respectively, at the date of such suspension and the assessment and requisition made by the Comptroller of the Currency thereon, and that a decree be made for the payment thereof out of the separate property held by the married women defendants in their own right, as each may be found indebted, with interest.

Mr. and Mrs. Cocke filed a demurrer to the bill for want of equity and also for multifariousness. The plaintiff then amended the bill by striking out the names of Flanagan and his wife as defendants; and in July, 1885, he filed a bill of revivor, based on the fact of the death of Mrs. Cocke in March, 1885.

The bill of revivor alleges that, when Mrs. Cocke died, she was a citizen of Kentucky, and was domiciled and resident therein; that she left a will whereby her husband was appointed her sole executor and her sole residuary legatee and devisee; that the will had been duly proved and recorded in the proper court in Kentucky; and that Mr. Cocke had accepted the terms of the will and taken upon himself the office of such executor. The bill prays for the revival of the suit against Mr. Cocke as devisee and legatee of his wife and as sole executor of her will, and for relief against him out of all assets received or held by him as devisee or legatee of his wife, or as executor of her will.

Mr. Cocke appeared and filed a demurrer to the bill of revivor, for want of equity. The cause was heard on the demurrer to the bill and the demurrer to the bill of revivor. The court sustained both of the demurrers, giving to the plaintiff time to amend his bill, and, he declining to do so, a decree was entered dismissing it. From that decree the plaintiff has appealed.

From the opinion of the court, accompanying the record, the ground of the dismissal appears to have been, that the bill was defective in not alleging that, at the time Mrs. Cocke became a stockholder, she had the capacity to become a stockholder,

But we think the bill is not open to this objection. It alleges that, at the time the bank suspended, Mrs. Cocke "was the owner" of the 100 shares. This is an allegation that she was then the lawful owner of those shares, and had lawfully become such owner, with the capacity to become such owner at the time she became such owner. It is consistent with this allegation, that she may have owned the shares before she married Mr. Cocke, or that, when she became such owner, if she was then the wife of Mr. Cocke, she had the right to become such owner by virtue of the laws of the State of Arkansas, where the bank was located, in connection with the provisions of the statutes of the United States in regard to national banks.

Section 4194 of the Digest of the Statutes of Arkansas, published in 1874 (chap. 93, p. 756), provides as follows:

"Sec. 4194. A married woman may bargain, sell, assign, and transfer her separate personal property, and carry on any trade or business, and perform any labor or services on her sole and separate account; and the earnings of any married woman from her trade, business, labor, or services shall be her sole and separate property, and may be used or invested by her in her own name; and she may alone sue or be sued in the courts of this State on account of the said property, business, or services."

Under this provision, if it was in force at the time of the transaction, it would seem that Mrs. Cocke, when a married woman, might lawfully have either subscribed for or taken an assignment of the shares, they being shares of a national bank in Arkansas, and the transaction being, therefore, governed by the statutes of Arkansas, unless, under special circumstances, a different rule ought to govern. (*Milliken* v. *Pratt*, 125 Mass., 374.)

As the bill alleges that Mrs. Cocke is possessed of property in her own right amply sufficient to pay the assessment, and as the prayer of the bill is for a decree for the payment of the amount of the assessment out of the separate property held by her in her own right, and as the bill of revivor prays for relief against Mr. Cocke out of the assets received by him as the legatee or devisee of his wife, or as executor of her will, the case is clearly one of equitable cognizance, because it does not appear that she could be sued at law, to reach her separate property. (3 *Pomeroy's Eq. Juris.*, § 1099.)

The original bill and bill of revivor are sufficient on their faces to call upon Mr. Cocke to answer them, and, when all the facts bearing upon the case are fully developed the rights of the parties can be properly adjudicated. For that reason we refrain from considering any of the other questions discussed at the bar.

The decree of the circuit court is reversed, and the case is remanded to that court, with a direction to overrule the demurrer to the original bill and the demurrer to the bill of revivor, and to take such further proceedings as may be proper and not inconsistent with this opinion.

CONCLUSION.

In presenting this report I gladly take occasion to bear testimony to the excellent spirit prevailing among the officers and directors of national banks all over the country, and to the intelligence and conscientiousness which they habitually display in the conduct of business.

Although the requirements of the national-bank laws are often rendered onerous by local conditions, and many of its restraints are not only irksome but sometimes in particular cases seem to be unreasonable, there exists everywhere as a rule a spirit of sincere and ready acquiescence. In the comparatively few cases where this spirit is wanting the power of the Comptroller to enforce compliance with law has been found to be ample, and its exercise has but in one case had to transcend the limits of a courteous but firm admonition. In that case the bank was closed and placed in the hands of a receiver, the president and cashier were arrested and indicted, and the property of the directors was attached.

For several years past, under the influence of the act of July 12, 1882, the national-bank system has been growing vigorously, and its benefits have been thus brought within reach of a constantly increasing number of people, and have been extended into communities where they were not previously enjoyed.

At present this healthy and desirable growth is checked and is in danger of being arrested by the scarcity and dearness of bonds. In the proper place in this report I have called especial attention to the value and capabilities of the bank-note feature of the system and have ventured to submit a plan for its preservation and extension into full utility. The subject is one of national importance, and yet it is also of definite pecuniary interest to each and every industrial worker in the country, however obscure his employment may seem or however secluded his location.

The functions performed by banks are essential to the free and full play of industrial activities, whether these are agricultural, mechanical, or professional. The products of all industries must be marketed in order that the workers may enjoy the fruits of their toil or the rewards of their skill, and without banks the marketing of the vast masses of the products of American industry would be simply impossible.

The banks as a body establish and maintain, ready for use at all times and to any extent required, a line of communication between the world's consumers and the remotest farmer on the Western plains or among the Southern forests. Break this line of communication and the abundance of the farm becomes a rotting incubus. Interrupt it, burden it with tolls or taxes, and the farmer loses in the price of his products or pays in the cost of what he buys more than the toll-gatherer or the tax-collector receives.

A great prejudice has been excited in agricultural sections against the national banks, because they are forbidden to lend money on real-estate securities. Never was there any prejudice more unreasonable and more harmful to those who entertain it than this prejudice.

In the first place, if national banks absorbed all the capital of the country or directed its employment and investment, not only their interests, but even their very existence would necessitate the setting aside of a large part of that capital for investment exclusively in real estate or in real-estate securities, because such investments are essential to the progress of every community.

But the national banks do not by any means occupy that position. Private capitalists, corporations, such as savings banks, insurance companies, loan and trust companies, farm and mortgage investment companies, abound; they possess and control more capital than the national banks, and for all these there can be no investment safer, more attractive, and more appropriate than real estate or its representative instruments.

The national banks, on the other hand, constitute a body of bankers exclusively devoted to the collection, the safe-keeping, and the employment in temporary loans of the floating capital of the country. If in any community the national-bank capital and deposits exceed what can be safely and profitably employed there in that way, the floating capital of that community is excessive and a part of it may with advantage be converted into fixed forms, but it should first be withdrawn from the national banks. These institutions are too expensive to be used as mere agencies for keeping bonds and stocks, and collecting interest quarterly or half yearly. Such misuse of a national bank is bad economy; it is as if a farmer should buy wagons and carriages for storing his crop instead of building a barn.

Again, to entertain a prejudice against national banks and to oppose the improvement and healthy extension of the system is unwise because we must have banks, and these are the best that have ever existed in this country or in any other. It is especially unwise on the part of farmers to entertain such prejudice because they are more dependent upon other people's floating capital than any other industrial class.

Miners, manufacturers, transportation companies, and other large employers keep a part of their capital in money, and depend upon the banks for only a moderate proportion of the cash funds needed to liquidate their transactions, but farmers can not afford to keep any amount of money idle while their crops are growing or their cattle are taking on flesh or their sheep and hogs are multiplying. It is more profitable for them to use all their own money in enlarging the scale of their operations; and, therefore, when their crops come to be harvested or their stock is ready to be driven to market, it is of supreme importance to them to be able to get the ready money for the purpose, either directly or through the medium of dealers in their products. Whether obtained directly or through merchants or drovers, the money essential to the marketing of the farm produce is supplied by the banks, and could not be supplied by them at that moment of supreme need if it had previously been lent to the farmers upon the security of their lands.

The banks that serve the farmers best are those that move their crops with least delay. A bank in an agricultural section that gets its funds tied up in long loans to farmers mistakes its office and vocation, and is as great an obstruction to local prosperity as a railroad would be that should hire all its freight cars out during the dull season for an employment that keeps them out of its reach and control beyond the season during which the community depends upon it to take away the produce of its year's labor, and to bring back the commodities essential to its winter's comfort and maintenance.

Very respectfully,

W. L. TRENHOLM.
Comptroller of the Currency.

Hon. JOHN G. CARLISLE,
Speaker of the House of Representatives.

[A]BSTRACT OF REPORTS OF THE NATIONAL BANKING ASSOCIATIONS OF THE UNITED STATES, SHOWING THEIR CONDITION AT THE CLOSE OF BUSINESS ON THURSDAY, OCTOBER 4, [illegible]

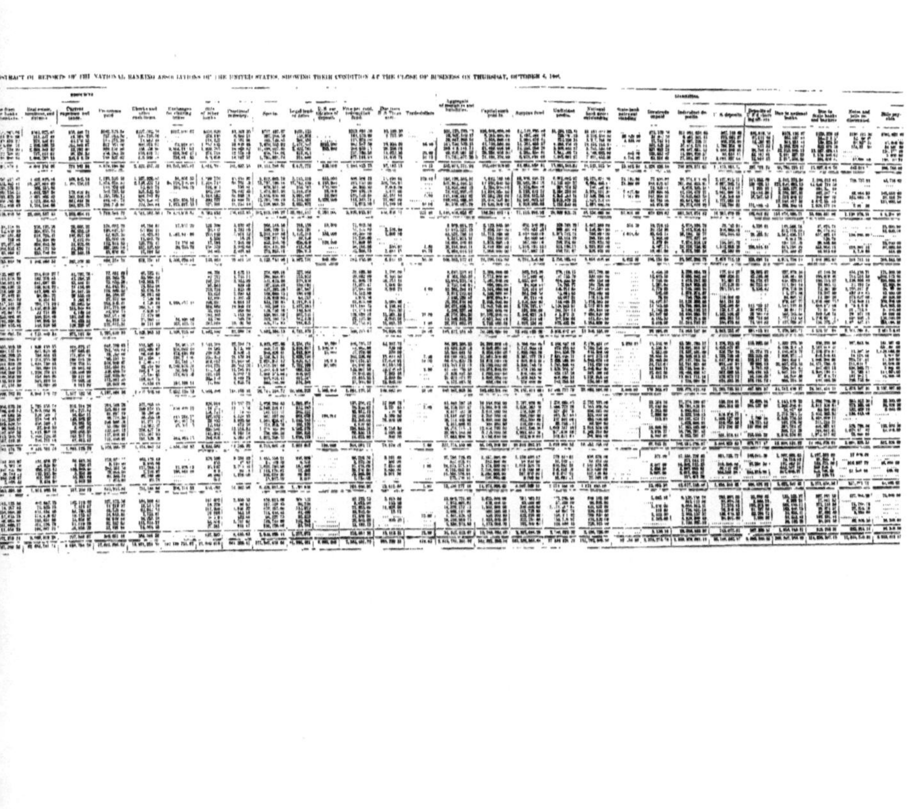

APPENDIX.

A DIGEST OF NATIONAL-BANK CASES.

CONTENTS.*

---

*Cases which turned upon a peculiar state of facts, and many which but reiterate settled principles, have been omitted; also, a few which are reported so badly or so meagerly that the precise points decided do not clearly appear.

XI. **Jurisdiction.**

(1) Jurisdiction of Federal courts prior to the act of July 12, 1882; (2) Jurisdiction of Federal courts subsequent to act of July 12, 1882; (3) Jurisdiction of State courts; (4) United States can not be subjected to jurisdiction of court; (5) Citizenship.

XII. **Suits.**

(1) By and against associations; (2) By shareholders; (3) By receivers; (4) By creditors of insolvent association; (5) For usury; (6) To enforce liability of shareholders; (7) Execution; (8) Attachments; (9) Abatement; (10) Estoppel; (11) Suits against liquidating associations; (12) Transitory and local suits; (13) Survival of suits.

XIII. **Evidence.**

(1) Certificates of Comptroller; (2) Evidence of insolvency; (3) Necessity for assessment by Comptroller.

XIV. **Crimes.**

(1) Under United States laws; (2) Under State laws; (3) Term "United States currency" in penal statutes.

I. CONSTITUTIONAL LAW.

1. POWERS OF CONGRESS:

(a) Congress has the constitutional power to incorporate banks. (*McCulloch* v *Maryland*, 4 *Wheat.*, 316; *Osborn* v. *Bank of the United States*, 9 *Wheat.*, 738.)

(b) Congress has power to clothe national banking associations, as to their contracts and dealings with the world, with any special immunities and privileges exempting them, in their trade and intercourse with others, from the laws and remedies applicable in like cases to other citizens. (*The Chesapeake Bank* v. *The First National Bank of Baltimore*, 40 *Md.*, 269.)

(c) Thus, the provision of the banking law that no attachment, injunction, or execution shall issue against a national banking association before final judgment in any suit, action, or proceeding in a State court is constitutional. (*Ibid.*)

(d) The tax imposed on State or national banks paying out the notes of individuals or State banks used for circulation is constitutional. (*Veazie Bank* v. *Fenno*, 8 *Wall.*, 533.)

(e) So is the tax imposed on them for paying out the circulating notes of municipal corporations. (*Merchants' National Bank of Little Rock* v. *United States*, 101 *U. S.*, 1.)

(*f*) Such a tax is not a direct tax within the meaning of the clause of the Constitution, which declares that "direct taxes shall be apportioned among the several States, according to their respective numbers." (*Veazie Bank* v. *Fenno, and Merchants' National Bank of Little Rock* v. *United States, supra.*)

(g) Congress having, in the exercise of undisputed constitutional powers, undertaken to provide a currency for the whole country, may secure the benefit of it to the people by appropriate legislation. (*Veazie Bank* v. *Fenno, supra.*)

(h) Congress has the power to divest the United States courts of their jurisdiction of suits by or against national banking associations. (*National Bank of Jefferson* v. *Fare et al., U. S. C. C. (E. D. Texas)*, 25 *Fed. Rep.*, 209.)

2. POWERS OF THE STATES:

(a) National banking associations, being instruments designed to aid the Government in the administration of a branch of the public service, can not be controlled by the States, except in so far as Congress may see proper to permit. (*Farmers and Mechanics' Bank* v. *Dearing*, 91 *U. S.*, 29.)

(b) No authority from the State is necessary to enable a State bank to convert itself into a national banking association. (*Casey* v. *Galli*, 94 *U. S.*, 673.)

(c) National banking associations located outside of a State are subject to its restraining acts prohibiting all corporations, not authorized by the law of the State, from keeping therein offices for the purpose of discount and deposit. (*National Bank of Fairhaven* v. *The Phœnix Warehousing Company*, 6 *Hun*, 71.)

(d) It is competent for a State by penal enactments to protect its citizens in their dealings with national banking associations located within the State. (*State* v. *Fuller*, 34 *Conn.*, 280; see also *Taxation and Jurisdiction.*)

II. POWERS AND LIABILITIES.

1. IMPLIED POWERS:

To the enumerated powers of national banking associations are to be superadded all the powers incidental to the business of banking. (*Pattison* v. *Syracuse National Bank*, 80 *N. Y.*, 82.)

2. AS TO COLLATERAL SECURITIES:

(a) A national banking association may take stock of a corporation as collateral security for a loan. (*Shoemaker* v. *The National Mechanics' Bank*, 2 *Abb. U. S.*, 416; *Canfield* v. *The State National Bank of Minneapolis*, *U. S. C. C. (Dist. Minn.)*, 1 *Northwestern Reporter*, 173.)

(b) And it may take for such purpose the stock of another national banking association. (*National Bank* v. *Case*, 99 *U. S.*, 628.)

NOTE.—But this point was not necessary to the decision of the case.

2. AS TO COLLATERAL SECURITIES—Continued.

(c) A national banking association may take a pledge of personal chattels as security for a loan. (*Pittsburgh Locomotive and Car Works* v. *State National Bank of Keokuk*, *U. S. C. C.* (*Eighth Circuit*, 1875), 2 *Cent. L. J.*, 692.)

(d) A national banking association may take as security for a loan the indorsement of a married woman, charging her separate estate. Such security is to be treated as personal security, within the meaning of the banking law, and not as a mortgage. (*Third National Bank* v. *Blake*, 73 *N. Y.*, 260.)

(e) A national banking association may take as collateral security for a loan a warehouse receipt for merchandise. (*Cleveland, Brown & Co.* v. *Shoeman*, 40 *Ohio St.*, 176.)

(f) A national banking association may take as security for a loan the stock of a corporation whose entire capital is vested in real estate. Such a loan does not amount to a lending upon mortgage. (*Baldwin* v. *Canfield*, 26 *Minn.*, 43.)

(g) An agreement by a national banking association to the effect that, in case a note discounted by it shall not be paid, a mortgage given by the maker to his indorser shall inure to the benefit of the association, is not inhibited by the national banking law. (*First National Bank* v. *Haire*, 36 *Iowa*, 443; see also *National Bank* v. *Matthews*, 98 *U. S.*, 621.)

(h) A national banking association having taken a mortgage on real estate to secure a debt previously contracted may, in order to protect itself, pay off a prior lien on the said real estate; and the lien which it thus acquires it may enforce. (*Ornn* v. *Merchants' National Bank*, 16 *Kans.*, 341; *Holmes* v. *Boyd*, 90 *Ind.*, 332.)

(i) Where a national banking association has taken collaterals to secure a loan, and, after the loan has been repaid, holds them to secure future advances, it is not a gratuitous bailee; and it is responsible for the loss of such collaterals occasioned by its lack of ordinary care and diligence, though at the time the bailor was not indebted to it. (*Third National Bank of Baltimore* v. *Boyd*, 44 *Md.*, 47.)

3. SPECIAL DEPOSITS:

(a) A national banking association may receive special deposits. The provision in section 5228, Revised Statutes, authorizing an association "to deliver special deposits" implies that it may receive them as a part of its legitimate business; and this implication is as effectual as an express declaration to the same effect would have been. (*National Bank* v. *Graham*, 100 *U. S.*, 699.)

(b) National banking associations have power to receive special deposits either gratuitously or otherwise. (*Pattison* v. *Syracuse National Bank*, 80 *N. Y.*, 82.)

(c) But the executive officers of an association can not bind it as a gratuitous bailee, unless they have a special authority from the board of directors so to do, or there exists a general custom or usage to that effect. (*First National Bank of Lyons* v. *Ocean National Bank*, 60 *N. Y.*, 278.)

4. GOVERNMENT SECURITIES:

(a) National banking associations can engage in the business of dealing in and exchanging Government securities. (*Van Leuven* v. *First National Bank*, 54 *N. Y.*, 671; *Yerkes* v. *National Bank of Port Jervis*, 69 *N. Y.*, 383; *Leach* v. *Hale*, 31 *Iowa*, 69.)

(b) And where an association receives United States bonds of one class for the purpose of having them converted into bonds of another class, it is not a mere mandatary, but is responsible for the failure to deliver the bonds on demand. (*Leach* v. *Hale*, *supra*.)

5. CERTIFIED CHECK:

A national banking association may "certify" a check. A "certified" check is not within the meaning of section 5183, Revised Statutes, which prohibits the issuing of post-notes or any notes to circulate as money other than such as are authorized by the national banking law. (*Merchants' National Bank* v. *State National Bank*, 10 *Wall.*, 604.)

6. PURCHASING CHECK:

A national bank may buy a check drawn upon another bank; and whether the check is payable to order or to bearer is immaterial. (*First National Bank of Rochester* v. *Harris*, 108 *Mass.*, 514.)

7. STOCKS:

(a) A national banking association, in the compromise of a claim growing out of its legitimate business, may take railroad stock. (*First National Bank of Charlotte* v. *National Exchange Bank of Baltimore*, 92 *U. S.*, 122.)

7. STOCKS—Continued.

(b) And when necessary to do so, it may pay the difference between the value of the stock and the amount of the claim. (*Ibid.*)

(c) A national banking association may take and hold the coupons of municipal bonds, and may maintain actions thereon. (*First National Bank of North Bennington* v. *Town of Bennington, U. S. C. C.* (*Dist. Vt.*), *Browne's N. B. Cas.*, 437; see also *Lyons* v. *Lyons National Bank*, 19 *Blatch.*, 279.)

8. DEPOSITS TO SECURE PERFORMANCE OF CONTRACT:

A national banking association may receive a deposit to be held by it as security for the faithful performance of a contract between the depositor and another. (*Bushnell* v. *The Chautauqua County National Bank*, 10 *Hun*, 378.)

NOTE.—But the court put the decision upon the further ground that even were the contract *ultra vires*, the association, having received the deposit, was estopped from setting up its want of power.

9. LOANS IN EXCESS OF ONE-TENTH CAPITAL:

(a) Sec. 5200, Revised Statutes, which provides that the total liabilities to any association of any person, etc., shall not exceed one-tenth part of the capital stock paid in, was intended only for the guidance of the association, and, though its franchises may be liable to forfeiture for violation of the law, the association may recover of the borrower the full amount of the loan. (*Gold Mining Company* v. *Rocky Mountain National Bank*, 96 *U. S.*, 640; *O'Hare* v. *Second National Bank of Titusville*, 77 *Penn. St.*, 96; *Shoemaker* v. *The National Mechanics' Bank*, 2 *Abb. U. S.*, 416; *Stewart* v. *National Union Bank of Maryland*, 2 *Abb. U. S.*, 424.)

(b) A note is not illegal because at the time it was discounted by the association the maker was indebted to the association in a sum equal to more than one-tenth part of its capital. (*O'Hare* v. *Second National Bank of Titusville, supra.*)

(c) And a court of equity will not enjoin an association, at the instance of the borrower, from transferring to innocent third persons notes and securities, on the ground that the notes represent part of a loan made in excess of 10 per cent. of the capital of the association. (*Elder* v. *First National Bank of Ottawa*, 12 *Kans.*, 238.)

(d) Where a State bank makes a loan to one person of an amount in excess of one-tenth part of its capital, and is afterward converted into a national bank, it may, after conversion, extend the time for payment of such loan without violating section 5200, Revised Statutes. (*Allen* v. *The First National Bank of Xenia*, 23 *Ohio St.*, 97.)

10. REAL ESTATE:

(a) Where a national banking association acquires real estate which it is not authorized to take, the conveyance to it is not void, but only voidable. And the title of the association to such real estate is good until assailed in a direct proceeding by the Government. (*Reynolds* v. *Crawfordsville Bank*, 112 *U. S.*, 405; see also *National Bank* v. *Matthews*, 98 *U. S.*, 621; *National Bank* v. *Whitney*, 103 *U. S.*, 99; *Swope* v. *Leffingwell*, 105 *U. S.*, 3; *Fortier* v. *New Orleans Bank*, 112 *U. S.*, 439.)

(b) The amount of real estate which a national banking association may purchase to secure a pre-existing debt is not limited to the exact amount of the debt, but as much may be purchased as is necessary to secure the debt due, so long as the security of such debt is the real object of the purchase. (*Upton* v. *National Bank of South Reading*, 120 *Mass.*, 153.)

(c) Where the purpose is to secure a debt previously contracted, a national banking association may take a conveyance of real estate worth more than the debt, and pay the difference between the debt and the value of the property. (*Libby* v. *Union National Bank*, 99 *Ill.*, 622.)

(d) Where a national banking association sells real estate it may take a mortgage thereon to secure the payment of the purchase-money. (*New Orleans National Bank* v. *Raymond*, 29 *La. Ann.*, 355.)

11. CERTIFICATES OF DEPOSIT:

National banking associations may issue certificates of deposit. Such certificates are not post-notes within the prohibition of section 5183, Revised Statutes. (*Hunt* v. *Appellant, Supreme Court of Mass., May* 7, 1886; *Riddle* v. *First National Bank, U. S. C. C.* (*W. D. Penn.*), 27 *Fed. Rep.*, 503.)

12. LIEN ON DIVIDENDS:

An association has an equitable lien upon dividends declared for any just debt due to it from the shareholders. (*Hager* v. *Union National Bank*, 63 *Me.*, 509.)

13. CONTRACTS AND OBLIGATIONS OF OLD CORPORATION:

(a) Where a State bank has been converted into a national banking association it may enforce all contracts made with it while a State corporation. (*City National Bank* v. *Phelps*, 97 *N. Y.*, 44.)

(b) And it is liable, after the conversion, for all the obligations of the old institution. (*Coffee* v. *The National Bank of Missouri*, 46 *Mo.*, 140; *Kelsey* v. *The National Bank of Crawford*, 69 *Penn. St.*, 426.)

(c) A national banking association organized as the successor of a State bank may take and hold the assets of the bank whose place it takes, though there was not in form a conversion from a State to a national corporation, but the organization of a new corporation. (*Bank* v. *McIntire*, 40 *Ohio St.*, 528.)

(d) And such association will be liable to the depositors of the former bank. (*Eans* v. *Exchange Bank*, 79 *Mo.*, 182.)

14. PLACE OF BUSINESS:

(a) The provision requiring "the usual business" of the association to be transacted "at an office or banking-house in the place specified in its organization certificate" must be construed reasonably; and a part of the legitimate business of the association which can not be transacted at the banking-house may be done elsewhere. (*Merchants' Bank* v. *State Bank*, 10 *Wall.*, 604.)

(b) Although the general business of a national banking association is to be transacted at its place of business, yet, if the association is fully advised of the facts, and does not object, and there is no fraud, its officers, when acting within the general scope of their authority, may bind it by acts done at another place. (*Burton* v. *Burley*, 9 *Biss.*, 253.)

15. CIRCULATING NOTES:

The circulating notes of a national banking association are valid, though they do not bear the imprint of the seal of the Treasury. Such imprint was intended to be simply evidence of the contract, and forms no part of the contract itself. (*United States* v. *Bennett*, 17 *Blatch.*, 357.)

16. BUSINESS OF LIQUIDATING ASSOCIATION:

After an association goes into liquidation there is no authority on the part of its officers to transact any business in its name so as to bind its shareholders, except that which is implied in the duty of liquidation, unless such authority has been expressly conferred by the shareholders. (*Richmond* v. *Irons*, 121 *U. S.*, 27.)

III. ULTRA VIRES.

1. DEALING IN STOCKS:

(a) A national banking association is not authorized to act as a broker or agent in the purchase of bonds and stocks. (*First National Bank of Allentown* v. *Hoch*, 89 *Penn St.*, 324; *Weckler* v. *The First National Bank of Hagerstown*, 42 *Md.*, 581.)

(b) A national banking association can not deal in stocks. The prohibition is to be implied from the failure to grant the power. (*First National Bank* v. *National Exchange Bank*, 92 *U. S.*, 122.)

NOTE.—But see as to its power to deal in Government securities, Powers, 4.

2. PURCHASING NEGOTIABLE PAPER:

A national banking association can not *purchase* negotiable paper. (*Lazear* v. *National Union Bank of Baltimore*, 52 *Md.*, 78; *First National Bank of Rochester* v. *Pierson*, 24 *Minn.*, 140; see also *Farmers and Mechanics' Bank* v. *Baldwin*, 23 *Minn.*, 198. But see *Smith* v. *The Exchange Bank of Pittsburgh*, 26 *Ohio St.*, 141.)

3. LENDING CREDIT:

(a) A national banking association can not lend its credit. (*Johnston* v. *Charlottesville National Bank*, 3 *Hughes*, 657; *Seligman* v. *Charlottesville National Bank*, 3 *Hughes*, 647.)

(b) A national banking association can not guaranty the paper of a customer *for his accommodation*. (*Seligman* v. *Charlottesville National Bank*, *supra*.)

(c) The accommodation paper of a national banking association is void in the hands of one who takes it with knowledge of its character. (*Johnston* v. *Charlottesville National Bank*, *supra*.)

4. MORTGAGES ON REAL ESTATE:

(a) National banking associations are by implication prohibited from taking mortgages on real estate as security for contemporaneous loans. (*National*

4. MORTGAGES ON REAL ESTATE—Continued.

Bank v. *Matthews*, 98 *U. S.*, 621; *Fowler* v. *Scully*, 72 *Penn. St.*, 456; *Kansas Valley National Bank* v. *Rowell*, 2 *Dill.*, 371; *Commonwealth Bank* v. *Clark*, 4 *Mo.*, 59; *Crocker* v. *Whitney*, 71 *N. Y.*, 161; *Fridley* v. *Bowen*, 87 *Ill.*, 151.)

(*b*) But where such security has been taken, no one but the Government can be heard to complain that the association has exceeded its powers. (*National Bank* v. *Matthews*, *supra*; *National Bank* v. *Whitney*, 103 *U. S.*, 99; *Swope* v. *Leffingwell*, 105 *U. S.*, 3; *Reynolds* v. *National Bank*, 112 *U. S.*, 405; *Fortier* v. *National Bank*, 112, *U. S.*, 439.)

NOTE.—These decisions overrule, on this point, *Kansas Valley National Bank* v. *Rowell*, 2 *Dill.*, 371; *Crocker* v. *Whitney*, *supra*; *Fowler* v. *Scully*, *supra*; *Matthews* v. *Skinker*, 62 *Mo.*, 329; *Woods* v. *People's National Bank of Pittsburgh*, 83 *Penn. St.*, 57; *Fridley* v. *Bowen*, *supra*.

5. WHEN ASSOCIATION CAN NOT SET UP WANT OF POWER:

Where a national banking association has entered into a contract which it was not authorized to make, a party who has enjoyed the benefit of such contract can not question its validity. (*Casey* v. *La Société de Credit Mobilier*, 2 *Woods*, 77; *German National Bank* v. *Meadowcroft*, 95 *Ill.*, 124.)

IV. STOCK.

1. PURCHASING ITS OWN STOCK:

Where a national banking association purchases shares of its own stock, and divides them among its directors, to whom the shares are transferred upon the stock books, the transaction is void, and no title passes. (*Meyers* v. *Valley National Bank*, *U. S. D. C.* (*E. Dist. Mo.*), 13 *National Bankruptcy Register*, 34.)

2. LIENS ON STOCK:

(*a*) A national banking association can not acquire a lien on the stock of a shareholder. And a by-law prohibiting a transfer until all liabilities of the shareholder to the association are discharged, or a provision to that effect in the certificates of stock, is void. (*Bullard* v. *National Bank*, 18 *Wall.*, 589; *Bank* v. *Lanier*, 11 *Wall.*, 369; *Conklin* v. *The Second National Bank*, 45 *N. Y.*, 655.)

(*b*) A national banking association can not take a pledge of its stock to secure a deposit made by it with another bank. Such a transaction amounts to a lending upon the security of its own shares. (*Bank* v. *Lanier*, *supra*.)

(*c*) Though a bank is prohibited from lending money upon the security of its own shares, yet if the shares have been sold and the proceeds applied to the payment of the debt, the courts will not aid the shareholder to recover the value of the shares. He can dispute the validity of the transaction only while the contract is executory, and the security still subsists in the possession of the ban k. (*National Bank of Xenia* v. *Stewart*, 107 *U. S.*, 676.)

3. MAY BE ATTACHED:

The stock of a shareholder indebted to it may be attached by the association and sold on execution. (*Hagar* v. *Union National Bank*, 63 *Me.*, 509.)

4. CAPITAL SET FREE BELONGS TO SHAREHOLDERS:

When a national banking association reduces its capital stock the amount of capital thus released belongs to the shareholders pro rata, and must be returned to them; and it can not be retained by the association for a surplus. (*Seeley* v. *New York National Exchange Bank*, 8 *Daly*, 400; *s. c.*, 4 *Abb. N. C.*, 61; affirmed, 78 *N. Y.*, 608.)

5. CONTRACTS TO GIVE SHARES FOR BUSINESS:

Where an association has made or ratified a contract to give a person a certain number of the shares of its stock, upon condition that he will continue to do his business with it, and derives the benefit from this contract, the other party may recover of the association the value of the shares. (*Rich* v. *State National Bank of Lincoln*, 7 *Nebr.*, 231.)

6. TRANSFER OF STOCK:

(*a*) The transfer of shares in national banking associations is not governed by different rules from those which are ordinarily applied to the transfer of shares in other corporate bodies. (*Johnson* v. *Laflin*, 103. *U. S.*, 800.)

(*b*) The entry of the transaction in the books of the association is required, not for the translation of the title, but for the protection of the parties, and others dealing with the association, and to enable it to know who are its stockholders. (*Ibid.*)

6. TRANSFER OF STOCK—Continued.

(c) A shareholder in a national bank, while it is a going concern, has the absolute right, in the absence of fraud, to make a bona fide and actual sale and transfer of his shares, at any time, to any person capable in law of purchasing and holding the same, and of assuming the transferrer's liabilities in respect thereto; and this right is not, in such cases, subject to the control of the directors or other stockholders. (*Johnson* v. *Laflin*, 5 *Dill.*, 65.)

(d) Under the pretense of prescribing the manner thereof, an association can not clog the transfer with useless restrictions. (*Johnson* v. *Laflin*, *supra.*)

(e) When a shareholder, acting in good faith, delivers his certificates of stock, with a blank power of attorney for making the transfer, and receives the purchase-money, the sale is complete and the title passes. (*Ibid.*)

(f) Where a cashier, who is intrusted by the directors with the duty of transferring the stock of the association, refuses, for insufficient reasons, to transfer shares, and the association subsequently becomes insolvent, the owner of the shares may maintain an action against the receiver for the injury sustained. (*Case* v. *Citizens' Bank*, 100 *U. S.*, 446.)

(g) Where a shareholder who has sold his stock has delivered to the bank the certificates of stock and a power of attorney with the request that the transfer be made upon the books of the bank, and has had no reason to suppose that such transfer was not made, he will not, should the bank afterward become insolvent, be held liable as a shareholder, although he still appears as such on the books of the bank. (*Whitney* v. *Butler*, 118 *U. S.*, 655.)

(h) But where the president of the bank is himself the purchaser of the stock then the delivery of the certificates and power of attorney to him with the request to make the transfer upon the books of the bank would not be sufficient to discharge the seller from liability as a stockholder. (*Richmond* v. *Irons* 121 *U. S.*, 27.)

7. SUBSCRIPTIONS TO INCREASE OF CAPITAL STOCK:

(a) Where one subscribes for shares in the increase of the capital of a national banking association in a certain amount, such subscription and payment are upon the implied condition that the increase shall be in the exact amount so fixed; and if such amount is changed, the subscriber may avoid the subscription and recover the amount paid in. (*Eaton* v. *Pacific Bank*, 144 *Mass.*, 260.)

(b) And the certificate of the Comptroller of the Currency that the amount of the increase in another sum has been paid in, which amount includes what was paid by the dissenting subscriber, will not be conclusive upon such subscriber. (*Ibid.*)

(c) But if such subscriber has assented to or ratified the change he will be held a shareholder. (*Delano* v. *Butler*, 118 *U. S.*, 634.)

8. SPECIFIC PERFORMANCE OF CONTRACT TO SELL:

A specific performance of a contract to sell the stock of a national banking association will not be enforced in favor of a purchaser who places his claim for equitable relief upon the ground that he desires to obtain control of the association. Such an object is contrary to public policy. (*Foll's Appeal*, 91 *Penn. St.*, 434.)

V. SHAREHOLDERS.

1. ESTOPPED TO DENY INCORPORATION:

A shareholder who has held himself out to the world as such is estopped to deny that the association was legally incorporated. (*Casey* v. *Galli*, 94 *U. S.*, 673; *Wheelock* v. *Kost*, 77 *Ill.*, 296.)

2. INDIVIDUAL LIABILITY:

(a) The question whether there is a deficiency of assets, and when it is necessary to enforce the individual liability of shareholders, is for the Comptroller to determine; and his decision in this matter is final and conclusive. (*Kennedy* v. *Gibson*, 8 *Wall.*, 498; *National Bank* v. *Case*, 99 *U. S.*, 628; *Casey* v. *Galli*, 94 *U. S.*, 673.)

(b) The amount contributed by each shareholder should bear the same proportion to the whole amount of the deficit as his own stock bears to the whole amount of the capital stock at its par value. And the solvent shareholders can not be made to contribute more than their proportion to make good the deficiency caused by the insolvency of other shareholders. (*United States* v. *Knox*, 102 *U. S.*, 422.)

2. INDIVIDUAL LIABILITY—Continued.

(c) A shareholder who disposes of his stock will continue to be liable thereon until the transfer is noted on the books of the association. (*Bowdell* v. *Farmers and Merchants' National Bank of Baltimore, U. S. C. C.* (*D. Md.*, 1877), *Browne's N. B. Cas.*, 147.)

(d) The individual liability of a shareholder adheres to his estate after his death until his place as a member of the association is taken by some new shareholder. (*Davis* v. *Weed, U. S. D. C.* (*Dist. Conn.*), *reported* 44 *Conn.*, 569.)

(e) The receiver has a valid claim against the estate generally of a deceased shareholder who died prior to the insolvency of the bank, but whose stock has not been transferred. (*Richmond* v. *Irons*, 121 U. S., 27; *Davis* v. *Weed, supra.*)

(f) And the fact that the title to the stock of a deceased shareholder vests in his administrator does not relieve the estate from the burden of an assessment. (*Davis* v. *Weed, supra.*)

(g) Nor will the fact that the administration is complete, and all the assets have been distributed, defeat an action brought to recover the assessment. (*Ibid.* But see *Witters* v. *Sowles.*)

(h) One who appears on the books of the association as the owner of shares of its stock is individually liable, though he hold the stock merely as collateral security. (*National Bank* v. *Case*, 99 *U. S.*, 628; *Moore* v. *Jones*, 3 *Woods*, 53; *Bowdell* v. *Farmers and Merchants' National Bank of Baltimore, supra; Hale* v. *Walker*, 31 *Iowa*, 344; *Wheelock* v. *Kost, supra.*)

(i) But where a pledgee, for the express purpose of avoiding a personal liability, and before the association becomes insolvent, or is in danger of insolvency, transfers the stock to an irresponsible person, he, the pledgee, will not be liable to contribute as a shareholder. (*Anderson* v. *Warehouse Company*, 111 *U. S.*, 479.)

(j) And where stock has been transferred as collateral security for a loan, *with the understanding that in case of default in the payment of the loan the shares shall be sold*, the transferee, upon default made, and before the bank closes its doors, may sell the stock for a nominal consideration, though his purpose be to avoid a personal liability; and such a transaction can not be set aside as a fraud upon the creditors of the association. (*Magruder* v. *Colston*, 44 *Md.*, 349.)

NOTE.—The court put the decision upon the ground that the sale was in pursuance of a stipulation which formed a part of the contract between the original owner and his transferee. See also *Holyoke Bank* v. *Burnham*, 11 *Cush.*, 187, upon the authority of which the Maryland case was decided.

(k) If the trusteeship of one who holds stock in trust does not appear upon the books of the association he will be individually liable. (*Davis* v. *Essex Baptist Society, U. S. D. C.* (*Dist. Conn.*), *reported* 44 *Conn.*, 582.)

(l) A transfer of shares for the purpose of avoiding liability, though made "out and out," is void. (*National Bank* v. *Case, supra; Bowden* v. *Santos*, 1 *Hughes*, 158.)

(m) And where a shareholder, who has knowledge of the insolvent condition of the bank, transfers his shares, without consideration, to a person unable to respond to the assessment, the transfer may be set aside and the individual liability of the transferer enforced. (*Bowden* v. *Johnson*, 107 *U. S.*, 251.)

(n) The real owner of the stock is liable as a stockholder, though when he purchased the stock he had it transferred upon the books to another. (*Davis* v. *Stevens*, 17 *Blatch.*, 259.)

NOTE.—The case of the owner of stock is thus different from that of a pledgee. (See *Anderson* v. *Warehouse Company, supra.*)

(o) Where shareholders have assessed themselves to the amount of the par value of the stock for the purpose of restoring impaired capital, the contributions made in pursuance of such assessment, though all used in paying the debts of the association, will not so operate as to discharge the shareholders from their individual liability. (*Delano* v. *Butler*, 118 *U. S.*, 634.)

(p) The individual liability of the shareholders of an insolvent association may be enforced for the purpose of paying all of its liabilities, and not merely for the purpose of paying its "debts," technically so called. (*Stanton* v. *Wilkeson*, 8 *Ben.*, 357.)

(q) The individual liability of the stockholders must be restricted in its meaning to such contracts, debts, and engagements of the association as have been duly contracted in the ordinary course of its business. And, therefore, creditors of an association who make settlements *after the association is put into liquidation* and receive from the president payment of their claims in paper of the association, or the individual notes of the president himself,

2. INDIVIDUAL LIABILITY—Continued.

indorsed or guaranteed in the name of the association, are not to be considered as creditors of the association entitled to subject the stockholders to individual liability; for these are new contracts. (*Richmond* v. *Irons*, 121 *U. S.*, 27.)

(*r*) The individual liability of the stockholders is enforcible only in behalf of all the creditors, and any security given by a stockholder for his liability in this respect should likewise be for the benefit of all the creditors. Accordingly, a mortgage of all the individual property of a stockholder, made after the bank has closed its doors, for the purpose of securing a single depositor, is void as against a judgment obtained against such stockholder in an action by the receiver to recover the amount of his individual liability. (*Gatch* v. *Fitch*, 34 *Fed. Rep.*, 566.)

(*s*) Where a married woman is by the State law capable of holding stock in a national bank in her own right, she is liable to an assessment upon her shares, though the law of the State does not authorize married women to bind themselves by contracts for the payment of money. The law annexes her obligations by its own force; no act or capacity to act on her part is required. (*Witters* v. *Sowles*, 35 *Fed. Rep.*, 640; *S. C.* 32 *Fed. Rep.*, 767.)

(*t*) While it is undoubtedly the rule as regards stockholders that one put upon the books as a stockholder without his consent can not be held for any liability in respect to such stock, yet where the person to whom the stock is transferred is a director of the bank, and is concerned in the management of its affairs, he must be presumed to have knowledge of the fact that the stock stood in his name, and, if he has not repudiated the transfer to himself, is liable as the holder of such stock. (*Brown* v. *Finn*, 34 *Fed. Rep.*, 124.)

(*u*) In such case the mere return of the dividends paid upon the stock to the person by whom the transfer was made will not be a sufficient repudiation thereof. (*Ibid.*)

3. WHEN LIABILITY DISQUALIFIES FROM VOTING:

The provision of section 5144, Revised Statutes, which disqualifies shareholders "whose liability is past due and unpaid," from voting at meetings of shareholders, applies only to liability for unpaid subscriptions for stock. (*United States, ex rel.* v. *Barry*, 36 *Fed. Rep.*, 246.)

VI. OFFICERS.

1. TENURE OF OFFICE:

(*a*) The officers of a national banking association can hold their positions only by the tenure specified in section 5136, Revised Statutes, viz, the pleasure of the board of directors. (*Harrington* v. *First National Bank of Chittenango*, *S. C. N. Y.*, 1873; *Thomp. N. B. Cas.*, 761; see also *Taylor* v. *Hutton*, 43 *Barb.*, 195.)

(*b*) Directors of national banking associations may remove the president, both under the law of Congress and the articles of association, where the latter so provide. The power exists though the association has adopted no by-laws. (*Taylor* v. *Hutton*, *supra.*)

2. BONDS OF OFFICERS:

(*a*) It is not necessary that national banking associations shall signify their approval of the official bonds of their officers by memoranda entered upon the journals or minutes of the directors. The acceptance is to be presumed from the retention of the bond, and from the fact that the officer is permitted to enter upon or continue in the discharge of his duties. (*Grover* v. *The Lebanon National Bank*, 10 *Bush*, 23.)

(*b*) Where the sureties of an officer can reasonably be presumed to have been deceived by the statement of the condition of the bank published just prior to the execution of the bond, and to have been led to think that there was no deficit, whereas there had been a misapplication of a large part of the funds by the officer whose bondsmen they became, which fact would have been ascertained had the directors exercised ordinary diligence, the sureties are discharged from their liability. (*Grover* v. *The Lebanon National Bank*, *supra.*)

3 DIRECTORS MUST ACT AS A BOARD:

The election of an individual as a director does not constitute him an agent of the corporation with authority to act separately and independently of his fellow members. It is the board duly convened and acting as a unit

3. DIRECTORS MUST ACT AS A BOARD—Continued.

that is made the representative of the association. The assent or determination of the members of the board acting separately and individually is not the assent of the corporation. The law proceeds upon the theory that the directors shall meet and counsel with each other, and that any determination affecting the association shall be arrived at and expressed only after a consultation at a meeting of the board, attended by at least a majority of its members. (*National Bank* v. *Drake*, 35 *Kans.*, 564.)

4. BORROWING MONEY OF ASSOCIATION:

An officer may, in the ordinary course of business, borrow money of the association. (*Blair* v. *First National Bank of Mansfield*, *U. S. C. C.* (*N. D. Ohio*, 1877, 10 *Chicago Legal News*, 84.)

5. LIABILITY FOR VIOLATIONS OF LAW:

(*a*) All directors who participate in and assent to a loan in excess of one-tenth of the capital of the bank, in violation of section 5200, Revised Statutes, will be liable to the bank for all damages sustained by it in consequence of such loan. (*Witters* v. *Sowles*, *U. S. C. C.* (*District of Vermont*), 31 *Fed. Rep.*, 1.)

(*b*) If a cashier, without authority from the directors so to do, makes a loan in excess of one-tenth of the capital of the association, he will be liable, in case of loss, for the amount of the excess. (*Second National Bank of Oswego* v. *Burt*, *XIV. New York Weekly Digest*, 290. Reversed in Court of Appeals on ground that transaction was discount of bill of exchange drawn against actually existing values, 93 *N. Y.*, 233).

(*c*) The directors of a national bank will not be held liable for loss occasioned to the bank through the frauds of a co-director in which they had no part, and which were perpetrated without their connivance or knowledge. It is not sufficient to charge them with liability that the frauds might have been prevented by the exercise on their part of a proper degree of supervision over the affairs of the bank. (*Movius* v. *Lee*, *U. S. C. C.* (*N. D. New York*), 30 *Fed. Rep.*, 298.)

6. DIRECTORS OF CONVERTED BANKS:

(*a*) When a State bank is converted into a national banking association all of the directors at the time will continue to be the directors of the association until others are appointed or elected, though some of them may not have joined in the execution of the articles of association and organization certificate. (*Lockwood* v. *The American National Bank*, 9 *R. I.*, 308.)

(*b*) And, *semble*, that the directors of a bank at the time of its conversion into a national banking association are not required to take the oath of directors. (*Ibid.*)

(*c*) But even were the oath required, a majority of all who were directors at the time of the conversion, and not merely a majority of those who take the oath, are necessary to constitute a quorum. (*Ibid.*)

7. RETIREMENT OF DIRECTORS:

(*a*) The law providing no particular mode by which a director is to resign from the board, an oral resignation would be as good as any. (*Movius* v. *Lee*, 30 *Fed. Rep.*, 298.)

(*b*) The president being the head of the board, a resignation to him is a resignation to the board. (*Ibid.*)

(*c*) A director is not prohibited from resigning during the year. The apparent purpose of the provision in regard to the term of office is to make it conform to the time of the new election, and not to absolutely require every director to serve the full term. (*Ibid.*)

VII. INTEREST.

1 WHAT INTEREST ASSOCIATIONS MAY TAKE:

(*a*) The provision in section 30 of the act of 1864 "that where, by the law of any State, a different rate is limited for banks of issue organized under State laws, the rate so limited shall be allowed for associations organized in any such State under the act," is enabling, and not restrictive; and, therefore, a national banking association in any State may stipulate for as high a rate of interest as by the laws of such State a natural person may, although State banks of issue are restricted to a less rate. (*Tiffany* v. *National Bank of the State of Missouri*, 18 *Wall.*, 409.)

1. WHAT INTEREST ASSOCIATIONS MAY TAKE—Continued.

(b) But it is not to be inferred from Tiffany v. National Bank of Missouri that whatever by the laws of the State is lawful for natural persons in acquiring title to negotiable paper by discount is lawful for national banks. (*National Bank* v. *Johnson*, 104 *U. S.*, 271.)

(c) The interest which a national banking association may charge is limited to the rate allowed to the banks of the State generally; and the fact that a few of the State banks are specially authorized to take a higher rate is not a warrant for a national banking association to do so. (*Duncan* v. *First National Bank of Mount Pleasant, U. S. D. C.* (*W. D. Penn.*, 1878), 11 *Bank. Mag.*, 787; *Gruber* v. *First National Bank*, 87 *Penn. St.*, 468.)

(d) Where the State law does not limit the rate of interest which may be charged on loans to corporations, a national banking association located in that State can not charge more than 7 per cent. interest on such loans: (*In re Wild*, 11 *Blatch.*, 243.)

(e) Where by the statutes of the State parties are authorized to contract for any rate of interest, national banking associations in that State may likewise contract for any rate, and are not limited to 7 per cent. (*Hinds* v. *Marmelejo*, 60 *Cal.*, 229; *National Bank* v. *Bruhn*, 64 *Tex.*, 571.)

2. ON CLAIMS AGAINST INSOLVENT AND LIQUIDATING ASSOCIATIONS:

(a) A depositor in a national banking association which has become insolvent is entitled to interest on his deposit. (*National Bank of Commonwealth* v. *Mechanics' National Bank*, 94 *U. S.*, 437.)

(b) He is entitled to interest from the date of the suspension of payments; and no demand upon the association is necessary. (*Chemical National Bank* v. *Bailey*, 12 *Blatch.*, 480.)

(c) Claims, when proved to the satisfaction of the Comptroller, are upon the same footing as if put in judgment, and therefore bear interest; and the fact that, under certain circumstances, there might be thus a compounding of interest will not defeat the right to interest. (*National Bank of Commonwealth* v. *Mechanics' National Bank, supra.*)

(d) But where a creditor has obtained judgment against an insolvent national banking association for the full amount of his claim and interest, he is not entitled to interest upon the face of the judgment, but only upon the amount of the claim at the time of the failure. (*White* v. *Knox*, 111 *U. S.*, 784.)

(e) The creditors of an insolvent national banking association in the hands of a receiver are entitled to interest on their claims during the period of administration. (*Chemical National Bank* v. *Bailey, supra.*)

(f) The assessments made by the Comptroller upon the shareholders of an insolvent association bear interest from the date of the order. (*Casey* v. *Galli*, 94 *U. S.*, 673.)

(g) In the case of book accounts in favor of depositors, interest begins to run against an association in liquidation from the date of the suspension of business. (*Richmond* v. *Irons*, 121 *U. S.*, 27.)

3. USURY:

(a) The usury laws of the States do not apply to national banking associations. (*Farmers and Mechanics' Bank* v. *Dearing*, 91 *U. S.*, 29; *Central National Bank* v. *Pratt*, 115 *Mass.*, 539; *First National Bank* v. *Garlinghouse*, 22 *Ohio St.*, 492; *Davis* v. *Randall*, 115 *Mass.*, 547; *Hintermister* v. *First National Bank*, 64 *N. Y.*, 212.)

(b) And the remedies provided by the State for the taking of usury can not be resorted to. (*Farmers and Mechanics' Bank* v. *Dearing*, *supra*; *Wiley* v. *Starbuck*, 44 *Ind.*, 298.)

(c) The taking of illegal interest by a national banking association does not render the contract void. (*Farmers and Mechanics' Bank* v. *Dearing*, *supra.*)

(d) It does not invalidate an indorsement or a guaranty of the notes upon which the usurious interest was paid. (*Oates* v. *First National Bank of Montgomery*, 100 *U. S.*, 239; *Lazear* v. *National Union Bank of Baltimore*, 52 *Md.*, 78.)

(e) But usury destroys the interest-bearing power of the obligation; and there will be no point of time from which it can bear interest. (*Lucas* v. *Government National Bank*, 78 *Penn.*, *St.*, 228.)

(f) The usury works a forfeiture of the entire interest accruing after maturity and before judgment, as well as that which accrues before maturity. (*Shunk* v. *The First National Bank of Galion*, 22 *Ohio St.*, 508.)

3. USURY—Continued.

(g) The discounting of business paper by a national banking association at a higher than the legal rate is usurious, though the law of the State fixes no limit to the rate which natural persons may take for the discount or purchase of such paper. (*Johnson* v. *National Bank of Gloversville*, 74 *N. Y.*, 329; affirmed in *National Bank* v. *Johnson*, 104 *U. S.*, 271.)

(h) By charging more than legal interest on overdrafts, a national banking association loses the right to recover any interest at all. (*Third National Bank of Philadelphia* v. *Miller*, 90 *Penn. St.*, 241.)

(i) The liabilities of antecedent parties to a note or bill will not be affected by the usurious character of the transaction between the payee and the association; and the association may recover the full amount of the note or bill from the maker or acceptor. (*Smith* v. *The Exchange Bank of Pittsburgh*, 26 *Ohio St.*, 141.)

(j) Usurious interest which has been paid to a national banking association can not be applied by way of payment or set-off in any action by the association to recover the amount of the loan. (*Barnet* v. *Muncie National Bank*, 98 *U. S.*, 555.)

(k) Nor can the penalty for taking the usurious interest be recovered by way of counter-claim in such action, but a separate action must be brought therefor. (*Ibid.*)

NOTE.—This case overrules portions of the decisions in *Lucas* v. *Government National Bank*, *supra*; *Overholt* v. *National Bank*, 82 *Penn. St.*, 490; *Cake* v. *The First National Bank of Lebanon*, 83 *Penn. St.*, 303.

(l) A director is not by reason of his position estopped from setting up the defense of usury in an action brought against him by the association. (*Bank of Cadiz* v. *Slemmons*, 34 *Ohio St.*, 142.)

(m) Where a national banking association has discounted notes for another bank at a usurious rate of interest, the fact that the other bank has charged illegal interest on those notes to its customers will not affect its right to set up the defense of usury in an action by the association. (*Third National Bank of Philadelphia* v. *Miller*, *supra*.)

(n) The amount which may be recovered from the association as a penalty is twice the amount of interest paid, and not simply twice the amount in excess of the legal rate. (*Crocker* v. *First National Bank of Chetopa*, *U. S. C. C.* (*Eighth Circuit*), 3 *Am. L. T.* [N. S.], 350; *Overholt* v. *National Bank of Mount Pleasant*, 82 *Penn. St.*, 490; see also *Barnet* v. *Muncie National Bank*, *supra*.)

VIII. INSOLVENCY.

1. NOT SUBJECT TO BANKRUPT ACT:

National banking associations were not subject to the bankrupt act while that act was in force. (*In re Manufacturers' National Bank*, 5 *Biss.*, 499.)

2. WHAT CONSTITUTES INSOLVENCY:

The term "insolvency," as used in section 5242, Revised Statutes, forbidding transfer of the assets of national banking associations after, or in contemplation of, such insolvency, has the same meaning as it had when applied to traders in the bankrupt act; that is, it does not mean an absolute inability of a debtor to pay his debt at some future time, upon a settlement and winding up of his affairs, but a present inability to pay in the ordinary course of business. (*Case* v. *Citizens' Bank of Louisiana*, 2 *Woods*, 23; *Market Bank* v. *Pacific National Bank*, 30 *Hun*, 50.)

3. ASSETS A TRUST FUND:

Upon the appointment of a receiver all the assets of the association become in his hands a trust fund which the statute of limitations does not touch or affect. (*Riddle* v. *First National Bank*, *U. S. C. C.* (*W. D. Penn.*), 27 *Fed. Rep.*, 503.)

NOTE.—But this point was not necessary to the decision of the case, for suits against insolvent corporations are by a law of Pennsylvania expressly excluded from the operation of the statute.

4. UNITED STATES HAS NO PRIORITY:

(a) Section 3466, which gives the United States a priority for all claims it has against insolvent debtors, does not apply to the case of an insolvent national banking association. (*Cook County National Bank* v. *United States*, 107 *U. S.*, 445.)

(b) And as against the proceeds of the bonds deposited to secure circulation the United States can set off no claim, except for money advanced to redeem the notes. (*Ibid.*)

4. UNITED STATES HAS NO PRIORITY—Continued.

(c) And upon the failure of an association its five per cent. redemption fund can not be retained by the Treasurer to pay taxes due to the United States, but the fund passes to the Comptroller as an asset of the association. (*Jackson* v. *United States*, 20 *Ct. Cls.*, 298.)

5. CLAIMS FOR TORTS:

Claims arising out of the non-feasance or malfeasance of the association should be paid ratably with the debts, technically so called. (*Turner* v. *The First National Bank of Keokuk et al.*, 26 *Iowa*, 562.)

6. PREFERENCES:

(a) A preference, to be within the meaning of section 5242, Revised Statutes, must be given to an existing creditor to secure a pre-existing debt. A transfer by an insolvent bank to secure a contemporaneous loan is not a violation of the law. (*Casey* v. *La Société de Crédit Mobilier*, 2 *Woods*, 77.)

(b) The insolvency need be in the contemplation of the bank only. It need not be known to the person to whom the transfer is made. (*Case* v. *Citizens' Bank of Louisiana*, *supra*.)

(c) After the directors of an insolvent association have voted to close its doors, any transfer of assets whereby a creditor secures a preference must be presumed to be made with an intent to prefer. (*National Security Bank* v. *Price*, 22 *Fed. Rep.*, 697.)

(d) Where the officers of an association which is in danger of insolvency, *for the purpose and in the expectation of preventing a failure*, make a pledge of securities to a depositor to induce him not to withdraw his deposit, such a pledge is not a preference within the meaning of section 5242, Revised Statutes, and will not be set aside when the association afterward is declared insolvent. (*Roberts* v. *Hill*, 23 *Fed. Rep.*, 311.)

(e) Where an insolvent association receives a deposit a short time before closing its doors, its officers knowing of the insolvency at the time, the receipt of such deposit is a fraud upon the depositor, and no title passes to the association; and, therefore, the depositor may reclaim the whole amount of the deposit; and as he claims under his original title, and not under a transfer from the association, such reclamation does not amount to a preference. (*Cragie et al.* v. *Hadley*, 99 *N. Y.*, 131.)

(f) But a creditor will not have a lien upon the funds of the association because checks given in settlement of balances were fraudulent, and were given at a time when the bank was hopelessly insolvent, and its officers were contemplating flight. (*Citizens' National Bank* v. *Dowd*, 35 *Fed. Rep.*, 340.)

7. BASIS FOR ESTIMATION OF DIVIDENDS:

In estimating the dividends to be paid out of the assets of an insolvent association, the value of the claims at the time when the insolvency is declared is to be taken as the basis of distribution. (*White* v. *Knox*, 111 *U. S.*, 784.)

8. SET-OFF:

(a) A person liable upon a note to an insolvent national bank may set off against his indebtedness the amount of his deposit with the bank. (*Platt* v. *Bentley*, *Thom. N. B. Cas.*, 758.)

(b) But a debtor can not set off the amount of a deposit assigned to him after the act of insolvency committed. (*The Venango National Bank* v. *Taylor*, 56 *Penn. St.*, 14.)

(c) Where a note has not matured when the bank which has discounted it becomes insolvent, the maker, in an action against him by the receiver, can not set off the amount of his deposit with the bank at the time of the insolvency. (*Armstrong* v. *Scott*, 36 *Fed. Rep.*, 63.)

9. CLAIM FOR BREACH OF CONTRACT OF LEASE:

Where a national bank has leased a banking house for a long term of years, and subsequently becomes insolvent, but during the time it continued business had not defaulted in paying the rent, the lessor has no claim against the receiver by reason of the insolvency or dissolution of the corporation or the forfeiture of its franchises, or by the refusal of the receiver to take under the contract, and pay the rent. (*Fidelity Safe Deposit and Trust Co.* v. *Armstrong*, 35 *Fed. Rep.*, 567.)

IX. RECEIVERS.

1. OFFICER OF THE UNITED STATES:

A receiver, when appointed by the Comptroller, with the concurrence of the Secretary, is an officer of the United States. (*Stanton* v. *Wilkeson*, 8 *Ben.*, 357.)

2. WHOM HE REPRESENTS:

He represents the bank, its stockholders, and its creditors; but he does not in any sense represent the Government. (*Case* v. *Terrell*, 11 *Wall.*, 199.)

3. HOW FAR SUBJECT TO COMPTROLLER'S ORDERS:

(*a*) The clause of section 50, act of 1864, which prescribes that the receiver shall be "under the direction of the Comptroller," means only that he shall be subject to the Comptroller's direction, not that he shall not act without orders. He may bring suit to collect assets without having been instructed to do so by the Comptroller. (*Bank* v. *Kennedy*, 17 *Wall.*)

(*b*) The receiver of a national bank is the instrument of the Comptroller, and may be removed by him. (*Kennedy* v. *Gibson*, 8 *Wall.*, 505.)

4. POWER OF COURTS TO APPOINT:

(*a*) The power of the Comptroller to appoint a receiver is not exclusive; it does not oust the courts of equity of their authority in the matter; and therefore, a court of competent jurisdiction may place the bank in the hands of a receiver in cases where, according to the rules of equity, it may pursue such a course with regard to insolvent corporations generally. (*Irons* v. *Manufacturers' National Bank*, 6 *Biss.*, 301; *Wright* v. *Merchants' National Bank*, 1 *Flippin*, 561.)

(*b*) Where a bank has gone into voluntary liquidation, and the Comptroller has no power to appoint a receiver, a proper court, in a case where such action is necessary to protect the interests of a creditor, will appoint a receiver for it. (*Irons* v. *Manufacturers' National Bank*, *supra.*)

5. DEBTORS OF ASSOCIATION CAN NOT QUESTION LEGALITY OF APPOINTMENT:

The legality of the appointment of the receiver can not be questioned by the debtors of the bank when sued by him. The bank may move to have the appointment set aside, but the debtors can not. (*Cadle* v. *Baker*, 20 *Wall.*, 650; see also *Platt* v. *Beebe*, 57 *N. Y.*, 339.)

6. RECEIVER'S DECISION NOT FINAL:

The decision of a receiver rejecting a claim is not final. The claimant still has the right to sue. (*Bank of Bethel* v. *Pahquioque Bank*, 14 *Wall.*, 383.)

7. SALE BY:

(*a*) The receiver can not sell the real or personal property of the bank without an order from a court of competent jurisdiction. (*Ellis* v. *Little*, 27 *Kans.*, 707.)

(*b*) Nor can he sell upon terms in conflict with the order. (*Ibid.*)

(*c*) And under an order permitting him to sell the property of the bank he can not exchange, trade, or barter it for other property. (*Ibid.*)

(*d*) A sale made by a receiver under order of a court is to all intents and purposes a judicial sale. (*In re Third National Bank*, 9 *Biss.*, 535.)

8. CONTRACTS OF:

(*a*) As the power of a receiver of a national bank appointed by the Comptroller is limited, a person dealing with him in his official capacity is bound as a matter of law to have knowledge of his authority to act, and if contracts and agreements are entered into with the receiver in excess of his authority as conferred by law, the parties contract at their own peril, and the estate of the bank can not be charged for the default or inability of a receiver acting outside of his functions as receiver and beyond the duties which it involves. (*Ellis* v. *Little*, 27 *Kans.*, 707.)

(*b*) The receiver can not charge the estate of the bank by any executory contract, unless authorized so to do by the provisions of the national banking law, and the order of a court of competent jurisdiction obtained upon the terms of said law. (*Ibid.*)

9. EXPENSES OF RECEIVERSHIP FOR ASSOCIATIONS WHICH HAVE GONE INTO LIQUIDATION:

Where, after an association bank has gone into liquidation, a receiver is appointed at the instance of the creditors, the expenses of such receivership must be paid by the creditors. The shareholders can not be made individually liable for such expenses. (*Richmond* v. *Irons.*)

X. TAXATION.

1. WHAT MAY BE TAXED:

(a) A State can not tax the capital stock of a national bank, as such. The tax must be assessed upon the shares of the different stockholders. (*Collins* v. *Chicago*, 4 *Biss.*, 472.)

(b) The entire interests of the shareholders may be taxed without any deduction for that portion of the capital which is invested in United States securities. (*Van Allen* v. *The Assessors*, 3 *Wall.*, 573.)

(c) New shares issued by a national banking association can not be taxed until the increase of capital has been approved by the Comptroller of the Currency. (*Charleston* v. *People's National Bank*, 5 *S. C.*, 103.)

(d) The manifest intention of the law is to permit the State in which a national bank is located to tax, subject to the limitations prescribed, all the shares of its capital stock without regard to their ownership; and, therefore, a national bank may be taxed upon the shares which it holds in another national bank. (*Bank of Redemption* v. *Boston*, 126 *U. S.*, 60.)

(e) The undivided surplus of a national banking association, unless invested in Federal securities, may be lawfully taxed by the State. (*North Ward National Bank of Newark* v. *City of Newark*, 10 *Vroom*, 380; *First National Bank* v. *Peterborough*, 56 *N. H.*, 38.)

(f) But, of course, if the surplus is taken into consideration in estimating the taxable value of the shares, it is not to be taxed separately. (*North Ward National Bank* v. *City of Newark*, *supra*.)

NOTE.—But it has been held in Maryland that the stock of an association represents its whole property, and where a tax is assessed upon the shares a separate tax upon the real or personal estate amounts to double taxation; and, therefore, where the organic laws of the State prohibit double taxation, such a tax upon the property of an association is void. (*County Commissioners* v. *Farmers and Mechanics' National Bank*, 48 *Md.*, 117; see also *National State Bank* v. *Young*, 25 *Iowa*, 311, wherein it was held that the States could tax only the shares *eo nomine* and the real estate.)

(g) The surplus fund of a national banking association is not excluded in the valuation of its shares for taxation. (*Strafford National Bank* v. *Dover*, 59 *N. H.*, 316.)

(h) Where shares of stock are assessed at their actual cash value without any deduction for the real estate owned by the association the real estate should not be taxed *eo nomine*. (*Commissioners of Rice County* v. *Citizens' National Bank of Faribault*, 23 *Minn.*, 280.)

(i) The States can not tax the circulating notes of national banking associations. (*Horne* v. *Greene*, 52 *Miss.*, 452; Contra *Board of Commissioners* v. *Elston*, 32 *Ind.*, 27; see also *Ruffin* v. *Board of Commissioners*, 69 *N. C.*, 498; *Lily* v. *The Commissioners*, 69 *N. C.*, 300.)

2. RATE:

(a) Where the State banks are taxed upon their capital, no tax can be imposed upon the shares of national banking associations; for as the capital of the State banks may consist of the bonds of the United States, which are exempt from State taxation, a tax on capital is not equivalent to a tax on shares. (*Van Allen* v. *The Assessors*, 3 *Wall.*, 573; *Bradley* v. *The People*, 4 *Wall.*, 459.)

(b) But though the tax upon the State banks is not *eo nomine* a tax on shares, *yet if it is equivalent to such a tax* the shares in the national banking associations located in that State may be taxed. (*Frazer* v. *Seibern*, 16 *Ohio St.*, 614; *Van Slyke* v. *State*, 23 *Wis.*, 656; *Boynoll* v. *State*, 25 *Wis.*, 112.)

(c) When by local legislation different rates are prescribed for different classes of moneyed capital, the rate imposed upon shares of national banks should approximate as closely as may be to the rate imposed upon other moneyed capital of the same or similar class, viz, shares of State banks. (*City National Bank* v. *Paducah*, *U. S. C. C.* (*Sixth Circuit*, 1877), 5 *Cent. L. J.*, 347.)

(d) Congress meant no more than to require of the States as a condition to the exercise of the power to tax the shares in national banks, that they should, as far as they had the capacity, tax in like manner the shares of banks of issue of their own creation. (*Lionberger* v. *Rouse*, 9 *Wall.*, 468.)

(e) Therefore, where a State has previously contracted with the banks which it has chartered that they shall not be taxed above a certain rate, a tax upon national-bank shares at a greater rate is not invalid, if this rate is not greater than that assessed upon all the moneyed capital within the State, except that of the State banks. (*Ibid.*)

2. RATE—Continued.

(f) Any system of assessment of taxes which exacts from the owner of the shares of a national banking association a larger sum in proportion to the actual value of those shares than it does from other moneyed capital, valued in like manner, taxes the shares at a greater rate, notwithstanding that the percentage of tax on the valuation is the same as that applied to other moneyed capital. (*Pelton* v. *Commercial National Bank*, 101 *U. S.*, 143.)

3. VALUATION:

(a) In estimating the value of the shares for the purpose of taxation reference may be had to all the property and values of the bank. (*Saint Louis National Bank* v. *Papin*, *U. S. C. C.* (*Eighth Circuit*), 3 *Cent. L. J.*, 669.)

(b) If no excessive valuation is complained of, and a correct result is arrived at, equity will not restrain the collection of a tax because the method of computation was erroneous. (*Ibid.*)

(c) The shares may be valued for taxation at an amount exceeding their face value, if this amount is not at a greater rate than the valuation set upon other moneyed capital in the State. (*Hepburn* v. *School Directors*, 23 *Wall.*, 480.)

(d) Under the statute of New York, shares in national banking associations should be taxed at their real or market value. (*People* v. *The Commissioners of Taxes and Assessments*, 94 *U. S.*, 415.)

(e) Where shares in national banking associations are purposely valued proportionally higher than the other moneyed capital in the State, the assessment is void. (*Pelton* v. *National Bank*, 101 *U. S.*, 143.)

(f) And the collection of what is in excess of the rate imposed on the other moneyed capital may be enjoined. (*Ibid.*)

(g) It is not required that the States should abandon systems of taxation of their own banks, or of money in the hands of their other corporations, which they may think the most wise and efficient modes of taxing their own corporate organizations, in order to make that taxation conform to the system of taxing the national banks upon the shares of their stock in the hands of the shareholders; all that is necessary is, that the system of State taxation of its own citizens, of its own banks, and of its own corporations shall not work a discrimination unfavorable to the holders of the shares of the national banks. (*Davenport Bank* v. *Davenport*, 123 *U. S.*, 83.)

4. EXEMPTIONS:

(a) The intention of Congress was that the rate of taxation of the shares should be the same as, or not greater than, the tax upon the moneyed capital of the individual citizen which is *subject and liable to taxation*. (*People* v. *The Commissioners*, 4 *Wall.*, 244.)

(b) Therefore, it is not a ground of objection to the validity of a tax on shares that, while deductions for United States bonds are made from the personal estates of individuals and the capital of State corporations, no deductions are made on account of the capital of national banking associations invested in such bonds. (*Ibid.*)

(c) The fact that by the statutes creating them, which statutes were passed prior to the national banking law, State banks are entirely exempt from taxation, will not render a tax upon the shares of national banking associations void. (*City of Richmond* v. *Scott*, 48 *Ind.*, 568.)

(d) And a State tax upon shares in national banking associations is not rendered invalid by an exemption of the shares of other corporations the capital of which consists of property required to be listed for taxation, as such. (*McIver* v. *Robinson*, 53 *Ala.*, 456.)

(e) Merely a partial exemption of other moneyed capital will not invalidate a tax upon shares in national banking associations. (*Hepburn* v. *School Directors*, 23 *Wall.*, 480.)

(f) But though Congress did not contemplate that there should be an absolute equality (which in the nature of things is impossible), yet it did intend that there should be a substantial equality; and, therefore, if the exemptions in favor of other moneyed capital are so palpable as to show that there is a serious discrimination against capital invested in the shares of national banking associations, the tax will be declared unlawful. (*Boyer* v. *Boyer*, 113 *U. S.*, 690.)

(g) A State law which does not permit a deduction to be made from the assessed value of bank shares for all debts due by the holder thereof, while authorizing such a deduction to be made from the assessed value of moneyed capital otherwise invested, is void. (*People ex rel. Williams* v. *Weaver*, 100 *U. S.*, 539, reversing *S. C.*, 67 *N. Y.*, 516, and overruling *People* v. *Dolan*, 36 *N. Y.*, 59.)

4. EXEMPTIONS—Continued.

(h) The main purpose of Congress in fixing limits to State taxation on investments in the shares of national banks, was to render it impossible for the State, in levying such a tax, *to create and foster an unequal and unfriendly competition, by favoring institutions or individuals carrying on similar business and operations and investments of a like character;* and the language of the law is to be read in the light of this policy. And, therefore, the exemption of shares of stock in corporations, *the business of which does not come into competition with that of the national banks* (*e. g.*, railroad companies, mining companies, manufacturing companies, and insurance companies) does not invalidate a tax upon national-bank shares. Capital thus employed is not "moneyed capital" within the meaning of the act of Congress. (*Mercantile Bank* v. *New York*, 121 *U. S.*, 138.)

(i) Bonds issued by a State, or under its authority by its public municipal bodies, although they undoubtedly represent moneyed capital, yet as from their nature they are not ordinarily the subject of taxation, are not within the reason of the rule established by Congress for the taxation of national-bank shares, and the fact that the State exempts them from taxation does not deprive it of the right to tax shares of stock of national banks in the State. (*Ibid.*)

(j) Although deposits in savings banks constitute moneyed capital in the hands of individuals within the terms of any definition which can be given of that phrase, yet they are not within the meaning of the act of Congress in such a sense as to require that, if they are exempted from taxation, shares of stock in national banks must thereby also be exempted from taxation; for it can not be supposed that savings banks come into any possible competition with national banks. (*Ibid.*)

5. COLLECTION OF TAX FROM THE ASSOCIATION:

(a) A State tax upon shares is valid, though the tax is collected from the bank. (*National Bank* v. *Commonwealth*, 9 *Wall.*, 353.)

(b) And the State may require the banks to pay a tax rightfully laid upon the shares. (*Ibid.*)

(c) And where the tax on shares is payable by the association the collection of the tax may be enforced by distraint of its property. (*First National Bank* v. *Douglas County*, 3 *Dill.*, 330.)

(d) But where the tax laws of the State make the bank the *mere agent* for paying the tax on shares, and direct it to retain so much of the dividends as will answer that purpose, other agents being required to pay taxes for their principals only when they have under their control the property, money, or credit of such principals, the bank can not be made liable unless it has the control of the property, etc., of its shareholders, or has dividends in its possession, or has failed to retain them. (*Hershire* v. *The First National Bank*, 35 *Iowa*, 272.)

6. LICENSE TAX:

(a) National banking associations can not be subjected to a license or privilege tax. (*Mayor* v. *First National Bank of Macon*, 59 *Ga.*, 648; *City of Carthage* v. *First National Bank of Carthage*, 71 *Mo.*, 508; *National Bank of Chattanooga* v. *Mayor*, 8 *Heiskell*, 814.)

(b) A State law prohibiting the establishment of banking companies in the State without authority of the legislature was not intended to apply to banking corporations created by authority of Congress, since such corporations may be legally established in the State without the consent of the legislature. (*Stetson* v. *City of Bangor*, 56 *Me.*, 274.)

7. POWERS OF TAXING OFFICERS:

(a) Municipal officers can not assess a tax upon the shares of national banking associations until authorized to do so by some law of the State. (*Stetson* v. *City of Bangor*, 56 *Me.*, 274.)

(b) The officers of a national banking association can not be compelled to exhibit to the taxing officers of a State the books of the association showing the deposits of its customers. (*First National Bank of Youngstown* v. *Hughes*, *U. S. C. C.* (*N. D. Ohio*, 1878), *Browne's N. B. Cas.*, 176.)

(c) A national banking association is not exempt from examination by internal-revenue officers when it has in its possession any articles subject to an internal-revenue tax. Such an examination is not the exercise of a visitorial power, and, therefore, is not prohibited by the provision of section 5241, Revised Statutes, that the national banks shall not be subject to any visitorial powers except those authorized by the national-bank act or vested in the courts of justice. (*United States* v. *Rhawn*, *U. S. D. C.* (*E. D. Penn.*), *Thomp. N. B. Cas.*, 358.)

7. POWERS OF TAXING OFFICERS—Continued.

(d) Where by the tax laws of a State a perpetual lien for taxes attaches to property only by virtue of a levy thereon, and such levy is not made prior to the insolvency of the bank, the taxing officers of the State will be restrained, at the instance of the receiver, from levying upon the property of an insolvent national bank, and selling it, for the purpose of collecting a tax. (*Woodward* v. *Ellsworth*, 4 *Colo.*, 580.)

(e) A State may require the cashiers of national banking associations located within its territory to transmit lists of the shareholders to the taxing officers of the various towns in which the shareholders reside. (*Waite* v. *Dowley*, 94 *U. S.*, 527.)

8. ENFORCEMENT OF TAXES:

A tax duly assessed upon shares may be enforced in accordance with the general laws of the State on that subject. (*Weld* v. *City of Bangor*, 59 *Me.*, 416.)

9. LOCATION OF ASSOCIATION FOR TAXING PURPOSES:

An association which opens an office for the purpose of receiving deposits in another place than that in which it was organized does not become "located" in that place for purposes of taxation. (*National State Bank of Camden* v. *Pierce*, *U. S. C. C.* (*E. D. Penn.*), 18 *Alb. L. J.*, 16.)

XI. JURISDICTION.

NOTE.—The jurisdiction of the Federal courts in national-bank cases was very materially changed by the proviso to the fourth section of the act of July 12, 1882. The proviso is as follows:

"*Provided, however*, That the jurisdiction for suits hereafter brought by or against any association established under any law providing for national banking associations, except suits between them and the United States, or its officers and agents, shall be the same as, and not other than, the jurisdiction for suits by or against banks not organized under any law of the United States which do or might do banking business where such national banking associations may be doing business when such suits may be begun. And all laws and parts of laws of the United States inconsistent with this proviso be, and the same are hereby, repealed."

The jurisdiction of the United States circuit courts in suits by or against national banks is thus defined by section 4, act March 3, 1887:

"SEC. 4. That all national banking associations established under the laws of the United States shall, for the purposes of all actions by or against them, real, personal, or mixed, and all suits in equity, be deemed citizens of the States in which they are respectively located; and in such cases the circuit and district courts shall not have jurisdiction other than such as they would have in cases between individual citizens of the same State."

"The provisions of this section shall not be held to affect the jurisdiction of the courts of the United States in cases commenced by the United States or by direction of any officer thereof, or cases for winding up the affairs of any such bank."

1. JURISDICTION OF FEDERAL COURTS PRIOR TO THE ACT OF JULY 12, 1882:

(a) National banking associations may sue in the Federal courts. The word "by" was omitted from section 57 of the act of 1864 by mistake. (*Kennedy* v. *Gibson*, 8 *Wall.*, 505.)

(b) A national banking association may sue and be sued in the circuit court for the district in which the association is located, irrespective of the amount in controversy and the citizenship of the parties. (*County of Wilson* v. *National Bank*, 103 *U. S.*, 770; *Mitchell* v. *Walker*, *U. S. C. C.* (*W. D. Penn.*, 1879), *Browne's N. B. Cas.*, 180; *Commercial Bank of Cleveland* v. *Simmons*, *U. S. C. C.* (*W. D. Ohio*), 10 *Alb. L. J.*, 155.)

(c) But where the amount in controversy does not exceed five hundred dollars, the association can not sue in a Federal court outside of the district in which it is established. (*Saint Louis National Bank* v. *Brinkman*, *U. S. C. C.* (*D. Kans.*), 1 *Fed. Rep.*, 45.)

(d) A national banking association located in one State may bring an action in the circuit court of the United States sitting within another State against a citizen of that State. (*Manufacturers' National Bank* v. *Baack*, 8 *Blatch.*, 147.)

1. JURISDICTION OF FEDERAL COURTS PRIOR TO THE ACT OF JULY 12, 1882—Continued.

(*e*) When a national bank is sued in a Federal court the suit must be brought in the district in which the bank is located. And service upon an officer of the bank in another district will not give the court of that district jurisdiction of the cause. (*Maine* v. *Second National Bank of Chicago*, 8 *Biss.*, 26.)

(*f*) A United States district court has jurisdiction of a suit in equity by or against a national banking association located within the district. (*First National Bank of Pittsburgh* v. *Pittsburgh and Castle Shannon Railroad Company*, 1 *Fed. Rep.*, 190.)

(*g*) A circuit court has no jurisdiction of a suit by a private person to compel the Comptroller of the Currency and the Treasurer of the United States to disclose what disposition has been made of the United States bonds deposited with the Treasurer by a national banking asssociation, and for a decree directing those officers as to their duty regarding such bonds. (*Van Antwerp* v. *Hulburd*, 7 *Blatch.*, 425; *Van Antwerp* v. *Hulburd*, 8 *Blatch.*, 282.)

(*h*) Section 380 Revised Statutes, which provides that "all suits and proceedings arising out of the provisions of law governing national banking associations, in which the United States or any of its officers or agents shall be parties, shall be conducted by the district attorneys of the several districts under the direction and supervision of the Solicitor of the Treasury," does not enlarge the jurisdiction of the circuit court, and can not be held to confer jurisdiction in such suits or proceedings upon a court not having, independently of this section, authority to entertain them. (*Van Antwerp* v. *Hulburd*, 7 *Blatch.*, 426 *supra*).

(*i*) National banking associations, being corporations organized under the laws of the United States, are entitled as such to remove into the circuit courts of the United States suits brought against them in the State courts. (*Cruikshank* v. *Fourth National Bank*, 21 *Blatch.*, 322; see also *Removal Cases*, 115 *U. S.*, 1.)

(*j*) A United States district court has jurisdiction to authorize a receiver to compromise a debt. (*Matter of Platt*, 1 *Ben.*, 534.)

(*k*) An action at common law to recover a debt due to the bank may be instituted by a receiver in a United States district court, he being an officer of the United States within the meaning of section 563, Revised Statutes. (*Platt* v. *Beach*, 2 *Ben.*, 303; *Stanton* v. *Wilkeson*, 8 *Ben.*, 357.)

(*l*) The power of a national banking association to take a mortgage upon real estate is a question which the party raising it should be permitted to litigate in a Federal court; and he should not be sent into the State courts to try this question on the distribution of surplus moneys in a foreclosure suit, or in a suit brought by the party holding the alleged invalid mortgage. (*In re Duryea*, *U. S. D. C.* (*S. D. N. Y.*), 17 *National Bankruptcy Register*, 495.)

2. JURISDICTION OF FEDERAL COURTS SUBSEQUENT TO ACT OF JULY 12, 1882:

(*a*) The tenth subdivision of section 629, Revised Statutes, which confers upon the circuit court of the United States jurisdiction of all suits by or against any national banking association established in the district for which the court is held, has been repealed by the proviso to section 4 of the act of July 12, 1882. (*National Bank of Jefferson* v. *Fare et al.*, *U. S. C. C.* (*E. D. Tex.*), 25 *Fed. Rep.*, 200.)

(*b*) The object of this proviso was to deprive the United States courts of jurisdiction of suits by or against national banking associations in all cases where banks organized under State laws could not likewise sue or be sued in such courts. (*National Bank of Jefferson* v. *Fare et al.*, *supra.*)

(*c*) But the proviso does not affect the right of the receiver of an insolvent association to sue in a Federal court. (*Hendee* v. *Connecticut and P. R. R. Co.*, 26 *Fed. Rep.*, 677.)

(*d*) Nor would the act of July 12, 1882, take from the circuit court jurisdiction of a suit brought against a director for negligent performance of his duties; for as such suit rests upon the requirements of the United States laws, and by-laws made pursuant thereto, it is a case arising under the laws of the United States. (*Witters v. Foster*, *U. S. C. C.* (*D. Vt.*), 28 *Fed. Rep.*, 737.)

3. JURISDICTION OF STATE COURTS:

(*a*) State courts have jurisdiction of suits by and against national banking associations. (*Bank of Bethel* v. *Pahquioque Bank*, 14 *Wall.*, 383; see also *Ordway* v. *Central National Bank*, 47 *Md.*, 217, and *Claflin* v. *Houseman*, 93 *U. S.*, 130.)

3. JURISDICTION OF STATE COURTS—Continued.

(*b*) Where a national banking association is sued in a State court the suit must be brought in the city or county in which the bank is located. (*Cadle* v. *Tracey*, 11 *Blatch.*, 101; *Crocker* v. *Maine National Bank*, 101 *Mass.*, 240.)

NOTE.—But the New York court of appeals has held that the provision of the national banking law as to the jurisdiction of State courts is permissive only, and not mandatory, and that a State court, in a proper case, may entertain a proceeding against a national bank located in another State. (*Cooke* v. *The State National Bank of Boston*, 52 *N. Y.*, 96; *Robinson* v. *National Bank of New Berne*, 81 *N. Y.*, 385; see also *Adams* v. *Daunis*, 29 *La. Ann.*, 315.) And in *Talmage* v. *Third National Bank*, 27 *Hun*, 61, the supreme court of New York said: "The words of restriction to the place where said 'association is situated' apply to the county and municipal courts and not to the State courts. In the State courts of general jurisdiction a national banking association can be sued whenever an individual can be for the same cause." In *Cooke* v. *The State National Bank*, Chief Judge Church questioned the constitutional right of Congress to deprive the State courts of jurisdiction in such cases.

(*c*) A State court can entertain an action brought to recover of a national banking association the penalty for taking usury. (*Ordway* v. *The Central National Bank*, 47 *Md.*, 217; *Hade* v. *McVay*, 31 *Ohio St.*, 231; *Bletz* v. *Columbia National Bank*, 87 *Penn. St.*, 87.)

(*d*) The State courts have jurisdiction of an action brought by a shareholder on behalf of himself and other shareholders to recover of the directors of an insolvent association damages for injuries resulting from their negligence and misconduct. (*Brinckerhoff* v. *Bostwick*, 88 *N. Y.*, 52.)

(*e*) A State court has no power to make an order directing the receiver of a national bank, who has been appointed by the Comptroller of the Currency, to pay a judgment obtained against the bank before the receiver was appointed. (*Ocean National Bank* v. *Carll*, 7 *Hun*, 237.)

(*f*) State courts have no jurisdiction of the case of an embezzlement of the funds of the association by one of its officers. (*Commonwealth* v. *Felton*, 101 *Mass.*, 204; *Commonwealth, ex rel. Torrey* v. *Ketner*, 92 *Penn. St.*, 372.)

(*g*) The defense of usury may be set up in action brought in a State court. (*National Bank of Winterset* v. *Eyre*, 52 *Iowa*, 114.)

4. UNITED STATES CAN NOT BE SUBJECTED TO JURISDICTION OF COURT:

Neither the Comptroller nor the receiver by putting in an appearance to a suit can subject the United States to the jurisdiction of a court. (*Case* v. *Terrell*, 11 *Wall.*, 199.)

5. CITIZENSHIP:

A national banking association is for jurisdictional purposes a citizen of the State in which it is located. (*Davis* v. *Cook*, 9 *Nev.*, 134.)

XII. SUITS.

1. BY AND AGAINST ASSOCIATIONS:

(*a*) Suit may be brought against a national banking association though it is in the hands of a receiver. (*Bank of Bethel* v. *Pahquioque Bank*, 14 *Wall.*, 383; *Security National Bank* v. *National Bank of the Commonwealth*, 2 *Hun*, 287; *Green* v. *The Wallkill National Bank*, 7 *Hun*, 63.)

(*b*) Where the tax on shares is collected from the association it may bring a suit to enjoin the collection of an illegal tax. (*Cummings* v. *National Bank*, 101 *U. S.*, 153; *Pelton* v. *Commercial National Bank*, 101 *U. S.*, 143; *Boyer* v. *Boyer*, 113 *U. S.*, 143.)

(*c*) A State law authorizing national banking associations which have been converted from State banks to use the name of the original corporation for the purpose of prosecuting and defending suits is not in conflict with the national banking law, and therefore proceedings based upon a judgment obtained before the conversion may be instituted by such association in its former corporate name. (*Thomas* v. *Farmers' Bank of Maryland*, 46 *Md.*, 43.)

(*d*) A national banking association is a foreign corporation within the meaning of a State statute requiring corporations created by the laws of any other State or country to give security for costs before prosecuting a suit in the courts of the State. (*National Park Bank* v. *Gunst*, 1 *Abb. N. C.*, 292.)

(*e*) As a national banking association can acquire no title to *negotiable* paper purchased by it, it can maintain no action thereon in a State where the person suing must be owner of the paper. (*First National Bank of Rochester* v. *Pierson*, 24 *Minn.*, 140.)

1. BY AND AGAINST ASSOCIATIONS—Continued.

(*f*) But in a State where the holder may sue without respect to the ownership an association may bring suit upon paper so acquired. (*National Pemberton Bank* v. *Porter*, 125 *Mass.*, 333; *Atlas National Bank* v. *Savery*, 127 *Mass.*, 75.)

(*g*) Suits brought by a receiver can not be settled or compounded upon an order of the Comptroller; this can be done only with the authority of the court. (*Case* v. *Small*, 2 *Woods*, 78.)

2. BY SHAREHOLDERS:

(*a*) A shareholder of a national banking association can not maintain an action against the directors to recover damages sustained for neglect and mismanagement of the affairs of the association, whereby it became insolvent and its stock was rendered worthless. Such an action can be brought only by the corporation itself. (*Conway* v. *Halsey*, 15 *Vroom*, 462.)

(*b*) But where the receiver refuses to bring an action against negligent directors to recover the amount which the shareholders have been compelled to contribute to pay the debts of the association, an action against such directors may be brought by a shareholder on behalf of himself and the other shareholders. (*Nelson* v. *Burrows*, 9 *Abb. N. C.*, 280.)

(*c*) And when the receiver is a director, and one of the parties charged with misconduct and against whom a remedy is sought, the action may be brought by a shareholder on behalf of himself and the other shareholders. (*Brinckerhoff* v. *Bostwick*, 88 *N. Y.*, 52.)

3. BY RECEIVERS:

(*a*) A receiver may sue either in his own name or the name of the bank. (*National Bank* v. *Kennedy*, 17 *Wall.*, 19.)

(*b*) Suits and proceedings under the act in which the United States or their officers or agents are parties, whether commenced before or after the appointment of a receiver, are to be conducted by the district attorney under the direction of the Solicitor of the Treasury. (*Bank of Bethel* v. *Pahquioque Bank*, 14 *Wall.*, 383.)

(*c*) But section 380, Revised Statutes, is directory merely, and the employment of private counsel by the receiver can not be made a ground of defense to a suit brought by him. (*Ibid.*)

(*d*) Receivers may sue in the courts of the United States by virtue of the act, without reference to the locality of their personal citizenship.

(*e*) The provisions of the codes that every action must be brought in the name of the real party in interest, except in the case of the trustee of an express trust, or of a person authorized by statute to sue, does not apply to the receiver of a national banking association suing in a Federal court held in a State which has adopted the code procedure; for the right of the receiver to sue is derived from the national banking law. (*Stanton* v. *Wilkeson*, 8 *Ben.*, 357.)

(*f*) Under section 1001 of the Revised Statutes no bond for the prosecution of the suit, or to answer in damages or costs, is required on writs of error or appeals issuing from or brought to the Supreme Court of the United States by direction of the Comptroller of the Currency in suits by or against insolvent national banking associations, or the receivers thereof. (*Pacific National Bank* v. *Mixter*, 114 *U. S.*, 463.)

4. BY CREDITORS OF INSOLVENT ASSOCIATION:

The creditors of an insolvent association must seek their remedy through the Comptroller, in the mode prescribed by the statute; they can not proceed directly in their own names against the stockholders or debtors of the bank. (*Kennedy* v. *Gibson*, 8 *Wall.*, 498.)

5. FOR USURY:

(*a*) The penalty for all illegal interest paid to a national banking association within two years prior to the commencement of proceedings may be recovered in a single action, whether the amount was in one payment or in several. (*Hintermister* v. *First National Bank*, 64 *N. Y.*, 212.)

(*b*) Where a bankrupt has paid usurious interest, his assignee may bring an action against the association to recover the penalty. (*Wright* v. *First National Bank of Greensburgh*, *U. S. C. C.* (*Dist. Ind.*, 1878); *Crocker* v. *First National Bank of Chetopa*, *U. S. C. C.* (*Eighth Circuit*, 1876); 3 *Am. L. T.*, *N. S.*, 350.)

(*c*) The party who paid the usurious interest is the only party to the note who is entitled to sue for the penalty. (*Lazear* v. *National Union Bank of Maryland*, 52 *Md.*, 78.)

6. TO ENFORCE LIABILITY OF SHAREHOLDERS:

(a) When the full personal liability of shareholders is to be enforced the action must be at law. (*Kennedy* v. *Gibson*, 8 *Wall.*, 505; *Casey* v. *Galli*, 94 *U. S.*, 673.)

(b) And it may be at law though the assessment is not for the full value of the shares; for, since the sum each shareholder must contribute is a certain, exact sum, there is no necessity for invoking the aid of a court of equity. (*Bailey* v. *Sawyer*, 4 *Dill.*, 463.)

(c) But the suit may be in equity. (*Kennedy* v. *Gibson*, *supra.*)

7. EXECUTION:

A judgment against a national bank in the hands of a receiver only establishes the validity of the claim; the plaintiff can have no execution on such judgment, but must wait pro-rata distribution. (*Bank of Bethel* v. *Pahquioque Bank*, 14 *Wall.*, 383.)

8. ATTACHMENTS:

(a) When a creditor attaches the property of an insolvent bank he can not hold such property against the claim of a receiver appointed after the attachment suit was commenced. Such creditor must share pro rata with all others. (*First National Bank of Selma* v. *Colby*, 21 *Wall.*, 609; *Harvey* v. *Allen*, 16 *Blatch.*, 29.)

(b) No State court can issue an attachment against the funds of a national bank. Although the provision forbidding attachments was evidently made to secure equality among the general creditors in the division of the proceeds of the property of an insolvent bank, its operation is by no means confined to cases of actual or contemplated insolvency; but the remedy is taken away altogether and can not be used under any circumstances. The effect of the provision in section 5242, Revised Statutes, is to write into all State attachment laws an exception in favor of national banks, and all such laws must be read as if they contained an exception in favor of national banks. (*Pacific National Bank* v. *Mixter*, 124 *U. S.*, 721.)

NOTE.—This case overrules the decision of the New York Court of Appeals in *Robinson* v. *National Bank of New Berne* (81 *N. Y.*, 385), where it was held that the national banking law does not prohibit attachments against the property of national banks, except in cases where an act of insolvency has been committed or is contemplated. See also *National Shoe and Leather Bank* v. *Mechanics' National Bank*, 89 *N. Y.*, 467; *Raynor* v. *Pacific National Bank*, 93 *N. Y.*, 371; *Southwick* v. *First National Bank of Memphis*, 7 *Hun*, 96.

(c) Nor can an attachment be issued by a circuit court of the United States; for as by the law of Congress all power of issuing attachments against national banks before judgment has been eliminated from State statutes, there can be no laws of the State providing for such a remedy on which the circuit court can act. (*Ibid.*)

9. ABATEMENT:

An action brought by the creditor of a national bank is abated by a decree of a district or circuit court dissolving the corporation and forfeiting its franchises. (*First National Bank of Selma* v. *Colby*, 21 *Wall.*, 609.)

10. ESTOPPEL:

(a) A shareholder against whom suit is brought to recover the assessment made upon him by the Comptroller will not be permitted to deny the existence of the association, or that it was legally incorporated. (*Casey* v. *Galli*, 94 *U. S.*, 673.)

(b) Where one sued by a national bank is accustomed to deal with it, as such, and does so deal with it in respect to the matter in suit, he is estopped from denying its incorporation. (*National Bank of Fairhaven* v. *The Phœnix Warehousing Company*, 6 *Hun*, 71.)

11. SUITS AGAINST LIQUIDATING ASSOCIATIONS:

A national bank which has gone into voluntary liquidation will continue to exist as a body corporate for the purpose of suing and being sued until its affairs are completely settled. (*National Bank* v. *Insurance Company*, 104 *U. S.*, 54; *Ordway* v. *Central National Bank*, 47 *Md.*, 217.)

12. TRANSITORY AND LOCAL SUITS:

The provision of the banking law (section 5198 Revised Statutes) which requires that actions brought against national banking associations in State courts shall be brought in the county or city in which the association is located, applies only to transitory actions; it was not intended to apply to actions local in their character. (*Casey* v. *Adams*, 102 *U. S.*, 66.)

13. SURVIVAL OF SUITS:

Whether a suit against a director for negligent performance of his duties, as required by the statutes of the United States and the by-laws of the association, will survive against the executor or administrator depends upon State laws. (*Witters* v. *Foster*, *U. S. C. C.* (*Dist. Vt.*), 25 *Fed. Rep.*, 737.)

XIII. EVIDENCE.

1. CERTIFICATES OF COMPTROLLER:

(*a*) The certificate of the Comptroller of the Currency that an association has complied with all the provisions required to be complied with before commencing the business of banking is admissible in evidence upon a plea of *nul tiel corporation;* and such certificate, together with proof that the association has been acting as a national banking association for a long time, is amply sufficient evidence to establish, at least, prima facie, the existence of the corporation. (*Mix* v. *The National Bank of Bloomington*, 91 *Ill.*, 20; see also *Merchants' National Bank of Bangor* v. *Glendon*, 120 *Mass.*, 97.)

(*b*) The certificate of the Comptroller that the association has complied with all the provisions of law touching the organization of associations removes any objection which might otherwise have been made to the evidence upon which he acted. (*Casey* v. *Galli*, 94 *U. S.*, 673; *Thatcher* v. *West River National Bank*, 10 *Mich.*, 196.)

(*c*) And in a suit against the association or its shareholders such certificate of the Comptroller is conclusive as to the completeness of the organization. (*Casey* v. *Galli*, *supra.*)

(*d*) A letter from the Comptroller directing the receiver to institute suit, if not objected to at the time, is sufficient evidence that the Comptroller has decided that the enforcement of the individual liability of the shareholders is necessary. (*Bowden* v. *Johnson*, 107 *U. S.*, 251.)

2. EVIDENCE OF INSOLVENCY:

(*a*) It is not necessary that the facts upon which the Comptroller bases his action in appointing a receiver should be established by what is *competent legal evidence;* but he is left to be satisfied as best he can be, under the peculiar circumstances of each case, of the facts and the necessity for the exercise of his authority. (*Platt* v. *Beebe*, 57 *N. Y.*, 330.)

(*b*) A return of *nulla bona* upon an execution issued against the property of national bank is proof of its insolvency. (*Wheelock* v. *Kost*, 77 *Ill.*, 296.)

3. NECESSITY FOR ASSESSMENT BY COMPTROLLER:

It is not essential, in an action to enforce the individual liability of the shareholders of an insolvent national banking association, to aver and prove that the assessment was necessary; for the decision of the Comptroller on this point is conclusive. (*Strong* v. *Southworth*, 8 *Ben.*, 331; *Kennedy* v. *Gibson*, 8 *Wall.*, 505; *Casey* v. *Galli*, 94 *U. S.*, 673.)

XIV. CRIMES.

1. UNDER UNITED STATES LAWS:

(*a*) The willful misapplication of the moneys and funds of a national banking association, made an offense by section 5209, Revised Statutes, must be for the use or benefit of the party charged or of some person or company other than the association. (*United States* v. *Britton*, 107 *U. S.*, 655.)

(*b*) The exercise of official discretion in good faith, without fraud, for the advantage or the supposed advantage of the association is not punishable; but if official action be taken in bad faith, for personal advantage and with fraudulent intent, it is punishable. (*United States* v. *Fish*, 24 *Fed. Rep.*, 585.)

(*c*) It is not necessary that the officer should personally misapply the funds of the association. He will be guilty as a principal offender though he merely procures or causes the misapplication. (*Ibid.*)

(*d*) A loan in bad faith, with intent to defraud the association, is a willful misapplication within the meaning of the statute. (*Ibid.*)

(*e*) It is no defense to a charge of embezzlement, abstraction, or misapplication of the funds of a national banking association that the funds were used with the knowledge and consent of the president and some of the directors. The intent to defraud is to be conclusively presumed from the commission of the offense. (*United States* v. *Taintor*, 11 *Blatch.*, 374.)

1. UNDER UNITED STATES LAWS—Continued.

(*f*) Where the president charged as a trustee with the administration of the funds of the bank in his hands, converts them to his own use without authority for so doing, he embezzles and abstracts them within the meaning of section 5209, Revised Statutes. (*In the matter of Van Campen*, 2 *Ben.*, 419.)

(*g*) If, with intent to defraud the association, an officer allows a firm in which he is a member to overdraw its account, he will be guilty of misapplying the funds of the association. (*Ibid.*)

(*h*) As the national banking law makes the embezzlement, abstraction, or willful misapplication of the funds of a national banking association merely a misdemeanor, a person who procures such an offense to be committed can not be punished under a State statute which provides that a person who procures a felony to be committed may be indicted and convicted of a substantive felony. (*Commonwealth* v. *Felton*, 101 *Mass.*, 204.)

(*i*) An indictment charging defendants with aiding and abetting a director in a willful misapplication of the money of an association must state facts to show that there has been such misapplication committed by the director. (*United States* v. *Warner*, *U. S. C. C.* (*S. D. N. Y.*), *Feb.* 13, 1886, 26 *Fed. Rep.*, 616.)

(*j*) Allowing the withdrawal of the deposit of one indebted to the association can not be charged as a misapplication of the money of the association. (*United States* v. *Britton*, 108 *U. S.*, 193.)

(*k*) It is not a willful misapplication of the moneys of the association within the meaning of section 5209, Revised Statutes, for a president who is insolvent to procure the discounting by the association of his note not well secured. (*Ibid.*)

(*l*) To constitute the offense of a willful misapplication of the moneys, funds, or credits of the association within section 5209, Revised Statutes, it is not necessary that the person charged with the offense should have been previously in the actual possession of such moneys, funds, and credits under or by virtue of any trust, duty, or employment committed to him. Nor is it necessary to the commission of this offense that the officer making the willful misapplication should derive any personal benefit therefrom. When the funds or assets of the bank are unlawfully taken from its possession, and afterward willfully misapplied by converting them to the use of any person other than the bank, with intent to injure and defraud, the offense as described in the statute is committed. (*United States* v. *Harper*, 33 *Fed. Rep.*, 471.)

(*m*) This criminal act may be done directly and personally, or it may be done indirectly through the agency of another. If the officer charged with it has such control, direction, and power of management by virtue of his relation to the bank as to direct an application of its funds in such manner and under such circumstances as to constitute the offense of willful misapplication, and actually makes such direction, or causes such misapplication to be made, he is equally as guilty as if it was done by his own hands. (*Ibid.*)

(*n*) Any entry on the books of the bank which is intentionally made to represent what is not true or what does not exist, with intent either to deceive its officers, or defraud the association, is a false entry within the meaning of the statute. (*United States* v. *Harper*, 33 *Fed. Rep.*, 471.)

(*o*) It may be made personally or by direction.

(*p*) The erasure of figures already written in the books of a national bank, and the substitution of other figures which falsify the state of the account, constitute a "false entry" within the meaning of section 5209, Revised Statutes, by which it is declared to be a misdemeanor to make "any false entry in any book, report, or statement of the association with intent to injure or defraud," etc. (*United States* v. *Crecelius*, 34 *Fed. Rep.*, 30.)

(*q*) Where false entries are made by a clerk at the direction of the president, the latter is a principal. (*In the matter of Van Campen*, *supra*; *United States* v. *Fish*, *supra*.)

(*r*) Prior to the act of February 26, 1881, a notary public holding his commission under a State had no authority to administer the oath required by section 5211, Revised Statutes; and, therefore, a cashier who made oath before such notary to a false statement of the condition of his association was not guilty of perjury. (*United States* v. *Curtis*, 107 *U. S.*, 671.)

(*s*) To constitute the offense of willful abstraction by an officer, defined by the statute, it is necessary that the money or funds of the association should be withdrawn by the officer or by his direction; that such taking or withdrawing should be without the knowledge or consent of the bank, or of its

1. UNDER UNITED STATES LAWS—Continued.

board of directors, that the money or funds so taken or withdrawn should be converted to the officer's own use, or for the benefit and advantage of some person other than the association, and that this should be done with intent to injure and defraud the association. (*United States* v. *Harper*, 33 *Fed. Rep.*, 471.)

2. UNDER STATE LAWS:

(*a*) An officer of a national banking association can not be punished under State laws for embezzling the funds of the association. (*Commonwealth ex rel. Torrey* v. *Ketner*, 92 *Penn. St.*, 372; *Commonwealth* v. *Felton*, 101 *Mass.*, 204.)

(*b*) But where the offense committed by an officer is properly a larceny of the funds, and not an embezzlement, he may be indicted under a State law. (*Commonwealth* v. *Barry*, 116 *Mass.*, 1.)

(*c*) And an officer may be punished under State laws for making false entries in the books of the association with intent to defraud it. (*Luberg* v. *Commonwealth*, 94 *Penn. St.*, 85.)

(*d*) The officers of a national banking association may be prosecuted under State statutes for fraudulent conversion of the property of individuals deposited with, and in the custody of, the association. (*Commonwealth* v. *Tenney*, 97 *Mass.*, 50; *State* v. *Fuller*, 34 *Conn.*, 280,)

3. TERM "UNITED STATES CURRENCY" IN PENAL STATUTE:

The circulating notes of national banking associations are included in the phrase "United States currency" when used in a penal statute. (*State* v. *Gasting*, 23 *La. Ann.*, 1609.)

A DIGEST OF RECENT DECISIONS IN BANKING LAW.

BANKS AND BANKING.

CONSTITUTIONAL PROVISION:

The term "banking powers," as used in the constitution of the State of Ohio, has a restricted meaning, and relates only to the powers of making and issuing paper money, or, at most, to powers exercised by associations organized to deal in money, including the making and issuing of bills and notes intended to circulate as money. (*Dearborn* v. *Bank*, 42 *Ohio State*, 617.)

POWER OF SAVINGS BANK TO BORROW MONEY:

A savings bank having the usual powers of such an institution may borrow money in the course of its legitimate business, and may make and indorse negotiable paper for the money so borrowed. (*Fifth Ward Savings Bank* v. *First National Bank*, 48 *N. J. Law*, 513.)

WRONGFUL PAYMENT TO AGENT:

S. drew his check for $5,000 on the People's Bank of New York, payable to the order of the United States Trust Company, and delivered it to C. with verbal instructions to deposit it to his (S.'s) credit with the trust company. C. delivered the check to the trust company, but, instead of doing as directed, requested and received from the company a certificate of deposit payable to himself as trustee of S., and shortly thereafter drew the money and converted it to his own use. Held, that the trust company was not authorized in paying the money to C., and was liable to the executors of S. for the amount. The use of the company's name as payee of the check indicated the drawer's intention to lodge the moneys in its custody and place them under its control, and nothing further than this was inferable from the language of the check. (*Sims* v. *United States Trust Company*, 103 *N. Y.*, 472.)

NOTE.—Upon the trial, evidence of a custom to make such payments was submitted to the jury; but the evidence was conflicting, and the jury found against the existence of the custom. (*Id.*)

EVIDENCE OF CUSTOM TO BORROW MONEY:

In order to show that the borrowing of money was within the scope of the ordinary and customary business of a firm doing a banking business, evidence that such is the custom of the banks in the same place is admissible. (*Crain et al.* v. *National Bank*, 114 *Ill.*, 516.)

PAYMENTS THROUGH CLEARING-HOUSE:

(*a*) Where, by the rules of a clearing-house, checks not good are to be returned by the banks receiving them to the banks from which they are received as soon as the fact that they are not good is discovered, *and in no case to be retained after a certain hour*, yet when by mistake as to a matter of fact a bank has delayed to return a check until after the hour so fixed, it may demand repayment of the other bank, *if in the interval between the time fixed by the rule and the time of the actual return the latter bank has not changed its position, as, for instance, by paying over the amount of the check to the person who had deposited it for collection.* (*Merchants' Bank* v. *Bank of Commonwealth*, 139 *Mass.*, 213.)

(*b*) But in such case the recovery could be only the difference between the sum which the depositor has to his credit and the amount of the check; notwithstanding that, by the course of dealing between banks in the clearing-house association, the ordinary custom is to return the check as not good when there is not money enough to pay it in full; for the clearing-house rules not having been complied with by the return of the check within the

PAYMENTS THROUGH CLEARING-HOUSE—Continued.

time fixed, these rules can not control in determining how much shall be returned after payment of it has been made. (*Merchants' Bank* v. *Bank of Commonwealth*, 139 *Mass.*, 513.)

NOTE.—Under a similar rule of the Chicago Clearing-House it has been held by the United States circuit court for the northern district of Illinois that no such mistake could be corrected after the time allowed by the rule. Blodgett., J., said: "If parties competent to contract within what time they may correct mistakes in their dealings with each other have so contracted, it seems to me the courts have no right to override or disregard such an agreement. If a mistake which is discovered within an hour or within ten minutes after the expiration of the time limited by the agreement for its correction may be corrected, I can see no reason why it can not be corrected a week afterward, or whenever it is discovered." (*Preston* v. *Bank*, 23 *Fed. Rep.*, 179.)

(*c*) Where a check received through the clearing-house by the bank on which it was drawn was placed upon the file and entered in the journal, but subsequently, and before 1 o'clock of the same day (the time within which checks not good are by the rules of the clearing required to be returned), was sent back to the bank from which it was received: Held, that the filing and entry in the journal did not operate as a payment or acceptance of the check so as to deprive the bank of the right to return it. (*German National Bank* v. *Farmers' Deposit National Bank*, 118 *Penn. St.*, 294.)

PASS-BOOK:

(*a*) The duty of a depositor in respect to examining his pass-book and reporting any mistake to the bank is such as that which prudent men usually bestow on the examination of such accounts. (*Leather Manufacturers' Bank* v. *Morgan*, 117 *U. S.*, 96.)

(*b*) And by neglecting to make an examination of his pass-book within a reasonable time, a depositor may estop himself from afterward questioning its correctness. (*Ibid.*)

DUTIES AND LIABILITIES OF BANKS MAKING COLLECTIONS:

(*a*) Where a certified check is left with a bank for collection the collecting bank does not discharge its duty by forwarding that check to the bank on which it is drawn; and if it does so forward the check, and loss results, it will be liable for such loss. (*Drovers' National Bank* v. *Provision Co.*, 117 *Ill.*, 100.)

(*b*) Nor would it in any case be a sufficient discharge of the duty of the collecting bank to forward the check to the bank on which it is drawn. (*Merchants' National Bank* v. *Goodman*, 109 *Penn. St.*, 422.)

NOTE.—In Indig *v.* National City Bank, 80 N. Y., 100, it was said that when there are no indorsers to charge, sending the check through the mail to the bank on which it is drawn is a good presentment. (*See also Heywood* v. *Pickering*, *L. R.*, 93 *B.*, 428.)

(*c*) Where paper is received by a bank in the ordinary course of business for collection, such bank will be responsible for the neglect or misconduct of any sub-agent employed by it in the business of making the collection. (*Simpson* v. *Walby*, *Supreme Ct. Mich.*, 1886, 30 *N. W. Rep.*, 199.)

NOTE.—The same rule has recently been adopted by the Territorial court of Montana. (*Power* v. *First National Bank*, 6 *Mont.*, 251.)

This is now the rule in the Supreme Court of the United States (*Exchange National Bank* v. *Third National Bank*, 112 *U. S.*, 276); in England (*Mackersy* v. *Ramsay*, 9 *Cl. and Fin.*, 818); in New York (*Ayrault* v. *Pacific Bank*, 47 *N. Y.*, 570); in New Jersey (*Titus* v. *Mechanics' Bank*, 35 *N. J. Law*, 588); in Pennsylvania (*Wingate* v. *Mechanics' Bank*, 10 *Penn. St.*, 104); in Ohio *Reeves* v. *State Bank*, 8 *Ohio St.*, 465); in Indiana (*Tyson* v. *State Bank*, 6 *Blackf.*, 225); in Michigan (*Simpson* v. *Walby*, *supra*), and in Montana.

In other jurisdictions the rule prevails that the bank is only bound to transmit the paper to a suitable agent at the place of payment for that purpose, and when a suitable sub-agent is thus employed, in good faith, the collecting bank is not liable for his neglect or default. This is the rule in Massachusetts (*Fabens* v. *Mercantile Bank*, 23 *Pick.*, 330; *Dorchester Bank* v. *New England Bank*, 1 *Cush.*, 177); in Maryland (*Jackson* v. *Union Bank*, 6 *Har. and Johns.*, 146); in Connecticut (*Lawrence* v. *Stonington Bank*, 6 *Conn.*, 521; *East Haddam Bank* v. *Scovil*, 12 *Conn.*, 303); in Missouri (*Daly* v. *Butchers and Drovers' Bank*, 56 *Mo.*, 94); in Illinois (*Ætna Insurance Co.* v. *Alton City Bank*, 25 *Ill.*, 243); in Tennessee (*Bank of Louisville* v. *First*

DUTIES AND LIABILITIES OF BANKS MAKING COLLECTIONS—Continued.

National Bank, 8 *Baxter*, 101); in Iowa (*Guelich* v. *National State Bank*, 56 *Iowa*, 434); in Wisconsin (*Stacy* v. *Dane County Bank*, 12 *Wis.*, 629; *Vilas* v. *Bryants*, *Wis.*, 702).

BANKERS' LIEN AND RIGHT OF SET-OFF:

(*a*) Where a customer deposited with his bankers a policy of life insurance to secure any indebtedness of his to them then due, or which should thereafter become due, not exceeding at any one time the sum of £4,000: Held, that the bankers had no lien for any indebtedness of the customer in excess of £4,000; for as the express terms of the deposit limited the security to that amount, it would be inconsistent with those terms that the bank should hold the policy for something more. (*Earl of Strathmore* v. *Vane*, *L. R.*, 33 *Ch. Div.*, 586.)

(*b*) Where agents deposit money in bank for the benefit of their principals, and the purpose of the deposit is known to the bank, the deposit is impressed with a trust, and the bank can not charge against it any indebtedness of the agents, *even with their consent*. (*Baker et al.* v. *New York National Bank*, 100 *N. Y.*, 31.)

(*c*) The general rule is that a bank has the right to set off as against a deposit only where the person who is both depositor and debtor stands in both these characters alike, in precisely the same relation, and on precisely the same footing toward the bank, and hence an individual deposit can not be set off against a partnership debt. (*International Bank* v. *Jones*, 119 *Ill.*, 407.)

(*d*) And notwithstanding that it is the duty of a partner to pay the firm's debt to the bank, still, inasmuch as the bank could not set off the firm debt against his deposit, he could lawfully appropriate such deposit to the payment of a *bona fide* creditor of his own. (*Id.*)

STATUTE OF LIMITATIONS:

(*a*) Where notes deposited with a bank as collateral security for a line of discounts are paid, it is the duty of the bank to carry the proceeds to the credit of the borrower's account, when he will occupy the position of depositor; and then, as to any part of such proceeds, the rule will apply, that when a deposit is made in bank the statute of limitations does not begin to run until demand is made. (*Humphrey* v. *National Bank of Clearfield*, 113 *Penn. St.*, 417.)

(*b*) Whenever demand is made by presentation of a genuine check in the hands of a person entitled to receive its amount, for a portion of the amount on deposit, and payment is refused, a cause of action immediately arises in favor of the drawer; and as to the amount specified in the check the statute of limitations begins to run from that time. (*Viets* v. *Union National Bank of Troy*, 101 *N. Y.*, 564.)

(*c*) Although it is a general rule that a bank in accepting and paying a check drawn by a customer is generally held to know the signature, and if a forged check is paid by it it will not be heard to assert a mistake as to the signature, yet where one in whose favor a forged check is drawn *takes it under suspicious circumstances, and gives it credit by indorsing his own name thereon*, and collects the money on it, the bank may recover the amount from him. (*Rouvant* v. *San Antonio National Bank*, 63 *Tex.*, 610.)

(*d*) The statute of limitations begins to run against a banker's certificate of deposit drawn "payable on the return of this certificate properly indorsed" (which is the same thing as payable on demand) from the date of the same, and no special demand is necessary to put the statute in motion. (*Curran* v. *Witter*, 68 *Wis.*, 16.)

NOTE.—The same is held in Michigan (*Tripp* v. *Curtenius*, 36 *Mich.*, 496) and in California (*Brummagin* v. *Tallant*, 29 *Cal.*, 503). In other States it is held that such a certificate is not due until presented for payment, and hence that the statute of limitations does not commence to run against it until such presentation. This is the rule in New York (*Payne* v. *Gardiner*, 29 *N. Y.*, 146; *Munger* v. *Albany City National Bank*, 85 *N. Y.*, 589); in Maryland (*Fell's Point Savings Inst.* v. *Weedon*, 18 *Md.*, 320), and in Vermont (*Bellows Falls Bank* v. *Rutland Co. Bank*, 40 *Vt.*, 377).

BANK OFFICERS.

POWERS OF OFFICERS:

(*a*) The treasurer of a savings bank is an officer of much more limited powers than the cashier of a commercial bank. His duties more nearly resemble

POWERS OF OFFICERS—Continued.

those of the paying and receiving tellers of banks. He can not, simply in virtue of his office as treasurer, create obligations which will be binding upon the bank, as by indorsement of notes, or transfer to a purchaser a promissory note belonging to the bank. (*Fifth Ward Savings Bank* v. *First National Bank*, 48 *N. J. Law*, 513.)

(*b*) A cashier of a bank may, *without authority from the board of directors*, employ an attorney to collect outstanding debts due the bank; and this though the bank has regularly retained counsel. His authority in this respect is incidental to his duty to collect. (*Root* v. *Olcott*, 49 *Hun*, 536.)

(*c*) Knowledge acquired by the cashier of a bank *in his capacity as an officer of another corporation* can not be imputed to the bank, unless he communicated that knowledge to some one or more of the other officers of the bank. (*Wilson* v. *Second National Bank of Pittsburgh*, 7 *Att. Rep.*, 145.)

(*d*) Where a president of a bank takes other promissory notes in settlement for notes over-due, he is not performing the duties of the directors respecting discounts, but is a mere agent, and whatever he does within the apparent scope of his authority to obtain the new security is binding upon the bank when it accepts and holds the security. (*Cake* v. *Pottsville Bank*, 116 *Penn. St.*, 264.)

(*e*) Evidence is not admissible to show a custom of bankers and brokers to receive cashiers' checks and drafts drawn in favor of their own banks upon New York banks as cash upon transactions with the cashier individually, for no usage, however common and well recognized, can be invoked to justify a banker in taking money or negotiable paper known to belong to the principal in payment of the agent's debt. (*Anderson* v. *Kissam*, 35 *Fed. Rep.*, 699.)

(*f*) Whenever an officer of a bank offers paper of the bank under circumstances which show that he has made it officially for his private use, the party dealing with him must take notice of his want of authority, and can not treat it as the obligation of the bank unless he can prove the existence of some special and extraordinary authority on the part of such officer. (*Anderson* v. *Kissam*, *supra*.)

CASHIER'S BOND:

(*a*) The sureties on a cashier's bond will not be discharged by an increase of the capital stock of the bank when this increase is made under the authority of a provision of the law under which the bank is organized. The bond must be understood and read in the light of the law existing at the time it was made; and the parties must have contemplated that the bank would enlarge its business by all lawful ways and means, not going beyond a banking business. (*Lionberger* v. *Krieger*, 88 *Mo.*, 160.)

(*b*) The cashier's bond will not be invalidated by the fact that he is not a director, though the law under which the bank is organized provides that the cashier shall be chosen from among the directors. (*Id.*)

LIABILITY OF DIRECTOR:

(*a*) Where a director and member of the finance committee of a savings bank, acting with the president, invests the funds of the institution contrary to the provisions of the law by which it is governed, he will be liable for the loss on such investment. (*Williams* v. *McDonald*, 42 *N. J. Eq.*, 392.)

(*b*) And in such case it is not essential, in order to charge him with liability for the loss, to show that he acted fraudulently, or that he derived any benefit from the loan; it is sufficient that there was a culpable lack of prudence, or failure to exercise with ordinary care his functions as *quasi* trustee of the funds of the bank, by reason of which loss was sustained. (*Id.*)

(*c*) Directors of a bank are trustees for depositors as well as stockholders. They are bound to the observance of ordinary care and diligence, and are hence liable for injuries resulting to depositors from a failure to exercise such care and diligence. (*Delano* v. *Case*, 121 *Ill.*, 247; *S. C.*, 17 *Bradw.*, 531.)

(*d*) A depositor can maintain an action at law against the directors for loss resulting to him by reason of the neglect of the directors to use due care and diligence. (*Ibid.*)

BUSINESS PAPER.

CONSTITUTIONAL PROVISIONS:

(*a*) It is not unconstitutional for a State to enact a law making the liabilities of signers of commercial paper made and payable within its limits entirely different from the laws of other States respecting such liabilities, and by

CONSTITUTIONAL PROVISIONS—Continued.

statute change absolutely the operation of the law merchant, so far as it affects contracts made and to be performed within that State. (*Shoe and Leather National Bank* v. *Wood*, 142 *Mass.*, 563.)

(*b*) A provision in a State law requiring that the words "given for a patent right" shall be inserted in every promissory note executed in consideration of the sale and transfer of a patent right is constitutional. (*New* v. *Walker*, 108 *Ind.*, 365.)

(*c*) This provision is in the nature of a police regulation. But independent of this consideration it is valid, because it simply prescribes what shall be written in a promissory note given for a particular class of property. (*Id.*)

BILLS DRAWN IN ANOTHER COUNTRY:

Where bills of exchange were drawn in France by a domiciled Frenchman, in the French language, but according to the English form, on an English company, by which they were duly accepted: Held, that the bills were to be regarded as English bills, at least so far as the acceptor was concerned, and that their negotiability could not be attacked by the company on the ground that the indorsement of the drawer was not a good indorsement according to the French law. (*In re Marseilles Extension Railway and Land Company*, *L. R.* 30 *Ch. Div.*, 598.)

NOTES GIVEN FOR PATENT RIGHTS:

(*a*) Where a State statute requires that notes for which the consideration is the assignment of a patent right shall contain the words "given for a patent right," notes issued in violation of such provision will be unenforcible as between the parties, and when in the hands of a purchaser with notice of the nature of the consideration. (*New* v. *Walker*, 108 *Ind.*, 365.)

(*b*) But they will not be void in the hands of an innocent purchaser unless the statute, either expressly or by necessary implication, declares them to be void. But this the Indiana statute (section 6055 R. S.) does not do. (*Id.*)

NOTE.—Similar statutes in Pennsylvania and Ohio have received the same construction. (*Haskell* v. *Jones*, 86 *Penn. St.*, 173; *Tod* v. *Wick*, 36 *Ohio St.*, 370.)

INCOMPLETE INSTRUMENT:

Where one signs and delivers a note in blank to be used as security, the law implies that he means to become liable upon a completed and perfected note, and so far as the same is, at the time of his signature, an incomplete and imperfect instrument, he is held to have authorized the filling of such blank by the agent intrusted with the note for use; but nothing more than this is implied. And, therefore, if a matter of special agreement (*e. g.*, a provision for a special rate of interest) is crowded into it, there being no blank space left for such insertion, the alteration is material, and discharges the indorser. (*Weyerhauser* v. *Dun*, 100 *N. Y.*, 150.)

SUNDAY CONTRACT:

Where a note is signed on Sunday, but not delivered until Monday, it is not open to the objection that it is a Sunday contract; for a promissory note becomes a contract from the time of its delivery. (*Bell* v. *Mohin*, 69 *Iowa*, 408.)

NOTE PAYABLE ON DEMAND:

Although the principle laid down in the case of Merritt *v.* Todd (23 N. Y., 28), has been criticised in later cases, it has been acquiesced in too long as the law of New York to be open to question or dispute. That principle is that a promissory note payable on demand, with interest, is a continuing security; so that the holder may make demand when he pleases, and is not chargeable with neglect if he does not make it within any particular time, *and an indorser on such note remains liable until an actual demand.* (*Parker et al.* v. *Stroud*, 98 *N. Y.*, 379.)

A note payable "on call" is the same as payable "on demand." (*Mobile Savings Bank* v. *McDonnell*, 80 *Ala.*, 83.)

PROMISE TO PAY FORGED NOTE:

An oral promise to pay a note by one whose signature has been forged to the note is nothing more than an oral promise to pay the debt of another, and is ineffectual to bind the promissor. (*Smith* v. *Tramel*, 68 *Iowa*, 488.)

AUTHORITY AND LIABILITY OF AGENT:

(*a*) Where a bill drawn upon him by his principal is accepted by an agent by signing his own name thereto, with the addition of words describing him-

AUTHORITY AND LIABILITY OF AGENT—Continued.

self as agent and giving the name of his principal, he will be individually liable upon such acceptance; and he will not be allowed to show that the acceptance was intended to charge only his principal. (*Robinson* v. *Kanawha Valley Bank*, 44 *Ohio*, 441.)

(*b*) Where a note ran "we promise to pay," and was signed "Pioneer Mining Company, John E. Mason, sup't," parol evidence was held admissible, in a suit by the payee, to show that the note was given as that of the company, and not as the note of the company *and* Mason. (*Bean* v. *Pioneer Mining Co.*, 66 *Cal.*, 451.)

(*c*) Where a bill of exchange, drawn on a firm, was accepted by one of the partners by signing the name of the firm and adding his own underneath: Held, that the acceptance was that of the firm, and that the individual partner was not separately liable. (*Edwards* v. *Barned, L. R.*, 32, *Ch. Div.*, 447.)

(*d*) In the case of a non-trading partnership, in order to subject the firm to liability upon a bill or note executed by one partner in its name, a course of conduct, or usage, or other facts sufficient to warrant the conclusion that the acting partner had been invested by his copartners with the requisite authority must appear, or that the firm has ratified the act by receiving the benefit of it. (*Pearse* v. *Cole*, 53 *Conn.*, 53.)

(*e*) Where a note was made payable to "the order of T. W. Woollen, Attorney-General:" Held, that the words "Attorney-General" were merely descriptive of the individual, and that as the persons in giving the note had executed a commercial instrument, fair on its face and complete in all its parts, they could not, as against a *bona fide* holder, set up the defense that the payee had no right to transfer it. (*Walke* v. *Kuhne*, 109 *Ind.*, 313.)

(*f*) A note was drawn in the following form:

$1061.24.

DETROIT, MICHIGAN, *August* 4, 1880.

Four (4) months after date we promise to pay to the order of Geo. Moebs, Sec. & Treas., ten hundred sixty-one and $\frac{24}{100}$ dollars, at Merchants and Manufacturers' National Bank, value received.

PENINSULAR CIGAR CO.
GEO. MOEBS, SEC. & TREAS.

Indorsed: Geo. Moebs, Sec. & Treas.

Held, that the indorsement purported to be that of the Peninsular Cigar Company; that it was not ambiguous, and that, therefore, evidence was not admissible to show that it was the intention of the indorser to bind himself personally by the indorsement. (*Falk* v. *Moebs*, 127, *U. S.*, 597.)

CONSIDERATION:

(*a*) One dollar is a mere nominal consideration, and therefore not sufficient to constitute the holder of a note a purchaser for value. (*Proctor* v. *Cole*, 104 *Ind.*, 373.)

(*b*) An agreement to pay one-half the proceeds that may be realized upon a note is a venture approaching very near a wagering contract; at all events, it is not such an agreement as will create a right against prior equities. (*Id.*)

(*c*) It is the law of New York that one who takes commercial paper upon a pre existing debt, without parting with any right or property of value, is not a *bona fide* holder for value who will be protected against the equities of third persons. (*Webster & Co.* v. *Howe Machine Co.*, 54 *Conn.*, 394.)

NOTE.—See for this the following New York cases: *Coddington* v. *Bay*, 20 *Johns.*, 637; *Stalker* v. *McDonald*, 6 *Hill*, 93; *McBride* v. *Farmers' Bank of Salem*, 26 *N. Y.*, 450; *Comstock* v. *Hier*, 73 *N. Y.*, 269. For the contrary rule see *Swift* v. *Tyson*, 16 *Peters* 1; *Railroad Company* v. *National Bank*, 102 *U. S.*, 14.

(*d*) An existing debt is a sufficient consideration to constitute a pledgee of a negotiable instrument a holder for value. (*Spencer* v. *Sloan*, 108 *Ind.*, 183.)

(*e*) The pledgee of negotiable securities received by him as collateral security for an antecedent debt is not a holder for value, and is not protected from antecedent equities. (*Appeal of the Leggett Spring and Axle Co.*, 111 *Penn. St.*, 291.)

NOTE.—The rule in the Supreme Court of the United States is in accordance with that in the Indiana case. (*Railroad Company* v. *National Bank*, 102 *U. S.*, 14.)

(*f*) If the compounding of a felony affected the consideration of a note *in any way, or such purpose entered into the consideration, or such motive actuated the*

CONSIDERATION—Continued,

maker in any respect, the contract is illegal. And, therefore, where H. and his wife had given their note to R., the employer of their son, to prevent R. from criminally prosecuting the son for theft, they could not recover from R. the amount which they had been compelled to pay to a *bona fide* purchaser of the note; and in such case the makers of the note could not set up that it was obtained from them by duress and undue influence; for such a right does not exist when the contract is tainted with a corrupt consideration. (*Haynes* v. *Rudd*, 102 *N. Y.*, 372.)

(*g*) If one becomes a *bona fide* holder for value of a bill before its acceptance, it is not essential to his right to enforce it against a subsequent acceptor that an additional consideration should proceed from him to the drawee. The holder does not trust wholly to the credit of the drawer. He believes and expects that the drawee will accept, and upon such belief and expectation he acts. (*Heuleremalte* v. *Morris*, 101 *N. Y.*, 63; *Credit Company* v. *Howe Machine Co.*, 54 *Conn.*, 357.)

(*h*) The promise of a husband who has borrowed money of his wife to pay it to her children is a consideration sufficient to constitute one of those children a *bona fide* holder of a note assigned to him by the husband. (*Proctor* v. *Cole*, 104 *Ind.*, 373.)

(*i*) Where the instrument to secure which negotiable securities are deposited as a pledge turns out to be a forgery, this circumstance will not defeat the title of the pledge to the securities; for these having in themselves a negotiable character, the pledgee does not need to make any other title to them than such as springs from a delivery for value. (*Fifth Ward Savings Bank* v. *First National Bank.*)

(*j*) Where a bank has discounted for the drawer drafts to which forged bills of lading are attached, the acceptors can not afterward defeat the claim of the bank on the ground that they accepted the drafts in the belief that the bills of lading were genuine. (*Goetz* v. *Bank of Kansas City*, 119 *U. S.*, 551.)

(*k*) After discounting the drafts the bank stands toward the acceptors in the position of an original lender, and can not be affected in its claim by the want of a consideration from the drawer for the acceptance or by the failure of such consideration. (*Id.*)

(*l*) To enable one of the makers of a joint note to set up the defense that as to him there was no consideration for it, he is not necessarily obliged to show that it was without consideration as to all the makers; for, though presumably all makers executed it at the same time, and upon ample consideration as to each and all, it is possible that one might have signed the note without any consideration for his contract running to him or to any one else. (*Moyer* v. *Round*, 102 *Ind.*, 301.)

PRESENTMENT AND NOTICE:

(*a*) As to every bill not payable on demand, the day on which payment is to be made to prevent dishonor is to be determined by adding three days of grace, where the bill itself does not otherwise provide, to the time of payment as fixed in the bill. Thus, where the acceptor had stated in his acceptance "Due 21st May," it was held that the bill was not due until three days after the 21st of May. The time named in the acceptance after the word "due" was to be regarded as the time of payment to which days of grace were to be added, and not as a date which included days of grace. (*Bell* v. *First National Bank of Chicago*, 115 *U. S.*, 373.)

(*b*) A draft drawn upon a bank, and purporting to be drawn upon funds deposited, and payable on demand, is to be regarded as a banker's check. And where such a draft is payable at a different place from that in which it is negotiated, the holder should, as a general rule, forward it for presentment on the day on which it is received, or on the next succeeding day; and although this general rule may be varied by the particular circumstances of the case, the presentment must be made, in every instance, with all the dispatch and diligence consistent with the transaction of other commercial matters. Therefore, where the holders retained a draft for several days in their possession, for no other reason than that they chose to send it through a local bank with which they did business, and it did not suit their convenience to deposit it at an earlier date: Held, that they could not recover against the indorsers. (*Northwestern Coal Company* v. *Bowman & Co.*, 69 *Iowa*, 150.)

(*c*) And in such case it makes no difference as between the indorsee and his indorser that the drawer had no funds on deposit with the bank at the time the draft was drawn. (*Id.*)

PRESENTMENT AND NOTICE—Continued.

(*d*) Where notice of the dishonor of a draft was sent by the notary to the indorsers at Boone, Iowa, when their post-office address was Odebolt, in a different county: Held, that this was not a sufficient notice to fix their liability. (*The Northwestern Coal Company* v. *Bowman & Co.*, 69 *Iowa*, 150.)

(*e*) Where there was written upon a note "I hereby acknowledge the receipt of notice of protest on the within note," and this was signed by all the indorsers: Held, that the word "protest" included all acts necessary to hold indorsers, and the legal effect of the acknowledgment was to release the holder from any obligation to make demand or give notice. (*City Savings Bank* v. *Hopson*, 53 *Conn.*, 453.)

BONA FIDE HOLDER:

(*a*) Mere notice of facts such as would have put a prudent person upon inquiry is not sufficient to impeach the title of the holder of negotiable paper taken for value before maturity, and his right to recover can be defeated only by proof of such circumstances as show that he took the paper with knowledge of some infirmity in it, or with such suspicion with regard to its validity as that his conduct in taking it was fraudulent. (*National Bank of the Republic* v. *Young* 41 *N. J. Eq.*, 531; *Fifth Ward Savings Bank* v. *First National Bank*, 48 *N. J. Law*, 513; *Credit Co.* v. *Howe Machine Co.*, 54 *Conn.*, 357; *Morton & Bliss* v. *N. O. and Selma Railway Co.*, 79 *Ala.*, 590; *Mayes* v. *Robinson*, 93 Mo. 114.)

(*b*) Therefore, where the vice-president of a bank, who had negotiated a loan upon the paper of a corporation was advised by one of the officers of the corporation that it had outstanding a large amount of accommodation paper: Held, that this was not sufficient to defeat the claim of the bank as a bona fide holder of paper of the corporation discounted after such notice to the vice-president. (*National Bank of the Republic* v. *Young*, *supra.*)

(*c*) But in cases of this kind the burden of proof is on the holder to show that he took the instrument before maturity bona fide and for value. The mere possession of it, when it has been obtained or issued under such circumstances, is not enough. (*Id.*)

(*d*) But when he has shown that he became the holder of it before maturity and for value, in the due course of business, he has established all the facts that are necessary to fulfill the burden of proof laid upon him, and from these facts the law will imply that he is a bona fide holder, unless there should be circumstances from which bad faith may be inferred. (*Id.*)

(*e*) The bad faith in the taker of negotiable paper which will defeat a recovery by him must be something more than a failure to inquire into the consideration upon which it is made or accepted, because of rumors of general reputation as to the bad character of the maker or drawer. (*Goetz* v. *Bank of Kansas City*, 119 *U. S.*, 551.)

(*f*) The failure to pay interest on coupon bonds as it becomes due does not dishonor them before maturity so as to subject them to antecedent equities in the hands of otherwise innocent purchasers for value. (*Morton & Bliss* v. *N. O. and Selma Railway Co.*, 79 *Ala.*, 590.)

(*g*) Where a negotiable bond or other negotiable instrument is taken in such a way that the purchaser is not affected by antecedent equities, a mortgage given to secure payment is likewise protected against such latent defenses. (*Spence* v. *Mobile and Montgomery Railway Co.*, 79 *Ala.*, 576.)

NOTE.—The contrary is held in Ohio and Illinois. (See *Bailey* v. *Smith*, 14 *Ohio St.*, 396; *Kleeman* v. *Frisbie*, 63 *Ill.*, 462.)

(*h*) Where the condition of a bond is that the principal shall become due and payable upon the failure to pay any of the coupons as they become due, *after demand made*, the fact that the bonds have so become due and payable, as it rests upon an extrinsic matter, foreign to the face of the paper, and which does not dishonor it upon its face, does not of itself operate to charge the purchaser with knowledge that the bonds have been dishonored. The law does not in such case charge him with knowledge of the fact, unless he either knows it, or exhibits bad faith by intentionally avoiding a knowledge of it. And mere neglect to inquire whether there has been a demand made is not evidence conclusive of a fraudulent intent. (*Morton & Bliss* v. *N. O. and Selma Railway Co.*, 79 *Ala.*, 590.)

(*i*) Where a State repeals the law under which it had become the indorser of the bonds of a corporation, and by which provision was made for the payment of the bonds in the event of a default of payment by the corporation as maker, such action—whether or not it was an open repudiation by the State of its liability as indorser of the bonds, such as to dishonor them *ipso facto*—was at least sufficient to put the purchaser on inquiry, and charge him

BONA FIDE HOLDER—Continued.

with notice of the fact that there was something wrong about the bonds, especially when taken in connection with another fact—that, at the time of such repeal, several years of overdue coupons remained unpaid, and were attached to the bonds. (*Morton & Bliss* v. *New Orleans and Selma Railway Company, supra.*)

(*j*) By the law of Kentucky, promissory notes in the hands of an indorsee are subject to any defense, discount, or offset that the maker had or might have had against the payee before notice of the assignment. (*Shoe and Leather National Bank* v. *Wood*, 142 *Mass.*, 536. See *Gen. Sts. of Kentucky* c. 22, *secs.* 6, 22.)

(*k*) A note transferred as collateral security for an existing debt, and upon no new consideration, is open to all defenses which could have been made against the payee. (*Haden* v. *Lehman*, 83 *Ala.*, 243.)

(*l*) As the rights of the parties are to be determined by the relation they sustain to the contract to be performed, and not by the nature of the security given for its performance, one who is a bona fide holder of a note for value before maturity (under the rule that gross negligence in taking negotiable instruments is not sufficient to let in the defenses of prior parties) is in equal measure the bona fide holder of a deed of trust given to secure such note, and in determining the question as to such deed of trust, the rules governing the transfer of commercial paper should obtain, and not the rules applicable in the case of a purchase of real estate. (*Mayes* v. *Robinson*, 93 *Mo.*, 114.)

CHECKS:

(*a*) A check in the usual form, not accepted or certified by its cashier to be good, does not constitute a transfer of any money to the credit of the holder; it is simply an order which may be countermanded, and payment forbidden by the drawer at any time before it is actually cashed. It creates no lien on the money which the holder can enforce against the bank. It does not of itself operate as an equitable assignment. (*Florence Mining Company* v. *Brown*, 124 *U. S.*, 385.)

(*b*) Where, by the law of a State the drawing of a check by a depositor amounts to an assignment of his deposit *pro tanto*, that result will follow where the check is upon a bank in that State, *though the check is drawn in another State in which* this peculiar rule as to the effect of drawing a check does not prevail. (*Bank of America* v. *Indiana Banking Company*, 114 *Ill.*, 483.)

(*c*) A check becomes no valid claim upon the funds against which it is drawn until the bank is notified of its existence. (*Laclede Bank* v. *Schuler*, 120 *U. S.*, 511.)

(*d*) And however the doctrine that a check is an appropriation of the amount for which it is drawn of the funds of the drawer in the possession of the bank may operate to secure an equitable interest in the funds after notice given to the bank (a question which the court expressly stated it did not undertake to decide), yet the bank, so far as concerns itself and its duties and obligations in regard to the fund, remains unaffected by the execution of the check until notice has been given to it, or demand of payment made upon it. (*Id.*)

(*e*) Although the practice of drawing instruments in sets for the payment of money is generally confined to foreign bills of exchange, yet there is nothing in the purpose or effect of that practice which would render it inapplicable under all circumstances to checks. And, therefore, the character of an instrument as a check is not destroyed by the fact that it contains the words "original" and "second unpaid." These words do not make the instrument payable conditionally. (*Merchants' National Bank* v. *Betzinger*, 188 *Ill.*, 484.)

(*f*) Whenever demand is made by presentation of a genuine check in the hands of a person entitled to receive its amount, for a portion of the amount on deposit, and payment is refused, a cause of action immediately arises in favor of the drawer; and as to the amount specified in the check the statute of limitations begins to run from that time. (*Viets* v. *Union National Bank of Troy*, 101 *N. Y.*, 564.)

(*g*) Where, by the law of a State the drawing of a check by the depositor operates as the assignment of the deposit *pro tanto*, a bank in such State upon which process of garnishment has been served should be allowed credit for the amount paid upon checks of the depositor drawn *before such service though not presented for payment until after such service.* (*Bank of America* v. *Indiana Banking Co.*, 114 *Ill.*, 483.)

(*h*) But for no credit for checks paid after service, and which do not appear to have been drawn before. (*Id.*)

CHECKS—Continued:

(*i*) A fraudulent change in the date of a check, whereby the time for its payment is accelerated, is an alteration which vitiates the instrument. (*Crawford* v. *West Side Bank*, 100 *N. Y.*, 50.)

(*j*) If a bank pay a check so altered, it can not charge the amount against the account of the drawer. (*Id.*)

(*k*) And holding the check until its true date will not entitle the bank to charge it to the drawer, for the possibility that the check could ever become a legal liability in the hands of any person was destroyed by the fraudulent alteration. (*Id.*)

(*l*) An indorsee of a bank check, taking it six months after date, for a valuable consideration and without notice, the funds against which it was drawn still remaining with the bank, is protected against any right of set-off, existing between the maker and the payee. (*Bull* v. *Bank of Kasson*, 123 *U. S.*, 105.)

(*m*) Where a bank certifies *for the drawer* a check made payable to the drawer's own order, it incurs no liability to any subsequent holder until the check is indorsed by the drawer. (*Lynch* v. *First National Bank of Jersey City*, 107 *N. Y.*, 179.)

NOTE.—It was held by the same court in *Freund v. Importers and Traders' Bank* (76 *N. Y.*, 352) that a certification by the bank of a check in the hands of a holder who had purchased it for value from the payee, but which had not been indorsed by him, rendered the bank liable to such holder for the amount thereof. Distinguishing these two cases the court pointed out that in the earlier case the bank by certifying the check took, as it had the right to do, the risk of the title which the holder claimed to have acquired from the payee, and entered into a contract with the holder by which it accepted the check, and promised to pay it to him, notwithstanding it lacked the indorsement provided for, while in the case under consideration the certification was made *at the request of the drawer* and was subject to the condition imposed by him, plainly written in the check, that it should not thereafter be payable except by his indorsement.

(*n*) In the absence of an agreement to the contrary, a check or promissory note of either the debtor or a third person, received for a debt, is merely conditional payment, that is, satisfaction of the debt, if and when paid; but the acceptance of such check or note implies an undertaking of due diligence in presenting it for payment, etc., and if the party from whom it is received sustains loss by want of such diligence it will be held to operate as actual payment. (*Kilpatrick* v. *B. & L. Ass.*, 119 *Penn. St.*, 30.)

CERTIFICATE OF DEPOSIT:

A certificate of deposit in the ordinary form of such instruments is in substance and legal effect, a negotiable promissory note. (*Curran* v. *Witter*, 68 *Wis.*, 16.)

PAPER OF CORPORATIONS:

(*a*) A corporation engaged in business has implied power to make negotiable paper for use within the scope of its business, but it has no power, express or implied, to become a party to bills or notes for the accommodation of others, and such paper is valid and enforcible only in the hands of a holder taking the same before maturity *bona fide* and without notice. (*National Bank of Republic* v. *Young*, 41 *N. J. Eq.*, 531.)

(*b*) The general doctrine of the law is that where a corporation has powers under any circumstances to issue negotiable paper, a *bona fide* holder has a right to presume that the paper was issued under the circumstances which give the requisite authority, and such paper is no more liable to be impeached for any infirmity in the hands of such a holder than any other commercial paper. And this doctrine is applied to commercial paper made by a corporation for the accommodation of a third person when in the hands of a *bona fide* holder who has discounted it before maturity on the faith of its being business paper. (*Id.*)

(*c*) As corporations may accept drafts for some purposes, and as the purpose for which a draft is drawn does not ordinarily appear on its face, the question as to all parties with notice is, Was it drawn for a legitimate purpose? As to all others the implied inquiry is, Is the holder a *bona fide* holder for value? (*Credit Company* v. *Howe Machine Co.*, 54 *Conn.*, 357.)

(*d*) Although it is a correct proposition that persons dealing in the commercial paper of a corporation are bound to take notice of the limits of the corporate power in this respect, yet a distinction is to be observed *between the terms of the power and the circumstances under which it is exercised*. Parties

PAPER OF CORPORATIONS—Continued:

must take notice of the former, but they are not required to have knowledge of the latter. And, therefore, a purchaser of such paper, when the same has been accepted by the proper officer of the corporation, is not bound to inquire whether it was issued in the legitimate exercise of the officer's power to so bind the corporation, for this he has the right to presume. (*Credit Company* v. *Howe Machine Co.*, 54 *Conn.*, 357.)

(*e*) The fact that bonds of a private corporation were sold in violation of a restriction in the charter as to the price can not be set up to defeat the claim of a *bona fide* holder of such bonds. (*Ellsworth* v. *St. L., A. & T. R. R. Co.*, 98 *N. Y.*, 553.)

(*f*) When a corporation gives its promissory note in pursuance of a contract, which is afterward performed on his part by the payee, the corporation can not, in a suit upon the note, set up that the contract was *ultra vires*. (*Main* v. *Casserly*, 67 *Cal.*, 127.)

PROVISIONS WHICH DESTROY NEGOTIABILITY:

(*a*) Where a note was made payable twelve months after date, but contained a further provision "that the payee or his assigns may extend the time of payment thereof from time to time indefinitely, as he or they may see fit": Held, that the latter provision, as it made the time of payment uncertain and indefinite, destroyed the negotiable character of the instrument. (*Gidden* v. *Henry*, 104 *Ind.*, 278.)

(*b*) Where a note contained the following stipulation: "This note is given in consideration of, and is subject to one certain contract existing between S. B. J. Bryant and Jacob Haas, of even date with this": Held, that this provision destroyed the negotiable character of the instrument, and that the assignee took it subject to all existing equities. (*McComas* v. *Haas*, 107 *Ind.*, 512.)

(*c*) A note containing a power of attorney, which, in effect, authorizes a confession of judgment *at any time* after date is not negotiable. (*Richards* v. *Barlow*, 140 *Mass.*, 218.)

(*d*) A provision in a note for the payment of an attorney's fee in case suit should be brought thereon destroys the negotiability of the instrument. (*Chase* v. *Whitmore*, 68 *Cal.*, 545.)

(*e*) But an agreement inserted in a note to pay "all costs of collection, including 10 per cent. attorney's fees," does not render the note non-negotiable. This stipulation does not make the amount which the maker is to pay uncertain, for the promise to pay a fee of 10 per cent. excludes the possibility that the makers could be compelled to pay a fee more or less than that amount, and as to the costs, as they must necessarily fall upon the losing party, the stipulation as to them is to be regarded as mere surplusage. (*Schlesinger* v. *Arline* (*U. S. C. C., S. D. Georgia*), 31 *Fed. Rep.*, 648.)

NOTE.—As to whether a provision for the payment of an attorney's fee will render a note non-negotiable, the authorities are conflicting. That it will have this effect has been decided in Pennsylvania (*Woods* v. *North*, 84 *Penn. St.*, 407; Missouri (*First National Bank* v. *Gay*, 63 *Mo.*, 33); Minnesota (*Jones* v. *Radatz*, 27 *Minn.*, 240); Wisconsin (*First National Bank* v. *Larsen*, 60 *Wis.*, 206); North Carolina (*First National Bank* v. *Bynum*, 84 *N. C.*, 24); and in the United States circuit court for the district of Minnesota, 14 *Fed. Rep.*, 705. The contrary rule prevails in Indiana (*Stoneman* v. *Pyle*, 35 *Ind.*, 103; *Wyant* v. *Pattorf*, 37 *Ind.*, 512); Iowa (32 *Iowa*, 184); Kansas (*Seaton* v. *Scoville*, 18 *Kans.*, 433); Louisiana (*Dietrich* v. *Baylie*, 23 *La. Ann.*, 767); Nebraska (*Heard* v. *Dubuque Bank*, 8 *Nebr.*, 10).

In neither class of cases is any distinction taken between provisions for a fee at a fixed percentage and a provision to pay a "reasonable attorney's fee" or simply "an attorney's fee." The courts which sustain the negotiability of notes containing such provisions, rest their decisions in the main upon the ground that so long as the amount payable is certain up to the time of maturity and dishonor, it is not essential that after that time, when the instrument has for other reasons become non-negotiable the certainty as to the amount should continue (see *Stoneman* v. *Pyle*, *supra*, and *Wyant* v. *Pattorf*, *supra*). The courts which hold that such provisions destroy the certainty essential to commercial instruments follow the reasoning of Sharswood, J., in *Woods* v. *North*, *supra* In that case the stipulation was to pay "five per cent. collection fee if not paid when due." In the course of his opinion Judge Sharswood said: "It is a mistake to suppose that if this note was unpaid at maturity the five per cent. would be payable to the holder by the parties. It must go into the hands of an attorney for collection. It is not a sum necessarily payable. The phrase 'collection fee' necessarily implies this. Not only so, but this amount of percentage can

PROVISIONS WHICH DESTROY NEGOTIABILITY—Continued.

not be arbitrarily determined by the parties. It must be only what would be a reasonable compensation to an attorney for collection. This, in reason and usage of the legal profession, depends upon the amount of the note. * * * How then can this note be said to be certain as to its amount, or an amount unaffected by any contingency? Interest and cost of protest, after non-payment at maturity, are necessary legal incidents of the contract, and the insertion of them in the body of the note would not affect its negotiability. But a collateral agreement, as here, depending, too, as it does, upon its reasonableness, to be determined by the verdict of a jury, is entirely different. * * * If this collateral agreement may be introduced with impunity, what may not be?"

(*f*) The negotiability of an instrument will not be destroyed by the use of the term "in current funds;" for since the issue of legal-tender notes, the meaning of such term is that payment is to be made in whatever is receivable and current by law as money, whether in the form of notes or coin. (*Bull* v. *Bank of Kasson*, 123 *U. S.*, 105.)

DEFENSES:

(*a*) In a suit upon a promissory note evidence is not admissible to show that the note was given upon an understanding between the parties that it should not be of any force. (*Davy* v. *Kelly*, 66 *Wis.*, 452.)

(*b*) The drawer of a bill of exchange will not be permitted to show that at the time the instrument was drawn there was verbal agreement that he should not be held liable thereon as drawer. (*Cummings* v. *Kent*, 44 *Ohio St.*, 92.)

(*c*) Although it is the rule in Iowa that when there is a blank indorsement of a promissory note, a different contract from that which in such case is implied by law may be established by parol evidence, yet this rule will not be extended further so as to allow it to be shown by parol that no contract of any description was entered into or intended by such indorsement. (*Geneser* v. *Wissner*, 69 *Iowa*, 119.)

(*d*) Where the payee of a promissory note is sued as indorser thereon, he may show by parol evidence that when he wrote his name on the note the note had already been paid, and that he put his name thereto at the request of the holder merely as evidence of the payment. (*Spencer* v. *Sloan*, 108 *Ind.*, 183.)

(*e*) Where a promissory note has been given in part payment of a house, the maker of the note may, as against the purchaser of the note with notice of the facts, set up as a defense to it the damages sustained by him by reason of the false and fraudulent representations of the vendor as to the condition of one of the walls. (*Applegarth* v. *Robertson*, 65 *Md.*, 493.)

(*f*) The rule early established in Pennsylvania, that an indorser of a negotiable instrument is not a competent witness to invalidate it, is still adhered to in that State. It has not been changed by legislation. (*John's Adm'r* v. *Pardee*, 109 *Penn. St.*, 545.)

INDICIA OF OWNERSHIP:

(*a*) Where by the laws of the State a married woman can not transfer, *without the written or oral assent of her husband*, shares of stock held by her in a corporation, and she delivers to her husband the certificates of stock and a power of attorney in blank, and such stock is pledged by the husband, but the power of attorney *is not accompanied by written evidence of the assent of the husband*, a transferee from the pledgee is put upon inquiry, and his title to the stock can be no better than that which by the assent of the husband the pledgee had; for in such case, all the indicia of ownership are not conferred upon the pledgee. (*Leiper's Appeal*, 109 *Penn.*, 377.)

(*b*) If the true owner of a negotiable note overdue, or a non-negotiable note, clothes another with the usual evidences of ownership, or with the full power of disposition, and third persons are led into dealing with such apparent owner, they will be protected in their dealings. This is upon the principle that where one of two innocent parties must suffer for the wrongful act of another, the loss must fall upon him who put the wrong-doer in the position to do the wrongful act. (*Nenhoff* v. *O'Reilly*, 93 *Mo.*, 164.)

AMOUNT WHICH PLEDGEE MAY RECOVER:

Where negotiable instruments have been transferred as collateral security by one who is not a *bona fide* holder for value, the pledgee, if he has taken the instruments in good faith for value before maturity, will still be allowed to prove against the maker of the instruments for the full amount thereof; but the amount of his recovery can not exceed the debt for the security of which the instruments were pledged, and interest. (*Morton & Bliss* v. *New Orleans and Selma Railway Company*, 79 *Ala.*, 590.)

TABLE SHOWING, BY STATES AND TERRITORIES, THE ESTIMATED POPULATION OF EACH ON JUNE 1, 1888, AND THE AGGREGATE CAPITAL, SURPLUS, UNDIVIDED PROFITS, AND INDIVIDUAL DEPOSITS OF NATIONAL AND STATE BANKS, LOAN AND TRUST COMPANIES, AND SAVINGS AND PRIVATE BANKS IN THE UNITED STATES ON JUNE 30, 1888; THE AVERAGE OF THESE PER CAPITA OF POPULATION, AND THE PER-CAPITA AVERAGES OF SUCH RESOURCES IN EACH CLASS OF BANKS AND IN ALL.

States and Territories.	Estimated population June 1, 1888.*	All banks.		National banks.	State banks.	Loan and trust companies.	Savings banks.	Private banks.
		Capital, etc.	Average per capita.	Average per capita.	Average per capita.	Average per capita.	Average per capita.	Average per capita.
Maine	669,400	$66,510,496	$99.36	$35.66	....	$1.80	$61.58	$0.32
New Hampshire	375,200	73,918,144	197.01	87.37	$0.28	1.07	157.39	....
Vermont	334,000	34,122,503	102.16	48.33	....	....	53.83	....
Massachusetts	2,076,000	639,142,605	307.87	131.07	....	23.60	152.59	.61
Rhode Island	331,300	111,978,926	337.99	122.46	9.68	29.70	176.15	....
Connecticut	704,900	176,676,326	250.64	84.42	9.67	6.13	149.96	.46
New York	5,715,100	1,448,485,300	253.44	84.38	31.73	33.44	103.28	.62
New Jersey	1,343,900	96,674,083	71.93	43.57	3.39	....	23.47	1.50
Pennsylvania	4,971,700	469,163,521	94.37	59.20	8.28	12.42	12.19	2.28
Delaware	168,400	11,553,060	68.60	42.36	5.62	....	20.61	....
Maryland	1,081,100	87,477,119	80.91	43.07	6.37	....	31.29	.18
District of Columbia	224,800	11,272,382	50.25	46.04	....	....	4.21	....
Virginia	1,770,400	31,203,474	17.62	8.60	8.63	....	....	.30
West Virginia	784,200	7,708,545	9.83	7.07	2.76	....	....	....
North Carolina	1,701,200	10,038,740	5.91	3.81	1.54	....	.13	.43
South Carolina	1,268,600	12,109,535	9.54	5.52	.76	....	3.00	.17
Georgia	1,870,500	27,972,504	14.95	4.99	8.38	....	1.15	.43
Florida	346,900	4,045,583	11.66	10.13	....	....	....	1.52
Alabama	1,506,200	14,124,288	9.37	6.42	1.08	....	....	1.87
Mississippi	1,414,700	6,885,606	4.87	2.16	2.61	....	....	.10
Louisiana	1,134,700	28,470,000	25.09	16.62	7.49	....	.72	.24
Texas	2,373,200	35,973,128	15.15	12.74	....	....	....	2.41
Arkansas	1,116,900	5,170,809	4.63	3.17	.85	....	....	.61
Kentucky	1,944,200	69,280,211	35.64	16.36	18.45	....	....	.83
Tennessee	1,796,100	28,618,518	15.93	12.07	3.87	....	....	....
Ohio	3,681,000	173,604,141	47.16	32.15	1.54	....	10.18	3.29
Indiana	2,278,700	56,517,108	24.80	17.04	2.33	....	1.24	3.29
Illinois	3,576,000	178,639,393	49.96	36.38	....	3.10	3.98	6.55
Michigan	2,060,800	90,148,028	43.74	24.13	4.44	....	13.43	1.73
Wisconsin	1,555,600	60,758,467	39.06	16.50	17.71	....	....	4.75
Iowa	2,025,400	74,712,040	36.88	17.10	5.98	.05	7.13	5.71
Minnesota	1,125,200	75,641,381	67.22	38.98	19.53	2.50	3.53	2.08
Missouri	2,572,800	125,579,107	48.81	14.21	20.21	1.51	....	8.88
Kansas	1,654,600	64,475,049	38.96	10.39	10.54	3.80	....	5.23
Nebraska	852,800	43,673,831	51.21	34.25	6.90	2.30	....	7.76
Colorado	419,400	23,470,669	55.96	51.50	....	....	....	4.46
Nevada	83,200	944,221	11.34	7.67	....	....	....	3.67
California	1,150,400	225,652,814	194.63	24.90	86.72	....	73.47	9.54
Oregon	261,400	9,261,289	35.43	33.93	....	....	....	1.50
Arizona	80,100	748,650	9.35	3.00	....	....	....	6.35
Dakota	351,100	14,843,837	42.28	29.18	3.40	3.17	....	6.42
Idaho	52,500	1,438,138	27.39	23.45	....	....	....	3.94
Montana	59,200	14,130,757	238.69	203.99	8.26	....	....	26.44
New Mexico	147,900	3,026,578	20.46	18.64	....	....	....	1.82
Utah	200,500	6,651,976	33.17	19.51	....	....	2.70	10.96
Washington	137,700	10,446,016	75.86	60.17	....	....	....	15.69
Wyoming	35,600	3,960,974	111.26	77.81	....	....	....	33.45
Total	61,304,000	4,766,909,263	77.64	34.76	10.13	5.65	24.61	2.46

* The estimate of population was prepared, at special request, by Mr. Jos. S. McCoy, acting Government actuary.

NUMBER OF BANKS ORGANIZED, IN LIQUIDATION, AND IN OPERATION, WITH THEIR CAPITAL, BONDS ON DEPOSIT, AND CIRCULATION ISSUED, REDEEMED, AND OUTSTANDING ON OCTOBER 31, 1888.

States and Territories.	Banks.			Capital stock paid.	U. S. bonds on deposit.	Circulation.		
	Organized.	In liquidation.	In operation.			Issued.	Redeemed.	Outstanding.*
Maine	85	10	75	$10,560,000	$5,005,950	$35,905,700	$28,885,282	$7,020,418
New Hampshire	54	5	49	6,205,000	3,764,800	23,106,505	18,618,500	4,488,005
Vermont	63	14	49	7,506,000	3,241,400	31,848,720	27,093,964	4,254,756
Massachusetts	268	16	252	96,640,500	28,472,650	300,410,955	257,311,076	43,099,879
Rhode Island	64	4	60	20,284,050	4,031,800	63,265,955	54,684,167	8,581,788
Connecticut	97	13	84	24,104,370	9,102,250	83,922,280	71,362,764	12,559,516
Eastern States	631	62	569	165,440,920	53,618,850	537,960,115	457,955,753	80,004,362
New York	428	106	322	86,753,710	26,931,250	274,590,025	238,262,811	36,327,214
New Jersey	97	11	86	13,328,000	6,704,750	50,586,130	42,406,086	8,000,044
Pennsylvania	365	52	313	67,211,311	18,269,000	189,684,045	158,944,449	30,739,596
Delaware	18	......	18	2,128,985	1,685,200	6,961,975	5,281,938	1,680,037
Maryland	52	3	49	14,559,000	1,408,950	37,368,720	32,043,507	5,325,213
Dist. Columbia	13	5	8	1,827,000	910,000	5,097,600	4,313,888	783,712
Middle States	973	177	796	185,890,566	55,099,150	564,288,495	481,342,679	82,945,816
Virginia	40	14	26	3,846,300	1,353,850	11,899,480	10,174,961	1,724,519
West Virginia	27	8	19	2,066,000	592,050	7,401,410	6,260,823	1,140,617
North Carolina	23	5	18	2,366,000	720,000	6,416,470	5,496,741	919,729
South Carolina	18	2	16	1,774,200	523,500	5,403,925	4,747,228	656,697
Georgia	31	6	25	3,411,000	804,500	7,968,990	6,739,767	1,229,223
Florida	15	2	13	895,510	280,000	448,750	211,077	237,673
Alabama	25	3	22	3,561,080	826,600	4,932,770	3,916,033	1,016,737
Mississippi	14	2	12	1,105,000	332,500	517,380	244,269	273,111
Louisiana	17	4	13	3,425,000	1,418,800	10,491,950	8,596,928	1,895,022
Texas	106	6	100	11,784,850	2,624,000	6,352,090	3,832,089	2,520,001
Arkansas	10	3	7	950,000	422,500	1,283,220	920,663	362,557
Kentucky	83	14	69	13,644,400	3,262,000	33,672,495	28,031,142	5,641,353
Tennessee	58	16	42	7,716,000	1,512,000	10,930,810	9,169,161	1,761,649
Southern States	467	85	382	56,544,840	14,768,300	107,740,070	88,341,462	19,398,588
Missouri	80	30	50	12,881,000	919,000	16,898,915	14,481,657	2,417,258
Ohio	304	85	219	41,063,000	12,910,600	98,761,160	81,352,878	17,408,282
Indiana	156	60	96	11,884,500	4,809,800	51,091,825	44,230,043	6,861,782
Illinois	248	66	182	29,930,000	5,674,000	50,340,035	43,495,830	6,844,205
Michigan	154	44	110	14,060,000	2,936,000	27,699,000	23,620,875	4,078,125
Wisconsin	92	32	60	5,605,000	1,690,000	12,617,680	10,530,593	2,087,087
Iowa	180	50	130	10,224,000	2,998,000	21,735,500	18,181,677	3,553,823
Minnesota	77	21	56	13,938,200	2,034,200	11,826,980	9,795,426	2,031,554
Kansas	185	25	160	13,002,650	3,210,250	7,743,860	4,719,923	3,023,937
Nebraska	116	10	106	9,325,000	1,978,250	5,800,010	3,998,195	1,801,815
Western States	1,592	423	1,169	162,013,250	39,126,000	304,574,965	254,377,067	50,197,898
Nevada	3	1	2	282,000	69,500	239,400	192,093	47,307
Oregon	27	......	27	2,300,000	519,800	1,004,350	927,400	76,950
Colorado	43	9	34	3,455,000	1,000,000	4,413,810	3,393,182	1,020,628
Utah	10	3	7	900,000	300,000	1,523,700	1,153,851	369,849
Idaho	7	......	7	440,000	117,800	434,980	338,775	96,205
Montana	22	5	17	1,975,000	500,000	1,713,620	1,247,791	465,829
Wyoming	9	......	9	1,175,000	298,750	526,140	334,505	191,635
New Mexico	10	1	9	900,000	307,500	1,448,270	1,139,648	308,622
Dakota	70	11	59	3,775,000	1,005,000	2,144,770	1,218,701	926,069
Washington	27	3	24	1,800,000	398,750	1,196,140	587,723	608,417
Arizona	4	3	1	100,000	25,000	95,160	69,040	26,120
California	42	4	38	8,175,000	2,028,750	3,680,890	1,906,035	1,774,855
Pacific States & Territories	274	40	234	25,397,000	6,580,450	19,922,200	12,400,724	6,522,566
Add for mutilated notes	......	......	......	......	......	......	......	127,020
Total currency banks	......	......	......	......	......	1,533,585,935	1,294,510,705	239,099,230
Add gold banks	......	......	......	......	......	3,465,240	3,276,253	188,987
United States	3,937	†787	3,150	596,114,076	170,008,350	1,537,051,175	1,297,792,958	239,365,237

*Including $87,018,909 for which lawful money has been deposited with the Treasurer of the United States to retire an equal amount of circulation which has not been presented for redemption.

† One bank restored to solvency and resumed business, making total going banks, 3,151.

NATIONAL-BANK CURRENCY ISSUED, REDEEMED, AND OUTSTANDING FOR THE YEAR ENDING OCTOBER 31, 1888.

Denomination of notes on each plate.	Amount.	Total.	Ones.	Twos.	Fives.	Tens.	Twenties.	Fifties.	One hundreds.	Five hundreds.	One thousands.
Issued, including those canceled:											
$5—$5—$5—$5	$18,419,160				$18,419,160						
$10—$10—$10—$10	146,760					$146,760					
$10—$10—$10—$20	24,663,550					14,798,130	$9,865,420				
$20—$20—$20—$20	57,440						57,440				
$20—$20—$20—$50	57,200						31,200	$26,000			
$20—$20—$50—$100	17,100						3,600	4,500	$9,000		
$50—$50	37,000							37,000			
$50—$100	7,084,950							2,361,650	4,723,300		
$100—100	46,800								46,800		
Total		$50,529,960.00			18,419,160	14,944,890	9,957,660	2,429,150	4,779,100		
Canceled:*											
$5—$5—$5—$5	148,280				148,280						
$10—$10—$10—$10	9,920					9,920					
$10—$10—$10—$20	607,750					364,650	243,100				
$50—$100	52,350							17,450	34,900		
$100—$100	43,200								43,200		
Total		861,500.00			148,280	374,570	243,100	17,450	78,100		
Actual issues to banks from October 31, 1887, to November 1, 1888		49,668,460.00			18,270,680	14,570,320	9,714,560	2,411,700	4,701,600		
Total issues to banks prior to November 1, 1887		1,483,917,475.00	$23,167,677	$15,495,038	502,277,620	427,627,990	266,022,900	92,480,650	137,514,600	$11,962,000	$7,369,000
Total issues to banks since organization		1,533,585,935.00	23,167,677	15,495,038	520,548,500	442,198,310	275,737,460	94,892,350	142,215,600	11,962,000	7,369,000
Total redeemed and destroyed		1,294,541,113.00	22,783,281	15,298,872	453,086,540	364,436,000	218,803,920	81,230,400	119,872,000	11,706,500	7,320,000
Total whole notes outstanding		239,044,822.00	384,396	196,166	67,461,960	77,76 ,710	56,930,540	13,661,950	22,343,600	255,500	49,000
Total fractions outstanding		24,408.20									
Total national-bank currency outstanding†		239,069,230.20									

* National-bank currency canceled is such as has never been issued, but is left on hand in the vaults in this office by banks which extend their corporate existence, fail, or go into voluntary liquidation. † Exclusive of gold notes, $188,957; amount due banks for mutilated notes, $127,020.

NUMBER AND DENOMINATIONS OF NATIONAL-BANK NOTES ISSUED AND REDEEMED AND THE NUMBER OF EACH DENOMINATION OUTSTANDING, ON OCTOBER 31, IN EACH YEAR FROM 1868 TO 1888.

	Ones.	Twos.	Fives.	Tens.	Twenties.	Fifties.	One hundreds.	Five hundreds.	One thousands.
1868:									
Issued	8,896,576	2,978,160	23,106,728	7,915,914	2,219,322	355,181	267,350	13,486	4,746
Redeemed....	254,754	73,176	482,132	142,359	36,355	17,256	15,583	1,759	1,846
Outstanding..	8,641,822	2,904,984	22,624,596	7,773,555	2,182,967	337,925	251,767	11,727	2,900
1869:									
Issued	9,589,160	3,209,388	23,676,760	8,094,645	2,269,764	363,523	274,799	13,668	4,769
Redeemed....	904,013	232,224	985,940	272,495	71,655	28,859	25,968	2,585	2,415
Outstanding..	8,685,147	2,977,164	22,690,820	7,821,150	2,198,109	334,664	248,831	11,083	2,354
1870:									
Issued	10,728,727	3,590,157	24,636,720	8,413,244	2,370,056	378,482	284,460	13,926	4,779
Redeemed....	2,568,703	667,733	1,737,983	484,135	129,185	47,845	43,599	3,952	3,263
Outstanding..	8,160,024	2,922,424	22,898,737	7,929,109	2,240,871	330,637	240,861	9,974	1,516
1871:									
Issued	12,537,657	4,195,791	28,174,940	9,728,375	2,779,392	433,426	321,163	14,642	4,843
Redeemed....	5,276,057	1,493,326	3,276,374	933,445	245,361	82,972	76,287	6,017	4,005
Outstanding..	7,261,600	2,702,465	24,898,566	8,794,930	2,534,031	350,454	244,876	8,625	838
1872:									
Issued	14,297,360	4,782,628	31,933,348	11,253,452	3,225,688	497,199	367,797	15,621	4,933
Redeemed....	7,919,389	2,408,389	5,960,667	1,699,702	438,852	126,180	110,989	7,867	4,315
Outstanding..	6,377,971	2,374,239	25,972,681	9,553,750	2,786,836	371,019	256,808	7,754	618
1873:									
Issued	15,524,189	5,195,111	34,894,456	12,560,399	3,608,219	559,722	416,590	16,496	5,148
Redeemed....	9,891,606	3,120,723	9,141,963	2,573,079	653,071	168,976	144,057	9,658	4,530
Outstanding..	5,632,583	2,074,388	25,752,493	9,987,320	2,955,148	390,746	272,533	6,838	618
1874:									
Issued	16,548,259	5,539,113	39,243,136	13,337,076	3,962,109	666,950	492,482	17,344	5,240
Redeemed ...	11,143,606	3,555,019	13,041,605	3,912,707	1,171,608	231,556	196,572	11,676	4,683
Outstanding..	5,404,653	1,984,094	26,201,531	9,424,369	2,790,501	435,394	295,910	5,668	557
1875:									
Issued	18,046,176	6,039,752	47,055,184	17,410,507	5,296,064	884,165	645,838	18,476	5,530
Redeemed....	14,092,126	4,616,632	24,926,771	7,608,532	2,204,464	381,037	299,428	14,471	5,048
Outstanding..	3,954,050	1,423,120	22,128,413	9,801,975	3,091,600	503,128	346,410	4,005	482
1876:									
Issued	18,849,264	6,307,448	51,783,528	20,008,652	6,086,492	985,615	710,900	18,721	5,539
Redeemed....	15,556,708	5,124,546	32,382,056	10,369,214	3,052,246	515,784	395,785	16,217	5,272
Outstanding..	3,292,556	1,182,902	19,401,472	9,639,438	3,034,246	469,831	315,115	2,504	267
1877:									
Issued	20,616,024	6,896,968	56,816,848	22,266,064	6,776,253	1,079,781	767,317	20,022	5,668
Redeemed....	16,815,568	5,555,526	38,115,868	12,434,779	3,703,528	634,679	479,317	17,615	5,411
Outstanding..	3,800,456	1,341,442	18,700,980	9,831,285	3,072,725	445,102	288,000	2,407	257
1878:									
Issued	22,478,415	7,517,765	61,191,288	24,157,293	7,344,167	1,147,578	812,903	20,210	6,204
Redeemed....	18,194,196	6,026,692	42,683,433	13,859,149	4,133,178	728,222	541,859	18,895	5,900
Outstanding..	4,284,219	1,491,073	18,507,855	10,298,144	3,210,989	419,356	271,044	1,315	304
1879:									
Issued	23,167,677	7,747,519	65,578,440	25,904,223	7,869,951	1,211,761	830,720	20,570	6,340
Redeemed....	19,660,477	6,501,279	45,996,076	14,930,599	4,437,343	785,263	561,604	19,287	6,057
Outstanding..	3,507,200	1,246,240	19,582,364	10,973,624	3,432,608	426,498	269,116	1,283	283
1880:									
Issued	23,167,677	7,747,519	69,131,976	27,203,168	8,266,398	1,253,865	879,490	20,763	6,363
Redeemed....	20,875,215	6,943,889	49,149,824	15,821,110	4,684,820	825,499	610,601	19,484	6,124
Outstanding..	2,292,462	803,630	19,982,152	11,382,058	3,581,578	428,366	268,889	1,279	239

NUMBER AND DENOMINATIONS OF NATIONAL-BANK NOTES ISSUED AND REDEEMED AND THE NUMBER OF EACH DENOMINATION OUTSTANDING, ETC.—Continued.

	Ones.	Twos.	Fives.	Tens.	Twenties.	Fifties.	One hundreds.	Five hundreds.	One thousands.
1881:									
Issued	23,167,677	7,747,519	73,612,504	29,477,519	8,040,817	1,357,574	950,712	21,950	7,144
Redeemed	21,838,555	7,286,434	53,516,488	17,346,635	5,084,992	891,890	660,202	20,486	6,943
Outstanding ..	1,329,112	461,085	20,096,016	12,130,884	3,855,825	465,684	290,510	1,464	201
1882:									
Issued	23,167,677	7,747,519	76,697,424	32,042,260	9,751,784	1,453,324	1,035,118	22,787	7,187
Redeemed	22,353,877	7,484,140	59,313,233	19,770,934	5,751,707	980,182	719,130	20,880	6,990
Outstanding ..	813,800	263,379	17,384,191	12,271,326	4,000,077	473,142	315,988	1,907	197
1883:									
Issued	23,167,677	7,747,519	83,447,208	34,544,080	10,578,846	1,556,009	1,114,722	23,163	7,277
Redeemed	22,593,909	7,570,903	65,142,567	22,712,355	6,424,638	1,090,703	789,125	21,367	7,092
Outstanding ..	573,768	176,616	18,304,641	11,831,731	4,154,208	465,306	325,597	1,796	185
1884:									
Issued	23,167,677	7,747,519	88,101,188	37,182,102	11,442,091	1,661,010	1,199,750	23,736	7,369
Redeemed	22,671,936	7,603,285	71,039,357	26,050,197	7,481,762	1,216,573	874,543	21,981	7,156
Outstanding ..	495,741	144,234	17,061,831	11,131,905	3,960,329	444,437	325,207	1,755	213
1885:									
Issued	23,167,677	7,747,519	93,208,400	39,804,001	12,318,173	1,758,533	1,287,686	23,924	7,369
Redeemed	22,731,963	7,628,877	76,817,066	29,382,872	8,563,797	1,345,762	971,922	22,727	7,238
Outstanding ..	435,714	118,642	16,391,334	10,421,129	3,754,376	412,771	315,764	1,197	131
1886:									
Issued	23,167,677	7,747,519	97,667,360	41,695,970	12,945,618	1,815,174	1,342,001	23,924	7,369
Redeemed	22,757,987	7,639,806	81,109,272	31,767,278	9,397,854	1,451,301	1,055,330	23,138	7,299
Outstanding ..	409,690	107,713	16,558,088	9,928,692	3,547,764	363,873	286,671	786	70
1887:									
Issued	23,167,677	7,747,519	100,455,524	42,762,799	13,301,145	1,849,613	1,375,146	23,924	7,369
Redeemed	22,776,403	7,646,720	85,170,819	33,799,928	10,091,941	1,536,143	1,127,452	23,293	7,305
Outstanding ..	391,274	100,799	15,284,705	8,962,871	3,209,204	313,470	247,694	631	64
1888:									
Issued	23,167,677	7,747,519	104,109,700	44,219,831	13,786,873	1,897,847	1,422,156	23,924	7,369
Redeemed	22,783,281	7,649,436	90,617,308	36,443,660	10,946,346	1,624,608	1,198,720	23,413	7,320
Outstanding ..	384,396	98,083	13,492,392	7,776,171	2,840,527	273,239	223,436	511	49

STATEMENT OF MONTHLY INCREASE OR DECREASE OF NATIONAL-BANK CIRCULATION FOR THE YEAR ENDING OCTOBER 31, 1888, PRECEDED BY QUARTERLY INCREASE OR DECREASE SINCE JANUARY 14, 1875.

	National-bank circulation.		Increase.	Decrease.
	Issued.	Retired.		
From Jan. 14 to Jan. 31, 1875	$537,580	$255,600	$281,980	....
For quarter ending—				
Apr. 30, 1875	4,409,220	3,336,804	1,072,416	....
July 31, 1875	4,124,165	5,423,930	....	$1,299,765
Oct. 31, 1875	1,915,710	5,553,971	....	3,638,261
Jan. 31, 1876	2,504,600	3,852,731	....	1,348,131
Apr. 30, 1876	877,580	5,425,539	....	4,547,959
July 31, 1876	1,107,110	9,663,984	....	8,556,874
Oct. 31, 1876	2,604,390	8,564,727	....	5,960,337
Jan. 31, 1877	3,188,630	4,759,015	....	1,570,385
Apr. 30, 1877	4,363,010	5,005,596	....	642,586
July 31, 1877	3,000,230	4,984,399	....	1,984,169
Oct. 31, 1877	5,754,160	3,516,321	2,237,839	....
Jan. 31, 1878	6,725,585	2,701,885	4,023,700	....
Apr. 30, 1878	3,036,760	1,906,721	1,130,039	....
July 31, 1878	4,252,980	3,453,080	797,900	....
Oct. 31, 1878	2,276,360	2,924,430	....	648,070
Jan. 31, 1879	3,087,060	747,327	2,340,733	....
Apr. 30, 1879	7,039,300	1,822,988	5,216,312	....
July 31, 1879	3,674,830	2,715,524	959,306	....
Oct. 31, 1879	9,122,300	1,754,558	7,367,742	....
Jan. 31, 1880	7,289,805	674,129	6,615,676	....
Apr. 30, 1880	3,163,820	1,555,766	1,608,054	....
July 31, 1880	1,748,660	2,427,398	....	678,738
Oct. 31, 1880	1,199,920	1,535,700	....	335,830
Jan. 31, 1881	2,234,780	1,361,534	873,246	....
Apr. 30, 1881	12,690,890	4,426,506	8,264,294	....
July 31, 1881	9,569,410	4,734,578	4,834,832	....
Oct. 31, 1881	6,484,550	3,182,551	3,301,999	....
Jan. 31, 1882	5,625,200	3,354,153	2,271,047	....
Apr. 30, 1882	2,991,400	4,414,865	....	1,423,465
July 31, 1882	4,651,740	5,741,456	....	1,089,716
Oct. 31, 1882	9,792,910	5,611,497	4,181,413	....
Jan. 31, 1883	4,588,850	4,927,020	....	338,170
Apr. 30, 1883	3,638,650	6,510,245	....	2,871,595
July 31, 1883	3,527,100	6,868,245	....	3,341,145
Oct. 31, 1883	2,755,600	6,369,273	....	3,613,673
Jan. 31, 1884	2,748,270	5,172,714	....	2,424,444
Apr. 30, 1884	2,052,294	8,430,804	....	6,378,510
July 31, 1884	2,778,960	7,883,997	....	5,105,037
Oct. 31, 1884	2,792,170	6,833,874	....	4,041,704
Jan. 31, 1885	1,265,520	7,842,055	....	6,576,535
Apr. 30, 1885	2,125,260	8,135,112	....	6,009,8[illegible]
July 31, 1885	2,160,110	5,731,673	....	3,571,563
Oct. 31, 1885	5,591,760	6,758,154	....	1,166,394
Jan. 31, 1886	7,751,794	5,581,261	2,170,533	....
Apr. 30, 1886	4,700,384	8,307,163	....	3,606,779
July 31, 1886	1,469,325	8,425,486	....	6,956,161
Oct. 31, 1886	1,566,700	6,468,227	....	4,901,527
Jan. 31, 1887	1,243,550	9,580,973	....	8,337,423
Apr. 30, 1887	2,961,775	11,014,057	....	8,052,282
July 31, 1887	2,936,670	11,307,718	....	8,371,048
Oct. 31, 1887	4,021,350	8,421,529	....	4,400,179
	203,133,747	268,048,903	59,560,061	124,475,307
November, 1887	1,687,897	3,845,055	....	2,157,158
December, 1887	2,039,803	3,393,874	....	1,354,071
January, 1888	2,416,929	4,951,230	....	2,534,301
February, 1888	1,889,790	5,010,081	....	3,120,291
March, 1888	2,855,660	5,412,719	....	2,557,059
April, 1888	3,009,966	4,582,779	....	1,572,813
May, 1888	2,910,246	5,684,642	....	2,774,396
June, 1888	2,122,695	5,570,022	....	3,447,327
July, 1888	1,155,590	3,860,521	....	2,704,931
August, 1888	492,355	3,678,093	....	3,185,738
September, 1888	251,020	3,063,105	....	2,812,085
October, 1888	306,390	4,536,570	....	4,230,180
	21,138,341	53,588,691	....	32,450,350
Total	224,272,088	321,637,684	59,560,061	156,925,657
Surrendered to this office and retired from Jan. 14, 1875, to Oct. 31, 1888	....	15,667,563	....	15,667,563
Grand total	224,272,088	337,305,247	59,560,061	172,593,220

TABLE SHOWING, BY STATES, THE AMOUNT OF NATIONAL-BANK CIRCULATION ISSUED, THE AMOUNT OF LAWFUL MONEY DEPOSITED IN THE UNITED STATES TREASURY TO RETIRE NATIONAL-BANK CIRCULATION FROM JUNE 20, 1874, TO OCTOBER 31, 1888, AND THE AMOUNT REMAINING ON DEPOSIT AT THE LATTER DATE.

States and Territories.	Additional circulation issued since June 20, 1874.	Lawful money deposited to retire national-bank circulation since June 20, 1874.				Lawful money on deposit with the United States Treasurer at date.
		For redemption of notes of liquidating banks.	To retire circulation under act of July 12, 1882.	To retire circulation under act of June 20, 1874.	Total deposits.	
Maine	$3,364,559	$786,300	$2,681,035	$3,418,840	$6,786,375	$2,491,522
New Hampshire	2,073,905	465,083	1,431,550	1,524,100	3,421,633	1,176,583
Vermont	3,776,015	1,059,277	1,916,642	4,380,503	7,356,422	1,630,892
Massachusetts	37,467,255	1,907,105	24,622,617	43,626,498	70,156,220	18,064,706
Rhode Island	5,152,955	257,768	6,010,801	7,890,641	14,159,210	4,431,648
Connecticut	8,257,000	993,381	6,480,097	10,387,810	17,861,288	4,905,959
New York	44,036,140	8,549,294	15,639,615	49,541,119	73,730,028	12,164,221
New Jersey	6,027,485	1,389,908	3,072,436	6,689,814	11,152,158	2,418,037
Pennsylvania	28,386,415	4,441,545	15,801,685	31,863,922	52,107,152	13,806,558
Delaware	914,810	....	458,645	231,750	690,395	328,212
Maryland	3,292,275	184,800	3,665,625	6,022,870	9,873,295	3,171,054
District of Columbia	565,150	455,664	76,310	741,860	1,273,834	146,344
Virginia	1,708,740	1,176,419	649,480	2,203,550	4,029,449	729,893
West Virginia	627,364	870,550	586,425	810,240	2,267,215	467,065
North Carolina	1,445,100	330,480	68,350	2,044,085	2,442,915	177,519
South Carolina	262,905	83,750	32,930	1,899,335	1,966,015	252,087
Georgia	936,060	330,925	429,720	1,496,075	2,256,720	377,603
Florida	278,970	19,210	....	7,790	27,000	10,305
Alabama	680,350	135,000	107,750	1,013,320	1,256,070	219,800
Mississippi	337,500	....	....	38,450	38,450	961
Louisiana	2,505,900	606,413	802,250	3,109,400	4,518,063	455,301
Texas	2,902,475	147,080	69,000	1,052,210	1,268,290	167,443
Arkansas	519,750	55,880	....	268,120	324,000	16,453
Kentucky	6,650,750	1,200,247	1,254,648	8,537,705	10,992,600	2,480,812
Tennessee	1,913,455	915,191	278,620	2,130,374	3,323,185	707,504
Missouri	3,508,385	1,273,795	586,419	6,070,911	7,931,125	1,001,790
Ohio	17,741,956	7,473,713	5,053,934	17,056,332	29,583,979	6,632,948
Indiana	7,581,090	5,180,860	1,255,924	11,245,666	17,691,450	2,591,817
Illinois	7,500,145	3,780,444	1,518,890	11,749,101	17,048,435	1,841,475
Michigan	4,923,170	2,882,605	374,524	5,493,816	8,750,945	1,089,700
Wisconsin	2,735,055	1,219,990	640,000	2,379,739	4,245,729	549,593
Iowa	4,399,179	1,749,513	604,845	4,497,683	6,852,041	743,[illegible]40
Minnesota	2,318,565	959,754	407,420	2,482,081	3,849,255	349,503
Kansas	3,154,580	881,391	50,900	893,520	1,825,811	174,18[illegible]
Nebraska	2,307,410	187,720	194,800	1,120,150	1,402,670	217,557
Nevada	76,950	....	....	13,500	13,500	1,543
Oregon	506,120	....	82,450	180,860	263,310	173,[illegible]90
Colorado	1,046,[illegible]80	347,475	186,490	428,310	962,275	78,413
Utah	488,150	161,191	....	379,050	540,241	8,239
Idaho	103,750	....	....	74,250	74,250	1,439
Montana	638,590	189,940	....	272,250	462,190	9,144
Wyoming	179,715	....	....	15,750	15,750	170
New Mexico	281,2[illegible]0	1[illegible],500	....	283,200	300,700	79,729
Dakota	1,258,915	133,330	....	295,905	429,235	68,572
Washington	840,850	40,500	....	374,600	415,100	73,887
Arizona	75,500	50,590	....	2,500	53,090	8,080
California	2,613,870	101,250	....	760,150	861,400	155,600
Lawful money deposited prior to June 20, 1874, and remaining at that date	....	....	....	....	3,[illegible]12,675	....
Total	*229,006,588	53,030,931	96,958,857	257,010,705	410,8[illegible]4,198	†180,[illegible]29,922

* This includes circulation issued under act of July 12, 1882.
† Exclusive of $188,987 on deposit to retire circulation of national gold banks.

STATEMENT SHOWING THE AMOUNT OF NATIONAL-BANK NOTES OUTSTANDING, THE AMOUNT OF LAWFUL MONEY ON DEPOSIT WITH THE TREASURER OF THE UNITED STATES TO REDEEM NATIONAL-BANK NOTES, AND THE KINDS AND AMOUNTS OF UNITED STATES BONDS ON DEPOSIT TO SECURE CIRCULATION AND PUBLIC DEPOSITS ON OCTOBER 31, 1888, WITH THE CHANGES DURING THE PRECEDING YEAR AND PRECEDING MONTH.

	October 31, 1887.	September 29, 1888.
NATIONAL-BANK NOTES.		
Total circulation.		
Total amount outstanding at the dates named	$271, 801, 274	$243, 409, 950
Additional circulation issued during the intervals:		
To new banks	2, 328, 110	103, 570
To banks increasing circulation	18, 810, 231	202, 820
Aggregate	292, 939, 615	243, 716, 340
Surrendered and destroyed during the intervals	53, 743, 365	4, 520, 090
Total amount outstanding October 31, 1888 *	239, 196, 250	239, 196, 250
Decrease in total circulation since October 31, 1887	32, 605, 024	....
Decrease in total circulation since September 29, 1888	....	4, 213, 700
Circulation based on United States bonds.		
Amount outstanding at the dates named	169, 215, 067	155, 364, 908
Additional issued during the intervals as above	21, 138, 341	306, 390
Aggregate	190, 353, 408	155, 671, 298
Retired during the intervals:		
By insolvent banks	173, 250	101, 250
By liquidating banks	630, 545	46, 645
By reducing banks	37, 183, 285	3, 157, 075
Total retired during the intervals	37, 987, 080	3, 304, 970
Outstanding against bonds October 31, 1888	152, 366, 328	152, 366, 328
Decrease in circulation since October 31, 1887	16, 848, 739	....
Decrease in circulation since September 29, 1888	....	2, 998, 580
*Circulation secured by lawful money.**		
Amount of outstanding circulation represented by lawful money on deposit with the Treasurer of the United States to redeem notes:		
Of insolvent national banks	958, 902	1, 099, 076
Of liquidating national banks	9, 792, 493	6, 552, 061
Of national banks reducing circulation under section 4 of the act of June 20, 1874	46, 756, 970	32, 446, 211
Of national banks retiring circulation under section 6 of the act of July 12, 1882	45, 077, 842	46, 732, 574
Total lawful money on deposit	102, 586, 207	86, 829, 922
Lawful money deposited in October, 1888	....	3, 318, 840
National-bank notes redeemed in October, 1888	....	4, 533, 960
Decrease in aggregate deposit since October 31, 1887	15, 756, 285	....
Decrease in aggregate deposit since September 29, 1888	....	1, 215, 120

	To secure circulating notes.	To secure public deposits.
United States registered bonds on deposit.		
Pacific Railroad bonds, 6 percents	$3, 468, 000	$1, 185, 000
Funded loan of 1891, 4½ percents	66, 121, 750	17, 813, 500
Funded loan of 1907, 4 percents	100, 413, 600	32, 513, 500
Funded loan of 1882, 3 percents	....	110, 000
Total on deposit October 31, 1888	170, 003, 350	51, 622, 000

* Circulation of national gold banks not included in the above, $188,987.

TABLE, BY STATES, TERRITORIES, AND RESERVE CITIES, EXHIBITING THE NUMBER OF BANKS IN EACH, WITH THEIR CAPITAL, MINIMUM AMOUNT OF BONDS REQUIRED BY LAW, BONDS ACTUALLY HELD, AND CIRCULATION OUTSTANDING THEREON ON OCTOBER 4, 1888.

States, Territories, and reserve cities.	No.	Capital.	United States bonds.		Circulation outstanding October 4, 1888.
			Minimum required.	Held October 4, 1888.	
Maine	75	$10,600,000	$2,015,000	$4,961,000	$4,403,033
New Hampshire	40	6,205,000	1,501,250	3,677,000	3,276,550
Vermont	40	7,566,000	1,541,500	3,614,000	3,227,765
Massachusetts	198	44,740,500	8,004,375	21,813,400	19,454,153
Boston	55	51,400,000	2,750,000	6,464,650	5,703,530
Rhode Island	60	20,284,050	2,439,250	5,143,900	4,589,032
Connecticut	84	24,104,370	3,468,325	8,832,600	7,871,452
Division No. 1	570	165,049,920	21,800,700	54,506,550	48,525,515
New York	270	35,042,700	7,687,415	18,098,050	16,121,838
New York City	46	49,100,000	2,287,500	7,920,000	6,603,465
Albany	6	1,750,000	300,000	948,000	780,390
New Jersey	85	13,318,350	2,677,088	6,716,250	5,992,912
Pennsylvania	246	33,502,291	7,214,330	14,050,300	12,336,796
Philadelphia	43	23,098,000	2,137,500	3,187,500	2,833,334
Pittsburgh	24	10,430,000	1,175,000	1,615,500	1,395,680
Division No. 2	720	166,241,401	23,478,833	52,544,600	46,154,405
Delaware	18	2,129,885	454,175	1,599,200	1,407,210
Maryland	31	2,816,700	691,250	1,311,000	1,138,690
Baltimore	17	11,713,260	850,000	900,000	790,890
District of Columbia	1	252,000	50,000	250,000	201,100
Washington	7	1,575,000	325,000	580,000	425,820
Virginia	26	3,846,300	772,750	1,155,000	1,025,920
West Virginia	20	1,966,000	502,500	725,000	626,460
Division No. 3	120	24,200,145	3,645,675	6,520,200	5,616,000
North Carolina	18	2,266,000	520,000	766,000	647,780
South Carolina	16	1,773,000	430,750	468,500	420,030
Georgia	24	3,361,000	652,750	969,500	860,150
Florida	13	896,000	224,247	280,000	194,750
Alabama	21	3,544,000	667,250	863,000	748,580
Mississippi	12	1,105,000	276,250	332,500	292,860
Louisiana	5	500,000	125,000	125,000	110,415
New Orleans	8	2,925,000	400,000	1,375,000	1,216,595
Texas	101	11,805,700	2,606,425	2,634,000	2,312,615
Arkansas	7	950,000	225,000	410,000	368,940
Kentucky	60	10,102,000	2,146,975	2,937,000	2,630,030
Louisville	9	3,651,500	450,000	500,000	440,890
Tennessee	42	7,715,000	1,147,500	1,421,500	1,253,520
Division No. 4	335	50,596,000	9,881,147	13,082,000	11,506,155
Ohio	197	24,390,000	5,415,000	9,476,300	8,430,451
Cincinnati	13	8,900,000	650,000	1,977,000	1,750,700
Cleveland	9	6,650,000	430,000	600,000	543,380
Indiana	94	11,084,500	2,646,125	4,573,800	4,084,375
Illinois	163	14,824,000	3,518,500	4,534,500	3,985,675
Chicago	10	15,250,000	950,000	1,100,000	744,420
Michigan	101	10,974,600	2,393,500	2,784,000	2,485,960
Detroit	8	4,000,000	400,000	400,000	343,280
Wisconsin	56	4,080,000	1,157,500	1,391,500	1,241,925
Milwaukee	3	850,000	150,000	300,000	270,000
Division No. 5	663	102,402,100	17,730,625	27,143,100	23,880,166
Iowa	120	10,148,000	2,437,000	3,082,500	2,752,533
Minnesota	56	13,064,500	1,547,375	1,784,800	1,585,360
Missouri	34	2,431,000	607,750	732,750	656,105
Saint Louis	4	3,200,000	200,000	360,000	324,000
Kansas City	10	6,600,000	500,000	500,000	450,000
Saint Joseph	2	300,000	75,000	100,000	89,990
Kansas	160	12,854,700	3,013,675	3,138,250	2,818,570
Nebraska	97	6,235,000	1,533,750	1,541,000	1,383,710
Omaha	7	3,050,000	325,000	325,000	291,900
Division No. 6	499	58,783,200	10,280,550	11,564,300	10,352,258

TABLE, BY STATES, TERRITORIES, AND RESERVE CITIES, EXHIBITING THE NUMBER OF BANKS IN EACH, WITH THEIR CAPITAL, ETC.—Continued.

States, Territories, and reserve cities.	No.	Capital.	United States bonds.		Circulation outstanding October 4, 1888.
			Minimum required.	Held October 4, 1888.	
Colorado	34	$3,457,800	$789,450	$1,071,500	$958,670
Nevada	2	282,000	70,500	70,500	63,410
California	35	5,475,000	1,106,250	1,276,250	1,103,570
San Francisco	3	2,700,000	150,000	650,000	575,650
Oregon	27	2,300,000	502,500	510,800	447,690
Arizona	1	100,000	25,000	25,000	22,500
Division No. 7	102	14,374,800	2,643,700	3,613,050	3,171,490
Dakota	58	3,625,000	906,250	937,500	839,100
Idaho	7	430,000	107,500	112,800	99,045
Montana	17	1,950,000	400,000	480,000	421,450
New Mexico	9	900,000	225,000	252,500	226,410
Utah	7	850,000	212,500	390,000	269,690
Washington	24	1,855,000	463,750	471,250	420,520
Wyoming	9	1,175,000	243,750	248,750	220,515
Division No. 8	131	10,785,000	2,558,750	2,893,400	2,496,730
United States	3,140	592,621,656	91,987,980	171,867,200	151,702,809

TABLE BY STATES, TERRITORIES, AND RESERVE CITIES, EXHIBITING THE NUMBER OF BANKS IN EACH, WITH CAPITAL OF $150,000 AND UNDER, FOR THE YEARS 1887 AND 1888, AND THE INCREASE OR DECREASE IN BANKS AND CAPITAL DURING THE INTERVAL.

States, Territories, and reserve cities.	October 5, 1887.		October 4, 1888.		Increase.		Decrease.	
	No.	Capital.	No.	Capital.	No.	Capital.	No.	Capital.
Maine	58	$5,110,000	61	$5,260,000	3	$150,000		
New Hampshire	41	4,405,000	41	4,405,000				
Vermont	36	3,566,000	36	3,566,000				
Massachusetts	87	10,177,500	87	10,177,500				
Boston								
Rhode Island	26	2,813,000	25	2,757,000			1	$56,000
Connecticut	29	3,204,340	33	3,673,300	4	468,960		
Division No. 1	277	29,275,840	283	29,838,800	7	618,960	1	56,000
New York	210	18,931,100	211	18,949,600	1	18,500		
New York City	1	150,000	1	150,000				
Albany								
New Jersey	53	4,814,220	57	5,108,350	4	294,130		
Pennsylvania	178	16,716,170	188	17,257,321	10	541,151		
Philadelphia	1	150,000	1	150,000				
Pittsburgh	1	100,000	1	100,000				
Division No. 2	444	40,861,550	459	41,715,331	15	853,781		
Delaware	13	970,800	14	1,016,700	1	45,900		
Maryland	28	2,145,000	28	2,165,000		20,000		
Baltimore								
District of Columbia								
Washington	1	100,000	1	100,000				
Virginia	17	1,441,000	18	1,491,000	1	50,000		
West Virginia	18	1,605,000	18	1,610,000		5,000		
Division No. 3	77	6,261,800	79	6,382,700	2	120,900		
North Carolina	12	1,062,280	13	1,116,000	1	53,720		
South Carolina	12	1,048,000	13	1,123,000	1	75,000		
Georgia	16	1,300,520	19	1,611,000	3	310,480		
Florida	8	500,000	13	890,000	5	390,000		
Alabama	12	1,010,100	13	1,068,100	1	58,000		
Mississippi	12	1,055,000	12	1,105,000		50,000		
Louisiana	4	300,000	4	300,000				
New Orleans								
Texas	79	6,559,750	85	7,225,700	6	665,950		
Arkansas	5	500,000	5	500,000				
Kentucky	36	3,773,000	36	3,787,000		14,000		
Louisville								
Tennessee	29	2,160,000	31	2,390,000	2	230,000		
Division No. 4	225	19,269,550	244	21,124,590	19	1,855,040		
Ohio	155	13,542,020	156	13,460,000	1			82,020
Cincinnati								
Cleveland								
Indiana	72	6,264,500	74	6,584,500	2	320,000		
Illinois	148	11,441,500	151	11,674,000	3	232,500		
Chicago								
Michigan	88	6,874,600	88	6,974,000		99,400		
Detroit								
Wisconsin	49	3,592,000	52	3,830,000	3	238,000		
Milwaukee								
Division No. 5	512	41,714,620	521	42,522,500	9	889,900		82,020
Iowa	122	8,450,000	123	8,548,000	1	98,000		
Minnesota	39	2,715,000	38	2,589,500			1	125,500
Missouri	34	2,317,280	33	2,231,000			1	86,280
Saint Louis								
Kansas City	1	140,000					1	140,000
Saint Joseph	1	100,000	1	100,000				
Kansas	131	8,530,800	151	10,254,700	20	1,723,900		
Nebraska	93	5,506,100	95	5,735,000	2	228,900		
Omaha	2	200,000	1	100,000			1	100,000
Division No. 6	423	27,959,180	443	29,558,200	23	2,050,800	4	451,780

TABLE BY STATES, TERRITORIES, AND RESERVE CITIES, EXHIBITING THE NUMBER OF BANKS IN EACH, WITH CAPITAL, ETC.—Continued.

States, Territories, and reserve cities.	October 5, 1887.		October 4, 1888.		Increase.		Increase.	
	No.	Capital.	No.	Capital.	No.	Capital.	No.	Capital.
Colorado	26	$1, 651, 850	27	$1, 757, 800	1	$105, 950	.....	....
Nevada	2	150, 000	1	82, 000	.....	....	1	$68, 000
California	21	1, 760, 000	24	2, 225, 000	3	465, 000	.....	....
San Francisco	.....	....	.....	....	.....	....	.....	....
Oregon	21	1, 295, 000	24	1, 410, 000	3	115, 000	.....	....
Arizona	1	100, 000	1	100, 000	.....	....	.....	....
Division No. 7	71	4, 956, 850	77	5, 574, 800	7	685, 950	1	68, 000
Dakota	62	3, 720, 000	58	3, 625, 000	.....	....	4	95, 000
Idaho	6	350, 000	7	430, 000	1	80, 000	.....	....
Montana	15	1, 225, 000	15	1, 200, 000	.....	....	.....	25, 000
New Mexico	9	850, 000	9	900, 000	.....	50, 000	.....	....
Utah	5	450, 000	5	450, 000	.....	....	.....	....
Washington	18	1, 280, 000	23	1, 655, 000	5	375, 000	.....	....
Wyoming	6	475, 000	7	575, 000	1	100, 000	.....	....
Division No. 8	121	8, 350, 000	124	8, 835, 000	7	605, 000	4	120, 000
United States	2, 150	178, 649, 390	2, 229	185, 551, 921	89	7, 680, 331	10	777, 800

TABLE BY STATES, TERRITORIES, AND RESERVE CITIES, EXHIBITING THE NUMBER OF BANKS IN EACH, WITH CAPITAL EXCEEDING $150,000, FOR THE YEARS 1887 AND 1888, AND THE INCREASE OR DECREASE IN BANKS AND CAPITAL DURING THE INTERVAL.

States, Territories, and reserve cities.	October 5, 1887.		October 4, 1888.		Increase.		Decrease.	
	No.	Capital.	No.	Capital.	No.	Capital.	No.	Capital.
Maine	14	$5, 380, 700	14	$5, 400, 000		$09, 300		
New Hampshire	8	1, 800, 000	8	1, 800, 000				
Vermont	13	4, 000, 000	13	4, 000, 000				
Massachusetts	111	34, 613, 000	111	34, 563, 000				$50, 000
Boston	54	50, 950, 000	55	51, 400, 000	1	450, 000		
Rhode Island	35	17, 527, 050	35	17, 527, 050				
Connecticut	54	21, 301, 070	51	20, 521, 070			3	780, 000
Division No. 1	280	133, 521, 820	267	133, 211, 120	1	519, 300	3	830, 000
New York	59	15, 793, 100	59	16, 093, 100		300, 000		
New York City	46	49, 000, 000	45	48, 950, 000			1	50, 000
Albany	6	1, 750, 000	6	1, 750, 000				
New Jersey	28	8, 210, 000	28	8, 210, 000				
Pennsylvania	59	10, 834, 970	58	10, 334, 970			1	500, 000
Philadelphia	42	22, 508, 000	42	22, 858, 000		350, 000		
Pittsburgh	22	10, 080, 000	23	10, 330, 000	1	250, 000		
Division No. 2	262	124, 176, 070	261	124, 526, 070	1	900, 000	2	550, 000
Delaware	4	1, 113, 185	4	1, 113, 185				
Maryland	3	651, 700	3	651, 700				
Baltimore	17	11, 713, 200	17	11, 713, 200				
District of Columbia	1	252, 000	1	252, 000				
Washington	6	1, 475, 000	6	1, 475, 000				
Virginia	8	2, 355, 300	8	2, 355, 300				
West Virginia	2	356, 000	2	356, 000				
Division No. 3	41	17, 916, 445	41	17, 916, 445				
North Carolina	6	1, 350, 000	5	1, 150, 000			1	200, 000
South Carolina	3	650, 000	3	650, 000				
Georgia	5	1, 750, 000	5	1, 750, 000				
Florida								
Alabama	8	2, 475, 000	8	2, 475, 000				
Mississippi								
Louisiana	1	200, 000	1	200, 000				
New Orleans	8	2, 925, 000	8	2, 925, 000				
Texas	12	3, 360, 000	15	4, 580, 000	3	1, 220, 000		
Arkansas	2	450, 000	2	450, 000				
Kentucky	23	5, 985, 000	24	6, 315, 000	1	330, 000		
Louisville	9	3, 551, 500	9	3, 651, 500		100, 000		
Tennessee	11	5, 300, 000	11	5, 325, 000		25, 000		
Division No. 4	88	27, 996, 500	91	29, 471, 500	4	1, 675, 000	1	200, 000
Ohio	37	9, 254, 000	41	10, 930, 000	4	1, 685, 000		
Cincinnati	15	10, 400, 000	13	8, 900, 000			2	1, 500, 000
Cleveland	9	6, 700, 000	9	6, 650, 000				50, 000
Indiana	21	5, 630, 000	20	5, 380, 000			1	250, 000
Illinois	12	2, 900, 000	12	3, 150, 000		250, 000		
Chicago	18	15, 050, 000	19	15, 250, 000	1	200, 000		
Michigan	12	3, 800, 000	13	4, 000, 000	1	200, 000		
Detroit	8	3, 883, 540	8	4, 000, 000		116, 460		
Wisconsin	4	850, 000	4	850, 000				
Milwaukee	3	650, 000	3	850, 000		200, 000		
Division No. 5	139	59, 117, 540	142	59, 969, 600	6	2, 652, 060	3	1, 800, 000
Iowa	6	1, 700, 000	6	1, 600, 000				100, 000
Minnesota	19	11, 025, 000	18	11, 375, 000		350, 000	1	
Missouri	1	200, 000	1	200, 000				
Saint Louis	5	3, 000, 000	4	3, 200, 000		200, 000	1	
Kansas City	7	5, 800, 000	10	6, 600, 000	3	800, 000		
Saint Joseph	1	200, 000	1	200, 000				
Kansas	8	2, 000, 000	9	2, 600, 000	1	600, 000		
Nebraska	2	500, 000	2	500, 000				
Omaha	6	2, 200, 000	6	2, 950, 000		750, 000		
Division No. 6	55	26, 625, 000	57	29, 225, 000	4	2, 700, 000	2	100, 000

TABLE BY STATES, TERRITORIES, AND RESERVE CITIES EXHIBITING THE NUMBER OF BANKS IN EACH, WITH CAPITAL, ETC.—Continued.

States, Territories, and reserved cities.	October 5, 1887.		October 4, 1888.		Increase.		Decrease.	
	No.	Capital.	No.	Capital.	No.	Capital.	No.	Capital.
Colorado	5	$1,100,000	7	$1,700,000	2	$600,000		
Nevada			1	200,000	1	200,000		
California	9	2,410,000	11	3,250,000	2	810,000		
San Francisco	3	2,700,000	3	2,700,000				
Oregon	2	500,000	3	950,000	1	450,000		
Arizona								
Division No. 7	19	6,710,000	25	8,800,000	6	2,000,000		
Dakota								
Idaho								
Montana	2	750,000	2	750,000				
New Mexico								
Utah	2	400,000	2	400,000				
Washington			1	200,000	1	200,000		
Wyoming	2	600,000	2	600,000				
Division No. 8	6	1,750,000	7	1,950,000	1	200,000		
United States	899	399,813,375	911	407,069,735	23	10,736,360	11	$3,480,000

NATIONAL BANKS THAT HAVE GONE INTO VOLUNTARY LIQUIDATION UNDER THE PROVISIONS OF SECTIONS 5220 AND 5221 OF THE REVISED STATUTES OF THE UNITED STATES, WITH THE DATES OF LIQUIDATION, THE AMOUNT OF THEIR CAPITAL, CIRCULATION ISSUED AND RETIRED, AND CIRCULATION OUTSTANDING, OCTOBER 31, 1888.

Name and location of bank.	Date of liquidation	Capital.	Circulation.		
			Issued.	Retired.	Outstanding.
First National Bank, Penn Yan, N. Y.*	Apr. 6, 1864	....	....	....	....
First National Bank, Norwich, Conn*	May 2, 1864	....	....	....	....
Second National Bank, Ottumwa, Iowa†	May 2, 1864	....	....	....	....
Second National Bank, Canton, Ohio†	Oct. 3, 1864	....	....	....	....
First National Bank, Lansing, Mich.†	Dec. 5, 1864	....	....	....	....
First National Bank, Columbia, Mo.	Sept. 19, 1864	$100,000	$90,000	$89,875	$125
First National Bank, Carondelet, Mo.	Mar. 15, 1865	30,000	25,500	25,389	111
First National Bank, Utica, N. Y.*	June 9, 1865	....	....	....	....
Pittston National Bank, Pittston, Pa.	Sept. 16, 1865	200,000	....	....	....
Fourth National Bank, Indianapolis, Ind.	Nov. 30, 1865	100,000	100,000	99,220	780
Berkshire National Bank, Adams, Mass.‡	Dec. 8, 1865	100,000	....	....	....
National Union Bank, Rochester, N. Y.	Apr. 26, 1866	400,000	192,500	191,363	1,137
First National Bank, Leonardsville, N. Y.	July 11, 1866	50,000	45,000	44,385	615
Farmers' National Bank, Richmond, Va.	Oct. 22, 1866	100,000	85,000	83,228	1,772
Farmers' National Bank, Waukesha, Wis.	Nov. 25, 1866	100,000	90,000	89,520	480
National Bank of Metropolis, Washington, D. C	Nov. 28, 1866	200,000	180,000	176,875	3,125
First National Bank, Providence, Pa.	Mar. 1, 1867	100,000	90,000	88,665	1,335
National State Bank, Dubuque, Iowa	Mar. 9, 1867	150,000	127,000	125,605	1,395
First National Bank of Newton, Newtonville, Mass	Mar. 11, 1867	150,000	130,000	128,646	1,354
First National Bank, New Ulm, Minn	Apr. 18, 1867	60,000	54,000	53,155	845
National Bank of Crawford County, Meadville, Pa	Apr. 19, 1867	300,000	....	....	....
Kittanning National Bank, Kittanning, Pa†	Apr. 29, 1867	200,000	....	....	....
City National Bank, Savannah, Ga†	May 28, 1867	100,000	....	....	....
Ohio National Bank, Cincinnati, Ohio	July 3, 1867	500,000	450,000	443,690	6,310
First National Bank, Kingston, N. Y.	Sept. 26, 1867	200,000	180,000	177,604	2,396
First National Bank, Bluffton, Ind	Dec. 5, 1867	50,000	45,000	44,564	436
National Exchange Bank, Richmond, Va.	Dec. 5, 1867	200,000	180,000	179,135	865
First National Bank, Skaneateles, N. Y.	Dec. 21, 1867	150,000	135,000	133,601	1,399
First National Bank, Jackson, Miss	Dec. 26, 1867	100,000	45,000	45,320	180
First National Bank, Downington, Pa.	Jan. 14, 1868	100,000	90,000	88,911	1,089
First National Bank, Titusville, Pa	Jan. 15, 1868	100,000	86,750	85,724	1,026
Appleton National Bank, Appleton, Wis.	Jan. 21, 1868	50,000	45,000	44,362	638
National Bank of Whitestown, N. Y.	Feb. 14, 1868	120,000	45,500	45,213	287
First National Bank, New Brunswick, N. J	Feb. 26, 1868	100,000	90,000	88,609	1,391
First National Bank, Cuyahoga Falls, Ohio	Mar. 4, 1868	50,000	45,000	44,421	579
First National Bank, Cedarburg, Wis	Mar. 23, 1868	100,000	90,000	89,437	563
Commercial National Bank, Cincinnati, Ohio	Apr. 28, 1868	500,000	345,950	343,365	2,585
Second National Bank, Watertown, N. Y.	July 21, 1868	100,000	90,000	88,800	1,200
First National Bank, South Worcester, N. Y	Aug. 4, 1868	175,500	157,400	155,731	1,669
National Mechanics and Farmers' Bank, Albany, N. Y	Aug. 4, 1868	350,000	314,950	312,890	2,060
Second National Bank, Des Moines, Iowa	Aug. 5, 1868	50,000	42,500	42,132	368
First National Bank, Steubenville, Ohio.	Aug. 8, 1868	150,000	135,000	132,982	2,018
First National Bank, Plumer, Pa	Aug. 25, 1868	100,000	87,500	86,047	1,453
First National Bank, Danville, Va.	Sept. 30, 1868	50,000	45,000	44,615	385
First National Bank, Dorchester, Mass.	Nov. 23, 1868	150,000	132,500	130,384	2,116
First National Bank, Oskaloosa, Iowa	Dec. 17, 1868	75,000	67,500	66,960	540
Merchants and Mechanics' National Bank, Troy, N. Y.	Dec. 31, 1868	300,000	184,750	183,030	1,720
National Savings Bank, Wheeling, W. Va	Jan. 7, 1869	100,000	90,000	89,320	680
First National Bank, Marion, Ohio	Jan. 12, 1869	125,000	109,850	108,864	986
National Insurance Bank, Detroit, Mich	Feb. 26, 1869	200,010	85,000	84,423	577
National Bank of Lansingburg, N. Y.	Mar. 6, 1869	150,000	135,000	133,620	1,380
National Bank of North America, New York, N. Y	Apr. 15, 1869	1,000,000	333,000	330,530	2,470
First National Bank, Hallowell, Me.	Apr. 19, 1869	60,000	53,350	52,857	493
First National Bank, Clyde, N. Y.	Apr. 23, 1869	50,000	44,000	43,240	760
Pacific National Bank, New York, N. Y	May 10, 1869	422,700	134,900	134,012	948
Grocers' National Bank, New York, N. Y	June 7, 1869	300,000	85,250	84,866	384
Savannah National Bank, Savannah, Ga	June 22, 1869	100,000	85,000	84,395	605
First National Bank, Frostburg, Md.	July 30, 1869	50,000	45,000	44,732	268
First National Bank, La Salle, Ill.	Aug. 30, 1869	50,000	45,000	44,475	525

* New bank, with same title. † Never completed organization. ‡ Consolidated with another bank.

NATIONAL BANKS THAT HAVE GONE INTO VOLUNTARY LIQUIDATION UNDER THE PROVISIONS OF SECTIONS 5220 AND 5221 OF THE REVISED STATUTES, ETC.—Continued.

Name and location of bank.	Date of liquidation.	Capital.	Circulation.		
			Issued.	Retired.	Outstanding.
National Bank of Commerce, Georgetown, D. C	Oct. 28, 1869	$100,000	$90,000	$89,025	$975
Miners' National Bank, Salt Lake City, Utah	Dec. 2, 1869	150,000	135,000	133,842	1,158
First National Bank, Vinton, Iowa	Dec. 13, 1869	50,000	42,500	42,283	217
National Exchange Bank, Philadelphia, Pa	Jan. 8, 1870	300,000	175,750	173,519	2,231
First National Bank, Decatur, Ill	Jan. 10, 1870	100,000	85,250	84,184	1,066
National Union Bank, Owego, N. Y	Jan. 11, 1870	100,000	88,250	87,170	1,080
First National Bank, Berlin, Wis	Jan. 25, 1870	500,000	44,000	43,611	389
Central National Bank, Cincinnati, Ohio	Mar. 31, 1870	500,000	425,000	420,865	4,135
First National Bank, Dayton, Ohio	Apr. 9, 1870	150,000	135,000	133,752	1,248
National Bank of Chemung, Elmira, N. Y	June 10, 1870	100,000	90,000	89,448	552
Merchants' National Bank, Milwaukee, Wis	June 14, 1870	100,000	90,000	89,230	770
First National Bank, Saint Louis, Mo	July 16, 1870	200,000	179,990	178,543	1,447
Chemung Canal National Bank, Elmira, N. Y	Aug. 3, 1870	100,000	90,000	89,095	905
Central National Bank, Omaha, Nebr.*	Sept. 23, 1870	100,000	....	....	....
First National Bank, Clarksville, Va	Oct. 13, 1870	50,000	27,000	26,880	120
First National Bank, Burlington, Vt	Oct. 15, 1870	300,000	270,000	266,573	3,427
First National Bank, Lebanon, Ohio	Oct. 24, 1870	100,000	85,000	84,248	752
National Exchange Bank, Lansingburg, N. Y	Dec. 27, 1870	100,000	90,000	89,336	664
Muskingum National Bank, Zanesville, Ohio	Jan. 7, 1871	100,000	90,000	89,165	835
United National Bank, Winona, Minn	Feb. 15, 1871	50,000	45,000	44,540	460
First National Bank, Des Moines, Iowa	Mar. 25, 1871	100,000	90,000	89,198	802
Saratoga County National Bank, Waterford, N. Y	Mar. 28, 1871	150,000	135,000	133,913	1,087
State National Bank, Saint Joseph, Mo	Mar. 31, 1871	100,000	90,000	89,439	561
First National Bank, Fenton, Mich	May 2, 1871	100,000	49,500	48,998	502
First National Bank, Wellsburgh, W. Va	June 24, 1871	100,000	90,000	89,163	837
Clarke National Bank, Rochester, N. Y	Aug. 11, 1871	200,000	180,000	178,107	1,893
Commercial National Bank, Oshkosh, Wis	Nov. 22, 1871	100,000	90,000	89,188	812
Fort Madison National Bank, Fort Madison, Iowa	Dec. 26, 1871	75,000	67,500	66,940	560
National Bank of Maysville, Ky	Jan. 6, 1872	300,000	270,000	268,382	1,618
Fourth National Bank, Syracuse, N. Y	Jan. 9, 1872	105,500	91,700	90,738	962
American National Bank, New York, N. Y	May 10, 1872	500,000	450,000	443,450	6,550
Carroll County National Bank, Sandwich, N. H	May 24, 1872	0,000	45,000	44,373	627
Second National Bank, Portland, Me	June 24, 1872	100,000	81,000	79,749	1,251
Atlantic National Bank, Brooklyn, N. Y	July 15, 1872	200,000	165,000	163,420	1,580
Merchants and Farmers' National Bank, Quincy, Ill	Aug. 8, 1872	150,000	135,000	133,565	1,435
First National Bank, Rochester, N. Y	Aug. 9, 1872	400,000	206,100	203,629	2,471
Lawrenceburg National Bank, Indiana	Sept. 10, 1872	200,000	180,000	177,578	2,422
Jewett City National Bank, Jewett City, Conn	Oct. 4, 1872	60,000	48,750	48,152	598
First National Bank, Knoxville, Tenn	Oct. 22, 1872	100,000	80,910	79,974	936
First National Bank, Goshen, Ind	Nov. 7, 1872	115,000	103,500	102,136	1,364
Kidder National Gold Bank, Boston, Mass	Nov. 8, 1872	300,000	120,000	120,000	....
Second National Bank, Zanesville, Ohio	Nov. 16, 1872	154,700	138,140	136,318	1,822
Orange County National Bank, Chelsea, Vt	Jan. 14, 1873	200,000	180,000	177,206	2,794
Second National Bank, Syracuse, N. Y	Feb. 18, 1873	100,000	90,000	88,755	1,245
Richmond National Bank, Richmond, Ind.*	Feb. 28, 1873	230,000	207,000	207,000	....
First National Bank, Adams, N. Y	Mar. 7, 1873	75,000	66,900	65,920	980
Mechanics' National Bank, Syracuse, N. Y	Mar. 11, 1873	140,000	93,800	92,730	1,070
Farmers and Mechanics' National Bank, Rochester, N. Y	Apr. 15, 1873	100,000	83,250	82,179	1,071
Montana National Bank, Helena, Mont	Apr. 15, 1873	100,000	31,500	31,365	135
First National Bank, Havana, N. Y	June 3, 1873	50,000	45,000	44,285	715
Merchants and Farmers' National Bank, Ithaca, N. Y	June 30, 1873	50,000	45,000	44,215	785
National Bank of Cazenovia, N. Y	July 18, 1873	150,000	116,770	115,169	1,601
Merchants' National Bank, Memphis, Tenn	Aug. 30, 1873	250,000	225,000	222,053	2,947

*New bank, with same title.

NATIONAL BANKS THAT HAVE GONE INTO VOLUNTARY LIQUIDATION UNDER THE PROVISIONS OF SECTIONS 5220 AND 5221 OF THE REVISED STATUTES, ETC.—Continued.

Name and location of bank.	Date of liquidation.	Capital.	Circulation.		
			Issued.	Retired.	Outstanding.
Manufacturers' National Bank, Chicago, Ill	Sept. 25, 1873	$500,000	$438,750	$432,622	$6,128
Second National Bank, Chicago, Ill	Sept. 25, 1873	100,000	97,500	95,891	1,609
Merchants' National Bank, Dubuque, Iowa	Sept. 30, 1873	200,000	180,000	175,546	4,454
Beloit National Bank, Beloit, Wis	Oct. 2, 1873	50,000	45,000	44,256	744
Union National Bank, Saint Louis, Mo	Oct. 22, 1873	500,000	150,300	148,163	2,137
City National Bank, Green Bay, Wis	Nov. 20, 1873	50,000	45,000	44,110	890
First National Bank, Shelbina, Mo	Jan. 1, 1874	100,000	90,000	89,085	915
Second National Bank, Nashville, Tenn	Jan. 8, 1874	125,000	92,920	91,335	1,585
First National Bank, Oneida, N. Y	Jan. 13, 1874	125,000	110,500	108,700	1,800
Merchants' National Bank, Hastings, Minn	Feb. 7, 1874	100,000	90,000	88,235	1,765
National Bank of Tecumseh, Mich	Mar. 3, 1874	50,000	45,000	44,230	770
Gallatin National Bank, Shawneetown, Ill	Mar. 7, 1874	250,000	225,000	222,318	2,682
First National Bank, Brookville, Pa	Mar. 26, 1874	100,000	90,000	88,605	1,395
Citizens' National Bank, Sioux City, Iowa	Apr. 14, 1874	50,000	45,000	44,740	260
Citizens' National Bank, Charlottesville, Va	Apr. 27, 1874	100,000	90,000	88,899	1,101
Farmers' National Bank, Warren, Ill	Apr. 28, 1874	50,000	45,000	44,301	699
First National Bank, Medina, Ohio	May 6, 1874	75,000	45,000	44,036	964
Croton River National Bank, South East, N. Y	May 25, 1874	200,000	166,550	163,401	3,149
Merchants' National Bank of West Virginia, Wheeling, W. Va	July 7, 1874	500,000	450,000	443,712	6,288
Central National Bank, Baltimore, Md	July 15, 1874	200,000	180,000	178,351	1,649
Second National Bank, Leavenworth, Kans	July 22, 1874	100,000	90,000	87,666	2,334
Teutonia National Bank, New Orleans, La	Sept. 2, 1874	300,000	270,000	266,600	3,400
City National Bank, Chattanooga, Tenn	Sept. 10, 1874	170,000	148,001	146,379	1,622
First National Bank, Cairo, Ill	Oct. 10, 1874	100,000	90,000	88,370	1,630
First National Bank, Olathe, Kans	Nov. 9, 1874	50,000	45,000	44,564	436
First National Bank, Beverly, Ohio	Nov. 10, 1874	102,000	90,000	88,223	1,777
Union National Bank, La Fayette, Ind	Dec. 4, 1874	250,000	224,095	219,674	4,421
Ambler National Bank, Jacksonville, Fla.*	Dec. 7, 1874	42,500	....	....	....
Mechanics' National Bank, Chicago, Ill	Dec. 30, 1874	250,000	125,900	123,310	2,590
First National Bank, Evansville, Wis	Jan. 9, 1875	55,000	45,000	44,474	526
First National Bank, Baxter Springs, Kans	Jan. 12, 1875	50,000	36,000	35,585	415
People's National Bank, Pueblo, Colo	Jan. 12, 1875	50,000	27,000	26,793	207
National Bank of Commerce, Green Bay, Wis	Jan. 12, 1875	100,000	90,000	88,995	1,005
First National Bank, Millersburg, Ohio	Jan. 12, 1875	100,000	60,400	59,810	590
First National Bank, Staunton, Va	Jan. 22, 1875	100,000	90,000	88,777	1,223
National City Bank, Milwaukee, Wis	Feb. 24, 1875	100,000	60,000	58,825	1,175
Irasburg National Bank of Orleans, Irasburgh, Vt	Mar. 17, 1875	75,000	67,500	66,254	1,246
First National Bank, Pekin, Ill	Mar. 25, 1875	100,000	90,000	88,384	1,616
Merchants and Planters' National Bank, Augusta, Ga	Mar. 30, 1875	200,000	160,000	160,260	2,740
Monticello National Bank, Monticello, Iowa	Mar. 30, 1875	100,000	45,000	44,384	616
Iowa City National Bank, Iowa City, Iowa	Apr. 14, 1875	125,000	104,800	102,962	1,838
First National Bank, Wheeling, W. Va	Apr. 22, 1875	250,000	225,000	220,315	4,685
First National Bank, Mount Clemens, Mich	May 20, 1875	50,000	27,000	26,850	150
First National Bank, Knob Noster, Mo	May 29, 1875	50,000	43,800	43,383	417
First National Bank, Brodhead, Wis	June 24, 1875	50,000	45,000	44,372	628
Auburn City National Bank, Auburn, N. Y	June 26, 1875	200,000	141,300	138,467	2,833
First National Bank, El Dorado, Kans	June 30, 1875	50,000	45,000	44,452	548
First National Bank, Junction City, Kans	July 1, 1875	50,000	45,000	44,645	355
First National Bank, Chetopa, Kans	July 10, 1875	50,000	36,000	35,612	388
First National Bank, Golden, Colo	Aug. 25, 1875	50,200	27,000	26,788	212
National Bank of Jefferson, Wis	Aug. 26, 1875	60,000	54,000	52,807	1,193
Green Lane National Bank, Green Lane, Pa	Sept. 9, 1875	100,000	90,000	89,419	581
State National Bank, Topeka, Kans	Sept. 15, 1875	60,500	30,000	30,417	183

*No circulation.

NATIONAL BANKS THAT HAVE GONE INTO VOLUNTARY LIQUIDATION UNDER THE PROVISIONS OF SECTIONS 5220 AND 5221 OF THE REVISED STATUTES, ETC.—Continued.

Name and location of bank.	Date of liquidation.	Capital.	Circulation.		
			Issued.	Retired.	Outstanding.
Farmers' National Bank, Marshalltown, Iowa	Sept. 18, 1875	$50, 000	$27, 000	$26, 775	$225
Richland National Bank, Mansfield, Ohio	Sept. 25, 1875	150, 000	130, 300	127, 119	3, 181
Planters' National Bank, Louisville, Ky	Sept. 30, 1875	350, 000	315, 000	306, 755	8, 245
First National Bank, Gallatin, Tenn	Oct. 1, 1875	75, 000	45, 000	44, 490	510
First National Bank, Charlestown, W. Va	Oct. 2, 1875	100, 000	90, 000	88, 926	1, 074
People's National Bank, Winchester, Ill	Oct. 4, 1875	75, 000	67, 500	66, 628	872
First National Bank, New Lexington, Ohio	Oct. 12, 1875	50, 000	45, 000	44, 525	475
First National Bank, Ishpeming, Mich	Oct. 20, 1875	50, 000	45, 000	44, 087	913
Fayette County National Bank, Washington, Ohio	Oct. 26, 1875	100, 000	81, 280	80, 146	1, 134
Merchants' National Bank, Fort Wayne, Ind	Nov. 8, 1875	100, 000	46, 820	46, 055	765
Kansas City National Bank, Kansas City, Mo	Nov. 13, 1875	100, 000	65, 901	63, 796	1, 105
First National Bank, Schoolcraft, Mich	Nov. 17, 1875	50, 000	45, 000	43, 362	638
First National Bank, Curwensville, Pa	Dec. 17, 1875	100, 000	90, 000	87, 898	2, 102
National Marine Bank, Saint Paul, Minn	Dec. 28, 1875	100, 000	59, 710	58, 045	1, 665
First National Bank, Rochester, Ind	Jan. 11, 1876	50, 000	45, 000	43, 967	2, 033
First National Bank, Lodi, Ohio	Jan. 11, 1876	100, 000	90, 000	87, 867	2, 133
Iron National Bank, Portsmouth, Ohio	Jan. 19, 1876	100, 000	90, 000	88, 857	1, 143
First National Bank, Ashland, Nebr	Jan. 26, 1876	50, 000	45, 000	44, 495	505
First National Bank, Paxton, Ill	Jan. 28, 1876	50, 000	45, 000	44, 051	949
First National Bank, Bloomfield, Iowa	Feb. 5, 1876	50, 000	49, 500	48, 320	1, 180
Marietta National Bank, Marietta, Ohio	Feb. 16, 1876	150, 000	90, 000	87, 572	2, 428
Salt Lake City National Bank, Salt Lake City, Utah	Feb. 21, 1876	100, 000	45, 000	43, 958	1, 042
First National Bank, La Grange, Mo	Feb. 24, 1876	50, 000	45, 000	44, 324	676
First National Bank, Atlantic, Iowa	Mar. 7, 1876	50, 000	45, 000	44, 336	664
First National Bank, Spencer, Ind	Mar. 11, 1876	70, 000	63, 000	62, 272	728
National Currency Bank, New York, N. Y	Mar. 23, 1876	100, 000	45, 000	43, 610	1, 390
Caverna National Bank, Caverna, Ky	May 13, 1876	50, 000	45, 000	44, 505	495
City National Bank, Pittsburgh, Pa	May 25, 1876	200, 000	68, 929	66, 547	1, 382
National State Bank, Des Moines, Iowa	June 21, 1876	100, 000	50, 795	48, 988	1, 807
First National Bank, Trenton, Mo	June 22, 1876	50, 000	45, 000	44, 376	624
First National Bank, Bristol, Tenn	July 10, 1876	50, 000	45, 000	44, 530	470
First National Bank, Leon, Iowa	July 11, 1876	60, 000	45, 000	43, 818	1, 182
Anderson County National Bank, Lawrenceburgh, Ky	July 20, 1876	100, 000	45, 000	44, 560	440
First National Bank, Newport, Ind	Aug. 7, 1876	60, 000	45, 000	43, 798	1, 202
First National Bank, De Pere, Wis	Aug. 17, 1876	50, 000	31, 500	31, 174	326
Second National Bank, Lawrence, Kans	Aug. 23, 1876	100, 000	67, 500	66, 415	1, 085
Commercial National Bank, Versailles, Ky	Aug. 26, 1876	170, 000	153, 000	149, 855	3, 145
State National Bank, Atlanta, Ga	Aug. 31, 1876	200, 000	73, 725	71, 500	2, 225
Syracuse National Bank, Syracuse, N. Y	Sept. 25, 1876	200, 000	117, 961	113, 150	4, 811
First National Bank, Northumberland, Pa	Oct. 6, 1876	100, 000	62, 106	59, 783	2, 323
First National Bank, Lancaster, Mo	Nov. 14, 1876	50, 000	27, 000	26, 777	223
First National Bank, Council Grove, Kans	Nov. 28, 1876	50, 000	26, 500	26, 077	423
National Bank Commerce, Chicago, Ill	Dec. 2, 1876	250, 000	71, 465	69, 746	1, 719
First National Bank, Palmyra, Mo	Dec. 12, 1876	100, 000	46, 140	44, 630	1, 510
First National Bank, Newton, Iowa	Dec. 16, 1876	50, 000	45, 000	43, 299	1, 701
National Southern Kentucky Bank, Bowling Green, Ky	Dec. 23, 1876	50, 000	27, 000	26, 649	351
First National Bank, Monroe, Iowa	Jan. 1, 1877	60, 000	35, 700	35, 115	585
First National Bank, New London, Conn	Jan. 9, 1877	100, 000	38, 300	36, 161	2, 139
Winona Deposit National Bank, Winona, Minn	Jan. 28, 1877	100, 000	63, 285	63, 232	2, 053
First National Bank, South Charleston, Ohio	Feb. 24, 1877	100, 000	90, 000	87, 413	2, 587
Lake Ontario National Bank, Oswego, N. Y	Feb. 24, 1877	275, 000	66, 405	61, 868	4, 537
First National Bank, Sidney, Ohio	Feb. 26, 1877	52, 000	46, 200	44, 917	1, 283
Chillicothe National Bank, Ohio	Apr. 9, 1877	100, 000	53, 825	51, 555	2, 270
First National Bank, Manhattan, Kans	Apr. 13, 1877	52, 000	44, 200	43, 439	761
National Bank, Monticello, Ky	Apr. 23, 1877	60, 000	49, 500	47, 460	2, 040
First National Bank, Rockville, Ind	Apr. 25, 1877	200, 000	173, 000	168, 000	5, 000
Georgia National Bank, Atlanta, Ga	May 31, 1857	100, 000	45, 000	43, 374	1, 626
First National Bank, Adrian, Mich	June 11, 1877	100, 000	43, 500	42, 336	1, 164

NATIONAL BANKS THAT HAVE GONE INTO VOLUNTARY LIQUIDATION UNDER THE PROVISIONS OF SECTIONS 5220 AND 5221 OF THE REVISED STATUTES, ETC.—Continued.

Name and location of bank.	Date of liquidation.	Capital.	Circulation.		
			Issued.	Retired.	Outstanding.
First National Bank, Napoleon, Ohio	June 30, 1877	$50,000	$45,000	$43,804	$1,196
First National Bank, Lancaster, Ohio	Aug. 1, 1887	60,000	54,000	52,021	1,979
First National Bank, Minerva, Ohio	Aug. 24, 1877	50,000	45,000	44,107	893
Kinney National Bank, Portsmouth, Ohio	Aug. 28, 1877	100,000	90,000	88,235	1,765
First National Bank, Green Bay, Wis	Oct. 10, 1877	50,000	45,000	43,565	1,435
National Exchange Bank, Wakefield, R. I	Oct. 27, 1877	70,000	34,050	32,987	1,063
First National Bank, Union City, Ind	Nov. 10, 1877	50,000	45,000	43,565	1,435
First National Bank, Negaunee, Mich	Nov. 13, 1877	50,000	45,000	43,901	1,099
Tenth National Bank, New York, N. Y	Nov. 23, 1877	500,000	441,000	416,187	24,813
First National Bank, Paola, Kans	Dec. 1, 1877	50,000	44,350	43,223	1,127
National Exchange Bank, Troy, N. Y	Dec. 6, 1877	100,000	90,000	86,808	3,192
Second National Bank, La Fayette, Ind	Dec. 20, 1877	200,000	52,167	47,694	4,473
State National Bank, Minneapolis, Minn	Dec. 31, 1877	100,000	82,500	79,165	3,335
Second National Bank, Saint Louis, Mo	Jan. 8, 1878	200,000	53,055	47,913	5,142
First National Bank, Sullivan, Ind	Jan. 8, 1878	50,000	45,000	44,145	855
Rockland County National Bank, Nyack, N. Y	Jan. 10, 1878	100,000	89,000	86,106	2,894
First National Bank, Wyandotte, Kans	Jan. 19, 1878	50,000	45,000	44,095	905
First National Bank, Boone, Iowa	Jan. 22, 1878	50,000	32,400	31,355	1,045
First National Bank, Pleasant Hill, Mo	Feb. 7, 1878	50,000	45,000	43,854	1,146
National Bank of Gloversville, N. Y	Feb. 28, 1878	100,000	64,730	62,742	2,008
First National Bank, Independence, Mo	Mar. 1, 1878	50,000	27,000	25,051	1,949
National State Bank, Lima, Ind	Mar. 2, 1878	100,000	33,471	31,732	1,739
First National Bank, Tell City, Ind	Mar. 4, 1878	50,000	44,500	43,770	730
First National Bank, Pomeroy, Ohio	Mar. 5, 1878	200,000	75,713	70,932	4,781
Eleventh Ward National Bank, Boston, Mass	Mar. 14, 1878	200,000	89,400	86,995	2,405
First National Bank, Prophetstown, Ill	Mar. 19, 1878	50,000	45,000	44,369	631
First National Bank, Jackson, Mich	Mar. 26, 1878	100,000	88,400	85,055	3,345
First National Bank, Eau Claire, Wis	Mar. 30, 1878	60,000	38,461	37,427	1,034
First National Bank, Washington, Ohio	Apr. 5, 1878	200,000	69,750	65,825	3,925
First National Bank, Middleport, Ohio	Apr. 20, 1878	80,000	31,500	30,925	575
First National Bank, Streator, Ill	Apr. 24, 1878	50,000	40,500	39,865	635
First National Bank, Muir, Mich	Apr. 25, 1878	50,000	44,200	43,309	891
Kane County National Bank, Saint Charles, Ill	May 31, 1878	50,000	26,300	25,568	732
First National Bank, Carthage, Mo	June 1, 1878	50,000	44,500	43,550	950
Security National Bank, Worcester, Mass	June 5, 1878	100,000	49,000	47,480	1,520
First National Bank, Lake City, Colo	June 15, 1878	50,000	29,300	28,994	306
People's National Bank, Norfolk, Va	July 31, 1878	100,000	85,705	81,115	4,590
Topeka National Bank, Topeka, Kans	Aug. 7, 1878	100,000	89,300	84,819	4,481
First National Bank, Saint Joseph, Mo	Aug. 13, 1878	100,000	67,110	62,801	4,309
First National Bank, Winchester, Ind	Aug. 24, 1878	60,000	52,700	49,915	2,785
Muscatine National Bank, Muscatine, Iowa	Sept. 2, 1878	100,000	44,200	40,756	3,444
Traders' National Bank, Chicago, Ill	Sept. 4, 1878	200,000	43,700	39,440	4,260
Union National Bank, Rahway, N. J	Sept. 10, 1878	100,000	89,200	85,007	4,193
First National Bank, Sparta, Wis	Sept. 14, 1878	50,000	45,000	43,261	1,739
Herkimer County National Bank, Little Falls, N. Y	Oct. 11, 1878	200,000	178,300	169,543	8,757
Farmers' National Bank, Bangor, Me	Nov. 22, 1878	100,000	89,100	84,602	4,498
Pacific National Bank, Council Bluffs, Iowa	Nov. 30, 1878	100,000	45,000	43,445	1,555
First National Bank, Anamosa, Iowa	Dec. 14, 1878	50,000	44,500	41,847	2,653
Smithfield National Bank, Pittsburgh, Pa	Dec. 16, 1878	200,000	78,750	73,450	5,300
First National Bank, Buchanan, Mich	Dec. 21, 1878	50,000	27,000	26,395	605
First National Bank, Prairie City, Ill	Dec. 24, 1878	50,000	27,000	24,570	2,430
Corn Exchange National Bank, Chicago, Ill	Jan. 4, 1879	500,000	59,160	52,504	6,656
Franklin National Bank, Columbus, Ohio	Jan. 4, 1879	100,000	93,070	87,953	5,117
Traders' National Bank, Bangor, Me	Jan. 14, 1879	100,000	76,400	70,987	5,413
First National Bank, Gonic, N. H	Jan. 14, 1879	60,000	45,597	43,058	2,539
First National Bank, Salem, N. C	Jan. 14, 1879	150,000	128,200	120,540	7,660
First National Bank, Granville, Ohio	Jan. 14, 1879	50,000	34,365	32,139	2,226
Commercial National Bank, Petersburgh, Va	Jan. 14, 1879	120,000	99,800	91,968	7,832
First National Gold Bank, Stockton, Cal	Jan. 14, 1879	300,000	238,600	218,716	19,884
First National Bank, Sheboygan, Wis	Jan. 14, 1879	50,000	45,000	43,775	1,225
First National Bank, Boscobel, Wis	Jan. 21, 1879	50,000	43,900	42,517	1,383
National Marine Bank, Oswego, N. Y	Jan. 25, 1879	120,000	44,300	41,489	2,811

NATIONAL BANKS THAT HAVE GONE INTO VOLUNTARY LIQUIDATION UNDER THE PROVISIONS OF SECTIONS 5220 AND 5221 OF THE REVISED STATUTES, ETC.—Continued.

Name and location of bank.	Date of liquidation.	Capital.	Circulation.		
			Issued.	Retired.	Outstanding.
Central National Bank, Hightstown, N. J.	Feb. 15, 1879	$100,000	$32,400	$31,520	$880
Brookville National Bank, Brookville, Ind	Feb. 18, 1879	100,000	89,000	83,735	5,265
Farmers' National Bank, Centreville, Iowa	Feb. 27, 1879	50,000	41,500	40,578	922
First National Bank, Clarinda, Iowa	Mar. 1, 1879	50,000	45,000	44,029	971
Waterville National Bank, Waterville, Me	Mar. 3, 1879	125,000	110,300	104,234	6,066
First National Bank, Tremont, Pa	Mar. 4, 1879	75,000	64,600	59,415	5,185
First National Bank, Atlanta, Ill	Apr. 15, 1879	50,000	26,500	25,040	1,460
Union National Bank, Aurora, Ill	Apr. 22, 1879	125,000	82,000	76,765	5,235
National Bank of Menasha, Wis	Apr. 26, 1879	50,000	44,500	43,134	1,366
National Exchange Bank, Jefferson City, Mo	May 8, 1879	50,000	45,000	42,761	2,239
First National Bank, Hannibal, Mo	May 15, 1879	100,000	88,200	82,096	6,104
Merchants' National Bank, Winona, Minn	June 10, 1879	100,000	35,000	34,033	967
Farmers' National Bank, Keithsburgh, Ill.	July 3, 1879	50,000	27,000	25,610	1,390
First National Bank, Franklin, Ky	July 5, 1879	100,000	54,000	51,040	2,960
National Bank of Salem, Salem, Ind	July 8, 1879	50,000	44,400	43,495	905
Fourth National Bank, Memphis Tenn.	July 10, 1879	125,000	45,000	41,870	3,130
Bedford National Bank, Bedford, Ind	July 21, 1879	100,000	87,200	84,777	2,423
First National Bank, Afton, Iowa	Aug. 15, 1879	50,000	26,500	25,294	1,206
First National Bank, Deer Lodge, Mont.	Aug. 16, 1879	50,000	45,000	43,710	1,290
First National Bank, Batavia, Ill	Aug. 30, 1879	50,000	44,300	41,908	2,392
National Gold Bank and Trust Company, San Francisco, Cal	Sept. 1, 1879	750,000	40,000	28,230	11,770
Gainesville National Bank, Gainesville, Ala	Nov. 25, 1879	100,000	90,000	83,435	6,565
First National Bank, Hackensack, N. J.	Dec. 6, 1879	100,000	90,000	85,122	4,878
National Bank of Delavan, Delavan, Wis.	Jan. 7, 1880	50,000	27,000	25,090	1,910
Mechanics' National Bank, Nashville, Tenn	Jan. 13, 1880	100,000	90,000	80,400	9,600
Manchester National Bank, Manchester, Ohio	Jan. 13, 1880	50,000	48,303	44,893	3,410
First National Bank, Meyersdale, Pa	Mar. 5, 1880	50,000	30,600	29,770	830
First National Bank, Mifflinburgh, Pa	Mar. 8, 1880	100,000	90,000	82,565	7,435
National Bank of Michigan, Marshall, Mich	May 14, 1880	120,000	100,800	94,407	6,393
National Exchange Bank, Houston, Tex.	Sept. 10, 1880	100,000	31,500	29,111	2,389
Ascutney National Bank, Windsor, Vt.	Oct. 19, 1880	100,000	90,000	83,634	6,366
First National Bank, Seneca Falls, N. Y.	Nov. 23, 1880	60,000	54,000	52,248	1,752
First National Bank, Baraboo, Wis	Nov. 27, 1880	50,000	27,000	25,821	1,179
Bundy National Bank, New Castle, Ind.	Dec. 6, 1880	50,000	45,000	44,159	841
Vineland National Bank, Vineland, N. J.	Jan. 11, 1881	50,000	45,000	43,943	1,057
Ocean County National Bank, Tom's River, N. J	Jan. 11, 1881	100,000	119,405	109,550	9,855
Hungerford National Bank, Adams, N. Y.	Jan. 27, 1881	50,000	45,000	40,537	4,463
Merchants' National Bank, Minneapolis, Minn	Jan. 31, 1881	150,000	98,268	95,305	2,963
Farmers' National Bank, Mechanicsburgh, Ohio	Feb. 18, 1881	100,000	30,140	28,775	1,365
First National Bank, Green Spring, Ohio.	Feb. 18, 1881	100,000	45,000	43,433	1,567
First National Bank, Cannon Falls, Minn.	Feb. 21, 1881	50,000	45,000	43,540	1,460
First National Bank, Coshocton, Ohio	Feb. 21, 1881	50,000	53,058	51,063	1,995
Manufacturers' National Bank, Three Rivers, Mich	Feb. 25, 1881	50,000	45,000	43,466	1,534
First National Bank, Lansing, Iowa	Feb. 25, 1881	50,000	45,000	42,987	2,013
First National Bank, Watertown, N. Y.	May 26, 1881	100,000	75,510	66,905	8,605
First National Bank, Americus, Ga	June 17, 1881	60,000	45,000	43,446	1,554
First National Bank, Saint Joseph, Mich.	June 30, 1881	50,000	26,500	25,066	1,434
First National Bank, Logan, Ohio	July 8, 1881	50,000	45,000	43,015	1,985
First National Bank, Rochelle, Ill	Aug. 9, 1881	50,000	45,000	43,099	1,901
First National Bank, Shakopee, Minn	Aug. 10, 1881	50,000	45,000	42,625	2,375
National State Bank, Oskaloosa, Iowa	Aug. 13, 1881	50,000	81,665	75,815	5,850
First National Bank, Hobart, N. Y	Aug. 27, 1881	100,000	90,000	82,856	7,144
Attica National Bank, Attica, N. Y	Aug. 30, 1881	50,000	45,000	42,890	2,110
National Bank of Brighton, Boston, Mass	Oct. 4, 1881	300,000	270,000	249,958	20,042
Clement National Bank, Rutland, Vt.*	Aug. 1, 1881	100,000	....	....	....
First National Bank, Lisbon, Iowa	Nov. 1, 1881	50,000	45,000	43,320	1,680
First National Bank, Warsaw, Ind	Dec. 1, 1881	50,000	48,500	46,250	2,250
Brighton National Bank, Brighton, Iowa.	Dec. 15, 1881	50,000	45,000	43,168	1,832
Merchants' National Bank, Denver, Colo.	Dec. 24, 1881	120,000	72,000	63,720	8,280
Merchants' National Bank, Holly, Mich.	Dec. 31, 1881	50,000	45,000	43,195	1,805
First National Bank, Alliance, Ohio	Jan. 3, 1882	50,000	45,000	41,878	3,122

*New bank, with same title.

NATIONAL BANKS THAT HAVE GONE INTO VOLUNTARY LIQUIDATION UNDER THE PROVISIONS OF SECTIONS 5220 AND 5221 OF THE REVISED STATUTES, ETC.—Continued.

Name and location of bank.	Date of liquidation.	Capital.	Circulation.		
			Issued.	Retired.	Outstanding.
National Union Bank, New London, Conn	Jan. 10, 1882	$300,000	$112,818	$100,526	$12,292
National Bank of Royalton, Vt	Jan. 10, 1882	100,000	90,000	81,489	8,511
First National Bank, Whitehall, N. Y	Jan. 18, 1882	50,000	45,000	40,341	4,659
National Bank of Pulaski, Tenn	Jan. 23, 1882	70,000	43,700	39,146	4,554
First National Bank, Alton, Ill	Mar. 30, 1882	100,000	90,000	82,794	7,206
Havana National Bank, Havana, N. Y	Apr. 15, 1882	50,000	45,000	42,231	2,769
First National Bank, Brownsville, Pa	May 2, 1882	75,000	67,500	59,670	7,830
Second National Bank, Franklin, Ind	June 20, 1882	100,000	81,060	70,540	10,520
Merchants' National Bank, Georgetown, Colo	June 22, 1882	50,000	45,000	43,183	1,817
Commercial National Bank, Toledo, Ohio	July 6, 1882	100,000	90,000	84,820	5,180
Harmony National Bank, Harmony, Pa	July 7, 1882	50,000	45,000	41,080	3,920
First National Bank, Liberty, Ind	July 22, 1882	60,000	54,000	50,317	3,683
Manufacturers' National Bank, Amsterdam, N. Y	Aug. 1, 1882	80,000	72,000	66,760	5,240
First National Bank, Bay City, Mich	Nov. 8, 1882	400,000	156,100	141,892	14,208
First National Bank, Ripley, Ohio	Nov. 10, 1882	100,000	69,201	59,578	9,623
National Bank of State of New York, New York, N. Y	Dec. 6, 1882	800,000	397,004	365,757	31,247
First National Bank, Wellington, Ohio	Dec. 12, 1882	100,000	90,000	83,141	6,859
Second National Bank, Jefferson, Ohio	Dec. 26, 1882	100,000	90,000	79,228	10,772
First National Bank, Painesville, Ohio	Dec. 30, 1882	200,000	162,800	143,037	19,763
Saint Nicholas National Bank, New York, N. Y	Dec. 30, 1882	500,000	450,000	396,970	53,030
Fifth National Bank, Chicago, Ill	Dec. 30, 1882	500,000	29,700	20,547	9,153
First National Bank, Dowagiac, Mich	Jan. 3, 1883	50,000	45,000	41,868	3,132
First National Bank, Greenville, Ill	Jan. 9, 1883*	150,000	59,400	50,693	8,707
Merchants' National Bank, East Saginaw, Mich	Jan. 9, 1883	200,000	101,100	89,716	11,384
Logan County National Bank, Russellville, Ky	Jan. 9, 1883	50,000	40,050	37,650	2,400
National Bank of Vandalia, Ill	Jan. 11, 1883	100,000	90,000	78,250	11,750
Traders' National Bank, Charlotte, N. C	Jan. 16, 1883	50,000	38,800	35,933	2,867
First National Bank, Norfolk, Nebr	Feb. 3, 1883	45,000	11,240	10,100	1,140
First National Bank, Midland City, Mich.*	Feb. 5, 1883	30,000	....	....	....
Citizens' National Bank, New Ulm, Minn	Mar. 1, 1883	50,000	27,000	23,560	3,440
National Bank of Owen, Owenton, Ky	Mar. 5, 1883	56,000	48,900	43,150	5,750
Merchants' National Bank, Nashville, Tenn	June 30, 1883	300,000	141,200	113,590	27,610
Indiana National Bank, Bedford, Ind	Aug. 25, 1883	35,000	11,250	11,250	....
Stockton National Bank, Stockton, Cal	Oct. 1, 1883	100,000	90,000	78,930	11,070
Wall Street National Bank, New York, N. Y	Oct. 15, 1883	500,000	102,800	87,036	15,764
Commercial National Bank, Reading, Pa	Oct. 23, 1883	150,000	135,000	112,530	22,470
Corn Exchange National Bank, Chicago, Ill.*	Nov. 10, 1883	700,000	....	....	....
Farmers' National Bank, Sullivan, Ind	Dec. 24, 1883	50,000	45,000	36,710	8,290
City National Bank, La Salle, Ill	Jan. 8, 1884	100,000	22,500	15,550	6,950
Hunt County National Bank, Greenville, Tex	Jan. 22, 1884	68,250	17,300	12,530	4,770
Waldoboro' National Bank, Waldoboro', Me	Jan. 31, 1884	50,000	44,000	36,530	7,470
Third National Bank, Nashville, Tenn	Feb. 20, 1884	300,000	167,600	142,125	25,475
Madison County National Bank, Anderson, Ind	Mar. 25, 1884	50,000	45,000	39,770	5,230
First National Bank, Phœnix, Ariz	Apr. 7, 1884	50,000	11,240	9,700	1,540
Cobbossee National Bank, Gardiner, Me	Apr. 18, 1884	150,000	90,000	73,212	16,788
Mechanics and Traders' National Bank, New York, N. Y	Apr. 21, 1884	200,000	85,400	68,820	16,580
Princeton National Bank, Princeton, N. J	May 17, 1884	100,000	72,500	63,865	8,635
Kearsarge National Bank, Warner, N. H	June 30, 1884	50,000	23,586	20,914	2,672
Second National Bank, Lansing, Mich	July 31, 1884	50,000	40,000	30,561	9,439
First National Bank, Ellensburg, Wash	Aug. 9, 1884	50,000	13,500	10,670	2,830
German National Bank, Millerstown, Pa	Aug. 12, 1884	50,000	45,000	32,755	12,245
Exchange National Bank, Cincinnati, Ohio	Aug. 27, 1884	500,000	78,000	56,080	21,920
First National Bank, Rushville, Ill	Sept. 30, 1884	75,000	66,500	47,245	19,255
Mechanics' National Bank, Peoria, Ill	Oct. 4, 1884	100,000	72,000	52,538	19,462
First National Bank, Freeport, Pa	Oct. 10, 1884	50,000	44,200	32,020	12,180
Genesee County National Bank, Batavia, N. Y	Oct. 11, 1884	50,000	45,000	37,790	7,210

NATIONAL BANKS THAT HAVE GONE INTO VOLUNTARY LIQUIDATION UNDER THE PROVISIONS OF SECTIONS 5220 AND 5221 OF THE REVISED STATUTES, ETC.—Continued.

Name and location of bank.	Date of liquidation.	Capital.	Circulation.		
			Issued.	Retired.	Outstanding.
Valley National Bank, Red Oak, Iowa	Oct. 20, 1884	$50,000	$22,150	$16,840	$5,310
Merchants' National Bank, Bismarck, Dak	Oct. 28, 1884	73,000	22,500	17,900	4,600
Manufacturers' National Bank, Minneapolis, Minn	Nov. 1, 1884	300,000	45,000	31,460	13,540
Farmers and Merchants' National Bank, Uhrichsville, Ohio	Nov. 10, 1884	50,000	34,600	25,120	9,480
Metropolitan National Bank, New York, N. Y	Nov. 18, 1884	3,000,000	1,447,000	1,100,520	346,480
First National Bank, Grand Forks, Dak	Dec. 2, 1884	50,000	19,250	17,070	2,180
Iron National Bank, Gunnison, Colo	Dec. 8, 1884	50,000	11,250	8,550	2,700
Freehold National Banking Company, Freehold, N. J	Dec. 10, 1884	50,000	93,000	74,822	18,178
Albia National Bank, Albia, Iowa	Dec. 16, 1884	50,000	11,240	9,350	1,890
First National Bank, Carlinville, Ill	Dec. 16, 1884	50,000	22,450	18,592	3,858
Freeman's National Bank, Augusta, Me	Dec. 26, 1884	100,000	90,000	68,235	21,765
First National Bank, Kokomo, Ind	Jan. 1, 1885	250,000	45,000	34,820	10,180
First National Bank, Sabetha, Kans	Jan. 2, 1885	50,000	10,740	8,580	2,160
First National Bank, Wyoming, Ill	Jan. 13, 1885	50,000	11,200	7,500	3,700
First National Bank, Tarentum, Pa	Jan. 13, 1885	50,000	42,500	30,450	12,050
First National Bank, Walnut, Ill	Jan. 21, 1885	60,000	36,000	25,440	10,560
Farmers' National Bank, Franklin, Tenn	Jan. 24, 1885	50,000	10,740	8,240	2,500
Citizens' National Bank, Sabetha, Kans	Jan. 27, 1885	50,000	11,240	8,740	2,500
First National Bank, Tucson, Ariz	Jan. 31, 1885	100,000	28,100	24,160	3,940
Ripon National Bank, Ripon, Wis	Feb. 7, 1885	50,000	16,200	11,885	4,315
Farmers' National Bank, Franklin, Ohio	Apr. 1, 1885	50,000	27,350	21,350	6,000
First National Bank, Prescott, Ariz	Apr. 9, 1885	50,000	11,250	8,050	3,200
National Union Bank, Swanton, Vt	Apr. 28, 1885	50,000	43,800	31,770	12,030
German National Bank, Memphis, Tenn	May 6, 1885	175,300	120,100	81,818	38,282
Merchants and Farmers' National Bank, Shakopee, Minn	May 12, 1885	50,000	10,240	7,550	2,690
First National Bank, Superior, Wis	May 16, 1885	60,000	18,900	16,840	2,060
Shetucket National Bank, Norwich, Conn	May 18, 1885	100,000	72,000	53,213	18,787
Cumberland National Bank, Cumberland, R. I	June 5, 1885	125,000	106,200	78,475	27,725
First National Bank, Columbia, Tenn	July 14, 1885	100,000	66,800	44,513	22,287
Union National Bank, New York, N. Y	July 21, 1885	1,200,000	25,100	11,733	13,367
First National Bank, Centerville, Ind	Oct. 3, 1885	50,000	27,350	18,400	8,950
Manufacturers' National Bank, Appleton, Wis	Oct. 10, 1885	50,000	45,000	30,043	14,957
First National Bank, Plankinton, Dak	Oct. 21, 1885	50,000	11,250	6,760	4,490
Valley National Bank, Saint Louis, Mo	Dec. 4, 1885	250,000	44,900	25,220	19,740
First National Bank, Belton, Tex	Jan. 6, 1886	50,000	23,490	14,200	9,290
First National Bank, Granville, Ohio	Feb. 15, 1886	50,000	26,500	16,140	10,360
Concordia National Bank, Concordia, Kans	Mar. 12, 1886	50,000	11,240	7,410	3,830
Citizens' National Bank, Beloit, Wis	Mar. 22, 1886	50,000	11,240	6,920	4,320
First National Bank, Dayton, Wash	Mar. 24, 1886	50,000	13,490	10,520	2,970
First National Bank, Macomb, Ill	Apr. 14, 1886	100,000	89,520	48,194	41,326
First National Bank, Jesup, Iowa	Apr. 20, 1886	50,000	25,760	18,400	7,360
Dallas National Bank, Dallas, Tex	May 8, 1886	150,000	33,750	17,000	16,750
First National Bank, Lewiston, Ill	May 12, 1886	50,000	45,000	22,110	22,890
First National Bank, Cedar Rapids, Iowa	May 28, 1886	100,000	35,490	17,110	18,380
First National Bank, Socorro, N. Mex	July 31, 1886	50,000	15,500	8,120	7,380
Custer County National Bank, Broken Bow, Nebr	Aug. 9, 1886	50,000	11,240	11,240	....
Roanoke National Bank, Roanoke, Va	Sept. 16, 1886	50,000	11,250	6,040	5,210
First National Bank, Brownville, Nebr	Sept. 16, 1886	50,000	39,680	18,402	21,278
First National Bank, Leslie, Mich	Sept. 25, 1886	50,000	13,410	7,500	5,910
Mount Vernon National Bank, Mount Vernon, Ill	Oct. 11, 1886	51,100	45,000	22,495	22,505
National Bank of Piedmont, W. Va	Oct. 14, 1886	50,000	45,000	22,410	22,590
First National Bank, Saint Clair, Mich	Oct. 20, 1886	50,000	39,310	21,658	17,652
First National Bank, Milford, Mich	Oct. 21, 1886	50,000	45,000	20,840	24,160
National Bank of Kingwood, W. Va	Oct. 21, 1886	125,000	96,140	31,630	64,510
Merchants' National Bank, Lima, Ohio	Oct. 22, 1886	50,000	45,000	19,720	25,280
Hubbard National Bank, Hubbard, Ohio	Oct. 23, 1886	50,000	45,000	22,839	22,161
Commercial National Bank, Marshalltown, Iowa	Oct. 25, 1886	100,000	22,500	9,590	12,910
First National Bank, Indianapolis, Ind	Nov. 11, 1886	500,000	162,325	70,365	91,960
First National Bank, Concord, Mich	Nov. 27, 1886	50,000	11,250	6,570	4,680
Jamestown National Bank, Jamestown, Dak	Nov. 29, 1886	50,000	11,250	4,080	
First National Bank, Berea, Ohio	Dec. 1, 1886	50,000	45,000	22,794	

NATIONAL BANKS THAT HAVE GONE INTO VOLUNTARY LIQUIDATION UNDER THE PROVISIONS OF SECTIONS 5220 AND 5221 OF THE REVISED STATUTES, ETC.—Continued.

Name and location of bank.	Date of liquidation.	Capital.	Circulation.		
			Issued.	Retired.	Outstanding.
First National Bank, Allerton, Iowa	Dec. 6, 1886	$50,000	$11,250	$6,450	$4,800
Second National Bank, Hillsdale, Mich	Dec. 18, 1886	50,000	13,892	6,381	7,511
Topton National Bank, Topton, Pa	Dec. 28, 1886	50,000	18,000	7,060	10,940
First National Bank, Warsaw, Ill	Dec. 31, 1886	50,000	38,250	14,950	23,300
First National Bank, Hamburg, Iowa	Dec. 31, 1886	50,000	13,500	6,605	6,895
Darlington National Bank, Darlington, S. C	Feb. 10, 1887	100,000	22,500	12,430	10,070
Union National Bank, Cincinnati, Ohio	Feb. 14, 1887	500,000	237,230	114,052	123,178
Roberts National Bank, Titusville, Pa	Feb. 28, 1887	100,000	75,610	34,560	41,050
National Bank of Rahway, N. J	Mar. 9, 1887	100,000	42,500	17,754	24,746
Olney National Bank, Olney, Ill	Mar. 11, 1887	60,000	27,000	12,760	14,240
Metropolitan National Bank, Leavenworth, Kans	Mar. 15, 1887	100,000	22,500	8,890	13,610
Ontario County National Bank, Canandaigua, N. Y	Mar. 23, 1887	50,000	11,250	6,540	4,710
Winsted National Bank, Winsted, Conn	Apr. 12, 1887	50,000	11,250	5,350	5,900
Council Bluffs National Bank, Council Bluffs, Iowa	May 5, 1887	100,000	22,500	6,630	15,870
First National Bank, Homer, Ill	June 22, 1887	50,000	11,250	7,465	3,785
First National Bank, Beloit, Wis	June 30, 1887	50,000	11,250	4,940	6,310
Mystic National Bank, Mystic, Conn	July 7, 1887	52,450	47,205	20,046	27,159
Exchange National Bank, Louisiana, Mo	July 12, 1887	50,000	11,250	4,500	6,750
Exchange National Bank, Downs, Kans	Aug. 1, 1887	50,000	11,250	3,060	8,190
First National Bank, Tecumseh, Nebr	Nov. 3, 1887	50,000	11,700	4,380	7,320
Third National Bank, Saint Paul, Minn	Nov. 4, 1887	500,000	45,000	13,470	31,530
First National Bank, Marshall, Mo	Dec. 6, 1887	100,000	22,500	7,600	14,900
First National Bank, Greene, Iowa	Dec. 15, 1887	50,000	10,750	3,000	7,750
Fulton National Bank, New York, N. Y	Dec. 20, 1887	300,000	....	....	....
Fayetteville National Bank, Fayetteville, N. C	Dec. 31, 1887	200,000	39,580	13,749	25,831
National Bank of Somerset, Ky	Dec. 31, 1887	50,000	45,000	10,790	34,210
First National Bank, Richburgh, N. Y	Jan. 10, 1888	50,000	25,905	9,770	16,135
Scituate National Bank, North Scituate, R. I	Jan. 11, 1888	56,000	35,018	10,230	24,788
National Bank of Franklin, Ind	Jan. 31, 1888	50,000	11,250	3,635	7,615
First National Bank, Hampton, Iowa	Feb. 1, 1888	50,000	11,250	3,440	7,810
First National Bank, Greensburgh, Kans	Feb. 10, 1888	50,000	11,240	1,960	9,280
First National Bank, Central City, Nebr	Feb. 11, 1888	50,000	10,710	3,310	7,400
Duluth National Bank, Duluth, Minn	Feb. 20, 1888	300,000	45,000	9,140	35,860
Bismarck National Bank, Bismarck, Dak	Mar. 1, 1888	50,000	11,250	3,100	8,000
First National Bank, Ashton, Dak	Mar. 6, 1888	50,000	11,250	2,420	8,830
Citizens' National Bank, Sioux Falls, Dak	Apr. 24, 1888	50,000	11,250	1,730	9,520
First National Bank, Stanton, Mich	Apr. 30, 1888	50,000	11,250	2,400	8,700
First National Bank, Fairmont, Nebr	May 1, 1888	50,000	11,250	2,550	8,700
First National Bank, Greenleaf, Kans	May 9, 1888	50,000	11,250	1,340	9,910
National Bank Geneseo, Batavia, N. Y	May 21, 1888	75,000	44,434	7,090	37,344
Strong City National Bank, Strong City, Kans	May 26, 1888	50,000	11,250	1,900	9,350
Citizens' National Bank, Saginaw, Mich	June 1, 1888	100,000	45,000	5,960	39,040
Saugerties National Bank, Saugerties, N. Y	June 16, 1888	125,000	93,316	9,420	83,896
Hyde National Bank, Titusville, Pa	June 21, 1888	300,000	74,730	18,990	55,740
State National Bank, Omaha, Nebr	July 18, 1888	100,000	22,500	2,800	19,700
Cincinnati National Bank, Cincinnati, Ohio	Aug. 1, 1888	280,000	52,510	3,010	49,500
First National Bank, Worthington, Minn	Sept. 5, 1888	75,000	16,875	2,400	14,475
South Framingham National Bank, South Framingham, Mass	Sept. 8, 1888	100,000	21,720	1,350	20,370
First National Bank, Grass Valley, Cal	Sept. 18, 1888	50,000	11,250	....	11,250
First National Bank, Cawker City, Kans	Oct. 3, 1888	50,000	11,250	....	11,250
Merchants' National Bank, West Virginia, Morgantown, W. Va	Oct. 4, 1888	110,000	81,480	1,070	80,410
Total	....	64,779,700	38,457,315	34,897,466	3,559,849

NATIONAL BANKS THAT HAVE GONE INTO VOLUNTARY LIQUIDATION UNDER THE PROVISIONS OF SECTIONS 5220 AND 5221 OF THE REVISED STATUTES OF THE UNITED STATES, FOR THE PURPOSE OF ORGANIZING NEW ASSOCIATIONS WITH THE SAME OR DIFFERENT TITLE, WITH DATE OF LIQUIDATION, AMOUNT OF CAPITAL, CIRCULATION ISSUED, RETIRED, AND OUTSTANDING ON OCTOBER 31, 1888.

Name and location of bank.	Date of liquidation.	Capital.	Circulation.		
			Issued.	Retired.	Outstanding.
First National Bank, Rondout, N. Y.	Oct. 30, 1880	$300,000	$270,000	$248,577	$21,423
First National Bank, Huntington, Ind	Jan. 31, 1881	100,000	90,000	85,630	4,370
First National Bank, Indianapolis, Ind	July 5, 1881	300,000	279,248	248,404	30,844
First National Bank, Valparaiso, Ind	Apr. 24, 1882	50,000	45,000	42,131	2,869
First National Bank, Stillwater, Minn	Apr. 29, 1882	130,000	83,456	79,516	3,940
First National Bank, Chicago, Ill	Apr. 29, 1882	1,000,000	90,000	80,053	9,947
First National Bank, Woodstock, Ill	Apr. 30, 1882	50,000	45,000	41,940	3,060
Second National Bank, Cincinnati, Ohio	Apr. 28, 1882	200,000	180,000	159,950	20,050
Second National Bank, New York, N. Y.	Apr. 28, 1882	300,000	376,890	342,070	34,820
First National Bank, Portsmouth, N. H.	Apr. 29, 1882	300,000	286,000	259,653	26,347
First National Bank, Richmond, Ind	May 5, 1882	200,000	87,400	76,427	10,973
Second National Bank, Cleveland, Ohio	May 6, 1882	1,000,000	510,800	452,240	58,560
First National Bank, New Haven, Conn.	May 6, 1882	500,000	355,310	325,890	29,420
First National Bank, Akron, Ohio	May 2, 1882	100,000	114,822	99,983	14,839
First National Bank, Worcester, Mass	May 4, 1882	300,000	252,000	231,753	20,247
First National Bank, Barre, Mass	May 9, 1882	150,000	135,000	122,041	12,959
First National Bank, Davenport, Iowa	May 9, 1882	100,000	45,000	39,068	5,932
First National Bank, Kendallville, Ind	May 12, 1882	150,000	90,000	81,218	8,782
First National Bank, Cleveland, Ohio	May 13, 1882	300,000	266,462	233,661	32,801
First National Bank, Youngstown, Ohio.	May 15, 1882	500,000	441,529	405,513	36,016
First National Bank, Evansville, Ind	May 15, 1882	500,000	442,870	395,165	47,705
First National Bank, Salem, Ohio	May 15, 1882	50,000	110,540	99,085	11,455
First National Bank, Scranton, Pa	May 18, 1882	200,000	45,000	37,470	7,530
First National Bank, Centreville, Ind	May 18, 1882	50,000	64,525	58,801	5,724
First National Bank, Fort Wayne, Ind	May 22, 1882	300,000	45,000	37,191	7,809
First National Bank, Strasburgh, Pa	May 22, 1882	100,000	79,200	72,107	7,093
First National Bank, Marietta, Pa	May 27, 1882	100,000	99,000	87,705	11,295
First National Bank, La Fayette, Ind	May 31, 1882	150,000	175,060	158,429	16,631
First National Bank, McConnelsville, Ohio	May 31, 1882	50,000	84,640	75,856	8,784
First National Bank, Milwaukee, Wis	May 31, 1882	200,000	229,170	206,132	23,038
Second National Bank, Akron, Ohio	May 31, 2882	100,000	102,706	91,976	10,730
First National Bank, Ann Arbor, Mich	June 1, 1882	100,000	85,078	77,143	7,935
First National Bank, Geneva, Ohio	June 1, 1882	100,000	90,000	79,050	10,950
First National Bank, Oberlin, Ohio	June 1, 1882	50,000	58,382	51,030	7,352
First National Bank, Philadelphia, Pa	June 10, 1882	1,000,000	799,800	695,190	104,610
First National Bank, Troy, Ohio	June 10, 1882	200,000	180,000	162,725	17,275
Third National Bank, Cincinnati, Ohio	June 14, 1882	800,000	609,500	539,830	69,670
First National Bank, Cambridge City, Ind	June 15, 1882	50,000	45,000	39,204	5,796
First National Bank, Lyons, Iowa	June 15, 1882	100,000	90,000	76,913	13,087
First National Bank, Detroit, Mich	June 17, 1882	500,000	336,345	310,668	25,677
First National Bank, Wilkes Barre, Pa.	June 20, 1882	375,000	337,500	301,645	35,855
First National Bank, Iowa City, Iowa	June 24, 1882	100,000	88,400	80,905	7,495
First National Bank, Nashua, N. H	June 24, 1882	100,000	90,000	79,668	10,332
First National Bank, Johnstown, Pa	June 24, 1882	60,000	54,000	48,165	5,835
First National Bank, Pittsburgh, Pa	June 29, 1882	750,000	594,000	527,890	66,110
First National Bank, Terre Haute, Ind.	June 29, 1882	200,000	141,575	124,438	17,137
First National Bank, Hollidaysburgh, Pa	June 30, 1882	50,000	45,000	41,425	3,575
First National Bank, Bath, Me	June 30, 1882	200,000	180,000	161,683	18,317
First National Bank, Janesville, Wis	June 30, 1882	125,000	121,050	108,020	13,030
First National Bank, Michigan City, Ind	June 30, 1882	100,000	45,000	43,358	1,642
First National Bank, Monmouth, Ill	July 3, 1882	75,000	45,000	42,474	2,526
First National Bank, Marion, Iowa	July 11, 1882	50,000	45,000	41,894	3,106
First National Bank, Marlborough, Mass	Aug. 3, 1882	200,000	180,000	163,521	16,479
National Bank of Stanford, Ky	Oct. 3, 1882	150,000	135,000	123,260	11,740
First National Bank, Sandusky, Ohio	Oct. 6, 1882	150,000	90,000	77,951	12,049
First National Bank, Sandy Hill, N. Y.	Dec. 31, 1882	50,000	45,000	39,942	5,058
First National Bank, Lawrenceburgh, Ind	Feb. 24, 1883	100,000	90,000	81,505	8,495
First National Bank, Cambridge, Ohio	Feb. 24, 1883	100,000	80,800	70,616	10,184
First National Bank, Oshkosh, Wis	Feb. 24, 1883	100,000	47,800	44,220	3,580
First National Bank, Grand Rapids, Mich	Feb. 24, 1883	400,000	155,900	144,870	11,030
First National Bank, Delphos, Ohio	Feb. 24, 1883	50,000	45,000	40,633	4,367
First National Bank, Freeport, Ill	Feb. 24, 1883	100,000	53,500	49,870	3,630
First National Bank, Elyria, Ohio	Feb. 24, 1883	100,000	90,000	79,540	10,460
First National Bank, Troy, N. Y.	Feb. 24, 1883	300,000	229,550	207,111	22,439

NATIONAL BANKS THAT HAVE GONE INTO VOLUNTARY LIQUIDATION UNDER THE PROVISIONS OF SECTIONS 5220 AND 5221 OF THE REVISED STATUTES, ETC.—Continued.

Name and location of bank.	Date of liquidation.	Capital.	Circulation.		
			Issued.	Retired.	Outstanding.
Second National Bank, Detroit, Mich...	Feb. 24, 1883	$1,000,000	$303,700	$317,387	$46,313
Second National Bank, Peoria, Ill	Feb. 24, 1883	100,000	90,000	71,718	18,282
National Fort Plain Bank, Fort Plain, N. Y	Feb. 24, 1883	200,000	174,300	154,651	19,649
Logansport National Bank, Logansport, Ind........	Dec. 1, 1883	100,000	16,850	13,700	3,150
National Bank of Birmingham, Ala.....	May 14, 1884	50,000	45,000	38,527	6,473
First National Bank, Westfield, N. Y...	June 1, 1884	50,000	42,800	33,656	9,144
First National Bank Independence, Iowa	Oct. 31, 1884	100,000	90,000	70,210	19,790
First National Bank, Sturgis, Mich	Dec. 31, 1884	50,000	43,850	35,519	8,331
National Bank of Rutland, Vt	Jan. 13, 1885	500,000	238,700	184,444	54,256
Kent National Bank, Chestertown, Md..	Feb. 12, 1885	50,000	18,200	13,490	4,710
National Fulton County Bank, Gloversville, N. Y........	Feb. 20, 1885	150,000	135,000	102,966	32,034
First National Bank, Centralia, Ill......	Feb. 25, 1885	80,000	70,600	49,340	21,260
National Exchange Bank, Albion, Mich.	Feb. 28, 1885	75,000	30,600	21,163	9,437
First National Bank, Paris, Mo..........	Mar. 31, 1885	100,000	89,155	61,025	28,130
First National Bank, Yakima, Wash....	June 20, 1885	50,000	14,650	10,360	4,290
First National Bank, Flint, Mich	June 30, 1885	200,000	122,500	85,172	37,328
Total........	....	17,570,000	12,430,713	10,995,380	1,435,333

NAMES OF BANKS IN LIQUIDATION UNDER SECTION 7, ACT JULY 12, 1882, WITH DATE OF EXPIRATION OF CHARTER, CIRCULATION ISSUED, RETIRED, AND OUTSTANDING OCTOBER 31, 1888.

Name and location of bank.	Date of liquidation.	Capital.	Circulation.		
			Issued.	Retired.	Outstanding.
First National Bank, Pontiac, Mich	Dec. 31, 1881	$50,000	$88,890	$79,565	$9,325
First National Bank, Washington, Iowa	Apr. 11, 1882	100,000	88,565	79,768	8,797
First National Bank, Fremont, Ohio	May 22, 1882	100,000	90,000	80,216	9,784
Second National Bank, Dayton, Ohio	May 26, 1882	300,000	262,941	231,130	31,811
First National Bank, Girard, Pa	June 1, 1882	100,000	90,000	82,085	7,915
First National Bank, Xenia, Ohio	Feb. 24, 1883	120,000	108,000	93,900	14,100
First National Bank, Peru, Ill	Feb. 24, 1883	100,000	45,000	37,436	7,564
First National Bank, Elmira, N. Y	Feb. 24, 1883	100,000	90,000	79,550	10,450
First National Bank, Chittenango, N. Y	Feb. 24, 1883	150,000	135,000	126,369	8,631
First National Bank, Eaton, Ohio	July 4, 1884	50,000	44,300	32,990	11,310
First National Bank, Leominster, Mass	July 5, 1884	300,000	244,400	201,450	42,950
First National Bank, Winona, Minn	July 21, 1884	50,000	44,200	37,364	6,836
American National Bank, Hallowell, Me	Sept. 10, 1884	75,000	67,500	53,955	13,545
First National Bank, Attica, Ind	Oct. 28, 1884	56,000	50,400	42,265	8,135
Citizens' National Bank, Indianapolis, Ind	Nov. 11, 1884	300,000	87,800	62,253	25,547
First National Bank, North East, Pa	Dec. 23, 1884	50,000	24,550	19,427	5,123
First National Bank, Galva, Ill	Jan. 2, 1885	50,000	36,000	26,154	9,846
First National Bank, Thorntown, Ind	Jan. 13, 1885	50,000	43,740	31,550	12,190
Muncie National Bank, Muncie, Ind	Jan. 28, 1885	200,000	161,000	117,436	43,564
Merchants' National Bank, Evansville, Ind	Feb. 6, 1885	250,000	90,800	65,761	25,039
Saybrook National Bank, Essex, Conn	Feb. 20, 1885	100,000	61,200	48,650	12,550
Union National bank, Albany, N. Y	Mar. 7, 1885	250,000	144,400	119,825	24,575
Battenkill National Bank, Manchester, Vt	Mar. 21, 1885	75,000	57,700	42,958	14,742
First National Bank, Owosso, Mich	Apr. 14, 1885	60,000	47,700	27,345	20,355
Coventry National Bank, Anthony, R. I	Apr. 17, 1885	100,000	89,000	66,945	22,055
State National Bank, Keokuk, Iowa	May 23, 1885	150,000	45,000	27,810	17,190
Tolland County National Bank, Tolland, Conn	June 6, 1885	100,000	44,100	31,646	12,454
City National Bank, Hartford, Conn	June 9, 1885	550,000	90,000	63,828	26,172
West River National Bank, Jamaica, Vt	Aug. 17, 1885	60,000	54,000	38,719	15,281
National Bank, Lebanon, Tenn	Aug. 30, 1885	50,000	24,550	11,040	12,910
Greene County National Bank, Springfield, Mo	Feb. 8, 1886	100,000	22,500	5,247	17,253
Union Stock Yards National Bank, Chicago, Ill	Feb. 20, 1886	500,000	45,000	9,765	35,235
Total		4,646,000	2,618,236	2,075,002	543,234

NAMES OF BANKS IN LIQUIDATION UNDER SECTION 7, ACT JULY 12, 1882, WITH DATE OF EXPIRATION OF CHARTER, CIRCULATION ISSUED, RETIRED, AND OUTSTANDING, SUCCEEDED BY ASSOCIATIONS WITH THE SAME OR DIFFERENT TITLE, OCTOBER 31, 1888.

Name and location of bank.	Date of liquidation.	Capital.	Circulation.		
			Issued.	Retired.	Outstanding.
First National Bank, Kittanning, Pa	July 2, 1882	$200,000	$199,500	$176,510	$22,990
National Bank of Beaver County, New Brighton, Pa	Nov. 12, 1884	200,000	97,300	73,187	24,113
National Bank, Beaver Dam, Wis	Dec. 24, 1884	50,000	41,100	33,089	8,011
Merchants' National Bank, Cleveland, Ohio	Dec. 27, 1884	800,000	228,100	166,176	61,924
Union National Bank, Chicago, Ill	Dec. 29, 1884	1,000,000	62,800	38,240	24,560
First National Bank, Le Roy, N. Y	Jan. 2, 1885	150,000	135,000	103,844	31,156
Evansville National Bank, Evansville, Ind	Jan. 3, 1885	800,000	543,050	383,142	159,908
National Albany Exchange Bank, Albany, N. Y	Jan. 10, 1885	300,000	243,900	190,030	53,870
National Bank, Galena, Ill	Jan. 11, 1885	100,000	55,900	39,294	16,606
National State Bank, La Fayette, Ind	Jan. 16, 1885	300,000	615,000	576,002	38,998
First National Bank, Knoxville, Ill	Jan. 16, 1885	60,000	43,600	32,412	11,188
Farmers' National Bank, Ripley, Ohio	Jan. 17, 1885	100,000	87,400	61,880	25,520
City National Bank, Grand Rapids, Mich	Jan. 21, 1885	300,000	45,000	35,580	9,420
Lee County National Bank, Dixon, Ill	Jan. 21, 1885	100,000	41,500	32,867	8,633
Fort Wayne National Bank, Fort Wayne, Ind	Jan. 25, 1885	350,000	257,300	181,072	76,228
National Exchange Bank, Tiffin, Ohio	Mar. 1, 1885	125,000	50,500	34,543	15,957
National Bank, Malone, N. Y	Mar. 9, 1885	200,000	65,900	47,484	18,416
Jefferson National Bank, Steubenville, Ohio	Mar. 21, 1885	150,000	132,000	90,942	41,058
First National Bank, Battle Creek, Mich	Mar. 28, 1885	100,000	89,200	57,160	32,040
Central National Bank, Danville, Ky	Mar. 28, 1885	200,000	180,000	119,784	60,216
Knox County National Bank, Mount Vernon, Ohio	Apr. 1, 1885	75,000	53,200	36,592	16,608
First National Bank, Houghton, Mich	Apr. 18, 1885	100,000	45,000	31,282	13,718
National Bank, Fort Edward, N. Y	Apr. 22, 1885	100,000	88,900	67,135	21,765
National Bank, Salem, N. Y	May. 4, 1885	100,000	86,100	63,015	23,085
National Exchange Bank, Seneca Falls, N. Y	May. 6, 1885	100,000	88,400	66,392	22,008
Trumbull National Bank, Warren, Ohio	July 5, 1885	150,000	132,400	80,770	51,630
Attleborough National Bank, North Attleborough, Mass	July 17, 1885	100,000	84,300	60,478	23,822
American National Bank, Detroit, Mich	July 24, 1885	400,000	251,500	166,820	84,680
First National Bank, Paris, Ill	Aug. 12, 1885	125,000	111,500	67,820	43,680
First National Bank, Saint John, Mich	Aug. 14, 1885	50,000	21,000	13,590	7,410
Second National Bank, Pontiac, Mich	Sept. 1, 1885	100,000	43,000	30,057	12,943
Raleigh National Bank of North Carolina, Raleigh, N. C	Sept. 5, 1885	400,000	123,900	80,315	43,585
First National Bank, Danville, Ky	Sept. 22, 1885	150,000	130,500	80,399	50,101
Total		7,535,000	4,474,350	3,317,903	1,156,447

NATIONAL BANKS THAT HAVE BEEN PLACED IN THE HANDS OF RECEIVERS, AT DATE OF FAILURE, CAUSE OF FAILURE, DIVIDENDS PAID WHILE SOLVENT, REDEEM CIRCULATION, THE AMOUNT REDEEMED, AND THE AMOUNT OUTSTANDING

	Name and location of bank.	Organization.				Total dividends paid during existence as a national banking association.	
		Charter number.	Date.	Capital.	Surplus	Amount.	Per cent.
1	First National Bank, Attica, N. Y	199	Jan. 14, 1864	$50,000	....	Law requiring dividend reports from banks went into effect March 3, 1869.	......
2	Venango National Bank, Franklin, Pa	1176	May 20, 1865	300,000	....		......
3	Merchants' National Bank, Washington, D. C	627	Dec. 14, 1864	200,000	....		......
4	First National Bank, Medina, N. Y	229	Feb. 3, 1864	50,000	....		......
5	Tennessee National Bank, Memphis, Tenn	1225	June 5, 1865	100,000	....		......
6	First National Bank, Selma, Ala	1537	Aug. 24, 1865	100,000	$1,780		......
7	First National Bank, New Orleans, La	162	Dec. 18, 1863	500,000	....		......
8	National Unadilla Bank, Unadilla, N. Y	1403	July 17, 1865	150,000	....		......
9	Farmers and Citizens' National Bank, Brooklyn, N. Y	1223	June 5, 1865	300,000	....		......
10	Croton National Bank, New York, N. Y	1556	Sept. 9, 1865	200,000	....		......
11	First National Bank, Bethel, Conn	1141	May 15, 1865	60,000	2,236		......
12	First National Bank Keokuk, Iowa	80	Sept. 9, 1863	50,000	....		......
13	National Bank of Vicksburg, Miss	803	Feb. 14, 1865	50,000	....		......
14	First National Bank, Rockford, Ill	429	May 20, 1864	50,000	....		......
15	First National Bank of Nevada, Austin, Nev	1331	June 23, 1865	155,000	465	$7,500	4.9
16	Ocean National Bank, New York, N. Y	1232	June 6, 1865	1,000,000	....	421,052	42.1
17	Union Square National Bank, New York, N. Y	1691	Mar. 13, 1869	250,000	....	....	......
18	Eighth National Bank, New York, N. Y	384	Apr. 16, 1864	250,000	....	140,000	56
19	Fourth National Bank, Philadelphia, Pa	286	Feb. 26, 1864	100,000	....	....	......
20	Waverly National Bank, Waverly, N. Y	1192	May 29, 1865	106,100	9,424	24,403	23
21	First National Bank, Fort Smith, Ark	1631	Feb. 6, 1866	50,000	....	18,000	36
22	Scandinavian National Bank, Chicago, Ill	1978	May 7, 1872	250,000	....	....	......
23	Walkill National Bank, Middletown, N. Y	1473	July 21, 1865	175,000	....	103,250	59
24	Crescent City National Bank, New Orleans, La	1937	Feb. 15, 1872	500,000	....	25,000	5
25	Atlantic National Bank, New York, N. Y	1388	July 1, 1865	300,000	50,472	183,000	61
26	First National Bank, Washington, D. C	26	July 16, 1863	500,000	....	805,000	161
27	National Bank of Commonwealth, New York, N. Y	1372	July 1, 1865	750,000	....	429,250	57.2
28	Merchants' National Bank, Petersburgh, Va	1548	Sept. 1, 1865	140,000	....	134,200	95.9
29	First National Bank, Petersburgh, Va	1378	July 1, 1865	120,000	....	97,770	81.5
30	First National Bank, Mansfield, Ohio	436	May 24, 1864	100,000	....	102,660	102.6
31	New Orleans National Banking Association, New Orleans, La	1825	May 27, 1871	600,000	....	108,000	18
32	First National Bank, Carlisle, Pa	21	June 29, 1863	50,000	....	42,000	84
33	First National Bank, Anderson, Ind	44	July 31, 1863	50,000	....	31,150	62.3
34	First National Bank, Topeka, Kans	1660	Aug. 23, 1866	50,000	....	46,000	92
35	First National Bank, Norfolk, Va	271	Feb. 23, 1864	100,000	....	90,500	90.5
36	Gibson County National Bank, Princeton, Ind	2066	Nov. 30, 1872	50,000	....	6,000	12
37	First National Bank of Utah, Salt Lake City, Utah	1695	Nov. 15, 1869	100,000	....	125,000	125
38	Cook County National Bank, Chicago, Ill	1845	July 8, 1871	300,000	....	53,333	17.8
39	First National Bank, Tiffin, Ohio	900	Mar. 16, 1865	100,000	....	108,279	108.2
40	Charlottesville National Bank, Charlottesville, Va	1468	July 19, 1865	100,000	....	149,245	149.2
41	Miners' National Bank, Georgetown, Colo	2199	Oct. 30, 1874	150,000	....	4,500	3
42	Fourth National Bank, Chicago, Ill.*	276	Feb. 24, 1864	100,000	....	184,008	184
43	First National Bank, Bedford, Iowa	2208	Sept. 18, 1875	50,000	....	....	......
44	First National Bank, Osceola, Iowa	1776	Jan. 26, 1871	50,000	....	23,500	46.1

* Formerly in voluntary liquidation.

TOGETHER WITH THEIR CAPITAL AND SURPLUS AT DATE OF ORGANIZATION AND CIRCULATION ISSUED, LAWFUL MONEY DEPOSITED WITH THE TREASURER TO ON OCTOBER 31, 1888.

Failures.				Lawful money deposited.	Circulation.			
Capital.	Surplus.	Receiver appointed.	Cause of failure.		Issued.	Redeemed.	Outstanding.	
$50,000	....	Apr. 14, 1865	W	$44,000	$44,000	$43,751	$249	1
300,000	....	May 1, 1866	U	85,000	85,000	84,774	226	2
200,000	....	May 8, 1866	U	180,000	180,000	179,314	686	3
50,000	$2,288	Mar. 13, 1867	T	40,000	40,000	39,756	244	4
100,000	20,435	Mar. 21, 1867	V	90,000	90,000	89,688	312	5
100,000	4,788	Apr. 30, 1867	B	85,000	85,000	84,557	443	6
500,000	37,003	May 20, 1867	Q	180,000	180,000	178,766	1,234	7
120,000	....	Aug. 20, 1867	W	100,000	100,000	99,770	230	8
300,000	32,000	Sept. 6, 1867	U	253,900	253,900	252,694	1,206	9
200,000	....	Oct. 1, 1867	G	180,000	180,000	179,641	359	10
60,000	4,610	Feb. 28, 1868	N	26,300	26,300	26,095	205	11
100,000	20,000	Mar. 3, 1868	Q	90,000	90,000	89,624	376	12
50,000	5,000	Apr. 24, 1868	N	25,500	25,500	25,429	71	13
50,000	1,400	Mar. 15, 1869	B	45,000	45,000	44,688	312	14
250,000	5,580	Oct. 14, 1869	U	129,700	129,700	128,641	1,059	15
1,000,000	150,000	Dec. 13, 1871	V	800,000	800,000	791,917	8,083	16
200,000	....	Dec. 15, 1871	U	50,000	50,000	49,689	311	17
250,000	40,000	Dec. 15, 1871	F	243,393	243,393	240,721	2,672	18
200,000	33,005	Dec. 20, 1871	U	179,000	179,000	177,500	1,500	19
106,100	27,130	Apr. 23, 1872	U	71,000	71,000	70,032	968	20
50,000	2,509	May 2, 1872	V	45,000	45,000	44,485	515	21
250,000	....	Dec. 12, 1872	B	135,000	135,000	134,546	454	22
175,000	17,000	Dec. 31, 1872	B	118,900	118,900	117,487	1,413	23
500,000	3,045	Mar. 18, 1873	M	450,000	450,000	447,000	3,000	24
300,000	56,000	Apr. 28, 1873	A	100,000	100,000	98,630	1,370	25
500,000	108,000	Sept. 19, 1873	M	450,000	450,000	441,079	8,921	26
750,000	56,027	Sept. 22, 1873	V	234,000	234,000	230,382	3,618	27
400,000	18,302	Sept. 25, 1873	R	360,000	360,000	354,080	5,920	28
200,000	11,801	Sept. 25, 1873	R	179,200	179,200	176,110	3,090	29
100,000	16,000	Oct. 18, 1873	P	90,000	90,000	88,586	1,414	30
600,000	14,161	Oct. 23, 1873	W	360,000	360,000	354,000	6,000	31
50,000	25,000	Oct. 24, 1873	U	45,000	45,000	44,315	685	32
50,000	23,839	Nov. 23, 1873	V	45,000	45,000	44,095	905	33
100,000	7,000	Dec. 16, 1873	P	90,000	90,000	88,641	1,359	34
100,000	3,000	June 3, 1874	G	95,000	95,000	93,310	1,690	35
50,000	1,000	Nov. 28, 1874	X	43,800	43,800	43,390	410	36
150,000	18,719	Dec. 10, 1874	V	118,191	118,191	116,769	1,422	37
500,000	80,000	Feb. 1, 1875	V	285,100	285,100	282,398	2,702	38
100,000	20,000	Oct. 22, 1875	E	45,000	45,000	43,759	1,241	39
200,000	22,234	Oct. 28, 1875	U	146,585	146,585	143,675	2,910	40
150,000	968	Jan. 24, 1876	V	45,000	45,000	44,460	540	41
200,000	....	Feb. 1, 1876	V	85,700	85,700	82,283	3,417	42
30,000	....	Feb. 1, 1876	N	27,000	27,000	26,300	700	43
50,000	10,000	Feb. 25, 1876	V	45,000	45,000	44,291	709	44

NATIONAL BANKS THAT HAVE BEEN PLACED IN THE HANDS OF RECEIVERS,

	Name and location of bank.	Organization.				Total dividends paid during existence as a national banking association.	
		Charter number.	Date.	Capital.	Surplus.	Amount.	Per cent.
45	First National Bank, Duluth, Minn	1954	Apr. 6, 1872	$50,000	....	$25,000	50
46	First National Bank, La Crosse, Wis	1313	June 20, 1865	50,000	....	31,500	63
47	City National Bank, Chicago, Ill	818	Feb. 18, 1865	250,000	....	182,500	73
48	Watkins National Bank, Watkins, N. Y	456	June 2, 1864	75,000	....	85,450	113.9
49	First National Bank, Wichita, Kans	1913	Jan. 2, 1872	50,000	....	36,975	73.9
50	First National Bank, Greenfield, Ohio*	101	Oct. 7, 1863	50,000	....	80,300	160.6
51	National Bank of Fishkill, N. Y	971	Apr. 1, 1865	200,000	$36,205	143,000	71.5
52	First National Bank, Franklin, Ind	50	Aug. 5, 1863	60,000	....	222,319	370.5
53	Northumberland County National Bank, Shamokin, Pa	689	Jan. 9, 1865	67,000	2,976	670,000	1000
54	First National Bank, Winchester, Ill	1484	July 25, 1865	50,000	....	71,750	143.5
55	National Exchange Bank, Minneapolis, Minn	719	Jan. 16, 1865	50,000	....	124,000	248
56	National Bank of State of Missouri, Saint Louis Mo	1665	Oct. 30, 1866	3,410,300	....	....	......
57	First National Bank, Delphi, Ind	1949	Mar. 25, 1872	100,000	....	45,000	45
58	First National Bank, Georgetown, Colo	1991	May 31, 1872	50,000	....	....	......
59	Lock Haven National Bank, Lock Haven, Pa	1273	June 14, 1865	120,000	15,000	153,600	128
60	Third National Bank, Chicago, Ill	236	Feb. 5, 1864	120,000	....	1,035,000	862.5
61	Central National Bank, Chicago, Ill	2047	Sept. 18, 1872	200,000	....	38,000	19
62	First National Bank, Kansas City, Mo	1612	Nov. 23, 1865	100,000	1,000	540,500	540.5
63	Commercial National Bank, Kansas City, Mo	1995	June 3, 1872	100,000	7,214	25,000	25
64	First National Bank, Ashland Pa.*	403	Apr. 27, 1864	60,000	....	187,181	311.9
65	First National Bank, Tarrytown, N. Y	364	Apr. 5, 1864	50,000	....	132,250	264.5
66	First National Bank, Allentown, Pa.*	161	Dec. 16, 1863	100,000	....	....	......
67	First National Bank, Waynesburgh, Pa.*	305	Mar. 5, 1864	100,000	222	86,692	86.7
68	Washington County National Bank, Greenwich, N. Y	1266	June 13, 1865	200,000	....	205,940	102.9
69	First National Bank, Dallas, Tex	2157	July 16, 1874	100,000	....	45,750	45.7
70	People's National Bank, Helena, Mont	2105	May 13, 1873	100,000	....	10,000	10
71	First National Bank, Bozeman, Mont	2027	Aug. 14, 1872	50,000	....	20,000	40
72	Merchants' National Bank, Fort Scott, Kans.*	1927	Jan. 20, 1872	50,000	....	34,731	69.5
73	Farmers' National Bank, Platte City, Mo	2356	May 5, 1877	50,000	....	4,000	8
74	First National Bank, Warrensburgh, Mo	1856	July 31, 1871	50,000	....	57,750	115.5
75	German-American National Bank, Washington, D. C	2358	May 14, 1877	130,000	2,000	....	......
76	German National Bank, Chicago, Ill.*	1734	Nov. 15, 1870	250,000	....	....	......
77	Commercial National Bank, Saratoga Springs, N. Y	1227	June 6, 1865	100,000	11,872	113,000	113
78	Second National Bank, Scranton, Pa.*	49	Aug. 5, 1863	100,000	....	392,125	392.1
79	National Bank of Poultney, Vt	1200	May 31, 1865	100,000	....	92,000	92
80	First National Bank, Monticello, Ind	2208	Dec. 3, 1874	50,000	....	7,400	14.8
81	First National Bank, Butler, Pa	309	Mar. 11, 1864	50,000	....	139,000	278
82	First National Bank, Meadville, Pa	115	Oct. 27, 1863	70,000	....	248,400	354.8
83	First National Bank, Newark, N. J	52	Aug. 7, 1863	125,000	....	605,250	484.2
84	First National Bank, Brattleboro', Vt	470	June 30, 1864	100,000	....	387,000	387
85	Mechanics' National Bank, Newark, N. J	1251	June 9, 1865	500,000	251,802	1,198,000	239.6
86	First National Bank, Buffalo, N. Y	235	Feb. 5, 1864	100,000	....	287,500	287.5
87	Pacific National Bank, Boston, Mass	2373	Nov. 9, 1877	250,000	....	75,000	30
88	First National Bank, Union Mills, Union City, Pa	110	Oct. 23, 1863	50,000	....	91,955	183.9
89	Vermont National Bank, Saint Albans, Vt	1583	Oct. 11, 1865	200,000	....	186,000	93
90	First National Bank, Leadville, Colo	2420	Mar. 19, 1879	60,000	....	63,000	105
91	City National Bank, Lawrenceburgh, Ind.*	2889	Feb. 24, 1883	100,000	....	3,000	3
92	First National Bank, Saint Albans, Vt	269	Feb. 20, 1864	100,000	....	197,000	197
93	First National Bank, Monmouth, Ill	2751	July 7, 1882	75,000	....	15,000	20
94	Marine National Bank, New York, N. Y	1215	June 3, 1865	400,000	....	659,643	164.9
95	Hot Springs National Bank, Hot Springs, Ark	2887	Feb. 17, 1883	50,000	2,000	3,000	6

* Formerly in voluntary liquidation.

TOGETHER WITH THEIR CAPITAL AND SURPLUS, ETC.—Continued.

Failures.				Lawful money deposited.	Circulation.			
Capital.	Surplus.	Receiver appointed.	Cause of failure.		Issued.	Redeemed.	Outstanding.	
$100,000	....	Mar. 13, 1876	P	$45,000	$45,000	$44,358	$642	45
50,000	$25,000	Apr. 11, 1876	P	45,000	45,000	43,993	1,007	46
250,000	130,000	May 17, 1876	V	137,209	137,209	133,237	3,972	47
75,000	3,000	July 12, 1876	G	67,500	67,500	65,349	2,151	48
60,000	12,000	Sept. 23, 1876	B	43,200	43,200	42,434	766	49
50,000	10,000	Dec. 12, 1876	U	29,662	29,662	28,445	1,217	50
200,000	30,000	Jan. 27, 1877	B	177,200	177,200	172,256	4,944	51
132,000	28,538	Feb. 13, 1877	B	92,092	92,092	88,682	3,410	52
67,000	....	Mar. 12, 1877	M	60,300	60,300	58,415	1,885	53
50,000	17,135	Mar. 16, 1877	W	45,000	45,000	43,745	1,255	54
100,000	20,000	May 24, 1877	M	90,000	90,000	86,535	3,465	55
2,500,000	248,775	June 23, 1877	O	1,693,660	1,693,660	1,668,042	25,618	56
50,000	20,000	July 20, 1877	W	45,000	45,000	43,749	1,251	57
75,000	65,000	Aug. 18, 1877	U	45,000	45,000	43,775	1,225	58
120,000	8,000	Aug. 20, 1877	V	71,200	71,200	68,023	3,177	59
750,000	200,000	Nov. 24, 1877	V	597,840	597,840	560,997	36,813	60
200,000	10,000	Dec. 1, 1877	V	45,000	45,000	43,529	1,471	61
500,000	25,000	Feb. 11, 1878	X	44,940	44,940	41,130	3,810	62
100,000	6,392	Feb. 11, 1878	V	44,500	44,500	42,652	1,848	63
112,500	19,000	Feb. 28, 1878	V	75,554	75,554	70,269	5,285	64
100,000	25,000	Mar. 23, 1878	V	89,200	89,200	85,195	4,005	65
250,000	220,000	Apr. 15, 1878	N	78,641	78,641	73,883	4,758	66
100,000	....	May 15, 1878	V	69,345	69,345	68,410	935	67
200,000	24,000	June 8, 1878	P	114,220	114,220	109,929	4,291	68
50,000	5,000	June 8, 1878	V	29,800	29,800	29,025	775	69
100,000	8,000	Sept. 13, 1878	Q	89,300	89,300	86,741	2,559	70
50,000	7,000	Sept. 14, 1878	Q	44,400	44,400	43,445	955	71
50,000	13,500	Sept. 25, 1878	X	35,328	35,328	34,295	1,033	72
50,000	....	Oct. 1, 1878	N	27,000	27,000	26,425	575	73
100,000	10,600	Nov. 1, 1878	X	45,000	45,000	43,645	1,355	74
130,000	2,000	Nov. 1, 1878	P	62,500	62,500	61,660	840	75
500,000	125,000	Dec. 20, 1878	B	42,795	42,795	36,780	6,015	76
100,000	40,476	Feb. 11, 1879	X	86,900	86,900	83,844	3,056	77
200,000	70,000	Mar 15, 1879	X	91,465	91,465	85,143	6,322	78
100,000	4,000	Apr. 7, 1879	X	90,000	90,000	86,487	3,513	79
50,000	2,000	July 18, 1879	N	27,000	27,000	26,152	848	80
50,000	10,600	July 23, 1879	E	71,165	71,165	64,360	6,805	81
100,000	20,000	June 9, 1880	R	89,500	89,500	82,920	6,580	82
300,000	62,584	June 14, 1880	F	326,643	326,643	305,698	20,945	83
300,000	57,000	June 19, 1880	N	90,000	90,000	80,202	9,798	84
500,000	400,000	Nov. 2, 1881	C	449,900	449,900	407,033	42,867	85
100,000	50,000	Apr. 22, 1882	P	99,500	99,500	92,325	7,175	86
961,300	....	May 22, 1882	S	450,000	450,000	435,607	14,393	87
50,000	13,455	Mar. 24, 1883	S	43,000	43,000	39,690	3,310	88
200,000	25,000	Aug. 9, 1883	V	65,200	65,200	55,942	9,258	89
60,000	15,000	Jan. 24, 1884	B	53,000	53,000	47,865	5,135	90
100,000	....	Mar. 11, 1884	G	77,000	77,000	65,680	11,320	91
100,000	40,000	Apr. 22, 1884	P	89,980	89,980	74,578	15,402	92
75,000	15,000	Apr. 22, 1884	B	27,000	27,000	19,510	7,490	93
400,000	225,000	May 13, 1884	T	260,100	260,100	230,157	29,943	94
50,000	180	June 2, 1884	E	40,850	40,850	27,820	13,030	95

NATIONAL BANKS THAT HAVE BEEN PLACED IN THE HANDS OF RECEIVERS,

	Name and location of bank.	Organization.				Total dividends paid during existence as a national banking association.	
		Charter number.	Date.	Capital.	Surplus.	Amount.	Per cent.
96	Richmond National Bank, Richmond, Ind	2090	Mar. 5, 1873	$270,000	....	$274,000	101.5
97	First National Bank, Livingston, Mont	3006	July 16, 1883	50,000	....	....	......
98	First National Bank, Albion, N. Y	166	Dec. 22, 1863	50,000	....	170,500	341
99	First National Bank, Jamestown, Dak	2578	Oct. 25, 1881	50,000	....	....	......
100	Logan National Bank, West Liberty, Ohio	2942	May 7, 1883	50,000	....	4,000	8
101	Middletown National Bank, Middletown, N. Y	1276	June 14, 1865	200,000	$23,128	356,000	178
102	Farmers' National Bank, Bushnell, Ill	1791	Feb. 18, 1871	50,000	....	38,500	77
103	Schoharie County National Bank, Schoharie, N. Y	1510	Aug. 9, 1865	100,000	....	....	......
104	Exchange National Bank, Norfolk, Va	1137	May 13, 1865	100,000	....	337,500	337.5
105	First National Bank, Lake City, Minn	1740	Nov. 29, 1870	50,000	....	90,142	180.2
106	Lancaster National Bank, Clinton, Mass	583	Nov. 22, 1864	200,000	32,894	285,000	142.5
107	First National Bank, Sioux Falls, Dak	2465	Mar. 15, 1880	50,000	....	10,000	20
108	First National Bank, Wahpeton, Dak	2624	Feb. 2, 1882	50,000	....	12,000	24
109	First National Bank, Angelica, N. Y	564	Nov. 3, 1864	100,000	....	186,000	186
110	City National Bank, Williamsport, Pa	2139	Mar. 17, 1874	100,000	....	38,500	38.5
111	Abington National Bank, Abington, Mass. †	1386	July 1, 1865	150,000	15,000	307,382	204.9
112	First National Bank, Blair, Nebr	2724	June 7, 1882	50,000	....	23,000	46
113	First National Bank, Pine Bluff, Ark	2776	Sept. 18, 1882	50,000	....	....	......
114	Palatka National Bank, Palatka, Fla	3266	Nov. 20, 1884	50,000	....	....	......
115	Fidelity National Bank, Cincinnati, Ohio	3461	Feb. 27, 1886	1,000,000	....	2,784	.3
116	Henrietta National Bank, Henrietta, Tex	3022	Aug. 8, 1883	50,000	....	12,250	24.5
117	National Bank of Sumter, S. C	3082	Nov. 26, 1883	50,000	....	13,500	27
118	First National Bank, Dansville, N. Y	75	Sept. 4, 1863	50,000	....	75,825	151.6
119	First National Bank, Corry, Pa	665	Dec. 6, 1864	100,000	....	168,500	168.5
120	Stafford National Bank, Stafford Springs, Conn	686	Jan. 7, 1865	150,000	10,000	306,000	204
121	Fifth National Bank, St. Louis, Mo	2835	Dec. 12, 1882	200,000	....	75,000	37.5
122	Metropolitan National Bank, Cincinnati, Ohio	2542	July 12, 1881	500,000	....	215,000	43
123	First National Bank, Auburn, N. Y	231	Feb. 4, 1864	100,000	....	266,000	266
124	Commercial National Bank, Dubuque, Iowa	1801	Mar. 11, 1871	100,000	....	* 146,806	146.8
125	State National Bank, Raleigh, N. C	1682	June 17, 1868	100,000	....	....	......
126	Second National Bank, Xenia, Ohio	277	Feb. 24, 1864	60,000	....	278,000	453.3
127	Madison National Bank, Madison, Dak	3507	Dec. 7 1886	50,000	....	5,000	10
128	Lowell National Bank, Lowell, Mich	1280	June 14, 1865	50,000	....	159,494	318.9
	Total	......	....	22,108,400	484,600	16,376,700	74.7

* Formerly in voluntary liquidation.
† Restored to solvency.

A Defalcation of officers.
B Defalcation of officers and fraudulent management.
C Defalcation of officers and excessive loans to others.
D Defalcation of officers and depreciation of securities.
E Depreciation of securities.
F Excessive loans to others, injudicious banking, and depreciation of securities.
G Excessive loans to officers and directors and depreciation of securities.
H Excessive loans to officers and directors and investments in real estate and mortgages.
I Excessive loans to others and depreciation of securities.
J Excessive loans to others and investments in real estate and mortgages.
K Excessive loans and failure of large debtors.
L Excessive loans to officers and directors.

TOGETHER WITH THEIR CAPITAL AND SURPLUS, ETC.—Continued.

Failures.				Lawful money deposited.	Circulation.			
Capital.	Surplus.	Receiver appointed.	Cause of failure.		Issued.	Redeemed.	Outstanding.	
$250,000	$33,000	July 23, 1884	H	$158,900	$158,900	$124,525	$34,375	96
50,000	....	Aug. 25, 1884	X	11,240	11,240	9,605	1,635	97
100,000	20,000	Aug. 26, 1884	B	90,000	90,000	72,297	17,703	98
50,000	12,500	Sept. 13, 1884	E.	18,650	18,650	16,557	2,093	99
50,000	1,000	Oct. 18, 1884	P	23,400	23,400	17,440	5,900	100
200,000	40,000	Nov. 29, 1884	I	149,000	176,000	143,209	32,791	101
50,000	7,500	Dec. 17, 1884	L	44,000	44,000	35,487	8,513	102
50,000	15,000	Mar. 23, 1885	B	38,350	38,350	28,110	10,240	103
300,000	150,000	Apr. 9, 1885	O	228,200	228,200	169,328	58,872	104
50,000	10,000	Jan. 4, 1886	E	44,420	44,420	29,000	15,420	105
100,000	20,000	Jan. 20, 1886	B	72,360	72,360	46,224	26,136	106
50,000	30,447	Mar. 11, 1886	J	10,740	10,740	6,650	4,090	107
50,000	4,000	Apr. 8, 1886	J	8,120	17,120	8,120	9,000	108
100,000	20,100	Apr. 19, 1886	A	89,000	89,000	54,473	34,527	109
100,000	12,500	May 4, 1886	D	43,140	43,140	22,010	21,130	110
150,000	25,300	Aug. 2, 1886	L	108,870	131,370	25,425	105,945	111
50,000	11,000	Sept. 8, 1886	U	26,180	26,180	14,695	11,485	112
50,000	20,000	Nov. 20, 1886	V	15,030	26,280	15,030	11,250	113
50,000	....	June 3, 1887	V	19,210	19,210	9,245	9,965	114
1,000,000	50,000	June 27, 1887	B	10,000	90,000	9,997	80,003	115
50,000	8,000	Aug. 17, 1887	K	11,250	11,250	600	10,650	116
50,000	10,000	Aug. 24, 1887	A	11,250	11,250	910	10,340	117
50,000	15,000	Sept. 8, 1887	B	4,480	15,730	4,480	11,250	118
100,000	10,183	Oct. 11, 1887	V	29,379	73,829	23,672	50,157	119
200,000	24,000	Oct. 17, 1887	B	139,048	139,048	49,163	89,885	120
300,000	30,000	Nov. 15, 1887	F	....	44,430	....	44,430	121
1,000,000	180,000	Feb. 10, 1888	V	277,745	277,745	68,490	209,255	122
150,000	....	Feb. 20, 1888	R	19,046	44,400	18,100	26,300	123
100,000	20,000	Apr. 2, 1888	V	39,670	62,170	16,849	45,321	124
100,000	....	Apr. 11, 1888	B	....	22,500	....	22,500	125
150,000	14,000	May 9, 1888	V	48,470	48,470	8,325	40,145	126
50,000	3,000	June 23, 1888	S	....	11,250	....	11,250	127
50,000	10,000	Sept. 19, 1888	W	13,620	24,870	2,230	22,640	128
25,938,000	4,074,438	....	....	14,901,026	15,43[illegible],360	13,911,335	1,521,025	

M Failure of large debtors.
N Fraudulent management.
O Fraudulent management, excessive loans to officers and directors, and depreciation of securities.
P Fraudulent management and depreciation of securities.
Q Fraudulent management and injudicious banking.
R Fraudulent management, defalcation of officers, and depreciation of securities.
S Fraudulent management, injudicious banking, investments in real estate and mortgages, and depreciation of securities.
T Fraudulent management, excessive loans to officers and directors, and excessive loans to others.
U Injudicious banking.
V Injudicious banking and depreciation of securities.
W Injudicious banking and failure of large debtors.
X Investments in real estate and mortgages and depreciation of securities.

INSOLVENT NATIONAL BANKS, DATES OF ORGANIZATION, APPOINTMENT OF RE-
SYSTEM, WITH AMOUNTS OF NOMINAL AND ADDITIONAL ASSETS, AMOUNTS COL-
ON ASSETS, EXPENSES OF RECEIVERSHIP, CLAIMS PROVED, DIVIDENDS PAID,

	Name and location of bank.	Date of organization.	Capital stock.	Receiver appointed.
1	First National Bank, Attica, N. Y	Jan. 14, 1864	$50,000	Apr. 14, 1865
2	Venango National Bank, Franklin, Pa	May 20, 1865	300,000	May 1, 1866
3	Merchants National Bank, Washington, D. C	Dec. 14, 1864	200,000	May 8, 1866
4	First National Bank, Medina, N. Y	Feb. 3, 1864	50,000	Mar. 13, 1867
5	Tennessee National Bank, Memphis, Tenn	June 5, 1865	100,000	Mar. 21, 1867
6	First National Bank, Selma, Ala	Aug. 24, 1865	100,000	Apr. 30, 1867
7	First National Bank, New Orleans, La	Dec. 18, 1863	500,000	May 20, 1867
8	National Unadilla Bank, Unadilla, N. Y	July 17, 1865	120,000	Aug. 20, 1867
9	Farmers and Citizens' National Bank, Brooklyn, N. Y	June 5, 1865	300,000	Sept. 6, 1867
10	Croton National Bank, New York, N. Y	Sept. 9, 1865	200,000	Oct. 1, 1867
11	First National Bank, Bethel, Conn	May 15, 1865	60,000	Feb. 28, 1868
12	First National Bank, Keokuk, Iowa	Sept. 9, 1863	100,000	Mar. 3, 1868
13	National Bank of Vicksburg, Miss	Feb. 14, 1865	50,000	Apr. 24, 1868
14	First National Bank, Rockford, Ill	May 20, 1864	50,000	Mar. 15, 1869
15	First National Bank of Nevada, Austin, Nev	June 23, 1865	250,000	Oct. 14, 1869
16	Ocean National Bank, New York, N. Y	June 6, 1865	1,000,000	Dec. 13, 1871
17	Union Square National Bank, New York, N. Y	Mar. 30, 1869	200,000	Dec. 15, 1871
18	Eighth National Bank, New York, N. Y	Apr. 6, 1864	250,000	Dec. 15, 1871
19	Fourth National Bank, Philadelphia, Pa	Feb. 26, 1864	200,000	Dec. 20, 1871
20	Waverly National Bank, Waverly, N. Y	May 29, 1865	106,100	Apr. 23, 1872
21	First National Bank, Fort Smith, Ark	Feb. 6, 1866	50,000	May 2, 1872
22	Scandinavian National Bank, Chicago, Ill	May 7, 1872	250,000	Dec. 12, 1872
23	Wallkill National Bank, Middletown, N. Y	July 21, 1865	175,000	Dec. 31, 1872
24	Crescent City National Bank, New Orleans, La	Feb. 15, 1872	500,000	Mar. 18, 1873
25	Atlantic National Bank, New York, N. Y	July 1, 1865	300,000	Apr. 28, 1873
26	First National Bank, Washington, D. C	July 16, 1863	500,000	Sept. 19, 1873
27	National Bank of the Commonwealth, New York, N. Y	July 1, 1865	750,000	Sept. 22, 1873
28	Merchants' National Bank, Petersburgh, Va	Sept. 1, 1865	400,000	Sept. 2[illegible], 1873
29	First National Bank, Petersburgh, Va	July 1, 1865	200,000	Sept. 25, 1873
30	First National Bank, Mansfield, Ohio	May 24, 1864	100,000	Oct. 18, 1873
31	New Orleans National Banking Association, New Orleans, La	May 27, 1871	600,000	Oct. 23, 1873
32	First National Bank, Carlisle, Pa	July 7, 1863	50,000	Oct. 24, 1873
33	First National Bank, Anderson, Ind	July 31, 1863	50,000	Nov. 23, 1873
34	First National Bank, Topeka, Kans	Aug. 23, 1866	100,000	Dec. 16, 1873
35	First National Bank, Norfolk, Va	Feb. 23, 1864	100,000	June 3, 1874
36	Gibson County National Bank, Princeton, Ind	Nov. 30, 1872	50,000	Nov. 28, 1874
37	First National Bank of Utah, Salt Lake City, Utah	Nov. 15, 1869	150,000	Dec. 10, 1874
38	Cook County National Bank, Chicago, Ill	July 8, 1871	500,000	Feb. 1, 1875
39	First National Bank, Tiffin, Ohio	Mar. 16, 1865	100,000	Oct. 22, 1875
40	Charlottesville National Bank, Charlottesville, Va	July 19, 1865	200,100	Oct. 28, 1875
41	Miners' National Bank, Georgetown, Colo	Oct. 30, 1874	150,000	Jan. 24, 1876
42	Fourth National Bank, Chicago, Ill.*	Feb. 24, 1864	200,000	Feb. 1, 1876
43	First National Bank, Bedford, Iowa	Sept. 18, 1875	30,000	Feb. 1, 1876
44	First National Bank, Osceola, Iowa	Jan. 26, 1871	50,000	Feb. 25, 1876
45	First National Bank, Duluth, Minn	Apr. 6, 1872	100,000	Mar. 13, 1876
46	First National Bank, LaCrosse, Wis	June 20, 1865	50,000	Apr. 11, 1876
47	City National Bank, Chicago, Ill	Feb. 18, 1865	250,000	May 17, 1876
48	Watkins National Bank, Watkins, N. Y	June 2, 1864	75,000	July 12, 1876
49	First National Bank, Wichita, Kans	Jan. 2, 1872	60,000	Sept. 23, 1876
50	First National Bank, Greenfield, Ohio*	Oct. 7, 1863	50,000	Dec. 12, 1876
51	National Bank of Fishkill, N. Y	Apr. 1, 1865	200,000	Jan. 27, 1877
52	First National Bank, Franklin, Ind	Aug. 5, 1863	132,000	Feb. 13, 1877
53	Northumberland County National Bank, Shamokin, Pa	Jan. 9, 1865	67,000	Mar. 12, 1877
54	First National Bank, Winchester, Ill	July 25, 1865	50,000	Mar. 16, 1877
55	National Exchange Bank, Minneapolis, Minn	Jan. 16, 1865	100,000	May 24, 1877
56	National Bank of the State of Missouri, Saint Louis, Mo	Oct. 30, 1866	2,500,000	June 23, 1877
57	First National Bank, Delphi, Ind	Mar. 25, 1872	50,000	July 20, 1877
58	First National Bank, Georgetown, Colo	May 31, 1872	75,000	Aug. 18, 1877
59	Lock Haven National Bank, Lock Haven, Pa	June 14, 1865	120,000	Aug. 20, 1877
60	Third National Bank, Chicago, Ill	Feb. 5, 1864	750,000	Nov. 24, 1877
61	Central National Bank, Chicago, Ill	Sept. 18, 1872	200,000	Dec. 1, 1877
62	First National Bank, Kansas City, Mo	Nov. 23, 1865	500,000	Feb. 11, 1878
63	Commercial National Bank, Kansas City, Mo	June 3, 1872	100,000	Feb. 11, 1878
64	First National Bank, Ashland, Pa.*	Apr. 27, 1864	112,500	Feb. 28, 1878
65	First National Bank, Tarrytown, N. Y	Apr. 5, 1864	100,000	Mar. 23, 1878
66	First National Bank, Allentown, Pa.*	Dec. 16, 1863	250,000	Apr. 15, 1878
67	First National Bank, Waynesburgh Pa.*	Mar. 5, 1864	100,000	May 15, 1887
68	Washington County National Bank, Greenwich, N. Y	June 30, 1865	200,000	June 8, 1878
69	First National Bank, Dallas, Tex	July 16, 1874	50,000	June 8, 1878
70	Peoples' National Bank, Helena, Mont	May 13, 1873	100,000	Sept. 13, 1878
71	First National Bank, Bozeman, Mont	Aug. 14, 1872	50,000	Sept. 14, 1878
72	Merchants' National Bank, Fort Scott, Kans.*	Jan. 20, 1872	50,000	Sept. 25, 1878

CEIVER, AND CLOSING, SINCE THE ORGANIZATION OF THE NATIONAL BANKING LECTED FROM ALL SOURCES, LOANS PAID AND OTHER DISBURSEMENTS, LOSSES AND REMAINING ASSETS RETURNED TO STOCKHOLDERS.

Nominal assets at date of suspension.			Additional assets received since date of suspension.	Total assets.	Offsets allowed and settled.	Loss on assets compounded or sold under order of court.	Nominal value of assets returned to stockholders.	
Estimated good.	Estimated doubtful.	Estimated worthless.						
$50,823	$28,053	$115,538	$13,692	$208,106	$18,061	$114,236	....	1
83,713	57,029	818,154	27,741	986,637	69,445	796,107	....	2
....	800,929	....	....	800,929	....	686,665	....	3
16,424	2,029	101,073	5,400	126,925	....	93,638	....	4
50,000	393,412	....	26,579	471,991	....	380,383	....	5
116,422	96,556	78,415	57,732	349,125	6,845	179,804	....	6
853,148	276,400	701,116	156,575	1,987,239	58,645	929,289	....	7
36,748	69,857	86,856	19,449	212,910	....	132,806	....	8
1,175,656	121,688	272,757	121,017	1,691,113	55,342	400,903	....	9
255,235	144,903	65,301	21,572	487,071	30,641	187,586	....	10
39,486	4,809	83,830	12,212	140,337	1,570	70,122	....	11
98,240	79,652	125,057	13,426	316,375	83,454	123,409	....	12
21,584	40,959	23,569	....	94,112	4,008	57,938	....	13
7,000	811	....	80,871	88,182	274	....	....	14
129,721	497,292	91,412	42,236	760,661	317,742	219,750	....	15
1,867,641	....	942,283	124,832	2,934,756	285,736	1,254,358	....	16
364,973	....	91,355	11,895	468,223	101,719	....	$89,855	17
229,017	736,997	165,442	49,409	1,181,465	38,911	379,794	....	18
653,658	....	....	....	653,658	303,504	....	....	19
86,493	40,000	37,494	32,517	196,504	15,780	56,011	....	20
15,800	14,174	25,000	6,537	61,511	....	37,629	....	21
100,000	100,000	168,100	24,866	392,966	6,211	221,703	....	22
127,769	50,000	25,000	25,102	227,871	30,378	23,084	....	23
379,020	110,450	148,920	168,003	806,903	8,949	285,340	....	24
336,833	58,852	283,550	128,337	807,572	98,460	161,013	....	25
1,000,000	1,277,690	....	215,724	2,493,414	280,955	765,356	....	26
1,485,113	473,872	453,503	404,431	2,706,509	368,092	589,213	....	27
342,260	252,250	321,722	103,609	1,019,841	103,842	616,642	....	28
100,000	50,000	79,409	43,225	272,634	3,225	140,704	....	29
94,483	173,378	7,954	21,005	296,910	5,735	182,231	....	30
300,000	100,000	376,870	654,185	1,431,055	8,964	715,584	....	31
28,077	55,880	29,207	2,574	115,304	7,008	51,204	....	32
50,000	80,000	108,037	995,927	332,984	10,410	167,702	....	33
25,000	85,000	78,857	14,241	203,098	26,951	118,083	....	34
77,723	56,350	80,207	3,542	217,912	2,191	55,917	....	35
51,246	32,011	29,055	12,816	125,178	3,593	54,332	....	36
6,300	204,600	3,274	15,258	229,432	2,869	106,231	....	37
619,836	1,250,163	151,430	678,340	2,699,787	452,953	1,948,095	....	38
140,000	120,000	63,020	18,439	342,059	60,447	84,709	....	39
169,520	105,218	257,655	30,696	563,089	24,882	58,715	....	40
20,000	190,069	....	27,287	237,356	8,761	160,254	....	41
27,123	131,227	65,802	3,084	227,236	2,100	6,206	....	42
29,752	26,858	9,359	9,635	75,604	3,510	49,929	....	43
74,376	19,938	5,737	15,102	115,218	3,043	30,319	33,363	44
18,093	118,300	35,855	13,816	186,064	1,139	111,780	....	45
35,000	25,000	65,097	44,815	169,912	4,206	85,019	....	46
453,037	478,917	85,805	86,248	1,104,007	48,381	470,908	....	47
86,014	44,582	9,105	21,738	161,439	3,151	18,635	53,478	48
59,226	18,387	67,531	3,681	148,825	17,409	67,345	....	49
....	57,075	....	976	58,051	....	44,344	....	50
194,065	262,909	51,403	49,441	558,418	18,192	223,375	....	51
86,492	58,188	200,909	24,217	369,806	60,811	203,792	....	52
67,246	112,020	25,941	14,770	219,983	8,487	99,588	....	53
67,541	66,025	79,101	14,270	226,937	6,537	117,173	....	54
135,231	90,704	124,371	18,411	368,717	21,408	139,309	....	55
935,999	2,818,966	633,744	433,400	4,822,109	166,831	1,771,699	36,957	56
175,254	6,250	6,596	13,478	201,578	62,774	1,310	34,259	57
34,368	52,027	629,113	30,308	746,506	36,598	606,560	....	58
220,481	150,050	24,990	34,350	430,471	41,324	143,664	....	59
1,330,215	631,797	330,704	297,166	2,589,882	59,328	310,818	....	60
157,438	161,441	170,712	16,073	505,664	7,245	79,038	....	61
1,118,118	313,726	405,000	19,817	1,856,661	1,482,725	22,559	....	62
52,349	74,724	51,175	6,723	184,971	22,902	67,396	....	63
107,318	41,584	19,070	8,859	176,831	16,072	....	112,818	64
100,994	....	153,467	20,289	274,750	104,049	....	....	65
19,879	132,445	185,220	2,171	339,715	20,608	268,000	....	66
....	15,809	42,284	1,861	60,014	714	47,239	....	67
311,324	27,894	236,071	13,749	589,938	18,541	6,972	279,987	68
48,149	36,245	67,423	4,805	156,122	30,088	106,202	....	69
32,559	95,251	166,151	67,942	861,903	12,492	32,372	....	70
30,010	76,046	333	21,090	136,479	7,700	20,141	....	71
21,225	15,548	46,588	1,892	85,248	178	65,804	....	72

INSOLVENT NATIONAL BANKS, DATE OF ORGANIZATION, APPOINTMENT OF RE-
SYSTEM, WITH AMOUNTS OF NOMINAL AND ADDITIONAL ASSETS,

	Name and location of bank.	Date of organization.	Capital stock.	Receiver appointed.
73	Farmers' National Bank, Platte City, Mo	May 5, 1877	$50,000	Oct. 1, 1878
74	First National Bank, Warrensburgh, Mo	July 31, 1871	100,000	Nov. 1, 1878
75	German-American National Bank, Washington, D. C	May 14, 1877	130,000	Nov. 1, 1878
76	German National Bank, Chicago, Ill.*	Nov. 15, 1870	500,000	Dec. 20, 1878
77	Commercial National Bank, Saratoga Springs, N. Y	June 6, 1865	100,000	Feb. 11, 1879
78	Second National Bank, Scranton, Pa.*	Aug. 5, 1863	200,000	Mar. 15, 1879
79	National Bank of Poultney, Vt	May 31, 1865	100,000	Apr. 7, 1879
80	First National Bank, Monticello, Ind	Dec. 3, 1874	50,000	July 18, 1879
81	First National Bank, Butler, Pa	Mar. 11, 1864	50,000	July 23, 1879
82	First National Bank, Meadville, Pa	Oct. 27, 1863	100,000	June 9, 1880
83	First National Bank, Newark, N. J	Aug. 7, 1863	300,000	June 14, 1880
84	First National Bank, Brattleborough, Vt	June 30, 1864	300,000	June 19, 1880
85	Mechanics' National Bank, Newark, N. J	June 9, 1865	500,000	Nov. 2, 1881
86	First National Bank, Buffalo, N. Y	Feb. 5, 1864	100,000	Apr. 22, 1882
87	Pacific National Bank, Boston, Mass	Nov. 9, 1877	961,300	May 22, 1882
88	First National Bank of Union Mills, Union City, Pa	Oct. 23, 1863	50,000	Mar 24, 1883
89	Vermont National Bank, Saint Albans, Vt	Oct. 11, 1865	200,000	Aug. 9, 1883
90	First National Bank, Leadville, Colo	Mar. 19, 1879	60,000	Jan. 24, 1884
91	City National Bank, Lawrenceburgh, Ind.*	Feb. 24, 1883	100,000	Mar. 11, 1884
92	First National Bank, Saint Albans, Vt	Feb. 20, 1864	100,000	Apr. 22, 1884
93	First National Bank, Monmouth, Ill	July 7, 1882	75,000	Apr. 22, 1884
94	Marine National Bank, New York, N. Y	June 3, 1865	400,000	May 13, 1884
95	Hot Springs National Bank, Hot Springs, Ark	Feb. 17, 1883	50,000	June 2, 1884
96	Richmond National Bank, Richmond, Ind	Mar. 5, 1873	250,000	July 23, 1884
97	First National Bank, Livingston, Mont	July 16, 1883	50,000	Aug. 25, 1884
98	First National Bank, Albion, N. Y	Dec. 22, 1863	100,000	Aug. 26, 1884
99	First National Bank, Jamestown, Dak	Oct. 25, 1881	50,000	Sept. 13, 1884
100	Logan National Bank, West Liberty, Ohio	May 7, 1883	50,000	Oct. 18, 1884
101	Middletown National Bank, Middletown, N. Y	June 14, 1865	200,000	Nov. 29, 1884
102	Farmers' National Bank, Bushnell, Ill	Feb. 18, 1871	50,000	Dec. 17, 1884
103	Schoharie County National Bank, Schoharie, N. Y	Aug. 9, 1865	50,000	Mar. 23, 1885
104	Exchange National Bank, Norfolk, Va	May 13, 1865	300,000	Apr. 9, 1885
105	First National Bank, Lake City, Minn	Nov. 29, 1870	50,000	Jan. 4, 1886
106	Lancaster National Bank, Clinton, Mass	Nov. 22, 1864	100,000	Jan. 20, 1886
107	First National Bank, Sioux Falls, Dak	Mar. 15, 1880	50,000	Mar. 11, 1886
108	First National Bank, Wahpeton, Dak	Feb. 2, 1882	50,000	Apr. 8, 1886
109	First National Bank, Angelica, N. Y	Nov. 3, 1864	100,000	Apr. 10, 1886
110	City National Bank, Williamsport, Pa	Mar. 17, 1874	100,000	May 4, 1886
111	Abington National Bank, Abington, Mass.†	July 1, 1865	150,000	Aug. 2, 1886
112	First National Bank, Blair, Nebr	June 7, 1882	50,000	Sept. 8, 1886
113	First National Bank, Pine Bluff, Ark	Sept. 18, 1882	50,000	Nov. 20, 1886
114	Palatka National Bank, Palatka, Fla	Nov. 20, 1884	50,000	June 3, 1887
115	Fidelity National Bank, Cincinnati, Ohio	Feb. 27, 1886	1,000,000	June 27, 1887
116	Henrietta National Bank, Henrietta, Tex	Aug. 8, 1883	50,000	Aug. 17, 1887
117	National Bank of Sumter, S. C	Nov. 26, 1883	50,000	Aug. 24, 1887
118	First National Bank, Dansville, N. Y	Sept. 4, 1863	50,000	Sept. 8, 1887
119	First National Bank, Corry, Pa	Dec. 6, 1864	100,000	Oct. 11, 1887
120	Stafford National Bank, Stafford Springs, Conn	Jan. 7, 1865	200,000	Oct. 17, 1887
121	Fifth National Bank, Saint Louis, Mo	Dec. 6, 1882	300,000	Nov. 15, 1887
122	Metropolitan National Bank, Cincinnati, Ohio	June 23, 1881	1,000,000	Feb. 10, 1888
123	First National Bank, Auburn, N. Y	Jan. 13, 1864	150,000	Feb. 20, 1888
124	Commercial National Bank, Dubuque, Iowa	Mar. 4, 1871	100,000	Apr. 2, 1888
125	State National Bank, Raleigh, N. C	June 2, 1868	100,000	Mar. 31, 1888
126	Second National Bank, Xenia, Ohio	Jan. 1, 1864	150,000	May 9, 1888
127	Madison National Bank, Madison, Dak	Nov. 29, 1886	50,000	June 23, 1888
128	Lowell National Bank, Lowell, Mich	June 14, 1865	50,000	Sept. 19, 1888
	Total		25,958,900	

* Formerly in voluntary liquidation. † Restored to solvency.

CEIVER, AND CLOSING, SINCE THE ORGANIZATION OF THE NATIONAL BANKING AMOUNTS COLLECTED FROM ALL SOURCES, ETC.—Continued.

Nominal assets at date of suspension.			Additional assets received since date of suspension.	Total assets.	Offsets allowed and settled.	Loss on assets compounded or sold under order of court.	Nominal value of assets returned to stockholders.	
Estimated good.	Estimated doubtful.	Estimated worthless.						
$9,561	$18,691	$42,296	$1,944	$72,492	$10,947	$8,207	....	73
90,053	194,457	11,578	33,875	330,363	55,255	118,507	....	74
256,286	139,514	87,923	61,147	404,870	165,846	42,883	....	75
104,966	101,971	475,052	29,881	711,870	6,170	521,783	....	76
133,169	107,503	28,969	17,085	346,726	17,475	101,810	$60,059	77
264,906	101,178	104,858	47,591	518,535	36,737	203,982	72,754	78
68,078	97,257	18,384	19,560	203,279	3,358	25,729	77,502	79
23,646	6,734	4,374	15,017	49,771	8,411	64	....	80
12,617	134,716	34,737	27,503	209,603	11,920	106,562	....	81
115,012	22,545	12,863	·19,198	169,618	3,345	26,043	26,439	82
418,931	64,041	55,895	41,173	580,060	154,945	4,000	....	83
51,574	....	302,654	43,895	398,123	4,902	801	302,654	84
1,114,503	185,002	78,286	107,243	1,485,034	73,925	54,338	....	85
488,892	65,526	696,987	36,308	1,287,713	172,063	55,274	....	86
648,710	1,416,793	1,397,334	394,883	3,857,720	172,843	565,779	....	87
161,699	46,829	16,300	23,580	248,426	4,876	14,013	....	88
124,114	520,917	118,618	19,963	783,612	19,141	5,541	....	89
72,197	56,042	102,112	34,556	264,907	8,971	18,418	....	90
13,993	14,500	2,554	1,599	32,646	52	16,017	....	91
217,314	96,878	49,951	68,912	433,050	9,888	23,293	....	92
172,940	96,543	9,688	28,049	307,220	5,075	....	....	93
2,776,636	1,736,106	1,508,609	833,204	6,854,555	734,289	3,019	....	94
31,038	27,774	27,190	6,339	92,361	5,381	29,880	....	95
367,109	72,356	171,319	120,850	731,634	32,233	211,773	....	96
33,543	15,304	22,255	846	71,948	....	6,333	....	97
55,763	44,446	113,329	185,441	398,979	4,146	125,966	....	98
7,519	29,826	29,352	3,312	70,009	5	49,155	....	99
60,096	22,695	....	40,454	123,245	11,099	....	....	100
600,810	53,692	167,075	112,039	933,616	21,114	3,436	....	101
13,170	3,874	62,229	11,899	91,172	3,411	350	41,079	102
96,891	39,593	28,010	4,731	169,225	508	78,405	....	103
1,273,711	1,441,378	938,816	169,295	3,823,200	188,920	161,127	....	104
57,487	91,996	7,201	57,094	214,768	584	....	65,573	105
144,850	138,707	8,094	65,390	357,041	18,717	30,867	....	106
48,510	137,859	3,821	7,023	197,213	37,157	3,493	....	107
21,410	66,085	44,884	2,599	134,978	1,168	4,281	....	108
50,810	28,459	70,458	7,798	166,525	1,284	10,211	77,725	109
154,879	26,825	24,308	35,202	241,304	4,104	816	70,715	110
122,551	168,164	5,402	21,633	317,810	8,721	76,659	38,017	111
235,474	8,000	6,834	5,439	255,747	5,645	2,358	43,697	112
50,703	82,612	4,900	2,550	140,864	127	57,000	....	113
15,646	32,092	8,791	1,790	58,319	....	....	44,068	114
2,464,079	915,577	2,494,511	39,034	5,913,201	309,375	15,155	....	115
74,171	35,999	12,995	22,969	146,134	6,594	....	....	116
66,081	....	159	2,768	69,008	883	....	....	117
17,449	8,397	37,572	2,280	65,698	13,266	421	....	118
156,586	20,239	66,710	23,790	266,325	8,079	2,983	....	119
208,243	119,869	60,869	29,150	418,131	10,556	10,026	....	120
580,321	929,368	61,622	55,768	1,627,099	140,308	50,028	....	121
1,668,952	787,596	125,236	7,111	2,588,897	17,528	16,000	1,164,063	122
268,961	160,617	510,790	57,966	998,334	20,110	....	....	123
333,506	324,872	15,112	16,220	689,710	59,250	....	....	124
152,390	176,652	137,561	2,561	469,164	6,842	233	....	125
181,870	214,560	78,496	56,321	531,247	10,201	24,491	....	126
17,136	94,153	20,025	890	129,204	2,001	....	....	127
55,535	71,124	1,316	....	127,975	....	....	....	128
34,633,197	26,184,648	20,958,429	7,802,852	89,580,126	7,888,189	20,836,047	2,735,647	

INSOLVENT NATIONAL BANKS, DATE OF ORGANIZATION, APPOINTMENT OF RE- SYSTEM, WITH AMOUNTS OF NOMINAL AND ADDITIONAL ASSETS

	Nominal value of remaining assets.	Collected from assets.	Collected from assessment upon shareholders.	Total collections from all sources.	Loans paid and other disbursements.	Dividends paid.	Legal expenses.	Receiver's salary and other expenses.
1	....	$75, 209	$1, 104	$76, 373	....	$70, 811	....	$5, 562
2	....	120, 995	1, 245	122, 240	....	101, 387	$6, 403	14, 390
3	....	174, 264	16, 488	190, 752	$275	165, 709	11, 281	13, 427
4	....	33, 287	4, 000	37, 287	816	32, 305	1, 258	2, 908
5	....	91, 608	....	91, 608	935	65, 335	6, 182	19, 156
6	....	162, 386	7, 500	169, 886	507	132, 608	12, 247	24, 524
7	....	999, 305	38, 224	1, 037, 529	17, 477	684, 420	43, 183	92, 440
8	$200	79, 904	2, 125	82, 029	7, 054	58, 661	6, 678	9, 442
9	....	1, 234, 868	....	1, 234, 868	18, 655	1, 138, 870	28, 677	48, 066
10	....	268, 844	....	268, 844	72, 390	143, 307	17, 184	35, 983
11	....	68, 645	28, 935	97, 580	208	86, 787	5, 315	5, 320
12	....	159, 512	8, 936	168, 448	15, 507	134, 920	3, 977	14, 008
13	....	31, 566	....	31, 566	3, 786	16, 654	1, 773	9, 353
14	....	37, 908	....	37, 908	2, 926	29, 277	2, 705	3, 000
15	....	223, 169	....	223, 169	4, 932	163, 982	9, 091	45, 164
16	....	1, 394, 662	348, 961	1, 743, 623	203, 170	1, 326, 487	76, 048	137, 318
17	....	276, 649	....	276, 649	72, 365	175, 920	10, 437	16, 713
18	....	762, 760	136, 172	898, 932	596, 482	263, 065	9, 436	29, 766
19	....	350, 154	....	350, 154	....	342, 054	....	8, 100
20	....	124, 713	....	124, 713	2, 206	77, 568	3, 085	8, 264
21	....	23, 882	....	23, 882	....	15, 142	862	1, 878
22	....	162, 052	10, 079	172, 131	1, 300	143, 209	6, 037	21, 564
23	....	175, 409	42, 795	218, 204	6, 248	175, 430	16, 709	19, 817
24	....	512, 698	109, 707	622, 405	18, 964	540, 427	25, 376	28, 038
25	....	548, 099	228, 580	776, 679	35, 839	661, 816	27, 330	51, 445
26	....	1, 447, 103	5, 200	1, 452, 303	16, 393	1, 374, 330	24, 241	37, 128
27	....	1, 808, 304	....	1, 808, 304	740, 153	747, 428	13, 637	53, 287
28	....	209, 357	....	209, 357	20, 315	259, 487	728	18, 827
29	....	122, 645	19, 675	142, 320	4, 545	125, 667	250	11, 858
30	....	108, 944	11, 400	120, 344	....	107, 258	1, 270	11, 362
31	....	706, 507	303, 813	1, 010, 320	3, 630	802, 263	67, 569	76, 858
32	....	56, 942	....	56, 942	4, 350	46, 634	1, 267	4, 691
33	80, 420	74, 452	....	74, 452	....	57, 004	4, 718	12, 291
34	....	58, 064	2, 250	60, 314	14, 289	31, 668	6, 075	8, 278
35	67, 835	91, 969	37, 597	129, 566	559	101, 545	8, 232	19, 230
36	....	67, 251	....	67, 251	296	62, 646	....	4, 300
37	....	30, 332	....	30, 332	....	19, 002	1, 106	10, 164
38	....	298, 739	66, 535	365, 274	50, 921	228, 412	42, 067	37, 874
39	....	196, 903	....	196, 903	74, 896	108, 818	....	18, 680
40	291, 357	188, 135	93, 619	281, 754	2, 309	226, 308	21, 495	31, 642
41	....	42, 341	106, 451	148, 792	445	135, 707	3, 946	8, 604
42	196, 790	22, 080	11, 260	33, 340	....	18, 258	4, 731	10, 348
43	....	22, 165	1, 100	23, 265	....	12, 624	1, 367	9, 274
44	....	48, 488	....	48, 488	3, 938	34, 536	2, 077	7, 935
45	....	73, 145	42, 212	115, 357	3, 616	88, 697	8, 804	10, 005
46	....	80, 597	4, 510	85, 107	5, 385	65, 783	5, 060	8, 879
47	....	584, 718	58, 826	643, 544	63, 475	545, 593	13, 802	10, 880
48	....	86, 180	....	86, 180	1, 579	60, 647	592	13, 874
49	....	64, 071	15, 552	79, 623	16, 773	59, 121	2, 200	1, 529
50	....	13, 707	2, 664	16, 371	....	9, 456	2, 751	4, 164
51	....	321, 851	122, 127	443, 978	5, 000	388, 856	25, 040	25, 082
52	....	105, 703	91, 930	197, 633	520	178, 512	5, 146	9, 716
53	....	111, 908	43, 232	155, 140	4, 797	136, 474	966	12, 008
54	....	103, 227	8, 044	111, 271	8, 805	89, 715	2, 082	10, 609
55	....	207, 910	9, 540	217, 450	753	202, 753	1, 898	12, 046
56	....	2, 846, 622	245, 108	3, 091, 730	658, 784	2, 165, 388	79, 802	161, 036
57	....	103, 235	....	103, 235	4, 059	81, 941	2, 600	10, 019
58	....	103, 328	....	103, 328	....	73, 890	11, 987	17, 251
59	....	245, 483	47, 949	293, 432	7, 846	254, 647	6, 668	24, 271
60	893, 241	1, 326, 505	....	1, 326, 505	107, 402	1, 071, 774	11, 395	57, 512
61	274, 465	144, 916	65, 132	210, 048	....	177, 254	12, 077	14, 129
62	....	351, 377	....	351, 377	1, 701	316, 828	5, 444	27, 314
63	....	94, 613	....	94, 613	3, 048	52, 514	576	1, 604
64	....	47, 941	....	47, 941	....	33, 105	3, 974	5, 013
65	....	109, 801	16, 455	126, 256	....	107, 575	5, 540	13, 135
66	....	51, 107	54, 536	105, 643	1, 576	79, 725	11, 006	13, 336
67	....	12, 061	16, 447	28, 508	....	21, 710	2, 315	4, 483
68	....	284, 438	123, 430	407, 868	114, 220	262, 887	10, 129	4, 950
69	....	19, 742	16, 500	36, 242	....	29, 377	825	6, 040
70	250, 854	66, 185	23, 622	89, 807	9, 762	65, 368	1, 352	11, 476
71	30, 504	78, 134	1, 811	79, 945	2, 125	69, 038	634	8, 153
72	....	19, 266	2, 880	22, 146	272	16, 670	1, 488	3, 716
73	32, 510	20, 819	....	20, 819	1, 633	11, 803	850	3, 005
74	....	156, 601	16, 277	172, 878	47, 315	100, 870	3, 338	8, 176
75	160, 448	125, 693	52, 631	178, 054	52, 002	87, 260	10, 306	20, 964
76	....	183, 917	20, 257	204, 174	49, 406	182, 572	....	32, 136

CEIVER, AND CLOSING, SINCE THE ORGANIZATION OF THE NATIONAL BANKING AMOUNTS COLLECTED FROM ALL SOURCES, ETC.—Continued.

Balance in hands of Comptroller or receiver.	Amount returned to shareholders in cash.	Amount of assessment upon shareholders.	Amount of claims proved.	Dividends, per cent.	Interest dividends, per cent.	Finally closed.	
		$50,000	$122,089	58		Jan. 2, 1867	1
		300,000	434,531	23.37		Feb. 2, 1885	2
		200,000	669,513	24.70		May 14, 1883	3
		50,000	82,338	30.15		July 28, 1870	4
			376,392	17.333		Feb. 4, 1870	5
		100,000	289,467	46.60		Nov. 25, 1882	6
		500,000	1,119,313	79		Sept. 28, 1882	7
$199		120,000	127,801	45.00		Dec. 19, 1874	8
			1,191,500	98		Nov. 18, 1874	9
21		26,000	170,752	88.50		Aug. 15, 1872	10
		89,300	68,986	100	64	Apr. 7, 1881	11
27		100,000	205,256	68.33		Nov. 30, 1872	12
			33,870	49.20		Nov. 25, 1882	13
			60,874	41.90		Dec. 4, 1875	14
			170,012	92.70		May 16, 1884	15
		400,000	1,282,254	100	46	Apr. 20, 1882	16
	$1,214		157,120	100		Nov. 16, 1874	17
183		135,000	378,722	100		Sept. 1, 1875	18
			645,558	100		Feb. 13, 1872	19
	33,500		79,864	100		Oct. 2, 1877	20
	6,500		15,142	100		Jan. 3, 1870	21
21		125,000	254,901	57.46		Feb. 15, 1886	22
		52,500	171,468	100	30	Jan. 8, 1880	23
		350,000	657,020	84.83		June 1, 1881	24
249		300,000	597,885	100	50	Apr. 29, 1884	25
202		300,000	1,619,965	100		July 24, 1876	26
	247,799		796,905	100	100	Mar. 31, 1883	27
		400,000	992,636	34		May 1, 1876	28
		50,000	167,285	76		May 15, 1876	29
454		100,000	175,081	57.50		Nov. 30, 1883	30
		600,000	1,429,505	62		Mar. 21, 1887	31
			67,202	78.50		Dec. 6, 1882	32
430		50,000	144,406	39.50			33
4		45,000	55,372	58.80		Sept. 11, 1878	34
		100,000	176,601	57.50		June 2, 1883	35
			62,646	100		Sept. 18, 1876	36
			94,021	24.391		May 14, 1879	37
		500,000	1,795,992	14.941		Nov. 20, 1883	38
			237,824	66		Mar. 19, 1879	39
		200,000	376,756	62.50		Apr. 5, 1886	40
		150,000	177,512	76.50		June 2, 1884	41
12		34,000	35,801	51		Mar. 4, 1886	42
		50,000	56,457	22.50		Mar. 28, 1883	43
	12		34,535	100		Feb. 28, 1878	44
50	4,185	75,000	91,801	100	100	Jan. 31, 1881	45
		50,000	135,952	48.40		July 20, 1882	46
794		250,000	703,658	77.512		Feb. 28, 1885	47
	9,488		59,226	100	100	May 23, 1888	48
		60,000	97,464	70		July 14, 1880	49
		30,000	85,023	27		Nov. 25, 1882	50
		140,000	352,062	100	38.50	Aug. 11, 1884	51
	8,739	132,000	185,760	100	100	Sept. 14, 1881	52
		67,000	175,952	81.50		Jan. 18, 1883	53
		50,000	140,735	63.60		July 23, 1881	54
		53,000	227,355	80.179		June 10, 1880	55
	26,720	625,000	1,935,721	100	100	Mar. 26, 1888	56
	3,626		133,112	100	100	Oct. 15, 1881	57
200			106,356	37.6483		Oct. 5, 1885	58
		72,000	254,647	100		Mar. 3, 1882	59
18,422			1,061,508	100	100		60
6,588		200,000	298,324	60			61
			392,394	100		July 6, 1881	62
	36,871		75,175	100	100	Mar. 9, 1882	63
	5,849		29,204	100	100	Aug. 5, 1879	64
		35,000	118,371	90.50		June 20, 1882	65
		125,000	90,424	88		Mar. 9, 1885	66
		36,000	36,109	60		Sept. 7, 1883	67
	15,682	100,000	262,887	100		July 5, 1879	68
		50,000	77,104	38.10		Mar. 24, 1885	69
1,849		100,000	168,018	40			70
		21,500	70,191	98.35		Oct. 28, 1886	71
		17,000	27,801	60		Apr. 8, 1881	72
108	3,420		32,449	100	100	Oct. 10, 1879	73
	12,679	50,000	156,260	100	100	Mar. 15, 1881	74
7,432		130,000	282,370	50			75
		121,750	197,363	100	42.30	Mar. 1, 1884	76

INSOLVENT NATIONAL BANKS, DATE OF ORGANIZATION, APPOINTMENT OF RECEIVER, AMOUNTS OF NOMINAL AND ADDITIONAL ASSETS, AMOUNTS

	Nominal value of remaining assets.	Collected from assets.	Collected from assessment upon shareholders.	Total collections from all sources.	Loans paid and other disbursements.	Dividends paid.	Legal expenses.	Receiver's salary and other expenses.
77	....	$157, 782	....	$157, 782	$2, 021	$137, 428	$5, 385	$12, 119
78	....	205, 062	$54, 950	260, 012	57, 745	166, 587	10, 245	24, 551
79	....	96, 605	....	96, 605	53	88, 176	......	7, 517
80	$11, 877	29, 419	4, 677	34, 096	10	20, 758	1, 792	11, 296
81	....	91, 121	23, 001	114, 122	8, 420	82, 060	7, 167	16, 475
82	....	113, 791	....	113, 791	....	96, 176	3, 225	6, 739
83	93, 431	327, 684	267, 311	594, 995	7, 037	528, 305	13, 593	19, 600
84	....	89, 766	64, 655	154, 421	....	99, 847	2, 973	10, 832
85	117, 531	1, 239, 240	495, 550	1, 734, 790	....	1, 027, 538	26, 562	22, 819
86	604, 703	455, 674	13, 450	469, 124	1, 910	384, 735	41, 190	29, 844
87	2, 065, 048	1, 054, 055	629, 058	1, 683, 113	186, 021	1, 312, 093	60, 647	80, 078
88	84, 0[illegible]0	146, 007	8, 287	154, 294	....	118, 740	8, 162	16, 785
89	550, 550	208, 371	115, 204	323, 575	....	208, 450	10, 818	33, 144
90	118, 769	118, 749	4, 990	123, 739	5, 099	80, 864	5, 935	18, 223
91	....	16, 577	23, 732	40, 309	3, 392	26, 809	2, 223	7, 885
92	278, 431	121, 438	7, 898	129, 336	17, 307	72, 398	5, 227	15, 364
93	51, 869	250, 276	64, 150	314, 426	13, 349	225, 618	7, 931	17, 593
94	2, 040, 581	3, 176, 666	266, 424	3, 443, 090	429, 742	2, 684, 120	61, 448	105, 018
95	20, 339	36, 761	13, 569	50, 330	....	36, 527	3, 372	9, 995
96	214, 800	272, 828	73, 774	346, 602	62, 275	260, 190	4, 631	19, 363
97	42, 992	22, 623	18, 259	40, 882	....	18, 331	2, 532	11, 390
98	211, 487	57, 380	4, 200	61, 580	6, 359	....	16, 819	11, 771
99	....	20, 849	....	20, 849	6, 515	8, 807	52	5, 475
100	71, 283	40, 863	23, 500	64, 363	1, 893	41, 324	2, 993	8, 699
101	403, 392	503, 674	91, 149	594, 823	5, 967	520, 329	18, 216	15, 803
102	....	46, 332	50, 000	96, 332	....	86, 263	1, 825	8, 244
103	14, 190	76, 122	1, 400	77, 522	....	56, 131	2, 556	14, 111
104	1, 950, 736	1, 522, 417	161, 893	1, 684, 310	154, 603	1, 446, 091	37, 110	39, 936
105	....	148, 611	....	148, 611	231	131, 024	192	2, 314
106	102, 487	204, 970	....	204, 970	9, 020	119, 269	1, 484	12, 893
107	125, 778	30, 785	....	30, 785	4, 932	10, 208	1, 852	7, 942
108	105, 522	24, 007	35, 600	59, 607	625	49, 709	1, 131	7, 189
109	....	77, 305	....	77, 305	....	66, 394	1, 155	6, 607
110	....	165, 669	....	165, 669	16, 177	135, 574	1, 425	7, 321
111	....	198, 513	....	198, 513	....	117, 878	198	5, 208
112	....	204, 047	....	204, 047	106, 424	82, 946	324	4, 379
113	24, 884	58, 853	....	58, 853	....	37, 971	....	6, 478
114	....	14, 251	....	14, 251	82	9, 402	....	1, 348
115	3, 070, 889	1, 608, 782	....	1, 608, 782	13, 683	881, 048	15, 895	27, 947
116	57, 718	81, 827	....	81, 827	....	73, 939	1, 005	6, 205
117	3, 001	65, 124	16, 268	81, 392	....	60, 271	1, 512	2, 335
118	43, 747	8, 264	....	8, 264	....	....	2, 292	3, 099
119	159, 564	95, 699	....	95, 699	247	85, 993	305	2, 963
120	135, 742	261, 807	....	261, 807	859	255, 495	118	3, 161
121	611, 608	819, 155	....	819, 155	8, 473	767, 644	8, 524	15, 629
122	....	1, 391, 306	....	1, 391, 806	782, 390	400, 998	630	11, 572
123	735, 469	242, 755	....	242, 755	419	190, 613	538	5, 130
124	452, 752	177, 708	8, 000	185, 708	5, 810	158, 310	168	3, 595
125	385, 110	76, 079	....	76, 979	65	61, 428	850	2, 552
126	234, 803	201, 692	....	201, 692	513	238, 041	567	2, 988
127	131, 814	5, 389	....	5, 389	....	....	65	1, 736
128	127, 975	....	....	....	....	....	....	....
	19, 534, 598	38, 649, 700	5, 346, 171	43, 995, 871	5, 182, 932	33, 027, 451	1, 192, 337	2, 383, 871

AND CLOSING, SINCE THE ORGANIZATION OF THE NATIONAL BANKING SYSTEM, WITH COLLECTED FROM ALL SOURCES, ETC.—Continued.

Balance in hands of Comptroller or receiver.	Amount returned to shareholders in cash.	Amount of assessment upon shareholders.	Amount of claims proved.	Dividends, per cent.	Interest dividends, per cent.	Finally closed.	
....	$820	....	$128, 832	100	100	Jan. 17, 1881	77
....	884	$160, 000	132, 461	100	100	Apr. 24, 1880	78
....	850	....	81, 801	100	100	Aug. 1, 1881	79
$240	....	10, 000	21, 182	98	....	Feb. 6, 1883	80
....	....	50, 000	108, 385	81	....	Aug. 6, 1887	81
....	7, 651	....	93, 625	100	100	Feb. 4, 1882	82
1, 357	25, 103	300, 000	580, 502	100	100	Feb. 18, 1885	83
....	40, 769	75, 000	104, 740	100	100	Oct. 13, 1885	84
57, 851	....	500, 000	2, 730, 179	61. 25	....	....	85
11, 443	....	100, 000	804, 735	43	....	....	86
43, 674	....	961, 300	2, 465, 303	55	....	....	87
10, 607	....	50, 000	186, 993	65	....	....	88
11, 163	....	200, 000	401, 493	67. 50	....	....	89
13, 618	....	60, 000	202, 260	40	....	....	90
....	....	50, 000	46, 441	81. 10	....	Oct. 25, 1886	91
19, 040	....	100, 000	204, 521	25	....	....	92
49, 003	....	75, 000	237, 524	95	....	....	93
161, 862	....	400, 000	4, 476, 088	60	....	....	94
436	....	25, 000	36, 526	100	....	....	95
143	....	250, 000	365, 931	71	....	....	96
8, 009	....	32, 500	28, 350	75	....	....	97
26, 631	....	100, 000	158, 608	....	....	....	98
....	....	....	8, 181	100	100	Oct. 20, 1885	99
9, 434	....	50, 000	82, 618	50	....	....	100
34, 508	....	200, 000	650, 421	80	....	....	101
....	....	50, 000	86, 258	100	100	Feb. 10, 1888	102
4, 724	....	50, 000	140, 333	40	....	....	103
5, 070	....	300, 000	2, 895, 515	50	....	....	104
....	14, 850	....	127, 524	100	100	June 1, 1886	105
62, 304	....	....	171, 581	70	....	....	106
5, 851	....	....	51, 278	20	....	....	107
913	....	50, 000	110, 508	45	....	....	108
....	3, 149	....	63, 609	100	100	Mar. 2, 1888	109
....	5, 173	....	130, 772	100	100	Aug. 18, 1887	110
....	75, 229	....	116, 626	100	100	Feb. 17, 1887	111
....	10, 074	....	80, 452	100	100	Apr. 30, 1887	112
14, 404	....	50, 000	84, 383	45	....	....	113
....	3, 329	....	9, 379	100	100	Oct. 17, 1887	114
670, 209	....	....	3, 525, 213	25	....	....	115
678	....	....	82, 155	90	....	....	116
17, 274	....	19, 500	75, 550	80	....	....	117
2, 873	....	50, 000	141, 485	....	....	....	118
6, 191	....	60, 000	172, 950	50	....	....	119
2, 174	....	....	247, 920	100	100	Oct. 20, 1888	120
18, 885	....	....	959, 518	80	....	....	121
....	195, 716	....	308, 236	100	100	June 27, 1888	122
46, 055	....	....	766, 101	25	....	....	123
17, 825	....	100, 000	395, 770	40	....	....	124
12, 084	....	....	295, 626	20	....	....	125
19, 583	....	....	297, 551	80	....	....	126
3, 588	....	....	11, 708	....	....	....	127
....	....	....	....	....	....	....	128
1, 409, 082	799, 898	12, 555, 350	51, 924, 977	....	....	....	

LIABILITIES OF THE NATIONAL BANKS, AND THE RESERVE REQUIRED AND HELD AT THREE DATES IN THE YEARS 1884, 1885, 1886, 1887, and 1888.

STATES AND TERRITORIES EXCLUSIVE OF RESERVE CITIES.

Date.	No. of banks.	Net deposits.	Reserve required.	Reserve held.		Classification of reserve.			
				Amount.	Ratio to deposits.	Specie.	Other lawful money.	Due from agents.	Redemption fund.
		Millions.	*Millions.*	*Millions.*	*Per cent.*	*Millions.*	*Millions.*	*Millions.*	*Millions.*
Apr. 24, 1884	2,340	570.0	86.4	162.5	28.2	36.4	31.5	83.7	10.9
June 20, 1884	2,376	544.7	81.7	146.0	26.8	36.4	32.0	66.8	10.7
Sept. 30, 1884	2,417	535.8	80.4	156.3	29.2	35.2	30.9	79.7	10.5
May 6, 1885	2,432	540.3	81.1	171.0	31.6	40.7	30.2	90.0	10.1
July 1, 1885	2,442	552.2	82.8	170.3	30.8	40.1	28.1	92.1	10.0
Oct. 1, 1885	2,467	570.8	85.6	177.5	31.1	41.5	29.9	95.9	10.2
Mar. 1, 1886	2,518	596.1	89.4	181.6	30.4	45.1	27.7	98.9	9.8
June 3, 1886	2,552	611.7	91.8	181.6	29.7	49.1	29.7	93.5	9.3
Oct. 7, 1886	2,590	637.6	95.6	186.2	29.2	47.8	30.1	99.5	8.7
May 13, 1887	2,676	682.8	102.4	198.9	29.1	51.1	32.9	107.8	6.8
Aug. 1, 1887	2,724	683.0	102.4	189.5	27.7	48.9	31.3	102.6	6.6
Oct. 5, 1887	2,756	690.6	103.6	190.9	27.6	50.8	32.6	100.9	6.6
Apr. 30, 1888	2,809	707.5	106.1	193.9	27.4	51.0	33.8	102.8	6.4
June 30, 1888	2,829	711.8	106.8	199.2	28.0	49.1	31.5	112.2	6.3
Oct. 4, 1888	2,847	739.3	110.9	209.8	28.4	50.2	34.5	118.9	6.2

NEW YORK CITY.

Date.	No. of banks.	Net deposits.	Reserve required.	Amount.	Ratio to deposits.	Specie.	Other lawful money.	Due from agents.	Redemption fund.
Apr. 24, 1884	47	282.2	70.5	75.2	26.6	49.5	24.9	....	0.8
June 20, 1884	45	231.8	57.9	69.1	29.8	43.5	24.9	....	0.7
Sept. 30, 1884	44	254.9	63.7	90.8	35.6	63.1	27.0	....	0.7
May 6, 1885	44	297.7	74.4	123.5	41.5	96.5	26.4	....	0.6
July 1, 1885	45	312.7	78.2	132.8	42.5	96.5	37.5	....	0.6
Oct. 1, 1885	44	312.9	78.2	115.7	37.0	91.5	23.7	....	0.5
Mar. 1, 1886	45	323.6	80.9	101.2	31.3	77.2	23.5	....	0.5
June 3, 1886	45	296.8	74.2	89.9	30.3	57.9	31.5	....	0.4
Oct. 7, 1886	45	282.8	70.7	77.0	27.2	64.1	12.5	....	0.4
May 13, 1887	46	299.7	74.9	82.8	27.6	63.6	18.8	....	0.4
Aug. 1, 1887	46	294.0	73.5	82.6	28.1	65.0	17.2	....	0.4
Oct. 5, 1887	47	284.3	71.1	80.1	28.2	63.6	16.1	....	0.4
Apr. 30, 1888	46	316.7	79.2	94.8	29.9	69.4	25.0	....	0.4
June 30, 1888	46	338.4	84.6	102.7	30.3	73.4	28.8	....	0.4
Oct. 4, 1888	46	342.2	85.5	96.4	28.2	73.9	22.1	....	0.3

CHICAGO.

Date.	No. of banks.	Net deposits.	Reserve required.	Amount.	Ratio to deposits.	Specie.	Other lawful money.	Due from agents.	Redemption fund.
May 13, 1887	18	68.0	17.0	20.7	30.4	13.0	7.6	....	0.05
Aug. 1, 1887	18	66.3	16.6	22.0	33.1	14.6	7.2	....	0.05
Oct. 5, 1887	18	64.6	16.2	19.7	30.5	12.9	6.7	....	0.05
Apr. 30, 1888	18	71.3	17.8	21.2	29.7	13.4	7.8	....	0.05
June 30, 1888	19	71.8	18.0	22.5	31.4	14.1	8.4	....	0.05
Oct. 4, 1888	19	69.3	17.3	21.0	30.2	13.1	7.8	....	0.05

SAINT LOUIS.

Date.	No. of banks.	Net deposits.	Reserve required.	Amount.	Ratio to deposits.	Specie.	Other lawful money.	Due from agents.	Redemption fund.
May 13, 1887	5	9.1	2.2	3.3	36.4	1.5	1.8	....	0.03
Aug. 1, 1887	5	10.8	2.7	3.4	31.9	1.6	1.8	....	0.03
Oct. 5, 1887	5	10.3	2.6	2.7	26.4	1.3	1.3	....	0.03
Apr. 30, 1888	4	8.7	2.2	3.5	40.1	1.6	1.8	....	0.03
June 30, 1888	4	8.9	2.2	3.7	42.0	1.8	1.9	....	0.03
Oct. 4, 1888	4	7.9	2.0	2.1	27.1	1.0	1.1	....	0.02

LIABILITIES OF THE NATIONAL BANKS, AND THE RESERVE REQUIRED AND HELD AT THREE DATES, ETC.—Continued.

OTHER RESERVE CITIES.*

Date.	No. of banks.	Net deposits.	Reserve required.	Reserve held. Amount.	Reserve held. Ratio to deposits.	Classification of reserve. Specie.	Classification of reserve. Other lawful money.	Classification of reserve. Due from agents.	Classification of reserve. Redemption fund.
		Millions.	Millions.	Millions.	Per cent.	Millions.	Millions.	Millions.	Millions.
Apr. 24, 1884	202	338.0	84.5	104.1	30.8	28.8	33.3	38.8	3.2
June 20, 1884	204	302.8	75.7	91.1	30.1	29.7	29.9	28.4	3.1
Sept. 30, 1884	203	308.0	77.0	99.0	32.2	30.3	33.3	32.3	3.1
May 6, 1885	202	340.5	86.6	124.0	35.8	40.2	39.9	40.9	3.0
July 1, 1885	202	356.5	89.1	123.4	34.6	41.0	38.8	40.7	2.9
Oct. 1, 1885	203	364.5	91.1	122.2	33.5	41.9	35.0	42.4	2.9
Mar. 1, 1886	205	378.0	94.5	124.0	32.8	49.3	28.2	43.9	2.7
June 3, 1886	212	387.2	96.8	122.8	31.7	50.5	30.2	39.6	2.5
Oct. 7, 1886	217	381.5	95.4	118.9	29.9	44.5	26.0	41.3	2.2
May 13, 1887	210	345.1	86.3	106.1	30.7	38.0	26.4	40.2	1.4
Aug. 1, 1887	221	335.5	83.9	98.4	29.3	34.8	24.2	37.7	1.2
Oct. 5, 1887	223	338.5	84.6	100.7	29.7	36.3	23.2	40.0	1.2
Apr. 30, 1888	221	355.4	88.8	105.9	29.8	36.7	24.3	43.7	1.0
June 30, 1888	224	372.5	93.1	113.4	30.4	42.9	23.6	45.9	1.0
Oct. 4, 1888	224	384.9	96.2	116.9	30.4	40.0	24.4	51.5	0.9

SUMMARY.*

Date.	No. of banks.	Net deposits.	Reserve required.	Reserve held. Amount.	Reserve held. Ratio to deposits.	Classification of reserve. Specie.	Classification of reserve. Other lawful money.	Classification of reserve. Due from agents.	Classification of reserve. Redemption fund.
Apr. 24, 1884	2,589	1,196.2	241.4	341.8	28.6	114.7	89.7	122.5	14.9
June 20, 1884	2,625	1,079.3	215.3	306.2	28.4	109.6	86.8	95.2	14.5
Sept 30, 1884	2,664	1,098.7	221.1	346.1	31.6	128.6	91.2	112.0	14.3
May 6, 1885	2,678	1,184.5	242.1	418.5	35.3	177.4	96.5	130.9	13.7
July 1, 1885	2,689	1,221.4	250.1	426.5	34.9	177.6	102.6	132.8	13.5
Oct. 1, 1885	2,714	1,248.2	254.9	415.4	33.3	174.9	88.6	138.3	13.6
Mar. 1, 1886	2,768	1,297.6	264.8	406.8	31.3	171.6	79.4	142.8	12.9
June 3, 1886	2,809	1,295.7	262.8	394.2	30.4	157.5	91.6	133.0	12.2
Oct. 7, 1886	2,852	1,301.8	261.7	377.2	28.9	156.4	68.7	140.8	11.4
May 13, 1887	2,955	1,404.7	282.9	411.9	29.3	167.3	87.6	148.1	8.8
Aug. 1, 1887	3,014	1,389.7	279.1	396.0	28.5	165.1	82.3	140.3	8.3
Oct. 5, 1887	3,049	1,388.4	278.0	394.2	28.4	165.1	79.9	140.9	8.3
Apr. 30, 1888	3,098	1,459.6	294.1	419.3	28.7	172.1	92.9	146.5	7.9
June 30, 1888	3,120	1,502.5	304.7	441.5	29.4	181.3	94.3	158.1	7.8
Oct. 4, 1888	3,140	1,543.6	312.0	446.2	28.9	178.1	90.0	170.5	7.6

*Includes Chicago and Saint Louis up to 1887.

TABLE SHOWING, BY GEOGRAPHICAL DIVISIONS, THE RESERVE CITIES AND CENTRAL RESERVE CITIES, THE NUMBER OF BANKS IN OPERATION AT EVERY DATE ON WHICH REPORTS OF CONDITION HAVE BEEN MADE, FROM MARCH 11, 1882, TO OCTOBER 4, 1888, INCLUSIVE, TOGETHER WITH THE AMOUNT OF RESERVE REQUIRED AND THE AMOUNT HELD AT EACH OF THOSE DATES, AND THE CLASSIFICATION OF THE RESERVE HELD, SHOWING AMOUNTS AND PERCENTAGES IN EACH CASE.

[Division No. 1.—Maine, New Hampshire, Vermont, Massachusetts, Rhode Island, and Connecticut, excluding reserve cities.]

Dates.	No. of banks	Amount of reserve required, 15 per cent. of net deposits.	Reserve held.		Classification of reserve held.				
			Amount.	Ratio.	Lawful money (6 per cent.).		With reserve agents (9 per cent.).		Five per cent. redemption fund.
					Amount.	Ratio.	Amount.	Ratio.	
1882.				Per ct.		Per ct.		Per ct.	
Mar. 11...	502	$14,962,799	$20,478,048	29.55	$7,223,511	7.24	$17,716,653	17.76	$4,538,454
May 19...	503	15,068,764	31,457,478	31.31	7,405,171	7.46	19,488,807	19.40	4,473,500
July 1....	504	15,505,375	29,835,966	28.86	7,585,378	7.34	17,833,751	17.25	4,416,842
Oct. 3.....	505	16,296,302	29,332,584	27.00	7,916,022	7.29	16,949,161	15.96	4,467,401
Dec. 30...	507	16,254,969	33,151,031	30.59	8,197,588	7.56	20,509,426	18.93	4,444,017
1883.									
Mar. 13...	507	15,342,235	28,288,564	27.06	7,552,020	7.38	16,299,167	15.94	4,437,377
May 1....	509	15,309,783	27,968,728	27.40	7,495,846	7.34	16,040,299	15.72	4,432,583
June 22 ..	510	15,369,906	28,844,230	28.15	7,685,718	7.50	16,722,029	16.32	4,436,483
Oct. 2.....	511	16,161,030	31,164,435	28.93	7,650,678	7.10	19,099,007	17.73	4,414,690
Dec. 31...	512	16,420,477	34,548,821	31.55	8,144,345	7.44	21,965,101	20.06	4,439,375
1884.									
Mar. 7....	514	15,959,007	32,510,901	30.56	7,875,750	7.40	20,374,517	19.15	4,260,634
Apr. 24...	514	16,081,733	31,256,427	27.15	8,138,314	7.59	18,787,103	17.52	4,331,010
June 20...	514	15,103,686	27,470,663	27.28	8,231,410	8.17	14,972,792	14.87	4,266,461
Sept. 30...	514	15,614,046	32,199,345	30.93	8,199,770	7.88	19,833,278	19.05	4,166,297
Dec. 20...	515	15,216,181	31,576,643	31.13	8,273,291	8.16	19,211,124	18.94	4,092,228
1885.									
Mar. 10...	514	15,553,913	33,503,396	32.37	8,416,089	8.12	21,146,721	20.39	3,990,086
May 6....	511	16,093,617	34,886,766	32.52	8,641,121	8.05	22,184,176	20.68	4,061,469
July 1....	512	16,589,066	34,507,448	31.31	8,951,595	8.10	21,637,813	19.58	4,008,040
Oct. 1	506	17,218,577	34,416,314	29.98	9,549,345	8.32	20,832,605	18.15	4,034,364
Dec. 24...	506	17,150,864	32,831,670	28.71	9,562,800	8.36	19,311,376	16.89	3,957,494
1886.									
Mar. 1....	507	17,185,207	32,588,870	28.44	9,772,588	8.53	18,969,980	16.56	3,846,302
June 3....	510	16,473,718	32,509,786	27.91	10,304,208	8.85	18,555,748	15.93	3,649,830
Aug. 27...	509	17,388,516	31,345,788	27.04	10,316,259	8.90	17,449,280	15.05	3,580,249
Oct. 7	510	18,295,909	35,702,441	29.22	10,335,491	8.47	21,995,854	18.03	3,431,096
Dec. 28...	511	17,815,957	33,220,308	27.98	10,888,002	9.17	19,338,200	16.28	3,002,236
1887.									
Mar. 4....	511	17,404,118	34,081,099	29.27	10,261,663	8.81	21,137,117	18.15	2,682,319
May 13...	513	17,918,113	33,354,311	27.92	10,470,249	8.77	20,384,444	17.06	2,499,618
Aug. 1....	512	17,228,499	28,645,014	24.94	10,202,657	8.88	16,106,365	14.02	2,335,072
Oct. 5.....	512	17,758,954	32,079,549	27.10	10,081,047	8.51	19,698,402	16.64	2,300,100
Dec. 7....	514	17,341,009	29,625,900	25.64	10,316,702	8.92	17,045,118	14.74	2,264,080
1888.									
Feb. 14 ...	514	18,229,528	33,096,440	27.23	9,937,033	8.18	20,928,085	17.22	2,230,122
Apr. 30...	514	18,287,862	32,928,907	27.01	10,402,520	8.53	20,330,966	16.68	2,195,415
June 30. ..	515	18,929,571	35,172,829	27.87	10,047,520	7.96	22,986,251	18.21	2,139,058
Oct. 4.....	515	19,889,593	36,547,994	27.56	10,745,705	8.11	23,704,062	17.88	2,098,167

TABLE SHOWING, BY GEOGRAPHICAL DIVISIONS, THE RESERVE CITIES AND CENTRAL RESERVE CITIES, THE NUMBER OF BANKS IN OPERATION, ETC.—Continued.

[Division No. 2.—New York, New Jersey, and Pennsylvania, excluding reserve cities.]

Dates.	No. of banks	Amount of reserve required, 15 per cent. of net deposits.	Reserve held.		Classification of reserve held.				
			Amount.	Ratio.	Lawful money (6 per cent.).		With reserve agents (9 per cent.).		Five per cent. redemption fund.
					Amount.	Ratio.	Amount.	Ratio.	
1882.				*Per ct.*		*Per ct.*		*Per ct.*	
Mar. 11...	507	$24,513,805	$47,919,202	29.32	$14,546,614	8.90	$30,249,865	18.51	$3,122,723
May 19...	514	24,825,600	49,038,897	29.63	15,827,208	9.56	30,100,831	18.19	3,110,858
July 1...	515	25,243,576	47,501,012	28.23	15,228,446	9.05	29,217,784	17.36	3,054,782
Oct. 3....	515	25,702,599	47,834,868	27.92	15,881,906	9.27	28,868,395	16.85	3,084,567
Dec. 30...	521	26,500,579	48,071,228	27.21	16,667,008	9.43	28,338,020	16.04	3,066,200
1883.									
Mar. 13...	525	26,151,831	48,307,519	27.71	15,232,686	8.74	30,026,506	17.22	3,048,327
May 1...	532	26,557,410	45,564,935	25.74	16,603,462	9.38	25,905,781	14.63	3,055,692
June 22...	537	26,409,027	50,817,552	28.86	16,240,341	9.22	31,528,884	17.91	3,048,327
Oct. 2.....	545	26,885,132	48,979,043	27.33	16,912,419	9.44	29,011,331	16.19	3,055,293
Dec. 31...	549	26,992,446	50,577,804	28.11	17,734,066	9.86	29,840,086	16.58	3,003,652
1884.									
Mar. 7....	550	27,003,470	53,829,445	29.90	16,983,453	9.43	33,924,115	18.84	2,921,877
Apr. 24...	554	27,240,954	53,358,232	29.38	18,854,082	10.38	31,556,160	17.38	2,947,990
June 20..	561	25,502,692	45,241,638	26.61	18,801,649	11.06	23,558,015	13.86	2,881,974
Sept. 30..	563	25,245,939	49,180,050	29.23	18,694,389	11.11	27,634,801	16.42	2,860,460
Dec. 20...	566	24,531,549	50,799,720	31.06	18,036,445	11.03	29,977,889	18.33	2,785,386
1885.									
Mar. 10...	559	25,258,857	55,463,538	32.94	18,925,754	11.24	33,766,909	20.05	2,770,785
May 6....	559	25,204,550	53,071,039	31.58	20,044,604	11.93	30,262,867	18.01	2,763,578
July 1....	561	25,615,062	51,945,847	30.42	19,178,305	11.23	30,033,212	17.59	2,734,330
Oct. 1....	557	26,291,732	56,170,958	32.05	20,055,448	11.44	33,297,308	19.00	2,818,202
Dec. 24..	567	26,843,401	58,345,580	32.60	18,913,441	10.57	36,653,591	20.48	2,778,548
1886.									
Mar. 1...	570	27,453,354	56,026,945	30.61	18,960,011	10.36	34,334,359	18.76	2,732,575
June 3....	571	27,533,873	54,618,391	29.75	20,795,357	11.33	31,241,898	17.02	2,581,136
Aug. 27...	572	28,253,322	56,916,208	30.21	20,185,336	10.71	34,176,300	18.14	2,554,572
Oct. 7.....	572	28,830,549	54,836,089	28.53	20,192,341	10.51	32,249,120	16.78	2,394,628
Dec. 28...	575	28,792,675	53,341,795	27.79	20,360,434	10.61	30,849,802	16.07	2,131,559
1887.									
Mar. 4....	576	29,020,465	54,867,767	28.36	19,405,628	10.03	33,449,031	17.29	2,012,508
May 13...	580	29,685,015	56,208,209	28.48	20,193,151	10.20	34,100,474	17.26	1,914,584
Aug. 1...	586	29,837,428	51,301,676	25.82	19,291,157	9.70	30,226,408	15.20	1,844,111
Oct. 5....	587	30,064,960	52,990,784	26.44	19,775,576	9.87	31,370,441	15.65	1,844,767
Dec. 7....	591	30,090,137	52,172,378	26.01	20,038,795	9.99	30,215,646	15.01	1,817,937
1888.									
Feb. 14...	593	31,181,582	57,520,460	27.67	20,111,377	9.67	33,617,574	17.13	1,791,509
Apr. 30..	596	31,422,827	55,782,017	26.63	20,936,380	9.99	33,066,277	15.78	1,779,360
June 30..	598	31,184,265	56,274,855	27.07	19,371,217	9.31	35,146,220	16.91	1,757,409
Oct. 4....	601	32,659,379	62,056,872	28.50	21,624,500	9.93	38,705,110	17.78	1,726,762

TABLE SHOWING, BY GEOGRAPHICAL DIVISIONS, THE RESERVE CITIES AND CENTRAL RESERVE CITIES, THE NUMBER OF BANKS IN OPERATION, ETC.—Continued.

[Division No. 3.—Delaware, Maryland, Virginia, West Virginia, and the District of Columbia, excluding reserve cities.]

Dates.	No. of banks	Amount of reserve required, 15 per cent. of net deposits.	Reserve held.		Classification of reserve held.				
			Amount.	Ratio.	Lawful money (6 per cent.). Amount.	Lawful money (6 per cent.). Ratio.	With reserve agents (9 per cent.). Amount.	With reserve agents (9 per cent.). Ratio.	Five per cent. redemption fund.
1882.				*Per ct.*		*Per ct.*		*Per ct.*	
Mar. 11...	73	$3,326,580	$6,300,888	28.41	$2,702,126	12.18	$3,212,987	14.49	$1,385,775
May 19...	74	3,229,343	5,840,228	27.16	2,867,270	13.32	2,597,775	12.07	381,183
July 1....	74	3,293,018	6,330,795	28.83	2,951,218	13.44	3,000,277	13.66	379,300
Oct. 3.....	76	3,600,294	7,027,363	29.28	2,883,425	12.01	3,752,436	15.63	391,502
Dec. 30...	77	3,559,250	6,432,974	27.11	2,943,333	12.40	3,098,400	13.06	391,241
1883.									
Mar. 13...	77	3,527,516	5,733,783	24.38	2,337,863	9.94	3,008,054	12.79	387,871
May 1....	77	3,528,471	5,790,224	24.61	2,713,896	11.54	2,691,467	11.44	384,861
June 22..	78	3,621,398	6,406,495	26.54	2,774,761	11.49	3,243,785	13.44	387,949
Oct. 2 ..	82	4,152,516	7,383,800	26.67	3,088,038	11.15	3,901,193	14.09	394,569
Dec. 31...	82	3,998,036	6,620,967	24.82	3,018,536	11.33	3,210,691	12.05	391,760
1884.									
Mar. 7....	83	3,877,353	6,822,590	26.36	2,873,867	11.12	3,582,688	13.86	366,035
Apr. 24...	83	3,812,038	6,446,814	25.37	3,045,651	11.98	3,027,832	11.91	373,331
June 20...	83	3,513,153	5,375,113	22.95	2,975,931	12.71	2,025,960	8.65	373,222
Sept. 30...	88	3,702,825	6,837,101	27,70	3,220,417	13.05	3,246,528	13.15	370,156
Dec. 20...	88	3,365,854	6,467,992	28.82	2,912,926	13.12	3,164,161	14.10	360,905
1885.									
Mar. 10...	88	3,361,044	6,282,532	28.04	3,048,637	13.58	2,895,186	12.92	343,709
May 6....	87	2,854,130	5,624,608	29.56	2,9[illegible]5,242	15.69	2,289,321	12.03	350,135
July 1....	87	2,919,436	5,311,397	27.29	2,758,277	14.17	2,199,965	11.30	353,155
Oct. 1.....	88	3,286,346	7,338,927	33.50	3,134,687	14.31	3,850,486	17.57	353,754
Dec. 24...	80	3,162,147	7,070,981	33.51	2,887,760	13.70	3,825,340	18.15	357,881
1886.									
Mar. 1....	89	3,163,328	6,579,113	31.20	3,079,948	14.60	3,153,202	14.95	345,963
June 3...	90	3,250,103	6,761,881	31.12	3,414,420	15.71	3,034,136	13.97	313,325
Aug. 27..	91	3,490,359	7,337,721	31.53	3,313,468	14.24	3,714,380	15.96	309,873
Oct. 7....	89	3,525,434	7,125,856	30.32	3,405,443	14.49	3,414,134	14.53	306,279
Dec. 28...	91	3,459,845	6,826,991	29.60	3,124,102	13.54	3,414,702	14.80	288,187
1887.									
Mar. 4....	91	3,541,988	6,685,225	28.31	3,061,122	12.96	3,370,568	14.27	253,535
May 13...	92	3,434,211	6,233,763	27.16	3,351,755	14.64	2,640,664	11.53	241,344
Aug. 1....	93	3,681,532	6,591,665	26.86	3,397,925	13.84	2,952,617	12.03	241,123
Oct. 5.....	94	3,789,907	6,641,421	26.29	3,402,471	13.47	3,004,141	11.89	234,809
Dec. 7....	94	3,748,997	6,728,437	26.92	3,329,960	13.32	3,157,971	12.64	240,476
1888.									
Feb. 14...	94	3,827,479	6,737,364	26.40	3,272,849	12.83	3,236,123	12.68	228,392
Apr. 30..	94	3,789,808	6,554,763	25.94	3,340,776	13.22	2,988,503	11.83	225,484
June 30..	95	3,902,911	6,688,570	25.71	3,320,174	12.76	3,150,750	12.11	217,646
Oct. 4....	96	4,364,275	8,474,938	29.13	3,672,305	12.62	4,582,280	15.75	220,353

TABLE SHOWING, BY GEOGRAPHICAL DIVISIONS, THE RESERVE CITIES AND CENTRAL RESERVE CITIES, THE NUMBER OF BANKS IN OPERATION, ETC.—Continued.

[Division No. 4.—North Carolina, South Carolina, Georgia, Florida, Alabama, Mississippi, Louisiana, Texas, Arkansas, Kentucky, and Tennessee, excluding reserve cities.]

Dates.	No. of banks	Amount of reserve required, 15 per cent. of net deposits.	Reserve held.		Classification of reserve held.				
			Amount.	Ratio.	Lawful money (6 per cent.).		With reserve agents (9 per cent.).		Five per cent. redemption fund.
					Amount.	Ratio.	Amount.	Ratio.	
1882.				Per ct.		Per ct.		Per ct.	
May 11...	141	$5,185,281	$10,013,832	28.97	$5,466,058	15.81	$3,758,544	10.87	$789,230
May 19...	144	4,915,890	10,118,504	30.87	5,419,385	16.51	3,006,752	11.02	702,367
July 1....	148	5,115,056	10,326,820	30.28	5,227,153	15.33	4,313,224	12.65	786,443
Oct. 3.....	154	5,266,274	9,392,645	26.75	4,771,326	13.50	3,827,425	10.90	793,894
Dec. 30 ...	159	5,978,914	12,718,655	31.91	6,340,182	15.91	5,584,656	14.01	793,817
1883.									
Mar. 13...	164	6,116,981	13,254,160	32.50	6,396,960	15.69	6,086,199	14.92	771,001
May 1 ...	169	6,190,892	12,890,743	31.23	6,543,434	15.85	5,555,724	13.46	791,585
June 22 ..	175	6,143,331	12,353,975	30.16	6,475,724	15.81	5,075,892	12.39	802,359
Oct. 2.....	191	6,267,968	10,275,182	24.59	6,589,276	15.77	3,887,690	9.30	798,216
Dec. 31 ...	197	6,761,077	12,940,873	28.71	6,968,150	15.46	5,170,209	11.48	802,505
1884.									
Mar. 7....	201	6,816,062	13,644,672	30.03	6,883,358	15.15	5,979,087	13.16	781,627
Apr. 24...	204	6,874,431	12,348,517	26.95	6,803,162	14.84	4,762,025	10.39	783,330
June 20 ..	208	6,449,163	11,364,136	26.43	6,826,409	15.88	3,782,006	8.80	755,721
Sept. 30 ..	210	6,042,804	11,168,565	27.72	6,334,635	15.72	4,087,448	10.15	746,482
Dec. 20 ...	220	6,491,216	14,560,732	33.67	7,007,016	16.19	6,806,367	15.73	747,349
1885.									
Mar. 10 ..	226	6,669,784	15,098,820	33.96	7,964,807	17.91	6,385,184	14.36	748,829
May 6....	229	6,483,405	13,065,477	30.23	7,563,398	17.50	4,765,739	11.03	736,340
July 1....	232	6,442,500	12,404,357	28.88	7,150,393	16.07	4,532,187	10.55	712,777
Oct. 1	232	6,388,330	11,874,404	27.88	6,826,279	16.03	4,322,638	10.15	725,487
Dec. 24 ...	235	7,142,014	15,834,011	33.25	8,001,784	16.80	7,141,940	15.00	690,287
1886.									
Mar. 1....	240	7,583,052	16,308,788	32.26	8,523,803	16.86	7,114,109	14.07	670,756
June 3....	245	7,493,063	15,598,452	31.23	8,103,413	16.23	6,863,106	13.74	626,843
Aug. 27...	251	7,301,490	13,956,920	28.67	7,650,309	15.72	5,699,062	11.71	607,488
Oct. 7	251	7,520,093	13,507,692	27.12	7,565,181	15.09	5,474,973	10.92	557,538
Dec. 28 ...	253	8,863,744	21,096,851	35.70	9,650,357	16.35	10,914,071	18.47	523,423
1887.									
Mar. 4....	265	9,951,682	22,483,366	33.89	10,265,065	15.62	11,607,039	17.50	511,262
May 13...	270	9,403,413	18,093,309	28.86	9,623,458	15.35	7,965,043	12.71	504,808
Aug. 1....	290	9,227,123	15,981,046	25.98	8,924,833	14.51	6,555,611	10.66	500,602
Oct. 5	296	9,183,326	16,341,034	26.69	9,728,521	15.89	6,100,154	9.96	512,359
Dec. 7	301	9,671,142	18,963,708	29.41	10,375,365	16.10	8,072,837	12.52	515,506
1888.									
Feb. 14 ...	305	10,241,743	21,109,205	30.92	11,248,310	16.47	9,353,121	13.70	507,774
Apr. 30 ...	307	9,775,180	17,945,763	27.54	9,916,320	15.22	7,522,773	11.54	506,670
June 30...	313	9,683,437	17,925,943	27.77	9,397,854	14.56	8,027,614	12.44	500,475
Oct. 4.....	318	9,543,970	16,380,467	25.74	9,557,311	15.02	6,338,284	9.96	484,872

TABLE SHOWING, BY GEOGRAPHICAL DIVISIONS, THE RESERVE CITIES AND CENTRAL RESERVE CITIES, THE NUMBER OF BANKS IN OPERATION, ETC.—Continued.

[Division No. 5.—Ohio, Indiana, Illinois, Michigan, and Wisconsin, excluding reserve cities.]

Dates.	No. of banks	Amount of reserve required, 15 per cent. of net deposits.	Reserve held.		Classification of reserve held.				
			Amount.	Ratio.	Lawful money (6 per cent.).		With reserve agents (9 per cent.).		Five per cent. redemption fund.
					Amount.	Ratio.	Amount.	Ratio.	
1882.				Per ct.		Per ct.		Per ct.	
Mar. 11...	503	$19,032,152	$27,890,100	29.78	$17,235,102	13.58	$18,689,978	14.78	$1,965,025
May 19...	512	18,777,697	37,819,405	30.22	17,572,569	14.04	18,358,481	14.67	1,888,355
July 1....	514	18,063,931	37,703,899	29.82	16,982,358	13.43	18,910,821	14.96	1,810,720
Oct. 3....	519	19,272,709	35,909,848	27.99	17,205,670	13.39	16,875,972	13.13	1,888,206
Dec. 30...	523	18,845,485	35,817,290	28.51	17,047,739	13.57	16,905,080	13.46	1,863,871
1883.									
Mar. 13...	530	19,081,960	36,507,835	27.17	16,401,301	12.89	18,281,364	14.38	1,825,170
May 1....	536	18,892,570	34,009,157	27.00	17,003,342	13.50	15,146,613	12.03	1,859,202
June 22...	544	18,680,838	32,831,223	25.14	15,616,973	12.54	15,394,648	12.36	1,819,607
Oct. 2.....	554	18,563,099	34,705,552	28.04	16,503,659	13.34	16,347,350	13.21	1,854,543
Dec. 31...	554	17,961,597	34,790,630	29.05	16,853,215	14.07	16,142,536	13.48	1,794,879
1884.									
Mar. 7....	558	17,808,933	34,832,320	29.34	16,461,984	13.87	16,636,811	14.01	1,733,525
Apr. 24...	560	17,392,601	32,294,594	27.81	16,913,978	14.59	13,623,182	11.75	1,757,484
June 20...	569	16,640,340	30,968,073	29.15	16,186,847	14.59	13,081,876	11.79	1,699,350
Sept. 30..	574	15,784,480	31,545,404	29.98	16,127,236	15.33	13,764,179	13.08	1,654,079
Dec. 20...	572	15,040,275	33,478,235	33.30	15,563,364	15.52	16,332,719	16.29	1,582,152
1885.									
Mar. 10...	567	15,800,692	36,876,180	35.07	16,882,609	16.03	18,475,898	17.54	1,517,679
May 6....	568	15,954,519	35,963,108	33.81	17,117,106	16.09	17,336,757	16.30	1,509,305
July 1....	567	16,118,869	36,102,087	33.65	15,936,895	14.83	18,738,134	17.45	1,487,958
Oct. 1....	570	16,501,187	37,477,345	34.07	17,019,462	15.47	18,934,890	17.21	1,522,993
Dec. 24...	570	16,497,191	36,226,910	32.93	16,050,698	14.59	18,653,616	16.96	1,522,596
1886.									
Mar. 1....	571	17,184,063	38,467,958	33.57	16,692,494	14.57	20,284,810	17.78	1,490,654
June 3....	575	17,452,850	36,082,622	31.53	17,849,509	15.34	17,426,446	14.98	1,406,667
Aug. 27...	582	18,315,951	41,364,412	33.88	17,118,272	14.02	22,867,315	18.73	1,378,825
Oct. 7....	580	18,438,101	39,891,410	32.45	17,974,624	14.62	20,594,220	16.75	1,322,566
Dec. 28...	576	18,828,474	40,251,058	32.07	18,082,037	14.41	20,974,170	16.71	1,193,051
1887.									
Mar. 4....	582	19,446,236	42,186,029	32.54	18,037,038	13.91	23,012,354	17.75	1,136,637
May 13...	584	20,082,778	41,866,938	31.27	19,111,570	14.27	21,673,404	16.19	1,081,958
Aug. 1....	594	20,814,218	44,475,533	32.05	18,401,230	13.26	25,021,687	18.03	1,052,616
Oct. 5.....	598	20,576,959	40,983,916	29.88	19,171,016	13.98	20,771,852	15.14	1,041,048
Dec. 7....	600	20,237,958	39,110,212	28.99	18,425,529	13.66	19,629,800	14.55	1,060,883
1888.									
Feb. 14...	603	20,788,469	40,918,158	29.52	18,290,041	13.20	21,600,663	15.59	1,027,454
Apr. 30...	606	20,795,516	39,175,386	28.26	18,809,677	13.61	19,298,656	13.92	1,067,053
June 30..	609	20,756,627	39,800,200	28.77	17,754,453	12.83	21,045,051	15.21	1,000,696
Oct. 4.....	611	21,297,373	42,224,353	29.74	18,466,510	13.01	22,763,433	16.03	994,409

TABLE SHOWING, BY GEOGRAPHICAL DIVISIONS, THE RESERVE CITIES AND CENTRAL RESERVE CITIES, THE NUMBER OF BANKS IN OPERATION, ETC.—Continued.

[Division No. 6.—Iowa, Minnesota, Missouri, Kansas, and Nebraska (Omaha transferred to division No. 9, October 5, 1887; Kansas City and Saint Joseph transferred to division No. 9, May 13, 1887), excluding reserve cities.]

Dates.	No. of banks.	Amount of reserve required, 15 per cent. of net deposits.	Reserve held.		Classification of reserve held.				
			Amount.	Ratio.	Lawful money (6 per cent.).		With reserve agents (9 per cent.).		Five per cent. redemption fund.
					Amount.	Ratio.	Amount.	Ratio.	
1882.				Per ct.		Per ct.		Per ct.	
Mar. 11	157	$6,541,424	$11,840,967	27.17	$5,710,125	13.11	$5,605,681	12.90	$465,161
May 19	165	6,707,034	12,348,739	27.62	5,557,107	12.43	6,823,635	14.14	467,997
July 1	171	6,945,887	12,102,356	26.33	5,865,877	12.67	5,806,168	12.68	460,311
Oct. 3	184	7,211,774	11,860,093	24.68	5,934,090	12.34	5,443,780	11.32	491,205
Dec. 30	197	7,314,811	12,985,546	26.63	6,513,480	13.35	5,975,158	12.25	496,908
1883.									
Mar. 13	207	7,692,300	13,786,065	26.88	6,048,070	11.79	7,237,137	14.11	500,858
May 1	216	8,007,308	13,928,636	26.09	6,926,476	12.98	6,496,862	12.17	505,298
June 22	227	8,660,010	16,331,528	28.26	6,739,738	11.66	9,100,816	15.75	490,974
Oct. 2	257	9,087,854	15,692,027	25.90	7,240,080	11.95	7,922,362	13.08	529,585
Dec. 31	270	9,269,439	16,068,106	26.00	7,756,806	12.55	7,788,201	12.60	523,099
1884.									
Mar. 7	287	9,365,600	16,334,768	26.16	7,297,414	11.69	8,526,486	13.66	510,868
Apr. 24	298	9,712,119	17,385,106	26.85	8,463,096	13.07	8,406,680	12.98	515,330
June 20	309	9,546,762	16,682,585	26.21	9,366,090	14.72	6,806,044	10.69	510,451
Sept. 30	329	9,158,231	16,305,178	26.70	8,130,878	13.32	7,677,976	12.58	494,324
Dec. 20	329	8,643,147	15,874,452	27.55	7,734,917	13.42	7,642,884	13.26	496,651
1885.									
Mar. 10	336	9,202,146	18,064,151	29.45	8,442,274	13.76	9,131,647	14.89	490,230
May 6	340	9,643,675	19,112,996	29.73	8,803,813	13.69	9,806,853	15.25	502,330
July 1	346	10,105,532	20,186,373	29.96	8,868,049	13.16	10,827,681	16.07	490,643
Oct. 1	359	10,526,279	19,159,727	27.30	8,896,805	12.68	9,768,829	13.92	494,093
Dec. 24	363	10,511,542	19,128,184	27.30	9,309,286	13.28	9,315,121	13.29	503,777
1886.									
Mar. 1	377	10,872,088	19,373,302	26.73	8,838,140	12.19	10,043,854	13.86	491,308
June 3	391	12,203,046	23,020,432	28.30	11,204,906	13.77	11,339,220	13.94	476,306
Aug. 27	404	12,349,300	24,464,027	29.72	10,229,545	12.43	13,747,424	16.70	487,053
Oct. 7	406	12,377,733	21,931,867	26.58	11,019,342	13.35	10,422,066	12.63	490,459
Dec. 28	418	12,811,418	23,053,002	26.99	11,752,951	13.76	10,848,107	12.70	451,944
1887.									
Mar. 4	427	14,184,873	27,752,343	29.35	11,860,366	12.54	15,441,590	16.33	450,387
May 13	428	13,368,183	26,723,837	29.99	12,010,369	13.48	14,290,849	16.04	422,619
Aug. 1	438	12,435,313	25,056,695	30.22	10,458,600	12.62	14,175,769	17.10	422,236
Oct. 5	455	12,258,402	22,367,310	27.37	10,275,484	12.57	11,660,633	14.27	431,193
Dec. 7	462	11,440,774	20,023,408	26.25	9,831,122	12.89	9,753,960	12.79	438,326
1888.									
Feb. 14	460	11,915,472	24,167,651	30.42	10,418,840	13.12	13,308,830	16.75	439,981
Apr. 30	468	12,191,175	24,237,974	29.80	10,851,912	13.35	12,924,379	15.90	441,683
June 30	471	12,423,419	25,363,096	30.62	10,547,101	12.73	14,367,358	17.35	449,537
Oct. 4	476	12,646,574	23,898,707	28.35	10,011,697	11.87	13,436,321	15.94	450,689

TABLE SHOWING, BY GEOGRAPHICAL DIVISIONS, THE RESERVE CITIES AND CENTRAL RESERVE CITIES, THE NUMBER OF BANKS IN OPERATION, ETC.—Continued.

[Division No. 7.—Colorado, Nevada, California, and Oregon, excluding reserve cities.]

Dates.	No. of banks	Amount of reserve required, 15 per cent. of net deposits.	Reserve held.		Classification of reserve held.				
					Lawful money (6 per cent.).		With reserve agents (9 per cent.).		Five per cent. redemption fund.
			Amount.	Ratio.	Amount.	Ratio.	Amount.	Ratio.	
1882.				Per ct.		Per ct.		Per ct.	
Mar. 11...	30	$2,576,675	$5,408,452	31.58	$2,542,858	14.83	$2,758,864	16.08	$106,730
May 10...	31	2,696,322	5,873,661	32.72	2,637,314	14.09	3,122,481	17.40	112,866
July 1....	32	2,693,926	5,682,235	31.60	2,400,625	13.72	3,100,475	17.34	112,135
Oct. 3....	32	2,868,124	6,241,813	32.09	2,794,278	14.63	3,330,785	17.44	116,750
Dec. 30...	33	2,871,064	6,379,306	33.37	3,166,266	16.56	3,096,181	16.20	116,909
1883.									
Mar. 13...	33	2,866,867	6,081,382	31.80	3,594,508	18.83	2,374,534	12.44	112,250
May 1....	34	2,890,642	5,487,840	28.51	3,133,202	16.28	2,240,755	11.64	113,883
June 22..	38	2,984,656	6,355,048	31.07	3,203,157	16.11	3,033,366	15.26	119,125
Oct. 2.....	43	3,206,008	5,839,540	27.35	3,098,370	14.51	2,619,307	12.27	121,863
Dec. 31...	42	3,241,147	6,447,703	29.88	3,558,027	16.50	2,763,101	12.80	126,575
1884.									
Mar. 7....	43	3,009,701	5,626,902	28.08	3,217,309	16.06	2,287,585	11.40	122,008
Apr. 24...	43	3,028,531	5,701,614	28.08	3,207,082	15.88	2,402,898	12.20	121,634
June 20..	45	2,748,621	5,492,650	29.97	3,664,908	20.00	1,717,837	9.37	109,914
Sept. 30..	46	2,660,548	5,798,350	32.69	3,346,017	18.86	2,341,155	13.20	111,187
Dec. 20...	47	2,560,777	5,524,939	32.36	3,180,260	18.63	2,239,427	13.12	105,252
1885.									
Mar. 10...	47	2,663,353	5,978,551	33.67	3,450,520	19.43	2,419,586	13.63	108,436
May 6....	49	2,683,438	5,699,692	31.86	3,336,534	18.65	2,256,198	12.61	106,960
July 1....	50	2,721,004	5,697,478	31.41	2,966,876	16.36	2,626,141	14.48	104,461
Oct. 1....	51	2,920,866	6,635,005	34.07	3,260,554	16.74	3,264,417	16.76	110,034
Dec. 24...	54	3,189,900	7,038,522	33.10	3,732,709	17.55	3,192,688	15.01	113,125
1886.									
Mar. 1....	57	3,329,624	7,520,982	33.92	3,947,515	17.78	3,465,653	15.61	116,814
June 3...	61	3,598,749	7,672,897	31.98	4,034,027	16.82	3,527,877	14.70	110,993
Aug. 27...	67	3,863,286	8,288,012	32.18	4,096,387	15.91	4,075,587	15.82	116,038
Oct. 7....	68	3,971,589	7,896,910	29.83	4,104,213	15.50	3,672,731	13.87	119,966
Dec. 28...	71	4,329,961	9,221,771	31.95	5,276,940	18.28	3,828,079	13.26	116,853
1887.									
Mar. 4....	71	4,674,444	10,280,339	33.02	5,672,302	18.20	4,504,028	14.45	113,008
May 13...	75	5,276,435	11,540,554	32.81	5,990,889	17.03	5,438,612	15.46	011,053
Aug. 1....	83	5,719,220	11,790,010	30.95	6,134,729	16.09	5,548,500	14.55	116,507
Oct. 5.....	86	6,330,097	13,784,605	32.66	7,276,703	17.24	6,385,306	15.13	122,606
Dec. 7....	86	6,291,325	12,882,230	30.71	7,540,479	17.98	5,218,778	12.44	122,973
1888.									
Feb. 14...	87	6,149,731	12,446,903	30.36	7,457,014	18.19	4,861,593	11.86	128,295
Apr. 30...	94	6,042,609	11,396,749	28.29	6,557,882	16.28	4,708,066	11.69	130,801
June 30..	96	5,924,963	11,634,948	29.46	6,338,182	16.05	5,171,147	13.09	125,619
Oct. 4....	98	6,036,317	12,503,944	31.07	6,338,048	15.75	6,034,811	15.00	131,085

TABLE SHOWING, BY GEOGRAPHICAL DIVISIONS, THE RESERVE CITIES AND CENTRAL RESERVE CITIES THE NUMBER OF BANKS IN OPERATION, ETC.—Continued.

[Division No. 8.—Arizona, Dakota, Montana, New Mexico, Utah, Washington, and Wyoming.]

Dates.	No. of banks.	Amount of reserve required, 15 per cent. of net deposits.	Reserve held.		Classification of reserve held.				
			Amount.	Ratio.	Lawful money (6 per cent.).		With reserve agents (9 per cent.).		Five per cent. redemption fund.
					Amount.	Ratio.	Amount.	Ratio.	
1882.				Per ct.		Per ct.		Per ct.	
Mar. 11	32	$1,144,970	$1,864,032	24.42	$1,234,034	16.17	$547,357	7.17	$82,641
May 19	38	1,340,349	2,242,753	25.10	1,346,771	15.07	803,072	8.99	92,910
July 1	38	1,379,900	2,335,024	25.38	1,265,644	13.76	970,470	10.55	98,920
Oct. 3	41	1,662,285	2,686,299	24.24	1,566,209	14.13	1,019,233	9.20	100,857
Dec. 30	48	1,815,318	3,276,376	27.07	1,893,011	15.64	1,276,446	10.55	106,919
1883.									
Mar. 13	54	1,857,414	3,171,854	25.62	1,944,893	15.71	1,118,433	9.03	108,528
May 1	55	2,072,505	3,196,343	23.13	1,946,749	14.09	1,139,293	8.25	110,301
June 22	60	2,234,510	3,787,433	25.42	1,946,924	13.07	1,726,181	11.59	114,328
Oct. 2	70	2,362,081	3,453,105	21.93	2,000,374	12.70	1,331,438	8.46	121,293
Dec. 31	74	2,280,534	3,746,760	24.64	2,450,974	16.12	1,177,548	7.75	118,244
1884.									
Mar. 7	78	2,206,520	3,406,474	23.16	2,332,136	15.85	955,815	6.50	118,523
Apr. 24	84	2,256,846	3,584,760	23.83	2,421,783	16.10	1,038,881	6.90	124,096
June 20	87	2,194,632	3,402,695	23.26	2,377,061	16.25	899,284	6.15	126,350
Sept. 30	87	2,162,177	3,263,041	22.64	2,077,673	14.41	1,066,754	7.40	118,614
Dec. 20	86	2,193,537	3,581,574	24.49	2,357,403	16.12	1,114,624	7.62	109,547
1885.									
Mar. 10	88	2,132,223	3,703,384	26.05	2,525,590	17.77	1,068,609	7.52	109,185
May 6	89	2,124,740	3,587,907	25.33	2,387,887	16.86	1,089,153	7.69	110,937
July 1	92	2,317,930	3,939,506	25.48	2,354,579	15.24	1,473,460	9.53	111,557
Oct. 1	94	2,492,432	4,420,239	26.60	2,600,691	15.65	1,704,733	10.26	114,815
Dec. 24	107	2,633,914	4,881,391	27.80	3,166,234	18.03	1,594,293	9.08	120,864
1886.									
Mar. 1	107	2,643,604	4,716,817	26.86	3,057,426	17.41	1,535,412	8.74	123,977
June 3	109	2,745,657	4,688,187	25.61	3,091,659	16.89	1,471,191	8.04	125,339
Aug. 27	113	2,615,777	5,173,780	29.67	3,135,269	17.98	1,913,185	10.97	125,335
Oct. 7	114	2,675,213	5,149,624	28.87	3,360,609	18.79	1,669,970	9.36	119,045
Dec. 28	111	2,852,550	5,258,108	27.65	3,560,333	18.70	1,577,946	8.25	119,829
1887.									
Mar. 4	121	3,019,568	4,961,765	24.65	3,418,756	16.98	1,421,601	7.06	121,408
May 13	125	3,258,730	4,782,756	22.02	3,357,718	15.46	1,303,545	6.00	121,493
Aug. 1	128	3,501,233	5,626,017	24.13	3,492,525	14.96	2,010,740	8.57	122,752
Oct. 5	128	3,630,696	5,730,545	23.68	3,715,196	15.35	1,888,860	7.80	126,489
Dec. 7	130	3,787,621	6,200,797	24.91	4,235,601	16.85	1,998,315	7.56	126,881
1888.									
Feb. 14	131	3,779,467	5,791,312	22.98	3,874,586	15.38	1,787,096	7.09	129,630
Apr. 30	130	3,824,485	5,935,373	23.28	3,887,031	15.25	1,919,790	7.53	127,652
June 30	130	3,972,180	6,292,050	23.76	3,874,153	14.63	2,289,537	8.65	128,360
Oct. 4	132	4,461,321	7,758,182	26.08	4,241,947	14.26	3,386,255	11.39	129,980

TABLE SHOWING, BY GEOGRAPHICAL DIVISIONS, THE RESERVE CITIES AND CENTRAL RESERVE CITIES, THE NUMBER OF BANKS IN OPERATION, ETC.—Continued.

[Division No. 9.—Reserve cities—Boston, Albany, Philadelphia, Pittsburgh, Baltimore, Washington, New Orleans, Louisville, Cincinnati, Cleveland, Chicago, Detroit, Milwaukee, Saint Louis, and San Francisco.]

Dates.	No. of banks	Amount of reserve required, 25 per cent. of net deposits.	Reserve held.		Classification of reserve held.				
					Lawful money (12½ per cent.).		With reserve agents (12½ per cent.).		Five per cent. redemption fund.
			Amount.	Ratio.	Amount.	Ratio.	Amount.	Ratio.	
1882.				Per ct.		Per ct.		Per ct.	
Mar. 11...	192	$77,032,003	$93,401,093	30.31	$54,818,246	17.79	$34,852,796	11.31	$3,730,051
May 19...	192	80,291,028	102,352,999	31.87	59,318,593	18.47	39,467,976	12.29	3,566,430
July 1...	193	81,760,651	95,874,953	29.32	57,206,564	17.49	35,233,042	10.77	3,435,347
Oct. 3....	193	79,694,500	89,143,583	27.96	52,413,086	16.44	33,213,032	10.42	3,517,465
Dec. 30...	195	77,095,866	95,051,887	30.82	54,211,536	17.58	37,282,190	12.09	3,558,161
1883.									
Mar. 13...	198	77,419,807	89,796,888	29.00	49,661,801	16.04	36,592,761	11.82	3,542,326
May 1....	199	78,644,546	91,787,852	29.18	54,129,582	17.21	34,090,027	10.84	3,568,243
June 22...	200	83,005,153	103,900,990	31.29	59,515,283	17.93	40,821,353	12.29	3,504,354
Oct. 2...	200	80,961,109	100,638,235	31.08	56,425,407	17.42	40,798,990	12.60	3,413,838
Dec. 31...	202	83,646,150	105,535,835	31.54	63,273,391	18.91	38,942,133	11.64	3,320,311
1884.									
Mar. 7....	202	85,297,591	111,255,631	32.61	61,563,512	18.04	46,437,308	13.61	3,254,811
Apr. 24...	202	84,514,593	104,165,958	30.81	62,160,250	18.39	38,827,197	11.49	3,178,511
June 20...	204	75,708,561	91,103,676	30.08	59,623,045	19.69	28,403,338	9.38	3,077,293
Sept. 30..	203	76,984,343	99,022,475	32.16	63,578,992	20.65	32,340,900	10.50	3,102,583
Dec. 20...	203	78,739,375	103,685,153	32.92	66,011,790	20.96	34,672,781	11.01	3,000,582
1885.									
Mar. 10...	202	83,462,537	118,522,306	35.50	74,383,404	22.28	41,172,443	12.33	2,966,459
May 6....	202	86,028,766	123,962,577	35.77	80,109,098	23.12	40,912,049	11.81	2,941,430
July 1....	202	89,118,594	123,423,045	34.62	79,828,139	22.39	40,661,809	11.41	2,933,097
Oct. 1....	203	91,118,639	122,186,751	33.52	76,907,632	21.10	42,402,600	11.63	2,876,510
Dec. 24...	202	91,151,185	117,043,608	32.1[illegible]	74,674,927	20.48	39,551,479	10.88	2,817,202
1886.									
Mar 1....	205	94,506,304	124,034,387	32.81	77,446,733	20.49	43,904,247	11.61	2,683,357
June 3...	212	96,810,237	122,784,157	31.71	80,738,933	20.85	39,567,423	10.22	2,477,801
Aug. 27...	215	93,802,959	110,584,456	29.42	68,232,506	18.19	40,072,689	10.68	2,279,261
Oct. 7....	217	95,363,719	113,951,757	29.88	70,489,135	18.48	41,271,509	10.82	2,191,113
Dec. 28...	218	94,305,102	112,821,235	29.91	70,633,785	18.72	40,371,942	10.70	1,815,508
1887.									
Mar. 4....	220	99,518,660	124,447,510	31.26	73,631,556	18.50	49,217,253	12.36	1,598,701
May 13*..	210	86,270,869	106,121,301	30.75	64,496,954	18.69	40,210,839	11.65	1,413,508
Aug. 1†...	221	83,889,166	98,389,974	29.32	59,504,534	17.73	37,672,349	11.23	1,213,090
Oct. 5.....	223	84,621,164	100,714,633	29.75	59,524,848	17.59	39,993,709	11.82	1,196,076
Dec. 7....	223	84,031,602	97,132,024	28.90	58,086,213	17.28	37,957,340	11.29	1,088,471
1888.									
Feb. 14...	222	88,281,912	107,045,750	30.31	61,380,008	17.38	44,647,555	12.63	1,018,187
Apr. 30...	221	88,841,975	105,914,479	29.80	61,211,749	17.22	43,718,493	12.30	984,237
June 30...	224	93,119,904	113,399,111	30.44	66,493,977	17.85	45,949,662	12.34	955,472
Oct. 4....	224	96,217,307	116,864,734	30.36	64,447,941	16.75	51,508,038	13.38	908,755

* Kansas City and Saint Joseph included from May 13, 1887, and Chicago and Saint Louis transferred to Division No 10.

† Omaha included from August 1, 1887.

TABLE SHOWING, BY GEOGRAPHICAL DIVISIONS, THE RESERVE CITIES AND CENTRAL RESERVE CITIES, THE NUMBER OF BANKS IN OPERATION, ETC.—Continued.

[Division No. 10.—Central reserve cities—New York, Chicago, and Saint Louis.]

Dates.	New York City.			Chicago.			Saint Louis.		
	No. of banks.	Amount of reserve required, 25 per cent. of net deposits.	Ratio of reserve held.	No. of banks.	Amount of reserve required, 25 per cent. of net deposits.	Ratio of reserve held.	No. of banks.	Amount of reserve required, 25 per cent. of net deposits.	Ratio of reserve held.
1882.			*Per ct.*			*Per ct.*			*Per ct.*
Mar. 11	50	$63,982,629	25.16	......	......	......	......	......	......
May 19	50	66,708,718	26.14	......	......	......	......	......	......
July 1	50	69,337,260	25.90	......	......	......	......	......	......
Oct. 3	50	63,503,245	25.30	......	......	......	......	......	......
Dec. 30	48	64,301,245	26.14	......	......	......	......	......	......
1883.									
Mar. 13	48	62,437,001	23.50	......	......	......	......	......	......
May 1	48	63,422,340	25.48	......	......	......	......	......	......
June 22	48	69,869,640	28.81	......	......	......	......	......	......
Oct. 2	48	66,735,374	26.53	......	......	......	......	......	......
Dec. 31	47	69,509,200	27.58	......	......	......	......	......	......
1884.									
Mar. 7	47	75,378,000	28.94	......	......	......	......	......	......
Apr. 24	47	70,540,863	26.65	......	......	......	......	......	......
June 20	45	57,948,702	29.82	......	......	......	......	......	......
Sept. 30	44	63,787,684	35.63	......	......	......	......	......	......
Dec. 20	44	68,335,552	38.29	......	......	......	......	......	......
1885.									
Mar. 10	44	73,191,705	40.12	......	......	......	......	......	......
May 6	44	74,436,136	41.48	......	......	......	......	......	......
July 1	45	78,181,211	42.47	......	......	......	......	......	......
Oct. 1	44	78,214,626	36.98	......	......	......	......	......	......
Dec. 24	45	75,516,839	32.76	......	......	......	......	......	......
1886.									
Mar. 1	45	80,887,727	31.28	......	......	......	......	......	......
June 3	45	74,187,977	30.28	......	......	......	......	......	......
Aug. 27	45	70,386,879	27.46	......	......	......	......	......	......
Oct. 7	45	70,697,561	27.24	......	......	......	......	......	......
Dec. 28	45	73,607,025	29.89	......	......	......	......	......	......
1887.									
Mar. 4	45	78,607,422	28.70	......	......	......	......	......	......
May 13	46	74,921,037	27.64	18	$16,903,940	30.41	5	$2,280,864	36.40
Aug. 1	46	73,497,514	28.11	18	16,570,934	33.14	5	2,710,600	31.80
Oct. 5	47	71,084,776	28.18	18	16,161,735	30.53	5	2,574,207	26.44
Dec. 7	47	72,370,059	27.18	18	15,537,512	28.80	4	1,999,375	29.79
1888.									
Feb. 14	46	80,277,202	30.29	18	16,167,806	31.68	4	2,202,808	34.05
Apr. 30	46	79,168,888	29.93	18	$17,822,500	20.75	4	2,177,175	40.11
June 30	46	84,608,091	30.34	19	17,961,506	31.37	4	2,217,845	42.10
Oct. 4	46	85,539,988	28.16	19	17,832,756	30.24	4	1,970,368	27.07

AVERAGE WEEKLY DEPOSITS, CIRCULATION, AND RESERVE OF THE NATIONAL BANKS OF NEW YORK CITY, AS REPORTED TO THE NEW YORK CLEARING-HOUSE, FOR THE MONTHS GIVEN, IN THE YEARS 1882, 1883, 1884, 1885, 1886, 1887, 1888.

Week ending—	Liabilities.			Reserve.			
	Circulation.	Net deposits.	Total.	Specie.	Legal tenders.	Total.	Ratio to liabilities.
							Per cent.
Sept. 2, 1882	$18,278,400	$271,999,400	$290,277,800	$49,775,400	$19,953,100	$69,728,500	24.02
Sept. 9, 1882	18,307,000	265,566,900	283,873,900	47,148,500	19,448,800	66,597,300	23.46
Sept. 16, 1882	18,357,500	263,736,700	282,094,200	48,571,500	18,691,500	67,263,000	23.84
Sept. 23, 1882	18,623,700	260,205,800	278,829,500	47,114,000	17,993,700	65,107,700	23.35
Sept. 30, 1882	18,768,100	251,858,100	270,644,200	44,925,500	18,389,000	63,314,500	23.25
Oct. 7, 1882	18,894,800	249,136,800	268,031,600	47,016,000	18,384,500	65,400,500	24.03
Oct. 14, 1882	18,732,000	249,629,700	268,361,700	48,281,000	18,002,700	66,283,700	24.70
Oct. 21, 1882	18,749,400	247,974,400	266,723,800	49,518,200	17,023,900	66,542,100	24.97
Oct. 28, 1882	18,764,500	247,575,400	266,339,900	48,374,200	17,204,700	65,578,900	24.77
Sept. 1, 1883	15,622,600	269,961,900	285,584,500	53,529,000	21,729,000	75,258,000	26.35
Sept. 8, 1883	15,527,000	268,805,500	284,332,500	52,601,400	21,074,500	73,675,900	25.91
Sept. 15, 1883	15,519,700	272,325,100	287,844,800	53,397,400	20,662,700	74,060,100	25.73
Sept. 22, 1883	15,394,600	271,728,200	287,122,800	49,360,600	22,443,300	71,803,900	25.01
Sept. 29, 1883	15,184,800	268,496,600	283,681,400	50,067,900	20,566,800	70,634,700	24.90
Oct. 6, 1883	15,069,100	265,592,500	280,661,600	51,586,700	20,122,500	71,709,200	25.51
Oct. 13, 1883	15,164,200	268,942,000	284,106,200	50,894,000	21,145,800	72,039,800	25.36
Oct. 20, 1883	15,252,900	262,635,700	277,888,600	47,262,900	20,719,700	67,982,600	24.47
Oct. 27, 1883	15,336,200	258,589,600	273,925,800	46,372,800	20,617,600	66,990,400	24.46
Sept. 6, 1884	14,221,000	251,527,200	265,748,200	64,899,900	25,060,800	89,960,700	33.85
Sept. 13, 1884	14,132,300	251,654,700	265,787,000	64,288,200	25,191,800	89,480,000	33.67
Sept. 20, 1884	14,081,400	254,141,200	268,222,600	65,409,500	25,268,000	90,677,500	33.81
Sept. 27, 1884	14,083,300	252,765,500	266,848,800	64,302,000	25,375,700	89,677,700	33.61
Oct. 4, 1884	13,578,400	256,696,800	270,275,200	67,470,600	25,817,300	93,287,900	34.52
Oct. 11, 1884	·12,884,700	261,801,600	274,686,300	68,922,500	27,654,100	96,576,600	35.16
Oct. 18, 1884	12,752,700	261,527,700	274,280,400	67,579,400	27,875,500	95,454,900	34.80
Oct. 25, 1884	12,910,900	261,405,400	274,316,300	67,638,000	27,354,200	94,992,200	34.63
Sept. 5, 1885	9,704,700	321,859,000	331,563,700	102,921,100	28,701,900	131,623,000	39.70
Sept. 12, 1885	9,753,300	320,910,000	330,663,300	100,255,300	28,842,300	129,097,600	39.04
Sept. 19, 1885	9,735,800	319,060,800	328,796,600	97,333,200	27,662,800	124,996,000	38.01
Sept. 26, 1885	9,808,000	316,767,000	326,575,000	95,037,900	26,014,800	121,052,000	37.07
Oct. 3, 1885	9,902,900	315,002,600	324,905,500	92,351,600	24,516,600	116,868,200	35.97
Oct. 10, 1885	9,921,200	315,596,200	325,517,400	93,642,500	23,002,000	116,644,500	35.83
Oct. 17, 1885	9,954,000	317,296,700	327,250,700	91,945,300	22,221,100	114,166,400	34.89
Oct. 24, 1885	10,006,000	313,767,200	323,773,200	87,309,100	21,059,800	108,368,900	33.47
Oct. 31, 1885	9,989,800	313,399,700	323,389,500	84,954,600	21,874,900	106,829,500	33.03
Sept. 4, 1886	8,059,200	283,366,700	291,425,900	61,371,600	19,071,400	80,443,000	27.60
Sept. 11, 1886	8,058,000	282,417,800	290,475,800	63,403,700	16,929,300	80,333,000	27.66
Sept. 18, 1886	8,104,800	281,466,500	289,571,300	63,823,900	15,876,700	79,700,600	27.52
Sept. 25, 1886	8,136,100	283,170,900	291,307,000	66,714,600	15,252,200	81,966,800	28.14
Oct. 2, 1886	8,161,800	282,295,800	290,457,600	64,111,700	14,607,700	78,719,400	27.10
Oct. 9, 1886	8,110,700	281,170,758	289,281,458	65,090,900	13,069,500	78,160,400	27.02
Oct. 16, 1886	8,215,900	295,713,900	303,929,800	65,028,600	13,133,100	78,161,700	25.72
Oct. 23, 1886	8,246,400	283,693,500	291,939,900	65,668,400	12,803,800	78,472,200	26.88
Oct. 30, 1886	8,234,900	284,522,500	292,757,400	66,188,100	13,177,200	79,365,300	27.11
Sept. 3, 1887	8,112,000	281,345,100	289,457,100	59,175,700	18,786,100	77,961,800	26.93
Sept. 10, 1887	8,115,600	279,915,600	288,031,200	58,851,300	17,769,000	76,620,300	26.60
Sept. 17, 1887	8,126,000	279,288,500	287,414,500	59,052,900	16,389,600	75,442,500	26.25
Sept. 24, 1887	8,235,300	278,573,000	286,808,300	60,635,900	16,259,600	76,895,500	26.81
Oct. 1, 1887	8,202,500	281,647,300	289,849,800	64,619,200	15,767,500	80,386,700	27.73
Oct. 8, 1887	8,186,800	285,703,700	293,890,500	64,317,500	16,269,700	80,587,200	27.42
Oct. 15, 1887	8,199,100	289,861,500	298,060,600	64,663,100	16,885,400	81,548,500	27.36
Oct. 22, 1887	8,216,200	289,542,800	297,759,000	64,918,700	16,735,800	81,654,500	27.42
Oct. 29, 1887	8,115,100	289,601,900	297,717,000	66,005,800	17,542,400	83,548,200	28.06
Nov. 5, 1887	8,046,100	289,954,700	298,000,800	64,639,800	17,810,700	82,450,500	27.67
Nov. 12, 1887	8,033,700	288,289,700	296,323,400	63,791,600	18,070,800	81,862,400	27.63
Sept. 1, 1888	7,770,400	341,477,200	349,247,600	73,344,200	30,687,300	104,031,500	29.79
Sept. 8, 1888	7,850,400	336,495,600	344,346,000	69,844,500	28,797,600	98,642,100	28.65
Sept. 15, 1888	7,892,900	312,995,600	320,888,500	69,723,700	28,238,900	97,962,600	30.53
Sept. 22, 1888	7,927,700	333,959,700	341,887,400	70,054,900	26,320,600	96,375,500	28.02
Sept. 29, 1888	6,836,400	336,016,200	342,852,600	74,146,500	24,994,100	99,140,600	28.92
Oct. 6, 1888	6,515,300	349,506,800	356,022,100	74,411,300	23,204,300	97,615,600	27.42
Oct. 13, 1888	6,516,700	337,755,000	344,271,700	73,901,500	22,017,800	95,919,300	27.86
Oct. 20, 1888	6,488,700	343,953,000	350,441,700	81,457,700	21,386,800	102,844,500	29.35
Oct. 27, 1888	6,481,500	343,818,200	350,297,700	81,212,600	21,329,800	102,542,400	29.27
Nov. 3, 1888	6,363,200	343,587,300	349,950,500	80,140,200	21,700,800	101,841,000	29.10

11028—CUR 88——13

STATE OF THE LAWFUL-MONEY RESERVE OF THE NATIONAL BANKS AS

STATES AND

	Dates.	No. of banks.	Net deposits.	Reserve required.
1	Oct. 3, 1882	2,026	$545,842,660	$81,880,301
2	Dec. 30, 1882	2,065	554,245,520	83,140,300
3	Mar. 13, 1883	2,097	550,892,283	82,637,104
4	May 1, 1883	2,128	556,309,464	83,440,581
5	June 22, 1883	2,160	560,731,870	84,112,683
6	Oct. 2, 1883	2,253	577,880,812	86,685,088
7	Dec. 31, 1883	2,260	579,512,711	86,930,753
8	Mar. 7, 1884	2,314	573,619,524	86,046,715
9	Apr. 24, 1884	2,340	575,995,025	86,399,253
10	June 20, 1884	2,376	544,600,331	81,690,049
11	Sept. 30, 1884	2,417	535,807,406	80,371,110
12	Dec. 20, 1884	2,417	520,283,576	78,042,536
13	Mar. 10, 1885	2,425	537,613,418	80,642,012
14	May 6, 1885	2,432	540,281,214	81,042,182
15	July 1, 1885	2,442	552,196,593	82,829,489
16	Oct. 1, 1885	2,467	570,838,327	85,625,749
17	Dec. 24, 1885	2,485	580,879,155	87,131,873
18	Mar. 1, 1886	2,518	596,051,483	89,407,722
19	June 3, 1886	2,552	611,733,790	91,760,069
20	Aug. 27, 1886	2,589	623,886,736	93,583,010
21	Oct. 7, 1886	2,590	637,564,136	95,634,620
22	Dec. 28, 1886	2,612	651,697,492	97,754,624
23	Mar. 4, 1887	2,644	675,355,824	101,303,374
24	May 13, 1887	2,676	682,815,855	102,420,878
25	Aug. 1, 1887	2,724	682,963,777	102,444,566
26	Oct. 5, 1887	2,750	690,022,007	103,503,301
27	Dec. 7, 1887	2,778	684,059,721	102,608,958
28	Feb. 14, 1888	2,787	707,423,152	106,113,472
29	Apr. 30, 1888	2,809	707,530,018	106,129,502
30	June 20, 1888	2,827	711,846,213	106,777,362
31	Oct. 4, 1888	2,847	739,325,350	110,898,803

RESERVE

	Dates.	No. of banks.	Net deposits.	Reserve required.
1	Oct. 3, 1882	243	572,791,257	143,197,814
2	Dec. 30, 1882	243	565,948,445	141,487,111
3	Mar. 13, 1883	246	559,431,070	139,857,768
4	May 1, 1883	247	568,267,546	142,066,886
5	June 22, 1883	248	611,259,171	152,814,793
6	Oct. 2, 1883	248	590,785,930	147,696,483
7	Dec. 31, 1883	249	612,621,435	153,155,350
8	Mar. 7, 1884	249	642,682,644	160,670,660
9	Apr. 24, 1884	249	620,221,832	155,055,456
10	June 20, 1884	249	534,629,056	133,657,263
11	Sept. 30, 1884	247	562,888,105	140,722,026
12	Dec. 20, 1884	247	588,299,710	147,074,927
13	Mar. 10, 1885	246	626,616,971	156,654,242
14	May 6, 1885	246	644,259,607	161,064,902
15	July 1, 1885	247	669,199,214	167,299,805
16	Oct. 1, 1885	247	677,333,060	169,333,265
17	Dec. 24, 1885	247	666,672,097	166,668,024
18	Mar. 1, 1886	250	701,576,125	175,394,031
19	June 3, 1886	257	683,992,858	170,998,214
20	Aug. 27, 1886	260	656,759,355	164,189,838
21	Oct. 7, 1886	262	664,245,121	166,061,280
22	Dec. 28, 1886	263	671,648,508	167,912,127
23	Mar. 4, 1887	265	712,504,329	178,126,082
24	May 13, 1887	270	721,609,242	180,407,310
25	Aug. 1, 1887	266	706,708,847	176,677,212
26	Oct. 5, 1887	263	697,767,889	174,441,972
27	Dec. 7, 1887	262	695,790,194	173,947,548
28	Feb. 14, 1888	266	747,718,913	186,929,728
29	Apr. 30, 1888	289	752,040,152	188,010,038
30	June 30, 1888	293	791,629,383	197,907,346
31	Oct. 4, 1888	293	804,241,438	201,060,359

SHOWN BY THEIR REPORTS FROM OCTOBER 3, 1882, TO OCTOBER 4, 1888.

TERRITORIES.

Reserve held.		Classification of reserve held.					
Amount.	Ratio to liabilities.	Specie.	Legal tenders.	United States certificates of deposit.	Due from reserve agents.	Redemption fund with Treasurer.	
$150, 351, 513	27. 5	$30, 024, 280	$28, 318, 646	$610, 000	$80, 064, 196	$11, 334, 382	1
158, 832, 406	28. 7	31, 005, 496	31, 038, 111	635, 000	84, 783, 017	11, 279, 882	2
155, 131, 167	28. 2	30, 072, 360	28, 871, 031	565, 000	84, 431, 394	11, 191, 382	3
148, 836, 606	26. 7	31, 414, 155	30, 367, 252	585, 000	75, 216, 795	11, 253, 404	4
157, 726, 089	28. 1	31, 055, 220	29, 053, 116	575, 000	85, 823, 001	11, 219, 153	5
157, 493, 584	27. 2	31, 253, 104	30, 245, 600	585, 000	84, 119, 738	11, 290, 052	6
167, 741, 600	28. 6	33, 178, 820	32, 605, 200	610, 000	88, 057, 473	11, 200, 080	7
167, 008, 072	29. 1	33, 471, 053	29, 850, 218	595, 000	92, 207, 704	10, 815, 097	8
162, 466, 064	28. 2	36, 352, 084	30, 944, 464	550, 000	83, 664, 761	10, 954, 155	9
145, 097, 562	26. 8	36, 407, 051	31, 448, 254	575, 000	66, 843, 814	10, 723, 443	10
156, 304, 733	29. 2	35, 238, 175	30, 392, 840	500, 000	79, 652, 119	10, 521, 599	11
161, 864, 287	31. 1	34, 587, 231	29, 943, 391	565, 000	86, 489, 195	10, 279, 470	12
175, 030, 558	32. 6	38, 852, 602	30, 134, 197	665, 000	95, 280, 830	10, 088, 839	13
171, 011, 833	31. 6	40, 736, 009	29, 508, 036	635, 000	89, 991, 054	10, 141, 074	14
170, 245, 483	30. 8	40, 065, 640	27, 473, 329	635, 000	92, 068, 593	10, 002, 921	15
177, 470, 804	31. 1	41, 467, 335	29, 375, 936	500, 000	95, 934, 541	10, 172, 992	16
181, 357, 249	31. 2	42, 195, 802	28, 808, 910	530, 000	99, 687, 965	10, 044, 572	17
181, 591, 775	30. 4	45, 138, 994	27, 257, 991	475, 000	98, 901, 430	9, 818, 351	18
181, 552, 648	29. 6	49, 082, 209	29, 256, 191	465, 000	93, 450, 713	9, 289, 535	19
188, 847, 786	30. 2	47, 370, 313	28, 214, 619	460, 000	103, 642, 532	9, 160, 322	20
188, 191, 889	29. 2	47, 824, 967	29, 672, 277	460, 000	99, 493, 068	8, 741, 577	21
192, 278, 974	29. 5	50, 326, 819	31, 879, 137	500, 000	101, 746, 037	7, 826, 981	22
203, 307, 527	30. 1	50, 884, 172	30, 643, 368	555, 000	113, 943, 928	7, 281, 059	23
198, 863, 737	29. 1	51, 145, 531	32, 418, 634	545, 000	107, 857, 035	6, 897, 537	24
189, 537, 562	27. 7	48, 955, 455	30, 878, 201	470, 000	102, 597, 807	6, 636, 000	25
190, 919, 164	27. 6	50, 821, 078	32, 129, 936	475, 000	100, 879, 879	6, 613, 271	26
185, 803, 160	27. 2	51, 696, 357	31, 997, 316	520, 000	95, 002, 425	6, 587, 062	27
201, 787, 492	28. 5	51, 835, 866	32, 264, 784	510, 000	110, 693, 685	6, 483, 157	28
193, 936, 932	27. 4	50, 988, 350	33, 260, 054	515, 000	102, 759, 410	6, 414, 118	29
199, 159, 891	28. 0	49, 123, 698	31, 021, 956	505, 000	112, 183, 937	6, 324, 800	30
209, 844, 936	28. 4	50, 188, 336	33, 789, 747	680, 000	118, 950, 556	6, 236, 317	31

CITIES.

Amount.	Ratio to liabilities.	Specie.	Legal tenders.	United States certificates of deposit.	Due from reserve agents.	Redemption fund with Treasurer.	
153, 537, 856	26. 8	72, 883, 489	34, 004, 871	8, 035, 000	33, 213, 032	4, 481, 464	1
162, 387, 772	28. 7	75, 331, 663	37, 440, 310	7, 840, 000	37, 282, 190	4, 493, 609	2
148, 706, 922	26. 6	67, 800, 006	31, 977, 037	7, 840, 000	36, 502, 761	4, 407, 118	3
156, 419, 122	27. 5	72, 193, 111	37, 882, 216	7, 835, 000	34, 090, 027	4, 411, 768	4
184, 362, 295	30. 2	84, 209, 176	44, 779, 342	10, 070, 000	40, 821, 353	4, 392, 424	5
171, 448, 008	29. 0	76, 504, 789	40, 437, 397	9, 375, 000	40, 798, 990	4, 271, 832	6
182, 221, 554	29. 7	81, 007, 329	47, 864, 497	10, 280, 000	38, 942, 133	4, 087, 595	7
198, 511, 843	30. 9	88, 609, 073	45, 987, 877	13, 450, 000	46, 437, 308	4, 027, 585	8
179, 371, 793	28. 9	78, 392, 023	46, 768, 164	11, 440, 000	38, 827, 197	3, 944, 410	9
160, 231, 029	30. 0	73, 254, 631	45, 468, 958.	9, 295, 000	28, 403, 338	3, 809, 102	10
189, 850, 706	33. 7	93, 371, 209	46, 651, 819	13, 700, 000	32, 340, 900	3, 786, 688	11
208, 349, 105	35. 4	105, 159, 848	46, 426, 164	18, 475, 000	34, 672, 781	3, 615, 312	12
235, 074, 313	37. 7	128, 263, 181	40, 883, 125	22, 095, 000	41, 172, 443	3, 560, 564	13
247, 455, 612	38. 4	136, 678, 750	47, 828, 963	18, 500, 000	40, 912, 049	3, 535, 850	14
256, 223, 121	38. 3	137, 546, 852	52, 228, 023	22, 285, 000	40, 661, 809	3, 501, 437	15
237, 894, 989	35. 1	133, 405, 237	40, 362, 183	18, 300, 000	42, 402, 609	3, 424, 960	16
215, 991, 777	32. 4	123, 158, 550	38, 686, 556	11, 235, 000	39, 551, 479	3, 360, 192	17
225, 227, 964	32. 1	126, 476, 925	39, 756, 805	11, 955, 000	43, 904, 247	3, 134, 897	18
212, 639, 672	31. 0	108, 377, 660	50, 400, 597	11, 385, 000	39, 567, 423	2, 908, 991	19
187, 891, 591	28. 6	101, 630, 179	35, 825, 132	7, 655, 000	40, 072, 689	2, 708, 591	20
190, 985, 722	28. 7	108, 502, 730	33, 140, 045	5, 395, 000	41, 271, 509	2, 616, 438	21
200, 813, 518	29. 9	116, 656, 737	35, 800, 691	5, 695, 000	40, 371, 942	2, 229, 148	22
214, 686, 473	30. 1	120, 704, 734	35, 584, 790	7, 090, 000	49, 217, 253	1, 990, 696	23
212, 950, 477	29. 5	116, 170, 136	47, 170, 454	7, 480, 000	40, 210, 839	1, 913, 048	24
206, 466, 135	29. 2	116, 148, 755	43, 599, 051	7, 340, 000	37, 672, 349	1, 705, 980	25
203, 201, 575	29. 1	114, 264, 376	41, 621, 319	5, 715, 000	39, 993, 709	1, 697, 171	26
196, 092, 726	28. 2	107, 544, 286	43, 364, 659	5, 645, 000	37, 957, 340	1, 581, 441	27
227, 815, 221	30. 5	121, 994, 748	50, 052, 886	9, 610, 000	44, 647, 555	1, 510, 032	28
225, 407, 142	30. 0	121, 085, 661	50, 314, 156	8, 815, 000	43, 718, 493	1, 473, 832	29
242, 342, 065	30. 6	132, 168, 579	50, 973, 687	11, 810, 000	45, 949, 062	1, 441, 037	30
236, 321, 317	29. 4	127, 799, 480	47, 300, 714	8, 385, 000	51, 508, 038	1, 319, 085	31

LAWFUL-MONEY RESERVE OF THE NATIONAL BANKS, AS SHOWN BY THE REPORTS

	Cities, States, and Territories.	No. of banks.	Deposits.	Reserve required, 25 per cent.	Reserve held.	Ratio of reserve.
						Per cent.
1	New York City	46	$342, 159, 954	$85, 539, 988	$96, 360, 786	28. 16
2	Chicago	19	69, 331, 024	17, 332, 756	20, 962, 421	30. 24
3	Saint Louis	4	7, 881, 231	1, 970, 308	2, 133, 376	27. 07
	Total of central reserve cities	69	419, 372, 209	104, 843, 052	119, 456, 583	28. 48
1	Boston	55	111, 893, 891	27, 973, 473	31, 442, 978	28. 10
2	Albany	6	10, 642, 314	2, 660, 578	3, 832, 064	36. 01
3	Philadelphia	43	93, 043, 199	23, 260, 800	27, 359, 870	29. 41
4	Pittsburgh	24	28, 470, 937	7, 117, 734	9, 542, 020	33. 51
5	Baltimore	17	20, 401, 455	5, 100, 361	6, 334, 208	31. 05
6	Washington	7	7, 344, 348	1, 836, 087	2, 739, 060	37. 29
7	New Orleans	8	12, 031, 639	3, 007, 910	3, 024, 021	25. 13
8	Louisville	9	7, 001, 993	1, 750, 498	1, 795, 037	25. 64
9	Cincinnati	13	27, 316, 129	6, 829, 032	8, 907, 727	32. 61
10	Cleveland	9	12, 983, 675	3, 245, 919	3, 921, 069	30. 20
11	Detroit	8	14, 270, 491	3, 567, 623	4, 427, 266	31. 02
12	Milwaukee	3	5, 850, 419	1, 462, 605	2, 074, 546	35. 46
13	Kansas City	10	14, 989, 302	3, 747, 325	5, 288, 400	35. 28
14	Saint Joseph	2	2, 686, 848	671, 712	848, 633	31. 58
15	Omaha	7	11, 879, 156	2, 969, 789	3, 945, 567	33. 21
16	San Francisco	3	4, 063, 433	1, 015, 858	1, 382, 130	34. 01
	Total of reserve cities	224	384, 869, 229	96, 217, 307	116, 864, 734	30. 36
	Total of all reserve cities	293	804, 241, 438	201, 060, 359	236, 321, 317	29. 38
				15 per cent.		
1	Maine	75	10, 958, 376	1, 643, 756	3, 437, 882	31. 37
2	New Hampshire	49	7, 229, 121	1, 084, 368	2, 139, 207	29. 59
3	Vermont	49	7, 126, 362	1, 068, 954	2, 016, 305	28. 29
4	Massachusetts	198	60, 127, 265	9, 019, 090	16, 069, 986	26. 73
5	Rhode Island	60	16, 595, 281	2, 489, 292	4, 022, 603	24. 25
6	Connecticut	84	30, 560, 888	4, 584, 133	8, 800, 921	28. 99
7	New York	270	93, 99, 325	14, 060, 899	25, 200, 989	26. 87
8	New Jersey	85	45, 543, 352	6, 831, 503	13, 288, 044	29. 18
9	Pennsylvania	246	78, 386, 514	11, 757, 977	23, 567, 339	30. 07
10	Delaware	18	4, 906, 203	735, 930	1, 784, 524	36. 37
11	Maryland	31	8, 086, 845	1, 213, 027	2, 288, 749	28. 30
12	District of Columbia	1	776, 227	116, 434	341, 204	43. 97
13	Virginia	26	11, 943, 257	1, 791, 489	2, 979, 576	24. 95
14	West Virginia	20	3, 382, 632	507, 395	1, 080, 795	31. 95
15	North Carolina	18	3, 406, 579	510, 987	764, 034	22. 45
16	South Carolina	16	3, 980, 355	597, 053	671, 288	16. 87
17	Georgia	24	4, 802, 070	720, 310	1, 134, 876	23. 63
18	Florida	13	2, 160, 808	324, 121	578, 146	26. 76
19	Alabama	21	4, 877, 086	731, 563	1, 415, 414	29. 02
20	Mississippi	12	1, 381, 586	207, 238	412, 907	29. 89
21	Louisiana	5	955, 681	143, 352	254, 361	26. 63
22	Texas	100	15, 685, 484	2, 352, 823	5, 097, 546	32. 50
23	Arkansas	7	2, 306, 780	346, 017	565, 507	24. 51
24	Kentucky	60	11, 794, 203	1, 769, 130	3, 004, 843	25. 48
25	Tennessee	42	12, 275, 841	1, 841, 376	2, 480, 945	20. 21
26	Ohio	107	43, 171, 990	6, 475, 799	12, 917, 236	29. 92
27	Indiana	94	24, 884, 485	3, 732, 673	7, 953, 678	31. 96
28	Illinois	163	38, 007, 718	5, 701, 158	12, 035, 045	31. 66
29	Michigan	101	22, 354, 505	3, 353, 176	6, 035, 826	27. 00
30	Wisconsin	56	13, 563, 781	2, 034, 567	3, 282, 567	24. 20
31	Iowa	129	21, 845, 468	3, 276, 820	5, 928, 905	27. 14
32	Minnesota	56	29, 557, 038	4, 433, 556	7, 450, 667	25. 21
33	Missouri	34	4, 510, 120	676, 518	1, 403, 672	31. 12
34	Kansas	160	17, 534, 605	2, 630, 191	6, 181, 390	35. 25
35	Nebraska	97	10, 863, 257	1, 629, 489	2, 934, 073	27. 01
36	Colorado	34	18, 436, 216	2, 765, 432	6, 484, 580	35. 17
37	Nevada	2	395, 707	59, 356	82, 873	20. 94
38	California	35	14, 820, 235	2, 223, 035	4, 559, 446	30. 77
39	Oregon	27	6, 589, 960	988, 494	1, 377, 015	20. 90
40	Arizona	1	132, 168	19, 825	26, 072	19. 73
41	Dakota	58	6, 311, 234	946, 685	1, 478, 033	23. 42
42	Idaho	7	896, 505	134, 476	260, 525	29. 06
43	Montana	17	9, 134, 781	1, 370, 217	2, 340, 145	25. 62
44	New Mexico	9	1, 862, 967	279, 445	543, 107	29. 15
45	Utah	7	3, 024, 769	453, 715	903, 022	29. 85
46	Washington	24	6, 676, 034	1, 001, 405	1, 605, 750	24. 05
47	Wyoming	9	1, 703, 686	255, 553	601, 519	35. 31
	Total of country banks	2, 847	739, 325, 350	110, 898, 802	209, 844, 956	28. 38
	United States	3, 140	1, 543, 566, 788	311, 959, 161	446, 166, 273	28. 90

OF THEIR CONDITION AT THE CLOSE OF BUSINESS ON OCTOBER 4, 1888.

Cash reserve.		Classification of reserve held.					
Required.	Held.	Specie.	Legal tenders.	United States certificates of deposit.	Due from reserve agents.	Redemption fund with Treasurer.	
$85, 104, 838	$96, 015, 636	$73, 797, 196	$17, 763, 440	$4, 455, 000	....	$345, 150	1
17, 283, 770	20, 013, 441	13, 071, 242	7, 793, 109	50, 000	....	48, 980	2
1, 054, 108	2, 117, 176	963, 497	964, 679	100, 000	....	16, 200	3
104, 432, 722	110, 046, 253	87, 830, 935	26, 520, 318	4, 605, 000	....	410, 330	
13, 842, 407	14, 555, 780	11, 408, 028	2, 822, 761	235, 000	$16, 598, 530	288, 650	1
1, 310, 806	1, 382, 875	979, 332	253, 543	150, 000	2, 410, 222	38, 967	2
11, 558, 708	17, 927, 261	12, 391, 700	4, 315, 561	1, 220, 000	9, 289, 225	143, 384	3
3, 522, 531	5, 274, 641	3, 240, 969	2, 033, 672	....	4, 104, 716	72, 672	4
2, 520, 032	4, 221, 943	2, 244, 841	1, 427, 102	550, 000	2, 071, 825	40, 500	5
907, 244	1, 712, 245	953, 586	638, 659	120, 000	1, 005, 215	21, 600	6
1, 473, 017	2, 144, 135	933, 121	1, 211, 014	....	818, 011	61, 875	7
804, 000	924, 737	342, 301	582, 436	....	847, 802	22, 498	8
3, 370, 034	4, 886, 368	869, 721	2, 616, 647	1, 400, 000	3, 932, 394	88, 965	9
1, 600, 324	2, 016, 826	988, 826	1, 013, 000	15, 000	1, 870, 973	27, 270	10
1, 774, 811	1, 897, 557	1, 089, 555	808, 002	....	2, 511, 700	18, 000	11
724, 552	967, 770	593, 184	374, 586	....	1, 003, 276	13, 500	12
1, 862, 413	3, 000, 413	1, 504, 628	1, 495, 785	....	2, 265, 547	22, 500	13
333, 611	340, 544	174, 374	166, 170	....	503, 590	4, 490	14
1, 477, 582	2, 040, 384	1, 022, 208	1, 018, 176	....	1, 890, 558	14, 625	15
403, 304	1, 154, 453	1, 142, 171	12, 282	....	108, 436	20, 250	16
47, 654, 276	64, 447, 941	39, 968, 545	20, 789, 396	3, 690, 000	51, 508, 038	908, 755	
152, 086, 998	183, 494, 194	127, 799, 480	47, 309, 714	8, 385, 000	51, 508, 038	1, 319, 085	
571, 044	968, 623	717, 498	251, 125	....	2, 255, 364	213, 895	1
368, 479	543, 261	397, 288	145, 973	....	1, 432, 866	163, 170	2
369, 314	610, 188	405, 734	204, 454	....	1, 260, 447	145, 070	3
3, 214, 601	4, 637, 110	2, 970, 553	1, 471, 557	195, 000	10, 450, 288	982, 588	4
909, 437	1, 271, 771	658, 748	613, 023	....	2, 536, 132	215, 700	5
1, 082, 796	2, 714, 812	1, 795, 932	918, 880	....	5, 768, 965	377, 144	6
5, 303, 356	9, 273, 120	5, 612, 604	3, 245, 516	415, 000	15, 121, 360	806, 509	7
2, 613, 204	4, 233, 316	1, 875, 038	2, 348, 278	10, 000	8, 756, 234	298, 494	8
4, 454, 487	8, 118, 064	5, 016, 657	3, 091, 407	10, 000	14, 827, 516	621, 750	9
265, 607	428, 315	208, 189	210, 126	10, 000	1, 224, 206	71, 913	10
403, 420	944, 690	536, 499	408, 191	....	1, 280, 583	54, 476	11
42, 074	269, 401	229, 271	40, 130	....	60, 643	11, 250	12
696, 538	1, 430, 051	618, 431	811, 620	....	1, 499, 380	50, 145	13
189, 040	539, 848	272, 925	266, 923	....	508, 378	32, 509	14
190, 607	466, 867	228, 899	237, 968	....	263, 298	34, 469	15
230, 788	476, 020	200, 048	275, 972	....	174, 286	20, 082	16
271, 722	881, 880	531, 924	349, 956	....	211, 989	41, 007	17
125, 220	266, 432	107, 338	159, 094	....	300, 643	11, 071	18
277, 791	825, 379	437, 392	387, 987	....	552, 950	37, 085	19
77, 090	335, 726	149, 680	186, 046	....	62, 669	14, 512	20
55, 001	200, 196	136, 949	63, 247	....	48, 541	5, 624	21
805, 054	3, 122, 551	1, 305, 386	1, 817, 165	....	1, 859, 806	115, 180	22
131, 027	261, 584	120, 750	140, 834	....	285, 473	18, 450	23
655, 800	1, 118, 437	550, 902	567, 535	....	1, 756, 777	129, 620	24
713, 449	1, 601, 339	836, 714	764, 625	....	821, 852	57, 754	25
2, 427, 601	6, 291, 082	3, 022, 828	3, 238, 154	30, 000	6, 218, 458	406, 796	26
1, 411, 775	3, 990, 268	2, 150, 522	1, 839, 746	....	3, 760, 174	203, 236	27
2, 200, 681	4, 452, 752	2, 621, 931	1, 820, 821	10, 000	7, 382, 839	109, 454	28
1, 292, 067	2, 290, 949	1, 385, 426	905, 523	....	3, 621, 869	123, 008	29
789, 061	1, 440, 559	949, 014	491, 545	....	1, 780, 093	61, 915	30
1, 257, 370	2, 717, 143	1, 626, 265	1, 090, 878	....	3, 078, 366	133, 306	31
1, 742, 881	3, 101, 412	2, 169, 217	932, 195	....	4, 272, 901	76, 354	32
257, 418	543, 636	281, 414	262, 222	....	827, 063	32, 973	33
906, 623	2, 522, 085	1, 238, 506	1, 283, 579	....	3, 520, 070	138, 635	34
624, 063	1, 127, 421	736, 498	390, 923	....	1, 737, 521	69, 331	35
1, 080, 886	2, 451, 545	1, 455, 536	996, 009	....	3, 984, 818	48, 217	36
22, 473	60, 099	55, 546	4, 553	....	19, 602	3, 172	37
866, 242	2, 799, 283	2, 616, 791	182, 492	....	1, 702, 732	57, 431	38
386, 491	1, 027, 121	940, 619	86, 502	....	327, 659	22, 265	39
7, 480	24, 947	15, 947	9, 000	....	....	1, 125	40
361, 805	839, 138	470, 615	368, 523	....	596, 721	42, 174	41
51, 700	207, 759	117, 511	90, 248	....	47, 091	5, 075	42
539, 437	1, 413, 329	870, 407	542, 922	....	905, 191	21, 625	43
107, 405	208, 858	124, 449	84, 409	....	323, 317	10, 932	44
174, 406	451, 651	396, 128	55, 523	....	433, 821	17, 550	45
302, 440	852, 306	749, 741	102, 565	....	733, 148	20, 305	46
97, 744	243, 959	210, 176	33, 783	....	346, 366	11, 194	47
41, 864, 904	84, 658, 083	50, 188, 336	33, 780, 747	680, 000	118, 950, 556	6, 236, 317	
193, 951, 992	268, 152, 277	177, 987, 816	81, 090, 461	9, 065, 000	170, 458, 594	7, 555, 402	

TABLE, BY STATES, TERRITORIES, AND RESERVE CITIES, EXHIBITING THE AMOUNT OF
OCTOBER, 1887, AND

OCTOBER, 1887.

	States.	Gold coin.	Gold Treasury certificates.	Gold clearing-house certificates.	Silver coin.		Silver Treasury certificates.	Total.
					Dollars.	Fractional.		
1	Maine	$600, 450. 02	$10, 500	....	$44, 263	$23, 141. 91	$15, 275	$693, 629. 93
2	New Hampshire	296, 886. 00	1, 300	....	56, 168	30, 038. 15	9, 582	394 034. 15
3	Vermont	314, 532. 13	9, 440	....	34, 720	20. 865. 45	8, 136	387, 693. 58
4	Massachusetts	2, 167, 416. 60	251, 450	....	347. 815	199, 767. 25	81, 504	3, 047, 952. 85
5	Boston	4, 926, 938. 23	4, 515, 530	....	157, 633	64, 060. 05	332, 515	9, 996, 676. 28
6	Rhode Island	462. 030. 20	60, 410	....	67, 074	40, 102. 32	45, 875	675, 491, 52
7	Connecticut	1, 263, 656. 05	205, 950	....	130, 912	104, 715. 57	43, 063	1, 748, 294. 62
	Division No. 1	10, 031 909. 23	5, 054, 640	....	838, 585	482, 088. 70	535, 950	16, 943, 772. 93
8	New York	3, 368, 827. 67	1, 114, 140	....	347, 509	252, 342. 48	116, 868	5, 199, 687. 15
9	New York City	8, 028, 172. 10	38, 270, 930	$16,186,000	469, 781	233, 183. 84	434, 862	63, 622, 928. 94
10	Albany	451, 231. 00	455, 350	....	14, 683	5, 227. 50	8, 700	935, 191. 50
11	New Jersey	1, 231, 881. 75	167, 460	....	253, 649	101, 609. 24	98, 441	1, 852, 443. 99
12	Pennsylvania	3, 612, 712. 85	282, 490	....	530, 348	107, 806, 49	145, 463	4, 774, 820. 34
13	Philadelphia	2, 921, 241. 00	132, 940	7, 685, 000	355, 894	189. 222. 47	274, 638	11, 558, 955. 47
14	Pittsburgh	1, 087, 180. 55	785, 610	....	102, 620	33, 645. 66	91, 244	2, 080, 318. 21
	Division No. 2.	21, 600, 755. 92	41, 208, 920	23, 871, 000	2, 080, 393	1, 013, 037. 08	1, 150, 219	90, 924, 325. 60
15	Delaware	180, 883. 44	22, 550	....	35, 021	20, 807. 77	14, 377	273, 639. 21
16	Maryland	273, 335. 87	44, 410	....	61, 224	34, 804. 86	27, 200	440, 974. 73
17	Baltimore	1, 367, 424. 50	555, 080	....	101, 972	43, 287. 83	62, 336	2, 130, 106. 33
18	Dist. of Columbia	83, 693. 50	70, 000	....	5. 370	1, 035. 25	8, 560	168, 658. 75
19	Washington	174, 938. 50	631, 550	....	10, 386	7, 135. 50	112, 324	945, 334. 00
20	Virginia	420, 820. 10	24, 140	....	66, 311	40, 241. 28	55, 328	606, 840. 38
21	West Virginia	228, 164. 48	9, 800	....	26, 309	9, 170. 68	2, 509	275, 962. 36
	Division No. 3	2, 729, 260. 39	1, 357, 530	....	315, 593	156, 492. 37	282, 634	4. 841, 509. 76
22	North Carolina	153, 759, 50	300	....	27, 613	11, 317. 88	2, 250	195, 240. 38
23	South Carolina	218, 953, 05	43, 240	....	39, 651	10, 719. 90	12, 737	325, 300, 05
24	Georgia	173, 167. 35	147, 690	....	81, 036	23, 224. 00	122, 199	547, 316. 35
25	Florida	42, 861. 80	640	....	54, 979	8, 321, 50	960	107, 762. 30
26	Alabama	210, 804. 80	36, 820	....	57, 583	10, 282. 85	49, 958	365, 448 65
27	Mississippi	26, 789. 50	18, 540	....	51, 953	7, 502. 63	48, 622	153, 407. 13
28	Louisiana	13. 729. 50	2. 800	....	26, 001	9, 738. 94	47, 384	99, 713. 44
29	New Orleans	246, 208. 50	72, 680	....	87, 076	5, 377. 75	364, 273	776, 215. 25
30	Texas	629, 859. 60	157, 720	....	243, 770	33, 542. 07	191, 703	1, 256, 594. 67
31	Arkansas	57, 111. 00	10, 170	....	25, 393	6, 435. 60	58, 570	166, 679. 60
32	Kentucky	391, 271. 25	45, 010	....	85, 494	17, 665. 76	17, 120	556. 561. 01
33	Louisville	220, 154. 50	7, 500	....	24, 431	2, 168. 58	8, 000	262, 254. 08
34	Tennessee	492, 190. 85	103, 770	....	150, 867	37, 035. 30	70, 686	863, 549. 15
	Division No. 4	2, 876, 861. 20	655, 940	....	965, 447	183, 332. 76	904, 462	5, 676, 042. 96
35	Ohio	2, 399, 305. 04	101, 430	....	260, 507	106, 273. 87	55, 540	2, 923, 055. 91
36	Cincinnati	282, 135. 82	261, 500	....	74, 575	29, 557. 50	15, 400	663, 168. 32
37	Cleveland	565, 345. 00	200, 000	....	48, 005	5, 029. 43	....	818, 379. 43
38	Indiana	2, 008, 434. 47	117, 450	....	254, 465	71, 926. 99	49, 210	2, 501, 486. 46
39	Illinois	2, 115, 668. 08	189, 250	....	230, 473	107, 022. 28	59, 162	2, 692, 576. 26
40	Chicago	9, 040, 388. 50	3, 430, 550	....	177, 607	52, 972. 24	256, 900	12, 958, 417. 74
41	Michigan	1, 377, 900. 45	38, 210	....	133, 854	62, 412. 22	23, 535	1, 635, 911. 67
42	Detroit	982, 324. 50	5, 680	....	50, 572	19, 801. 51	6, 289	1, 064, 667. 01
43	Wisconsin	862, 290. 15	8, 200	....	82, 628	36, 332. 51	6, 319	995, 859. 66
44	Milwaukee	399, 800. 00	110, 000	....	13, 168	5, 560. 00	5, 150	532, 678. 00
	Division No. 5	20, 032, 502. 91	4, 453, 360	....	1, 325, 854	496, 888. 55	477, 505	26, 786, 200. 46
45	Iowa	1, 214, 595. 55	91, 040	....	138, 440	64, 803. 73	31, 579	1, 540, 458. 28
46	Minnesota	2, 124, 645, 09	26, 000	....	165, 091	57, 812. 50	13, 729	2, 387, 277. 59
47	Missouri	255, 469. 18	12, 900	....	42, 719	9, 120. 00	3, 815	324, 023. 18
48	Saint Louis	757, 410. 19	391, 570	....	20, 400	8, 440. 25	160, 160	1, 338, 040. 44
49	Kansas City	1, 085, 952. 50	239, 320	....	80, 477	32, 620. 60	39, 394	1, 480, 764. 10
50	Saint Joseph	63, 122. 50	23, 820	....	16, 752	8, 168. 65	44, 521	156, 384. 15
51	Kansas	1, 155, 756. 41	43, 600	....	149, 933	40, 809. 10	69, 879	1, 460, 157. 51
52	Nebraska	654, 171. 90	15, 550	....	62, 323	24, 231. 32	11, 198	767, 474. 22
52	Omaha	766, 633. 35	20, 560	....	118, 702	17, 459. 56	24, 090	947, 444. 91
	Division No. 6	8, 077, 756. 07	864, 450	....	803, 897	263, 555. 71	308, 365	10, 408, 024. 38

EACH KIND OF COIN AND COIN CERTIFICATE HELD BY THE NATIONAL BANKS IN OCTOBER, 1888.

OCTOBER, 1888.

Total.	Silver Treasury certificates.	Silver coin.		Gold clearing-house certificates.	Gold Treasury certificates.	Gold coin.	States.	
		Fractional.	Dollars.					
$717, 497. 67	$35, 303	$28, 894. 91	$36, 088	....	$8, 400	$608, 811. 70	Maine	1
397, 288. 50	16, 432	28, 061. 80	71 483	....	7,780	272, 931. 70	New Hampshire..	2
405, 733. 85	5, 045	28, 023. 36	40, 823	....	7, 600	324, 242. 40	Vermont..........	3
2, 970, 552. 92	140, 102	200, 543. 74	315, 188	....	239, 520	2, 075, 139. 18	Massachusetts...	4
11, 498, 027. 85	693, 321	81, 047. 79	105, 087	....	6, 610. 800	3, 995, 172. 09	Boston.........	5
658, 748. 04	87, 102	44. 740. 69	59, 372	....	67, 670	390, 863, 35	Rhode Island....	6
1, 795, 931. 78	86, 480	103, 636. 67	134, 863	....	182, 770	1, 288, 182. 11	Connecticut	7
18, 413, 760. 61	1, 063, 845	515, 548. 93	766, 504	....	7, 133, 540	8, 964, 342. 08	Division No. 1.	
5, 612, 603. 78	255, 317	206, 313. 30	385. 126	....	1, 216, 790	3, 489, 057. 48	New York	8
73, 707, 196. 14	1, 771, 348	219, 845. 64	362, 213	....	64, 305, 120	7, 138, 669. 50	New York City	9
979, 331. 50	14, 000	8, 171. 00	18, 500	....	535, 700	402, 960. 50	Albany	10
1, 875, 037. 60	171, 323	107, 949. 01	194, 805	....	309, 470	1, 091, 490. 50	New Jersey......	11
5, 016, 656. 83	191, 152	251, 439. 41	541, 141	....	284, 100	3, 748, 764. 42	Pennsylvania....	12
12, 391, 700. 19	518. 152	169, 237. 19	346, 940	$8, 890, 000	172, 450	2, 264, 915. 00	Philadelphia...	13
3, 240, 969. 23	94, 708	38, 003. 53	154, 209	....	823, 100	2, 130, 858. 70	Pittsburgh.....	14
102, 913, 495. 27	3, 046, 000	1, 060, 959. 08	2, 003, 030	8, 890, 000	67, 046, 790	20, 266, 716, 19	Division No. 2.	
208, 188. 59	37, 694	29, 751. 09	46, 430	....	22, 640	131, 453. 50	Delaware	15
536. 499. 41	65, 154	35, 612. 29	69, 251	....	44, 180	322, 303. 12	Maryland.........	16
2, 244, 840. 80	249, 872	39, 337. 30	101, 658	....	468, 080	1, 385, 293. 50	Baltimore.....	17
229, 271. 50	6, 980	5, 260. 50	4, 060	....	116, 500	96, 471. 00	Dist. of Columbia.	18
953, 586. 50	192, 624	14, 974. 50	13, 165	....	531, 040	201, 783. 00	Washington ..	19
618, 431. 05	84, 470	42, 127. 05	87, 756	....	9, 480	394, 598. 00	Virginia	20
272, 925. 15	8, 300	9, 963. 02	19, 157	....	10, 400	225, 096. 13	West Virginia ...	21
5, 123, 745. 06	645, 303	177, 025. 81	341, 497	....	1, 202, 920	2, 756, 907. 25	Division No. 3.	
228, 800. 10	10	17, 418. 10	50, 873	....	....	160, 598. 00	North Carolina....	22
200, 948. 05	8, 503	19, 142. 05	63, 841	....	420	108, 983. 00	South Carolina....	23
531, 923. 66	116, 019	24, 005. 03	191, 526	....	55, 500	144, 273. 63	Georgia...........	24
107, 338. 39	1, 385	16, 552. 39	46, 408	....	3, 580	39, 353. 00	Florida	25
437, 392. 36	45, 293	13, 180. 36	52, 607	....	10, 520	306, 792. 00	Alabama...........	26
149, 080. 15	40, 185	8, 503. 65	32, 122	....	4, 000	64, 869. 50	Mississippi	27
136, 049. 05	76, 736	16, 668. 05	26, 565	....	4, 500	12, 480. 00	Louisiana.........	28
933, 120. 85	505, 643	61, 523. 85	114, 592	....	127, 920	123, 442. 00	New Orleans ..	29
1, 305, 380. 15	218, 363	49, 749. 95	416, 152	....	130, 500	481, 531. 20	Texas.............	30
120, 750 10	40, 210	7, 572. 10	25, 523	....	14, 270	33, 175. 00	Arkansas	31
550, 001. 69	36, 895	15, 984. 33	67, 570	....	41, 390	389, 062. 36	Kentucky.........	32
342, 300. 75	1, 400	5, 022. 75	43, 630	....	1, 500	290, 748. 00	Louisville.....	33
836, 713. 85	72, 270	30, 858. 85	215, 062	....	117, 100	392, 423. 00	Tennessee	34
5, 882, 304. 15	1, 163, 571	295, 181. 46	1, 346, 531	....	529, 200	2, 547, 730. 69	Division No. 4.	
3, 023, 827. 06	45, 973	116, 657. 86	292, 133	....	146, 640	2, 422, 423. 80	Ohio..............	35
809, 721. 25	156, 500	11, 671. 75	60, 552	....	271, 000	309, 997. 50	Cincinnati....	36
988, 826. 41	25, 000	14, 904. 91	39, 132	....	180, 000	729, 789. 50	Cleveland ...	37
2, 150, 521. 51	40, 376	62, 733. 89	205, 120	....	113, 250	1, 729, 041. 62	Indiana...........	38
2, 621, 931. 42	98, 538	104, 820. 92	247, 130	....	198, 920	1, 972, 502. 50	Illinois	39
13, 071, 241. 60	416, 725	254, 807. 10	215, 851	....	2, 426, 750	9, 757, 108. 50	Chicago	40
1, 385, 425. 60	20, 575	45, 064. 67	135, 933	....	29, 340	1, 154, 512. 93	Michigan	41
1, 089, 554. 86	12, 535	53, 500. 36	45, 385	....	5, 900	972, 174. 50	Detroit	42
949, 014. 41	11, 371	46, 524. 54	93, 807	....	12, 300	785, 011. 87	Wisconsin	43
593, 184. 00	8, 534	9, 040. 00	20, 233	....	100, 000	455, 377. 00	Milwaukee ...	44
26, 743, 248. 72	836. 147	719, 726. 00	1, 355, 276	....	3, 484, 100	20, 347, 039. 72	Division No. 5.	
1, 626, 264. 65	58, 700	74, 774. 07	176, 280	....	75, 080	1, 240, 734. 58	Iowa.............	45
2, 109, 216. 64	12, 160	91, 509. 40	203, 136	....	5, 880	1, 794, 471. 24	Minnesota	46
281, 414 51	8, 587	8, 621. 51	34, 539	....	9, 000	220, 667. 00	Missouri..........	47
962, 497. 00	92, 400	7, 878. 00	20, 000	....	355, 000	487, 219. 00	Saint Louis...	48
1, 504, 628. 47	87, 120	38, 738. 97	72, 817	....	251, 200	1, 054, 752. 50	Kansas City..	49
174, 373. 70	26, 327	3, 668. 70	4, 378	....	50, 260	89, 740. 00	Saint Joseph..	50
1, 238, 505. 90	63, 947	48, 451. 10	134, 328	....	24, 260	967, 519. 80	Kansas	51
736, 498. 30	32, 582	22, 980. 85	69, 256	....	15, 060	595, 725. 45	Nebraska	52
1, 022, 208. 22	11, 540	28, 685. 12	67, 536	....	32, 950	881, 497. 10	Omaha........	53
9, 715, 607. 39	393, 453	325, 307. 72	844, 270	....	820, 190	7, 332, 326. 67	Division No. 6.	

TABLE, BY STATES, TERRITORIES, AND RESERVE CITIES, EXHIBITING THE

OCTOBER, 1887—Continued.

	States.	Gold coin.	Gold Treasury certificates.	Gold clearing-house certificates.	Silver coin.		Silver Treasury certificates.	Total.
					Dollars.	Fractional.		
54	Colorado	$1,286,250.30	$13,070	....	$91,106	$24,962.17	$7,601	$1,422,989.47
55	Nevada	50,380.00	....	....	3,805	3,301.42	....	57,486.42
56	California	3,151,990.25	239,800	....	90,483	25,550.17	64,104	3,571,927.42
57	San Francisco	958,262.50	260	$110,000	18,100	3,855.90	....	1,090,478.40
58	Oregon	906,627.50	3,170	....	13,019	14,525.38	9,532	947,479.88
59	Arizona	18,535.00	....	....	450	366.95	....	19,351.95
	Division No. 7	6,371,745.55	256,300	110,000	217,863	72,561.99	81,237	7,109,707.54
60	Dakota	386,718.90	5,230	....	37,021	14,246.45	5,838	449,054.35
61	Idaho	42,750.00	120	....	3,007	810.40	2,001	48,847.40
62	Montana	643,104.95	49,110	....	37,016	10,558.35	19,714	760,193.30
63	New Mexico	84,496.50	1,250	....	9,943	3,853.90	....	99,543.40
64	Utah	230,277.50	50,660	....	12,000	5,829.70	7,875	307,242.20
65	Washington	447,269.25	4,180	....	30,235	7,853.70	4,836	494,373.95
66	Wyoming	226,900.65	....	....	4,624	3,807.50	684	236,016.15
	Division No. 8	2,061,607.75	110,550	....	135,736	46,969.00	41,008	2,395,870.75
	Total of U. S	73,782,489.62	53,961,690	23,981,000	6,683,368	2,715,526.76	3,961,380	165,085,454.38

AMOUNT OF EACH KIND OF COIN AND COIN CERTIFICATE, ETC.—Continued.

OCTOBER, 1888—Continued.

Total.	Silver Treasury certificates.	Silver coin.		Gold clearing-house certificates.	Gold Treasury certificates.	Gold coin.	States.	
		Fractional.	Dollars.					
$1, 455, 536. 21	$11, 698	$28, 736. 56	$74, 457	....	$6, 490	$1, 334, 134. 65	Colorado	54
53, 546. 50	285	2, 845. 00	5, 620	....	60	46, 727. 50	Nevada	55
2, 616, 790. 98	52, 220	42, 964. 08	113, 289	....	122, 180	2, 286, 137. 90	California	56
1, 142, 170. 82	....	15, 255. 32	14, 643	$180, 000	3, 650	928, 622. 50	San Francisco	57
940, 619. 30	20, 843	13, 979. 80	18, 034	....	12, 100	875, 572. 50	Oregon	58
15, 947. 10	....	1, 437. 10	500	....	....	14, 010. 00	Arizona	59
6, 226, 6 1. 00	85, 046	105, 237. 95	226, 552	180, 000	144, 570	5, 485, 205. 05	Division No. 7.	
470, 615. 00	9, 406	21, 154. 90	50, 879	....	17, 240	371, 845. 10	Dakota	60
117, 510. 85	6, 117	1, 217. 35	6, 762	....	1, 630	101, 784. 50	Idaho	61
8[illegible]0, 407. 00	32, 524	11, 744. 00	48, 580	....	40, 600	736, 950. 00	Montana	62
124, 448. 85	2, 100	4, 522. 35	8, 557	....	1, 000	108, 269. 50	New Mexico	63
396, 127. 75	5, 009	5, 597. 45	6, 213	....	55, 500	323, 808. 30	Utah	64
749, 740. 99	8, 895	7, 804. 29	42, 344	....	10, 700	679, 997. 70	Washington	65
210, 176. 00	792	4, 801. 40	4, 927	....	660	198, 992. 00	Wyoming	66
2, 939, 026. 44	64, 033	56, 844. 74	168, 271	....	127, 330	2, 521, 647. 70	Division No. 8.	
177, 087, 816. 64	7, 298, 208	3, 255, 891. 69	7, 051, 931	9, 070, 000	81, 088, 790	70, 222, 905. 95	Total of U. S ...	

ABSTRACT OF REPORTS OF EARNINGS AND DIVIDENDS OF NATIONAL BANKS

	States, Territories, and reserve cities.	No. of banks.	Capital stock.	Surplus.	Capital and surplus.	Gross earnings.
1	Maine	73	$10, 560, 000	$2, 426, 100. 48	$12, 986, 100. 48	$854, 581. 12
2	New Hampshire	49	6, 205, 000	1, 454, 176. 55	7, 659, 176. 55	475, 970. 63
3	Vermont	40	7, 116, 000	1, 597, 760. 13	8, 713, 760. 13	558, 620. 16
4	Massachusetts	198	44, 790, 500	14, 232, 518. 45	59, 023, 018. 45	3, 754, 239. 54
5	Boston	54	50, 950, 000	12, 592, 036. 30	63, 542, 036. 30	3, 724, 944. 84
6	Rhode Island	61	20, 340, 050	4, 278, 272. 41	24, 618, 322. 41	1, 200, 162. 54
7	Connecticut	83	24, 444, 370	6, 878, 905 17	31, 323, 275. 17	1, 727, 695. 94
	Division No. 1	567	164, 405, 920	43, 459, 769 49	207, 865, 689. 49	12, 296, 214. 77
8	New York	270	34, 614, 760	10, 349, 689. 39	44, 964, 449. 39	3, 884, 020. 88
9	New York City	47	49, 150, 000	31, 019, 319. 58	80, 169, 319. 58	8, 905, 914. 75
10	Albany	6	1, 750, 000	1, 246, 000. 00	2, 996, 000. 00	312, 848. 86
11	New Jersey	81	13, 108, 350	4, 650, 853. 11	17, 759, 203. 11	1, 576, 169. 07
12	Pennsylvania	237	33, 390, 340	11, 910, 384. 73	45, 300, 724. 73	3, 231, 967. 26
13	Philadelphia	43	22, 758, 000	10, 961, 303. 08	33, 719, 303. 08	2, 412, 147. 76
14	Pittsburgh	23	10, 180, 000	4, 705, 950. 50	14, 885, 950. 50	1, 085, 687. 28
	Division No. 2	707	164, 951, 450	74, 843, 500. 39	239, 794, 950. 39	21, 408, 755. 86
15	Delaware	17	2, 083, 985	814, 000. 00	2, 897, 985. 00	201, 731. 86
16	Maryland	31	2, 806, 700	920, 016. 40	3, 726, 716. 40	286, 441. 51
17	Baltimore	17	11, 713, 260	3, 543, 510. 62	15, 256, 770. 62	879, 620. 17
18	District of Columbia	1	252, 000	60, 000. 00	312, 000. 00	26, 478. 42
19	Washington	7	1, 575, 000	498, 500. 00	2, 073, 500. 00	193, 005. 66
20	Virginia	25	3, 796, 300	1, 488, 541. 93	5, 284, 841. 93	494, 936. 28
21	West Virginia	20	1, 961, 000	465, 690. 78	2, 426, 690. 78	188, 251. 22
	Division No. 3	118	24, 188, 245	7, 790, 259. 73	31, 978, 504. 73	2, 270, 465. 12
22	North Carolina	18	2, 426, 000	578, 287. 26	3, 004, 287. 26	232, 368. 31
23	South Carolina	15	1, 698, 000	784, 000. 00	2, 482, 000. 00	292, 077. 37
24	Georgia	21	3, 106, 000	994, 353. 65	4, 100, 353. 65	339, 491. 15
25	Florida	9	535, 000	76, 000. 00	611, 000. 00	93, 976. 59
26	Alabama	20	3, 344, 000	691, 586. 54	4, 035, 586. 54	401, 964. 78
27	Mississippi	12	1, 055, 000	190, 213. 12	1, 245, 213. 12	130, 142. 43
28	Louisiana	5	500, 000	60, 280. 02	560, 280. 02	69, 504. 75
29	New Orleans	8	2, 925, 000	1, 346, 000. 00	4, 271, 000. 00	492, 439. 75
30	Texas	91	10, 082, 700	2, 587, 724. 14	12, 670, 424. 14	1, 512, 125. 27
31	Arkansas	7	950, 000	169, 300. 00	1, 119, 300. 00	140, 062. 20
32	Kentucky	58	9, 708, 900	2, 338, 000. 71	12, 046, 900. 71	786, 113. 21
33	Louisville	9	3, 551, 500	953, 175. 36	4, 504, 675. 36	305, 006. 97
34	Tennessee	40	7, 485, 000	1, 535, 249. 88	9, 020, 249. 88	874, 264. 59
	Division No. 4	313	47, 367, 100	12, 304, 170. 68	59, 671, 270. 68	5, 669, 627. 37
35	Ohio	192	22, 902, 000	5, 233, 670. 24	28, 135, 670. 24	2, 262, 238. 41
36	Cincinnati	15	10, 180, 000	1, 880, 000. 00	12, 060, 000. 00	882, 386. 52
37	Cleveland	9	6, 700, 000	959, 000. 00	7, 659, 000. 00	505, 668. 00
38	Indiana	92	11, 844, 500	3, 560, 682. 94	15, 405, 182. 94	1, 358, 641. 49
39	Illinois	159	14, 291, 500	4, 749, 273. 46	19, 040, 773. 46	1, 728, 016. 95
40	Chicago	18	15, 050, 000	4, 727, 837. 65	19, 777, 837. 65	2, 280, 906. 60
41	Michigan	100	10, 722, 933	2, 353, 461. 46	13, 076, 394. 46	1, 261, 330. 13
42	Detroit	8	4, 000, 000	487, 000. 00	4, 487, 000. 00	509, 142. 14
43	Wisconsin	54	4, 550, 000	1, 248, 850. 81	5, 798, 850. 81	631, 250. 78
44	Milwaukee	3	650, 000	390, 000. 00	1, 040, 000. 00	146, 285. 60
	Division No. 5	650	100, 890, 933	25, 589, 776. 56	126, 480, 709. 56	11, 565, 866. 62
45	Iowa	127	10, 050, 000	2, 622, 310. 61	12, 672, 310. 61	1, 108, 750. 48
46	Minnesota	57	13, 490, 000	2, 548, 262. 39	16, 038, 262. 39	1, 420, 090. 01
47	Missouri	34	2, 431, 000	549, 523. 49	2, 980, 523. 49	270, 051. 49
48	Saint Louis	4	2, 700, 000	1, 040, 000. 00	3, 740, 000. 00	403, 710. 75
49	Kansas City	8	5, 975, 000	512, 000. 00	6, 487, 000. 00	659, 244. 77
50	Saint Joseph	2	300, 000	110, 000. 00	410, 000. 00	73, 361. 81
51	Kansas	138	10, 412, 100	1, 686, 436. 83	12, 098, 536. 83	1, 523, 912. 29
52	Nebraska	95	6, 065, 000	990, 439. 54	7, 055, 439. 54	849, 250. 11
53	Omaha	8	2, 400, 000	583, 500. 00	2, 983, 500. 00	369, 379. 87
	Division No. 6	473	53, 823, 100	10, 642, 472. 86	64, 465, 572. 86	6, 737, 760. 58

IN THE UNITED STATES FROM SEPTEMBER 1, 1887, TO MARCH 1, 1888.

Charged off.		Net earnings.	Dividends.	Ratios.			
Losses and premiums.	Expenses and taxes.			Net earnings to capital and surplus.	Dividends to capital and surplus.	Dividends to capital.	
$147, 820. 77	$180, 742. 06	$526, 018. 29	$405, 800. 00	4. 05	3. 12	3. 84	1
65, 625. 42	127, 212. 75	283, 132. 46	235, 050. 00	3. 70	3. 07	3. 79	2
52, 045. 42	149, 018. 22	837, 556. 52	265, 805. 00	4. 10	3. 05	3. 74	3
705, 251. 22	1, 293, 730. 34	1, 665, 248. 98	1, 579, 505. 00	2. 82	2. 08	3. 53	4
486, 439. 82	1, 352, 544. 95	1, 885, 960. 07	1, 450, 234. 40	2. 97	2. 28	2. 85	5
139, 705. 87	222, 398. 07	837, 908. 60	657, 164. 00	3. 40	2. 67	3. 23	6
671, 501. 21	424, 424. 43	631, 680. 30	833, 118. 50	2. 02	2. 66	3. 41	7
2, 358, 530. 73	3, 750, 079. 82	6, 187, 595. 22	5, 426, 177. 80	2. 98	2. 61	3. 30	
629, 058. 57	1, 427, 795. 18	1, 827, 107. 13	1, 385, 065. 72	4. 00	3. 08	4. 00	8
1, 545, 048. 62	3, 646, 178. 07	3, 714, 688. 06	2, 118, 155. 18	4. 63	2. 64	4. 31	9
95, 141. 54	188, 955. 80	83, 751. 52	93, 355. 00	2. 80	3. 18	5. 45	10
156, 092. 44	403, 030. 55	927, 040. 08	586, 234. 00	5. 22	3. 30	4. 47	11
518, 569. 86	894, 041. 62	1, 819, 355. 78	1, 261, 469. 10	4. 02	2. 79	3. 78	12
338, 360. 25	833, 233. 50	1, 240, 551. 01	831, 860. 00	3. 68	2. 47	3. 66	13
52, 540. 82	281, 979. 39	751, 167. 67	386, 750. 00	5. 05	2. 60	3. 80	14
3, 334, 812. 10	7, 710, 214. 11	10, 303, 729. 65	6, 604, 889. 00	4. 32	2. 78	4. 01	
17, 900. 73	59, 182. 99	124, 648. 14	98, 745. 95	4. 30	3. 41	4. 74	15
32, 635. 63	112, 228. 15	141, 577. 71	113, 616. 54	3. 80	3. 05	4. 05	16
151, 130. 88	268, 238. 26	460, 251. 03	408, 308. 30	3. 02	2. 68	3. 49	17
7, 000. 00	8, 194. 60	11, 283. 82	10, 080. 00	3. 62	3. 23	4. 00	18
15, 177. 61	77, 610. 22	100, 217. 83	50, 875. 00	4. 83	2. 45	3. 23	19
89, 276. 41	175, 721. 29	229, 938. 58	142, 692. 00	4. 35	2. 70	3. 70	20
46, 232. 68	71, 100. 35	70, 918. 19	80, 280. 00	2. 02	3. 31	4. 09	21
359, 353. 96	772, 275. 86	1, 138, 835. 30	904, 597. 79	3. 56	2. 83	3. 74	
20, 673. 64	91, 458. 30	120, 236. 37	91, 811. 55	4. 00	3. 06	5. 78	22
15, 300. 07	99, 261. 15	177, 456. 15	140, 490. 00	7. 15	5. 66	8. 27	23
18, 522. 59	149, 114. 84	176, 853. 72	119, 110. 00	4. 31	2. 90	3. 83	24
3, 034. 21	50, 387. 27	40, 556. 11	21, 000. 00	6. 64	3. 44	3. 93	25
70, 656. 04	137, 192. 65	104, 116. 00	111, 000. 00	4. 81	2. 75	3. 32	26
10, 544. 15	44, 073. 02	75, 525. 26	43, 000. 00	6. 07	3. 45	4. 08	27
6, 230. 90	22, 973. 95	40, 389. 90	8, 000. 00	7. 21	1. 43	1. 66	28
128, 640. 30	199, 596. 40	164, 203. 05	124, 750. 00	3. 84	2. 92	4. 26	29
290, 283. 94	487, 840. 11	725, 001. 22	570, 450. 00	5. 72	4. 57	5. 75	30
10, 841. 02	47, 361. 06	81, 859. 22	46, 000. 00	7. 31	4. 11	4. 84	31
85, 877. 37	244, 127. 30	456, 108. 54	350, 345. 00	3. 79	2. 91	3. 61	32
36, 950. 32	119, 411. 16	148, 645. 40	130, 500. 00	3. 30	2. 90	3. 08	33
54, 086. 23	264, 443. 21	355, 735. 15	309, 550. 00	6. 16	3. 43	4. 14	34
755, 701. 68	1, 957, 240. 42	2, 956, 685. 27	2, 075, 006. 55	4. 95	3. 48	4. 38	
401, 606. 03	774, 753. 12	1, 085, 619. 26	886, 116. 80	3. 86	3. 15	3. 87	35
207, 065. 04	388, 866. 84	285, 554. 64	332, 500. 00	2. 37	2. 76	3. 27	36
61, 207. 13	182, 037. 66	202, 423. 21	177, 000. 00	3. 43	2. 31	2. 64	37
200, 979. 16	463, 455. 46	691, 206. 87	467, 990. 00	4. 50	3. 04	3. 95	38
218, 200. 13	552, 797. 17	957, 010. 65	693, 300. 66	5. 03	3. 64	4. 65	39
184, 933. 78	731, 325. 17	1, 344, 647. 65	623, 000. 00	6. 80	3. 15	4. 14	40
103, 570. 31	393, 471. 73	764, 288 00	604, 321. 70	5. 84	4. 62	5. 64	41
56, 694. 25	230, 616. 43	221, 831. 46	154, 000. 00	4. 04	3. 43	3. 65	42
47, 707. 06	220, 737. 97	302, 785. 75	221, 250. 08	6. 26	3. 82	4. 86	43
36, 596. 51	71, 770. 65	37, 018. 44	42, 000. 00	3. 65	4. 04	6. 46	44
1, 519, 528. 40	4, 029, 852. 20	6, 016, 486. 02	4, 201, 549. 14	4. 76	3. 32	4. 16	
110, 173. 45	401, 675. 29	590, 010. 71	565, 391. 88	4. 71	4. 46	5. 63	45
172, 083. 01	371, 343. 24	876, 663. 76	560, 625. 00	5. 47	3. 50	4. 16	46
9, 303. 49	114, 572. 08	146, 176. 01	117, 476. 35	4. 00	3. 94	4. 83	47
105, 190. 56	207, 200. 07	91, 311. 12	80, 000. 00	2. 41	2. 14	2. 96	48
79, 602. 88	239, 940. 21	339, 701. 68	284, 000. 00	5. 24	3. 61	3. 92	49
36, 740. 26	21, 500. 11	16, 061. 44	10, 000. 00	3. 02	2. 43	3. 33	50
76, 819. 64	582, 379. 01	864, 713. 64	604, 787. 37	7. 15	5. 00	5. 81	51
57, 156. 29	323, 036. 18	409, 037. 61	342, 846. 30	6. 67	4. 86	5. 63	52
77, 312. 67	180, 688. 20	111, 379. 60	75, 000. 00	3. 73	2. 51	3. 13	53
723, 391. 16	2, 502, 414. 39	3, 511, 955. 03	2, 590, 076. 90	5. 43	4. 02	4. 81	

ABSTRACT OF REPORTS OF EARNINGS AND DIVIDENDS OF NATIONAL BANKS IN

	States, Territories, and reserve cities.	No. of banks.	Capital stock.	Surplus.	Capital and surplus.	Gross earnings.
54	Colorado	31	$2,785,000	$982,000.00	$3,767,000.00	$1,122,076.48
55	Nevada	2	150,000	60,000.00	210,000.00	33,010.87
56	California	28	3,805,000	848,548.67	4,653,548.67	714,072.68
57	San Francisco	3	2,700,000	266,871.44	2,966,871.44	269,831.69
58	Oregon	23	1,815,000	241,550.00	2,056,550.00	317,778.68
	Division No. 7	87	11,255,000	2,398,970.11	13,653,970.11	2,398,270.40
59	Arizona	1	100,000	5,000.00	105,000.00	18,903.13
60	Dakota	62	3,725,000	751,942.03	4,476,942.03	543,151.82
61	Idaho	6	350,000	58,000.00	408,000.00	61,366.13
62	Montana	17	1,975,000	501,250.00	2,476,250.00	388,815.25
63	New Mexico	9	850,000	176,910.60	1,026,910.60	122,041.66
64	Utah	7	850,000	382,278.00	1,232,278.00	129,442.85
65	Washington	19	1,330,000	269,816.53	1,599,816.53	284,839.10
66	Wyoming	8	1,075,000	223,030.78	1,298,030.78	126,744.41
	Division No. 8	129	10,255,000	2,368,227.94	12,623,227.94	1,675,304.35
	United States	3,044	577,136,748	179,397,147.76	756,533,895.76	64,022,265.07

THE UNITED STATES FROM SEPTEMBER 1, 1887, TO MARCH 1, 1888—Continued.

Charged off.		Net earnings.	Dividends.	Ratios.			
Losses and premiums.	Expenses and taxes.			Net earnings to capital and surplus.	Dividends to capital and surplus.	Dividends to capital.	
$112,835.07	$280,148.10	$720,092.65	$284,900.00	19.35	7.56	10.23	54
920.31	11,892.03	21,097.03	6,000.00	10.05	2.86	4.00	55
62,616.35	200,553.26	451,603.07	154,500.00	9.70	3.32	4.06	56
12,587.82	50,543.77	146,700.10	52,500.00	4.94	1.77	1.94	57
9,799.13	93,127.31	214,852.24	315,500.00	10.45	15.34	17.38	58
198,759.28	636,265.43	1,563,245.09	813,400.00	11.38	5.96	7.23	
625.00	4,468.83	13,809.30	6,000.00	13.15	5.71	6.00	59
62,299.06	209,065.20	271,787.50	140,000.00	6.07	3.34	4.02	60
3,074.46	26,542.56	31,749.11	17,000.00	7.78	4.16	4.86	61
46,045.23	138,017.66	204,152.30	83,500.00	8.24	3.37	4.23	62
29,701.34	56,812.36	35,437.96	32,500.00	3.46	3.16	3.62	63
17,034.67	46,136.84	65,071.34	46,000.00	5.33	3.73	5.41	64
4,713.42	72,914.06	207,210.72	56,750.00	12.95	3.55	4.27	65
28,307.39	65,492.63	32,944.30	21,500.00	2.00	1.66	2.54	66
193,090.57	619,451.04	862,702.74	412,850.00	6.82	3.27	4.03	
9,443,176.88	21,077,703.27	32,601,204.92	23,088,007.18	4.31	3.05	4.00	

ABSTRACT OF REPORTS OF EARNINGS AND DIVIDENDS OF NATIONAL BANKS

	States, Territories, and reserve cities.	No. of banks.	Capital stock.	Surplus.	Capital and surplus.	Gross earnings.
1	Maine	75	$10,710,000	$2,459,848.80	$13,169,848.80	$827,523.50
2	New Hampshire	49	6,205,000	1,471,914.46	7,676,914.46	470,785.70
3	Vermont	49	7,566,000	1,689,976.41	9,255,976.41	530,004.72
4	Massachusetts	198	44,790,500	14,229,540.98	59,020,040.98	3,008,444.83
5	Boston	54	50,950,000	13,134,514.00	64,084,514.00	4,061,494.84
6	Rhode Island	60	20,284,050	4,327,768.26	24,611,818.26	1,234,206.96
7	Connecticut	83	24,144,270	6,883,854.39	31,028,124.39	1,783,359.87
	Division No. 1	568	164,649,820	44,197,417.90	208,847,237.90	12,515,970.42
8	New York	272	35,079,760	10,715,946.26	45,795,706.26	4,088,804.01
9	New York City	46	49,100,000	31,661,363.26	80,761,363.26	8,783,965.69
10	Albany	6	1,750,000	1,240,000.00	2,990,000.00	280,063.13
11	New Jersey	83	13,196,530	5,086,931.73	18,283,461.73	1,648,885.92
12	Pennsylvania	246	33,715,340	12,291,033.16	46,006,373.16	3,332,941.53
13	Philadelphia	43	22,758,000	10,996,803.08	33,754,803.08	2,349,650.50
14	Pittsburgh	24	10,180,000	4,929,935.06	15,109,935.06	1,106,771.45
	Division No. 2	720	165,779,630	76,931,012.55	242,710,642.55	21,591,708.23
15	Delaware	17	2,083,985	831,300.00	2,915,285.00	201,354.63
16	Maryland	31	2,816,700	971,857.33	3,788,557.33	348,051.57
17	Baltimore	17	11,713,260	3,672,588.47	15,385,848.47	1,014,560.47
18	District of Columbia	1	252,000	60,000.00	312,000.00	24,115.38
19	Washington	7	1,575,000	532,000.00	2,107,000.00	246,097.09
20	Virginia	26	3,796,300	1,514,103.44	5,310,403.44	440,216.62
21	West Virginia	20	1,961,000	465,555.27	2,426,555.27	166,271.02
	Division No. 3	119	24,198,245	8,047,494.51	32,245,739.51	2,441,276.68
22	North Carolina	17	2,226,000	565,632.95	2,791,632.95	254,161.48
23	South Carolina	16	1,773,000	787,800.00	2,560,800.00	205,000.75
24	Georgia	23	3,236,000	1,035,460.30	4,271,460.30	393,070.44
25	Florida	11	700,000	80,820.00	780,820.00	121,014.39
26	Alabama	20	3,344,000	674,430.38	4,018,430.38	376,051.73
27	Mississippi	12	1,055,000	239,289.59	1,294,289.59	177,952.05
28	Louisiana	5	500,000	84,213.06	584,213.06	81,256.30
29	New Orleans	8	2,925,000	1,424,000.00	4,349,000.00	515,424.10
30	Texas	94	10,970,700	2,743,342.43	13,714,042.43	1,309,952.07
31	Arkansas	7	950,000	191,000.00	1,141,000.00	157,644.54
32	Kentucky	60	10,134,300	2,458,127.24	12,592,427.24	825,208.28
33	Louisville	9	3,551,500	958,514.96	4,510,014.96	306,385.33
34	Tennessee	41	7,680,000	1,613,154.88	9,293,154.88	831,662.17
	Division No. 4	323	49,045,500	12,864,785.79	61,910,285.79	5,735,383.72
35	Ohio	194	23,909,750	5,497,840.66	29,407,590.66	2,409,360.09
36	Cincinnati	14	9,180,000	1,700,500.00	10,880,500.00	1,172,903.80
37	Cleveland	9	6,630,000	1,000,000.00	7,630,000.00	640,999.97
38	Indiana	93	11,834,500	3,596,277.79	15,430,777.79	1,308,096.01
39	Illinois	162	14,574,000	4,576,616.88	19,150,616.88	1,808,871.62
40	Chicago	18	15,050,000	5,305,620.43	20,355,620.43	2,270,170.70
41	Michigan	100	10,874,600	2,457,498.09	13,332,098.09	1,157,216.80
42	Detroit	8	4,000,000	500,000.00	4,500,000.00	491,801.70
43	Wisconsin	54	4,550,000	1,317,217.80	5,867,217.80	595,421.75
44	Milwaukee	3	650,000	370,000.00	1,020,000.00	162,276.87
	Division No. 5	655	101,362,850	26,291,577.65	127,654,427.65	12,057,049.27
45	Iowa	128	10,100,000	2,696,710.12	12,796,710.12	1,229,513.38
46	Minnesota	56	12,420,000	2,535,462.39	14,955,462.39	1,407,018.95
47	Missouri	34	2,431,000	549,130.76	2,980,130.76	259,916.08
48	Saint Louis	4	3,200,000	640,000.00	3,840,000.00	351,628.67
49	Kansas City	8	6,050,000	585,000.00	6,635,000.00	604,569.60
50	Saint Joseph	2	300,000	110,000.00	410,000.00	76,590.41
51	Kansas	151	12,002,100	1,803,686.56	13,805,786.56	1,555,108.58
52	Nebraska	95	6,036,000	1,074,146.28	7,100,146.28	907,012.90
53	Omaha	8	2,500,000	658,000.00	3,158,000.00	370,572.42
	Division No. 6	486	55,098,100	10,682,745.11	65,780,845.11	6,830,926.55
54	Colorado	31	2,985,000	1,126,090.42	4,111,090.42	820,482.54
55	Nevada	2	250,000	90,000.00	340,000.00	54,535.06
56	California	34	4,015,000	991,828.74	5,009,828.74	883,740.26
57	San Francisco	3	2,700,000	310,000.00	3,010,000.00	216,964.99
58	Oregon	23	2,090,000	313,450.00	2,403,450.00	304,323.18
	Division No. 7	93	12,940,000	2,835,260.16	15,775,260.16	2,370,046.03

IN THE UNITED STATES FROM MARCH 1, 1888, TO SEPTEMBER 1, 1888.

Charged off.		Net earnings.	Dividends.	Ratios.			
Losses and premiums.	Expenses and taxes.			Net earnings to capital and surplus.	Dividends to capital and surplus.	Dividends to capital.	
$176,690.39	$180,930.49	$460,902.62	$405,800.00	3.57	3.08	3.79	1
40,037.61	120,925.42	309,822.67	240,050.00	4.01	3.13	3.87	2
27,658.19	161,467.24	340,969.29	260,305.00	3.68	2.81	3.44	3
714,360.23	1,116,265.93	1,777,818.67	1,495,225.00	3.01	2.53	3.34	4
431,676.05	1,513,256.30	2,116,502.49	1,459,250.00	3.30	2.28	2.86	5
166,889.44	235,784.49	831,593.03	657,127.25	3.38	2.67	3.24	6
425,509.18	465,279.02	802,571.67	831,824.60	2.92	2.08	3.45	7
1,982,821.09	3,703,908.89	6,739,240.44	5,349,581.85	3.23	2.56	3.25	
670,873.28	1,542,924.83	1,875,095.90	1,432,154.23	4.09	3.13	4.08	8
1,310,169.21	3,250,710.59	4,223,088.89	2,238,875.00	5.23	2.77	4.56	9
48,737.92	153,639.25	78,305.96	88,000.00	2.61	2.93	5.03	10
277,295.86	409,688.23	901,901.83	587,734.00	4.93	3.21	4.45	11
473,223.48	1,121,425.32	1,738,292.73	1,312,369.10	3.78	2.85	3.89	12
354,323.58	916,734.01	1,078,598.01	810,509.68	3.20	2.40	3.56	13
94,126.91	394,198.87	618,445.67	368,750.00	4.09	2.57	3.82	14
3,228,747.24	7,849,321.10	10,513,729.89	6,858,392.01	4.33	2.83	4.14	
11,410.94	56,401.27	133,542.42	98,445.95	4.58	3.41	4.72	15
28,119.00	110,519.60	209,412.97	117,918.00	5.53	3.11	4.19	16
129,574.80	310,097.68	574,896.99	429,110.87	3.74	2.79	3.66	17
3,173.30	10,241.55	10,700.53	10,080.00	3.43	3.23	4.00	18
65,025.10	79,697.62	101,975.27	50,875.00	4.84	2.41	3.23	19
68,647.79	181,486.11	199,082.72	144,022.00	3.58	2.71	3.79	20
22,538.24	55,319.47	88,413.31	62,230.00	3.64	2.56	3.17	21
328,489.17	803,763.30	1,309,024.21	912,681.82	4.06	2.83	3.77	
31,589.05	78,784.99	143,787.44	69,500.00	5.15	2.49	3.12	22
49,547.01	103,435.01	142,018.70	80,120.00	5.55	3.13	4.53	23
19,018.58	139,539.33	235,117.53	118,360.00	5.50	2.77	3.06	24
3,527.58	65,208.25	52,278.56	27,000.00	6.63	3.42	3.86	25
65,612.22	145,027.16	165,412.35	114,500.00	4.12	2.85	3.42	26
9,852.26	56,647.67	111,952.12	38,000.00	8.65	2.94	3.60	27
17,912.19	22,685.23	40,658.97	10,000.00	6.96	1.71	2.00	28
268,291.82	167,118.08	69,014.20	108,750.00	1.38	2.50	3.72	29
105,122.46	510,188.23	724,641.38	557,950.00	5.28	4.07	5.09	30
18,627.17	53,305.81	85,712.06	37,500.00	8.39	3.29	3.95	31
104,363.75	244,364.17	476,480.36	410,595.00	3.78	3.26	4.05	32
83,490.37	109,456.82	113,438.14	130,560.00	2.52	2.89	3.68	33
55,073.38	301,335.43	475,253.36	280,850.00	5.11	3.02	3.66	34
891,522.84	2,017,005.71	2,826,765.17	1,983,685.00	4.57	3.20	4.04	
340,921.92	824,998.93	1,243,409.14	877,230.99	4.22	2.08	3.66	35
217,093.00	538,138.73	397,621.17	310,000.00	3.65	2.85	3.38	36
83,935.50	218,903.08	338,161.39	182,000.00	4.42	2.38	2.74	37
314,447.16	402,357.73	562,191.12	490,537.38	3.65	3.18	4.14	38
277,059.86	689,405.73	842,406.03	756,330.00	4.40	3.95	5.19	39
200,202.00	938,409.54	1,140,559.16	553,000.00	5.60	2.71	3.67	40
137,945.49	359,701.89	650,509.48	481,074.00	4.05	3.61	4.42	41
19,452.07	231,321.53	211,027.50	158,000.00	4.69	3.51	3.95	42
23,541.35	218,502.40	353,288.00	264,075.00	7.26	5.43	5.80	43
3,082.70	71,551.05	87,643.12	132,000.00	8.59	12.94	20.31	44
1,617,682.55	4,608,430.61	5,835,036.11	4,204,247.37	4.57	3.29	4.15	
136,570.98	471,627.14	621,315.26	455,200.00	4.86	3.56	4.51	45
220,154.86	601,071.97	585,792.13	515,950.00	3.92	3.45	4.15	46
24,815.45	107,946.00	127,155.19	101,706.06	4.27	3.41	4.18	47
13,726.16	166,172.68	171,729.83	606,000.00	4.47	15.78	18.94	48
31,961.10	286,490.98	346,117.52	254,000.00	5.22	3.83	4.20	49
50,900.63	23,143.92	2,455.86	10,000.00	.60	2.44	3.33	50
104,309.13	611,529.13	839,205.32	503,176.00	6.04	4.05	4.67	51
30,225.06	415,227.27	461,559.67	330,755.60	6.49	4.65	5.48	52
71,007.88	214,500.11	94,004.43	85,000.00	2.98	2.69	3.40	53
683,822.15	2,897,709.20	3,240,335.20	2,921,787.66	4.94	4.44	5.30	
104,401.66	314,536.49	401,544.39	276,800.00	9.77	6.73	9.27	54
383.62	9,780.77	44,370.67	12,600.00	13.05	3.53	4.80	55
64,382.59	202,472.69	536,884.98	366,750.00	9.42	6.21	7.46	56
10,179.72	56,610.94	150,174.33	52,500.00	4.90	1.74	1.94	57
11,703.20	107,271.51	275,348.47	84,100.00	11.46	3.50	4.02	58
191,050.79	750,672.40	1,426,322.84	792,150.00	9.05	5.02	6.12	

ABSTRACT OF REPORTS OF EARNINGS AND DIVIDENDS OF NATIONAL BANKS IN

	States, Territories, and reserve cities.	No. of banks.	Capital stock.	Surplus.	Capital and surplus.	Gross earnings.
59	Arizona	1	$100,000	$0,000.00	$100,000.00	$15,105.32
60	Dakota	59	3,575,000	804,062.32	4,379,062.32	488,463.88
61	Idaho	6	350,000	85,000.00	435,000.00	50,300.30
62	Montana	17	1,975,000	506,000.00	2,481,000.00	361,014.77
63	New Mexico	9	850,000	185,225.03	1,035,225.03	109,361.75
64	Utah	7	850,000	417,150.00	1,267,150.00	139,719.53
65	Washington	22	1,690,000	322,750.00	2,012,750.00	326,687.44
66	Wyoming	8	1,075,000	237,500.00	1,312,500.00	95,582.25
	Division No. 8	129	10,465,000	2,566,688.25	13,031,688.25	1,583,233.33
	United States	3,093	583,539,145	184,416,990.02	767,956,135.02	65,125,686.23

THE UNITED STATES FROM MARCH 1, 1888, TO SEPTEMBER 1, 1888—Continued.

Charged off.		Net earnings.	Dividends.	Ratios.			
Losses and premiums.	Expenses and taxes.			Net earnings to capital and surplus.	Dividends to capital and surplus.	Dividends to capital.	
....	$4,702.40	$10,312.02	$6,000.00	9.40	5.50	6.00	59
$43,531.75	225,480.48	219,420.65	144,000.00	5.01	3.27	4.00	60
4,501.75	19,055.70	25,782.91	27,000.00	5.03	6.21	7.71	61
44,500.37	128,124.24	188,300.16	65,400.00	7.59	2.64	3.31	62
11,028.75	41,020.55	51,312.45	37,000.00	4.96	3.57	4.35	63
1,875.54	37,853.91	99,090.06	43,000.00	7.80	3.30	5.06	64
11,855.43	100,625.60	214,206.41	87,625.00	10.04	4.35	5.18	65
1,820.00	46,257.99	47,503.36	11,500.00	3.02	.88	1.07	66
119,286.48	697,110.90	850,857.95	420,525.00	6.58	2.96	3.68	
9,644,422.31	23,323,072.11	82,759,191.81	23,443,050.71	4.26	3.05	4.02	

EARNINGS AND DIVIDENDS OF THE NATIONAL BANKS, ARRANGED BY GEOGRAPHICAL DIVISIONS, FOR SEMI-ANNUAL PERIODS FROM SEPTEMBER 1, 1879, TO SEPTEMBER 1, 1888.

Geographical divisions.	No. of banks	Capital.	Surplus.	Dividends.	Net earnings.	Ratios.		
						Dividends to capital.	Dividends to capital and surplus.	Earnings to capital and surplus.
						Pr. ct.	Pr. ct.	Pr. ct.
Sept., 1879, to March, 1880:								
New England States...	546	$164, 820, 020	$37, 800, 312	$5, 409, 351	$5, 610, 287	3. 3	2. 7	2. 8
Middle States..........	640	169, 399, 170	51, 306, 583	7, 151, 166	9, 220, 826	4. 2	3. 2	4. 2
Southern States........	175	30, 432, 700	5, 210, 198	1, 246, 470	1, 278, 695	4. 1	3. 5	3. 6
Western States........	685	89, 428, 200	22, 840, 408	4, 314, 286	5, 042, 976	4. 8	3. 8	4. 5
Total	2, 046	454, 080, 090	117, 226, 501	18, 121, 273	21, 152, 784	4. 0	3. 2	3. 7
March, 1880, to Sept., 1880:								
New England States...	548	165, 380, 242	38, 450, 207	5, 858, 434	7, 413, 622	3. 5	2. 9	3. 6
Middle States..........	654	169, 343, 870	52, 702, 674	7, 120, 204	9, 805, 448	4. 2	3. 2	4. 1
Southern States........	176	30, 423, 700	5, 516, 336	1, 139, 203	1, 434, 102	3. 7	3. 2	4. 0
Western States........	694	89, 067, 250	23, 416, 343	4, 172, 359	5, 380, 078	4. 7	3. 7	4. 8
Total	2, 072	454, 215, 062	120, 145, 649	18, 290, 200	24, 033, 250	4. 0	3. 2	4. 2
Sept., 1880, to March, 1881:								
New England States...	550	165, 623, 120	38, 944, 841	5, 900, 861	6, 757, 787	3. 6	2. 9	3. 3
Middle States.........	657	170, 739, 045	53, 536, 248	6, 974, 934	9, 162, 771	4. 1	3. 1	4. 1
Southern States........	178	30, 448, 700	5, 898, 107	1, 264, 398	1, 905, 690	4. 2	3. 5	5. 2
Western States........	702	90, 634, 000	24, 102, 592	4, 737, 324	6, 625, 773	5. 3	4. 2	5. 8
Total	2, 087	456, 844, 865	122, 481, 788	18, 877, 517	24, 452, 021	4. 1	3. 3	4. 2
March, 1881, to Sept., 1881:								
New England States...	550	165, 373, 120	39, 878, 448	6, 005, 608	8, 106, 022	3. 6	2. 9	4. 0
Middle States..........	660	171, 560, 315	55, 747, 501	7, 558, 407	11, 925, 784	4. 4	3. 3	5. 3
Southern States........	181	30, 973, 950	6, 530, 694	1, 282, 120	2, 300, 624	4. 1	3. 4	6. 1
Western States........	709	91, 027, 100	25, 081, 751	4, 653, 833	6, 778, 112	5. 1	3. 9	5. 8
Total	2, 100	458, 934, 485	127, 238, 394	19, 499, 968	29, 170, 542	4. 3	3. 3	5. 0
Sept., 1881, to March, 1882:								
New England States...	553	162, 650, 870	40, 703, 776	5, 952, 275	7, 123, 339	3. 7	2. 9	3. 5
Middle States..........	666	171, 488, 315	57, 470, 278	7, 367, 409	10, 210, 373	4. 3	3. 2	4. 5
Southern States	188	31, 672, 700	6, 928, 882	1, 333, 715	1, 961, 220	4. 2	3. 5	5. 1
Western States........	730	94, 542, 600	26, 188, 953	5, 261, 976	7, 768, 661	5. 6	4. 3	6. 4
Total	2, 137	460, 354, 485	131, 291, 889	19, 915, 375	27, 083, 599	4. 3	3. 4	4. 6
March, 1882, to Sept., 1882:								
New England States...	555	165, 515, 870	41, 033, 206	5, 729, 842	6, 732, 530	3. 5	2. 8	3. 3
Middle States..........	678	173, 270, 315	58, 491, 696	7, 194, 528	9, 704, 251	4. 1	3. 1	4. 2
Southern States........	194	32, 212, 700	7, 503, 078	1, 289, 363	2, 062, 960	4. 0	3. 2	5. 2
Western States........	770	102, 948, 830	26, 542, 802	6, 662, 821	7, 737, 893	6. 5	5. 1	6. 0
Total	2, 197	473, 947, 715	133, 570, 981	20, 896, 558	26, 237, 635	4. 4	3. 4	4. 3
Sept., 1882, to March, 1883:								
New England States...	557	165, 653, 070	41, 341, 246	5, 819, 093	6, 200, 443	3. 5	2. 8	3. 0
Middle States..........	687	174, 375, 472	62, 118, 694	7, 542, 146	9, 900, 021	4. 3	3. 2	4. 2
Southern States	207	33, 963, 000	8, 228, 309	1, 405, 019	2, 198, 993	4. 1	3. 3	5. 2
Western States........	816	109, 099, 800	25, 881, 856	5, 518, 844	8, 133, 477	5. 1	4. 1	6. 0
Total	2, 267	483, 091, 342	137, 570, 105	20, 285, 102	26, 432, 934	4. 2	3. 3	4. 2
March, 1883, to Sept., 1883:								
New England States...	562	166, 793, 070	41, 727, 679	5, 861, 182	6, 651, 595	3. 5	2. 8	3. 2
Middle States..........	698	173, 915, 465	63, 453, 454	7, 556, 795	9, 960, 635	4. 3	3. 2	4. 2
Southern States	224	35, 085, 300	9, 084, 011	1, 415, 529	2, 433, 336	4. 0	3. 2	5. 4
Western States........	875	118, 246, 305	26, 967, 043	5, 560, 070	8, 528, 648	4. 7	3. 8	5. 9
Total	2, 359	494, 040, 140	141, 232, 187	20, 393, 576	27, 574, 214	4. 1	3. 2	4. 3
Sept., 1883, to March, 1884:								
New England States...	565	167, 478, 070	41, 863, 101	5, 726, 356	6, 095, 915	3. 4	2. 7	2. 9
Middle States..........	715	175, 317, 316	64, 841, 178	7, 639, 670	9, 520, 978	4. 4	3. 2	4. 0
Southern States	248	38, 214, 310	9, 854, 923	1, 700, 113	2, 950, 096	4. 4	3. 5	6. 1
Western States........	963	126, 959, 605	29, 041, 587	6, 016, 667	9, 418, 775	4. 7	3. 9	6. 0
Total	2, 491	507, 969, 300	145, 600, 849	21, 082, 806	27, 994, 764	4. 1	3. 2	4. 3

EARNINGS AND DIVIDENDS OF THE NATIONAL BANKS, ETC.—Continued.

Geographical divisions.	No. of banks	Capital.	Surplus.	Dividends.	Net earnings.	Ratios.		
						Dividends to capital.	Dividends to capital and surplus.	Earnings to capital and surplus.
						Pr. ct.	Pr. ct.	Pr. ct.
March, 1884, to Sept., 1884:								
New England States...	568	$167,000,370	$41,905,905	$5,551,603	$5,738,456	3.3	2.6	2.7
Middle States..........	723	175,767,355	64,580,406	7,089,673	8,198,912	4.0	2.9	3.4
Southern States	264	40,638,300	10,726,209	1,691,520	2,747,018	4.2	3.3	5.3
Western States	1,027	134,500,700	30,508,955	5,838,871	7,683,633	4.3	3.5	4.7
Total	2,582	518,005,725	147,721,475	20,171,667	24,368,019	3.9	3.0	3.7
Sept., 1884, to March, 1885:								
New England States...	567	167,400,370	41,413,826	5,661,537	4,388,812	3.4	2.7	2.1
Middle States..........	732	173,212,145	64,741,009	7,156,680	7,474,752	4.1	3.0	3.1
Southern States........	278	42,648,400	11,527,942	1,790,726	2,426,858	4.2	3.3	4.5
Western States	1,073	139,638,800	31,088,344	5,828,707	7,310,780	4.2	3.4	4.3
Total	2,650	522,899,715	148,771,121	20,437,650	21,601,202	3.9	3.0	3.2
March, 1885, to Sept., 1885:								
New England States ...	563	165,668,370	40,786,007	5,391,401	4,725,395	3.3	2.6	2.3
Middle States	731	172,907,352	64,247,888	6,953,332	7,297,159	4.0	2.9	3.1
Southern States	287	43,500,300	11,505,477	1,655,261	2,282,782	3.8	3.0	4.2
Western States	1,085	142,523,580	30,364,123	6,218,477	7,718,959	4.5	3.6	4.5
Total	2,666	524,599,602	146,903,495	20,218,471	22,024,295	3.9	3.0	3.3
Sept., 1885, to March, 1886:								
New England States ..	559	165,203,920	41,128,387	5,375,226	5,025,381	3.2	2.6	2.8
Middle States..........	738	172,435,295	67,583,809	7,044,535	9,484,324	4.0	2.9	3.9
Southern States	294	44,437,400	12,053,524	1,969,190	2,705,274	4.4	3.4	4.7
Western States.........	1,117	148,879,580	32,767,699	6,946,485	9,412,687	4.6	3.8	5.2
Total	2,708	530,956,195	153,532,919	21,335,436	27,527,666	4.0	3.1	4.0
March, 1886, to Sept., 1886:								
New England States...	563	165,352,320	41,581,845	5,338,635	6,736,479	3.2	2.5	3.2
Middle States..........	744	173,628,875	70,041,187	7,328,708	9,[illegible]89,135	4.2	3.0	4.0
Southern States.........	303	45,444,000	11,967,821	1,994,537	2,553,055	4.3	3.4	4.0
Western States.........	1,174	153,138,458	33,470,925	6,485,172	8,834,050	4.2	3.5	4.7
Total	2,784	537,563,648	157,064,778	21,147,142	27,912,719	3.9	3.0	4.0
Sept., 1886, to March, 1887:								
New England States ..	563	165,252,370	41,897,072	5,318,480	6,176,707	3.2	2.6	3.0
Middle States..........	754	175,873,735	73,445,033	7,574,627	12,072,419	4.[illegible]	3.0	4.8
Southern States.........	313	46,213,240	12,463,050	[illegible],[illegible]43,870	2,646,393	4.6	3.6	4.5
Western States.........	1,225	161,016,425	35,926,745	7,111,610	10,803,275	4.4	3.6	5.5
Total	2,885	548,355,770	163,731,900	22,148,587	31,698,794	4.0	3.1	4.5
March, 1887, to Sept., 1887:								
New England States...	566	164,837,370	43,118,790	5,355,787	7,224,781	3.2	2.6	3.5
Middle States..........	764	176,035,656	76,574,179	7,357,400	11,360,803	4.2	2.9	4.5
Southern States.........	343	51,515,315	13,247,285	2,137,328	3,268,073	4.1	3.3	5.0
Western States.........	1,269	165,556,200	38,314,299	7,153,305	10,953,427	4.3	3.5	5.4
Total	2,942	558,544,541	171,254,553	22,003,820	32,808,074	3.9	3.0	4.5
Sept., 1887, to March, 1888:								
New England States...	567	164,405,920	43,459,769	5,426,178	6,187,505	3.3	2.6	3.0
Middle States..........	780	183,382,395	80,679,527	7,346,515	11,201,708	4.0	2.8	4.2
Southern States.........	358	53,124,400	14,258,403	2,298,030	3,257,542	4.3	3.4	4.8
Western States.........	1,339	176,224,033	40,909,447	8,017,876	11,954,449	4.5	3.7	5.5
Total	3,044	577,136,748	179,307,147	23,088,607	32,601,294	4.0	3.0	4.3
March, 1888, to Sept., 1888:								
New England States...	568	164,649,820	44,107,418	5,349,582	6,739,240	3.2	2.6	3.2
Middle States	793	184,220,575	82,098,759	7,564,822	11,544,258	4.1	2.8	4.3
Southern States.........	369	54,803,800	14,844,534	2,189,937	3,105,[illegible]61	4.0	3.1	4.4
Western States.........	1,363	179,865,950	42,376,280	8,338,710	11,370,432	4.6	3.8	5.1
Total	3,093	583,529,145	184,416,901	23,443,051	32,759,192	4.0	3.0	4.3
General average ...	2,806	508,126,587	146,064,037	20,634,934	27,070,611	4.1	3.0	4.1

TABLE, BY STATES AND RESERVE CITIES, OF THE RATIOS TO CAPITAL, AND TO
FROM MARCH 1, 1884,

	States, Territories, and reserve cities.	Ratio of dividends to capital for six months ending—										Ratio of dividends to capital and surplus for six months ending—			
		March 1, 1884.	Sept. 1, 1884.	March 1, 1885.	Sept. 1, 1885.	March 1, 1886.	Sept. 1, 1886.	March 1, 1887.	Sept. 1, 1887.	March 1, 1888.	Sept. 1, 1888.	March 1, 1884.	Sept. 1, 1884.	March 1, 1885.	Sept. 1, 1885.
		P. ct.	P. ct.	P. ct.	P. ct.	P. ct.	P. ct.	P. ct.	P. ct.	P. ct.	P. ct.	P. ct.	P. ct.	P. ct.	P. ct.
1	Maine	4.1	4.1	4.1	4.3	4.3	4.1	3.5	3.8	3.8	3.8	3.3	3.3	3.3	3.5
2	New Hampshire	3.7	3.7	3.7	3.7	3.6	3.8	3.7	3.7	3.8	3.9	3.1	3.1	3.1	3.1
3	Vermont	3.9	3.8	3.6	3.2	3.5	3.4	3.4	3.5	3.7	3.4	3.2	3.2	3.0	2.7
4	Massachusetts	3.6	3.3	3.6	3.4	3.4	3.3	3.4	3.4	3.5	3.3	2.8	2.5	2.8	2.6
5	Boston	2.7	2.8	2.8	2.7	2.5	2.6	2.7	2.7	2.8	2.9	2.2	2.3	2.3	2.2
6	Rhode Island	3.4	3.3	3.3	3.2	3.1	3.1	3.2	3.2	3.2	3.2	2.9	2.7	2.8	2.7
7	Connecticut	3.9	3.8	3.7	3.6	3.6	3.7	3.6	3.7	3.4	3.4	3.1	3.0	2.9	2.8
8	New York	4.2	3.9	3.7	3.7	3.8	3.7	3.8	4.2	4.0	4.1	3.3	3.1	3.0	3.0
9	New York City	4.7	4.3	4.5	4.3	4.3	5.5	4.5	4.6	4.3	4.6	3.2	2.9	3.0	2.9
10	Albany	6.[illegible]	4.2	6.2	3.3	4.3	4.9	6.6	3.8	5.4	5.0	3.5	2.4	3.5	2.0
11	New Jersey	4.7	4.4	4.5	4.4	4.4	4.4	4.5	4.7	4.5	4.4	3.6	3.3	3.4	3.4
12	Pennsylvania	4.0	3.5	3.8	3.7	3.7	3.7	5.6	3.7	3.8	3.9	3.1	2.7	2.9	2.8
13	Philadelphia	4.7	4.6	4.6	4.6	4.5	4.4	4.1	4.0	3.7	3.6	3.1	3.0	3.0	3.0
14	Pittsburgh	3.8	3.7	3.8	3.7	3.6	3.6	3.6	3.8	3.8	3.8	2.9	2.7	2.8	2.7
15	Delaware	4.6	4.8	4.8	4.9	4.4	4.3	4.4	4.3	4.7	4.7	3.4	3.6	3.5	3.6
16	Maryland	4.4	4.5	4.2	4.1	4.6	4.3	4.3	4.7	4.0	4.2	3.4	3.4	3.2	3.1
17	Baltimore	3.7	3.8	3.8	3.7	3.7	3.7	3.6	3.7	3.5	3.7	3.0	3.0	3.0	2.9
18	District of Columbia	4.0	4.0	4.0	4.0	4.0	4.0	4.0	4.0	4.0	4.0	3.2	3.2	3.2	3.2
19	Washington	3.4	3.4	3.4	3.4	3.4	3.2	3.7	3.1	3.2	3.2	2.7	2.7	2.7	2.7
20	Virginia	5.7	4.0	4.2	4.0	4.9	3.2	3.7	3.7	3.8	3.8	4.3	3.0	3.0	2.9
21	West Virginia	4.1	3.7	3.9	3.7	3.9	3.7	3.9	3.5	4.1	3.2	3.2	3.0	3.1	2.9
22	North Carolina	3.9	3.3	4.5	3.7	4.3	3.8	3.9	3.0	3.8	3.1	3.2	2.7	3.6	3.0
23	South Carolina	4.3	4.0	4.3	4.3	4.0	7.3	4.3	3.8	8.3	4.5	3.1	2.8	3.0	3.0
24	Georgia	3.5	3.2	3.7	3.6	3.8	3.3	3.7	5.7	3.8	3.7	2.7	2.4	2.7	2.7
25	Florida	2.5	2.5	3.0	2.3	1.5	1.4	4.6	4.9	3.9	3.9	2.2	2.2	2.7	2.0
26	Alabama	3.8	3.6	4.5	4.4	3.9	4.8	4.3	3.8	3.3	3.4	3.2	3.0	3.9	3.8
27	Mississippi	7.4	2.8	5.4	3.1	7.3	3.3	5.0	2.8	4.1	3.6	7.0	2.6	5.1	2.8
28	Louisiana	4.0	4.0	4.0	4.0	4.0	4.0	4.0	3.0	1.6	2.0	3.8	3.8	3.7	3.7
29	New Orleans	6.6	3.6	4.1	3.0	3.7	3.5	5.5	3.5	4.3	3.7	4.8	2.7	3.0	2.8
30	Texas	5.0	5.7	5.5	3.3	5.9	4.4	7.0	4.6	5.7	5.1	3.7	4.3	4.2	2.5
31	Arkansas	5.8	4.4	4.4	3.8	4.0	3.9	5.4	14.6	4.8	3.0	5.0	3.3	3.2	3.0
32	Kentucky	3.6	4.1	3.6	3.8	3.7	3.8	3.8	4.0	3.6	4.0	3.0	3.5	3.0	3.2
33	Louisville	3.5	3.8	3.3	3.5	3.0	3.0	3.8	3.7	3.7	3.7	2.8	3.1	2.7	2.9
34	Tennessee	5.0	4.7	5.3	4.4	5.1	8.1	4.7	3.6	4.1	3.7	4.2	4.0	4.3	3.7
35	Ohio	4.0	4.0	3.8	3.7	3.7	3.7	3.8	4.1	3.9	3.7	3.3	3.3	3.1	3.0
36	Cincinnati	3.3	3.2	3.1	3.3	3.5	2.8	3.2	3.2	3.3	3.4	3.0	2.9	2.7	2.9
37	Cleveland	3.8	4.1	2.3	2.8	3.2	3.1	2.9	2.6	2.6	2.7	3.3	3.6	2.0	2.5
38	Indiana	4.1	3.9	3.7	4.0	4.3	4.4	4.9	4.2	3.9	4.1	3.2	3.1	2.9	3.6
39	Illinois	5.7	5.0	4.9	4.9	5.0	5.2	4.9	4.9	4.8	5.2	4.3	3.8	3.7	3.7
40	Chicago	3.7	4.7	4.9	4.3	4.0	3.8	4.0	3.5	4.1	3.7	2.9	3.6	3.9	3.5
41	Michigan	5.0	4.4	4.8	4.5	4.7	4.2	5.1	4.6	5.6	4.4	4.8	3.6	3.9	3.8
42	Detroit	4.2	4.2	4.6	4.7	4.7	3.7	4.2	3.6	3.8	3.9	3.9	3.9	4.2	4.3
43	Wisconsin	7.0	5.3	4.8	4.1	6.1	4.6	4.9	5.8	4.9	5.8	5.7	4.3	3.8	3.3
44	Milwaukee	4.9	6.5	6.5	4.9	8.0	6.4	4.0	6.5	6.5	20.3	3.2	4.2	4.2	3.2
45	Iowa	4.9	4.4	4.5	5.0	4.6	4.9	5.4	5.0	5.6	4.5	4.0	3.6	3.6	4.1
46	Minnesota	5.2	3.1	3.9	4.1	4.3	4.2	4.3	4.6	4.2	4.1	4.3	2.6	3.3	3.5
47	Missouri	4.2	4.1	3.5	8.7	4.8	3.9	3.7	4.7	4.8	4.2	3.5	3.4	2.9	7.4
48	Saint Louis	3.6	3.0	3.5	2.8	3.8	3.6	3.5	3.7	3.0	18.0	2.9	2.4	2.7	2.2
49	Kansas City	....	....	....	....	....	....	....	4.1	3.9	4.2	....	....	....	....
50	Saint Joseph	....	....	....	....	....	....	....	3.3	3.3	3.3	....	....	....	....
51	Kansas	7.4	8.8	3.9	5.6	5.2	4.9	5.8	5.3	5.8	4.7	6.2	7.7	3.4	4.8
52	Nebraska	5.9	4.9	4.9	5.3	5.8	5.2	5.4	6.4	5.6	5.5	5.0	4.2	4.2	4.5
53	Omaha	....	....	....	....	....	....	....	3.1	3.1	3.4	....	....	....	....
54	Colorado	7.0	10.0	9.6	7.0	7.7	7.2	7.9	8.2	10.2	9.3	4.8	6.5	6.0	4.7
55	Nevada	12.0	10.0	10.0	8.0	10.0	8.0	5.3	4.0	4.0	4.8	9.5	7.5	7.5	6.0
56	California	7.9	3.5	4.5	4.3	8.0	4.9	4.7	5.6	4.1	7.5	6.6	2.7	3.6	3.5
57	San Francisco	4.0	4.0	4.0	4.0	4.0	3.5	2.0	1.9	1.0	1.9	3.5	3.5	3.5	3.5
58	Oregon	10.8	6.0	5.8	5.6	4.6	3.8	5.0	3.3	17.4	4.0	9.6	5.4	5.3	5.1
59	Arizona	7.0	3.3	....	....	....	....	....	....	6.0	6.0	6.8	3.3	....	....
60	Dakota	3.0	4.6	4.9	4.0	4.9	3.1	3.7	4.1	4.0	4.0	2.4	3.8	4.1	3.3
61	Idaho	22.5	....	14.0	....	10.0	....	4.3	....	4.9	7.7	20.4	....	13.0	....
62	Montana	....	4.1	0.8	1.7	2.9	2.2	4.1	1.5	4.2	3.3	....	3.4	0.7	1.4
63	New Mexico	8.9	7.8	6.1	5.5	8.1	4.8	7.1	4.9	3.8	4.3	7.0	6.0	5.1	4.5
64	Utah	5.2	4.7	3.9	5.6	4.1	4.1	4.7	5.3	5.4	5.1	3.5	3.4	2.7	3.8
65	Washington	1.6	3.1	3.9	3.9	4.3	7.1	3.3	4.5	4.2	5.2	1.5	2.9	3.6	3.5
66	Wyoming	22.5	3.0	3.6	3.7	7.5	3.3	6.5	3.2	2.5	1.1	10.4	2.6	2.9	3.2
	Average	4.2	3.9	3.9	3.8	4.0	3.9	4.0	3.9	4.0	4.0	3.2	3.0	3.0	3.0

NOTE.—Figures printed in bold-face type in

CAPITAL AND SURPLUS, OF THE EARNINGS AND DIVIDENDS OF NATIONAL BANKS TO SEPTEMBER 1, 1888.

Ratio of dividends to capital and surplus for six months ending—						Ratio of earnings to capital and surplus for six months ending—										
March 1, 1886.	Sept. 1, 1886.	March 1, 1887.	Sept. 1, 1887.	March 1, 1888.	Sept. 1, 1888.	March 1, 1884.	Sept. 1, 1884.	March 1, 1885.	Sept. 1, 1885.	March 1, 1886.	Sept. 1, 1886.	March 1, 1887.	Sept. 1, 1887.	March 1, 1888.	Sept. 1, 1888.	
P. ct.	P. ct.	P. ct.	P. ct.	P. ct.	P. ct.	P. ct.	P. ct.	P. ct.	P. ct.	P. ct.	P. ct.	P. ct.	P. ct.	P. ct.	P. ct.	
3.5	3.2	2.9	3.1	3.1	3.1	2.4	2.3	2.9	3.3	4.1	3.4	1.8	3.9	4.0	3.6	1
3.0	3.1	3.0	3.0	3.1	3.1	3.9	2.9	3.7	3.0	3.8	3.7	4.0	4.2	3.7	4.0	2
2.9	2.9	2.9	2.9	3.0	2.8	3.3	2.6	2.0	2.3	3.6	3.3	3.7	3.5	4.1	3.7	3
2.6	2.5	2.6	2.6	2.7	2.5	2.9	3.0	2.2	2.5	2.5	3.0	2.0	3.8	2.8	3.0	4
2.1	2.1	2.2	2.1	2.3	2.3	2.5	2.4	1.4	1.7	2.5	3.0	2.8	3.8	3.0	3.3	5
2.6	2.5	2.6	2.7	2.7	2.7	3.3	3.3	2.2	2.5	2.6	3.4	3.4	3.5	3.4	3.4	6
2.8	2.8	2.8	2.9	2.7	2.7	3.3	2.7	2.1	2.4	3.2	3.6	3.3	2.9	2.0	2.9	7
3.0	2.9	3.0	3.3	3.1	3.1	3.5	4.0	2.9	3.2	4.1	3.9	4.4	4.2	4.1	4.1	8
2.8	3.2	2.8	2.8	2.6	2.8	3.6	2.3	2.9	3.0	4.4	4.6	5.9	5.6	4.6	5.2	9
2.5	2.4	3.8	2.2	3.2	2.0	4.1	2.4	4.1	1.0	1.6	2.4	5.4	4.4	2.8	2.6	10
3.3	3.3	3.4	3.4	3.3	3.2	4.7	4.0	3.3	3.2	4.0	4.9	5.1	5.0	5.2	4.9	11
2.8	2.7	3.8	2.8	2.8	2.8	4.5	3.9	3.7	3.1	3.6	3.5	4.6	3.7	4.0	3.8	12
2.9	2.8	2.7	2.7	2.5	2.4	4.4	4.1	2.7	3.4	3.4	3.6	3.9	3.7	3.7	3.2	13
2.6	2.6	2.6	2.7	2.6	2.6	4.3	3.9	3.3	2.6	3.5	3.7	4.2	4.6	5.0	4.1	14
3.3	3.2	3.2	3.1	3.4	3.4	4.9	3.8	5.0	4.4	4.4	3.9	4.5	4.6	4.3	4.6	15
3.5	3.2	3.2	3.5	3.0	3.1	4.4	4.4	3.6	3.5	4.0	3.6	4.1	3.9	3.8	5.5	16
2.9	2.9	2.8	2.8	2.7	2.8	3.9	3.9	3.8	2.7	3.4	3.0	4.0	2.8	3.0	3.7	17
3.2	3.2	3.2	3.2	3.2	3.2	2.8	3.6	3.6	3.6	4.0	3.9	3.8	3.7	3.6	3.4	18
2.6	2.5	2.9	2.4	2.4	2.4	4.4	3.7	1.5	4.3	3.1	4.5	5.1	4.8	4.8	4.8	19
3.7	2.4	2.7	2.7	2.7	2.7	6.3	5.2	3.8	4.7	3.6	3.2	4.1	4.1	4.3	3.6	20
3.1	2.9	3.1	2.8	3.3	2.6	3.9	3.9	3.1	2.5	3.7	3.4	3.2	3.3	2.9	3.6	21
3.4	2.5	3.2	2.5	3.1	2.5	4.2	4.6	3.7	2.9	3.6	2.9	4.2	3.6	4.0	5.1	22
2.8	5.0	3.0	2.6	5.7	3.1	6.6	6.7	3.3	3.9	4.3	3.6	4.1	5.3	7.1	5.5	23
2.9	2.5	2.8	4.3	2.9	2.8	5.5	4.8	3.8	4.3	2.4	5.7	3.5	5.5	4.3	5.5	24
1.4	1.3	4.2	4.4	3.4	8.4	6.2	6.9	4.6	7.3	5.2	4.4	6.1	7.7	6.6	6.6	25
3.3	3.4	3.6	3.2	2.7	2.8	3.9	3.3	4.9	6.0	6.8	4.7	7.0	11.4	4.8	4.1	26
6.6	3.0	4.9	2.4	3.4	2.9	5.8	8.9	5.4	9.2	7.0	8.8	6.1	9.0	6.1	8.6	27
3.6	3.6	3.6	2.8	1.4	1.7	6.3	5.9	4.2	5.4	5.0	3.8	4.3	8.0	7.2	7.0	28
2.6	2.6	4.1	2.6	2.9	2.5	6.5	5.1	2.9	4.2	3.0	2.1	4.4	4.8	3.8	1.4	29
4.5	3.3	5.4	3.6	4.6	4.1	12.3	8.5	8.0	4.3	6.2	6.7	5.7	4.5	5.7	5.3	30
3.9	3.1	4.2	13.0	4.1	3.3	8.4	12.0	5.2	4.2	4.9	6.5	6.4	7.9	7.3	8.4	31
3.0	3.1	3.1	3.2	2.9	3.3	4.4	4.4	4.1	3.9	5.6	4.1	3.7	3.6	3.8	3.8	32
2.9	2.8	3.0	3.0	2.9	2.9	4.4	3.8	2.5	3.1	3.6	4.7	3.0	3.2	3.3	2.5	33
4.2	6.9	3.9	3.0	3.4	3.0	7.8	5.4	5.3	4.9	5.6	5.8	5.7	6.4	6.2	5.1	34
3.1	3.1	3.1	3.3	3.1	3.0	4.5	3.4	3.5	2.9	3.5	3.5	3.7	4.2	3.9	4.2	35
3.1	2.4	2.7	2.7	2.8	2.8	3.7	2.9	3.2	3.4	3.6	3.5	4.1	6.5	2.4	3.6	36
2.8	2.7	2.6	2.3	2.3	2.4	5.0	2.4	2.2	4.0	3.7	3.2	3.9	3.7	3.4	4.4	37
3.4	3.4	3.8	3.2	3.0	3.2	4.2	3.4	3.3	3.7	5.9	3.8	4.3	4.2	4.5	3.6	38
3.8	3.0	3.7	3.7	3.6	3.9	5.1	5.2	5.0	4.4	5.0	4.7	5.3	4.5	5.0	4.4	39
3.7	3.1	3.2	2.8	3.1	2.7	6.1	5.7	1.6	5.2	5.9	5.1	6.4	7.0	6.8	5.6	40
3.9	3.5	4.3	3.8	4.6	3.6	6.3	4.0	4.3	4.1	4.6	5.2	5.5	5.3	5.8	4.9	41
4.2	3.3	3.8	3.2	3.4	3.5	6.7	5.6	5.0	4.9	8.6	4.8	5.0	4.7	4.9	4.7	42
4.8	3.6	3.9	4.5	3.8	5.4	6.5	5.0	4.8	4.7	5.6	5.0	5.7	6.6	6.3	7.3	43
5.2	4.2	2.5	4.0	4.0	12.0	6.0	5.6	1.3	5.4	7.4	6.6	5.2	5.7	3.6	8.6	44
3.7	4.0	4.3	4.0	4.5	3.6	5.9	5.1	4.9	4.7	4.7	4.3	5.1	5.2	4.7	4.9	45
3.7	3.6	3.6	3.9	3.5	3.4	7.9	4.3	4.6	4.0	4.9	4.3	6.8	4.3	5.5	3.9	46
4.0	3.3	3.2	3.8	3.9	3.4	6.6	5.5	5.5	6.4	5.0	4.8	5.8	5.1	4.9	4.3	47
2.9	2.9	2.6	2.7	2.1	15.8	5.0	3.8	3.7	3.6	3.5	4.7	3.6	5.0	2.4	4.5	48
.....	.....	.....	3.6	3.6	3.8	.....	.....	.....	.....	.....	.....	.....	8.4	5.2	5.2	49
.....	.....	.....	2.5	2.4	2.4	.....	.....	.....	.....	.....	.....	.....	3.8	3.9	0.6	50
4.5	4.2	5.0	4.5	5.0	4.0	10.7	9.2	7.5	8.1	7.6	7.7	9.0	6.7	7.1	6.0	51
5.0	4.3	4.5	5.5	4.9	4.6	11.3	7.3	7.5	7.2	6.8	3.1	7.2	7.2	6.7	6.5	52
.....	.....	.....	2.5	2.5	2.7	.....	.....	.....	.....	.....	.....	.....	3.5	3.7	3.0	53
5.3	5.3	5.8	6.0	7.6	6.7	15.4	8.7	8.1	5.1	6.7	6.3	9.1	8.4	19.3	9.8	54
7.5	6.1	4.4	3.2	2.9	3.5	12.4	12.6	8.5	8.6	8.0	9.2	5.8	6.7	10.0	13.0	55
7.1	3.9	3.8	4.6	3.3	6.2	7.7	6.1	7.6	6.5	6.5	6.3	7.0	7.3	9.7	9.4	56
3.4	3.0	1.8	1.8	1.8	1.7	4.6	3.5	2.1	3.3	3.5	3.1	2.7	3.2	4.9	5.0	57
4.2	3.5	4.7	3.0	15.3	3.5	10.5	10.6	9.8	11.7	11.5	7.1	9.5	11.8	10.4	11.5	58
.....	.....	.....	.....	5.7	5.5	9.0	1.8	1.4	.....	.....	.....	.....	.....	13.1	9.5	59
4.0	2.6	3.2	3.5	3.3	3.3	7.6	3.2	4.0	4.2	5.1	4.8	6.1	3.2	6.1	5.0	60
9.2	.....	40.0	.....	4.2	6.2	22.7	10.4	10.9	6.0	7.0	5.8	6.1	3.4	7.8	5.9	61
2.5	1.9	3.4	1.2	3.4	2.6	9.8	9.2	7.7	5.2	6.4	4.8	9.4	8.0	8.2	7.6	62
6.5	3.9	5.9	4.1	3.2	3.6	7.7	7.2	2.6	5.7	7.2	5.5	5.0	3.7	3.4	5.0	63
3.1	3.0	3.4	3.7	3.7	3.4	9.1	6.5	7.0	3.5	5.7	8.8	6.1	5.1	5.3	7.9	64
3.8	6.2	2.0	3.7	3.5	4.3	11.1	8.4	8.5	10.1	6.1	7.1	7.2	8.2	12.9	10.6	65
6.3	2.8	5.4	2.6	1.7	0.9	11.4	7.9	7.5	8.6	7.6	6.2	5.7	6.0	2.0	3.6	66
3.1	3.0	3.1	3.0	3.0	3.0	4.3	3.7	3.2	3.3	4.0	4.0	4.5	4.5	4.3	4.3	

column for 1884 and 1886 signify percentage of loss.

CLASSIFICATION OF THE LOANS AND DISCOUNTS OF THE NATIONAL BANKS IN THE RESERVE CITIES AND IN THE STATES AND TERRITORIES ON OCTOBER 4, 1888.

Cities, States and Territories.	No. of banks.	On single-name paper.	On United States bonds.	On other bonds and stocks.	All other loans.	Total.
New York City	46	$28,626,204.76	$2,132,159.50	$108,466,001.44	$153,271,025.45	$292,495,481.15
Chicago	19	14,155,000.90	359,296.04	9,631,824.99	41,129,615.37	65,275,737.30
Saint Louis	4	306,450.00	....	921,853.59	6,988,242.38	8,216,545.97
Boston	55	22,811,643.69	30,565.00	23,414,349.39	89,992,897.83	136,249,455.91
Albany	6	502,300.22	19,855.00	3,179,484.99	5,205,628.26	8,907,268.47
Philadelphia	43	16,976,123.58	85,200.00	14,672,898.00	59,932,015.23	91,666,236.81
Pittsburgh	24	1,140,053.01	13,150.00	3,004,431.57	27,436,695.37	31,594,329.95
Baltimore	17	6,218,236.00	600.00	3,509,914.14	18,408,001.98	28,136,752.72
Washington	7	70,019.22	10,164.50	1,140,480.03	3,027,970.20	4,248,633.95
New Orleans	8	642,972.61	....	2,440,566.33	7,897,910.84	10,981,449.78
Louisville	9	251,550.68	....	715,833.67	8,101,754.14	9,069,138.49
Cincinnati	13	4,307,374.00	75,000.00	2,095,721.98	14,866,482.14	21,344,578.12
Cleveland	9	1,185,580.00	....	2,237,067.38	13,427,135.24	16,849,782.62
Detroit	8	1,157,357.48	....	1,669,787.36	10,889,421.92	13,716,569.76
Milwaukee	3	610,352.88	....	568,361.56	3,005,364.91	4,184,079.35
Kansas City	10	3,134,821.92	1,200.00	422,438.44	11,104,785.08	14,663,245.44
Saint Joseph	2	420,630.45	....	7,205.00	1,321,908.35	1,749,743.80
Omaha	7	1,939,915.09	....	259,079.55	7,279,212.94	9,478,207.58
San Francisco	3	3,006,598.36	....	516,873.40	1,597,420.07	5,120,891.83
Total of cities	293	107,463,275.45	2,727,190.04	178,874,172.81	484,883,490.70	773,948,129.00
Maine	75	1,440,681.26	75,721.46	945,563.64	17,689,779.48	20,151,745.84
New Hampshire	49	898,170.73	77,678.00	1,215,939.86	7,900,392.48	10,092,181.07
Vermont	40	998,301.51	19,676.20	432,854.36	11,201,583.58	12,652,415.65
Massachusetts	198	17,312,848.64	45,077.00	6,212,429.50	70,991,934.09	94,562,289.23
Rhode Island	60	8,563,059.58	100.00	892,653.26	26,074,980.54	35,530,793.38
Connecticut	84	7,825,406.09	1,325.00	3,327,256.67	32,486,293.44	43,640,281.20
New York	270	9,231,218.87	69,515.22	6,773,267.69	84,815,618.91	100,889,620.69
New Jersey	85	3,472,736.30	150,075.00	6,271,995.50	32,120,593.98	42,016,000.78
Pennsylvania	246	6,537,501.37	2,004.86	1,460,057.07	75,103,182.00	83,102,745.30
Delaware	18	183,668.81	....	188,847.15	5,038,457.75	5,410,973.71
Maryland	31	332,760.44	200.00	304,787.33	7,024,579.01	7,662,327.08
District of Columbia	1	....	....	63,972.30	272,687.87	336,660.17
Virginia	26	596,172.82	....	587,155.38	9,871,334.27	11,054,662.47
West Virginia	20	150,368.18	50.00	300.00	3,979,109.19	4,129,827.37
North Carolina	18	372,426.11	....	99,039.44	4,711,060.58	5,182,526.13
South Carolina	16	202,502.21	....	249,340.16	5,400,623.76	5,852,466.13
Georgia	24	803,071.92	50.00	1,171,949.58	6,509,453.82	8,484,525.32
Florida	13	382,005.53	....	61,817.62	1,483,783.04	1,927,606.19
Alabama	21	1,188,911.49	....	637,114.91	5,558,025.23	7,384,051.63
Mississippi	12	251,586.26	....	279,902.06	2,019,389.70	2,550,878.62
Louisiana	5	294,746.16	42,695.22	....	922,113.99	1,259,555.37
Texas	100	5,411,362.77	....	239,838.22	17,313,377.02	22,964,578.01
Arkansas	7	202,756.61	2,500.00	233,742.18	2,311,421.35	2,750,420.14
Kentucky	60	1,390,578.64	615.25	462,159.31	16,461,788.94	18,315,142.14
Tennessee	42	4,050,409.25	....	2,105,754.71	13,354,679.39	19,510,843.35
Ohio	107	5,181,048.12	1,500.00	1,729,531.75	46,616,136.94	53,528,216.81
Indiana	94	3,160,437.94	17,450.81	614,303.07	23,916,821.68	27,709,014.10
Illinois	163	7,336,227.70	45,718.29	1,030,224.78	30,293,607.22	38,705,777.99
Michigan	101	5,135,897.50	932.23	334,621.23	23,189,401.32	28,660,852.28
Wisconsin	56	1,977,204.71	....	345,727.00	12,538,722.83	14,861,654.54
Iowa	129	5,888,271.35	....	449,444.99	19,643,334.86	25,981,051.20
Minnesota	56	13,563,805.17	....	1,574,303.51	21,486,973.74	36,625,142.42
Missouri	34	571,141.42	....	78,395.00	4,477,728.50	5,127,265.82
Kansas	160	3,025,637.83	....	112,556.14	19,612,696.01	22,750,889.98
Nebraska	97	2,282,960.94	....	102,483.61	12,463,936.32	14,849,380.87
Colorado	34	4,098,137.64	....	334,809.57	9,518,389.17	13,951,336.38
Nevada	2	257,440.92	....	31,705.37	306,055.51	595,201.80
California	35	2,615,447.59	4,000.00	1,140,313.80	10,599,242.96	14,359,004.35
Oregon	27	2,322,332.43	....	87,502.62	4,116,638.64	6,526,473.69
Arizona	1	42,045.80	....	....	102,875.22	144,921.02
Dakota	58	1,117,573.19	20,000.00	68,585.34	6,108,602.89	7,314,761.42
Idaho	7	224,331.74	....	2,389.14	415,329.50	642,050.38
Montana	17	2,369,454.81	....	83,528.74	6,145,337.68	8,598,321.23
New Mexico	9	499,546.90	....	61,358.51	1,185,386.17	1,746,291.58
Utah	7	700,710.12	....	78,653.47	1,628,148.97	2,407,512.56
Washington	24	949,041.01	....	93,262.23	5,001,494.53	6,043,797.77
Wyoming	9	558,632.99	....	11,631.42	1,823,756.72	2,394,021.13
Total of country bank	2,847	135,967,639.37	577,484.54	42,586,171.59	721,806,600.79	900,938,156.29
United States	3,140	243,430,914.82	3,304,674.58	221,460,344.40	1,206,690,351.49	1,674,886,285.29

CLEARINGS AND BALANCES OF THE BANKS OF NEW YORK CITY FOR THE WEEKS ENDING AT THE DATES GIVEN.

Week ending—	Clearings.	Balances.
Sept. 1, 1883	$645, 021, 540. 80	$20, 472, 980. 85
Sept. 8, 1883	739, 732, 997. 18	31, 195, 746. 65
Sept. 15, 1883	732, 316, 071. 00	30, 914, 820. 30
Sept. 22, 1883	700, 082, 400. 54	30, 061, 000. 19
Sept. 29, 1883	763, 567, 336. 28	30, 260, 285. 71
Oct. 6, 1883	759, 872, 865. 58	32, 844, 144. 42
Oct. 13, 1883	833, 065, 048. 88	31, 363, 439. 92
Oct. 20, 1883	919, 608, 026. 44	31, 917, 847. 61
Oct. 27, 1883	906, 319, 847. 51	31, 844, 418. 48
Nov. 3, 1883	817, 906, 284. 43	29, 708, 441. 71
Nov. 10, 1883	622, 487, 073. 40	28, 478, 167. 32
Nov. 17, 1883	783, 094, 022. 25	33, 519, 480. 15
Nov. 24, 1883	682, 451, 400. 44	28, 333, 263. 61
Sept. 6, 1884	463, 912, 628. 57	21, 278, 021. 75
Sept. 13, 1884	422, 613, 010. 74	22, 793, 219. 00
Sept. 20, 1884	492, 060, 873. 06	21, 412, 397. 53
Sept. 27, 1884	491, 357, 661. 20	22, 028, 008. 11
Oct. 4, 1884	554, 602, 698. 69	32, 658, 517. 10
Oct. 11, 1884	496, 582, 476. 56	26, 358, 572. 40
Oct. 18, 1884	518, 575, 214. 89	28, 696, 794. 93
Oct. 25, 1884	605, 195, 031. 55	27, 673, 214. 95
Nov. 1, 1884	458, 532, 508. 11	24, 225, 199. 59
Nov. 8, 1884	477, 210, 095. 35	28, 209, 501. 50
Nov. 15, 1884	527, 541, 755. 74	26, 823, 201. 26
Nov. 22, 1884	555, 711, 500. 01	26, 496, 003. 13
Nov. 29, 1884	450, 204, 007. 66	21, 292, 407. 63
Sept. 5, 1885	476, 800, 526. 79	22, 090, 787. 52
Sept. 12, 1885	484, 537, 657. 96	23, 909, 267. 46
Sept. 19, 1885	480, 733, 380. 21	24, 410, 868. 93
Sept. 26, 1885	471, 652, 048. 41	22, 078, 080. 63
Oct. 3, 1885	572, 076, 277. 07	30, 153, 232. 32
Oct. 10, 1885	650, 500, 540. 70	28, 402, 678. 38
Oct. 17, 1885	702, 090, 829. 74	29, 632, 037. 42
Oct. 24, 1885	828, 373, 048. 53	30, 475, 583. 77
Oct. 31, 1885	695, 214, 389. 87	29, 590, 574. 77
Nov. 7, 1885	775, 416, 016. 08	30, 751, 563. 50
Nov. 14, 1885	770, 244, 286. 61	27, 323, 721. 40
Sept. 4, 1886	485, 535, 545. 80	28, 387, 207. 77
Sept. 11, 1886	520, 437, 476. 86	21, 805, 163. 40
Sept. 18, 1886	500, 366, 097. 81	28, 050, 351. 78
Sept. 25, 1886	601, 723, 056. 06	25, 003, 758. 94
Oct. 2, 1886	744, 533, 107. 80	31, 285, 172. 88
Oct. 9, 1886	830, 726, 858. 70	29, 904, 285. 79
Oct. 16, 1886	774, 127, 054. 20	30, 052, 375. 09
Oct. 23, 1886	734, 566, 056. 19	27, 767, 549. 66
Oct. 30, 1886	625, 098, 001. 48	26, 007, 923. 82
Nov. 6, 1886	735, 600, 027. 03	31, 825, 400. 11
Nov. 13, 1886	704, 572, 284. 86	28, 665, 256. 87
Sept. 3, 1887	629, 026, 782. 87	29, 322, 367. 47
Sept. 10, 1887	562, 627, 925. 28	22, 320, 268. 73
Sept. 17, 1887	628, 634, 786. 18	31, 404, 534. 44
Sept. 24, 1887	659, 048, 314. 43	30, 974, 062. 00
Oct. 1, 1887	575, 717, 723. 42	31, 060, 309. 36
Oct. 8, 1887	676, 201, 491. 67	29, 825, 323. 74
Oct. 15, 1887	718, 896, 811. 23	31, 170, 113. 34
Oct. 22, 1887	742, 551, 452. 60	33, 330, 889. 58
Oct. 29, 1887	647, 590, 728. 82	29, 899, 361. 75
Nov. 5, 1887	706, 280, 830. 34	31, 289, 781. 13
Nov. 12, 1887	602, 240, 331. 60	23, 758, 351. 90
Sept. 1, 1888	501, 823, 033. 31	26, 231, 528. 08
Sept. 8, 1888	538, 170, 073. 22	34, 047, 518. 67
Sept. 15, 1888	643, 165, 583. 40	34, 285, 911. 38
Sept. 22, 1888	702, 313, 474. 79	33, 177, 504. 55
Sept. 29, 1888	635, 316, 704. 00	34, 537, 541. 08
Oct. 6, 1888	811, 518, 630. 80	38, 746, 427. 25
Oct. 13, 1888	722, 328, 037. 35	44, 039, 194. 77
Oct. 20, 1888	667, 165, 762. 02	38, 103, 870. 93
Oct. 27, 1888	683, 152, 608. 85	35, 700, 246. 00
Nov. 3, 1888	671, 136, 250. 14	34, 802, 960. 62
Nov. 10, 1888	*530, 072, 637. 58	*26, 376, 380. 51

* Five days.

ABSTRACT OF REPORTS OF CONDITION

OF

State Banks, Loan and Trust Companies, Savings and Private Banks,

1887-'88,

ARRANGED BY STATES AND TERRITORIES.

NOTE.—Under the heading "official" are placed reports from State officers, and under the heading "unofficial" reports from other sources.

ABSTRACT OF REPORTS OF CONDITION OF STATE BANKS AND LOAN AND

	Location.	Date of report.	No. of banks	RESOURCES. Loans on real estate.	Loans on personal and collateral security.	Loans and discounts.
	STATE BANKS—OFFICIAL.					
1	New Hampshire	Mar. 31, 1888	1	$50, 425	$41, 772	....
2	Rhode Island	Nov. 15, 1887	10	....	....	$2, 506, 813
3	Connecticut	July 1, 1888	8	....	....	4, 665, 078
4	New York	June 16, 1888	122	....	....	126, 414, 734
5	New Jersey	Dec. 31, 1887	8	....	....	3, 441, 820
6	Pennsylvania	Nov. —, 1887	77	3, 023, 100	22, 700, 204	....
7	Virginia	June 30, 1888	64	....	....	11, 002, 256
8	North Carolina	....do	10	768, 063	....	1, 993, 385
9	Louisiana	....do	6	....	....	3, 823, 470
10	Kentucky	....do	83	8, 811	182, 117	27, 409, 171
11	Ohio	Apr. 2, 1888	25	....	....	4, 254, 080
12	Indiana	Oct. 31, 1887	32	....	....	3, 741, 645
13	Michigan	July 2, 1888	31	....	....	7, 220, 790
14	Wisconsin	....do	64	....	....	18, 720, 018
15	Iowa	June 30, 1888	74	....	....	8, 850, 405
16	Minnesota	....do	61	....	....	16, 008, 397
17	Missouri	Apr. 30, 1888	238	3, 400, 367	46, 975, 323	....
18	Kansas	Dec. 1, '87, and June 30, '88	177	11, 075	207, 071	11, 439, 960
19	California	July 1, 1888	110	13, 459, 956	55, 572, 004	....
20	Montana	June 30, 1888	2	73, 835	113, 377	91, 481
	Total	....	1, 209	21, 404, 602	125, 881, 958	253, 163, 012
	STATE BANKS—UNOFFICIAL.					
1	Delaware	June 30, 1888	2	68, 250	309, 151	219, 097
2	Maryland	....do	9	62, 718	971, 931	3, 662, 841
3	West Virginia	....do	10	306, 936	1, 262, 260	58, 433
4	South Carolina	....do	8	147, 800	463, 200	310, 416
5	Georgia	....do	19	333, 012	3, 298, 454	5, 503, 488
6	Alabama	....do	7	1, 620	935, 356	333, 034
7	Mississippi	....do	14	15, 503	461, 093	1, 885, 383
8	Arkansas	....do	5	17, 000	508, 002	248
9	Tennessee	....do	38	86, 326	1, 523, 055	3, 378, 350
10	Nebraska	....do	69	956, 090	2, 065, 820	480, 541
11	Dakota	....do	23	91, 349	752, 696	110, 363
	Total	....	194	2, 087, 884	13, 512, 317	15, 952, 800
	Total, official and unofficial	....	1, 403	23, 492, 576	139, 394, 275	269, 115, 812
	LOAN AND TRUST COMPANIES—OFFICIAL.					
1	Maine	Nov. 1, 1887	5	208, 847	155, 557	418, 252
2	New Hampshire	Mar. 31, 1888	3	1, 586, 404	143, 242	....
3	Massachusetts	Oct. 31, 1887	11	9, 205, 141	9, 518, 512	18, 100, 955
4	Rhode Island	Nov. 15, 1887	2	1, 101, 295	4, 758, 203	....
5	Connecticut	July 1, 1888	8	....	....	2, 565, 057
6	New York	Jan. 1, 1888	21	8, 612, 790	118, 450, 617	6, 535, 456
7	Minnesota	June 30, 1888	6	1, 005, 122	52, 819	1, 014, 920
	Total	....	56	21, 719, 668	133, 078, 950	28, 634, 640
	LOAN AND TRUST COMPANIES—UNOFFICIAL.					
1	Pennsylvania	June 30, 1888	16	4, 319, 781	32, 527, 847	126, 144
2	Illinois	....do	6	1, 185, 015	8, 037, 790	2, 208
3	Iowa	....do	6	5, 097, 116	213, 129	131, 743
4	Missouri	....do	6	4, 000, 743	131, 420	12, 253
5	Kansas	....do	17	5, 082, 201	574, 791	30, 966
6	Nebraska	....do	6	3, 396, 476	255, 429	87, 507
7	Dakota	....do	7	605, 300	214, 537	34, 745
	Total	....	64	24, 886, 722	41, 954, 943	425, 716
	Total, official and unofficial	....	120	46, 606, 390	175, 033, 893	29, 060, 356

TRUST COMPANIES, FROM OFFICIAL AND UNOFFICIAL SOURCES, IN 1887–'88.

RESOURCES—continued.									
Overdrafts.	U. S. bonds.	State, county, municipal, etc., bonds.	R. R. bonds and stocks.	Bank stocks.	All other bonds and stocks.	Due from other banks and bankers.	Real estate, furniture, and fixtures.	Current expenses and taxes paid.	
....	....	$5,000	$2,500	$2,400	....	....	$3,454	....	1
....	$3,600	....	....	79,104	$152,248	$165,253	230,600	$4,570	2
$10,862	....	....	....	....	711,048	1,264,025	211,627	3,922	3
75,027	....	....	....	....	6,045,035	12,967,652	3,155,904	710,256	4
271	78,700	....	....	....	344,825	438,128	118,101	17,220	5
....	127,688	....	....	....	5,415,699	4,031,118	1,784,818	162,014	6
134,450	20,000	....	....	....	1,322,010	1,248,937	485,454	89,110	7
46,520	....	31,000	....	....	74,938	392,533	165,573	27,391	8
23	....	....	....	....	667,751	5,465	415,101	4,664	9
62,634	30,150	47,100	27,000	2,000	1,162,863	3,275,547	997,897	17,865	10
36,952	150,950	....	....	....	117,524	575,667	281,257	36,321	11
81,659	....	....	....	....	113,445	769,126	225,213	38,906	12
42,724	25,000	61,701	....	....	80,411	1,000,207	206,219	16,969	13
158,919	....	....	....	....	2,005,679	4,435,331	637,811	27,828	14
277,833	....	....	....	....	....	1,962,986	646,822	....	15
108,481	30,008	....	....	....	931,814	2,607,441	1,030,932	156,763	16
666,082	1,557,048	....	....	....	4,730,193	8,672,163	2,595,679	....	17
97,661	12,500	....	....	2,500	184,420	1,794,924	995,156	140,215	18
....	....	....	....	....	4,045,554	8,460,961	3,911,114	....	19
8,042	....	....	....	....	7,903	115,414	15,068	....	20
1,808,140	2,030,634	144,801	29,500	86,004	28,122,372	54,272,878	18,113,980	1,454,014	
....	....	....	43,275	2,506	146,226	115,516	85,113	6,844	1
....	35,000	222,162	438,720	51,500	166,212	380,765	612,693	32,543	2
2,000	....	....	....	....	93,500	260,326	71,706	4,708	3
466	....	14,751	22,000	....	12,030	82,500	22,416	13,433	4
47,463	....	11,750	3,410,048	....	717,811	986,407	302,693	69,664	5
10,795	....	....	....	18,700	225,663	191,494	110,206	8,996	6
11,731	32,000	77,056	15,647	....	88,970	620,830	188,256	33,003	7
24,336	....	23,187	....	....	697	181,555	28,780	699	8
26,361	....	20,984	8,600	50,628	282,187	740,704	170,463	48,727	9
48,976	....	2,430	....	....	208,205	764,512	399,082	76,804	10
21,513	....	....	....	9,625	19,101	206,600	80,276	18,543	11
193,641	67,000	372,320	3,938,380	133,049	1,960,611	4,505,328	2,132,674	314,144	
2,001,781	2,097,634	517,121	3,967,880	219,053	30,082,983	58,778,206	20,246,654	1,768,158	
....	3,520	33,128	132,006	100,244	33,474	14,721	16,287	7,784	1
....	....	....	....	....	11,922	146,526	....	236	2
....	2,183,432	1,146,201	6,957,012	204,167	1,330,777	915,386	875,888	104,728	3
....	732,137	802,000	1,388,950	73,000	....	166,000	94	1,200	4
4,603	1,101	....	....	....	885,127	677,476	294,173	2,463	5
....	10,516,850	....	....	....	19,161,588	11,632,715	5,946,340	....	6
138	6,262	....	35,460	60,577	18,465	203,315	514,340	22,646	7
4,741	22,443,398	1,981,329	8,513,428	437,988	21,441,353	13,756,139	7,647,122	139,117	
1,957	354,568	13,000	7,029,812	123,063	7,361,396	3,791,316	4,158,798	138,833	1
....	26,800	12,150	112,200	60,000	132,168	1,172,380	142,532	14,910	2
1,309	....	....	....	....	66,194	53,147	251,343	242	3
6,369	75,000	....	43,790	33,217	208,536	467,402	305,928	141,023	4
1,874	....	....	....	....	1,907,548	823,678	1,246,874	75,908	5
8,061	....	....	3,200	2,000	48,030	188,202	47,463	50,571	6
....	....	....	....	4,200	54,545	39,400	151,731	34,074	7
19,570	456,368	25,150	7,189,002	222,480	9,868,417	6,035,783	6,304,669	466,056	
24,311	22,899,766	2,006,479	15,702,430	660,468	31,309,770	19,791,922	13,951,791	605,173	

ABSTRACT OF REPORTS OF CONDITION OF STATE BANKS AND LOAN AND TRUST

	Location.	RESOURCES—continued.			LIABILITIES.	
		Cash and cash items.	Other resources.	Total.	Capital stock.	Surplus.
	STATE BANKS—OFFICIAL—continued.					
1	New Hampshire	$7, 481	....	$113, 032	$50, 000	$14, 549
2	Rhode Island	123, 615	$50, 801	3, 325, 604	1, 706, 685	....
3	Connecticut	468, 470	2	7, 335, 634	2, 390, 000	220, 000
4	New York	50, 073, 233	203, 387	199, 735, 318	24, 920, 700	8, 604, 102
5	New Jersey	286, 040	5, 849	4, 726, 044	1, 085, 000	207, 520
6	Pennsylvania	2, 846, 103	1, 225, 014	42, 006, 408	7, 852, 589	1, 988, 490
7	Virginia	899, 123	38, 475	16, 139, 815	3, 468, 739	781, 018
8	North Carolina	207, 117	54, 832	3, 851, 352	1, 095, 170	211, 890
9	Louisiana	3, 627, 371	72, 612	8, 616, 490	2, 117, 259	250, 000
10	Kentucky	4, 571, 784	187, 982	37, 982, 921	12, 507, 937	1, 900, 935
11	Ohio	534, 832	1, 758	5, 090, 241	1, 504, 100	228, 612
12	Indiana	557, 538	....	5, 527, 583	1, 742, 500	250, 136
13	Michigan	765, 141	3, 188	9, 521, 359	2, 071, 200	353, 349
14	Wisconsin	3, 054, 837	....	20, 040, 423	3, 821, 100	1, 301, 602
15	Iowa	830, 279	9, 802	12, 587, 127	4, 028, 743	561, 139
16	Minnesota	1, 925, 448	52	23, 450, 420	5, 733, 000	724, 775
17	Missouri	11, 053, 118	2, 910, 012	82, 586, 985	13, 430, 003	7, 467, 209
18	Kansas	3, 190, 778	182, 773	18, 250, 042	6, 569, 699	342, 328
19	California	15, 877, 705	5, 186, 226	106, 513, 610	30, 893, 903	12, 341, 586
20	Montana	64, 125	....	489, 245	150, 000	....
	Total	101, 054, 228	10, 241, 395	617, 807, 608	130, 288, 327	37, 928, 240
	STATE BANKS—UNOFFICIAL—cont'd.					
1	Delaware	16, 281	3	1, 012, 862	420, 000	48, 274
2	Maryland	553, 669	9, 156	7, 209, 000	2, 484, 480	372, 000
3	West Virginia	174, 138	750	2, 240, 867	453, 744	184, 223
4	South Carolina	71, 114	7	1, 110, 211	420, 000	54, 422
5	Georgia	1, 259, 656	4, 427, 823	20, 429, 169	7, 664, 477	2, 070, 200
6	Alabama	214, 808	3, 436	2, 054, 108	705, 625	64, 337
7	Mississippi	498, 431	13, 300	3, 042, 210	1, 070, 000	224, 373
8	Arkansas	146, 573	24	991, 101	268, 000	23, 500
9	Tennessee	840, 610	6, 323	7, 203, 014	2, 336, 000	246, 367
10	Nebraska	377, 519	1, 320	6, 282, 307	2, 201, 100	122, 684
11	Dakota	107, 830	6, 685	1, 424, 671	500, 425	35, 818
	Total	4, 260, 719	4, 468, 842	53, 899, 709	18, 643, 541	3, 446, 228
	Total, official and unofficial	105, 314, 947	14, 710, 237	671, 707, 317	154, 931, 868	41, 374, 468
	LOAN AND TRUST COMPANIES—OFFICIAL—continued.					
1	Maine	109, 206	67, 578	1, 300, 670	435, 000	5, 000
2	New Hampshire	36, 848	1, 420	1, 026, 658	400, 000	20, 000
3	Massachusetts	3, 785, 900	93, 246	54, 421, 345	5, 050, 000	1, 318, 016
4	Rhode Island	536, 909	280, 193	9, 840, 040	1, 500, 000	....
5	Connecticut	157, 636	....	4, 587, 726	1, 036, 000	155, 060
6	New York	6, 403, 530	3, 827, 335	200, 087, 230	16, 596, 100	13, 879, 978
7	Minnesota	32, 662	134, 852	3, 101, 587	1, 895, 500	76, 552
	Total	11, 062, 751	4, 404, 623	275, 265, 256	26, 913, 200	15, 454, 606
	LOANS AND TRUST COMPANIES—UNOFFICIAL—continued.					
1	Pennsylvania	6, 587, 002	688, 570	67, 222, 987	14, 106, 610	6, 350, 272
2	Illinois	1, 823, 532	6, 260	12, 728, 014	2, 470, 000	1, 005, 644
3	Iowa	141, 944	137, 143	6, 693, 304	1, 416, 000	107, 317
4	Missouri	9, 878	268, 757	5, 705, 012	2, 176, 700	344, 242
5	Kansas	38, 086	190, 594	10, 162, 605	3, 838, 600	576, 924
6	Nebraska	6, 354	175, 789	4, 278, 262	1, 390	176, 885
7	Dakota	117, 851	340, 685	1, 508, 037	924, 400	89, 481
	Total	8, 725, 547	1, 807, 798	108, 388, 231	26, 330, 310	8, 650, 765
	Total, official and unofficial	19, 788, 298	6, 212, 421	383, 653, 477	53, 243, 510	24, 105, 371

COMPANIES, FROM OFFICIAL AND UNOFFICIAL SOURCES, ETC.—Continued.

LIABILITIES—continued.								
Other undivided profits.	State-bank notes.	Dividends unpaid.	Individual deposits.	State, county, and municipal deposits.	Deposits of State, county, and municipal disbursing officers.	Due to other banks.	Other liabilities.	
....	$1,101	$1,145	$40,257	....	....	$3,986	....	1
$173,853	3,142	9,084	1,207,567	....	....	104,371	$2	2
218,533	9,550	44,885	3,085,003	....	....	407,057	....	3
7,660,521	8,005	....	140,043,155	....	$261,086	15,624,111	2,503,578	4
131,134	....	5,600	3,128,523	....	....	135,169	30,000	5
604,287	71,068	....	30,412,607	$721	....	402,397	284,251	6
380,071	....	83,188	10,653,301	....	....	250,034	510,564	7
128,158	....	4,028	1,181,422	....	....	215,060	1,014,704	8
317,308	8,582	49,113	5,810,800	....	....	54,830	2	9
1,307,006	19,732	389,577	19,919,044	....	....	1,011,780	686,910	10
90,467	....	1,052	3,837,018	....	....	172,708	156,224	11
....	....	148,140	3,804,201	....	....	29,443	44,112	12
105,664	....	19,780	6,530,253	....	....	54,995	287,118	13
....	....	....	22,429,400	....	....	....	1,488,231	14
309,323	....	....	7,107,008	....	....	400,014	....	15
619,405	....	43,305	14,702,727	....	....	1,012,487	423,037	16
180,507	....	....	54,038,807	....	....	7,100,964	320,405	17
642,801	....	16,451	9,887,858	....	....	107,338	632,507	18
....	....	....	48,300,118	....	....	5,525,515	443,488	19
8,570	....	....	330,675	....	....	....	....	20
13,647,688	121,244	810,347	387,017,523	721	261,086	32,891,630	8,834,793	
23,145	....	....	455,175	....	....	9,084	56,584	1
104,279	65	43,380	3,861,217	....	....	210,600	66,070	2
57,677	....	10,720	1,471,307	....	11,804	27,831	23,561	3
56,278	....	4,000	436,720	2,096	1,213	12,857	122,623	4
610,318	....	141,170	5,328,861	20,229	32,408	954,097	3,607,469	5
152,302	....	3,171	716,383	2,258	....	18,412	391,700	6
143,837	....	....	2,245,511	3,283	....	67,823	178,392	7
23,311	....	1,500	618,174	15,000	13,500	604	7,602	8
392,213	....	10,785	4,033,526	51,671	3,641	127,245	60,870	9
247,825	27,125	13,186	3,314,207	19,238	10,510	188,658	137,714	10
51,087	....	1,200	549,228	756	1,542	23,483	170,502	11
1,862,033	27,190	229,112	23,030,310	114,531	74,618	1,647,303	4,823,935	
15,510,620	148,434	1,045,459	410,047,843	115,252	335,704	34,538,942	13,658,728	
39,223	....	1,077	725,300	....	....	....	95,070	1
21,173	1,080,800	....	207,520	....	....	....	107,105	2
1,397,370	....	2,514	41,230,824	....	....	70,240	5,352,372	3
150,804	....	....	8,180,236	....	....	....	....	4
144,547	....	18,873	2,985,732	....	....	246,914	....	5
6,002,233	3,985,908	....	154,601,138	....	....	....	4,961,873	6
133,017	....	....	718,876	26,309	....	....	251,333	7
7,957,370	a5,066,708	22,464	208,739,626	26,309	....	317,154	10,767,813	
2,700,402	298,000	33,809	38,589,403	....	....	6,055	5,137,470	1
224,410	85,579	61,057	7,364,824	....	....	1,504,158	2,442	2
96,600	4,610,000	53,888	343,190	....	....	20,100	76,300	3
483,104	1,677,800	14,135	868,083	....	....	52,700	68,188	4
221,658	2,250,500	6	1,049,194	....	....	60,023	1,553,106	5
133,936	....	12,000	258,210	....	....	85,276	2,221,946	6
55,775	422,050	....	45,575	....	....	....	60,750	7
3,888,040	a9,353,829	175,855	49,138,468	....	....	1,729,811	9,120,223	
11,846,316	a14,420,537	198,319	257,878,114	26,309	....	2,046,965	19,888,036	

a Debenture bonds.

ABSTRACT OF REPORTS OF CONDITION OF STATE BANKS, 1872-'73 TO 1887-'88.

	1872-'73.*	1873-'74.	1874-'75.	1875-'76.	1876-'77.	1877-'78.	1878-'79.	1879-'80.
	— banks.	— banks.	551 banks.	633 banks.	592 banks.	475 banks.	616 banks.	620 banks.
Resources:								
Loans and discounts	$119,332,341	$154,377,672	$176,308,949	$178,963,496	$266,585,314	$169,391,427	$191,444,093	$206,821,194
Overdrafts	237,104	212,772	377,297	348,604	516,565	319,959	447,302	528,543
United States bonds	1,544,296	1,961,447	344,984	809,144	929,260	2,150,680	7,739,203	7,142,532
Other stocks, bonds, and mortgages	9,617,667	16,437,815	23,667,950	19,364,450	23,209,670	19,398,287	21,916,024	17,117,117
Due from banks	12,605,100	19,030,046	19,851,146	23,096,812	25,201,782	25,107,149	22,169,065	36,180,435
Real estate, furniture, and fixtures	3,269,233	5,372,185	9,905,657	8,561,224	12,609,100	11,092,118	14,264,835	14,227,927
Other resources	944,079	1,164,999	4,909,190	6,863,083	6,442,710	10,694,390	9,221,760	5,801,796
Expenses	886,348	1,284,344	1,353,066	1,559,404	1,211,416	914,726	801,005	878,696
Cash items	18,977,324	10,434,018	8,624,086	9,059,547	9,816,456	7,320,845	8,767,391	11,176,374
Specie	3,020,139	1,980,083	1,156,456	1,926,100	2,219,659	3,041,676	1,979,701	6,201,617
Legal-tender and other notes	8,447,776	25,126,706	26,740,215	27,623,988	34,415,712	28,480,374	37,088,961	48,828,255
Total	178,881,407	237,402,088	272,338,996	278,255,852	383,257,704	277,911,831	315,839,340	354,904,486
Liabilities:								
Capital stock	42,705,834	59,305,532	69,084,960	80,425,634	110,949,515	95,193,292	104,124,871	90,816,575
Circulation	174,714	153,432	177,653	388,397	387,661	368,298	389,542	283,308
Surplus	2,109,732	2,942,707	6,797,167	7,027,817	5,665,854	7,983,996	16,667,574	18,816,496
Undivided profits	10,027,668	12,363,205	9,002,133	10,457,346	18,283,567	11,693,064	5,666,221	6,721,615
Dividends unpaid	33,492	337,290	83,722	393,419	335,904	324,176	501,831	474,567
Deposits	110,754,034	137,594,961	165,871,439	157,928,658	226,654,538	142,764,491	166,958,229	208,751,611
Due to banks	8,838,355	14,241,604	10,530,844	13,307,398	9,412,876	10,348,911	15,093,069	18,462,707
Other liabilities	4,237,578	10,463,357	10,791,038	8,327,183	11,567,789	9,215,603	6,438,003	10,577,607
Total	178,881,407	237,402,058	272,338,996	278,255,852	383,257,704	277,911,831	315,839,340	354,904,486

*In compliance with a House resolution, making it one of the duties of the Comptroller of the Currency, the Annual Report for 1873 contained the first report of State and savings banks made to this Office, and was the first call of that character ever made upon State by Federal officer.

ABSTRACT OF REPORTS OF CONDITION OF STATE BANKS, 1872-'73 TO 1887-'88—Continued.

	1880-'81.	1881-'82.	1882-'83.	1883-'84.	1884-'85.	1885-'86.	1886-'87.	1887-'88.
	652 banks.	672 banks.	754 banks.	817 banks.	975 banks.	849 banks.	1,413 banks.	1,403 banks.
Resources:								
Loans and discounts	$250,819,420	$272,520,217	$322,358,227	$331,049,510	$347,880,520	$331,183,626	$135,854,364	$432,002,663
Overdrafts	1,335,310	1,196,369	1,392,961	1,262,725	1,349,998	1,169,388	2,395,610	2,001,781
United States bonds	12,048,452	8,739,172	5,287,606	2,337,705	2,994,806	4,392,421	2,530,166	2,097,034
Other stocks, bonds, and mortgages	24,904,903	19,780,527	22,083,304	31,452,019	32,644,859	27,194,693	30,544,699	34,787,037
Due from banks	46,657,328	49,919,183	58,709,516	48,836,689	59,062,405	49,747,429	64,774,881	58,778,206
Real estate, furniture, and fixtures	13,914,238	13,037,939	13,592,791	15,058,411	15,873,312	14,605,853	20,475,102	20,246,654
Other resources	10,542,266	12,306,578	9,943,706	7,671,876	5,791,111	8,224,886	15,237,643	14,710,237
Expenses	965,327	999,944	918,403	1,025,237	1,130,883	1,047,782	2,123,672	1,768,158
Cash items	16,900,325	18,546,073	35,118,379	28,219,414	25,972,922	51,668,218		
Specie	17,071,445	17,201,489	17,429,817	25,376,565	29,867,724	24,734,684	110,845,718	105,314,947
Legal-tender and other notes	23,797,046	24,586,682	25,302,316	28,787,615	30,994,221	14,726,940		
Total	418,956,060	438,834,173	512,137,026	521,077,766	553,562,761	528,695,920	684,781,845	671,707,317
Liabilities:								
Capital stock	92,922,525	91,808,213	102,454,861	110,020,351	125,258,240	109,611,596	141,000,377	154,931,868
Circulation	274,941	286,391	187,978	177,554	98,129	103,430	228,956	148,434
Surplus	20,976,167	23,148,050	25,762,738	31,484,942	30,669,575	27,813,508	33,519,720	41,374,468
Undivided profits	7,943,466	8,902,579	11,287,623	12,718,894	11,574,736	10,095,760	14,452,490	15,510,620
Dividends unpaid	567,171	481,858	442,652	473,735	493,926	430,699	749,749	1,045,459
Deposits	261,362,303	281,835,496	334,995,702	325,365,669	344,307,996	342,882,767	446,560,022	410,047,842
Due to banks	18,870,466	18,262,172	20,651,930	27,125,108	29,950,453	27,800,280	32,445,414	34,538,942
Other liabilities	16,039,021	14,109,414	16,353,542	13,712,513	11,209,706	9,957,880	10,825,117	14,109,684
Total	418,956,060	438,834,173	512,137,026	521,077,766	553,562,761	528,695,920	684,781,845	671,707,317

LOAN AND TRUST COMPANIES—OFFICIAL AND UNOFFICIAL.

AGGREGATE RESOURCES AND LIABILITIES OF LOAN AND TRUST COMPANIES FROM 1883-'84 TO 1887-'88.

Resources and liabilities.	1883-'84.	1884-'85.	1885-'86.	1886-'87.	1887-'88.
	35 banks.	40 banks.	42 banks.	58 banks.	120 banks.
Resources.					
Loans on real estate				$16, 269, 093	$46, 606, 200
Loans on pers'l and collat'l security	$158,016,009	$141, 542, 640	$156, 828, 458	36, 544, 018	175, 033, 803
Other loans and discounts				143, 282, 810	20, 000, 365
Overdrafts	367, 749	135, 010	410	12, 810	24, 311
United States bonds	23, 371, 084	25, 376, 400	27, 985, 658	28, 787, 717	22, 809, 706
State, county, and municipal bonds				178, 148	2, 000, 479
Railroad bonds and stocks	27, 879, 858	29, 750, 200	43, 816, 716	7, 400, 348	15, 702, 430
Bank stocks				132, 651	660, 468
Other stocks, bonds, and mortgages				36, 428, 878	31, 804, 770
Due from other banks and bankers	16, 517, 457	23, 458, 085	16, 160, 112	18, 705, 503	19, 791, 922
Real estate, furniture, and fixtures	6, 152, 771	8, 750, 291	9, 774, 575	11, 087, 272	13, 051, 701
Current expenses and taxes paid	209, 842	302, 032	664, 497	433, 509	605, 173
Gold coins					
Gold certificates	552, 192	1, 388, 065			
Silver coins					
Silver certificates			10, 644, 510	16, 822, 224	19, 768, 208
Legal tenders and nat'l-bank notes	3, 871, 000	8, 557, 706			
Checks and other cash items	88, 802	94, 072			
Other resources	2, 841, 937	9, 023, 654	3, 439, 646	2, 949, 767	6, 212, 421
Total	239, 871, 691	248, 380, 683	278, 314, 591	319, 125, 657	383, 653, 477
Liabilities.					
Capital stock	23, 938, 000	26, 428, 000	27, 044, 150	36, 855, 769	53, 248, 510
Surplus fund	10, 101, 544	10, 695, 084	21, 671, 152	15, 841, 793	24, 105, 371
Other undivided profits	9, 619, 067	8, 508, 000	2, 849, 549	11, 351, 526	11, 846, 316
Debenture bonds	....	....	....	....	14, 420, 537
Dividends unpaid	25, 282	10, 251	38, 900	581, 255	198, 310
Individual deposits	188, 745, 922	188, 417, 203	214, 063, 415	240, 100, 711	257, 878, 114
State, county, and municipal deposits	....	....	....	38, 084	20, 309
Deposits of State, county, and municipal disbursing officers	....	....	....	....	....
Due to other banks and bankers	761, 888	107, 803	102, 243	5, 606, 807	2, 046, 965
Other liabilities	6, 580, 388	14, 122, 662	11, 855, 182	9, 150, 622	19, 868, 036
Total	239, 871, 691	248, 380, 683	278, 314, 591	319, 125, 657	383, 653, 477

11028—CUR 88——15

ABSTRACT OF REPORTS OF CONDITION, FROM OFFICIAL AND UNOFFICIAL

	Location.	Date.	No. of banks.	RESOURCES.		
				Loans on real estate.	Loans on personal and collateral security.	Loans and discounts.
	MUTUAL—OFFICIAL.					
1	Maine	Nov. 1, 1887	55	$6,352,794	....	$5,833,770
2	New Hampshire	Mar. 31, 1888	69	27,429,608	$7,883,804	....
3	Vermont	June 30, 1888	19	8,197,111	1,521,356	145,139
4	Massachusetts	Oct. 31, 1887	173	119,792,832	81,256,585	9,056,736
5	Rhode Island	Nov. 15, 1887	37	23,331,736	9,932,831	....
6	Connecticut	Oct. 1, 1887	85	41,712,904	11,379,780	....
7	New York	Jan. 1, 1888	118	193,704,194	10,078,190	177,931
8	New Jersey	....do	24	....	10,287,115	2,162,997
9	District of Columbia	June 30, 1888	1	258,753	247,406	....
10	Ohio	Apr. 2, 1888	4	....	....	6,373,955
11	Indiana	Oct. 31, 1887	6	....	....	2,182,985
12	Minnesota	July 31, 1888	7	1,940,801	711,352	....
	Total		598	422,780,733	133,298,428	26,853,522
	STOCK—OFFICIAL.					
1	Vermont	June 30, 1888	10	1,994,180	768,485	74,190
2	North Carolina	....do	4	33,895	....	213,936
3	Louisiana	....do	1	....	....	594,522
4	Ohio	Apr. 2, 1888	22	....	....	6,749,970
5	Michigan	July 2, 1888	43	793,662	23,733	20,119,237
6	Iowa	June 30, 1888	42	....	....	11,728,081
7	California	July 1, 1888	23	53,707,274	7,508,289	....
	Total		145	56,589,011	8,300,507	39,479,936
	Total, mutual and stock		743	479,369,744	141,598,935	66,333,458
	MUTUAL—UNOFFICIAL.					
1	Pennsylvania	June 30, 1888	7	11,883,231	7,142,416	7,232,813
2	Delaware	Dec., '87, and May, '88	2	....	....	733,537
3	Maryland	June 30, 1888	17	4,508,335	3,688,511	592,164
4	Illinois	....do	4	657,791	264,763	12,970
	Total		30	17,049,357	11,095,690	8,571,484
	STOCK—UNOFFICIAL.					
1	Maryland	June 30, 1888	5	199,226	186,636	91,414
2	South Carolina	....do	6	241,026	255,033	963,673
3	Georgia	....do	5	364,186	282,665	103,084
4	Ohio	....do	6	2,584,716	4,372,524	....
5	Illinois	....do	5	1,008,834	7,141,931	845,837
6	Utah	....do	1	250,000	244,212	....
	Total		28	4,647,988	12,483,001	2,004,558
	Total, mutual and stock		58	21,697,345	23,578,691	10,576,042
	Total, all savings banks		801	501,067,089	165,177,626	76,900,500

SOURCES, OF MUTUAL AND STOCK SAVINGS BANKS IN 1887-'88.

RESOURCES—continued.									
Over-drafts.	U. S. bonds.	State, county, municipal, etc., bonds.	R. R. bonds and stocks.	Bank stocks.	All other bonds and stocks.	Due from other banks and bankers.	Real estate, furniture, and fixtures.	Current expenses and taxes paid.	
....	$1, 870, 754	$12, 433, 106	$8, 856, 055	$2, 120, 065	$1, 164, 632	....	$1, 233, 938	....	1
....	341, 030	7, 013, 430	8, 500, 701	2, 002, 522	4, 451, 003	$723, 082	600, 342	....	2
....	210, 000	2, 506, 02[illegible]	....	237, 880	....	414, 630	212, 277	....	3
....	8, 040, 378	31, 003, 672	24, 265, 901	26, 850, 920	....	8, 246, 910	4, 002, 502	....	4
....	3, 526, 000	5, 651, 863	8, 706, 520	2, 895, 173	....	....	2, 302, 180	....	5
....	2, 879, 705	17, 183, 804	20, 446, 320	6, 388, 275	....	....	4, 606, 113	....	6
....	132, 704, 100	201, 200, 769	....	....	....	33, 630, 607	7, 736, 103	....	7
....	10, 716, 170	....	....	....	4, 007, 051	....	1, 079, 636	....	8
....	200, 000	170, 000	....	....	....	14, 013	....	$7, 630	9
....	2, 255, 000	545, 065	....	....	7, 406, 726	770, 032	247, 658	16, 712	10
....	133, 832	130, 500	....	3, 000	....	....	121, 091	8, 048	11
$8, 475	55, 300	....	....	....	1, 052, 841	680, 245	95, 446	27, 033	12
8, 475	163, 542, 259	278, 530, 131	70, 865, 515	40, 587, 335	10, 072, 853	44, 480, 428	23, 287, 886	60, 252	
....	45, 630	908, 196	....	154, 275	....	238, 824	14, 788	....	1
92	....	5, 100	....	....	2, 000	28, 050	3, 450	3, 475	2
....	....	....	....	....	155, 416	....	....	....	3
8, 404	70, 000	86, 315	....	....	1, 040, 933	725, 586	341, 371	32, 264	4
50, 039	185, 200	1, 066, 445	....	....	887, 036	4, 005, 829	370, 722	125, 190	5
79, 439	....	....	....	....	....	1, 866, 478	387, 164	....	6
....	....	....	....	....	18, 847, 181	1, 096, 477	2, 016, 701	....	7
138, 574	300, 850	2, 066, 056	....	154, 275	20, 933, 466	7, 061, 244	3, 143, 196	160, 929	
147, 049	163, 843, 109	280, 625, 187	70, 865, 515	40, 741, 610	40, 006, 319	52, 450, 672	26, 431, 082	221, 181	
....	8, 866, 312	3, 628, 392	12, 018, 468	40, 824	3, 805, 418	1, 000, 869	1, 361, 018	105, 407	1
....	....	97, 500	136, 215	73, 136	2, 114, 762	....	240, 734	....	2
....	9, 787, 034	2, 733, 208	5, 440, 279	234, 462	4, 080, 304	157, 345	494, 826	112, 588	3
....	81, 470	6, 742	34, 891	59, 206	98, 495	152, 077	75, 281	3, 829	4
....	18, 734, 816	6, 465, 842	18, 629, 853	436, 628	11, 007, 979	1, 400, 291	2, 172, 450	221, 824	
....	....	4, 000	8, 000	7, 028	17, 710	20, 150	31, 121	991	1
....	50, 000	....	....	....	1, 735, 617	372, 373	100, 744	8, 740	2
400	....	36, 798	....	....	45, 008	27, 958	74, 579	7, 348	3
2, 424	359, 100	317, 298	306, 000	10, 000	430, 008	1, 363, 062	77, 007	15, 323	4
4, 676	540, 250	....	5, 000	....	1, 418, 845	1, 449, 047	86, 826	....	5
3, 583	....	....	....	....	....	17, 804	14, 025	....	6
11, 152	949, 350	358, 096	319, 000	17, 028	3, 647, 338	3, 252, 194	385, 802	32, 402	
11, 152	19, 684, 166	6, 823, 938	18, 949, 853	454, 556	14, 655, 317	4, 652, 485	2, 558, 301	254, 226	
158, 201	183, 527, 275	287, 449, 125	89, 715, 358	41, 196, 166	54, 661, 636	57, 103, 157	28, 989, 343	475, 407	

ABSTRACT OF REPORTS OF CONDITION, FROM OFFICIAL AND UNOFFICIAL

	Location.	RESOURCES—continued.			LIABILITIES.	
		Cash and cash items.	Other resources.	Total.	Capital stock.	Surplus.
	MUTUAL—OFFICIAL.					
1	Maine	$830, 299	$579, 192	$41, 283, 614	....	$1, 515, 531
2	New Hampshire	152, 868	*8	59, 249, 863	....	2, 237, 107
3	Vermont	101, 969	174, 730	13, 782, 474	....	390, 411
4	Massachusetts	611, 720	909, 384	317, 097, 499	....	5, 202, 170
5	Rhode Island	719, 896	1, 214, 319	58, 400, 527	....	50, 000
6	Connecticut	2, 740, 906	559, 087	107, 896, 912	....	3, 514, 772
7	New York	5, 776, 048	5, 390, 754	590, 458, 751	....	85, 249, 647
8	New Jersey	1, 505, 360	963, 695	31, 782, 024	....	2, 482, 120
9	District of Columbia	18, 250	28, 704	944, 965	....	....
10	Ohio	222, 345	30, 327	17, 885, 820	....	1, 176, 000
11	Indiana	333, 499	1, 650	2, 915, 805	....	182, 562
12	Minnesota	68, 509	237	4, 040, 259	....	151, 234
	Total	13, 081, 664	9, 861, 032	1, 246, 348, 513	....	102, 151, 623
	STOCK—OFFICIAL.					
1	Vermont	35, 849	12, 580	4, 247, 017	$475, 450	10, 000
2	North Carolina	12, 759	111	302, 868	86, 975	1, 056
3	Louisiana	61, 489	1	818, 418	100, 000	....
4	Ohio	409, 602	221, 038	9, 775, 558	1, 712, 400	223, 720
5	Michigan	985, 786	12, 088	28, 645, 467	3, 703, 702	345, 129
6	Iowa	563, 862	....	14, 625, 024	2, 637, 400	253, 755
7	California	2, 171, 722	319, 848	85, 727, 402	4, 404, 447	....
	Total	4, 333, 120	565, 681	144, 126, 854	13, 122, 434	833, 660
	Total mutual and stock	17, 414, 798	10, 426, 718	1, 390, 475, 367	13, 122, 434	102, 985, 283
	MUTUAL—UNOFFICIAL.					
1	Pennsylvania	2, 539, 608	13, 762	60, 638, 138	....	4, 052, 074
2	Delaware	23, 203	53, 219	3, 472, 305	....	281, 419
3	Maryland	374, 365	133, 037	33, 265, 458	....	290, 511
4	Illinois	70, 643	10, 004	1, 528, 162	....	174, 157
	Total	3, 007, 816	210, 022	98, 904, 063	....	4, 801, 161
	STOCK—UNOFFICIAL.					
1	Maryland	30, 148	13, 300	610, 624	184, 656	15, 600
2	South Carolina	240, 030	930	3, 908, 186	330, 540	222, 500
3	Georgia	29, 749	1, 270, 914	2, 243, 398	308, 000	57, 000
4	Ohio	121, 277	18, 967	9, 071, 556	1, 379, 691	605, 560
5	Illinois	710, 173	3	13, 221, 322	975, 000	927, 341
6	Utah	11, 309	....	541, 533	50, 000	22, 465
	Total	1, 142, 706	1, 304, 114	30, 556, 619	3, 227, 887	1, 850, 466
	Total mutual and stock	4, 150, 524	1, 514, 136	129, 460, 682	3, 227, 887	6, 651, 637
	Total all savings-banks	21, 565, 317	11, 940, 849	1, 519, 936, 049	16, 350, 321	109, 636, 940

SOURCES, OF MUTUAL AND STOCK SAVINGS BANKS IN 1887-'88—Continued.

LIABILITIES—continued.						No. of depositors.	Average amount due each.	
Other undivided profits.	Dividends unpaid.	Individual deposits.	Deposits of State, county, and municipal disbursing officers.	Due to other banks.	Other liabilities.			
$887,477	....	$28,810,043	....	....	$60,963	119,229	$325.58	1
2,878,828	....	51,949,079	....	....	104,789	139,967	385.80	2
382,214	....	14,069,847	....	....	2	46,694	278.61	3
8,611,746	....	302,948,024	....	....	314,959	944,778	320.66	4
2,016,982	....	55,363,283	....	$43,835	56,427	120,144	460.81	5
....	....	102,189,934	....	....	2,192,206	278,415	367.04	6
....	....	505,017,751	....	....	191,353	1,325,062	381.12	7
....	....	29,000,189	....	....	180,706	105,695	274.42	8
31,006	....	923,958	....	....	1	9,443	97.84	9
265,514	....	16,444,306	....	....	....	42,336	388.42	10
641	....	2,645,967	....	....	86,635	11,205	236.14	11
31,074	....	3,780,366	....	2,300	a668,385	16,962	223.22	12
16,046,382	....	1,124,148,947	....	46,135	3,955,426	3,160,130	355.73	
119,347	....	3,592,219	....	....	50,001	10,826	331.81	1
7,582	$600	127,180	....	3,681	73,788	1,448	87.83	2
49,140	180	661,098	....	....	1	2,330	284.28	3
115,903	1,209	7,609,974	....	73,017	39,335	23,922	318.11	4
689,115	21,449	22,043,806	....	544,579	387,627	88,529	250.16	5
286,374	....	11,268,079	....	170,416	....	36,004	312.96	6
3,053,527	....	77,718,534	....	48,624	502,360	106,263	731.38	7
4,320,907	23,438	123,923,896	....	840,317	1,053,112	269,328	460.12	
20,367,379	23,438	1,248,072,843	....	895,452	5,008,538	3,429,458	363.93	
1,064,600	....	55,400,516	....	....	51,858	197,095	280.58	1
....	....	3,187,886	....	....	....	13,524	235.72	2
910,907	....	32,044,508	....	....	10,502	120,055	264.93	3
24,182	....	1,240,614	....	22,321	b57,888	14,632	85.40	4
1,999,779	....	91,951,524	....	22,321	120,248	346,806	265.14	
10,892	838	368,579	....	....	21,039	1,935	190.48	1
127,689	42	3,243,811	....	9,756	33,848	8,800	368.61	2
28,022	1,943	1,761,282	....	37,053	49,496	11,939	147.52	3
209,691	2,225	7,748,104	....	16,784	10,001	15,491	500.17	4
303,890	9,000	10,581,210	$10,080	73,444	337,727	19,862	532.73	5
....	....	469,067	....	....	1	4,000	117.26	6
692,184	14,050	24,172,183	10,080	137,037	452,132	62,027	389.70	
2,691,963	14,050	116,123,707	10,080	159,358	581,380	408,833	284.03	
23,059,342	37,488	1,364,196,550	10,080	1,054,810	5,589,948	3,838,291	355.41	

a Includes $459,008 commercial deposits, $150,000, the capital of two banks, and $59,007 dividends unpaid.

b Includes $55,000, the capital of two banks which claim to be mutual.

ABSTRACT OF REPORTS OF CONDITION, FROM OFFICIAL

	Location.	Date of report.	No. of banks	RESOURCES.		
				Loans on real estate.	Loans on personal and collateral security.	Loans and discounts.
	OFFICIAL.					
1	North Carolina	June 30, 1888	10	$06, 776	....	$080, 100
2	Wisconsin	July 2, 1888	73	....	....	4, 774, 473
3	Missouri	Apr. 30, 1888	91	504, 107	$5, 174, 076	....
4	California	July 1, 1888	30	1, 828, 317	6, 715, 610	....
5	Wyoming	June 30, 1888	9	4, 500	377, 108	362, 203
	Total		212	2, 433, 700	12, 266, 824	5, 822, 935
	UNOFFICIAL.					
1	Maine	June 30, 1888	2	....	132, 075	13, 000
2	Massachusetts	do	5	....	422, 035	288, 141
3	Connecticut	do	3	21, 400	15, 615	236, 062
4	New York	do	30	815, 210	554, 384	1, 110, 681
5	New Jersey	do	6	82, 118	739, 017	714, 237
6	Pennsylvania	do	39	405, 152	2, 805, 405	4, 018, 531
7	Maryland	do	3	23, [illegible]00	57, 924	78, 542
8	Virginia	do	3	11, 030	360, 641	26, 979
9	South Carolina	do	3	23, 502	62, 250	21, 246
10	Georgia	do	8	53, 931	284, 808	22, 100
11	Florida	do	7	15, 385	269, 232	26, 148
12	Alabama	do	6	134, 400	242, 903	806, 878
13	Mississippi	do	2	....	....	104, 854
14	Louisiana	do	2	1, 300	140, 077	....
15	Texas	do	26	313, 559	1, 802, 695	1, 484, 481
16	Arkansas	do	7	17, 583	281, 100	34, 419
17	Kentucky	do	13	2, 100	818, 301	473, 840
18	Ohio	do	69	1, 063, 080	6, 752, 243	676, 348
19	Indiana	do	39	355, 944	3, 758, 887	443, 537
20	Illinois	do	120	1, 335, 252	13, 662, 194	2, 522, 072
21	Michigan	do	53	366, 240	1, 062, 891	908, 564
22	Wisconsin	do	3	32, 655	8, 740	60, 302
23	Iowa	do	134	585, 038	5, 165, 392	1, 701, 741
24	Minnesota	do	30	154, 104	1, 570, 791	523, 116
25	Missouri	do	5	74, 277	316, 133	11, 550
26	Kansas	do	123	200, 385	4, 228, 610	1, 158, 536
27	Nebraska	do	125	104, 308	4, 118, 466	351, 351
28	Colorado	do	16	97, 207	527, 263	613, 448
29	Nevada	do	2	....	198, 129	....
30	California	do	3	....	66, 370	1, 420
31	Oregon	do	7	56, 587	201, 173	13, 777
32	Arizona	do	4	16, 450	198, 174	63, 640
33	Dakota	do	63	103, 517	1, 232, 805	80, 350
34	Idaho	do	1	4, 800	7, 200	20, 000
35	Montana	do	2	....	16, 023	1, 174, 008
36	New Mexico	do	3	33, 165	103, 755	10, 652
37	Utah	do	6	105, 618	1, 317, 545	44, 867
38	Washington	do	9	201, 363	680, 278	372, 221
39	Wyoming	do	2	....	....	30, 886
	Total		991	7, 140, 309	54, 340, 185	20, 972, 444
	Total, official and unofficial		1, 203	9, 574, 009	66, 607, 009	26, 795, 379

AND UNOFFICIAL SOURCES, OF PRIVATE BANKS IN 1888.

RESOURCES—continued.									
Over-drafts.	U. S. bonds.	State, county, municipal, etc., bonds.	R. R. bonds and stocks.	Bank stocks.	All other bonds and stocks.	Due from other banks and bankers.	Real estate, furniture, and fixtures.	Current expenses and taxes paid.	
$27,933	....	$300	....	....	$94,212	$120,774	$74,042	$3,419	1
148,479	$240,855	....	....	....	....	1,122,089	370,707	32,729	2
270,301	85,452	....	....	....	130,093	2,035,864	459,810	....	3
....	....	....	....	....	520,101	171,040	720,637	....	4
18,964	....	1,431	....	....	22,674	226,331	44,410	5,616	5
405,707	326,307	1,731	....	....	737,080	3,682,698	1,678,696	41,764	
....	....	....	....	....	10,000	39,068	2,800	2,284	1
....	500	....	$203,614	$25,728	32,433	240,000	4,000	4,931	2
561	....	....	3,000	....	11,802	58,820	....	1,729	3
15,899	58,100	4,000	12,940	1,000	200,956	509,908	185,796	11,938	4
....	....	16,605	86,510	....	45,372	212,820	71,335	15,323	5
78,723	36,000	....	343,771	74,715	367,936	1,668,077	280,715	47,800	6
46	....	....	....	....	6,020	14,878	25,051	361	7
36,175	....	....	80,000	8,290	15,244	58,521	34,006	4,351	8
....	....	....	....	1,500	18,280	25,263	64,033	500	9
6,057	....	29,000	40,600	2,000	11,935	44,781	356,148	5,147	10
8,181	....	....	....	....	3,000	93,002	33,658	2,818	11
6,939	....	44,646	21,800	97,600	941,405	305,290	244,049	12,037	12
1,828	....	....	825	....	5,900	16,346	8,495	2,803	13
55,500	....	....	....	....	3,225	28,032	21,639	841	14
170,580	....	....	20,094	3,000	178,317	709,443	504,878	18,732	15
5,281	....	....	....	5,000	1,000	189,770	21,188	6,604	16
18,408	....	....	36,636	10,979	43,176	198,901	24,280	4,728	17
69,816	100,905	10,800	184,885	113,714	148,342	1,388,275	623,327	73,646	18
24,755	890,320	43,500	....	31,580	228,458	1,014,988	394,644	23,816	19
298,473	164,000	463,280	130,209	79,208	419,589	3,523,239	1,377,089	140,543	20
7,502	11,000	12,000	2,000	6,500	29,688	476,794	328,835	34,265	21
....	....	....	....	....	500	18,078	3,300	30	22
244,700	38,000	....	....	72,644	149,457	1,898,342	1,105,141	104,605	23
57,485	....	....	....	4,000	42,803	529,286	208,270	38,838	24
5,669	....	....	....	1,000	149,352	64,471	20,752	1,122	25
118,437	1,994	....	1,000	124,049	231,331	1,058,907	1,048,750	95,501	26
107,319	....	330	100	13,000	31,737	1,042,821	679,214	108,066	27
28,287	....	....	....	....	27,543	346,128	96,101	23,390	28
79,131	....	....	....	....	25,005	15,551	21,806	1,569	29
....	....	....	....	....	....	32,582	33,718	4,570	30
8,285	....	....	....	....	....	35,839	24,369	2,081	31
19,893	....	70,090	....	....	48,145	40,572	24,643	3,435	32
31,259	....	....	....	4,240	45,461	301,553	209,608	39,902	33
....	....	....	....	....	75,000	....	44,200	....	34
5,080	....	....	....	....	....	140,947	25,305	10,028	35
5,284	....	339	....	....	358	62,144	15,050	921	36
58,381	....	....	....	....	33,774	408,527	44,527	8,174	37
27,936	....	65,483	....	15,750	90,715	398,629	86,574	8,095	38
....	....	....	....	....	....	11,116	4,280	515	39
1,606,619	1,392,415	700,673	1,168,584	695,402	3,680,009	17,218,193	8,431,014	866,808	
2,072,386	1,718,722	702,404	1,168,584	695,492	4,417,689	20,900,891	10,110,310	908,572	

ABSTRACT OF REPORTS OF CONDITION, FROM OFFICIAL AND

	Location.	RESOURCES—continued.			LIABILITIES.	
		Cash and cash items.	Other resources	Total.	Capital.	Surplus.
	OFFICIAL.					
1	North Carolina	$68, 689	$15, 617	$1, 163, 931	$247, 000	$39, 450
2	Wisconsin	752, 238	17, 318	7, 458, 978	972. 978	....
3	Missouri	1, 142, 320	26, 799	9, 829, 512	1, 370, 241	892, 447
4	California	1, 614, 857	235, 357	11, 815, 549	3, 793, 092	....
5	Wyoming	112, 669	3	1, 175, 909	329, 325	71, 051
	Total	3, 690, 773	295, 094	31, 443, 969	6, 712, 636	1, 002, 948
	UNOFFICIAL.					
1	Maine	13, 936	....	213, 223	60, 000	....
2	Massachusetts	83, 205	15, 000	1, 320, 187	420, 000	166, 544
3	Connecticut	34, 964	1, 560	885, 073	56, 285	....
4	New York	188, 742	145, 594	3, 851, 233	903, 738	296, 986
5	New Jersey	148, 481	11, 696	2, 143, 523	346, 214	127, 500
6	Pennsylvania	812, 315	32, 223	11, 761, 323	1, 286, 843	912, 376
7	Maryland	8, 525	433	215, 880	133, 408	498
8	Virginia	29, 002	1, 917	666, 796	110, 000	15, 400
9	South Carolina	11, 102	3, 469	231, 174	161, 353	5, 567
10	Georgia	33, 648	7, 890	897, 705	600, 898	25, 000
11	Florida	82, 202	5, 067	539, 383	129, 164	12, 929
12	Alabama	193, 728	503, 037	3, 613, 772	273, 500	428, 316
13	Mississippi	22, 875	1	163, 926	52, 000	11, 100
14	Louisiana	17, 342	22, 903	291, 768	167, 000	19, 923
15	Texas	670, 709	227, 105	6, 230, 202	2, 833, 509	98, 670
16	Arkansas	122, 905	28, 072	713, 012	219, 500	9, 448
17	Kentucky	84, 732	4, 551	1, 720, 632	520, 180	36, 456
18	Ohio	1, 213, 122	152, 685	12, 661, 312	2, 492, 534	665, 534
19	Indiana	874, 109	39, 802	8, 124, 346	2, 264, 609	248, 148
20	Illinois	2, 408, 111	929, 453	27, 453, 307	5, 067, 412	2, 370, 644
21	Michigan	305, 431	142, 963	3, 754, 670	1, 087, 687	139, 002
22	Wisconsin	13, 521	168	133, 293	12, 000	5, 303
23	Iowa	971, 624	126, 512	12, 164, 285	4, 174, 133	617, 723
24	Minnesota	200, 639	47, 414	3, 376, 946	919, 652	200, 797
25	Missouri	49, 475	2, 003	695, 824	200, 000	32, 000
26	Kansas	831, 317	135, 341	9, 294, 158	3, 834, 127	404, 471
27	Nebraska	438, 777	17, 387	7, 103, 476	2, 492, 202	365, 730
28	Colorado	205, 612	558	1, 965, 627	474, 897	59, 737
29	Nevada	40, 593	6, 168	387, 952	168, 700	29, 362
30	California	55, 971	1	194, 632	99, 573	....
31	Oregon	41, 071	34, 406	417, 588	187, 900	12, 961
32	Arizona	62, 988	3	548, 644	100, 000	50, 000
33	Dakota	194, 520	143, 310	2, 455, 525	1, 130, 824	118, 458
34	Idaho	1, 800	64, 000	217, 000	50, 000	25, 000
35	Montana	208, 485	3	1, 580, 774	119, 320	50, 620
36	New Mexico	35, 911	5	270, 584	105, 800	4, 720
37	Utah	134, 248	6, 019	2, 216, 050	270, 811	1, 003, 372
38	Washington	286, 254	164	2, 242, 762	488, 515	15, 000
39	Wyoming	4, 316	1	51, 114	30, 000	....
	Total	11, 136, 398	2, 850, 484	132, 269, 287	34, 129, 438	8, 585, 290
	Total, official and unofficial	14, 827, 171	3, 154, 578	163, 713, 256	40, 842, 074	9, 588, 238

UNOFFICIAL SOURCES, OF PRIVATE BANKS IN 1888—Continued.

LIABILITIES—continued.								
Other undivided profits.	State-bank notes.	Dividends unpaid.	Individual deposits.	State, county, and municipal deposits.	Deposits of State, county, and municipal disbursing officers.	Due to other banks.	Other liabilities.	
$33, 817			$101, 026			$15, 707	$123, 931	1
554, 281			5, 742, 445			180, 518	2, 750	2
			7, 014, 060			454, 261	07, 804	3
596, 838			6, 477, 331			744, 460	203, 828	4
24, 274			715, 381		$11, 732	4, 023	20, 213	5
1, 209, 210			20, 353, 852		11, 732	1, 404, 909	748, 622	
6, 597			146, 026					1
50, 666			626, 414			20, 000	30, 563	2
2, 007			268, 804			24, 087	32, 000	3
67, 935		$2, 075	2, 259, 153	$1, 740	1, 940	95, 679	221, 078	4
78, 896		486	1, 470, 806	28, 220	12, 500	38, 620	40, 691	5
204, 471		1, 734	8, 932, 477		10, 300	185, 522	227, 000	6
967			63, 102				17, 815	7
27, 326			986, 825		24, 842	27, 041	76, 062	8
			43, 513		3, 383	8, 754	8, 604	9
9, 638			171, 672	1, 153		31, 519	57, 825	10
12, 843		300	374, 885	5, 016		1, 780	2, 400	11
704, 850			1, 315, 060		15, 213	154, 847	631, 308	12
7, 628			73, 161		861	4, 074	14, 502	13
6, 202			82, 642			16, 000	1	14
224, 307		781	2, 590, 754	30, 000	10, 764	65, 806	375, 401	15
16, 542			437, 820		28, 730	731	201	16
24, 273		8	1, 010, 810			76, 321	30, 575	17
310, 287		10, 611	8, 037, 624	5, 000	30, 930	105, 033	298, 720	18
100, 747		10, 081	4, 803, 064		204, 574	102, 292	114, 831	19
458, 677		12, 639	15, 335, 137	1, 885, 404	222, 128	1, 742, 241	358, 045	20
70, 920		5, 884	2, 278, 518		6, 914	21, 630	144, 121	21
904			107, 340		6, 517		1, 220	22
302, 379		7, 357	6, 368, 870	115, 390	148, 410	45, 670	274, 353	23
93, 469		4, 220	1, 706, 211	69, 964	07, 734	75, 649	120, 250	24
3, 834		5, 000	447, 835		6, 904	751		25
329, 870		14, 383	4, 084, 059	144, 674		128, 155	353, 510	26
312, 118	$21, 000	5, 246	3, 447, 089	81, 770	55, 000	115, 231	206, 992	27
76, 241			1, 250, 405		10, 486	49, 906	34, 865	28
5, 472			102, 272			55, 408	26, 648	29
7, 878			81, 030			5, 250	1	30
5, 989		25	185, 612	17, 640		5, 964	1, 407	31
10, 201			288, 407			27, 878	12, 068	32
132, 483		3, 702	874, 716	33, 301	13, 672	12, 728	135, 546	33
120, 000			12, 000				10, 000	34
29, 530			1, 305, 804			15, 469	2	35
4, 234			154, 345			1, 483	2	36
22, 087		10	804, 021		3, 006	12, 782	955	37
38, 368			1, 019, 370		40, 100	40, 568	811	38
4, 524			16, 540				50	39*
4, 080, 538	21, 000	84, 658	74, 524, 990	2, 419, 440	1, 032, 307	3, 496, 470	3, 875, 147	
5, 289, 748	21, 000	84, 658	94, 878, 842	2, 419, 440	1, 064, 039	4, 901, 448	4, 623, 769	

SAVINGS BANKS—OFFICIAL AND UNOFFICIAL.*

AGGREGATE RESOURCES AND LIABILITIES OF SAVINGS BANKS FROM 1883-'84 TO 1887-'88.

Resources and liabilities.	1883-'84.	1884-'85.	1885-'86.	1886-'87.	1887-'88.
	636 banks.	646 banks.	638 banks.	684 banks.	801 banks.
Resources.					
Loans on real estate	$358, 086, 040	$389, 953, 928	$418, 372, 642	$457, 441, 666	$501, 007, 089
Loans on pers'l and collat'l security	141, 457, 111	133, 716, 902	127, 677, 702	145, 553, 135	165, 177, 626
Other loans and discounts	....	....	....	37, 904, 817	76, 909, 500
Overdrafts	....	....	....	90, 125	158, 201
U. S. bonds	196, 226, 202	191, 980, 698	197, 171, 307	180, 248, 754	183, 527, 275
State, county, and municipal bonds	222, 218, 066	228, 993, 250	241, 051, 536	215, 764, 815	287, 449, 125
R. R. bonds and stocks	50, 994, 579	59, 585, 489	63, 511, 735	74, 408, 931	89, 715, 358
Bank stocks	37, 929, 754	38, 460, 603	39, 029, 813	40, 067, 680	41, 196, 166
Other stocks, bonds, and mortgages	....	....	....	50, 684, 227	54, 661, 636
Due from other banks and bankers	52, 358, 971	46, 125, 014	43, 689, 103	55, 109, 727	57, 103, 157
Real estate, furniture, and fixtures	34, 467, 276	32, 174, 810	30, 984, 883	29, 639, 750	28, 989, 343
Current expenses and taxes paid	156, 044	166, 636	142, 717	1, 761, 450	475, 407
Gold coins					
Gold certificates					
Silver coins					
Silver certificates	14, 079, 452	13, 423, 064	19, 757, 941	18, 005, 235	21, 565, 317
Legal tenders and nat'l-bank notes					
Checks and other cash items					
Other resources	69, 166, 581	68, 445, 304	79, 451, 562	70, 980, 412	11, 940, 849
Total	1, 177, 740, 919	1, 203, 025, 698	1, 260, 840, 941	1, 377, 660, 724	1, 519, 936, 049
Liabilities.					
Capital stock	....	....	....	10, 090, 866	16, 350, 321
Surplus fund	82, 895, 717	88, 647, 315	96, 924, 117	119, 695, 310	109, 636, 940
Other undivided profits	16, 904, 753	13, 106, 359	15, 326, 391	7, 204, 933	23, 050, 342
Dividends unpaid	....	....	....	1[illegible]3, 386	37, 488
Individual deposits	1, 073, 294, 955	1, 095, 172, 147	1, 141, 530, 578	1, 235, 736, 069	1, 364, 196, 550
State, county, and municipal deposits	....	....	....	....	....
Deposits of State, county, and municipal disbursing officers	....	....	....	....	10, 680
Due to other banks and bankers	....	....	....	90, 788	1, 054, 810
Other liabilities	5, 145, 494	6, 090, 877	7, 059, 855	4, 649, 372	5, 589, 918
Total	1, 177, 740, 919	1, 203, 025, 698	1, 260, 840, 941	1, 377, 660, 724	1, 519, 936, 049

* Official only prior to 1886-'87.

TABLE, BY STATES, OF THE AGGREGATE DEPOSITS OF SAVINGS BANKS, WITH THE NUMBER OF THEIR DEPOSITORS AND THE AVERAGE AMOUNT DUE TO EACH, IN 1886-'87 AND 1887-'88.

States.	1886-'87.			1887-'88.		
	Number of depositors.	Amount of deposits.	Average to each depositor.	Number of depositors.	Amount of deposits.	Average to each depositor.
Maine	114,691	$37,216,071	$324.47	119,229	$38,819,643	$325.58
New Hampshire	132,714	50,822,702	382.94	139,967	53,939,079	385.36
Vermont	53,810	15,587,050	289.67	57,520	16,002,006	288.03
Massachusetts	906,039	291,107,000	321.40	944,778	302,948,624	320.66
Rhode Island	119,159	53,284,821	447.18	120,144	55,363,283	460.81
Connecticut	266,888	97,424,820	365.01	278,415	102,189,934	367.04
New York	1,264,535	482,486,730	381.55	1,325,062	505,017,751	381.12
New Jersey	98,137	27,482,135	280.04	105,895	29,060,189	274.42
Pennsylvania	156,722	42,219,000	269.39	197,695	55,469,516	280.58
Delaware	12,744	2,771,302	217.46	13,524	3,187,886	235.72
Maryland	59,565	19,020,002	319.33	122,890	32,413,087	263.75
District of Columbia	8,245	834,524	101.22	9,443	923,958	97.84
North Carolina	*377	11,307	30.00	1,448	127,186	87.83
South Carolina	....	....	....	8,800	3,243,811	368.61
Georgia	....	....	....	11,939	1,761,282	147.52
Louisiana	....	....	....	2,336	664,008	284.28
Ohio	*41,059	15,065,650	366.93	*81,749	31,802,484	389.02
Indiana	9,933	2,312,013	232.75	11,205	2,645,967	236.14
Illinois	*28,038	14,061,258	501.51	*34,494	11,830,854	342.98
Michigan	....	....	....	*88,529	22,943,806	259.16
Iowa	*39,638	9,969,019	251.50	*36,004	11,268,079	312.96
Minnesota	15,474	3,402,950	219.91	16,962	3,786,366	223.22
Utah	....	....	....	4,000	469,067	117.26
California	*90,245	70,077,890	776.52	*106,263	77,718,534	731.38
Total	3,418,013	1,235,247,371	361.39	3,838,291	1,364,196,550	355.41

*Partially estimated.

TABLE SHOWING THE GROWTH OF SAVINGS BANKS, AS INDICATED BY DEPOSITS, IN THE STATES NAMED, IN 1830, 1840, AND 1850 TO 1887-88.*

Date.	California.	Maine.	N. Hampshire.	Vermont.	Massachusetts.	Rhode Island.	Connecticut.	New York.	New Jersey.
1830 ..	....	....	$250,000	....	$2,500,000	$200,000	$350,060	$2,023,304	....
1840 ..	....	....	750,000	....	5,810,554	500,000	1,500,000	5,431,000	....
1850 ..	....	....	1,041,543	$199,370	13,000,024	1,405,545	5,406,444	20,832,072	....
1851 ..	....	....	1,776,768	282,217	15,554,089	1,007,233	6,098,158	24,006,509	....
1852 ..	....	....	2,009,617	407,188	18,401,308	2,474,109	8,135,010	27,541,023	....
1853 ..	....	....	2,507,900	704,000	23,370,102	3,308,769	8,883,307	32,824,177	....
1854 ..	....	....	3,222,261	901,789	25,036,858	4,104,091	10,006,131	33,453,781	....
1855 ..	....	$867,131	3,341,256	897,407	27,296,217	4,834,312	10,844,933	26,012,713	....
1856 ..	....	919,571	3,537,363	897,432	30,373,447	5,797,857	12,162,136	41,099,502	....
1857 .	....	968,325	3,748,285	875,900	33,015,757	6,079,053	12,562,504	41,422,672	....
1858 ..	....	968,194	3,588,658	810,050	33,914,972	6,340,621	14,052,181	48,194,847	....
1859 ..	....	923,397	4,138,822	940,846	39,424,419	7,705,771	16,565,284	58,178,160	....
1860 ..	....	1,539,257	4,800,024	1,111,532	45,054,236	9,163,760	19,377,670	67,440,397	....
1861 ..	....	1,708,961	5,590,652	1,231,940	44,785,439	9,282,879	19,983,959	64,083,119	....
1862 ..	....	1,876,165	5,653,535	1,348,833	50,403,074	9,560,441	23,140,930	76,538,183	....
1863 ..	....	2,641,476	6,560,308	1,678,201	56,883,828	11,128,713	26,054,802	93,786,384	$5,500,000
1864 ..	....	3,672,975	7,661,738	1,952,500	62,557,604	12,815,007	29,142,288	111,737,763	6,570,839
1865 ..	$7,005,062	3,356,828	7,831,335	1,708,531	59,936,482	13,533,002	27,310,013	115,472,566	6,450,357
1866 ..	10,358,888	3,946,433	7,857,001	1,589,854	67,732,204	17,751,713	31,224,404	131,769,074	7,020,186
1867 ..	17,365,597	5,598,600	10,463,418	1,815,602	80,431,583	21,413,647	36,283,400	151,127,609	9,431,807
1868 ..	23,818,533	8,032,246	13,541,584	2,046,321	94,838,336	24,408,635	41,803,681	169,808,078	11,545,526
1869 ..	28,893,645	10,839,955	16,379,857	2,601,940	112,119,016	27,067,072	47,904,834	194,360,217	15,428,910
1870 ..	30,555,909	16,597,888	18,759,461	2,745,770	135,745,097	30,708,501	55,297,705	230,749,408	20,001,951
1871 ..	44,235,610	22,787,802	21,472,120	3,172,525	163,704,077	36,289,703	62,717,814	267,905,826	25,231,311
1872 ..	51,431,326	26,154,333	24,700,774	3,836,224	184,797,313	42,583,538	68,523,307	285,286,621	28,754,482
1873 ..	57,833,373	29,556,523	29,071,114	4,478,842	202,195,343	46,617,183	70,769,407	285,520,085	30,666,534
1874 ..	69,026,603	31,051,963	28,829,376	5,011,831	217,452,120	48,771,501	73,783,802	303,935,649	32,044,840
1875 ..	70,062,568	30,757,651	30,214,585	6,004,604	234,974,001	51,311,331	76,875,049	319,260,202	32,727,342
1876-7	31,185,600	26,662,150	30,963,047	6,815,829	243,340,043	50,542,272	78,524,172	319,716,864	29,318,543
1877-8	70,984,764	25,708,472	28,780,549	6,722,691	244,596,614	48,103,119	77,214,372	312,823,058	16,353,275
1878-9	57,846,025	21,104,503	26,282,136	6,753,105	209,860,631	42,806,657	72,515,468	299,074,639	15,194,562
1879-0	47,719,829	20,978,140	28,204,791	7,348,812	206,378,709	43,095,534	72,842,443	310,258,591	17,470,014
1880-1	49,954,333	23,277,676	32,097,734	8,066,007	218,047,022	44,755,625	76,518,571	353,029,657	19,863,638
1881-2	53,208,780	26,474,555	36,181,187	9,830,157	230,444,470	46,771,723	80,522,301	387,832,8[illegible]3	25,321,713
1882-3	56,507,163	29,503,890	39,124,815	10,686,041	241,311,302	48,320,672	84,942,410	412,147,213	27,344,035
1883-4	59,464,726	31,371,869	42,091,507	11,061,056	252,607,593	50,127,806	88,098,384	431,080,010	29,323,428
1884-5	58,943,903	32,913,835	43,827,350	11,2[illegible]8,285	263,720,147	51,079,101	90,614,023	437,107,501	24,017,917
1885-6	60,435,919	35,111,600	47,331,919	11,723,075	274,998,413	51,816,390	92,481,425	457,030,250	25,835,780
1886-7	70,077,893	37,215,072	50,822,702	15,587,050	291,197,000	53,284,821	97,424,820	482,486,730	27,482,135
1887-8	77,718,534	38,819,643	53,939,079	16,602,000	302,948,624	55,303,283	102,180,934	505,017,751	29,000,180

Date.	Pennsylvania.	Delaware.	Maryland.	Dist. of Columbia.	North Carolina.	South Carolina.	Georgia.	Louisiana.	Ohio.
1876-7	$17,577,468	....	$19,543,907	....	....	....	....	....	$10,041,720
1877-8	17,923,825	....	19,739,200	$382,905	....	....	....	$1,932,330	8,623,245
1878-9	19,923,951	....	19,981,300	280,009	....	....	....	2,009,835	8,790,811
1879-0	23,956,285	....	....	307,992	....	....	....	....	9,710,771
1880-1	26,895,205	....	23,824,354	462,930	....	....	....	....	10,902,052
1881-2	29,913,605	....	25,989,874	518,532	....	....	....	....	12,417,317
1882-3	32,347,733	....	27,205,225	690,400	....	....	....	....	12,909,606
1883-4	34,031,154	....	28,336,934	622,304	....	....	....	....	....
1884-5	35,362,660	....	28,603,083	731,733	....	....	....	....	12,005,008
1885-6	37,530,870	....	30,512,992	703,943	....	....	....	....	12,823,374
1886-7	42,219,099	$2,771,392	19,020,963	834,524	$11,307	....	....	....	15,065,659
1887-8	55,469,516	3,187,886	32,413,087	923,958	127,180	$3,243,811	$1,701,282	664,008	31,802,484

Date.	Indiana.	Illinois.	Michigan.	Iowa.	Minnesota.	Utah.
1876-'77	$1,986,025	....	....	....	$280,146	....
1877-'78	....	....	....	....	....	....
1878-'79	....	....	....	....	....	....
1879-'80	....	....	....	....	....	....
1880-'81	1,330,056	....	....	....	....	....
1881-'82	....	....	....	....	....	....
1882-'83	1,755,256	....	....	....	....	....
1883-'84	2,108,428	....	....	....	....	....
1884-'85	2,171,009	....	....	....	3,105,926	....
1885-'86	....	....	....	....	3,654,528	....
1886-'87	2,312,013	$14,061,258	....	$9,060,010	3,801,650	....
1887-'88	2,615,907	11,830,854	$22,943,806	11,268,079	3,786,366	$409,067

* For the years 1830 to 1875 inclusive, from E. W. Keyes' History of Savings Banks in the United States; for later years from returns compiled in this Bureau.

PRIVATE BANKS—OFFICIAL AND UNOFFICIAL.

AGGREGATE RESOURCES AND LIABILITIES OF PRIVATE BANKS IN 1887 AND 1888.

Resources and liabilities.	1887.	1888.
	1,001 banks.	1,203 banks.
Resources.		
Loans on real estate	$17, 688, 540	$9, 574, 069
Loans on personal and collateral security	63, 774, 934	66, 607, 009
Other loans and discounts	21, 365, 262	26, 705, 379
Overdrafts	1, 858, 778	2, 072, 380
United States bonds	4, 351, 656	1, 718, 722
State bonds	356, 234	702, 404
Railroad bonds and stocks	2, 904, 872	1, 168, 584
Bank stocks	502, 091	695, 492
Other stocks, bonds, and mortgages	6, 743, 050	4, 417, 689
Due from other banks and bankers	22, 226, 065	20, 900, 801
Real estate, furniture, and fixtures	9, 757, 816	10, 110, 310
Current expenses and taxes paid	751, 547	908, 572
Gold coins Gold certificates Silver coins Silver certificates Legal tenders and national-bank notes	15, 663, 724	14, 827, 171
Other resources	3, 530, 870	3, 154, 578
Total	174, 478, 330	163, 713, 256
Liabilities.		
Capital	40, 079, 438	40, 842, 074
Surplus fund	12, 238, 065	9, 588, 238
Other undivided profits	5, 925, 835	5, 289, 748
State-bank notes outstanding	2, 155	21, 000
Dividends unpaid	170, 053	84, 658
Individual deposits	96, 580, 457	94, 878, 842
State, county, and municipal deposits	946, 192	2, 419, 440
Deposits of State, county, and municipal disbursing officers	1, 158, 903	1, 064, 039
Due to other banks and bankers	5, 818, 151	4, 901, 448
Other liabilities	11, 564, 066	4, 623, 769
Total	174, 478, 330	163, 713, 256

REPORT OF THE CONDITION OF THE NATIONAL SAVINGS BANK OF THE DISTRICT OF COLUMBIA, AT WASHINGTON, D. C., AT THE CLOSE OF BUSINESS ON THE 4TH DAY OF OCTOBER, 1888.

DR. CR.

RESOURCES.			LIABILITIES.		
Loans and discounts (see schedule)		$558, 201. 98	Undivided profits		$13, 251. 80
United States bonds on hand (par value), 4 per cents		200, 000. 00	Individual deposits subject to check	$957, 363. 45	
Other stocks, bonds, and mortgages (market value, see schedule)		170, 000. 00	Time certificates of deposit	1, 000. 00	
Due from State and private banks and bankers (see schedule)		3, 821. 35			958, 363. 45
Current expenses and taxes paid		3, 730. 75			
Premium (market value) on bonds		28, 000. 00			
Checks and other cash items (see schedule)		2, 777. 28			
Bills of other banks		60. 00			
Fractional paper currency, nickels, and cents		23. 89			
Specie, viz:					
Gold coin	$90. 00				
Silver coin	370. 00				
Silver Treasury certificates	1, 440. 00				
		1, 900. 00			
Legal-tender notes		2, 500. 00			
Total		971, 015. 25	Total		971, 015. 25

SCHEDULES.

Loans and discounts.

On mortgages and other real-estate security	$319, 383. 86
On United States bonds (demand loans)	4, 200. 00
On other stocks, bonds, etc. (demand loans)	234, 618. 12
	558, 201. 98

Other stocks, bonds, and mortgages.

50,000 District of Columbia 5s	$50, 000. 00
50,000 District of Columbia 6s	50, 000. 00
40,000 District of Columbia 3.65s	40, 000. 00
30,000 Georgia 7s	30, 000. 00
Total	170, 000. 00

I, Benjamin P. Snyder, president of the National Savings Bank of the District of Columbia, do solemnly swear that the above statement is true, to the best of my knowledge and belief.

BENJAMIN P. SNYDER,
President.

DISTRICT OF COLUMBIA,
City of Washington:

Sworn to and subscribed before me this 8th day of October, 1888.
[SEAL.]

GEO. W. BRAGG,
Notary Public.

Correct. Attest:

ANDREW WYLIE,
M. G. EMERY,
LEWIS CLEPHANE,
ZENAS C. ROBBINS,
Directors.

The highest rate of interest paid by the bank is 2 per cent.
Number of depositors October 1, 1888, 9,852.

AGGREGATE RESOURCES AND LIABILITIES

OF

THE NATIONAL BANKS

FROM

OCTOBER, 1863, TO OCTOBER, 1888.

AGGREGATE RESOURCES AND LIABILITIES OF THE NATIONAL

1863.

Resources.	JANUARY.	APRIL.	JULY.	OCTOBER 5.
				66 banks.
Loans and discounts	....	....	....	$5,466,088.33
U. S. bonds and securities	....	....	....	5,662,600.00
Other items	....	....	....	106,009.12
Due from nat'l and other b'ks	....	....	....	2,625,597.05
Real estate, furniture, etc	....	....	....	177,565.69
Current expenses	....	....	....	53,808.92
Premiums paid	....	....	....	2,503.69
Checks and other cash items	....	....	....	492,138.58
Bills of nat'l and other banks	....	....	....	764,725.00
Specie and other lawful mon'y	....	....	....	1,446,607.62
Total	....	....	....	16,797,644.00

1864.

	JANUARY 4.	APRIL 4.	JULY 4.	OCTOBER 3.
	139 banks.	307 banks.	467 banks.	508 banks.
Loans and discounts	$10,666,095.60	$31,593,943.43	$70,746,513.33	$93,238,657.92
U. S. bonds and securities	15,112,250.00	41,175,150.00	92,530,500.00	108,064,400.00
Other items	74,571.48	432,059.95	842,017.73	1,434,739.76
Due from national banks	....	4,699,479.56	15,[illegible]	10,965,720.47
Due from other b'ks and b'krs	*4,786,124.58	8,537,908.94	17,[illegible]	14,051,396.31
Real estate, furniture, etc	381,144.00	755,696.41	1,[illegible]	2,[illegible]
Current expenses	118,854.43	352,720.77	50[illegible]	1,021,569.02
Checks and other cash items	577,507.92	2,651,916.96	5,05[illegible]	7,640,169.14
Bills of nat'l and other banks	895,521.00	1,660,000.00	5,344,[illegible]	4,68[illegible]
Specie and other lawful mon'y	5,018,622.57	22,961,411.64	42,283,[illegible]	44,801,497.48
Total	37,630,691.58	114,820,287.66	252,273,[illegible]	297,108,[illegible]

1865.

	JANUARY 2.	APRIL 3.	JULY 3.	OCTOBER 2.
	638 banks.	907 banks.	1,294 banks.	1,513 banks.
Loans and discounts	$166,448,718.00	$252,404,208.07	$362,442,743.08	$487,170,136.29
U. S. bonds and securities	176,578,750.00	277,619,900.00	391,744,850.00	427,731,300.00
Other items	3,294,883.27	4,275,769.51	12,569,120.38	19,048,513.15
Due from national banks	30,820,175.44	40,963,243.47	76,977,539.59	89,978,980.55
Due from other b'ks and b'krs	19,836,072.83	22,554,636.57	26,078,028.01	17,393,232.25
Real estate, furniture, etc	4,083,226.12	6,525,118.80	11,231,257.28	14,703,281.77
Current expenses	1,053,725.84	2,298,025.65	2,338,775.56	4,539,525.11
Premiums paid	1,323,023.56	1,823,291.84	2,243,210.31	2,585,501.06
Checks and other cash items	17,837,496.77	29,681,394.13	41,314,904.50	72,309,854.44
Bills of nat'l and other banks	14,275,153.00	13,710,370.00	21,651,826.00	16,247,241.00
Specie	4,481,937.68	6,659,660.47	9,437,060.40	18,072,012.59
Legal tenders and frac'l cur'y	72,535,504.07	112,999,320.59	168,426,166.55	189,988,496.28
Total	512,568,666.68	771,514,939.10	1,126,455,481.66	1,359,768,074.49

* Including amount due from national banks.

1863.

BANKS FROM OCTOBER, 1863, TO OCTOBER, 1888.

Liabilities.	JANUARY.	APRIL.	JULY.	OCTOBER 5.
				66 banks.
Capital stock	....	....	....	$7,188,393.00
Undivided profits	....	....	....	128,030.06
Individual and other deposits	....	....	....	8,497,081.84
Due to nat'l and other banks*	....	....	....	981,178.59
Other items	....	....	....	2,360.51
Total	....	....	....	16,797,644.00

1864.

	JANUARY 4.	APRIL 4.	JULY 4.	OCTOBER 3.
	139 banks.	307 banks.	467 banks.	508 banks.
Capital stock	$14,740,522.00	$42,204,474.00	$75,213,945.00	$86,782,802.00
Surplus fund	....	....	1,129,910.22	2,010,286.10
Undivided profits	432,827.81	1,625,656.87	3,094,330.11	5,982,392.22
National b'knotes outstanding	30,155.00	9,797,975.00	25,825,665.00	45,260,504.00
Individual and other deposits	19,450,492.53	51,274,914.01	119,414,239.03	122,166,536.40
Due to nat'l and other banks*	2,153,779.38	6,814,930.40	27,382,006.37	34,862,384.81
Other items	822,914.86	3,102,337.38	213,708.02	43,289.77
Total	37,630,601.58	114,820,287.06	252,273,803.75	297,108,195.30

1865.

	JANUARY 2.	APRIL 3.	JULY 3.	OCTOBER 2.
	638 banks.	907 banks.	1,294 banks.	1,513 banks.
Capital stock	$135,618,874.00	$215,326,023.00	$325,834,558.00	$393,157,206.00
Surplus fund	8,663,311.22	17,318,942.65	31,303,565.64	38,713,380.72
Undivided profits	12,283,812.65	17,809,307.14	23,159,408.17	32,350,278.19
National b'knotes outstanding	66,769,375.00	98,896,488.00	131,452,158.00	171,321,903.00
Individual and other deposits	183,479,636.98	262,961,473.13	398,357,559.59	500,910,873.22
United States deposits	37,764,729.77	57,630,141.01	58,032,720.67	48,170,381.31
Due to national banks	30,619,175.57	41,301,031.16	78,261,045.64	90,044,837.08
Due to other b'ks and bankers*	37,104,130.62	59,692,581.64	79,591,594.93	84,155,161.27
Other items	205,620.87	578,951.37	462,871.02	944,053.70
Total	512,568,650.68	771,514,939.10	1,126,455,481.66	1,359,768,074.49

* Including State bank circulation outstanding.

AGGREGATE RESOURCES AND LIABILITIES OF THE NATIONAL

1866.

Resources.	JANUARY 1.	APRIL 2.	JULY 2.	OCTOBER 1.
	1,582 banks.	1,612 banks.	1,634 banks.	1,644 banks.
Loans and discounts	$500, 650, 109. 10	$528, 080, 526. 70	$550, 353, 094. 17	$603, 314, 704. 83
U.S. b'ds dep'd to secure circ'n	298, 376, 850. 00	315, 850, 300. 00	326, 483, 350. 00	331, 843, 200. 00
Other U.S. b'ds and securities	142, 003, 500. 00	125, 625, 750. 00	121, 152, 950. 00	94, 974, 650. 00
Oth'r stocks, b'ds, and mortg's	17, 483, 753. 18	17, 379, 738. 92	17, 565, 911. 46	15, 887, 490. 00
Due from national banks	93, 254, 551. 02	87, 564, 329. 71	96, 696, 482. 66	107, 650, 174. 18
Due from other b'ks and b'k'rs	14, 658, 229. 87	13, 682, 345. 12	13, 982, 613. 23	15, 211, 117. 16
Real estate, furniture, etc	15, 436, 296. 16	15, 895, 564. 46	16, 730, 923. 62	17, 134, 002. 58
Current expenses	3, 193, 717. 78	4, 927, 599. 79	3, 032, 716. 27	5, 311, 253. 35
Premiums paid	2, 423, 918. 02	2, 233, 516. 31	2, 398, 872. 26	2, 493, 773. 47
Checks and other cash items	89, 837, 684. 50	105, 490, 619. 36	96, 077, 134. 53	103, 684, 249. 21
Bills of national and other b'ks	20, 406, 442. 00	18, 279, 816. 00	17, 866, 742. 00	17, 437, 779. 00
Specie	19, 205, 018. 75	17, 529, 778. 42	12, 629, 376. 30	9, 226, 831. 82
Legal tenders and fract'l cur'y	187, 846, 548. 82	189, 867, 852. 52	201, 425, 041. 63	205, 793, 578. 76
Total	1, 404, 776, 010. 29	1, 442, 407, 737. 31	1, 476, 395, 208. 13	1, 526, 002, 804. 42

1867.

	JANUARY 7.	APRIL 1.	JULY 1.	OCTOBER 7.
	1,648 banks.	1,642 banks.	1,636 banks.	1,642 banks.
Loans and discounts	$608, 771, 799. 61	$597, 648, 286. 53	$588, 450, 396. 12	$609, 675, 214. 61
U.S. b'ds dep'd to secure circ'n	339, 570, 700. 00	338, 863, 650. 00	337, 684, 250. 00	338, 640, 150. 00
U.S. b'ds dep'd to sec're dep'ts	36, 185, 950. 00	38, 465, 800. 00	38, 368, 950. 00	37, 862, 100. 00
U.S. b'ds and sec'ties on hand	52, 949, 300. 00	46, 639, 400. 00	45, 633, 700. 00	42, 460, 800. 00
Oth'r stocks, b'ds, and mortg's	15, 073, 737. 45	20, 194, 875. 21	21, 452, 615. 43	21, 507, 881. 42
Due from national banks	92, 552, 206. 29	94, 121, 186. 21	92, 308, 911. 87	95, 217, 610. 14
Due from other b'ks and b'k'rs	12, 996, 157. 40	10, 737, 392. 90	9, 663, 322. 82	8, 389, 226. 47
Real estate, furniture, etc	18, 925, 315. 51	19, 625, 893. 81	19, 800, 905. 86	20, 639, 708. 23
Current expenses	2, 822, 675. 18	5, 693, 784. 17	3, 249, 153. 31	5, 297, 494. 13
Premiums paid	2, 860, 398. 85	3, 411, 325. 56	3, 338, 600. 37	2, 764, 186. 35
Checks and other cash items	101, 430, 220. 18	87, 951, 405. 13	128, 312, 177. 79	134, 603, 231. 51
Bills of national banks	10, 263, 718. 00	12, 873, 785. 00	16, 138, 769. 00	11, 841, 104. 00
Bills of other banks	1, 176, 142. 00	825, 748. 00	531, 267. 00	333, 209. 00
Specie	19, 726, 043. 20	11, 444, 529. 15	11, 128, 672. 98	12, 798, 044. 40
Legal tenders and fract'l cu'y	104, 872, 371. 64	92, 861, 254. 17	102, 534, 613. 46	100, 550, 849. 01
Compound-interest notes	82, 047, 250. 00	84, 065, 790. 00	75, 488, 220. 00	56, 888, 250. 00
Total	1, 511, 222, 985. 40	1, 465, 451, 105. 84	1, 494, 084, 526. 01	1, 499, 469, 060. 17

1868.

	JANUARY 6.	APRIL 6.	JULY 6.	OCTOBER 5.
	1,642 banks.	1,643 banks.	1,640 banks.	1,643 banks.
Loans and discounts	$616, 603, 479. 89	$628, 029, 347. 65	$655, 729, 546. 42	$657, 668, 847. 83
U.S. b'ds dep'd to secure circ'n	339, 064, 200. 00	339, 686, 650. 00	339, 569, 100. 00	340, 487, 050. 00
U.S. b'ds dep'd to sec're dept's	37, 315, 750. 00	37, 446, 000. 00	37, 853, 150. 00	37, 360, 150. 00
U.S. b'ds and sec'ties on hand	44, 164, 500. 00	45, 958, 550. 00	43, 068, 350. 00	36, 817, 600. 00
Oth'r stocks, b'ds, and mortg's	19, 365, 864. 77	19, 874, 384. 33	20, 007, 327. 42	20, 693, 406. 40
Due from national banks	99, 311, 446. 60	95, 900, 606. 35	114, 434, 097. 93	102, 278, 547. 77
Due from other b'ks and b'k'rs	8, 480, 199. 74	7, 074, 207. 44	8, 642, 456. 72	7, 848, 822. 24
Real estate, furniture, etc	21, 125, 665. 68	22, 082, 570. 25	22, 699, 829. 70	22, 747, 875. 18
Current expenses	2, 986, 893. 86	5, 428, 460. 25	2, 938, 519. 04	5, 278, 911. 22
Premiums paid	2, 464, 536. 96	2, 660, 106. 09	2, 432, 074. 37	1, 819, 815. 50
Checks and other cash items	109, 390, 266. 37	114, 993, 036. 23	124, 076, 097. 71	143, 241, 394. 99
Bills of national banks	16, 655, 572. 00	12, 573, 514. 00	13, 210, 179. 00	11, 842, 974. 00
Bills of other banks	261, 269. 00	196, 106. 00	342, 550. 00	222, 668. 00
Fractional currency	1, 927, 876. 78	1, 825, 610. 16	1, 863, 358. 91	2, 262, 791. 97
Specie	20, 981, 601. 45	18, 373, 943. 22	20, 755, 919. 04	13, 003, 713. 39
Legal-tender notes	114, 306, 491. 00	84, 390, 219. 00	100, 166, 100. 00	92, 453, 475. 00
Compound-interest notes	39, 997, 030. 00	38, 917, 490. 00	19, 473, 420. 00	4, 513, 730. 00
Three per cent. certificates	8, 245, 000. 00	24, 255, 000. 00	44, 905, 000. 00	59, 080, 000. 00
Total	1, 502, 647, 644. 10	1, 499, 668, 920. 07	1, 572, 167, 076. 26	1, 559, 621, 773. 49

BANKS FROM OCTOBER, 1863, TO OCTOBER, 1888—Continued.

1866.

Liabilities.	JANUARY 1. 1,582 banks.	APRIL 2. 1,612 banks.	JULY 2. 1,634 banks.	OCTOBER 1. 1,644 banks.
Capital stock	$403, 357, 346. 00	$409, 273, 534. 00	$414, 270, 493. 00	$415, 472, 369. 00
Surplus fund	43, 000, 370. 78	44, 687, 810. 54	50, 151, 991. 77	53, 359, 277. 64
Undivided profits	28, 972, 493. 70	30, 964, 422. 73	29, 286, 175. 45	32, 593, 486. 69
National b'k notes outstand'g	213, 239, 530. 00	248, 886, 282. 00	267, 798, 678. 00	280, 253, 818. 00
State bank notes outstanding	45, 449, 155. 00	33, 800, 865. 00	19, 996, 163. 00	9, 748, 025. 00
Individual deposits	522, 507, 829. 27	534, 734, 950. 33	533, 338, 174. 25	564, 616, 777. 64
U. S. deposits	29, 747, 236. 15	29, 150, 729. 82	36, 038, 185. 03	30, 420, 819. 80
Dep'ts of U.S. disb'sing officers	....	....	3, 066, 892. 22	2, 979, 955. 77
Due to national banks	94, 709, 074. 15	89, 067, 501. 54	96, 496, 726. 42	110, 531, 957. 31
Due to other b'ks and bankers	23, 793, 584. 24	21, 841, 641. 35	25, 951, 728. 99	26, 986, 317. 57
Total	1, 404, 776, 619. 29	1, 442, 407, 737. 31	1, 476, 305, 208. 13	1, 526, 962, 804. 42

1867.

	JANUARY 7. 1,648 banks.	APRIL 1. 1,642 banks.	JULY 1. 1,636 banks.	OCTOBER 7. 1,642 banks.
Capital stock	$420, 229, 739. 00	$419, 399, 484. 00	$418, 558, 148. 00	$420, 073, 415. 00
Surplus fund	59, 992, 874. 57	60, 206, 013. 58	63, 232, 811. 12	66, 695, 587. 01
Undivided profits	26, 961, 382. 60	31, 131, 034. 39	30, 656, 222. 84	33, 751, 446. 21
National b'k notes outstand'g	291, 436, 749. 00	292, 788, 572. 00	291, 769, 553. 00	293, 887, 941. 00
State bank notes outstanding	6, 961, 499. 00	5, 460, 312. 00	4, 484, 112. 00	4, 092, 153. 00
Individual deposits	558, 699, 768. 06	512, 046, 182. 47	539, 599, 076. 10	540, 797, 837. 51
U. S. deposits	27, 284, 876. 93	27, 473, 005. 66	29, 838, 391. 53	23, 062, 119. 92
Dep's of U.S. disb'sing officers	2, 477, 509. 48	2, 650, 981. 39	3, 474, 192. 74	4, 352, 379. 43
Due to national banks	92, 761, 998. 43	91, 156, 890. 89	89, 821, 751. 60	99, 111, 240. 89
Due to other b'ks and bankers	24, 416, 588. 33	23, 138, 629. 46	22, 659, 267. 08	19, 644, 940. 20
Total	1, 511, 222, 985. 40	1, 465, 451, 105. 84	1, 494, 084, 526. 01	1, 499, 469, 060. 17

1868.

	JANUARY 6. 1,642 banks.	APRIL 6. 1,643 banks.	JULY 6. 1,640 banks.	OCTOBER 5. 1,643 banks.
Capital stock	$420, 260, 790. 00	$420, 676, 210. 00	$420, 105, 011. 00	$420, 634, 511. 00
Surplus fund	70, 586, 125. 70	72, 349, 119. 60	75, 840, 118. 94	77, 995, 761. 40
Undivided profits	31, 399, 877. 57	32, 861, 597. 08	33, 543, 223. 35	36, 095, 883. 98
National b'k notes outstand'g	294, 377, 390. 00	295, 336, 044. 00	294, 908, 264. 00	295, 769, 489. 00
State bank notes outstanding	3, 792, 013. 00	3, 310, 177. 00	3, 163, 771. 00	2, 906, 352. 00
Individual deposits	534, 704, 709. 00	532, 011, 480. 36	575, 842, 070. 12	580, 940, 820. 85
U. S. deposits	24, 305, 638. 02	22, 750, 342. 77	24, 603, 676. 96	17, 573, 250. 64
Dep'ts of U.S. disb'si'g officers	3, 208, 783. 03	4, 976, 682. 31	3, 499, 369. 99	4, 570, 478. 16
Due to national banks	98, 144, 669. 61	94, 073, 631. 25	113, 306, 346. 34	99, 414, 397. 28
Due to other b'ks and bankers	21, 867, 648. 17	21, 323, 636. 60	27, 355, 204. 56	23, 720, 829. 18
Total	1, 502, 647, 044. 10	1, 499, 668, 920. 97	1, 572, 167, 076. 26	1, 559, 021, 773. 49

AGGREGATE RESOURCES AND LIABILITIES OF THE NATIONAL

1869.

Resources.	JANUARY 4.	APRIL 17.	JUNE 12.	OCTOBER 9.
	1,628 banks.	1,620 banks.	1,619 banks.	1,617 banks.
Loans and discounts	$644, 945, 039. 53	$662, 084, 813. 47	$680, 347, 755. 81	$682, 883, 106. 97
U. S. bonds to secure circ'lat'n	338, 539, 950. 00	338, 379, 250. 00	338, 699, 750. 00	339, 480, 100. 00
U. S. bonds to secure deposits.	34, 538, 350. 00	29, 721, 350. 00	27, 625, 350. 00	18, 704, 000. 00
U. S. b'ds and sec'ties on hand.	35, 010, 600. 00	30, 226, 550. 00	27, 476, 650. 00	25, 903, 950. 00
Oth'r stocks, b'ds, and mortg's	20, 127, 732. 96	20, 074, 435. 09	20, 777, 560. 53	22, 250, 697. 14
Due from redeeming agents	65, 727, 070. 80	57, 554, 382. 55	62, 912, 636 82	56, 669, 562 84
Due from other national b'nks	36, 067, 316. 84	30, 520, 527. 89	35, 556, 504. 53	35, 393, 563. 47
Due from State b'ks and b'k'rs	7, 715, 719. 34	8, 075, 595. 60	9, 140, 010. 24	8, 700, 418. 57
Real estate, furniture, etc	23, 269, 838. 28	23, 798, 188. 13	23, 859, 271. 17	25, 169, 188 95
Current expenses	3, 265, 990. 81	5, 641, 195. 01	5, 820, 577 87	5, 646, 382. 96
Premiums paid	1, 654, 352. 70	1, 716, 210. 13	1, 809, 070 01	2, 092, 364. 85
Checks and other cash items.	142, 605, 984. 92	154, 137, 191. 23	161, 614, 852. 66	108, 809, 817. 37
Bills of other national banks.	14, 684, 799. 00	11, 725, 239. 00	11, 524, 447. 00	10, 776, 023. 00
Fractional currency	2, 280, 471. 06	2, 088, 545. 18	1, 804, 855. 53	2, 090, 727. 38
Specie	29, 626, 750. 26	9, 944, 532. 15	18, 455, 090, 48	23, 002, 405. 83
Legal-tender notes	88, 239, 300. 00	80, 875, 161. 00	80. 934, 119. 00	83, 719, 295. 00
Three per cent. certificates	52, 075, 000. 00	51, 190, 000. 00	49, 815, 000. 00	45, 845, 000. 00
Total	1, 540, 394, 266. 50	1, 517, 753, 107. 03	1, 564, 174, 410. 65	1, 497, 226, 604. 33

1870.

	JANUARY 22.	MARCH 24.	JUNE 9.	OCTOBER 8.	DECEMBER 28.
	1,615 banks.	1,615 banks.	1,612 banks.	1,615 banks.	1,648 banks.
Loans and discounts	$688, 875, 203. 70	$710, 848, 609. 39	$719, 341, 186. 06	$715, 928, 079. 81	$725, 515, 538. 40
Bonds for circulation	339, 350, 750 00	339, 251, 350. 00	338, 845, 200. 00	340, 857, 450. 00	344, 104, 200. 00
Bonds for deposits	17, 592, 000. 00	16, 102, 000. 00	15, 704, 000. 00	15, 381, 500. 00	15, 189, 500. 00
U. S. bonds on hand.	24, 677, 100 00	27, 292, 150. 00	28, 276, 600. 00	22, 323, 800. 00	23, 893, 300. 00
Other stocks and b'ds	21, 082, 412 00	20, 524, 294. 55	23, 300, 681. 87	23, 614, 721. 25	22, 686, 358. 59
Due from red'g ag'nts	71, 641. 486 05	73, 435, 117. 98	74, 635, 405. 61	66, 275, 668. 92	64, 805, 062. 88
Due from nat'l banks	31, 994, 600. 26	29. 510, 688. 11	36, 128, 750. 66	33, 948, 805. 65	37, 478, 166. 49
Due from State banks	9. 310, 560. 54	10, 238, 219. 85	10, 430, 781. 32	9, 202, 496. 71	9. 824, 144. 18
Real estate, etc	26, 002, 713. 01	26, 330, 701. 24	26, 593, 357. 00	27, 470, 746. 97	28, 021, 637. 44
Current expenses	3, 469, 588. 00	6, 683, 189. 54	6, 324, 955. 47	5, 871, 750. 02	6, 905, 073. 32
Premiums paid	2, 439, 591. 41	2, 680, 882. 39	3, 076, 456. 74	2, 491, 222. 11	3, 251, 648. 72
Cash items	111, 624, 822. 00	11, 267, 703. 12	11, 497, 534. 13	12, 536, 613. 57	13, 229, 403. 34
Cl'r'g-house exch'gs.	....	75, 317, 902. 22	83, 936, 515. 64	79, 089, 688. 39	76, 208, 707. 00
National bank notes.	15. 840. 669. 00	14, 226, 817. 00	16, 342, 582. 00	12, 512, 927. 00	17, 001, 846. 00
Fractional currency	2, 476, 966. 75	2, 285, 499. 03	2, 184, 714. 39	2. 078. 178. 05	2, 150, 522. 89
Specie	48, 345, 383. 72	37, 096, 543. 44	31, 099, 437. 78	18, 460, 011. 47	26, 307, 251. 59
Legal-tender notes	87, 708, 502. 00	84, 485, 978. 00	94, 573, 751. 00	79, 324, 577. 00	80, 580, 745. 00
Three per cent. cert'fs	43, 820, 000. 00	43, 570, 000. 00	43, 465, 000. 00	43, 345, 000. 00	41, 845, 000. 00
Total	1,546,261,357. 44	1,529,147,735. 85	1,565,756,909. 67	1,510,713,236. 92	1,538,998,105 93

1871.

	MARCH 18.	APRIL 29.	JUNE 10.	OCTOBER 2.	DECEMBER 16.
	1,688 banks.	1,707 banks.	1,723 banks.	1,767 banks.	1,790 banks.
Loans and discounts.	$767, 858, 490. 59	$779, 321, 828. 11	$789, 416, 568. 13	$831, 552, 210. 00	$818, 996, 311. 74
Bonds for circulation	351, 556, 700. 00	354, 427, 200 00	357, 388, 950. 00	364, 475, 800. 00	366. 840, 200. 00
Bonds for deposits	15. 231, 500. 00	15, 236, 500. 00	15, 250, 500. 00	28, 087, 500. 00	23, 155, 150. 00
U. S. bonds on hand	23, 011, 350. 00	22, 487, 950. 00	24, 200, 300. 00	17, 753, 650. 00	17, 675, 500. 00
Other stocks and b'ds	22, 763, 869. 20	22, 414, 659. 05	23, 132, 871. 05	24, 517, 059. 35	23, 061, 184. 20
Due from red'g ag'nts	83, 809, 188. 93	85, 061, 016. 31	93, 309, 246. 71	86, 878, 608. 84	77. 985, 600. 53
Due from nat'l banks	30, 201, 119. 99	38, 332, 679. 74	39, 636, 579. 35	43, 525, 362. 05	43, 313, 344. 78
Due from State banks	10, 271, 005. 34	11, 478, 174. 71	11, 853, 308. 60	12, 772, 669. 83	13, 069, 301. 40
Real estate, etc	28. 805, 814. 79.	29, 242, 762. 79	29 637, 999. 30	30, 089, 783. 85	30, 070, 330. 57
Current expenses	6 694, 014. 17	6, 764, 159. 73	6, 295, 099. 46	6, 153, 370. 29	7, 330, 424. 12
Premiums paid	3, 939, 995. 20	4, 414, 755. 40	5, 026, 583. 07	5, 500, 890. 17	5, 956, 073. 74
Cash items	11, 642, 644. 74	12, 749, 289. 84	13, 101, 497. 95	14, 058, 208. 80	13, 784. 424. 76
Cl'r'g-house exch'gs.	100, 693, 917. 54	130. 855, 698. 15	102, 091, 311. 75	101. 165, 854. 52	114, 538, 539 93
National bank notes	13, 137, 006. 00	16, 632, 323. 00	19. 101, 389. 00	14, 197, 653. 00	13, 085, 904 00
Fractional currency.	2. 103, 298. 16	2, 135, 763. 09	2 160, 713. 22	2, 095, 485. 79	2, 061, 600. 89
Specie	25, 709, 166. 64	22, 732, 027. 02	19, 924, 955. 16	13, 252, 998. 17	29, 595, 299 56
Legal-tender notes	91, 072, 349. 00	106. 219, 126. 00	122, 137, 660. 00	109, 414, 735. 00	93, 942, 707. 00
Three per cent. cert'fs	37, 570, 000. 00	33, 935, 000. 00	30, 690, 000. 00	25, 075, 000. 00	21, 400, 000. 00
Total	1,627,032,030. 28	1,694.440,012. 94	1,703,415,335. 65	1,730,566,899. 72	1,715,861,807. 22

BANKS FROM OCTOBER, 1863, TO OCTOBER, 1883—Continued.

1869.

Liabilities.	JANUARY 4.	APRIL 17.	JUNE 12.	OCTOBER 9.
	1,628 banks.	1,620 banks.	1,619 banks.	1,617 banks.
Capital stock	$419,040,931.00	$420,818,721.00	$422,659,260.00	$426,399,151.00
Surplus fund	81,169,936.52	82,653,989.10	82,218,576.47	86,165,334.32
Undivided profits	35,318,273.71	37,489,314.82	43,812,898.70	40,687,300.92
Nat'l bank notes outstanding	294,476,702.00	292,457,098.00	292,753,286.00	293,593,645.00
State bank notes outstanding	2,734,669.00	2,615,387.00	2,558,874.00	2,454,697.00
Individual deposits	568,530,934.11	547,922,174.91	574,307,382.77	511,400,196.63
U. S. deposits	13,211,850.19	10,114,328.32	10,301,907.71	7,112,646.67
Dep'ts U.S. disburs'g officers	3,472,884.90	3,005,131.61	2,454,048.99	4,516,648.12
Due to national banks	95,453,139.33	92,662,648.49	100,933,910.03	95,067,892.83
Due to State banks and b'k'rs	26,964,945.74	23,018,010.62	28,040,771.30	23,849,371.62
Notes and bills re-discounted	....	2,464,849.81	2,392,205.61	3,839,357.10
Bills payable	....	1,870,913.26	1,735,280.07	2,140,363.12
Total	1,540,394,266.50	1,517,753,167.03	1,564,174,410.65	1,497,226,004.33

1870.

	JANUARY 22.	MARCH 24.	JUNE 9.	OCTOBER 8.	DECEMBER 28.
	1,615 banks.	1,615 banks.	1,612 banks.	1,615 banks.	1,648 banks.
Capital stock	$426,074,954.00	$427,504,247.00	$427,235,701.00	$430,399,301.00	$435,356,004.00
Surplus fund	90,174,281.14	90,229,954.50	91,689,834.12	94,061,438.95	94,705,740.34
Undivided profits	34,300,430.80	43,109,471.62	42,861,712.59	38,608,618.91	46,056,428.55
Nat'l bank circulat'n	292,838,935.00	292,509,149.00	291,183,614.00	291,798,640.00	296,205,446.00
State bank circulat'n	2,351,993.00	2,279,469.00	2,222,793.00	2,138,548.00	2,091,799.00
Dividends unpaid	2,299,296.27	1,483,416.15	1,517,595.18	2,462,591.31	2,242,556.49
Individual deposits	546,236,881.57	516,058,085.26	542,261,563.18	501,407,586.90	507,368,618.67
U. S. deposits	6,750,139.19	6,424,421.25	10,677,873.92	6,807,978.49	6,074,407.90
Dep'ts U.S. dis. offic's	2,592,001.21	4,778,225.93	2,592,967.54	4,550,142.68	4,155,304.25
Due to national banks	108,351,300.33	109,667,715.95	115,456,491.84	109,348,292.45	100,090,414.53
Due to State banks	28,904,849.14	29,767,575.21	33,012,162.78	29,693,910.80	29,200,587.29
Notes re-discounted	3,842,542.30	2,462,647.40	2,741,843.53	3,843,577.67	4,612,131.08
Bills payable	1,543,753.49	2,873,357.40	2,302,756.09	4,592,609.76	4,838,667.83
Total	1,546,261,357.44	1,529,147,735.85	1,565,756,909.07	1,510,713,236.92	1,538,998,105.03

1871.

	MARCH 18.	APRIL 29.	JUNE 10.	OCTOBER 2.	DECEMBER 16.
	1,688 banks.	1,707 banks.	1,723 banks.	1,767 banks.	1,790 banks.
Capital stock	$444,232,771.00	$446,925,493.00	$450,330,841.00	$458,255,696.00	$460,225,866.00
Surplus funds	96,862,081.06	97,620,099.28	98,322,203.60	101,112,671.91	101,573,153.62
Undivided profits	43,883,857.64	44,776,030.71	45,535,227.79	42,008,714.38	48,630,925.81
Nat'l bank circulat'n	301,713,460.00	306,131,393.00	307,793,880.00	315,519,117.00	318,265,481.00
State bank circulat'n	2,035,800.00	1,982,580.00	1,968,058.00	1,921,056.00	1,886,538.00
Dividends unpaid	1,263,767.70	2,235,248.46	1,408,628.25	4,540,194.61	1,393,427.98
Individual deposits	561,190,830.41	611,025,174.16	602,110,758.16	600,868,486.55	596,586,487.51
U. S. deposits	6,314,957.81	6,521,572.92	6,265,167.94	20,511,935.98	14,829,525.65
Dep'ts U.S. dis. offic's	4,813,016.66	3,757,873.84	4,893,907.25	5,393,598.89	5,399,108.34
Due to national b'nks	118,904,865.84	128,037,409.17	135,167,847.69	131,730,713.04	118,657,614.16
Due to State banks	37,311,519.13	36,113,200.67	41,219,802.06	40,211,971.07	38,116,950.67
Notes re-discounted	3,256,896.42	3,573,723.02	3,120,039.09	3,964,552.57	4,922,455.78
Bills payable	5,248,206.01	5,740,964.77	5,278,973.72	4,528,191.12	5,374,302.67
Total	1,627,032,030.28	1,694,440,012.94	1,703,415,335.65	1,730,566,899.72	1,715,861,897.22

AGGREGATE RESOURCES AND LIABILITIES OF THE NATIONAL

1872.

Resources.	FEBRUARY 27.	APRIL 19.	JUNE 10.	OCTOBER 3.	DECEMBER 27.
	1,814 banks.	1,843 banks	1,853 banks.	1,919 banks.	1,940 banks.
Loans and discounts	$839, 665, 077. 91	$844, 902, 253. 49	$871, 531, 448. 67	$877, 197, 923. 47	$885, 653, 449. 62
Bonds for circulation	370, 924, 700. 00	374, 428, 450. 00	377, 029, 700. 00	382, 046, 400. 00	384, 458, 500. 00
Bonds for deposits..	15, 870, 000. 00	15, 169, 000. 00	15, 409, 950. 00	15, 479, 750. 00	16, 304, 750. 00
U. S. bonds on hand	21, 323, 150. 00	19, 292, 100. 00	16, 458, 250. 00	12, 142, 550. 00	10, 306, 100. 00
Other stocks and b'ds	22, 838, 388. 80	21, 538, 914. 06	22, 270, 610. 47	23, 533, 151. 73	23, 100, 557. 29
Due from red'g ag'nts	89, 518, 329. 93	82, 120, 017. 24	91, 564, 269. 53	80, 717, 071. 30	86, 401, 459. 44
Due from nat'l banks	38, 282, 905. 86	36, 097, 592. 81	39, 468, 323. 39	34, 486, 593. 87	42, 707, 613. 54
Due from State banks	12, 209, 822. 68	12, 299, 716. 94	13, 014, 265. 26	12, 976, 878. 01	12, 008, 843. 54
Real estate, etc	30, 637, 676. 75	30, 809, 274. 98	31, 123, 843. 21	32, 276, 498. 17	33, 014, 796. 83
Current expenses ...	6, 265, 655. 13	7, 026, 041. 23	6, 719, 794. 90	6, 310, 428. 79	8, 454, 803. 97
Premiums paid......	6, 308, 821. 86	6, 544, 279. 29	6, 616, 174. 75	6, 546, 848. 52	7, 097, 847. 86
Cash items..........	12, 143, 403. 12	12, 461, 171. 40	13, 458, 753. 80	14, 916, 784. 34	13, 696, 723. 85
Clear'g-house exch'gs	93, 154, 319. 74	114, 195, 966. 36	88, 592, 800. 16	110, 086, 315. 37	90, 145, 482. 72
National-bank notes.	15, 552, 087. 00	18, 492, 832. 00	16, 253, 560. 00	15, 787, 296. 00	19, 070, 322. 00
Fractional currency.	2, 278, 143. 24	2, 143, 249. 29	2, 069, 404. 12	2, 151, 747. 88	2, 270, 576. 32
Specie..............	25, 507, 825. 32	24, 433, 899. 46	24, 256, 644. 14	10, 229, 756. 79	19, 047, 336. 45
Legal-tender notes ..	97, 865, 400. 00	105, 732, 455. 00	122, 994, 417. 00	105, 121, 104. 00	102, 922, 369. 00
U.S.cer'fs of deposit	....	....	....	6, 710, 000. 00	12, 650, 000. 00
Three per cent.cert'fs	18, 980, 000. 00	15, 365, 000. 00	12, 005, 000. 00	7, 140, 000. 00	4, 185, 000. 00
Total............	1,719,415,057. 34	1,743,652,213. 55	1,770,837,269. 40	1,755,857,098. 24	1,773,556,532. 43

1873.

	FEBRUARY 28.	APRIL 25.	JUNE 13.	SEPTEMBER 12.	DECEMBER 26.
	1,947 banks.	1,962 banks.	1,968 banks.	1,976 banks.	1,976 banks.
Loans and discounts.	$913, 265, 189. 67	$912, 064, 267. 31	$925, 557, 682. 42	$944, 220, 116. 34	$856, 816, 555. 06
Bonds for circulation	384, 675, 050. 00	386, 763, 800. 00	388, 080, 300. 00	388, 330, 400. 00	389, 384, 400. 00
Bonds for deposits ..	15, 035, 000. 00	16, 235, 000. 00	15, 935, 000. 00	14, 805, 000. 00	14, 815, 200. 00
U. S. bonds on hand	10, 436, 950. 00	9, 613, 550. 00	9, 789, 400. 00	8, 824, 850. 00	8, 630, 850. 00
Other stocks and b'ds	22, 063, 306. 20	22, 449, 146. 04	22, 912, 415. 63	23, 709, 034. 53	24, 358, 125. 06
Due from red'g ag'nts	95, 773, 077. 10	88, 815, 557. 80	97, 143, 326. 94	96, 134, 120. 66	73, 032, 046. 87
Due from nat'l banks	39, 483, 700. 09	38, 671, 088. 63	43, 328, 792. 29	41. 413, 680. 06	40, 404, 757. 97
Due from State banks	13, 595, 679. 17	12, 883, 353. 37	14, 073, 287. 77	12, 022, 873. 41	11, 185, 253. 08
Real estate, etc......	34, 023, 057. 77	34, 210, 878. 07	34, 820, 562. 77	34, 661, 823. 21	35, 556, 746. 48
Current expenses ...	6, 977, 831. 35	7, 410, 045. 87	7, 154, 211. 69	6, 985, 436. 99	8, 678, 270. 39
Premiums paid......	7, 205, 259. 67	7, 559, 987. 67	7, 890, 962. 14	7, 752, 843. 87	7, 987, 107. 14
Cash items	11, 761, 711. 50	11, 425, 209. 00	13, 036, 482. 58	11, 433, 913. 22	12, 321, 972. 80
Clear'g-house exch'gs	131, 386, 860. 95	94, 132, 125. 24	91, 918, 526. 59	88, 926, 003. 53	62, 881, 342. 16
National-bank notes.	15, 998, 779. 00	19, 310, 202. 00	20, 394, 772. 00	16, 103, 842. 00	21, 403, 179. 00
Fractional currency.	2, 289, 680. 21	2, 198, 973. 37	2, 197, 559. 84	2, 302, 775. 26	2, 287, 454. 03
Specie..............	17, 777, 673. 53	16, 868, 808. 74	27, 950, 086. 72	19, 868, 469. 45	26, 907, 037. 58
Legal-tender notes..	97, 141, 909. 00	100, 605, 287. 00	106, 381, 491. 00	92, 522, 662. 00	108, 719, 506. 00
U.S.cert'fs of deposit	18, 460, 000. 00	18, 370, 000. 00	22, 365, 000. 00	20, 610, 000. 00	24, 010, 000. 00
Three per cent.cert'fs	1, 805, 000. 00	710, 000. 00	305, 000. 00	....	....
Total..........	1,839,152,715. 21	1,800,303,280. 11	1,851,234,860. 38	1,830,627,845. 53	1,720,380,303. 61

1874.

	FEBRUARY 27.	MAY 1.	JUNE 26.	OCTOBER 2.	DECEMBER 31.
	1,975 banks.	1,978 banks.	1,983 banks.	2,004 banks.	2,027 banks.
Loans and discounts	$897, 859, 600. 46	$923, 347 030. 79	$926, 195, 671. 70	$954, 394, 791. 59	$955, 862, 580. 51
Bonds for circulation	380, 614, 700. 00	380, 240, 100. 00	390, 281, 700. 00	383, 254, 800. 00	382, 976, 200. 00
Bonds for deposits ..	14, 600, 200. 00	14, 890, 200. 00	14, 890, 200. 00	14, 691, 700. 00	14, 714, 000. 00
U. S. bonds on hand	11, 043, 400. 00	10, 152, 000. 00	10, 456, 900. 00	13, 313, 550. 00	15, 290, 300. 00
Other stocks and b'ds	25, 305, 736. 24	25, 460, 460. 20	27, 010, 727. 48	27, 807, 826. 92	28, 313, 473. 12
Due from res've ag'ts	101, 502, 861. 58	94, 017, 603. 31	97, 871, 517. 06	83, 885, 126. 94	80, 488, 831. 45
Due from nat'l banks	36, 624, 001. 30	41, 291, 015. 24	45, 770, 715. 59	39, 695, 309. 47	48. 100, 842. 62
Due from State banks	11, 496, 711. 47	12, 374, 391. 28	12, 469, 592. 33	11, 196, 611. 73	11, 655, 573. 07
Real estate, etc......	36, 043, 741. 50	36, 708, 066. 39	37, 270, 876. 51	38, 112, 926. 52	39, 190, 683. 04
Current expenses ...	6, 998, 875. 75	7, 547, 203. 05	7, 550, 125. 20	7, 658, 738. 82	5, 510, 566. 47
Premiums paid......	8, 741, 028. 77	8, 680, 370. 84	8, 563, 262. 27	8, 376, 659. 07	8, 626, 112. 16
Cash items	10, 269, 955. 50	11, 949, 020. 71	10, 496, 257. 00	12, 296, 416. 77	14, 005, 517. 33
Clear'g-house exch'gs	62, 768, 119. 19	94, 877, 796. 52	63, 896, 271. 31	97, 383, 687. 11	112, 995, 317. 55
National-bank notes.	20, 003, 251. 00	20, 673, 452. 00	23, 527, 991. 00	18, 450, 013. 00	22, 532, 336. 00
Fractional currency.	2, 309, 919. 73	2, 187, 186. 69	2, 263, 898. 92	2, 224, 943. 12	2, 392, 668. 74
Specie	33, 365, 863. 58	32, 569, 969. 26	22, 326, 207. 27	21, 240, 945. 23	22, 436, 761. 04
Legal-tender notes..	102, 717, 563. 00	101, 692, 930. 00	103, 108, 350. 00	80, 021, 946. 00	82, 604, 791. 00
U.S.cert'fs of deposit	37, 235, 000. 00	40, 135, 000. 00	47, 780, 000. 00	42, 825, 000. 00	33, 670, 000. 00
Dep. with U. S. Treas	....	....	91, 250. 00	20, 349, 950. 15	21, 043, 084. 36
Total..........	1,808,500,529. 16	1,867,802,796. 28	1,851,840,913. 64	1,877,180,942. 44	1,902,409,638. 46

BANKS FROM OCTOBER, 1863, TO OCTOBER, 1888—Continued.

1872.

Liabilities.	FEBRUARY 27.	APRIL 19.	JUNE 10.	OCTOBER 3.	DECEMBER 27.
	1,814 banks.	1,843 banks.	1,853 banks.	1,919 banks.	1,940 banks.
Capital stock........	$464,081,744.00	$467,924,318.00	$470,543,301.00	$479,629,174.00	$482,606,252.00
Surplus fund........	103,787,082.02	104,312,525.81	105,181,943.28	110,257,516.45	111,410,248.98
Undivided profits ...	43,310,344.46	46,428,590.90	50,234,298.33	46,623,784.50	50,762,411.80
Nat'l bank circulation	321,634,675.00	325,305,752.00	327,092,752.00	333,495,027.00	336,289,285.00
State bank circulation	1,830,563.00	1,763,885.00	1,700,935.00	1,567,143.00	1,511,396.00
Dividends unpaid ...	1,451,746.29	1,501,014.45	1,454,044.06	3,149,749.61	1,356,934.48
Individual deposits..	593,645,666.16	620,775,265.78	618,801,619.49	613,290,671.45	598,114,679.26
U. S. deposits........	7,114,893.47	6,355,722.95	6,993,014.77	7,853,772.41	7,863,894.93
Dep'ts U.S.dis.officers	5,024,699.44	3,416,371.16	5,463,953.48	4,563,833.79	6,136,597.74
Due to national banks	128,627,494.44	120,755,565.86	132,804,924.02	110,047,347.67	124,218,392.83
Due to State banks..	39,025,165.44	35,005,127.84	39,878,826.42	33,789,083.82	34,794,963.37
Notes rediscounted..	3,818,686.01	4,225,622.04	4,745,178.22	5,549,431.88	6,545,059.78
Bills payable........	6,062,806.01	5,821,551.76	5,942,479.34	6,040,562.66	6,946,416.17
Total..........	1,710,415,657.34	1,743,652,213.55	1,770,837,269.40	1,755,857,098.24	1,773,556,532.43

1873.

	FEBRUARY 28.	APRIL 25.	JUNE 13.	SEPTEMBER 12.	DECEMBER 26.
	1,947 banks.	1,962 banks.	1,968 banks.	1,976 banks.	1,976 banks.
Capital stock........	$484,551,811.00	$487,891,251.00	$490,109,801.00	$491,072,616.00	$490,266,611.00
Surplus fund........	114,681,048.73	115,805,574.57	116,847,454.62	120,314,499.20	120,961,267.01
Undivided profits ...	48,578,045.28	52,415,348.46	55,306,154.69	54,515,131.76	58,375,100.43
Nat'l bank circulation	336,292,459.00	338,163,864.00	338,788,504.00	339,081,799.00	341,320,256.00
State bank circulation	1,368,271.00	1,280,208.00	1,224,470.00	1,188,853.00	1,130,585.00
Dividends unpaid ...	1,465,993.60	1,462,336.77	1,400,491.00	1,402,547.69	1,269,474.74
Individual deposits .	656,187,551.61	616,848,358.25	641,121,775.27	622,685,563.29	540,510,602.78
U. S. deposits........	7,044,848.34	7,890,057.73	8,691,001.03	7,829,327.73	7,680,375.26
Dep'ts U.S.dis.officers	5,835,696.60	4,425,750.14	6,416,275.10	8,098,560.13	4,705,593.36
Due to national banks	134,231,842.95	126,631,926.24	137,856,085.67	133,672,732.94	114,996,666.54
Due to State banks..	38,124,803.85	36,036,433.18	40,741,788.47	39,298,148.14	36,598,076.29
Notes rediscounted.	5,117,810.59	5,403,043.38	5,515,900.67	5,987,512.36	3,811,487.80
Bills payable........	5,672,532.75	7,059,128.39	7,215,157.04	5,480,554.09	7,754,187.41
Total..........	1,839,152,715.21	1,800,303,280.11	1,851,234,860.38	1,830,627,845.53	1,729,380,303.61

1874.

	FEBRUARY 27.	MAY 1.	JUNE 26.	OCTOBER 2.	DECEMBER 31.
	1,975 banks.	1,978 banks.	1,983 banks.	2,004 banks.	2,027 banks.
Capital stock........	$490,859,101.00	$490,077,001.00	$491,003,711.00	$493,765,121.00	$495,802,481.00
Surplus fund........	123,497,347.20	125,561,081.23	126,239,308.41	128,958,106.84	130,485,641.37
Undivided profits ...	50,236,919.88	54,331,713.13	58,332,965.71	51,484,437.32	51,477,629.33
Nat'l bank circulation	339,602,955.00	340,267,649.00	338,538,743.00	333,225,298.00	331,193,159.00
State bank circulation	1,078,988.00	1,049,286.00	1,009,021.00	964,567.00	860,417.00
Dividends unpaid ...	1,291,055.63	2,259,129.91	1,242,474.81	3,516,276.99	6,088,845.01
Individual deposits..	595,350,334.90	649,286,298.05	622,863,154.44	669,068,995.88	682,846,607.45
U. S. deposits........	7,276,959.87	7,994,422.27	7,322,830.85	7,302,153.58	7,492,307.78
Dep'ts U.S.dis.officers	5,034,624.46	3,297,689.24	3,238,639.20	3,927,828.27	3,579,722.94
Due to national banks	138,435,388.39	135,640,418.24	143,033,822.25	125,102,049.93	129,188,671.42
Due to State banks..	48,112,223.40	48,683,924.34	50,227,426.18	50,718,007.87	51,629,602.36
Notes rediscounted..	3,448,828.92	4,581,420.38	4,436,256.22	4,197,372.25	6,365,652.97
Bills payable........	4,275,002.51	4,772,662.59	4,352,560.57	4,950,727.51	5,398,900.83
Total..........	1,808,500,520.16	1,867,802,706.28	1,851,840,913.64	1,877,180,942.44	1,902,409,638.46

AGGREGATE RESOURCES AND LIABILITIES OF THE NATIONAL

1875.

Resources.	MARCH 1.	MAY 1.	JUNE 30.	OCTOBER 1.	DECEMBER 17.
	2,029 banks.	2,046 banks.	2,076 banks.	2,088 banks.	2,080 banks.
Loans and discounts	$956, 485, 930. 35	$971, 835, 298. 74	$972, 926, 532. 14	$984, 691, 434. 40	$962, 571, 807. 70
Bonds for circulation	380, 682, 650. 00	378, 026, 900. 00	375, 127, 900. 00	370, 321, 700. 00	363, 618, 100. 00
Bonds for deposits	14, 492, 200. 00	14, 372, 200. 00	14, 147, 200. 00	14, 097, 200. 00	13, 981, 500. 00
U. S. bonds on hand	18, 062, 150. 00	14, 297, 650. 00	12, 753, 000. 00	13, 989, 950. 00	16, 009, 550. 04
Other stocks and b'ds	28, 268, 841. 69	29, 102, 197. 10	32, 010, 316. 18	33, 505, 045. 15	31, 657, 960. 52
Due from res've ag'ts	89, 991, 175. 34	80, 620, 878. 75	80, 788, 903. 73	85, 701, 259. 82	81, 402, 682. 27
Due from nat'l banks	44, 720, 394. 11	46, 039, 507. 57	48, 513, 388. 80	47, 028, 700. 18	44, 831, 801. 48
Due from State banks	12, 724, 243. 97	12, 094, 086. 39	11, 625, 617. 15	11, 963, 768. 90	11, 805, 551. 48
Real estate, etc	39, 430, 952. 12	40, 312, 285. 99	40, 969, 020. 40	42, 366, 647. 65	41, 583, 311. 34
Current expenses	7, 790, 581. 86	7, 706, 700. 42	4, 992, 044. 34	7, 841, 213. 05	9, 218, 455. 47
Premiums paid	9, 006, 880. 92	8, 434, 453. 14	8, 742, 393. 83	8, 670, 091. 18	9, 442, 801. 54
Cash items	11, 734, 762. 42	13, 122, 145. 88	12, 433, 100. 43	12, 758, 872. 03	11, 238, 725. 72
Clear'g-house exch'gs	81, 127, 796. 39	116, 970, 819. 05	88, 924, 025. 93	75, 142, 863. 45	67, 886, 967. 04
Bills of other banks	18, 909, 397. 00	19, 504, 640. 00	24, 201, 961. 00	18, 528, 837. 00	17, 166, 190. 00
Fractional currency	3, 008, 592. 12	2, 702, 320. 44	2, 620, 504. 26	2, 595, 031. 78	2, 901, 023. 10
Specie	16, 667, 106. 17	10, 620, 361. 64	18, 959, 582. 30	8, 050, 329. 73	17, 070, 905. 90
Legal-tender notes	78, 508, 170. 00	84, 015, 028. 00	87, 492, 895. 00	76, 458, 734. 00	70, 725, 077. 00
U. S. cert'fs of deposit	37, 200, 000. 00	38, 615, 000. 00	47, 310, 000. 00	48, 810, 000. 00	31, 005, 000. 00
Due from U. S. Treas	21, 007, 919. 76	21, 454, 422. 29	19, 640, 785. 52	19, 686, 960. 30	19, 202, 256. 68
Total	1,869,819,753. 22	1,909,847,891. 40	1,913,239,201. 16	1,882,209,307. 62	1,823,469,752. 44

1876.

	MARCH 10.	MAY 12.	JUNE 30.	OCTOBER 2.	DECEMBER 22.
	2,091 banks.	2,089 banks.	2,091 banks.	2,089 banks.	2,082 banks.
Loans and discounts	$950, 205, 555. 02	$930, 895, 085. 34	$933, 686, 530. 45	$931, 304, 714. 06	$929, 066, 408. 42
Bonds for circulation	354, 547, 750. 00	344, 537, 350. 00	339, 141, 750. 00	337, 170, 400. 00	336, 705, 300. 00
Bonds for deposits	14, 216, 500. 00	14, 128, 000. 00	14, 328, 000. 00	14, 098, 000. 00	14, 757, 000. 00
U. S. bonds on hand	25, 910, 650. 00	26, 577, 000. 00	30, 842, 300. 00	33, 142, 150. 00	31, 937, 950. 00
Other stocks and b'ds	30, 425, 430. 43	30, 905, 195. 82	32, 482, 805. 75	34, 445, 157. 16	31, 565, 914. 50
Due from res've ag'ts	99, 068, 800. 35	86, 700, 083. 97	87, 989, 900. 00	87, 326, 950. 48	83, 789, 174. 05
Due from nat'l banks	42, 341, 542. 07	44, 328, 000. 40	47, 417, 029. 03	47, 525, 089. 98	44, 011, 064. 07
Due from State banks	11, 180, 562. 15	11, 262, 193. 00	10, 989, 507. 95	12, 061, 283. 08	12, 415, 811. 97
Real estate, etc	41, 937, 617. 25	42, 183, 958. 78	42, 722, 415. 27	43, 121, 942. 01	43, 498, 445. 49
Current expenses	8, 296, 207. 85	6, 820, 578. 35	5, 025, 549. 38	6, 987, 644. 40	9, 818, 422. 88
Premiums paid	10, 946, 713. 15	10, 414, 347. 28	10, 621, 634. 03	10, 715, 251. 16	10, 811, 300. 00
Cash items	9, 517, 808. 86	9, 693, 186. 37	11, 724, 502. 67	12, 043, 139. 68	10, 658, 709. 26
Clear'g-house exch'gs	58, 863, 182. 43	56, 806, 632. 63	75, 328, 878. 84	87, 870, 817. 06	68, 027, 016. 40
Bills of other banks	18, 536, 502. 00	20, 347, 904. 00	20, 398, 422. 00	15, 910, 315. 00	17, 521, 663. 00
Fractional currency	3, 215, 594. 30	2, 771, 886. 26	1, 987, 807. 44	1, 417, 203. 66	1, 146, 741. 94
Specie	29, 077, 345. 85	21, 714, 594. 36	25, 218, 400. 92	21, 360, 767. 42	32, 999, 647. 89
Legal-tender notes	76, 768, 446. 00	79, 858, 661. 00	90, 836, 876. 00	84, 250, 847. 00	66, 221, 400. 00
U. S. cert'fs of deposit	30, 805, 000. 00	27, 380, 000. 00	27, 955, 000. 00	29, 170, 000. 00	26, 095, 000. 00
Due from U. S. Treas	18, 479, 112. 79	16, 911, 680. 20	17, 063, 407. 65	16, 743, 695. 40	16, 359, 491. 73
Total	1,834,369,941. 70	1,793,306,002. 78	1,825,760,907. 28	1,827,205,307. 61	1,787,407,098. 76

1877.

	JANUARY 20.	APRIL 14.	JUNE 22.	OCTOBER 1.	DECEMBER 28.
	2,083 banks.	2,073 banks.	2,078 banks.	2,080 banks.	2,074 banks.
Loans and discounts	$920, 561, 018. 65	$911, 946, 833. 88	$901, 731, 416. 03	$891, 920, 593. 54	$881, 856, 744. 87
Bonds for circulation	337, 590, 700. 00	339, 658, 100. 00	337, 754, 100. 00	336, 810, 950. 00	343, 869, 550. 00
Bonds for deposits	14, 782, 000. 00	15, 084, 000. 00	14, 971, 000. 00	14, 903, 000. 00	13, 538, 000. 00
U. S. bonds on hand	31, 988, 650. 00	32, 964, 250. 00	32, 344, 050. 00	30, 088, 700. 00	28, 479, 800. 00
Other stocks and b'ds	31, 819, 930. 20	32, 554, 504. 44	35, 053, 755. 29	34, 485, 905. 21	32, 169, 491. 03
Due from res've ag'ts	88, 698, 308. 85	84, 942, 718. 41	82, 132, 099. 96	73, 284, 133. 12	75, 960, 067. 27
Due from nat'l banks	44, 844, 016. 88	42, 027, 778. 81	44, 507, 303. 63	45, 217, 246. 82	44, 123, 924. 07
Due from State banks	13, 080, 900. 81	11, 911, 437. 86	11, 240, 849. 79	11, 415, 761. 60	11, 479, 945. 65
Real estate, etc	43, 704, 335. 47	44, 736, 549. 09	44, 818, 722. 07	45, 229, 983. 25	45, 511, 932. 25
Current expenses	4, 131, 516. 48	7, 842, 266. 86	7, 910, 804. 84	6, 915, 702. 50	8, 958, 903. 00
Premiums paid	10, 991, 714. 50	10, 404, 505. 12	10, 320, 674. 34	9, 219, 174. 62	8, 841, 939. 09
Cash items	10, 295, 404. 19	10, 410, 023. 87	10, 099, 088. 46	11, 074, 587. 50	10, 205, 050. 49
Clear'g-house exch'gs	81, 117, 889. 04	85, 159, 422. 74	57, 861, 481. 18	74, 525, 215. 80	64, 664, 415. 01
Bills of other banks	18, 418, 727. 00	17, 942, 603. 00	20, 182, 948. 00	15, 531, 467. 00	20, 312, 692. 00
Fractional currency	1, 238, 228. 08	1, 114, 820. 00	1, 055, 123. 61	900, 805. 47	778, 084. 78
Specie	48, 709, 267. 55	27, 070, 037. 78	21, 335, 996. 00	22, 658, 820. 31	32, 907, 750. 70
Legal-tender notes	72, 089, 710. 00	72, 351, 573. 00	78, 004, 386. 00	66, 920, 084. 00	70, 568, 248. 00
U. S. cert'fs of deposit	25, 470, 000. 00	32, 100, 000. 00	44, 430, 000. 00	32, 410, 000. 00	26, 515, 000. 00
Due from U. S. Treas	16, 441, 509. 08	16, 201, 040. 84	17, 032, 574. 00	16, 021, 753. 01	16, 493, 577. 08
Total	1,818,174,517. 08	1,796,003,275. 20	1,774,352,833. 81	1,741,084,063. 84	1,737,205,145. 79

BANKS FROM OCTOBER, 1863, TO OCTOBER, 1888—Continued.

1875.

Liabilities.	MARCH 1.	MAY 1.	JUNE 30.	OCTOBER 1.	DECEMBER 17.
	2,029 banks.	2,046 banks.	2,076 banks.	2,088 banks.	2,086 banks.
Capital stock	$496, 272, 901. 00	$498, 717, 143. 00	$501, 568, 563. 50	$504, 829, 769. 00	$505, 485, 865. 00
Surplus fund	131, 249, 079. 47	131, 604, 008. 66	133, 169, 094. 79	134, 356, 076. 41	133, 085, 422. 30
Undivided profits	51, 650, 243. 62	55, 907, 619. 95	52, 160, 104. 68	52, 964, 953. 50	59, 204, 957. 81
Nat'l bank circulation	324, 525, 349. 00	323, 321, 230. 00	318, 148, 406. 00	318, 350, 379. 00	314, 979, 451. 00
State bank circulation	824, 876. 00	815, 229. 00	786, 844. 00	772, 348. 00	752, 722. 00
Dividends unpaid	1, 601, 255. 48	2, 501, 742. 39	6, 105, 519. 34	4, 003, 534. 00	1, 353, 396. 80
Individual deposits	647, 735, 879. 60	695, 347, 677. 70	686, 478, 630. 48	664, 579, 619. 39	618, 517, 245. 74
U. S. deposits	7, 971, 932. 75	6, 797, 972. 00	6, 714, 328. 70	6, 507, 531. 59	6, 652, 556. 67
Dep'ts U. S. dis. officers	5, 330, 414. 16	2, 766, 387. 41	3, 459, 061. 80	4, 271, 195. 19	4, 232, 550. 87
Due to national banks	137, 735, 121. 44	127, 280, 034. 02	138, 914, 828. 39	120, 810, 081. 00	119, 843, 665. 44
Due to State banks	55, 294, 663. 64	53, 037, 562. 69	55, 714, 055. 18	49, 918, 530. 95	47, 048, 174. 56
Notes re-discounted	4, 841, 600. 20	5, 671, 031. 44	4, 261, 464. 45	5, 254, 453. 66	5, 257, 160. 61
Bills payable	4, 786, 436. 57	6, 079, 632. 94	5, 758, 290. 85	6, 590, 234. 43	7, 056, 583. 64
Total	1,869,819,753. 22	1,909,647,891. 40	1,913,239,201. 16	1,882,209,307. 62	1,823,469,752. 44

1876.

	MARCH 10.	MAY 12.	JUNE 30.	OCTOBER 2.	DECEMBER 22.
	2,091 banks.	2,089 banks.	2,091 banks.	2,089 banks.	2,082 banks.
Capital stock	$504, 818, 666. 00	$500, 982, 006. 00	$500, 393, 796. 00	$499, 802, 232. 00	$497, 482, 016. 00
Surplus fund	133, 091, 739. 50	131, 795, 199. 94	131, 897, 197. 21	132, 202, 282. 00	131, 390, 664. 67
Undivided profits	51, 177, 031. 26	49, 039, 278. 75	46, 609, 341. 51	46, 445, 215. 59	52, 327, 715. 08
Nat'l bank circulation	307, 476, 155. 00	300, 252, 085. 00	294, 444, 678. 00	291, 544, 020. 00	292, 011, 575. 00
State bank circulation	714, 539. 00	667, 060. 00	658, 938. 00	628, 847. 00	608, 548. 00
Dividends unpaid	1, 405, 829. 06	2, 325, 523. 51	6, 116, 679. 30	3, 848, 705. 64	1, 286, 540. 28
Individual deposits	620, 674, 211. 05	612, 355, 096. 59	641, 432, 886. 08	651, 385, 210. 19	619, 350, 223. 06
U. S. deposits	6, 606, 394. 90	8, 493, 878. 18	7, 667, 722. 07	7, 256, 801. 42	6, 727, 155. 14
Dep'ts U. S. dis. officers	4, 313, 915. 45	2, 505, 273. 30	3, 392, 939. 48	3, 746, 781. 58	4, 749, 615. 39
Due to national banks	139, 407, 880. 06	127, 880, 045. 04	131, 702, 164. 87	131, 535, 969. 04	122, 351, 818. 09
Due to State banks	54, 002, 131. 54	46, 706, 960. 52	51, 403, 995. 50	48, 250, 111. 03	48, 685, 392. 14
Notes re-discounted	4, 631, 882. 57	4, 653, 400. 08	3, 867, 622. 24	4, 464, 407. 31	4, 553, 158. 76
Bills payable	6, 049, 566. 31	5, 650, 126. 87	6, 173, 006. 03	6, 154, 784. 21	5, 882, 672. 15
Total	1,834,369,941. 70	1,793,306,002. 78	1,825,760,967. 28	1,827,265,367. 61	1,787,407,093. 76

1877.

	JANUARY 20.	APRIL 14.	JUNE 22.	OCTOBER 1.	DECEMBER 28.
	2,083 banks.	2,073 banks.	2,078 banks.	2,080 banks.	2,074 banks.
Capital stock	$493, 634, 011. 00	$489, 684, 645. 00	$481, 044, 771. 00	$479, 467, 771. 00	$477, 128, 771. 00
Surplus fund	130, 224, 169. 02	127, 793, 320. 52	124, 714, 072. 93	122, 776, 121. 24	121, 618, 455. 32
Undivided profits	37, 456, 530. 32	45, 609, 418. 27	50, 508, 351. 70	44, 572, 678. 72	51, 530, 910. 18
Nat'l bank circulation	292, 851, 351. 00	294, 710, 313. 00	290, 002, 057. 00	291, 874, 236. 00	299, 240, 475. 00
State bank circulation	581, 242. 09	535, 963. 00	521, 611. 00	481, 738. 00	470, 540. 00
Dividends unpaid	2, 448, 909. 70	1, 853, 974. 79	1, 398, 101. 52	3, 623, 703. 43	1, 404, 178. 34
Individual deposits	659, 891, 909. 76	641, 772, 528. 08	636, 267, 529. 20	616, 403, 987. 12	604, 512, 514. 52
U. S. deposits	7, 234, 696. 96	7, 584, 267. 72	7, 187, 431. 67	7, 972, 714. 75	6, 529, 031. 09
Dep'ts U. S. dis. officers	3, 108, 316. 55	3, 076, 878. 70	3, 710, 167. 20	2, 376, 983. 02	3, 780, 759. 43
Due to national banks	130, 293, 566. 36	125, 422, 444. 43	121, 443, 601. 23	115, 028, 954. 38	115, 773, 660. 58
Due to State banks	49, 965, 770. 27	48, 604, 820. 09	46, 352, 583. 90	46, 577, 439. 88	44, 807, 958. 79
Notes re-discounted	4, 000, 063. 82	3, 985, 459. 75	2, 953, 128. 58	3, 791, 219. 47	4, 654, 784. 51
Bills payable	6, 483, 320. 92	5, 909, 241. 94	6, 249, 426. 88	6, 137, 116. 83	5, 843, 107. 03
Total	1,818,174,517. 68	1,796,603,275. 20	1,774,352,833. 81	1,741,084,663. 84	1,737,295,145. 79

AGGREGATE RESOURCES AND LIABILITIES OF THE NATIONAL

1878.

Resources.	MARCH 15. 2,063 banks.	MAY 1. 2,059 banks.	JUNE 29. 2,056 banks.	OCTOBER 1. 2,053 banks.	DECEMBER 6. 2,055 banks.
Loans and discounts.	$854, 750, 708. 87	$847, 620, 392. 49	$835, 078, 133. 13	$833, 988, 450. 59	$826, 017, 451. 87
Bonds for circulation	343, 871, 350. 00	345, 256, 350. 00	347, 332, 100. 00	347, 556, 650. 00	347, 812, 300. 00
Bonds for deposits ..	13, 329, 000. 00	19, 536, 000. 00	28, 371, 000. 00	47, 936, 850. 00	49, 110, 800. 00
U. S. bonds on hand.	34, 881, 600. 00	33, 615, 700. 00	40, 479, 900. 00	46, 785, 600. 00	44, 255, 850. 00
Other stocks and b'ds	34, 674, 307. 21	34, 697, 320. 53	36, 694, 996. 24	36, 850, 534. 82	35, 816, 810. 47
Due from res've agt's	86, 016, 990. 78	71, 331, 219. 27	78, 875, 055. 92	85, 083, 418. 51	81, 733, 137. 00
Due from nat'l banks	39, 602, 105. 87	40, 546, 522. 72	41, 897, 858. 89	41, 492, 918. 75	43, 144, 220. 68
Due from State banks	11, 683, 050. 17	12, 413, 579. 10	12, 232, 316. 30	12, 314, 698. 11	12, 259, 856. 09
Real estate, etc	45, 702, 363. 73	45, 901, 536. 93	46, 153, 409. 35	46, 702, 476. 26	46, 728, 147. 36
Current expenses ...	7, 786, 572. 42	7, 239, 365. 78	4, 718, 618. 66	6, 272, 566. 73	7, 608, 128. 83
Premiums paid......	7, 806, 252. 00	7, 574, 255. 95	7, 335, 454. 49	7, 134, 735. 68	6, 978, 768. 71
Cash items	10, 107, 583. 76	10, 989, 440. 78	11, 525, 376. 07	10, 982, 432. 89	9, 985, 004. 21
Clear'g-house exch'gs	66, 408, 965. 23	95, 525, 134. 28	87, 498, 287. 82	82, 372, 537. 88	61, 998, 286. 11
Bills of other banks.	16, 250, 569. 00	18, 363, 335. 00	17, 063, 576. 00	16, 929, 721. 00	19, 392, 281. 00
Fractional currency.	697, 398. 86	661, 044. 69	610, 084. 25	515, 661. 04	496, 864. 34
Specie...............	54, 729, 558. 02	46, 023, 756. 06	29, 251, 469. 77	30, 688, 606. 59	34, 355, 250. 36
Legal-tender notes ..	64, 034, 972. 00	67, 245, 975. 00	71, 643, 402. 00	64, 428, 600. 00	64, 672, 762. 00
U. S. cert'fs of deposit	20, 605, 000. 00	20, 905, 000. 00	36, 905, 000. 00	32, 690, 000. 00	32, 520, 000. 00
Due from U. S. Treas.	16, 257, 608. 08	16, 364, 030. 47	16, 798, 667. 02	16, 543, 674. 36	17, 940, 918. 84
Total..........	1,729,465,956. 90	1,741,898.959. 05	1,750,464,706. 51	1,767,279,133. 21	1,742,826,837. 37

1879.

	JANUARY 1. 2,051 banks.	APRIL 4. 2,048 banks.	JUNE 14. 2,048 banks.	OCTOBER 2. 2,048 banks.	DECEMBER 12. 2,052 banks.
Loans and discounts.	$823, 906, 763. 08	$814, 653, 422. 69	$835, 875, 012. 36	$878, 503, 097. 45	$933, 543, 661. 93
Bonds for circulation	347, 118, 300. 00	348, 487, 700. 00	352, 208, 000. 00	357, 313, 300. 00	364, 272, 700. 00
Bonds for deposits...	66, 507, 350. 00	309, 348, 450. 00	257, 038, 200. 00	18, 204. 650. 00	14, 788, 800. 00
U. S. bonds on hand .	44, 257, 250. 00	54, 601, 750. 00	62, 180, 300. 00	52, 942, 100. 00	40, 677, 500. 00
Other stocks and b'ds	35, 569, 400. 93	36, 747, 129. 40	37, 617, 015. 13	39, 671, 916. 50	38, 836, 369. 80
Due from res've agt's	77, 925, 068. 68	74, 003, 830. 40	93, 443, 463. 95	107, 023, 546. 81	102, 742, 452. 54
Due from nat'l banks	44, 161, 948. 46	39, 143, 388. 00	48, 102, 531. 93	46, 692, 994. 78	55, 352, 459. 82
Due from State banks	11, 892, 540. 26	10, 535, 252. 09	11, 258, 520. 45	13, 630, 772. 63	14, 425, 072. 00
Real estate, etc......	47, 091, 964. 70	47, 461, 614. 54	47, 706, 108. 26	47, 817, 169. 36	47, 992, 332. 99
Current expenses ...	4, 033, 024. 67	6, 693, 668. 43	6, 913, 430. 46	6, 111, 256. 56	7, 474, 082. 10
Premiums paid......	6, 300, 048. 85	6, 609, 390. 80	5, 674, 497. 80	4, 332, 419. 63	4, 150, 836. 17
Cash items..........	13, 564, 550. 25	10, 011, 294. 64	10, 209, 082. 43	11, 306, 132. 48	10, 377, 272. 77
Clear'g-house exch'gs	100, 035, 237. 82	63, 712, 445. 55	83, 152, 359. 49	112, 964, 964. 25	112, 172, 677. 95
Bills of other banks.	19, 535. 588. 00	17, 068, 505. 00	16, 685, 484. 00	16, 707, 550. 00	16, 406, 218. 00
Fractional currency.	475, 538. 50	467, 177. 47	446, 217. 26	396, 065. 06	374, 227. 02
Specie...............	41, 499, 757. 32	41, 148, 563. 41	42, 333, 287. 44	42, 173, 731. 23	79, 013, 041. 59
Legal-tender notes ..	70, 561, 233. 00	64, 461, 231. 00	67, 059, 152. 00	69, 196, 696. 00	54, 715, 096. 00
U. S. cert'fs of deposit	28, 915, 000. 00	21, 885, 000. 00	25, 180, 000. 00	26, 770, 000. 00	10, 860. 000. 00
Due from U. S. Treas.	17, 175, 435. 13	17, 029, 121. 31	16, 620, 986. 20	17, 029, 065. 45	17, 054, 816. 40
Total..........	1,800,592,002. 25	1,984,068,936. 58	2,019,884,549. 16	1,868,787,428. 10	1,925,229,617. 08

1880.

	FEBRUARY 21. 2,061 banks.	APRIL 23. 2,075 banks.	JUNE 11. 2,076 banks.	OCTOBER 1. 2,090 banks.	DECEMBER 31. 2,095 banks.
Loans and discounts.	$974, 295, 360. 70	$992, 970, 828. 10	$994, 712, 646. 41	$1,040,977,267.53	$1,071,356,141.79
Bonds for circulation	361, 901, 700. 00	361, 274, 650. 00	359, 512, 050. 00	357,789,350.00	358,042,550.00
Bonds for deposits...	14, 917, 000. 00	14, 722, 000. 00	14, 727, 000. 00	14,827,000.00	14,726,500.00
U. S. bonds on hand.	30, 798, 000. 00	29, 509, 600. 00	28, 605, 800. 00	28,793,400.00	25,016,400.00
Other stocks and b'ds	41, 223, 583 ·33	42, 494, 927. 73	41, 947, 345. 75	48,863,150.22	48,628,372.77
Due from res've agt's	117, 701, 386. 81	103, 964. 229. 84	115, 935, 008. 27	134,562,778. 70	126,155,014.40
Due from nat'l banks	53, 230, 034. 03	54, 493, 405. 09	56, 578, 444. 69	63,023,796.84	69,079,326.15
Due from State banks	14, 501, 152. 51	13, 293, 775. 94	13, 861, 582. 77	15,881,107.74	17,111,241.03
Real estate, etc......	47, 815, 915. 77	47, 808, 207. 09	47, 979, 244. 53	48,045,832.54	47,784,461.47
Current expenses ...	6, 404, 743. 54	7, 007, 404. 19	6, 778, 829. 19	6,386,182.01	4,442,440.02
Premiums paid......	3, 908, 059. 27	3, 791, 703. 33	3, 702, 354. 60	3,488,470.11	3,288,602.63
Cash items	10, 320, 274. 51	9, 857, 645. 34	9, 980, 179. 32	12,720,002.10	14,713,929.02
Clear'g-house exch'gs	166, 736, 402. 64	99, 357, 056. 41	122, 300, 409. 45	121,095,249.72	220,733,904.59
Bills of other banks.	15, 369, 257. 00	21, 064, 504. 00	21, 908, 193. 00	18,210,943.00	21,549,307.00
Fractional currency.	397, 187. 23	395, 747. 67	387, 226. 13	367,171.73	389,921.75
Specie...............	89, 442, 051. 75	86, 429, 732. 21	99, 506, 505. 26	109,346,509.49	107,172,900.92
Legal-tender notes ..	55, 229, 408. 00	61, 048, 941. 00	64, 470, 717. 00	56,640,458.00	59,216,934 00
U. S. cert'fs of deposit	10, 760, 000. 00	7, 890, 000. 00	12, 510, 000. 00	7.655,000.00	6,150,000.00
Due from U. S. Treas.	16, 994, 381. 37	17, 226, 060. 01	16, 999, 083. 78	17,103,866.00	17,125,822.37
Total..........	2,038,066,498. 46	1,974,600,472. 95	2,035,493,280. 15	2,105,786,625.82	2,241,683,829.01

BANKS FROM OCTOBER, 1863, TO OCTOBER, 1888—Continued.

1878.

Liabilities.	MARCH 15.	MAY 1.	JUNE 29.	OCTOBER 1.	DECEMBER 6.
	2,063 banks.	2,050 banks.	2,056 banks.	2,053 banks.	2,055 banks.
Capital stock........	$473,952,541.00	$471,971,627.00	$470,393,366.00	$466,147,436.00	$464,874,996.00
Surplus fund	120,870,290.10	119,231,126.13	118,178,530.75	116,897,779.98	116,402,118.84
Undivided profits ...	45,040,851.85	43,938,961.98	40,482,522.64	40,936,213.58	44,040,171.84
Nat'l bank circulat'n	300,926,284.00	301,884,704.00	299,621,059.00	301,888,092.00	303,324,733.00
State bank circulat'n	439,339.00	426,504.00	417,808.00	413,913.00	400,715.00
Dividends unpaid ...	1,207,472.68	1,930,669.58	5,466,350.52	3,118,389.91	1 473,784.86
Individual deposits..	602,882,585.17	625,479,771.12	621,632,160.06	620,236,176 82	598,805,775.56
U. S. deposits........	7,243,253.29	13,811,474.14	22,686,619.67	41,654,812.08	40,209,825.72
Dep's U.S.dis.officers	3,004,064.90	2,392,281.61	2,903,531.99	3,342,794.73	3,451,436.56
Due to national banks	123,230,448.50	109,720,396.70	117,845,405.88	122,496,513.92	120,261,774.54
Due to State banks..	43,979,239.39	44,006,551.05	43,360,527.86	42,636,703.42	41,767,755.07
Notes re-discounted.	2,465,390.79	2,834,012.00	2,453,839.77	3,007,324.85	3,228,132.03
Bills payable........	4,215,196.23	4,270,879.74	5,022,894.37	4,502,982.92	4,525,617.45
Total..........	1,729,465,056.00	1,741,808,959.05	1,750,464,706.51	1,767,279,133.21	1,742,826,837.37

1879.

	JANUARY 1.	APRIL 4.	JUNE 14.	OCTOBER 2.	DECEMBER 12.
	2,051 banks.	2,048 banks.	2,048 banks.	2,048 banks.	2,052 banks.
Capital stock........	$462,031,396.00	$455,611,362.00	$455,244,415.00	$454,067,365.00	$454,498,515.00
Surplus fund.......	116,200,863.52	114,823,316.49	114,321,375.87	114,786,528.10	115,429,031.93
Undivided profits ...	36,836,269.21	40,812,777.59	45,802,845.82	41,300,941.40	47,573,820.75
Nat'l bank circulat'n	303,506,470.00	304,467,139.00	307,328,695.00	313,786,342.00	321,949,154.00
State bank circulat'n	388,368.00	352,452.00	339,927.00	325,954.00	322,502.00
Dividends unpaid ...	5,816,348.82	2,158,516.79	1,309,059.13	2,658,337.46	1,305,480.45
Individual deposits..	643,337,745.26	598,822,694.02	648,934,141.42	719,737,568.89	755,459,966.01
U. S. deposits........	59,701,222.90	303,463,505.69	248,421,340.25	11,018,862.74	6,923,323.97
Dep's U.S.dis.officers	3,556,801.25	2,089,189.44	3,082,320.67	3,469,600.02	3,893,217.43
Due to national banks	118,311,635.60	110,481,176.98	137,360,091.60	149,200,257.16	152,484,079.44
Due to State banks..	44,035,787.56	43,709,770.14	50,498,064.54	52,022,453.99	59,232,391.93
Notes re-discounted .	2,926,434.95	2,224,491.91	2,226,390.39	2,205,015.54	2,116,484.47
Bills payable........	3,942,659.18	4,452,544.48	4,510,876.47	4,208,201.89	4,041,649.70
Total..........	1,800,502,002.25	1,984,068,936.53	2,019,884,549.16	1,868,787,428.19	1,925,229,617.08

1880.

	FEBRUARY 21.	APRIL 23.	JUNE 11.	OCTOBER 1.	DECEMBER 31.
	2,061 banks.	2,075 banks.	2,076 banks.	2,090 banks.	2,095 banks.
Capital stock........	$454,548,585.00	$456,097,935.00	$455,909,565.00	$457,553,985.00	$458,540,085.00
Surplus fund........	117,044,043.03	117,299,350.09	118,102,014.11	120,518,583.43	121,824,629.03
Undivided profits ...	42,803,804.95	48,226,087.61	50,443,645.45	46,139,690.24	47,046,741.64
Nat'l bank circulat'n	320,303,874.00	320,759,472.00	318,088,562.00	317,350,036.00	317,484,496.00
State bank circulat'n	303,452.00	299,790.00	290,738.00	271,045.00	258,499.00
Dividends unpaid ...	1,365,001.91	1,542,447.98	1,330,179.85	3,452,504.17	6,198,238.38
Individual deposits..	848,926,599.86	791,555,059.63	833,701,034.20	873,537,637.07	1,006,452,852.82
U. S. deposits........	7,856,781.07	7,925,988.37	7,680,905.47	7,548,538.67	7,898,100.94
Dep's U.S.dis.officers	3,069,880.74	3,220,606.64	3,026,757.34	3,344,386.62	2,489,501.01
Due to national banks	170,245,061.08	157,209,759.14	171,462,131.23	192,124,705.10	192,413,205.78
Due to State banks..	65,439,334.51	63,317,107.96	67,938,795.35	75,735,677.06	71,185,817.08
Notes re-discounted .	1,918,788.88	2,616,900.55	2,258,544.72	3,178,232.50	3,354,697.18
Bills payable........	4,181,280.53	4,529,967.98	5,260,417.43	5,031,604.96	4,636,876.05
Total..........	2,038,066,498.46	1,974,600,472.95	2,035,493,280.15	2,105,786,625.82	2,241,683,829.91

AGGREGATE RESOURCES AND LIABILITIES OF THE NATIONAL

1881.

Resources.	MARCH 11. 2,094 banks.	MAY 6. 2,102 banks.	JUNE 30. 2,115 banks.	OCTOBER 1. 2,132 banks.	DECEMBER 31. 2,164 banks.
Loans and discounts.	$1,073,786,749.70	$1,093,640,383.18	$1,144,988,949.45	$1,173,796,083.09	$1,169,177,557.16
Bonds for circulation	339,811,950.00	352,653,500.00	358,287,500.00	363,385,500.00	368,735,700.00
Bonds for deposits ..	14,851,500.00	15,240,000.00	15,265,000.00	15,540,000.00	15,715,000.00
U. S. bonds on hand .	46,626,150.00	44,116,500.00	48,584,950.00	40,860,750.00	31,884,000.00
Other stocks and b'ds	49,545,154.92	52,908,123.98	58,049,292.63	61,952,402.95	62,663,218.93
Due from res've ag'ts	120,820,691.09	128,017,627.03	156,258,637.05	132,968,183.12	123,530,465.75
Due from nat'l banks	62,295,517.84	63,176,225.07	75,703,599.78	78,505,446.17	77,633,902.77
Due from State banks	17,032,261.64	16,938,734.56	18,850,775.34	19,306,826.62	17,644,704.62
Real estate, etc	47,525,790.02	47,791,348.36	47,834,060.20	47,329,111.16	47,445,050.46
Current expenses...	7,810,930.83	6,096,109.78	4,235,911.19	6,731,936.48	4,617,101.04
Premiums paid	3,530,516.71	4,024,763.60	4,115,980.01	4,138,485.71	3,891,728.72
Cash items..........	10,144,682.87	11,826,603.16	13,534,227.31	14,831,879.30	17,337,964.78
Clear'g-house exch'gs	147,761,543.96	196,633,558.01	143,960,236.84	189,222,255.95	217,214,627.10
Bills of other banks.	17,733,032.00	25,120,933.00	21,631,932.00	17,732,712.00	24,190,534.00
Fractional currency	386,560.63	386,950.21	372,140.23	373,945.96	366,361.52
Specie	105,156,195.24	122,628,562.08	128,638,927.50	114,334,736.12	113,680,639.60
Legal-tender notes ..	52,158,439.00	62,516,296.00	58,728,713.00	53,158,441.00	60,104,387.00
U. S. cert's of deposit	6,120,000.00	8,045,000.00	9,540,000.00	6,740,000.00	7,930,000.00
Due from U. S. Treas	17,015,269.83	18,456,600.14	17,251,868.22	17,472,595.96	18,097,923.40
Total	2,140,110,944.78	2,270,226,817.76	2,325,832,700.75	2,358,387,391.59	2,381,890,866.85

1882.

	MARCH 11. 2,187 banks.	MAY 19. 2,224 banks.	JULY 1. 2,239 banks.	OCTOBER 3. 2,269 banks.	DECEMBER 30. 2,308 banks.
Loans and discounts.	$1,182,661,609.53	$1,189,094,830.35	$1,208,932,655.92	$1,243,203,210.08	$1,230,456,213.97
Bonds for circulation	367,333,700.00	360,153,800.00	355,789,550.00	357,631,750.00	357,047,650.00
Bonds for deposits ..	16,093,000.00	15,920,000.00	15,920,000.00	16,111,000.00	16,344,000.00
U. S. bonds on hand.	28,523,450.00	29,662,700.00	27,242,550.00	21,314,750.00	15,492,150.00
Other stocks and b'ds	64,430,686.18	65,274,999.32	66,691,399.56	66,168,916.04	66,998,620.36
Due from res've agt's	117,452,719.75	124,180,945.23	118,455,012.38	113,277,227.87	122,066,106.75
Due from nat'l banks	68,301,645.12	66,883,512.75	75,306,970.74	68,516,841.06	76,073,227.76
Due from State banks	15,921,432.07	16,890,174.92	16,344,688.66	17,105,468.44	18,405,748.49
Real estate, etc	47,073,247.45	46,956,574.28	46,425,351.40	46,537,066.41	46,903,408.41
Current expenses...	8,494,036.21	6,774,571.86	3,030,464.69	7,238,270.17	5,130,505.53
Premiums paid	3,762,382.59	5,062,314.52	5,404,224.35	6,515,155.03	6,472,585.82
Cash items..........	13,308,120.70	12,295,256.96	20,166,927.35	14,784,025.21	16,281,315.67
Clear'g-house exch'gs	162,088,077.94	107,270,094.71	150,114,220.08	208,366,540.08	155,051,194.81
Bills of other banks.	19,440,089.00	25,326,186.00	21,405,758.00	20,689,425.00	25,344,775.00
Fractional currency.	389,508.07	390,236.36	373,725.83	396,367.64	401,314.70
Specie	109,984,111.04	112,415,806.73	111,694,262.54	102,857,778.27	106,427,159.40
Legal-tender notes..	56,633,572.00	65,969,532.00	64,019,518.00	63,313,517.00	68,478,421.00
U.S. cert's of deposit.	9,445,000.00	10,395,000.00	11,045,000.00	8,645,000.00	8,475,000.00
Due from U. S. Treas	17,720,701.07	17,099,385.14	16,830,407.40	17,161,367.94	17,954,069.42
Total	2,309,057,088.72	2,277,924,911.13	2,344,342,686.90	2,399,833,676.84	2,360,793,467.09

1883.

	MARCH 13. 2,343 banks.	MAY 1. 2,375 banks.	JUNE 22. 2,417 banks.	OCTOBER 2. 2,501 banks.	DECEMBER 31. 2,529 banks.
Loans and discounts	$1,249,114,879.43	$1,262,339,981.87	$1,285,591,902.19	$1,309,244,781.64	$1,307,491,250.34
Bonds for circulation	354,746,500.00	354,480,250.00	354,002,900.00	351,412,850.00	345,595,800.00
Bonds for deposits ..	16,799,000.00	16,949,000.00	17,116,000.00	17,081,000.00	16,846,000.00
U. S. bonds on hand .	17,850,100.00	15,870,000.00	16,978,150.00	13,593,050.00	13,151,250.00
Other stocks and b'ds	68,428,685.67	68,340,590.79	68,552,073.03	71,114,031.11	71,609,421.62
Due from res've ag'ts	121,024,154.60	109,306,838.23	126,646,954.62	124,918,728.71	126,999,606.92
Due from nat'l banks	67,263,503.86	68,477,918.02	66,164,638.21	65,714,229.44	77,902,785.07
Due from State banks	16,093,341.72	19,382,129.33	19,451,498.16	18,260,275.05	19,402,047.12
Real estate, etc	47,063,305.68	47,155,909.80	47,502,163.52	48,337,665.02	49,540,760.35
Current expenses ...	8,949,615.28	7,754,958.86	8,829,278.26	6,808,327.30	4,878,318.44
Premiums paid	7,420,939.84	7,798,445.04	8,079,726.01	8,064,073.60	8,647,252.98
Cash items..........	11,360,731.07	15,461,050.16	11,109,701.18	13,581,040.94	17,401,804.43
Clear'g-house exch'gs	107,790,065.17	145,990,998.18	90,792,075.08	96,353,211.76	134,545,273.98
Bills of other banks.	19,739,526.00	22,655,833.00	26,279,856.00	22,675,447.00	28,809,609.00
Fractional currency.	431,931.15	446,318.94	456,447.36	443,951.12	427,754.35
Specie	97,962,366.34	103,607,266.32	115,354,394.62	107,817,983.53	114,276,158.04
Legal-tender notes ..	60,848,068.00	68,256,468.00	73,832,458.00	70,672,997.00	80,559,796.00
U. S. cert's of deposit	8,405,000.00	8,420,000.00	10,685,000.00	9,970,000.00	10,840,000.00
Due from U. S. Treas	16,726,451.30	17,497,694.31	17,407,906.20	16,586,712.60	16,865,938.85
Total	2,298,918,165.11	2,360,192,235.85	2,364,833,122.44	2,372,656,364.82	2,445,880,917.49

BANKS FROM OCTOBER, 1863, TO OCTOBER, 1888—Continued.

1881.

Liabilities.	MARCH 11.	MAY 6.	JUNE 30.	OCTOBER 1.	DECEMBER 31.
	2,094 banks.	2,102 banks.	2,115 banks.	2,132 banks.	2,164 banks.
Capital stock........	$458, 254, 935. 00	$459, 039, 205. 00	$460, 227, 835. 00	$463, 821, 985. 00	$465, 859, 835. 00
Surplus fund	122, 470, 990. 73	124, 405, 926. 91	126, 679, 517. 97	128, 140, 617. 75	129, 867, 493. 92
Undivided profits...	54, 072, 225. 49	54, 906, 090. 47	54, 684, 137. 16	56, 372, 190. 92	54, 221, 816. 10
Nat'l bank circulation	298, 590, 802. 00	309, 737, 193. 00	312, 223, 352. 00	320, 200, 069. 00	325, 018, 161. 00
State bank circulat'n	252, 765. 00	252, 647. 00	242, 967. 00	244, 399. 00	241, 701. 00
Dividends unpaid...	1, 402, 118. 43	2, 617, 134. 07	5, 871, 595. 59	3, 836, 445. 84	6, 372, 737. 13
Individual deposits..	933, 392, 430. 75	1, 027, 040, 514. 10	1, 031, 731, 043. 42	1, 070, 997, 431. 71	1, 102, 679, 163. 71
U. S. deposits	7, 381, 149. 25	9, 504, 081. 25	8, 971, 826. 73	8, 476, 689. 74	8, 796, 678. 73
Dep's U.S. dis. officers	3, 839, 324. 77	3, 371, 512. 48	3, 272, 610. 45	3, 631, 803. 41	3, 595, 726. 83
Due to national banks	181, 677, 285. 37	191, 250, 091. 90	223, 503, 034. 19	205, 862, 945. 80	197, 252, 326. 01
Due to State banks..	71, 579, 477. 47	80, 700, 506. 06	91, 035, 590. 05	89, 047, 471. 00	79, 380, 429. 38
Notes re-discounted.	2, 016, 203. 05	2, 908, 370. 45	2, 220, 053. 02	3, 091, 165. 30	4, 122, 472. 79
Bills payable........	4, 581, 231. 47	4, 493, 544. 77	5, 169, 128. 57	4, 064, 077. 12	4, 482, 325. 25
Total..........	2, 140, 110, 944. 78	2, 270, 226, 817. 76	2, 325, 832, 700. 75	2, 358, 387, 391. 59	2, 381, 890, 866. 85

1882.

	MARCH 11.	MAY 19.	JULY 1.	OCTOBER 3.	DECEMBER 30.
	2, 187 banks.	2,224 banks.	2,239 banks.	2,269 banks.	2,308 banks.
Capital stock........	$460, 390, 232. 00	$473, 819, 124. 00	$477, 184, 390. 00	$483, 104, 213. 00	$484, 883, 492. 00
Surplus fund........	130, 924, 139. 66	129, 233, 358. 24	131, 079, 251. 16	131, 977, 450. 77	135, 930, 969. 31
Undivided profits...	60, 475, 704. 98	62, 345, 199. 19	52, 128, 817. 73	61, 180, 310. 53	55, 343, 816. 94
Nat'l bank circulation	323, 651, 577. 00	315, 671, 236. 00	308, 921, 898. 00	314, 721, 215. 00	315, 230, 925 00
State bank circulat'n	241, 527. 00	241, 319. 00	235, 173. 00	221, 177. 00	207, 273. 00
Dividends unpaid...	1, 418, 119. 12	1, 950, 554. 83	6, 634, 372. 20	3, 153, 836. 30	6, 805, 057. 82
Individual deposits..	1, 036, 595, 098. 20	1, 001, 687, 693. 74	1, 066, 707, 248. 75	1, 122, 472, 682. 46	1, 066, 901, 719. 85
U. S. deposits.......	8, 853, 242. 16	9, 741, 133. 36	9, 817, 224. 44	8, 817, 411. 21	9, 022, 303 56
Dep's U.S. dis. officers	3, 372, 363. 96	3, 403, 252. 88	2, 867, 385. 63	3, 627, 846. 72	3, 786, 202. 20
Due to national banks	187, 433, 824. 90	192, 067, 865. 26	194, 868, 025. 46	180, 075, 749. 77	194, 491, 260. 60
Due to State banks..	78, 359, 675. 85	78, 911, 787. 20	84, 066, 023. 66	79, 885, 052. 22	77, 031, 165. 82
Notes re-discounted.	3, 912, 992. 38	3, 754, 044. 38	4, 195, 210. 90	5, 747, 014. 68	6, 703, 164. 45
Bills payable........	4, 428, 531. 51	5, 008, 343. 00	5, 637, 665. 88	4, 848, 517. 18	3, 856, 056. 54
Total..........	2, 399, 057, 088. 72	2, 277, 924, 911. 13	2, 344, 342, 686. 90	2, 399, 833, 676. 84	2, 360, 793, 467. 09

1883.

	MARCH 13.	MAY 1.	JUNE 22.	OCTOBER 2.	DECEMBER 31.
	2,343 banks.	2, 375 banks.	2,417 banks.	2,501 banks.	2,529 banks.
Capital stock........	$490 456, 932. 00	$493, 963, 069. 00	$500, 298, 312. 00	$509, 699, 787. 00	$511, 837, 575. 00
Surplus fund	136, 922, 884. 44	137, 775, 004. 39	138, 331, 002. 06	141, 991, 789. 18	144, 800, 252. 13
Undivided profits...	59, 340, 913. 64	60, 739, 878. 85	68, 354, 157. 15	61, 560, 652. 04	58, 787, 945. 91
Nat'l bank circulation	312, 778, 053. 00	313, 549, 093. 00	311, 963, 303 00	310, 517, 857. 00	304, 944, 131. 00
State bank circulat'n	200, 770. 00	198, 162. 00	189, 253. 00	184, 357. 00	181, 121. 00
Dividends unpaid...	1, 389, 092. 96	2, 849, 629. 87	1, 454, 232. 01	3, 229, 226. 31	7, 082, 682. 28
Individual deposits..	1, 004, 111, 400. 55	1, 007, 962, 238. 35	1, 043, 137, 703. 11	1, 049, 437, 700. 57	1, 106, 453, 008. 23
U. S. deposits	9, 613, 873. 33	11, 624, 894. 57	10, 130, 757. 88	10, 183, 190. 95	10, 026, 777. 79
Dep's U.S. dis. officers	3, 787, 225, 31	3, 618, 114. 79	3, 743, 326. 56	3, 080, 250. 28	3, 708, 862. 04
Due to national banks	191, 296, 859. 14	180, 445, 876. 92	194, 150, 676. 43	186, 828, 676. 27	200, 807, 280. 06
Due to State banks..	80, 251, 968. 26	78, 544, 128. 82	84, 744, 666. 35	83, 602, 073. 01	84, 776, 421. 00
Notes re-discounted.	5, 101, 458. 69	5, 557, 183. 60	5, 197, 514. 12	7, 387, 537. 40	8, 248, 562. 07
bills payable	3, 660, 724. 79	3, 364, 061. 60	3, 137, 250. 77	4, 053, 252. 81	4, 106, 297. 78
Total..........	2, 298, 918, 165. 11	2, 360, 192, 235. 85	2, 364, 833, 122. 44	2, 372, 656, 364. 82	2, 445, 880, 917. 49

AGGREGATE RESOURCES AND LIABILITIES OF THE NATIONAL

1884.

Resources.	MARCH 7.	APRIL 24.	JUNE 20.	SEPTEMBER 30.	DECEMBER 20.
	2,503 banks.	2,589 banks.	2,625 banks.	2,664 banks.	2,664 banks.
Loans and discounts	$1,321,548,289.02	$1,333,433,230.54	$1,260,862,035.96	$1,245,294,093.37	$1,234,202,226.44
Bonds for circulation	339,816,150.00	337,342,900.00	334,346,350.00	327,435,000.00	317,586,050.00
Bonds for deposits	16,850,000.00	17,135,000.00	17,060,000.00	16,840,000.00	16,740,000.00
U. S. bonds on hand	18,672,250.00	15,500,400.00	14,143,000.00	13,579,000.00	12,305,000.00
Other stocks and b'ds	73,155,084.00	73,424,815.97	72,572,306.93	71,363,477.40	73,449,352.07
Due from res've ag'ts	138,705,012.74	122,401,057.08	95,247,152.62	111,993,019.65	121,161,976.80
Due from nat'l banks	64,638,322.58	68,031,200.90	64,891,670.13	66,335,544.57	60,459,884.45
Due from State banks	17,937,976.35	18,145,827.01	16,306,500.01	15,833,982.98	18,329,012.01
Real estate, etc	49,418,805.02	49,007,126.87	50,149,083.90	49,900,880.91	49,889,030.06
Current expenses	7,813,880.50	8,054,206.82	8,866,558.09	6,913,508.85	9,070,906.14
Premiums paid	8,742,601.42	9,826,386.76	10,605,343.49	11,632,631.68	11,923,447.15
Cash items	11,383,792.57	11,237,975.71	11,382,202.60	13,103,008.55	11,924,152.89
Cl'g-house loan cert's	....	....	10,335,000.00	1,690,000.00	1,670,000.00
Clear'g-house exc'gs	68,403,373.30	83,531,472.58	69,408,913.13	66,257,118.15	75,106,055.05
Bills of other banks	23,485,124.00	26,525,120.00	23,386,695.00	23,258,854.00	22,377,905.00
Fractional currency	491,007.76	489,802.51	473,046.06	469,023.89	456,778.26
Specie	122,080,127.33	114,744,707.09	100,061,682.11	128,609,474.73	139,747,079.53
Legal-tender notes	75,847,005.00	77,712,628.00	76,917,212.00	77,044,059.00	76,369,555.00
U. S. cert's of deposit	14,045,000.00	11,900,000.00	9,870,000.00	14,200,000.00	10,040,000.00
Due from U. S. Treas.	16,465,785.66	17,408,976.58	17,022,909.34	17,739,906.28	15,442,300.52
Total	2,390,500,638.51	2,396,813,834.92	2,282,598,742.96	2,279,493,880.07	2,297,143,474.27

1885.

	MARCH 10.	MAY 6.	JULY 1.	OCTOBER 1.	DECEMBER 24.
	2,671 banks.	2,678 banks.	2,689 banks.	2,714 banks.	2,732 banks.
Loans and discounts	$1,232,327,453.09	$1,241,450,040.79	$1,257,055,547.92	$1,306,143,990.46	$1,343,517,559.06
Bonds for circulation	313,106,200.00	312,168,500.00	310,102,200.00	307,657,050.00	304,776,750.00
Bonds for deposits	16,815,000.00	16,740,000.00	17,607,000.00	17,457,000.00	18,012,000.00
U. S. bonds on hand	14,607,650.00	14,709,250.00	14,588,800.00	14,329,400.00	12,665,750.00
Other stocks and b'ds	75,152,919.35	75,019,208.99	77,249,159.42	77,495,230.25	77,533,841.38
Due from res've ag'ts	136,462,273.26	130,903,103.77	132,733,904.34	138,378,515.15	139,239,444.80
Due from nat'l banks	66,442,054.87	67,800,656.57	77,220,972.29	78,967,097.86	79,152,300.07
Due from State banks	17,572,822.65	17,348,938.11	17,180,008.40	17,087,801.44	18,553,916.46
Real estate, etc	49,099,501.42	49,886,378.87	50,729,896.08	51,293,801.16	51,963,062.01
Current expenses	7,877,320.27	7,096,268.06	3,533,750.49	6,853,392.72	9,410,971.01
Premiums paid	12,330,437.00	12,358,982.70	12,090,663.41	12,511,333.41	11,802,199.86
Cash items	11,228,856.82	11,270,626.48	17,214,373.52	14,347,479.53	12,810,187.04
Cl'g-house loan cert's	1,530,000.00	1,430,000.00	1,380,000.00	1,110,000.00	630,000.00
Clear'g-house exc'gs	59,085,781.90	72,250,120.30	113,158,075.32	84,926,730.70	92,351,296.77
Bills of other banks	22,013,314.00	26,217,171.00	23,465,388.00	23,062,705.00	23,178,052.00
Fractional currency	510,529.96	513,200.12	489,927.18	477,055.17	415,082.04
Trade dollars	....	....	....	1,005,703.69	1,070,961.77
Specie	167,115,873.07	177,433,119.30	177,012,402.02	174,872,572.54	165,354,352.37
Legal-tender notes	71,017,322.00	77,336,999.00	79,701,352.00	69,738,119.00	67,585,466.00
U. S. cert's of deposit	22,760,000.00	10,135,000.00	22,920,000.00	18,800,000.00	11,765,000.00
Due from U. S. Treas.	15,070,935.80	15,473,270.84	14,617,807.02	14,807,114.24	14,981,021.79
Total	2,312,744,247.35	2,340,682,452.90	2,421,852,016.47	2,432,913,002.38	2,457,675,256.13

1886.

	MARCH 1.	JUNE 3.	AUGUST 27.	OCTOBER 7.	DECEMBER 28.
	2,708 banks.	2,809 banks.	2,849 banks.	2,852 banks.	2,875 banks.
Loans and discounts	$1,367,705,252.80	$1,398,552,099.71	$1,421,547,109.22	$1,450,957,054.93	$1,470,157,081.19
Bonds for circulation	296,661,400.00	279,414,400.00	270,315,850.00	258,498,050.00	228,384,350.00
Bonds for deposits	18,637,000.00	18,810,000.00	19,084,900.00	20,105,900.00	21,040,900.00
U. S. bonds on hand	16,580,050.00	12,535,550.00	14,308,050.00	12,326,500.00	10,570,200.00
Other stocks and b'ds	80,227,388.98	83,347,119.93	82,439,901.64	81,825,206.40	81,431,000.60
Due from res've ag'ts	142,805,686.91	133,027,136.53	143,715,221.45	140,704,570.01	142,117,979.28
Due from nat'l banks	70,933,570.67	77,632,108.47	78,001,411.58	80,520,615.77	88,271,697.90
Due from State banks	18,834,235.88	17,720,924.26	18,387,215.76	20,140,256.27	21,405,427.08
Real estate, etc	52,262,718.07	53,117,564.42	53,834,583.58	54,000,070.94	54,763,530.37
Current expenses	7,705,850.57	8,681,072.33	5,837,175.21	7,438,741.12	10,283,007.79
Premiums paid	12,237,089.15	13,298,269.23	13,041,463.72	14,303,529.55	15,100,021.67
Cash items	15,135,538.48	12,181,455.80	10,408,981.58	13,277,160.64	13,218,973.44
Cl'g-house loan cert's	505,000.00	205,000.00	85,000.00	....	....
Clear'g-house exc'gs	99,923,656.84	76,140,830.60	62,474,605.90	95,536,941.15	70,525,126.02
Bills of other banks	20,503,303.00	25,129,038.00	21,602,661.00	22,734,085.00	26,132,830.00
Fractional currency	470,175.18	452,361.94	451,308.89	434,220.93	447,833.09
Trade dollars	1,681,530.65	1,713,381.35	1,857,041.56	1,880,704.55	1,827,364.20
Specie	171,615,910.39	167,459,870.40	149,000,402.10	156,387,006.00	166,983,556.01
Legal-tender notes	67,014,886.00	79,656,788.00	64,030,751.00	62,812,322.00	67,739,828.00
U. S. cert's of deposit	12,430,000.00	11,850,000.00	8,115,000.00	5,855,000.00	6,195,000.00
5% fund with Treas.	12,953,248.20	12,198,526.43	11,808,912.52	11,358,014.07	10,056,128.30
Due from U. S. Treas	1,513,019.07	1,416,802.00	1,590,303.36	2,592,042.94	975,376.96
Total	2,494,337,129.41	2,474,544,481.89	2,453,000,030.07	2,513,854,751.17	2,507,753,012.95

BANKS FROM OCTOBER, 1863, TO OCTOBER, 1888—Continued.

1884.

Liabilities.	MARCH 7.	APRIL 24.	JUNE 20.	SEPTEMBER 30.	DECEMBER 20.
	2,563 banks.	2,589 banks.	2,625 banks.	2,664 banks.	2,664 banks.
Capital stock	$515,725,005.00	$518,471,844.00	$522,515,996.00	$524,271,345.00	$524,089,065.00
Surplus fund	145,741,079.90	146,047,958.07	145,763,416.17	147,055,037.85	146,867,119.06
Undivided profits	63,644,861.56	67,450,450.00	70,597,487.21	63,234,237.62	70,711,360.95
Nat'l bank circulati'n	298,791,610.00	297,506,243.00	295,175,334.00	289,775,123.00	280,107,043.00
State bank circulati'n	180,580.00	180,576.00	179,666.00	179,053.00	174,645.00
Dividends unpaid	1,422,901.91	1,415,880.58	1,384,086.71	3,686,160.33	1,331,421.54
Individual deposits	1,046,050,167.90	1,060,778,388.06	979,020,349.63	975,243,795.14	987,649,055.68
U. S. deposits	9,956,875.24	11,233,495.77	10,520,759.44	10,367,909.02	10,655,803.72
Dep's U. S. dis. offic'rs	3,856,461.66	3,588,980.50	3,064,326.13	3,703,804.34	3,749,969.85
Due to national banks	207,461,179.63	192,868,942.31	155,785,354.44	173,979,140.80	187,296,348.30
Due to State banks	88,406,363.89	86,778,138.85	70,480,617.11	72,406,206.85	72,572,384.43
Notes re-discounted	6,234,202.32	7,290,284.58	11,343,505.55	11,008,505.07	8,433,724.67
Bills payable	2,968,740.50	3,193,635.20	4,262,244.57	4,580,862.15	3,415,524.07
Cl'g-house loan cert's	....	....	11,895,000.00	....	....
Total	2,390,500,638.51	2,396,813,834.02	2,282,508,742.90	2,279,493,880.07	2,297,143,474.27

1885.

	MARCH 10	MAY 6.	JULY 1.	OCTOBER 1.	DECEMBER 24.
	2,671 banks.	2,678 banks.	2,689 banks.	2,714 banks.	2,732 banks.
Capital stock	$524,255,151.00	$525,195,577.00	$526,273,602.00	$527,524,410.00	$529,360,725.00
Surplus fund	145,907,800.02	145,103,776.01	146,523,799.94	146,624,642.06	150,155,549.52
Undivided profits	60,296,452.56	60,184,358.12	52,229,946.61	59,335,519.11	69,229,645.82
Nat'l bank circulati'n	274,054,157.00	273,703,047.00	269,147,690.00	268,869,597.00	267,430,837.00
State bank circulati'n	162,581.00	144,498.00	144,489.00	136,808.00	133,932.00
Dividends unpaid	1,301,937.73	2,577,236.08	6,414,263.98	3,508,325.38	1,360,977.27
Individual deposits	996,501,647.40	1,035,802,188.56	1,106,376,516.80	1,102,372,450.35	1,111,429,914.98
U. S. deposits	11,006,919.47	11,690,707.52	10,095,974.68	11,552,621.08	12,058,768.36
Dep's U.S. dis. offic'rs	3,039,646.40	3,330,522.70	3,027,218.02	2,714,300.37	3,005,783.11
Due to national banks	205,877,203.09	199,081,104.40	203,032,800.05	213,534,005.08	216,564,533.96
Due to State banks	82,190,567.43	81,066,092.25	88,847,454.78	86,115,061.25	85,060,162.27
Notes re-discounted	6,299,722.15	5,736,012.02	5,864,000.85	8,432,702.61	9,032,828.24
Bills payable	1,850,462.10	2,167,333.33	2,074,250.76	2,191,380.16	1,951,508.60
Total	2,312,744,247.35	2,346,682,452.99	2,421,852,016.47	2,432,013,002.38	2,457,675,250.13

1886.

	MARCH 1.	JUNE 3.	AUGUST 27.	OCTOBER 7.	DECEMBER 28.
	2,768 banks.	2,809 banks.	2,849 banks.	2,852 banks.	2,875 banks.
Capital stock	$533,360,615.00	$539,109,201.72	$545,522,508.00	$548,240,730.00	$550,698,675.00
Surplus fund	152,872,340.01	153,642,934.86	157,003,875.60	157,249,190.87	159,573,479.21
Undivided profits	50,376,381.80	67,662,886.02	62,211,505.63	66,503,494.72	79,298,286.13
Nat'l bank circulati'n	256,072,158.00	244,893,097.00	238,273,685.00	228,672,610.00	202,078,287.00
State bank circulati'n	133,931.00	132,470.00	128,336.00	125,002.00	115,352.00
Dividends unpaid	1,534,905.58	1,526,776.66	1,863,303.62	2,227,810.59	1,500,345.06
Individual deposits	1,152,660,492.06	1,146,246,011.43	1,113,459,187.35	1,172,968,308.64	1,169,716,418.13
U. S. deposits	12,414,566.52	13,670,721.76	14,205,027.74	13,842,023.69	13,705,700.73
Dep's U.S. dis. offic'rs	3,010,018.72	2,798,864.55	2,884,865.62	2,721,276.77	4,276,257.85
Due to national ba'ks	210,778,171.80	204,405,273.11	218,327,437.33	218,395,950.54	223,842,279.46
Due to State banks	92,683,570.46	90,501,102.81	90,366,354.90	90,246,483.31	91,254,533.23
Notes re-discounted	8,376,095.20	8,718,911.71	7,948,698.27	10,594,176.50	9,150,345.79
Bills payable	1,174,874.29	1,145,240.26	1,381,095.01	2,067,693.48	2,444,958.36
Total	2,401,337,120.44	2,474,544,481.89	2,453,666,930.07	2,513,854,751.17	2,507,753,012.95

AGGREGATE RESOURCES AND LIABILITIES OF THE NATIONAL

1887.

Resources.	MARCH 4.	MAY 13.	AUGUST 1.	OCTOBER 5.	DECEMBER 7.
	2,909 banks.	2,955 banks.	3,014 banks.	3,049 banks.	3,070 banks.
Loans and discounts	$1,515,534,074.67	$1,560,201,810.73	$1,560,371,741.05	$1,587,540,133.76	$1,583,941,484.96
Bonds for circulation	211,537,150.00	200,452,300.00	189,032,050.00	189,083,100.00	186,431,900.00
Bonds for deposits	22,076,000.00	24,990,500.00	26,402,000.00	27,757,000.00	42,203,000.00
U. S. bonds on hand	9,721,450.00	8,157,250.00	7,808,000.00	6,014,350.00	6,988,550.00
Other stocks and b'ds	87,441,034.86	88,031,124.15	88,374,837.99	88,831,009.96	90,775,413.31
Due from res've ag'ts	163,161,181.37	148,067,874.43	140,270,155.75	140,873,587.98	132,959,765.34
Due from nat'l banks	86,460,829.09	105,576,841.99	99,487,767.80	93,302,413.04	98,227,065.30
Due from State banks	21,725,805.99	22,746,190.43	20,952,187.86	22,103,677.18	21,995,356.41
Real estate, etc	55,128,000.78	55,729,098.76	36,954,623.58	57,968,159.71	58,825,168.10
Current expenses	8,064,292.40	7,781,151.97	5,158,940.80	8,253,890.72	10,600,817.35
Premiums paid	15,537,721.22	16,806,431.83	17,353,130.17	17,288,771.35	18,797,205.79
Cash items	13,308,520.04	13,065,663.79	16,914,070.02	14,691,373.38	13,336,455.77
Clear'g-house exc'gs	80,239,194.59	86,829,363.73	128,211,028.48	88,775,457.09	85,097,380.41
Bills of other banks	22,235,206.00	25,188,137.00	22,962,737.00	21,937,884.00	23,447,294.00
Fractional currency	577,878.03	556,186.75	564,266.72	540,594.50	554,906.55
Trade dollars	1,803,601.40	184,203.08	63,071.97	509.25	328.00
Specie	171,678,906.15	167,315,065.62	165,104,210.28	165,085,454.38	159,240,043.48
Legal-tender notes	66,228,158.00	70,595,088.00	74,477,342.00	73,751,255.00	75,361,975.00
U. S. cert's of deposit	7,615,000.00	8,025,000.00	7,810,000.00	6,190,000.00	6,165,000.00
5% fund with Treas.	9,280,755.33	8,810,585.35	8,341,988.77	8,310,442.35	8,108,503.20
Due from U. S. Treas.	1,856,195.13	1,113,554.81	660,818.42	985,410.14	1,068,117.43
Total	2,581,143,115.05	2,529,314,022.42	2,637,276,167.72	2,620,193,475.59	2,624,186,330.55

1888.

Resources.	FEBRUARY 14.	APRIL 30.	JUNE 30.	OCTOBER 4.
	3,077 banks.	3,098 banks.	3,120 banks.	3,140 banks.
Loans and discounts	$1,584,170,370.51	$1,606,397,923.95	$1,628,124,564.83	$1,684,180,024.27
Bonds for circulation	181,845,450.00	181,042,950.00	177,513,900.00	171,867,200.00
Bonds for deposits	56,863,000.00	56,643,000.00	55,788,000.00	54,208,000.00
U. S. bonds on hand	6,450,500.00	7,639,350.00	7,830,150.00	6,507,050.00
Other stocks and bonds	94,153,088.97	95,296,917.07	96,265,812.31	99,752,403.73
Due from reserve agents	155,341,240.86	146,477,902.83	158,133,508.31	170,458,593.83
Due from national banks	93,080,082.48	95,519,102.26	101,080,774.90	99,821,000.57
Due from State banks	21,880,009.60	22,709,703.01	22,714,258.27	23,767,260.53
Real estate, etc	59,360,247.85	60,111,356.86	61,101,833.19	62,634,791.74
Current expenses	6,531,237.71	9,843,637.81	5,085,313.21	8,498,758.28
Premiums paid	19,779,498.56	19,501,481.06	18,003,434.54	17,615,898.02
Cash items	12,255,978.69	14,644,675.77	16,855,801.15	15,071,024.30
Clearing-house exchanges	78,418,037.29	117,270,706.86	74,220,763.69	102,439,751.67
Bills of other banks	23,145,206.00	24,434,212.00	21,343,405.00	201,600,818.00
Fractional currency	683,148.93	662,722.27	632,002.42	684,268.41
Trade dollars	437.59	351.15	371.76	419.05
Specie	173,830,614.62	172,074,011.19	181,292,270.76	178,097,816.64
Legal-tender notes	82,317,670.00	84,574,210.00	81,995,643.00	81,099,461.00
U. S. certificates of deposit	10,120,000.00	9,330,000.00	12,315,000.00	8,955,000.00
5% fund with Treasurer	7,993,180.22	7,887,950.36	7,765,837.16	7,555,401.72
Due from U. S. Treasurer	1,240,035.56	1,301,033.74	1,236,075.66	935,799.31
Total	2,664,366,304.44	2,732,423,198.19	2,731,448,016.16	2,815,751,141.07

BANKS FROM OCTOBER, 1863, TO OCTOBER, 1888—Continued.

1887.

Liabilities.	MARCH 4.	MAY 13.	AUGUST 1.	OCTOBER 5.	DECEMBER 7.
	2,909 banks.	2,955 banks.	3,014 banks.	3,049 banks.	3,070 banks.
Capital stock	$555, 351, 765. 00	$565, 629, 068. 45	$571, 648, 811. 00	$578, 462, 765. 00	$580, 733, 094. 42
Surplus fund	164, 337, 132. 72	167, 411, 521. 03	172, 348, 398. 99	173, 913, 440. 97	175, 246, 408. 26
Undivided profits	67, 248, 949. 16	70, 153, 368. 11	62, 294, 634. 02	71, 451, 167. 02	79, 899, 218. 06
Nat'l bank circulat'n	186, 231, 498. 00	176, 771, 539. 00	166, 025, 058. 00	167, 283, 343. 00	164, 904, 094. 00
State bank circulat'n	106, 100. 00	93, 716. 00	98, 697. 00	98, 689. 00	98, 676. 50
Dividends unpaid	1, 441, 628. 17	1, 977, 314. 40	2, 239, 929. 40	2, 405, 127. 83	1, 343, 963. 08
Individual deposits	1, 224, 925, 698. 26	1, 266, 570, 537. 67	1, 285, 076, 078. 58	1, 249, 477, 126. 05	1, 235, 757, 941. 59
U. S. deposits	15, 233, 909. 94	17, 556, 485. 93	19, 186, 712. 77	20, 392, 284. 03	38, 416, 270. 87
Dep's U. S. dis. offic'rs	4, 277, 187. 61	8, 779, 735. 14	4, 074, 903. 02	4, 831, 666. 14	4, 316, 024. 05
Due to national ba'ks	249, 337, 482. 40	244, 575, 545. 12	235, 966, 022. 46	227, 401, 984. 15	223, 088, 927. 85
Due to State banks	103, 012, 552. 48	102, 089, 438. 03	103, 003, 508. 14	102, 004, 625. 08	98, 809, 344. 06
Notes re-discounted	7, 556, 837. 10	10, 132, 799. 64	11, 125, 236. 08	17, 312, 806. 39	16, 268, 247. 74
Bills payable	2, 082, 374. 21	2, 567, 953. 30	2, 985, 967. 60	4, 886, 430. 43	5, 105, 112. 57
Total	2, 581, 143, 115. 05	2, 629, 314, 022. 42	2, 637, 276, 167. 72	2, 620, 193, 475. 50	2, 624, 180, 330. 55

1888.

Liabilities.	FEBRUARY 14.	APRIL 30.	JUNE 30.	OCTOBER 4.
	3,077 banks.	3,098 banks.	3,120 banks.	3,140 banks.
Capital stock	$582, 194, 263. 75	$585, 449, 487. 75	$588, 384, 018. 25	$592, 621, 656. 04
Surplus fund	179, 533, 475. 38	180, 053, 507. 27	183, 106, 435. 70	185, 520, 564. 08
Undivided profits	66, 606, 930. 87	78, 106, 768. 91	70, 206, 173. 07	77, 434, 426. 23
National bank circulation	159, 750, 193. 50	158, 897, 572. 00	155, 313, 353. 50	151, 702, 809. 50
State bank circulation	98, 652. 50	94, 876. 50	82, 372. 50	82, 334. 50
Dividends unpaid	1, 534, 314. 51	1, 766, 496. 41	7, 381, 894. 42	2, 378, 275. 70
Individual deposits	1, 251, 957, 844. 42	1, 309, 731, 015. 16	1, 292, 342, 471. 28	1, 350, 320, 861. 11
U. S deposits	55, 193, 899. 10	51, 601, 454. 69	54, 679, 648. 03	52, 140, 502. 07
Deposits U. S. dis. officers	4, 255, 362. 02	4, 789, 093. 63	3, 090, 052. 65	3, 993, 900. 51
Due to national banks	241, 038, 490. 03	237, 056, 040. 91	248, 248, 440. 03	260, 007, 968. 00
Due to State banks	105, 539, 405. 53	104, 502, 068. 21	109, 871, 372. 41	114, 936, 397. 15
Notes and bills re-discounted	12, 866, 722. 85	12, 724, 238. 71	13, 096, 110. 55	17, 305, 750. 01
Bills payable	3, 796, 739. 99	4, 400, 076. 04	4, 055, 068. 27	6, 615, 813. 47
Total	2, 664, 366, 304. 44	2, 732, 423, 198. 19	2, 731, 448, 010. 16	2, 815, 751, 341. 07

A SUMMARY

OF THE

STATE AND CONDITION

OF

THE NATIONAL BANKS

ON

DECEMBER 7, 1887, FEBRUARY 14, APRIL 30, JUNE 30, AND OCTOBER 4, 1888.

Arranged by States, Territories, and Reserve Cities.

NOTE.—The abstract of each State is exclusive of any reserve city therein.

Abstract of reports since October 5, 1887,

MAINE.

Resources.	DECEMBER 7. 74 banks.	FEBRUARY 14. 75 banks.	APRIL 30. 75 banks.	JUNE 30. 75 banks.	OCTOBER 4. 75 banks.
Loans and discounts	$18, 898, 502. 00	$18, 477, 001. 20	$18, 673, 708. 56	$18, 910, 036. 77	$20, 192, 140. 20
Bonds for circulation	5, 508, 500. 00	5, 533, 500. 00	5, 493, 500. 00	5, 208, 500. 00	4, 961, 000. 00
Bonds for deposits	170, 000. 00	170, 000. 00	170, 000. 00	170, 000. 00	170, 000. 00
U. S. bonds on hand	400. 00	500. 00	400. 00	....	100. 00
Other stocks and b'ds	867, 273. 83	804, 678. 85	884, 745. 18	911, 211. 49	912, 617. 38
Due from res've ag'ts	1, 434, 674. 81	1, 083, 091. 88	1, 379, 080. 42	1, 519, 072. 14	2, 255, 364. 43
Due from nat'l banks	513, 180. 02	446, 243. 90	452, 754. 45	517, 091. 97	536, 705. 45
Due from State banks	14, 678. 15	5 755. 78	11, 040. 50	26, 771. 20	26, 843. 66
Real estate, etc	511, 008. 00	516, 200. 88	512. 833. 00	543, 942 05	544, 027. 05
Current expenses	77, 060. 39	30, 706. 53	58, 504. 36	20, 089. 58	55, 446. 71
Premiums paid	263, 850. 98	256, 528. 99	252, 314. 55	219, 474. 06	182, 324. 58
Cash items	107, 302. 00	183, 532. 20	185, 325. 06	193, 530. 14	227, 502. 58
Clear'g-house exch'gs	73, 756. 90	88, 825. 54	102, 376. 06	89, 152. 17	117, 090. 07
Bills of other banks	353, 861. 00	203, 140. 00	304, 153. 00	263, 681. 00	350, 020 00
Fractional currency	3, 343. 48	4, 035. 21	4, 021. 35	3, 232. 16	3, 563. 65
Trade dollars	....	....	....	....	....
Specie	709, 727. 64	727, 020. 00	714, 082. 07	679, 292. 08	717, 407. 07
Legal-tender notes	211, 082. 00	193, 720. 00	221, 413. 00	206, 310. 00	251, 125. 00
U. S. cert's of deposit	....	....	....	....	....
5 % fund with Treas.	239, 286. 27	230, 097. 50	237, 047. 00	220, 912. 00	213, 891. 50
Due from U. S. Treas	7, 050. 00	7, 000. 00	3, 716. 33	9, 140. 33	6, 100. 00
Total	30, 055, 234. 07	30, 063, 820. 24	29, 661, 107. 68	29, 715, 254. 65	31, 725, 703. 53

NEW HAMPSHIRE.

	49 banks.	49 banks.	49 banks.	49 banks.	49 banks.
Loans and discounts	$9, 583, 071. 30	$9, 303, 100. 26	$9, 401, 184. 20	$9, 052, 860. 02	$10, 150 394. 19
Bonds for circulation	3, 919, 500. 00	3, 919, 500. 00	3, 869, 500. 00	3, 827, 000. 00	3, 677, 000. 00
Bonds for deposits	450, 000 00	450, 000. 00	450, 000. 00	450, 000. 00	450, 000. 00
U. S. bonds on hand	6, 000. 00	6, 000. 00	6, 000. 00	....	100. 00
Other stocks and b'ds	1, 775, 207. 41	1, 822, 704. 83	1, 936, 517. 36	1, 882, 308. 71	1, 839, 575. 58
Due from res've ag'ts	1, 084, 087. 02	1, 082, 042. 58	1, 144, 018. 50	1, 297, 400. 13	1, 432, 866. 35
Due from nat'l banks	183, 313. 26	140, 510. 13	124, 135. 74	175, 595. 42	221, 800. 97
Due from State banks	58, 490. 12	48, 416. 47	47, 327. 98	47, 418. 32	43, 990. 69
Real estate, etc	211, 608. 48	202, 144. 84	202, 310. 34	200, 845. 20	211, 337. 49
Current expenses	56, 083. 80	40, 806. 07	53, 552. 08	38, 218. 42	48, 388. 30
Premiums paid	205, 963. 00	266, 795. 16	269, 152. 08	255, 083. 33	247, 043. 50
Cash items	181, 968. 34	158, 060. 35	106, 288. 11	164, 410. 32	106, 716. 59
Clear'g-house exch'gs	....	....	....	....	....
Bills of other banks	238, 665. 00	198, 697. 00	249, 592. 00	210, 410. 00	279, 140. 00
Fractional currency	4, 658. 75	5, 897. 57	7, 117. 60	6, 325. 85	6, 686. 11
Trade dollars	....	5. 00	....	....	....
Specie	416, 484. 46	364, 409. 74	444, 004. 22	360, 607. 28	307, 288. 50
Legal-tender notes	132, 899. 00	117, 411. 00	142, 502. 00	128, 240. 00	145, 073. 00
U. S. cert's of deposit	....	....	....	....	....
5 % fund with Treas.	174, 022. 50	175, 012. 50	174, 302. 50	170, 917. 50	163, 170. 00
Due from U. S. Treas.	3, 475. 00	17, 250. 00	20. 00	2. 543. 00	4, 717. 90
Total	18, 771, 759. 63	18, 409, 454. 40	18, 717, 423. 60	18, 879, 043. 10	19, 507, 189. 17

VERMONT.

	49 banks.	49 banks.	49 banks.	49 banks.	49 banks.
Loans and discounts	$13, 075, 357. 05	$12, 026, 899. 40	$12, 704, 021. 32	$12, 584, 804. 38	$12, 800, 451. 86
Bonds for circulation	3, 814, 000. 00	3, 764, 000. 00	3, 764, 000. 00	3, 680, 000. 00	3, 614, 000. 00
Bonds for deposits	188, 000. 00	438, 000. 00	438, 000. 00	438, 000. 00	438, 000. 00
U. S. bonds on hand	127, 450. 00	128, 300. 00	148, 300. 00	149, 400. 00	127, 050. 00
Other stocks and b'ds	806, 214. 22	768, 973. 78	706, 410. 98	850, 810. 08	924, 787. 56
Due from res've ag'ts	818, 636. 42	968, 790. 06	870, 842. 57	1, 161, 338. 51	1, 200, 446. 83
Due from nat'l banks	179, 542. 63	250, 008. 30	153, 510. 98	150, 437. 51	227, 895. 75
Due from State banks	36, 375. 00	46, 210. 52	45, 917. 94	48, 045. 66	49, 410. 22
Real estate, etc	229, 145. 06	228, 470. 17	229, 100. 80	228, 464. 29	224. 434. 01
Current expenses	62, 202. 50	25, 634. 84	51, 206. 29	46, 048. 82	48, 150. 56
Premiums paid	150, 381. 48	188, 118. 70	191, 553. 08	182, 214 46	185, 271. 59
Cash items	71, 088. 73	61, 662. 35	61, 633. 54	92, 678. 01	73, 612. 48
Clear'g-house exch'gs	....	....	....	....	....
Bills of other banks	127, 227. 00	117, 190. 00	104, 252. 00	133, 339. 00	118, 427. 00
Fractional currency	4, 117. 98	4, 695. 60	4, 912. 14	4, 261. 70	4, 561. 94
Trade dollars	....	....	....	....	....
Specie	430, 010. 11	417, 154. 26	369, 711. 80	394, 724. 39	405, 733. 85
Legal-tender notes	178, 952. 00	166, 040. 00	184, 405. 00	190, 606. 00	204, 454. 00
U. S. cert's of deposit	....	....	....	....	....
5 % fund with Treas.	149, 489. 50	154, 050. 00	162, 100. 00	146, 017. 55	145, 670. 00
Due from U. S. Treas.	210. 00	2, 900. 00	1, 800. 00	....	....
Total	20, 440, 300. 88	20, 357, 725. 07	20, 277, 837. 53	20, 506, 150. 80	20, 847, 906. 63

arranged by States and reserve cities.

MAINE.

Liabilities.	DECEMBER 7.	FEBRUARY 14.	APRIL 30.	JUNE 30.	OCTOBER 4.
	74 banks.	75 banks.	75 banks.	75 banks.	75 banks.
Capital stock	$10, 585, 352. 42	$10, 635, 000. 00	$10, 660, 000. 00	$10, 660, 000. 00	$10, 660, 000. 00
Surplus fund	2, 406, 284. 88	2, 426, 282. 08	2, 427, 208. 34	2, 451, 776. 56	2, 549, 905. 80
Undivided profits	1, 504, 643. 97	1, 247, 080. 70	1, 403, 725. 84	1, 278, 040. 77	1, 394, 133. 81
Nat'l-bank circulation	4, 867, 403. 00	4, 821, 508. 00	4, 814, 555. 00	4, 593, 263. 00	4, 403, 033. 00
State-bank circulation	....	....	....	....	....
Dividends unpaid	36, 400. 00	51, 013. 03	52, 637. 10	271, 861. 75	71, 570. 38
Individual deposits	9, 706, 720. 44	9, 817, 916. 57	9, 348, 523. 18	9, 480, 280. 52	11, 064, 653. 05
U. S. deposits	55, 381. 31	63, 109. 00	70, 018. 83	63, 321. 86	67, 119. 69
Dep'ts U.S.dis.officers	77, 555. 77	87, 019. 16	78, 788. 81	74, 540. 20	81, 649. 38
Due to national banks	538, 529. 22	476, 003. 38	396, 563. 00	302, 029. 10	576, 166. 87
Due to State banks	166, 358. 74	186, 343. 02	106, 318. 73	89, 580. 61	120, 376. 16
Notes re-discounted	152, 615. 76	183, 650. 06	185, 033. 04	100, 749. 47	196, 448. 30
Bills payable	17, 904. 46	66, 044. 34	117, 135. 12	289, 801. 63	531, 022. 09
Total	30, 055, 234. 97	30, 003, 820. 24	29, 661, 107. 68	29, 715, 254. 65	31, 725, 703. 53

NEW HAMPSHIRE.

	49 banks.	49 banks.	49 banks.	49 banks.	49 banks.
Capital stock	$6, 205, 000. 00	$6, 205, 000. 00	$6, 205, 000. 00	$6, 205, 000. 00	$6, 205, 000. 00
Surplus fund	1, 454, 780. 45	1, 454, 251. 55	1, 459, 010. 85	1, 466, 054. 79	1, 497, 364. 46
Undivided profits	720, 405. 58	607, 394. 73	713, 285. 71	689, 002. 43	735, 093. 15
Nat'l-bank circulation	3, 400, 650. 00	3, 478, 795. 00	3, 406, 045. 00	3, 378, 500. 00	3, 276, 520. 00
State-bank circulation	6, 829. 00	6, 829. 00	6, 829. 00	6, 829. 00	6, 829. 00
Dividends unpaid	17, 949. 66	25, 370. 44	33, 488. 81	84, 603. 13	34, 803. 36
Individual deposits	5, 504, 387. 98	5, 255, 070. 25	5, 508, 728. 70	5, 650, 514. 24	6, 361, 001. 44
U. S. deposits	333, 516. 60	330, 444. 38	328, 407. 27	415, 929. 82	375, 093. 97
Dep'ts U.S.dis.officers	134, 745. 36	156, 902. 17	136, 097. 62	60, 485. 30	97, 144. 06
Due to national banks	498, 764. 46	529, 080. 48	612, 018. 58	586, 343. 23	602, 197. 88
Due to State banks	250, 776. 20	297, 508. 27	266, 629. 92	307, 777. 91	243, 211. 25
Notes re-discounted	39, 616. 34	51, 302. 13	11, 192. 34	8, 732. 86	12, 300. 00
Bills payable	24, 279. 00	10, 000. 00	30, 000. 00	11, 110. 30	....
Total	18, 771, 750. 63	18, 400, 454. 40	18, 717, 423. 80	18, 879, 043. 10	19, 507, 169. 17

VERMONT.

	49 banks.	49 banks.	49 banks.	49 banks.	49 banks.
Capital stock	$7, 566, 000. 00	$7, 566, 000. 00	$7, 566, 000. 00	$7, 566, 000. 00	$7, 566, 000. 00
Surplus fund	1, 572, 213. 75	1, 597, 771. 57	1, 597, 886. 60	1, 608, 386. 60	1, 690, 476. 41
Undivided profits	812, 489. 40	586, 311. 42	764, 733. 03	691, 683. 39	732, 229. 34
Nat'l-bank circulation	3, 401, 985. 00	3, 351, 215. 00	3, 319, 515. 00	3, 261, 600. 00	3, 227, 765. 00
State-bank circulation	3, 500. 00	3, 434. 00	3, 434. 00	3, 434. 00	3, 434. 00
Dividends unpaid	8, 076. 59	16, 818. 10	9, 380. 54	119, 558. 15	11, 743. 94
Individual deposits	6, 339, 889. 26	6, 311, 125. 06	5, 978, 572. 77	6, 217, 034. 44	6, 607, 226. 21
U. S. deposits	181, 722. 30	457, 217. 52	408, 787. 28	471, 288. 22	466, 258. 00
Dep'ts U.S.dis.officers	8, 706. 07	9, 197. 47	12, 170. 25	7, 579. 71	13, 295. 92
Due to national banks	393, 030. 82	255, 512. 32	374, 800. 78	278, 283. 56	203, 254. 83
Due to State banks	82, 206. 73	63, 625. 04	61, 950. 68	98, 266. 50	130, 324. 57
Notes re-discounted	48, 290. 71	100, 406. 67	67, 597. 00	77, 878. 23	60, 957. 51
Bills payable	20, 029. 25	30, 000. 00	50, 000. 00	45, 187. 50	45, 000. 00
Total	20, 440, 309. 88	20, 357, 725. 07	20, 277, 837. 53	20, 506, 150. 39	20, 847, 966. 63

Abstract of reports since October 5, 1887, arranged

MASSACHUSETTS.

Resources.	DECEMBER 7.	FEBRUARY 14.	APRIL 30.	JUNE 30.	OCTOBER 4.
	198 banks.	198 banks.	198 banks.	199 banks.	198 banks.
Loans and discounts.	$91, 587, 597. 64	$90, 932, 518. 57	$91, 522, 664. 58	$92, 291, 101. 68	$94, 674, 951. 93
Bonds for circulation.	23, 892, 900. 00	22, 890, 900. 00	22, 690, 900. 00	22, 190, 000. 00	21, 813, 400. 00
Bonds for deposits...	300, 000. 00	1, 575, 000. 00	1, 575, 000. 00	1, 575, 000. 00	1, 575, 000. 00
U. S. bonds on hand..	131, 250. 00	129, 750. 00	120, 850. 00	118, 650. 00	93, 850. 00
Other stocks and b'ds	4, 519, 352. 70	4, 487, 148. 45	4, 437, 551. 59	4, 502, 577. 17	4, 608, 443. 57
Due from res've ag'ts.	7, 129, 932. 33	8, 362, 540. 66	9, 123, 805. 71	9, 145, 601. 26	10, 450, 288. 04
Due from nat'l banks.	1, 292, 339. 18	973, 337. 07	1, 049, 683. 45	1, 045, 948. 75	987, 174. 40
Due from State banks	271, 366. 46	171, 575. 76	188, 839. 63	137, 410. 10	163, 696. 21
Real estate, etc	2, 261, 460. 55	2, 286, 119. 62	2, 317, 544. 98	2, 316, 329. 68	2, 326, 666. 23
Current expenses....	548, 651. 26	477, 581. 03	206, 183. 73	239, 578. 37	243, 889. 67
Premiums paid......	1, 044, 776. 81	1, 119, 631. 44	1, 030, 342. 11	968, 902. 87	912, 563. 06
Cash items	745, 720. 93	690, 535. 67	731, 859. 39	1, 007, 288. 23	890, 974. 07
Clear'g-house exch'gs	53, 899. 65	63, 129. 04	65, 879. 76	78, 428. 99	69, 918. 05
Bills of other banks..	1, 286, 285. 00	1, 144, 832. 00	1, 008, 745. 00	1, 072, 239. 00	1, 252, 635. 00
Fractional currency.	40, 383. 95	45, 523. 50	41, 718. 47	39, 106. 66	39, 030. 46
Trade dollars........	....	1. 00	6. 00	5. 00	6. 00
Specie	3, 029, 526. 68	2, 870, 846. 44	2, 888, 126. 84	2, 858, 510. 93	2, 970, 552. 92
Legal-tender notes ..	1, 185, 597. 00	1, 190, 806. 00	1, 349, 900. 00	1, 273, 792. 00	1, 471, 557. 00
U. S. cert's of deposit.	200, 000. 00	200, 000. 00	195, 000. 00	195, 000. 00	195, 000. 00
5 % fund with Treas.	1, 061, 495. 50	1, 019, 845. 50	1, 008, 195. 50	979, 505. 60	982, 587. 50
Due from U. S. Treas.	51, 444. 11	43, 980. 00	82, 830. 00	31, 892. 50	28, 355. 00
Total...........	140, 633, 979. 69	140, 675, 601. 75	141, 635, 621. 74	142, 157, 768. 79	145, 750, 539. 11

CITY OF BOSTON.

Resources.	DECEMBER 7.	FEBRUARY 14.	APRIL 30.	JUNE 30.	OCTOBER 4.
	54 banks.	54 banks.	54 banks.	54 banks.	55 banks.
Loans and discounts.	$125, 029, 621. 35	$130, 175, 453. 77	$127, 936, 199. 45	$134, 833, 892. 39	$136, 312, 847. 61
Bonds for circulation	8, 788, 150. 00	7, 338, 150. 00	7, 258, 150. 00	6, 937, 650. 00	6, 464, 650. 00
Bonds for deposits ..	3, 505, 000. 00	4, 955, 000. 00	4, 955, 000. 00	4, 655, 000. 00	4, 455, 000. 00
U. S. bonds on hand..	48, 350. 00	7, 400. 00	41, 200. 00	66, 600. 00	53, 050. 00
Other stocks and b'ds	2, 868, 346. 06	3, 449, 888. 65	3, 367, 281. 15	3, 575, 835. 46	3, 534, 675. 45
Due from res've ag'ts.	13, 141, 793. 19	14, 955, 074. 11	15, 193, 186. 27	14, 378, 022. 54	16, 598, 529. 64
Due from nat'l banks.	11, 584, 037. 74	11, 300, 662. 08	10, 744, 938. 82	12, 093, 085. 15	12, 221, 419. 01
Due from State banks	208, 178. 72	195, 140. 50	617, 977. 43	245, 737. 16	273, 219. 99
Real estate, etc	2, 924, 493. 58	2, 909, 550. 51	2, 868, 616. 68	2, 871, 706. 82	2, 893, 349. 52
Current expenses....	658, 075. 83	1, 002, 163. 98	167, 833. 80	441, 576. 72	33, 292. 60
Premiums paid......	873, 258. 76	954, 214. 20	958, 848. 15	879, 778. 53	809, 154. 86
Cash items	436, 872. 86	284, 009. 29	519, 539. 07	927, 956. 69	336, 550. 90
Clear'g-house exch'gs	9, 522, 820. 87	8, 881, 471. 36	11, 509, 708. 16	10, 311, 766. 18	9, 864, 113. 03
Bills of other banks..	1, 016, 216. 00	1, 161, 178. 00	1, 122, 014. 00	1, 054, 229. 00	1, 099, 765. 00
Fractional currency	17, 881. 56	22, 986. 06	18, 768. 41	17, 093. 88	16, 869. 02
Trade dollars........	....	....	....	....	....
Specie	8, 515, 027. 18	9, 330, 501. 15	9, 541, 241. 77	10, 265, 675. 86	11, 498, 027. 85
Legal-tender notes ..	2, 865, 676. 00	2, 331, 872. 00	2, 070, 429. 00	2, 187, 934. 00	2, 822, 701. 00
U. S. cert's of deposit.	325, 000. 00	885, 000. 00	495, 000. 00	675, 000. 00	235, 000. 00
5 % fund with Treas.	374, 601. 75	330, 181. 75	317, 671. 75	312, 159. 25	288, 659. 25
Due from U. S. Treas.	269, 820. 00	188, 010. 00	75, 570. 00	46, 002. 00	28, 250. 00
Total...........	193, 663, 221. 45	200, 657, 917. 01	199, 788, 194. 11	206, 777, 663. 62	209, 839, 184. 73

RHODE ISLAND.

Resources.	DECEMBER 7.	FEBRUARY 14.	APRIL 30.	JUNE 30.	OCTOBER 4.
	61 banks.	61 banks.	60 banks.	60 banks.	60 banks.
Loans and discounts.	$34, 922, 019. 77	$34, 635, 004. 63	$34, 520, 432. 97	$34, 800, 469. 32	$35, 568, 742. 23
Bonds for circulation.	5, 183, 900. 00	5, 168, 900. 00	5, 168, 900. 00	5, 168, 900. 00	5, 143, 900. 00
Bonds for deposits...	150, 000. 00	150, 000. 00	150, 000. 00	150, 000. 00	150, 000. 00
U. S. bonds on hand..	130, 050. 00	47, 150. 00	51, 400. 00	46, 530. 00	45, 050. 00
Other stocks and b'ds	1, 537, 896. 22	1, 565, 617. 56	1, 478, 554. 19	1, 439, 295. 65	1, 482, 885. 99
Due from res've ag'ts.	1, 728, 566. 01	2, 383, 227. 23	1, 846, 354. 25	2, 534, 709. 46	2, 536, 132. 23
Due from nat'l banks.	830, 361. 18	892, 151. 10	764, 959. 89	846, 835. 16	1, 124, 848. 14
Due from State banks	41, 246. 94	61, 909. 03	58, 929. 93	44, 907. 51	22, 708. 02
Real estate, etc	668, 759. 32	698, 154. 81	720, 309. 07	710, 204. 15	717, 144. 61
Current expenses....	117, 980. 58	79, 960. 35	106, 091. 55	58, 077. 22	96, 454. 33
Premiums paid......	413, 761. 90	379, 121. 65	372, 807. 62	361, 829. 81	354, 283. 39
Cash items	147, 909. 49	181, 027. 74	154, 937. 03	164, 528. 29	170, 431. 32
Clear'g-house exch'gs	301, 786. 01	373, 095. 61	374, 291. 74	575, 222. 09	418, 300. 47
Bills of other banks..	308, 226. 00	318, 132. 00	371, 250. 00	290, 927. 00	274, 718. 00
Fractional currency.	11, 765. 65	14, 418. 15	12, 254. 58	11, 498. 44	12, 578. 80
Trade dollars........	5. 00	3. 00	4. 00	14. 00	20. 00
Specie	695, 193. 26	666, 007. 11	651, 017. 49	646, 765. 49	658, 748. 04
Legal-tender notes ..	626, 314. 00	589, 121. 00	610, 640. 00	574, 921. 00	613, 023. 00
U. S. cert's of deposit.	....	....	....	....	....
5% fund with Treas.	232, 175. 50	220, 670. 50	223, 575. 50	227, 035. 50	215, 700. 50
Due from U. S. Treas.	13, 062. 50	18, 862. 50	49, 662. 50	43, 152. 50	15, 022. 50
Total...........	48, 000, 988. 33	48, 352, 533. 97	47, 686, 372. 31	48, 698, 952. 50	49, 620, 691. 57

by States and reserve cities—Continued.

MASSACHUSETTS.

Liabilities.	DECEMBER 7.	FEBRUARY 11.	APRIL 30.	JUNE 30.	OCTOBER 4.
	198 banks.	198 banks.	198 banks.	190 banks.	198 banks.
Capital stock	$44, 790, 500. 00	$44, 790, 500. 00	$44, 790, 500. 00	$44, 820, 005. 00	$44, 710, 500. 00
Surplus fund	14, 203, 975. 17	14, 253, 059. 21	14, 211, 044. 83	14, 226, 686. 53	14, 301, 455. 57
Undivided profits	4, 938, 885. 61	5, 031, 288. 15	4, 440, 094. 55	5, 012, 511. 40	4, 385, 438. 40
Nat'l-bank circulation	21, 090, 083. 00	20, 213, 059. 00	20, 158, 814. 00	19, 719, 114. 00	19, 454, 153. 00
State-bank circulation	....	....	....	....	....
Dividends unpaid	122, 065. 85	113, 249. 64	227, 335. 02	298, 785. 19	551, 423. 23
Individual deposits	52, 320, 485. 16	51, 978, 259. 28	53, 501, 613. 58	53, 713, 000. 66	57, 814, 224. 14
U. S. deposits	285, 981. 03	1, 035, 262. 64	1, 707, 948. 93	1, 708, 381. 25	1, 706, 254. 33
Dep'ts U. S. dis. officers	18, 136. 83	56, 052. 12	1, 465. 75	2, 233. 17	645. 53
Due to national banks	2, 242, 717. 73	1, 939, 874. 10	1, 991, 380. 70	2, 281, 073. 98	2, 205, 226. 82
Due to State banks	210, 770. 73	211, 001. 63	328, 288. 83	250, 201. 28	322, 914. 30
Notes re-discounted	366, 370. 58	443, 095. 98	260, 226. 46	108, 813. 33	173, 313. 90
Bills payable	35, 000. 00	10, 000. 00	10, 000. 00	10, 000. 00	34, 989. 80
Total	140, 633, 979. 69	140, 675, 601. 75	141, 636, 621. 74	142, 157, 768. 79	145, 750, 530. 11

CITY OF BOSTON.

	54 banks.	54 banks.	54 banks.	54 banks.	55 banks.
Capital stock	$50, 950, 000. 00	$50, 950, 000. 00	$50, 950, 000. 00	$51, 150, 000. 00	$51, 400, 000. 00
Surplus fund	12, 652, 035. 50	12, 652, 535. 50	13, 134, 513. 80	13, 059, 513. 80	13, 209, 256. 20
Undivided profits	4, 547, 546. 19	5, 966, 354. 33	4, 028, 737. 34	5, 099, 419. 98	3, 939, 833. 47
Nat'l-bank circulation	7, 808, 005. 00	6, 540, 610. 00	6, 476, 380. 00	6, 205, 280. 00	5, 703, 530. 00
State-bank circulation	....	....	....	....	....
Dividends unpaid	43, 733. 45	27, 719. 70	76, 752. 28	47, 262. 96	353, 625. 79
Individual deposits	79, 838, 623. 43	82, 818, 189. 13	83, 950, 607. 78	85, 013, 023. 98	86, 487, 601. 52
U. S. deposits	3, 735, 112. 34	5, 223, 749. 76	5, 227, 850. 31	4, 906, 458. 91	4, 088, 829. 90
Dep'ts U. S. dis. officers	37, 409. 39	34, 687. 02	34, 253. 16	52, 373. 84	38, 796. 48
Due to national banks	25, 929, 752. 80	28, 046, 434. 25	25, 661, 282. 05	30, 590, 850. 75	32, 515, 805. 13
Due to State banks	7, 930, 913. 29	8, 202, 907. 32	10, 241, 811. 30	10, 395, 473. 40	11, 207, 629. 04
Notes re-discounted	....	....	....	....	....
Bills payable	130, 000. 00	104, 700. 00	6, 000. 00	240, 000. 00	150, 157. 20
Total	193, 663, 221. 45	200, 057, 017. 01	199, 788, 194. 11	206, 777, 663. 62	209, 839, 184. 73

RHODE ISLAND.

	61 banks.	61 banks.	60 banks.	60 banks.	60 banks.
Capital stock	$20, 340, 050. 00	$20, 284, 050. 00	$20, 284, 050. 00	$20, 284, 050. 00	$20, 284, 050. 00
Surplus fund	4, 257, 984. 72	4, 285, 701. 74	4, 306, 733. 38	4, 322, 023. 96	4, 363, 658. 81
Undivided profits	2, 068, 759. 75	1, 952, 672. 98	2, 110, 754. 62	1, 880, 635. 51	1, 942, 209. 79
Nat'l-bank circulation	4, 629, 582. 00	4, 565, 722. 00	4, 574, 247. 00	4, 562, 812. 00	4, 580, 032. 00
State-bank circulation	890. 00	890. 00	890. 00	890. 00	885. 00
Dividends unpaid	84, 358. 57	104, 413. 95	89, 993. 72	306, 559. 63	130, 653. 87
Individual deposits	14, 085, 063. 93	14, 370, 163. 13	13, 891, 230. 90	14, 082, 885. 64	14, 998, 920. 57
U. S. deposits	74, 012. 98	130, 036. 80	107, 163. 15	98, 897. 50	80, 010. 85
Dep'ts U. S. dis. officers	62, 243. 81	25, 413. 55	38, 070. 94	29, 177. 49	53, 042. 81
Due to national banks	1, 570, 075. 78	1, 694, 170. 79	1, 100, 060. 53	1, 600, 676. 27	2, 013, 227. 25
Due to State banks	852, 966. 70	930, 297. 03	1, 156, 348. 29	1, 405, 072. 09	1, 150, 400. 62
Notes re-discounted	....	....	6, 775. 00	....	....
Bills payable	35, 000. 00	....	10, 152. 78	83, 752. 50	5, 000. 00
Total	48, 000, 988. 33	48, 352, 583. 97	47, 686, 372. 31	48, 608, 952. 59	49, 620, 691. 57

Abstract of reports since October 5, 1887, arranged

CONNECTICUT.

Resources.	DECEMBER 7. 83 banks.	FEBRUARY 14. 83 banks.	APRIL 30. 83 banks.	JUNE 30. 83 banks.	OCTOBER 4. 84 banks.
Loans and discounts	$42, 478, 106. 18	$42, 918, 885. 80	$42, 071, 059. 11	$42, 967, 841. 80	$43, 818, 391. 06
Bonds for circulation	9, 616, 100. 00	9, 370, 100. 00	9, 220, 900. 00	8, 935, 100. 00	8, 832, 600. 00
Bonds for deposits	1, 388, 000. 00	2, 938, 000. 00	2, 938, 000. 00	2, 038, 000. 00	3, 038, 000. 00
U. S. bonds on hand	153, 150. 00	163, 150. 00	113, 150. 00	53, 100. 00	155, 150. 00
Other stocks and b'ds	3, 350, 895. 14	3, 333, 714. 99	3, 408, 138. 79	3, 576, 900. 32	3, 795, 756. 73
Due from res've ag'ts	4, 848, 621. 42	6, 148, 383. 41	5, 960, 861. 17	7, 327, 169. 34	5, 768, 965. 17
Due from nat'l banks	2, 368, 241. 96	2, 702, 182. 46	3, 014, 326. 96	3, 061, 688. 98	1, 938, 572. 87
Due from State banks	240, 563. 59	246, 450. 76	336, 000. 15	407, 887. 82	316, 000. 64
Real estate, etc	1, 479, 274. 63	1, 510, 306. 29	1, 530, 108. 47	1, 556, 045. 36	1, 686, 295. 15
Current expenses	269, 542. 88	137, 320. 90	240, 337. 87	88, 481. 08	201, 499. 78
Premiums paid	802, 830. 38	1, 001, 011. 00	922, 820. 04	820, 049. 17	788, 527. 62
Cash items	298, 035. 90	287, 925. 28	854, 944. 08	516, 775. 08	426, 669. 38
Clear'g-house exch'gs	215, 218. 19	334, 109. 26	316, 012. 81	376, 252. 74	234, 843. 65
Bills of other banks	674, 103. 00	585, 830. 00	703, 589. 00	600, 683. 00	639, 090. 00
Fractional currency	17, 968. 90	22, 837. 04	19, 304. 49	21, 696. 19	18, 347. 57
Trade dollars	45. 00	57. 00	55. 00	45. 95	54. 15
Specie	1, 709, 594. 45	1, 759, 052. 05	1, 722, 604. 51	1, 711, 498. 76	1, 795, 931. 78
Legal-tender notes	700, 503. 00	672, 755. 00	909, 028. 00	818, 153. 00	918, 880. 00
U. S. cert's of deposit	....	....	....	....	....
5 % fund with Treas	407, 611. 41	419, 044. 50	400, 393. 75	394, 609. 50	377, 144. 00
Due from U. S. Treas	21, 907. 30	20, 801. 00	33, 046. 00	31, 369. 75	14, 636. 75
Total	71, 220, 452. 33	74, 581, 334. 75	75, 140, 783. 22	76, 204, 357. 88	74, 762, 377. 20

NEW YORK.

	272 banks.	271 banks.	272 banks.	272 banks.	270 banks.
Loans and discounts	$100, 324, 493. 54	$98, 548, 487. 17	$100, 532, 093. 43	$100, 005, 461. 05	$101, 262, 149. 67
Bonds for circulation	19, 468, 550. 00	18, 878, 550. 00	18, 780, 550. 00	18, 400, 050. 00	18, 098, 050. 00
Bonds for deposits	1, 177, 000. 00	2, 567, 000. 00	2, 367, 000. 00	2, 567, 000. 00	2, 467, 000. 00
U. S. bonds on hand	870, 900. 00	869, 800. 00	873, 400. 00	751, 950. 00	665, 450. 00
Other stocks and b'ds	8, 682, 670. 86	9, 010, 111. 61	8, 815, 139. 21	8, 581, 888. 55	8, 071, 591. 98
Due from res've ag'ts	13, 665, 003. 38	15, 071, 854. 17	13, 916, 876. 85	15, 122, 845. 95	15, 121, 360. 21
Due from nat'l banks	2, 742, 327. 15	2, 772, 108. 67	3, 071, 399. 73	3, 231, 752. 76	2, 611, 638. 00
Due from State banks	704, 328. 30	678, 032. 54	721, 223. 60	601, 798. 46	690, 213. 87
Real estate, etc	3, 459, 720. 88	3, 380, 829. 14	3, 405, 806. 99	3, 398, 521. 54	3, 410, 823. 86
Current expenses	697, 418. 17	352, 729. 83	588, 236. 60	371, 509. 11	466, 902. 14
Premiums paid	1, 311, 445. 37	1, 375, 035. 73	1, 367, 873. 72	1, 324, 063. 41	1, 193, 516. 10
Cash items	1, 728, 610. 50	1, 367, 836. 87	1, 966, 133. 76	1, 800, 925. 98	1, 567, 029. 85
Clear'g-house exch'gs	48, 928. 01	45, 093. 47	54, 620. 07	42, 402. 62	61, 856. 55
Bills of other banks	1, 292, 187. 00	1, 263, 038. 00	1, 207, 002. 00	1, 161, 350. 00	1, 399, 776. 00
Fractional currency	40, 456. 45	46, 168. 92	45, 989. 65	39, 438. 83	45, 850. 87
Trade dollars	138. 14	161. 94	66. 50	87. 01	176. 40
Specie	5, 192, 967. 92	5, 440, 201. 34	5, 310, 149. 36	5, 020, 260. 20	5, 612, 603. 78
Legal-tender notes	3, 106, 609. 00	3, 271, 436. 00	3, 079, 177. 00	2, 952, 674. 00	3, 245, 516. 00
U. S. cert's of deposit	260, 000. 00	250, 000. 00	270, 000. 00	270, 000. 00	415, 000. 00
5 % fund with Treas	860, 196. 75	838, 023. 75	838, 810. 58	811, 798. 05	806, 500. 25
Due from U. S. Treas	59, 020. 68	77, 749. 48	113, 755. 74	28, 912. 48	15, 490. 64
Total	165, 684, 093. 00	166, 108, 228. 65	167, 527, 263. 81	166, 764, 789. 00	168, 128, 506. 07

NEW YORK CITY.

	47 banks.	46 banks.	46 banks.	46 banks.	46 banks.
Loans and discounts	$258, 201, 928. 14	$267, 805, 004. 72	$264, 780, 220. 51	$276, 693, 049. 29	$292, 771, 593. 11
Bonds for circulation	9, 405, 000. 00	9, 420, 000. 00	9, 420, 000. 00	9, 420, 000. 00	7, 920, 000. 00
Bonds for deposits	8, 970, 000. 00	11, 400, 000. 00	10, 500, 000. 00	10, 070, 000. 00	8, 440, 000. 00
U. S. bonds on hand	678, 030. 00	566, 000. 00	2, 303, 500. 00	3, 026, 300. 00	1, 384, 350. 00
Other stocks and b'ds	16, 625, 775. 37	17, 540, 603. 57	18, 155, 040. 03	18, 125, 273. 65	19, 202, 856. 09
Due from res've ag'ts	....	....	....	....	....
Due from nat'l banks	25, 707, 282. 01	19, 598, 570. 72	23, 016, 241. 91	24, 223, 566. 55	22, 745, 739. 80
Due from State banks	2, 348, 259. 67	2, 534, 648. 19	2, 700, 014. 23	2, 730, 786. 06	2, 823, 465. 81
Real estate, etc	10, 524, 561. 00	10, 196, 414. 44	10, 253, 682. 24	10, 244, 799. 94	10, 247, 888. 09
Current expenses	1, 096, 572. 55	517, 273. 20	1, 127, 077. 46	145, 352. 12	1, 308, 158. 03
Premiums paid	1, 747, 669. 50	2, 148, 410. 68	2, 258, 142. 31	2, 450, 261. 06	1, 876, 678. 80
Cash items	1, 901, 542. 15	1, 503, 767. 38	2, 631, 776. 95	3, 003, 015. 54	2, 136, 322. 72
Clear'g-house exch'gs	54, 461, 861. 01	45, 590, 292. 58	83, 718, 631. 64	34, 467, 391. 19	68, 110, 358. 48
Bills of other banks	1, 890, 162. 00	1, 900, 024. 00	2, 960, 348. 00	2, 451, 197. 00	1, 348, 742. 00
Fractional currency	27, 026. 81	52, 061. 34	51, 881. 81	54, 439. 82	68, 761. 59
Trade dollars	....	....	....	....	....
Specie	58, 577, 806. 83	71, 302, 678. 36	69, 414, 603. 75	73, 420, 414. 94	73, 907, 106. 14
Legal-tender notes	17, 871, 132. 00	22, 640, 579. 00	21, 001, 354. 00	23, 444, 696. 00	17, 763, 440. 00
U. S. cert's of deposit	1, 815, 000. 00	2, 920, 000. 00	3, 065, 000. 00	5, 400, 000. 00	4, 345, 000. 00
5 % fund with Treas	416, 025. 00	414, 900. 00	412, 650. 00	406, 370. 00	345, 150. 00
Due from U. S. Treas	176, 651. 70	295, 297. 81	444, 044. 20	548, 652. 32	336, 766. 03
Total	473, 045, 305. 74	488, 356, 455. 99	530, 103, 209. 04	500, 328, 565. 48	537, 082, 466. 51

by States and reserve cities—Continued.

CONNECTICUT.

Liabilities.	DECEMBER 7.	FEBRUARY 14.	APRIL 30.	JUNE 30.	OCTOBER 4.
	83 banks.	83 banks.	83 banks.	83 banks.	84 banks.
Capital stock	$24,444,370.00	$24,344,370.00	$24,344,370.00	$24,144,370.00	$24,194,370.00
Surplus fund	6,010,032.82	6,850,550.75	6,860,554.62	6,875,854.39	6,924,891.66
Undivided profits	2,134,928.10	1,580,755.81	1,994,774.77	1,513,830.52	1,902,603.57
Nat'l-bank circulation	8,517,523.00	8,108,725.00	8,108,805.50	7,859,057.50	7,871,452.50
State-bank circulation	4,785.00	4,785.00	4,785.00	4,764.00	4,764.00
Dividends unpaid	55,714.90	59,029.40	63,224.39	450,437.09	63,314.01
Individual deposits	23,828,571.83	26,281,463.74	25,745,044.08	26,973,403.78	27,505,287.12
U. S. deposits	1,468,198.61	3,105,271.11	2,003,084.64	3,098,397.70	3,091,337.08
Dep'ts U. S. dis. officers	11,969.51	11,639.09	513,045.88	13,724.14	12,949.45
Due to national banks	2,958,304.08	3,258,042.88	3,012,289.08	4,315,956.00	2,617,356.30
Due to State banks	636,962.05	641,344.86	939,062.98	945,562.76	394,050.82
Notes re-discounted	199,122.43	205,447.99	59,842.28	3,000.00	40,000.00
Bills payable	50,000.00	40,000.00	....	....	140,000.00
Total	71,220,452.33	74,581,334.75	75,140,783.22	76,204,357.88	74,762,377.20

NEW YORK.

Liabilities.	DECEMBER 7.	FEBRUARY 14.	APRIL 30.	JUNE 30.	OCTOBER 4.
	272 banks.	271 banks.	272 banks.	272 banks.	270 banks.
Capital stock	$34,872,260.00	$34,774,760.00	$35,142,760.00	$35,067,760.00	$35,042,760.00
Surplus fund	10,134,596.98	10,465,192.82	10,481,839.39	10,662,071.48	10,806,446.26
Undivided profits	7,177,800.90	5,072,593.78	6,791,953.61	6,459,806.71	6,805,005.97
Nat'l-bank circulation	17,328,183.00	16,700,838.00	16,564,258.00	16,209,200.50	16,121,838.50
State-bank circulation	24,191.00	24,191.00	24,191.00	24,191.00	24,191.00
Dividends unpaid	62,380.53	91,118.38	77,401.15	396,304.81	77,400.02
Individual deposits	88,508,094.23	89,803,102.86	88,358,500.85	87,521,597.13	90,774,453.80
U. S. deposits	1,107,733.87	2,579,887.82	2,578,777.51	2,501,228.92	2,437,011.11
Dep'ts U. S. dis. officers	114,157.73	108,231.95	104,745.06	112,906.62	145,353.89
Due to national banks	4,170,527.06	4,024,750.20	4,785,025.28	5,039,083.87	3,842,575.98
Due to State banks	1,350,139.07	1,365,400.34	1,409,115.18	1,355,997.79	1,286,015.01
Notes re-discounted	711,765.69	403,281.81	1,117,445.12	1,188,472.30	710,737.91
Bills payable	122,262.86	94,856.68	87,590.70	134,907.87	45,716.62
Total	165,684,093.00	166,108,228.65	167,527,263.81	166,764,789.00	168,128,506.07

NEW YORK CITY.

Liabilities.	DECEMBER 7.	FEBRUARY 14.	APRIL 30.	JUNE 30.	OCTOBER 4.
	47 banks.	46 banks.	46 banks.	46 banks.	46 banks.
Capital stock	$49,150,000.00	$48,850,000.00	$49,100,000.00	$49,100,000.00	$49,100,000.00
Surplus fund	30,620,762.28	30,957,244.78	31,053,819.78	31,636,319.78	31,661,363.26
Undivided profits	11,257,387.91	10,035,525.30	11,970,354.17	9,492,100.76	12,415,018.27
Nat'l-bank circulation	8,155,992.00	7,747,982.00	7,886,887.00	7,767,480.00	6,693,465.00
State-bank circulation	24,362.00	24,360.00	24,360.00	24,360.00	24,360.00
Dividends unpaid	132,352.05	157,750.46	306,518.38	1,478,829.19	188,922.67
Individual deposits	226,090,463.43	226,421,547.78	271,145,644.69	240,473,296.45	261,464,825.90
U. S. deposits	9,181,672.40	12,035,007.80	11,058,553.72	10,568,844.85	8,667,282.14
Dep'ts U. S. dis. officers	313,030.29	174,226.27	176,903.78	162,073.37	139,820.54
Due to national banks	101,335,423.07	113,281,712.07	110,625,196.82	111,199,076.02	123,096,685.15
Due to State banks	36,783,860.29	38,071,009.53	36,694,070.70	38,426,193.06	43,630,714.58
Notes re-discounted	....	....	....	....	....
Bills payable	....	....	....	....	....
Total	473,045,305.74	488,356,435.90	530,103,209.04	500,328,565.48	537,082,466.51

Abstract of reports since October 5, 1887, arranged

CITY OF ALBANY.

Resources.	DECEMBER 7.	FEBRUARY 14.	APRIL 30.	JUNE 30.	OCTOBER 4.
	6 banks.	6 banks.	6 banks.	6 banks.	6 banks.
Loans and discounts.	$8,077,910.96	$8,167,235.78	$8,084,234.46	$8,583,401.22	$8,908,201.87
Bonds for circulation.	1,148,000.00	1,148,000.00	1,148,000.00	948,000.00	948,000.00
Bonds for deposits...	150,000.00	150,000.00	150,000.00	150,000.00	150,000.00
U.S. bonds on hand..	....	....	....	....	....
Other stocks and b'ds	327,154.23	275,354.22	239,441.00	341,226.00	309,040.10
Due from res've ag'ts.	1,381,507.40	1,708,120.50	2,728,158.01	1,885,805.48	2,410,222.27
Due from nat'l banks	870,263.57	777,072.12	802,015.73	1,201,485.27	960,074.38
Due from State banks	69,704.40	64,023.01	193,684.00	60,564.32	110,575.91
Real estate, etc	332,585.61	355,724.54	380,805.48	380,700.60	368,155.66
Current expenses....	....	....	....	....	....
Premiums paid......	163,565.00	150,505.00	158,905.00	103,370.00	103,370.00
Cash items	96,589.53	73,275.41	129,300.47	71,791.81	52,491.74
Clear'g-house exch'gs	116,690.77	114,269.78	115,245.44	119,577.02	103,760.10
Bills of other banks..	111,612.00	116,477.00	125,028.00	113,541.00	104,466.00
Fractional currency.	785.66	958.89	678.95	449.08	750.81
Trade dollars.......	....	....	....	....	....
Specie	684,403.20	884,642.80	924,420.50	1,035,083.50	979,331.50
Legal-tender notes ..	142,902.00	112,867.00	107,000.00	270,332.00	253,543.00
U.S. cert's of deposit	200,000.00	150,000.00	150,000.00	150,000.00	150,000.00
5% fund with Treas.	51,657.50	47,508.61	49,604.50	42,657.50	38,966.80
Due from U.S. Treas.	2,049.51	3,530.00	1,040.00	1,819.60	2,000.00
Total..........	13,927,600.43	14,310,414.68	15,661,342.14	15,465,871.85	15,954,804.23

NEW JERSEY.

	81 banks.	82 banks.	83 banks.	84 banks.	85 banks.
Loans and discounts	$40,815,284.80	$40,517,388.29	$41,022,524.19	$40,702,329.25	$42,002,341.26
Bonds for circulation	6,837,100.00	6,820,000.00	6,842,100.00	6,804,000.00	6,716,250.00
Bonds for deposits ..	950,000.00	1,950,000.00	1,950,000.00	1,950,000.00	1,950,000.00
U.S. bonds on hand..	175,500.00	54,700.00	43,200.00	15,050.00	14,050.00
Other stocks and b'ds	4,155,407.03	3,850,703.88	3,855,376.14	3,903,576.26	4,810,848.38
Due from res've ag'ts	5,094,622.48	7,234,084.37	6,535,082.24	6,808,748.70	8,750,234.00
Due from nat'l banks	1,569,872.55	1,617,205.61	1,760,256.14	1,835,150.81	1,681,849.63
Due from State banks	223,058.22	365,874.46	290,464.71	256,644.34	260,758.23
Real estate, etc......	1,710,334.11	1,728,923.73	1,772,646.50	1,809,800.22	1,842,253.68
Current expenses....	308,373.32	150,362.17	222,058.40	130,018.50	173,820.04
Premiums paid......	596,008.40	607,924.12	651,868.62	619,180.62	580,737.10
Cash items	846,736.86	1,178,824.47	1,083,243.22	1,270,916.32	921,522.65
Clear'g-house exch'gs	....	....	....	....	....
Bills of other banks..	560,714.00	485,010.00	408,944.00	416,902.00	482,208.00
Fractional currency.	23,514.66	25,284.29	24,126.24	25,130.40	24,802.35
Trade dollars........	2.00	5.00	15.00	....	....
Specie	1,760,705.01	1,722,755.88	1,751,207.36	1,612,019.52	1,875,037.60
Legal-tender notes ..	1,995,947.00	1,943,800.00	2,000,844.00	1,667,216.00	2,348,278.00
U.S. cert's of deposit.	30,000.00	30,000.00	20,000.00	10,000.00	10,000.00
5% fund with Treas.	297,858.45	301,688.45	303,080.05	302,704.05	298,404.20
Due from U.S. Treas.	15,080.00	17,249.70	11,300.00	14,010.00	5,431.00
Total..........	68,566,114.88	70,672,110.33	70,554,517.77	70,290,667.13	74,842,997.02

PENNSYLVANIA.

	238 banks.	241 banks.	241 banks.	245 banks.	246 banks.
Loans and discounts.	$80,833,208.11	$80,201,657.65	$82,425,580.62	$81,014,507.95	$83,360,337.07
Bonds for circulation	15,126,300.00	15,066,300.00	14,878,800.00	14,726,300.00	14,059,300.00
Bonds for deposits ..	480,000.00	830,000.00	830,000.00	830,000.00	830,000.00
U.S. bonds on hand..	507,150.00	552,250.00	521,800.00	491,000.00	540,000.00
Other stocks and b'ds	9,882,200.40	9,905,007.03	10,604,736.17	10,909,497.90	11,372,241.18
Due from res've ag'ts	10,855,900.21	13,811,695.86	12,614,318.07	13,159,684.41	14,827,515.73
Due from nat'l banks.	2,734,687.31	3,015,524.50	3,754,956.74	3,644,576.10	2,624,659.37
Due from State banks	1,127,390.83	1,222,163.24	1,522,556.70	1,503,210.01	1,101,625.59
Real estate, etc......	3,761,207.95	3,857,618.08	3,807,842.21	3,900,188.77	3,891,866.83
Current expenses....	373,147.63	335,666.62	761,754.17	393,235.75	554,698.05
Premiums paid......	1,348,006.94	1,355,430.72	1,329,382.27	1,279,835.00	1,255,700.12
Cash items	826,107.89	800,203.57	845,865.16	992,375.36	984,587.00
Clear'g-house exch'gs	....	....	....	....	....
Bills of other banks..	1,173,500.00	1,145,822.00	1,315,678.00	1,097,424.00	1,140,692.00
Fractional currency.	49,679.80	64,211.94	50,949.19	57,747.67	61,049.24
Trade dollars........	15.65	38.50	16.30	....	5.00
Specie	4,911,449.15	4,785,632.67	5,036,253.01	4,875,105.45	5,016,658.83
Legal-tender notes ..	2,871,056.00	2,657,512.00	3,458,000.00	2,933,874.00	3,091,407.00
U.S. cert's of deposit.	10,000.00	10,000.00	10,000.00	10,000.00	10,000.00
5% fund with Treas.	659,882.25	656,700.83	642,468.45	642,905.61	621,759.48
Due from U.S. Treas	39,058.23	38,247.88	66,216.80	29,015.94	33,161.84
Total..........	137,570,205.85	139,811,758.09	144,546,834.04	142,516,404.01	145,486,464.02

by States and reserve cities—Continued.

CITY OF ALBANY.

Liabilities.	DECEMBER 7.	FEBRUARY 14.	APRIL 30.	JUNE 30.	OCTOBER 4.
	6 banks.	6 banks.	6 banks.	6 banks.	6 banks.
Capital stock	$1,750,000.00	$1,750,000.00	$1,750,000.00	$1,750,000.00	$1,750,000.00
Surplus fund	1,243,000.00	1,246,000.00	1,246,000.00	1,246,000.00	1,274,000.00
Undivided profits	268,235.03	194,095.41	233,532.55	250,892.80	228,374.57
Nat'l-bank circulation	1,014,160.00	995,870.00	1,020,510.00	760,500.00	780,390.00
State-bank circulation	....	....	....	....	....
Dividends unpaid	907.26	8,022.85	11,428.75	13,294.15	12,303.01
Individual deposits	6,270,825.97	6,938,856.30	8,065,864.08	8,551,745.92	8,670,285.48
U. S. deposits	148,860.27	140,477.32	146,732.04	145,963.55	148,414.07
Dep'ts U.S.dis.officers	1,130.73	522.68	3,548.15	2,098.71	1,395.93
Due to national banks	2,859,032.27	2,688,080.95	2,532,078.89	2,439,055.09	2,593,177.69
Due to State banks	371,358.89	337,989.03	651,046.48	305,121.03	490,523.48
Notes re-discounted	....	....	....	....	....
Bills payable	....	....	....	....	....
Total	13,927,609.42	14,310,414.63	15,661,342.14	15,465,871.85	15,954,864.23

NEW JERSEY.

	81 banks.	82 banks.	83 banks.	84 banks.	85 banks.
Capital stock	$13,098,350.00	$13,123,350.00	$13,173,350.00	$13,221,390.00	$13,318,350.00
Surplus fund	4,514,267.09	4,870,853.11	4,906,353.11	5,017,546.08	5,155,431.73
Undivided profits	2,549,348.02	1,910,160.53	2,242,232.14	2,053,271.76	2,158,354.01
Nat'l-bank circulation	6,114,271.00	6,060,496.50	5,962,016.50	5,994,741.50	5,992,911.50
State-bank circulation	8,358.00	8,402.00	7,827.00	7,827.00	7,827.00
Dividends unpaid	44,039.06	67,142.24	51,230.51	204,050.47	109,098.85
Individual deposits	37,974,941.48	39,075,395.55	38,571,053.53	38,261,375.40	42,138,479.17
U. S. deposits	941,944.89	2,045,705.19	2,038,862.23	2,040,174.23	2,041,098.70
Dep'ts U.S.dis.officers	11,004.77	11,100.96	17,885.82	14,102.81	16,080.30
Due to national banks	2,083,806.45	2,847,100.37	2,791,389.53	2,507,454.27	3,204,307.31
Due to State banks	409,581.72	441,027.72	374,874.84	454,112.47	407,287.50
Notes re-discounted	55,000.00	52,386.06	191,833.56	182,521.08	49,804.95
Bills payable	160,000.00	150,000.00	225,000.00	248,500.00	183,000.00
Total	68,586,114.88	70,072,119.33	70,554,517.77	70,299,067.13	74,842,907.02

PENNSYLVANIA.

	238 banks.	241 banks.	241 banks.	245 banks.	246 banks.
Capital stock	$33,615,340.00	$33,526,475.00	$33,631,910.00	$33,525,340.00	$33,502,201.04
Surplus fund	11,651,810.31	11,878,000.15	11,940,654.15	12,187,861.87	12,316,112.53
Undivided profits	3,537,780.58	3,258,033.14	4,309,012.33	3,485,027.41	4,306,389.74
Nat'l-bank circulation	13,333,145.00	13,193,500.00	13,031,566.00	12,782,692.00	12,336,796.00
State-bank circulation	4,745.00	4,745.00	1,548.00	1,548.00	1,543.00
Dividends unpaid	214,922.43	173,977.19	136,294.42	290,970.36	147,368.41
Individual deposits	70,838,847.94	72,810,813.03	76,177,533.45	75,132,302.54	78,535,049.38
U. S. deposits	471,440.94	789,907.78	818,306.40	827,884.26	826,500.60
Dep'ts U.S.dis.officers	11,078.01	10,121.32	28,748.13	17,853.00	18,287.53
Due to national banks	3,071,981.04	3,374,870.12	3,697,410.03	3,011,693.97	2,719,886.62
Due to State banks	391,692.96	414,884.55	459,379.58	428,887.40	284,086.10
Notes re-discounted	302,482.36	312,421.98	228,206.34	243,270.32	352,063.30
Bills payable	35,490.28	57,990.28	85,506.03	10,490.28	50,490.25
Total	137,570,265.85	139,811,758.09	144,546,834.04	142,516,494.01	145,486,464.62

Abstract of reports since October 5, 1887, arranged

CITY OF PHILADELPHIA.

Resources.	DECEMBER 7.	FEBRUARY 14.	APRIL 30.	JUNE 30.	OCTOBER 4.
	43 banks.	43 banks.	43 banks.	43 banks.	43 banks.
Loans and discounts	$83, 428, 797. 20	$82, 307, 852. 57	$84, 370, 326. 15	$86, 608, 601. 00	$91, 678, 393. 95
Bonds for circulation	2, 737, 500. 00	2, 737, 500. 00	3, 187, 500. 00	3, 187, 500. 00	3, 187, 500. 00
Bonds for deposits	700, 000. 00	1, 350, 000. 00	1, 350, 000. 00	1, 350, 000. 00	1, 400, 000. 00
U. S. bonds on hand	10, 100. 00	1, 100. 00	1, 100. 00	1, 100. 00	1, 100. 00
Other stocks and b'ds	3, 332, 673. 48	4, 128, 564. 17	4, 022, 043. 86	3, 975, 847. 58	3, 944, 291. 78
Due from res've ag'ts	6, 602, 776. 40	8, 182, 687. 63	8, 734, 954. 39	8, 199, 049. 75	9, 289, 225. 04
Due from nat'l banks	6, 139, 823. 16	5, 631, 544. 52	7, 246, 106. 22	7, 080, 418. 27	5, 849, 540. 43
Due from State banks	910, 406. 59	1, 051, 146. 35	1, 162, 862. 97	1, 203, 061. 62	1, 168, 395. 68
Real estate, etc	3, 401, 516. 82	3, 505, 825. 82	3, 485, 834. 05	3, 504, 491. 09	3, 525, 364. 65
Current expenses	208, 709. 55	415, 804. 97	620, 780. 06	320, 046. 18	642, 844. 20
Premiums paid	470, 341. 85	510, 132. 07	514, 362. 32	514, 905. 54	484, 046. 74
Cash items	544, 575. 32	644, 587. 89	658, 936. 20	808, 353. 46	620, 138. 07
Clear'g-house exch'gs	8, 331, 052. 44	7, 350, 644. 38	7, 734, 385. 20	14, 524, 526. 97	8, 678, 951. 75
Bills of other banks	543, 828. 00	417, 731. 00	514, 479. 00	367, 548. 00	399, 777. 00
Fractional currency	42, 477. 17	45, 145. 06	33, 815. 17	37, 775. 52	43, 848. 71
Trade dollars	....	....	....	....	....
Specie	10, 812, 359. 76	9, 985, 282. 74	9, 965, 269. 78	15, 576, 009. 28	12, 391, 700. 10
Legal-tender notes	4, 558, 333. 00	4, 176, 243. 00	4, 190, 008. 00	4, 083, 926. 00	4, 315, 561. 00
U. S. cert's of deposit	1, 000, 000. 00	2, 020, 000. 00	2, 040, 000. 00	2, 540, 000. 00	1, 220, 000. 00
5 % fund with Treas.	123, 133. 74	123, 133. 24	138, 513. 74	143, 383. 74	143, 383. 74
Due from U. S. Treas.	30, 317. 21	27, 100. 00	66, 374. 00	40, 467. 40	27, 807. 00
Total	134, 117, 721. 78	134, 612, 025. 41	140, 037, 646. 06	154, 066, 410. 30	149, 002, 869. 03

CITY OF PITTSBURGH.

	23 banks.	23 banks.	23 banks.	24 banks.	24 banks.
Loans and discounts	$31, 733, 910. 13	$31, 158, 069. 90	$32, 183, 130. 81	$32, 188, 927. 54	$31, 665, 005. 94
Bonds for circulation	1, 765, 500. 00	1, 765, 500. 00	1, 565, 500. 00	1, 615, 500. 00	1, 615, 500. 00
Bonds for deposits	600, 000. 00	800, 000. 00	800, 000. 00	800, 000. 00	800, 000. 00
U. S. bonds on hand	2, 150. 00	2, 600. 00	200. 00	....	3, 850. 00
Other stocks and b'ds	330, 106. 80	349, 940. 87	311, 750. 82	336, 558. 70	332, 769. 68
Due from res've ag'ts	2, 323, 621. 87	2, 900, 800. 72	2, 680, 328. 00	3, 314, 483. 87	4, 194, 715. 50
Due from nat'l banks	1, 008, 898. 81	1, 418, 869. 74	1, 296, 137. 43	1, 747, 431. 31	1, 808, 287. 83
Due from State banks	212, 312. 54	201, 840. 82	233, 589. 66	349, 103. 85	222, 898. 49
Real estate, etc	1, 498, 807. 2[illegible]	1, 520, 984. 59	1, 524, 302. 30	1, 640, 959. 88	1, 714, 184. 66
Current expenses	122, 098. 83	85, 000. 53	174, 008. 17	79, 133. 59	183, 324. 73
Premiums paid	177, 340. 86	223, 809. 71	219, 269. 71	217, 885. 86	216, 535. 86
Cash items	254, 270. 11	212, 416. 86	213, 258. 19	338, 068. 27	229, 288. 84
Clear'g-house exch'gs	1, 282, 472. 46	1, 278, 133. 38	1, 626, 779. 06	1, 929, 811. 29	1, 475, 017. 65
Bills of other banks	468, 497. 00	307, 280. 00	392, 228. 00	308, 257. 00	525, 701. 00
Fractional currency	9, 879. 83	12, 636. 89	10, 405. 36	11, 066. 86	11, 253. 48
Trade dollars	28. 00	28. 00	28. 00	25. 00	40. 00
Specie	3, 270, 878. 06	3, 001, 589. 30	2, 970, 635. 40	3, 149, 283. 70	3, 240, 960. 23
Legal-tender notes	1, 766, 863. 00	1, 775, 817. 00	1, 941, 684. 00	1, 970, 755. 00	2, 033, 972. 00
U. S. cert's of deposit	....	....	....	....	....
5 % fund with Treas.	79, 422. 50	79, 422. 50	70, 422. 50	72, 672. 50	72, 672. 50
Due from U. S. Treas.	35, 076. 20	20, 643. 94	5, 890. 00	13, 205. 00	14, 180. 00
Total	47, 011, 134. 20	47, 274, 483. 84	48, 225, 548. 31	50, 173, 129. 22	50, 359, 867. 29

DELAWARE.

	17 banks.	17 banks.	17 banks.	18 banks.	18 banks.
Loans and discounts	$4, 925, 715. 88	$4, 918, 087. 30	$4, 077, 123. 58	$4, 934, 673. 17	$5, 415, 498. 52
Bonds for circulation	1, 596, 700. 00	1, 596, 700. 00	1, 586, 700. 00	1, 590, 200. 00	1, 599, 200. 00
Bonds for deposits	50, 000. 00	50, 000. 00	50, 000. 00	50, 000. 00	50, 000. 00
U. S. bonds on hand	....	....	....	....	....
Other stocks and b'ds	256, 173. 14	261, 845. 25	261, 524. 20	250, 716. 79	237, 430. 76
Due from res've ag'ts.	722, 131. 46	633, 782. 06	623, 805. 26	707, 241. 09	1, 224, 296. 41
Due from nat'l banks	179, 336. 80	176, 741. 25	254, 323. 20	243, 364. 56	107, 541. 63
Due from State banks	47, 124. 80	64, 264. 89	66, 699. 79	76, 707. 59	38, 178. 91
Real estate, etc	264, 468. 37	263, 707. 04	265, 030. 84	266, 436. 89	270, 137. 26
Current expenses	36, 962. 37	13, 808. 74	30, 945. 01	31, 764. 79	29, [illegible]. 22
Premiums paid	129, 004. 24	120, 077. 50	127, 715. 00	129, 771. 25	124, 652. 29
Cash items	54, 570. 05	42, 335. 61	41, 502. 03	51, 097. 85	46, 764. 07
Clear'g-house exch'gs	26, 141. 43	17, 164. 38	50, 689. 04	30, 097. 36	17, 957. 29
Bills of other banks	72, 120. 00	61, 886. 00	100, 697. 00	90, 688. 00	124, 398. 00
Fractional currency	2, 072. 05	2, 081. 14	2, 950. 53	2, 711. 24	3, 632. 87
Trade dollars	....	....	....	....	....
Specie	281, 054. 68	250, 720. 55	274, 728. 70	223, 867. 38	268, 188. 59
Legal-tender notes	129, 179. 00	140, 023. 00	171, 421. 00	143, 567. 00	210, 126. 00
U. S. cert's of deposit	10, 000. 00	10, 000. 00	10, 000. 00	10, 000. 00	10, 000. 00
5 % fund with Treas	71, 099. 50	69, 649. 50	69, 079. 50	69, 650. 00	71, 912. 50
Due from U. S. Treas.	2, 110. 00	24, 030. 00	22, 550. 00	13, 620. 00	....
Total	8, 856, 863. 86	8, 726, 504. 21	8, 987, 490. 77	8, 925, 175. 86	9, 900, 011. 22

by States and reserve cities—Continued.

CITY OF PHILADELPHIA.

Liabilities.	DECEMBER 7. 43 banks.	FEBRUARY 14. 43 banks.	APRIL 30. 43 banks.	JUNE 30. 43 banks.	OCTOBER 4. 43 banks.
Capital stock	$22, 758, 000. 00	$22, 758, 000. 00	$22, 758, 000. 00	$22, 758, 000. 00	$23, 008, 000. 00
Surplus fund	10, 856, 303. 08	10, 880, 303. 08	10, 926, 303. 08	10, 966, 803. 08	10, 081, 803. 08
Undivided profits	1, 706, 221. 98	2, 095, 074. 03	2, 932, 163. 52	2, 167, 833. 37	2, 928, 870. 21
Nat'l-bank circulation	2, 372, 880. 00	2, 429, 494. 00	2, 828, 904. 00	2, 822, 279. 00	2, 833, 321. 00
State-bank circulation	....	....	....	....	....
Dividends unpaid	80, 870. 81	44, 250. 46	33,090. 51	82, 054. 47	48, 701. 00
Individual deposits	70, 581, 273. 59	75, 713, 806. 11	78, 028, 971. 06	91, 304, 051. 94	85, 084, 061. 87
U. S. deposits	681, 017. 59	1, 406, 129. 70	1, 411, 288. 09	1, 407, 208. 90	1, 371, 061. 10
Dep'ts U. S. dis. officers	....	....	....	....	....
Due to national banks	15, 162, 208. 50	15, 164, 708. 53	15, 845, 461. 05	17, 976, 138. 15	17, 188, 817. 50
Due to State banks	3, 678, 907. 23	4, 063, 350. 50	4, 202, 704. 25	4, 582, 041. 30	4, 837, 353. 05
Notes re-discounted	....	....	....	....	....
Bills payable	150, 000. 00	50, 000. 00	150, 000. 00	....	125, 000. 00
Total	134, 117, 721. 78	134, 612, 025. 41	140, 037, 046. 06	154, 066, 410. 30	149, 002, 869. 03

CITY OF PITTSBURGH.

Liabilities.	23 banks.	23 banks.	23 banks.	24 banks.	24 banks.
Capital stock	$10, 180, 000. 00	$10, 180, 000. 00	$10, 180, 000. 00	$10, 370, 150. 00	$10, 430, 000. 00
Surplus fund	4, 415, 034. 80	4, 705, 950. 50	4, 780, 950. 50	4, 880, 035. 06	4, 910, 035. 06
Undivided profits	1, 146, 406. 53	846, 035. 98	1, 062, 668. 50	814, 113. 05	1, 103, 599. 44
Nat'l-bank circulation	1, 563, 910. 00	1, 530, 450. 00	1, 370, 040. 00	1, 405, 030. 00	1, 395, 080. 00
State-bank circulation	....	....	....	....	....
Dividends unpaid	81, 274. 00	70, 170. 00	69, 280. 75	199, 574. 00	85, 870. 00
Individual deposits	24, 470, 539. 93	24, 343, 098. 20	25, 557, 061. 74	26, 728, 330. 04	26, 273, 810. 02
U. S. deposits	344, 202. 57	665, 273. 05	702, 781. 92	718, 665. 50	713, 708. 82
Dep'ts U. S. dis. officers	263, 061. 16	210, 906. 98	105, 861. 47	128, 605. 37	171, 880. 83
Due to national banks	2, 570, 167. 78	2, 843, 003. 26	2, 080, 782. 04	3, 053, 044. 01	3, 233, 380. 40
Due to State banks	1, 781, 240. 36	1, 800, 415. 51	1, 504, 125. 98	1, 803, 030. 52	2, 024, 171. 28
Notes re-discounted	178, 182. 07	37, 224. 36	70, 395. 41	50, 419. 58	7, 810. 38
Bills payable	5, 000. 00	5, 000. 00	5, 000. 00	5, 000. 00	....
Total	47, 011, 134. 20	47, 274, 483. 84	48, 225, 548. 31	50, 173, 120. 22	50, 359, 867. 29

DELAWARE.

Liabilities.	17 banks.	17 banks.	17 banks.	18 banks.	18 banks.
Capital stock	$2, 083, 985. 00	$2, 083, 985. 00	$2, 083, 985. 00	$2, 113, 985. 00	$2, 129, 885. 00
Surplus fund	800, 350. 06	814, 000. 00	824, 000. 00	824, 000. 00	831, 300. 00
Undivided profits	268, 300. 00	188, 707. 46	255, 250. 44	202, 770. 45	270, 764. 39
Nat'l-bank circulation	1, 420, 570. 00	1, 390, 340. 00	1, 391, 870. 00	1, 377, 280. 00	1, 407, 210. 00
State-bank circulation	574. 50	574. 50	574. 50	574. 50	574. 50
Dividends unpaid	7, 208. 50	14, 703. 10	8, 975. 45	12, 041. 40	10, 210. 45
Individual deposits	3, 908, 703. 55	3, 817, 331. 84	3, 940, 124. 18	3, 903, 414. 51	4, 978, 196. 79
U. S. deposits	41, 086. 77	41, 007. 92	41, 855. 41	39, 881. 08	39, 742. 94
Dep'ts U. S. dis. officers	3, 288. 83	3, 992. 08	3, 144. 50	2, 871. 53	4, 726. 01
Due to national banks	285, 011. 12	304, 328. 31	389, 440. 08	327, 229. 12	183, 566. 76
Due to State banks	16, 979. 89	13, 214. 00	7, 100. 02	10, 825. 27	37, 825. 78
Notes re-discounted	11, 115. 64	15, 200. 00	35, 170. 20	14, 700. 00	....
Bills payable	....	....	....	5, 000. 00	15, 000. 00
Total	8, 856, 863. 86	8, 726, 504. 21	8, 987, 496. 77	8, 925, 175. 86	9, 900, 011. 22

Abstract of reports since October 5, 1887, arranged

MARYLAND.

Resources.	DECEMBER 7.	FEBRUARY 14.	APRIL 30.	JUNE 30.	OCTOBER 4.
	31 banks.	31 banks.	31 banks.	31 banks.	31 banks.
Loans and discounts	$6,915,533.69	$6,893,167.65	$7,076,339.54	$7,371,808.40	$7,708,401.06
Bonds for circulation	1,517,000.00	1,517,000.00	1,517,000.00	1,367,000.00	1,311,000.00
Bonds for deposits	230,000.00	280,000.00	280,000.00	280,000.00	280,000.00
U. S. bonds on hand	54,300.00	57,500.00	87,300.00	37,300.00	39,300.00
Other stocks and b'ds	830,533.50	811,435.52	859,707.02	881,343.71	990,953.65
Due from res've ag'ts	906,363.39	1,135,605.65	930,143.39	891,317.46	1,289,582.69
Due from nat'l banks	331,627.88	466,450.62	458,088.95	336,314.89	535,794.47
Due from State banks	72,627.09	57,253.41	53,907.29	38,324.51	52,859.39
Real estate, etc	346,633.34	346,027.80	351,878.34	353,171.08	368,035.74
Current expenses	67,640.16	27,603.59	54,356.48	30,623.69	66,232.28
Premiums paid	149,873.61	149,102.79	152,269.07	140,262.24	136,087.55
Cash items	32,265.61	50,043.31	41,614.24	83,944.13	63,990.11
Clear'g-house exch'gs					
Bills of other banks	48,402.00	61,528.00	83,640.00	83,959.00	66,837.00
Fractional currency	4,159.77	4,627.10	5,079.65	5,569.15	4,702.05
Trade dollars					
Specie	466,176.58	477,260.77	505,651.34	476,152.00	536,409.41
Legal-tender notes	314,000.00	376,000.00	386,753.00	400,515.00	408,101.00
U. S. cert's of deposit					
5% fund with Treas	64,757.50	63,861.59	59,127.00	52,687.59	54,476.00
Due from U. S. Treas	5,710.00	2,550.00	10,240.00	10,958.00	2,510.00
Total	12,447,724.11	12,780,016.80	12,863,704.40	12,841,311.75	13,015,532.40

CITY OF BALTIMORE.

	17 banks.	17 banks.	17 banks.	17 banks.	17 banks.
Loans and discounts	$26,091,532.08	$26,013,483.70	$27,342,082.68	$27,067,028.57	$28,179,375.54
Bonds for circulation	1,900,000.00	1,900,000.00	1,450,000.00	930,000.00	900,000.00
Bonds for deposits	550,000.00	550,000.00	550,000.00	550,000.00	550,000.00
U. S. bonds on hand					
Other stocks and b'ds	939,723.12	930,887.41	923,887.41	903,787.41	880,257.43
Due from res've ag'ts	1,875,407.18	1,940,504.57	1,625,520.21	1,809,268.73	2,071,824.78
Due from nat'l banks	1,978,532.73	1,319,172.03	1,334,665.72	1,980,095.03	1,667,134.79
Due from State banks	284,297.89	217,504.32	262,847.48	233,657.00	280,461.62
Real estate, etc	790,530.07	792,446.29	803,234.41	891,524.41	918,724.41
Current expenses	177,776.69	62,190.77	144,970.73	50,772.03	146,097.18
Premiums paid	60,784.38	58,684.38	58,446.88	43,175.00	42,937.50
Cash items	86,747.26	80,051.15	80,104.04	112,101.10	54,821.81
Clear'g-house exch'gs	1,340,511.21	886,921.69	1,569,196.40	1,783,038.73	1,387,845.00
Bills of other banks	347,793.00	309,084.00	269,077.00	243,832.00	270,449.00
Fractional currency	11,071.86	6,578.53	4,807.05	5,620.17	7,014.42
Trade dollars					
Specie	2,507,145.00	2,531,243.65	2,128,940.88	2,137,678.70	2,244,840.86
Legal-tender notes	1,240,285.00	1,281,447.00	998,821.00	1,452,521.00	1,427,102.00
U. S. cert's of deposit	700,000.00	2,030,000.00	960,000.00	1,210,000.00	530,000.00
5% fund with Treas	85,500.00	85,500.00	65,250.00	42,750.00	40,500.00
Due from U. S. Treas	31,000.00	22,850.00	2,280.00		1,000.00
Total	41,088,727.47	41,027,648.49	40,574,740.91	41,558,905.78	41,621,280.34

DISTRICT OF COLUMBIA.

	1 bank.	1 bank.	1 bank.	1 bank.	1 bank.
Loans and discounts	$337,717.12	$323,247.51	$300,001.08	$314,994.61	$336,912.49
Bonds for circulation	250,000.00	250,000.00	250,000.00	250,000.00	250,000.00
Bonds for deposits					
U. S. bonds on hand	151,200.00	151,200.00	151,200.00	151,200.00	151,200.00
Other stocks and b'ds	192,930.00	200,287.18	210,762.18	208,762.18	208,762.18
Due from res've ag'ts	63,625.54	97,507.41	65,555.26	60,664.42	60,643.24
Due from nat'l banks	6,341.41	31,437.67	10,233.05	10,432.05	11,581.12
Due from State banks	502.03	967.35	1,361.75	626.89	710.86
Real estate, etc	23,000.00	23,000.00	23,000.00	23,000.00	23,000.00
Current expenses	5,977.97	1,764.76	5,563.03	44.85	3,812.09
Premiums paid	32,357.18	25,000.00	25,000.00	25,000.00	25,000.00
Cash items	5,653.00	1,776.65	11,611.05	16,109.21	11,081.79
Clear'g-house exch'gs					
Bills of other banks	4,080.00	4,000.00	3,255.00	4,605.00	4,550.00
Fractional currency	44.08	52.18	43.71	11.15	18.24
Trade dollars					
Specie	197,791.25	207,117.50	220,422.45	223,403.75	220,271.50
Legal-tender notes	70,500.00	95,000.00	48,523.00	38,565.00	40,130.00
U. S. cert's of deposit					
5% fund with Treas	11,250.00	11,250.00	11,250.00	11,250.00	11,250.00
Due from U. S. Treas					
Total	1,372,970.48	1,413,608.21	1,337,781.55	1,333,671.11	1,367,923.51

by States and reserve cities—Continued.

MARYLAND.

Liabilities.	DECEMBER 7.	FEBRUARY 14.	APRIL 30.	JUNE 30.	OCTOBER 4.
	31 banks.	31 banks.	31 banks.	31 banks.	31 banks.
Capital stock	$2,806,700.00	$2,816,700.00	$2,816,700.00	$2,816,700.00	$2,816,700.00
Surplus fund	902,096.40	920,016.40	920,016.40	960,900.33	971,857.33
Undivided profits	360,587.13	264,576.54	362,690.01	320,053.07	369,307.84
Nat'l-bank circulation	1,348,835.00	1,335,020.00	1,318,330.00	1,185,075.00	1,138,690.00
State-bank circulation	....	....	....	....	....
Dividends unpaid	25,346.09	17,221.53	15,955.89	47,464.38	30,154.90
Individual deposits	6,390,192.37	6,768,813.51	6,729,084.32	6,692,264.13	7,815,526.91
U. S. deposits	198,000.00	301,942.50	308,000.00	308,000.00	308,000.00
Dep'ts U.S.dis.officers	....	....	....	....	....
Due to national banks	303,535.88	276,621.23	303,057.70	327,758.87	312,116.49
Due to State banks	47,809.48	52,762.91	69,385.37	61,550.85	68,170.02
Notes re-discounted	44,001.76	26,312.18	19,884.71	65,044.52	....
Bills payable	25,000.00	....	....	55,000.00	85,000.00
Total	12,447,724.11	12,780,016.80	12,863,704.40	12,841,311.75	13,915,532.49

CITY OF BALTIMORE.

	17 banks.	17 banks.	17 banks.	17 banks.	17 banks.
Capital stock	$11,713,260.00	$11,713,260.00	$11,713,260.00	$11,713,260.00	$11,713,260.00
Surplus fund	3,544,400.00	3,565,400.00	3,665,400.00	3,833,400.00	3,840,000.00
Undivided profits	1,322,172.68	973,975.50	1,268,077.73	884,871.58	1,165,742.24
Nat'l-bank circulation	1,695,560.00	1,694,180.00	1,275,880.00	848,640.00	790,890.00
State-bank circulation	16,543.00	16,543.00	16,541.00	4,056.00	4,048.00
Dividends unpaid	51,407.60	63,481.64	45,971.80	229,005.18	65,683.18
Individual deposits	18,522,509.31	18,940,151.16	18,877,221.84	19,340,044.78	19,169,550.77
U. S. deposits	541,711.56	548,309.70	563,123.93	532,515.58	551,848.43
Dep'ts U.S.dis.officers	24,224.07	27,736.02	23,670.03	40,638.65	20,325.52
Due to national banks	3,129,291.07	3,000,419.67	3,120,332.95	3,547,082.67	3,542,436.72
Due to State banks	527,647.58	484,191.80	504,001.63	576,391.34	657,492.48
Notes re-discounted	....	....	....	....	100,000.00
Bills payable	....	....	....	....	....
Total	41,088,727.47	41,027,648.49	40,574,740.91	41,558,905.78	41,621,280.34

DISTRICT OF COLUMBIA.

	1 bank.	1 bank.	1 bank.	1 bank.	1 bank.
Capital stock	$252,000.00	$252,000.00	$252,000.00	$252,000.00	$252,000.00
Surplus fund	60,000.00	60,000.00	60,000.00	60,000.00	60,000.00
Undivided profits	66,665.83	53,653.93	63,682.99	54,250.84	65,114.49
Nat'l-bank circulation	201,040.00	206,350.00	209,650.00	211,000.00	201,100.00
State-bank circulation	....	....	....	....	....
Dividends unpaid	2,740.00	3,128.00	3,008.00	12,616.00	2,940.00
Individual deposits	775,074.76	832,528.07	736,273.05	736,255.14	777,837.46
U. S. deposits	....	....	....	....	....
Dep'ts U.S.dis.officers	....	....	....	....	....
Due to national banks	15,449.89	5,947.61	13,167.51	7,481.62	8,802.78
Due to State banks	....	....	....	58.51	128.78
Notes re-discounted	....	....	....	....	....
Bills payable	....	....	....	....	....
Total	1,372,970.48	1,413,608.21	1,337,781.55	1,333,671.11	1,367,923.51

Abstract of reports since October 5, 1887, arranged

CITY OF WASHINGTON.

Resources.	DECEMBER 7.	FEBRUARY 14.	APRIL 30.	JUNE 30.	OCTOBER 4.
	7 banks.	7 banks.	7 banks.	7 banks.	7 banks.
Loans and discounts	$4, 090, 540. 34	$3, 809, 490. 45	$3, 999, 663. 28	$4, 221, 576. 92	$4, 255, 631. 32
Bonds for circulation	680, 000. 00	680, 000. 00	680, 000. 00	680, 000. 00	580, 000. 00
Bonds for deposits	150, 000. 00	150, 000. 00	150, 000. 00	150, 000. 00	150, 000. 00
U. S. bonds on hand	739, 400. 00	736, 100. 00	740, 500. 00	739, 600. 00	814, 700. 00
Other stocks and b'ds	356, 310. 62	305, 522. 00	440, 451. 69	451, 700. 95	460, 646. 53
Due from res've ag'ts	482, 034. 28	784, 561. 04	987, 963. 61	1, 035, 504. 13	1, 005, 214. 98
Due from nat'l banks	228, 173. 04	215, 035. 18	412, 059. 21	301, 071. 52	403, 091. 42
Due from State banks	21, 168. 09	20, 022. 12	11, 025. 78	42, 657. 36	27, 077. 03
Real estate, etc	617, 482. 28	651, 030. 50	659, 890. 09	654, 583. 28	659, 042. 30
Current expenses	59, 181. 77	14, 324. 83	49, 207. 00	8, 104. 08	34, 922. 06
Premiums paid	185, 978. 36	184, 871. 74	125, 529. 40	123, 095. 23	112, 934. 65
Cash items	105, 606. 59	94, 824. 97	142, 223. 12	123, 255. 49	125, 770. 47
Clear'g-house exch'gs	71, 414. 98	54, 214. 81	50, 743. 53	101, 946. 97	74, 134. 80
Bills of other banks	26, 342. 00	29, 284. 00	59, 091. 00	25, 427. 00	17, 704. 00
Fractional currency	9, 227. 60	8, 345. 68	7, 340. 22	6, 316. 82	7, 604. 60
Trade dollars	....	....	....	....	....
Specie	803, 376. 09	807, 077. 50	890, 200. 25	801, 105. 75	953, 586. 50
Legal-tender notes	513, 126. 00	450, 444. 00	443, 210. 00	515, 703. 00	638, 650. 00
U. S. cert's of deposit	120, 000. 00	130, 000. 00	130, 000. 00	90, 000. 00	120, 000. 00
5 % fund with Treas	25, 735. 50	26, 756. 50	26, 100. 00	26, 100. 00	21, 600. 00
Due from U. S. Treas	2, 727. 08	2, 611. 08	....	2, 065. 00	....
Total	9, 288, 535. 52	9, 389, 422. 08	9, 084, 030. 17	10, 099, 942. 50	10, 408, 409. 04

VIRGINIA.

Resources.	DECEMBER 7.	FEBRUARY 14.	APRIL 30.	JUNE 30.	OCTOBER 4.
	25 banks.	25 banks.	25 banks.	25 banks.	26 banks.
Loans and discounts	$10, 551, 739. 21	$10, 705, 772. 08	$10, 810, 870. 49	$10, 027, 353. 17	$11, 100, 287. 46
Bonds for circulation	1, 352, 500. 00	1, 202, 500. 00	1, 202, 500. 00	1, 202, 500. 00	1, 165, 000. 00
Bonds for deposits	1, 550, 000. 00	1, 700, 000. 00	1, 700, 000. 00	1, 700, 000. 00	1, 700, 000. 00
U. S. bonds on hand	9, 200. 00	9, 200. 00	9, 200. 00	....	....
Other stocks and b'ds	873, 856. 18	819, 327. 00	820, 417. 79	828, 530. 12	900, 323. 19
Due from res've ag'ts	1, 008, 561. 46	1, 076, 782. 27	1, 052, 005. 64	1, 195, 224. 53	1, 400, 379. 90
Due from nat'l banks	647, 715. 07	523, 177. 33	404, 825. 80	542, 041. 68	623, 858. 22
Due from State banks	297, 388. 46	300, 346. 32	236, 193. 54	254, 207. 00	200, 952. 42
Real estate, etc	395, 445. 00	404, 814. 15	422, 702. 11	421, 766. 11	426, 122. 55
Current expenses	131, 441. 15	30, 630. 47	101, 371. 68	27, 579. 29	81, 900. 71
Premiums paid	301, 008. 08	334, 376. 70	329, 176. 70	307, 527. 43	321, 966. 06
Cash items	212, 440. 56	230, 787. 75	224, 284. 14	476, 880. 82	357, 127. 69
Clear'g-house exch'gs	38, 636. 77	53, 038. 87	17, 355. 93	14, 810. 44	26, 733. 72
Bills of other banks	264, 016. 00	170, 103. 00	181, 610. 00	169, 077. 00	158, 570. 00
Fractional currency	5, 332. 30	5, 069. 19	6, 132. 10	5, 782. 87	3, 006. 68
Trade dollars	1. 80	1. 80	1. 80	1. 80	1. 80
Specie	567, 141. 92	524, 249. 04	525, 004. 01	542, 307. 65	618, 431. 05
Legal-tender notes	775, 144. 00	634, 740. 00	694, 686. 00	779, 508. 00	811, 620. 00
U. S. cert's of deposit	....	....	....	....	....
5 % fund with Treas	59, 492 50	51, 582. 16	52, 952. 16	50, 402. 00	50, 144. 66
Due from U. S. Treas	10. 66	4, 249. 62	2, 490. 62	8, 007. 77	550. 00
Total	19, 191, 081. 32	18, 701, 547. 75	18, 903, 855. 51	19, 455, 001. 68	20, 114, 966. 11

WEST VIRGINIA.

Resources.	DECEMBER 7.	FEBRUARY 14.	APRIL 30.	JUNE 30.	OCTOBER 4.
	20 banks.	20 banks.	20 banks.	20 banks.	20 banks.
Loans and discounts	$4, 062, 744. 02	$4, 029, 907. 75	$4, 084, 107. 82	$4, 086, 601. 16	$4, 144, 023. 05
Bonds for circulation	761, 250. 00	761, 250. 00	761, 250. 00	761, 250. 00	725, 000. 00
Bonds for deposits	75, 000. 00	75, 000. 00	75, 000. 00	75, 000. 00	75, 000. 00
U. S. bonds on hand	14, 500. 00	14, 500. 00	14, 500. 00	17, 000. 00	17, 000. 00
Other stocks and b'ds	78, 518. 28	78, 765. 03	79, 453. 32	76, 395. 32	78, 814. 27
Due from res've ag'ts	307, 288. 86	294, 446. 41	316, 938. 81	296, 301. 42	508, 378. 96
Due from nat'l banks	240, 142. 96	252, 183. 37	240, 029. 84	230, 772. 22	297, 500. 83
Due from State banks	52, 143. 33	52, 607. 85	51, 455. 00	71, 093. 78	65, 808. 47
Real estate, etc	233, 341. 98	232, 342. 97	232, 367. 07	233, 579. 01	235, 780. 08
Current expenses	48, 223. 73	17, 370. 01	37, 515. 10	27, 923. 20	20, 540. 19
Premiums paid	60, 358. 79	52, 737. 96	52, 136. 77	48, 098. 05	45, 650. 65
Cash items	17, 072. 31	17, 437. 50	18, 401. 72	24, 027. 14	17, 104. 53
Clear'g-house exch'gs	....	....	....	....	....
Bills of other banks	72, 854. 00	71, 873. 00	70, 709. 00	66, 652. 00	90, 865. 00
Fractional currency	1, 724. 02	2, 100. 07	2, 335. 83	2, 068. 15	2, 033. 03
Trade dollars	22. 00	26. 00	....	16. 00	48. 70
Specie	291, 795. 69	301, 136. 83	271, 961. 07	272, 556. 40	272, 925. 15
Legal-tender notes	227, 107. 00	253, 601. 00	231, 625. 00	214, 630. 00	266, 923. 00
U. S. cert's of deposit	....	....	....	....	....
5 % fund with Treas	33, 877. 43	32, 049. 20	33, 076. 25	33, 656. 25	32, 568. 75
Due from U. S. Treas	2, 054. 83	2, 004. 70	6, 553. 20	7, 103. 70	2, 883. 45
Total	6, 580, 010. 23	6, 539, 400. 25	6, 588, 562. 39	6, 544, 882. 80	6, 908, 043. 13

by States and reserve cities—Continued.

CITY OF WASHINGTON.

Liabilities.	DECEMBER 7.	FEBRUARY 14.	APRIL 30.	JUNE 30.	OCTOBER 4.
	7 banks.	7 banks.	7 banks.	7 banks.	7 banks.
Capital stock	$1,575,000.00	$1,575,000.00	$1,575,000.00	$1,575,000.00	$1,575,000.00
Surplus fund	461,203.75	518,500.00	533,500.00	540,500.00	567,000.00
Undivided profits	245,235.73	154,659.48	210,329.31	168,861.20	209,314.68
Nat'l-bank circulation	532,910.00	522,520.00	517,270.00	512,410.00	425,820.00
State-bank circulation	....	....	....	....	....
Dividends unpaid	1,953.50	3,083.50	2,183.00	25,332.00	3,379.00
Individual deposits	6,111,055.92	6,275,830.49	6,828,051.08	6,940,541.66	7,278,316.29
U. S. deposits	96,871.09	122,058.64	142,933.83	143,353.21	154,581.72
Dep'ts U.S.dis.officers	....	....	....	....	....
Due to national banks	151,132.75	137,645.01	125,528.52	130,792.16	190,111.20
Due to State banks	30,672.78	17,625.66	24,240.43	29,152.27	39,886.66
Notes re-discounted	....	....	....	....	....
Bills payable	62,500.00	62,500.00	25,000.00	25,000.00	25,000.00
Total	9,288,535.52	9,380,422.98	9,984,039.17	10,090,942.50	10,408,409.64

VIRGINIA.

Liabilities.	DECEMBER 7.	FEBRUARY 14.	APRIL 30.	JUNE 30.	OCTOBER 4.
	25 banks.	25 banks.	23 banks.	25 banks.	26 banks.
Capital stock	$3,796,300.00	$3,796,300.00	$3,796,300.00	$3,796,300.00	$3,846,300.00
Surplus fund	1,424,892.31	1,488,541.93	1,488,541.93	1,513,541.93	1,516,103.44
Undivided profits	677,352.73	348,058.13	513,923.44	355,626.85	513,190.13
Nat'l-bank circulation	1,100,390.00	1,079,800.00	1,075,040.00	1,068,540.00	1,025,920.00
State-bank circulation	....	....	....	....	....
Dividends unpaid	3,235.65	6,400.34	3,233.34	102,053.79	3,867.15
Individual deposits	9,404,023.41	9,084,798.21	8,931,780.01	9,710,924.54	10,176,756.98
U. S. deposits	1,492,751.22	1,608,899.90	1,579,942.48	1,630,620.85	1,542,038.20
Dep'ts U.S.dis.officers	96,643.12	138,484.66	137,423.69	98,058.92	230,444.61
Due to national banks	482,354.32	492,942.98	444,420.86	403,096.09	513,206.30
Due to State banks	412,240.26	418,169.95	436,794.56	378,749.68	555,968.12
Notes re-discounted	162,798.30	288,461.65	245,605.20	153,489.03	110,901.14
Bills payable	40,000.00	40,000.00	250,850.00	184,000.00	80,000.00
Total	19,191,981.32	18,791,547.75	18,903,855.51	19,455,001.68	20,114,966.11

WEST VIRGINIA.

Liabilities.	DECEMBER 7.	FEBRUARY 14.	APRIL 30.	JUNE 30.	OCTOBER 4.
	20 banks.	20 banks.	20 banks.	20 banks.	20 banks.
Capital stock	$1,961,000.00	$1,961,000.00	$1,961,000.00	$1,961,000.00	$1,966,000.00
Surplus fund	464,870.98	455,452.86	454,775.59	459,049.88	457,987.73
Undivided profits	158,343.36	74,560.70	144,682.10	136,109.56	156,731.07
Nat'l-bank circulation	672,170.00	672,835.00	670,655.00	669,965.00	626,460.00
State-bank circulation	....	....	....	....	....
Dividends unpaid	15,159.00	21,138.00	16,656.00	38,243.00	19,891.00
Individual deposits	2,997,186.17	3,028,921.55	3,031,166.70	2,984,533.99	3,371,105.58
U. S. deposits	75,000.00	82,500.00	82,500.00	82,500.00	82,500.00
Dep'ts U.S.dis.officers	....	....	....	....	....
Due to national banks	158,447.38	155,775.64	131,250.30	127,981.14	174,389.67
Due to State banks	54,733.54	49,815.15	67,406.70	48,218.17	48,915.03
Notes re-discounted	22,079.80	31,715.35	24,775.00	28,196.15	3,720.00
Bills payable	1,029.00	5,686.00	3,686.00	8,186.00	343.00
Total	6,580,019.23	6,539,400.25	6,588,562.39	6,544,882.89	6,908,043.13

Abstract of reports since October 5, 1887, arranged

NORTH CAROLINA.

Resources.	DECEMBER 7.	FEBRUARY 14.	APRIL 30.	JUNE 30.	OCTOBER 4.
	19 banks.	18 banks.	17 banks.	17 banks.	18 banks.
Loans and discounts	$4,987,652.67	$4,810,926.50	$4,753,184.04	$4,938,792.15	$5,245,311.65
Bonds for circulation	953,500.00	903,500.00	878,500.00	753,500.00	766,000.00
Bonds for deposits	100,000.00	100,000.00	150,000.00	150,000.00	150,000.00
U. S. bonds on hand	....	....	....	....	....
Other stocks and b'ds	314,062.84	341,615.32	298,095.67	320,727.07	307,877.89
Due from res've ag'ts	473,869.67	757,461.98	485,598.95	416,158.54	263,298.30
Due from nat'l banks	370,432.13	289,480.30	268,146.34	226,603.47	244,077.77
Due from State banks	109,709.65	102,206.49	80,242.28	50,407.50	122,062.97
Real estate, etc	299,509.93	287,525.02	234,311.22	220,035.24	234,018.37
Current expenses	67,782.25	22,566.92	48,536.37	24,790.50	41,792.76
Premiums paid	90,271.22	81,334.39	88,884.39	77,396.89	77,851.89
Cash items	39,401.57	47,075.14	38,773.95	42,192.48	40,122.41
Clear'g-house exch'gs	....	....	....	....	....
Bills of other banks	101,246.00	190,518.00	111,805.00	77,754.00	84,791.50
Fractional currency	2,547.21	2,030.69	1,855.23	2,050.15	3,421.64
Trade dollars	9.50	17.10	42.15	70.00	....
Specie	201,973.21	260,220.70	269,685.40	242,282.16	228,890.10
Legal-tender notes	271,482.00	250,569.00	321,741.00	229,179.00	237,968.00
U. S. cert's of deposit	....	....	....	....	....
5 % fund with Treas	41,221.25	38,917.00	37,497.40	32,507.00	34,469.50
Due from U. S. Treas	2,646.20	1,827.55	6,971.80	1,704.40	1,290.00
Total	8,427,977.30	8,503,122.00	8,074,471.19	7,854,150.55	8,083,253.81

SOUTH CAROLINA.

	16 banks.	16 banks.	16 banks.	16 banks.	16 banks.
Loans and discounts	$4,376,673.83	$4,703,414.00	$5,229,371.45	$5,484,153.77	$5,969,976.44
Bonds for circulation	612,250.00	537,250.00	548,500.00	493,500.00	468,500.00
Bonds for deposits	500,000.00	575,000.00	675,000.00	675,000.00	675,000.00
U. S. bonds on hand	24,100.00	24,100.00	29,100.00	28,100.00	28,100.00
Other stocks and b'ds	872,343.53	933,633.07	921,897.18	972,664.78	815,497.06
Due from res've ag'ts	852,893.20	736,111.91	173,418.97	294,397.93	174,285.52
Due from nat'l banks	363,590.70	314,257.80	157,120.27	160,840.40	161,071.04
Due from State banks	130,067.07	81,003.13	103,096.73	93,473.57	143,578.29
Real estate, etc	168,589.99	188,546.10	194,344.90	181,684.26	182,276.83
Current expenses	72,087.48	17,353.86	67,464.32	82,328.92	43,268.25
Premiums paid	64,688.75	66,766.25	68,649.07	56,782.50	58,503.75
Cash items	107,221.20	67,074.97	43,523.67	42,760.64	55,968.43
Clear'g-house exch'gs	....	....	....	....	....
Bills of other banks	104,182.00	121,832.00	70,120.00	37,039.00	82,212.00
Fractional currency	1,615.54	2,741.55	3,517.54	1,696.40	4,763.13
Trade dollars	....	....	....	....	....
Specie	204,370.30	386,415.80	406,042.40	264,040.15	200,948.05
Legal-tender notes	439,768.00	452,987.00	240,623.00	225,741.00	275,972.00
U. S. cert's of deposit	....	....	....	....	....
5 % fund with Treas	26,088.25	23,613.25	24,456.50	22,206.50	20,082.00
Due from U. S. Treas	160.00	5,498.80	11,500.00	1,550.00	6,100.00
Total	9,031,619.46	9,237,599.52	8,962,352.00	9,123,968.62	9,361,193.99

GEORGIA.

	21 banks.	22 banks.	22 banks.	23 banks.	24 banks.
Loans and discounts	$7,489,536.16	$7,339,989.61	$7,209,844.39	$7,415,379.67	$8,062,050.32
Bonds for circulation	988,500.00	951,000.00	951,000.00	964,500.00	969,500.00
Bonds for deposits	150,000.00	150,000.00	150,000.00	150,000.00	150,000.00
U. S. bonds on hand	....	....	....	....	....
Other stocks and b'ds	261,477.65	380,050.91	372,519.41	340,916.10	345,312.65
Due from res've ag'ts	276,720.50	436,948.02	487,509.18	300,023.70	211,980.05
Due from nat'l banks	327,328.01	286,516.41	221,041.24	192,348.28	338,168.50
Due from State banks	260,828.79	260,117.12	159,927.23	194,807.97	350,012.61
Real estate, etc	460,719.07	466,444.05	469,581.29	480,226.09	481,687.63
Current expenses	104,303.71	29,055.81	87,527.03	76,193.34	63,884.81
Premiums paid	80,197.86	82,679.65	80,548.40	77,835.90	75,652.59
Cash items	140,825.98	132,610.50	161,430.60	104,141.51	185,503.71
Clear'g-house exch'gs	....	....	....	....	....
Bills of other banks	203,281.00	334,630.00	252,222.00	163,028.00	197,291.00
Fractional currency	3,592.14	4,386.39	4,505.52	5,033.09	3,932.99
Trade dollars	....	....	....	....	....
Specie	515,967.85	549,910.27	528,702.83	476,726.41	523,773.66
Legal-tender notes	417,643.00	435,005.00	366,253.00	368,805.00	358,106.00
U. S. cert's of deposit	....	....	....	....	....
5 % fund with Treas	42,832.50	42,794.50	41,544.50	42,333.40	41,006.70
Due from U. S. Treas	2,054.85	6,452.60	21,050.30	21,004.84	30,373.14
Total	11,734,379.97	11,908,680.84	11,565,206.91	11,483,923.30	12,088,251.36

by States and reserve cities—Continued.

NORTH CAROLINA.

Liabilities.	DECEMBER 7.	FEBRUARY 14.	APRIL 30.	JUNE 30.	OCTOBER 4.
	19 banks.	18 banks.	17 banks.	17 banks.	18 banks.
Capital stock	$2,476,000.00	$2,297,013.75	$2,226,000.00	$2,226,000.00	$2,266,000.00
Surplus fund	544,490.66	526,287.26	520,287.26	554,087.26	562,242.99
Undivided profits	343,605.56	239,830.88	291,754.54	253,514.04	270,110.15
Nat'l-bank circulation	701,510.00	709,440.00	735,770.00	634,870.00	647,780.00
State-bank circulation	....	....	....	....	....
Dividends unpaid	5,368.00	3,013.50	3,155.50	34,005.50	4,858.10
Individual deposits	3,694,203.61	4,250,220.12	3,723,549.64	3,438,516.36	3,320,001.79
U. S. deposits	53,182.45	70,436.00	110,838.07	134,805.90	127,514.37
Dep'ts U.S.dis.officers	29,566.62	26,214.07	40,400.80	29,436.69	29,902.92
Due to national banks	164,985.51	118,462.42	127,749.78	129,444.15	227,970.54
Due to State banks	67,393.79	66,107.41	53,866.69	60,033.13	42,140.24
Notes re-discounted	221,605.77	114,596.59	223,008.91	327,547.52	454,133.71
Bills payable	36,005.38	14,000.00	....	30,000.00	121,500.00
Total	8,427,977.30	8,503,122.00	8,074,471.19	7,854,150.55	8,083,253.81

SOUTH CAROLINA.

	16 banks.	16 banks.	16 banks.	16 banks.	16 banks.
Capital stock	$1,723,000.00	$1,728,000.00	$1,773,000.00	$1,773,000.00	$1,773,000.00
Surplus fund	778,800.00	788,827.82	784,000.00	787,000.00	787,800.00
Undivided profits	708,234.36	702,429.72	826,524.40	841,425.33	797,755.79
Nat'l-bank circulation	538,065.00	469,370.00	479,305.00	442,130.00	420,030.00
State-bank circulation	....	....	....	....	....
Dividends unpaid	9,031.50	15,809.50	12,128.00	27,994.50	12,015.50
Individual deposits	4,097,704.92	4,471,105.52	3,694,509.92	3,605,717.41	3,095,982.88
U. S. deposits	509,718.98	593,472.17	673,102.63	699,702.02	690,320.91
Dep'ts U.S.dis.officers	41,034.89	30,704.35	51,120.73	29,561.94	42,240.86
Due to national banks	173,329.98	232,096.76	298,300.84	140,280.29	350,304.66
Due to State banks	288,530.53	176,608.68	205,423.67	204,948.75	166,079.86
Notes re-discounted	72,000.00	20,000.00	99,783.72	277,122.58	712,210.53
Bills payable	2,160.30	....	65,000.00	205,000.00	503,175.00
Total	9,031,619.46	9,237,590.52	8,062,358.00	9,123,906.82	9,361,193.90

GEORGIA.

	21 banks.	22 banks.	22 banks.	23 banks.	24 banks.
Capital stock	$3,106,000.00	$3,166,000.00	$3,176,000.00	$3,236,000.00	$3,361,000.00
Surplus fund	951,731.71	994,353.65	994,358.05	1,007,853.05	1,055,400.30
Undivided profits	645,345.15	404,411.28	643,933.99	600,427.30	616,930.28
Nat'l bank circulation	872,000.00	823,100.00	831,730.00	820,810.00	860,150.00
State-bank circulation	....	....	....	....	....
Dividends unpaid	2,103.00	5,041.50	3,822.00	3,250.00	4,240.00
Individual deposits	4,903,751.17	5,128,305.78	4,700,614.36	4,393,344.09	4,813,247.98
U. S. deposits	118,462.14	110,793.42	90,700.00	90,263.62	91,694.21
Dep'ts U.S.dis.officers	37,046.71	32,885.65	82,975.47	81,071.90	90,178.47
Due to national banks	343,387.95	287,143.37	215,320.17	244,168.38	438,620.01
Due to State banks	351,707.19	303,828.11	237,763.09	248,387.24	190,714.27
Notes re-discounted	393,885.95	453,218.10	508,074.22	610,737.13	1,136,006.89
Bills payable	8,000.00	100,000.00	80,000.00	30,000.00	330,000.00
Total	11,734,379.07	11,908,080.84	11,565,290.91	11,483,923.30	12,988,251.86

Abstract of reports since October 5, 1887, arranged

FLORIDA.

Resources.	DECEMBER 7.	FEBRUARY 14.	APRIL 30.	JUNE 30.	OCTOBER 4.
	11 banks.	11 banks.	11 banks.	13 banks.	13 banks.
Loans and discounts	$1,600,806.00	$1,724,705.84	$1,737,998.83	$2,100,291.54	$1,970,954.55
Bonds for circulation	230,000.00	230,000.00	280,000.00	280,000.00	280,000.00
Bonds for deposits	100,000.00	200,000.00	200,000.00	200,000.00	200,000.00
U.S. bonds on hand				1,000.00	
Other stocks and b'ds	98,002.76	111,853.39	113,513.75	100,408.36	119,267.42
Due from res've ag'ts	156,622.44	284,196.75	438,445.75	353,023.54	360,642.52
Due from nat'l banks	75,401.86	142,001.91	217,407.39	210,443.06	82,095.50
Due from State banks	62,803.94	63,449.47	74,139.53	60,552.68	100,486.23
Real estate, etc	108,663.54	115,838.00	143,560.78	156,407.30	160,919.22
Current expenses	22,916.25	18,171.51	27,692.26	34,272.95	28,416.00
Premiums paid	37,532.78	53,035.90	50,580.28	63,546.54	62,345.92
Cash items	19,799.77	22,283.50	27,694.28	23,811.85	24,652.04
Clear'g-house exch'gs					
Bills of other banks	77,849.00	117,215.00	105,957.00	94,091.00	97,664.00
Fractional currency	1,474.11	1,322.33	1,166.14	1,057.46	939.39
Trade dollars					
Specie	76,060.37	98,055.58	131,206.77	147,291.33	107,338.39
Legal-tender notes	138,856.00	172,120.00	170,660.00	198,175.00	150,094.00
U.S. cert's of deposit					
5 % fund with Treas.	8,779.00	10,328.97	10,198.97	11,505.97	11,071.47
Due from U.S. Treas.	730.57			4,000.00	1,000.00
Total	2,816,449.29	3,364,578.15	3,680,311.73	4,048,778.58	3,725,480.65

ALABAMA.

Resources.	DECEMBER 7.	FEBRUARY 14.	APRIL 30.	JUNE 30.	OCTOBER 4.
	20 banks.	20 banks.	20 banks.	21 banks.	21 banks.
Loans and discounts	$7,630,795.21	$6,558,958.54	$6,751,746.64	$7,026,055.87	$7,450,418.85
Bonds for circulation	900,500.00	900,500.00	900,500.00	913,000.00	863,000.00
Bonds for deposits	100,000.00	250,000.00	300,000.00	300,000.00	300,000.00
U.S. bonds on hand					
Other stocks and b'ds	855,430.16	926,514.04	840,083.83	842,100.68	859,067.51
Due from res've ag'ts	609,702.11	801,578.46	703,780.49	708,668.14	552,950.49
Due from nat'l banks	510,353.06	625,720.13	531,129.89	351,276.60	270,538.29
Due from State banks	162,072.38	237,877.09	246,709.69	194,622.11	210,669.26
Real estate, etc	382,573.61	388,375.18	397,574.14	412,633.32	443,080.83
Current expenses	110,160.20	47,465.28	93,639.51	79,547.61	58,541.35
Premiums paid	119,273.53	123,020.30	125,551.53	125,598.40	119,889.03
Cash items	89,761.14	94,542.03	47,297.73	31,665.32	45,016.18
Clear'g-house exch'gs					
Bills of other banks	216,843.00	219,216.00	239,582.00	154,554.00	210,754.00
Fractional currency	3,214.29	3,601.55	2,231.40	1,040.28	1,625.00
Trade dollars	1.00	7.00	2.00	6.00	4.00
Specie	378,977.80	480,436.64	364,851.65	408,336.48	437,392.36
Legal-tender notes	442,695.00	503,546.00	440,789.00	295,620.00	387,987.00
U.S. cert's of deposit					
5 % fund with Treas.	40,022.50	38,622.50	37,072.50	40,072.50	37,085.00
Due from U.S. Treas.	2,763.24	673.24	6,750.79	2,988.49	3,666.24
Total	12,555,159.16	12,299,654.88	12,047,901.79	11,889,586.00	12,261,204.41

MISSISSIPPI.

Resources.	DECEMBER 7.	FEBRUARY 14.	APRIL 30.	JUNE 30.	OCTOBER 4.
	12 banks.	12 banks.	12 banks.	12 banks.	12 banks.
Loans and discounts	$2,512,630.80	$2,086,420.55	$2,317,364.94	$2,248,282.47	$2,646,803.78
Bonds for circulation	320,000.00	320,000.00	320,000.00	320,000.00	332,500.00
Bonds for deposits					
U.S. bonds on hand		30,000.00	30,000.00	30,000.00	60,000.00
Other stocks and b'ds	67,357.12	29,280.27	51,102.93	59,586.54	75,784.26
Due from res've ag'ts	254,608.65	481,573.48	366,598.56	239,208.43	62,668.90
Due from nat'l banks	81,100.18	225,491.00	104,180.20	96,474.78	71,051.09
Due from State banks	75,797.60	99,988.28	48,298.43	41,702.29	37,032.91
Real estate, etc	47,628.50	47,455.94	52,909.94	53,026.44	60,695.22
Current expenses	36,396.67	16,063.02	39,703.69	19,337.95	28,555.40
Premiums paid	35,800.65	36,484.48	35,314.48	32,780.57	38,168.07
Cash items	26,596.66	36,886.44	15,567.69	15,630.07	34,102.83
Clear'g-house exch'gs					
Bills of other banks	14,111.00	20,905.00	18,528.00	20,065.00	13,651.00
Fractional currency	362.80	928.08	1,365.94	1,369.64	2,090.43
Trade dollars					
Specie	168,623.85	243,024.70	168,445.65	144,180.83	149,680.15
Legal-tender notes	158,224.00	234,771.00	161,387.00	133,952.00	186,046.00
U.S. cert's of deposit					
5 % fund with Treas.	13,643.57	13,913.57	13,839.50	13,459.50	14,512.00
Due from U.S. Treas.		2,486.85	4,100.00	2,650.00	
Total	3,812,881.63	3,924,672.06	3,748,706.86	3,401,715.51	3,814,242.04

by States and reserve cities—Continued.

FLORIDA.

Liabilities.	DECEMBER 7.	FEBRUARY 14.	APRIL 30.	JUNE 30.	OCTOBER 4.
	11 banks.	11 banks.	11 banks.	13 banks.	13 banks.
Capital stock	$640,000.00	$672,820.00	$700,000.00	$894,200.00	$896,900.00
Surplus fund	66,680.00	70,000.00	80,000.00	86,000.00	98,820.00
Undivided profits	67,106.76	57,571.14	82,492.90	95,345.75	78,793.77
Nat'l-bank circulation	145,730.00	184,100.00	170,760.00	170,070.00	194,750.00
State-bank circulation	....	....	....	....	....
Dividends unpaid	40.00	509.00	54.00	6,514.00	1,261.00
Individual deposits	1,642,112.73	2,058,096.76	2,334,821.59	2,440,216.23	2,048,955.82
U. S. deposits	96,988.51	102,355.43	108,309.57	107,453.41	147,529.60
Dep'ts U.S. dis. officers	2,790.77	105,444.57	99,491.28	100,330.45	60,725.40
Due to national banks	45,207.06	67,362.81	61,875.58	65,348.20	113,281.16
Due to State banks	17,124.95	24,015.11	28,506.81	62,540.54	20,985.11
Notes re-discounted	62,668.51	6,243.33	5,000.00	14,700.00	22,394.79
Bills payable	36,000.00	10,000.00	....	....	32,000.00
Total	2,816,449.29	3,304,578.15	3,080,311.73	4,048,776.58	3,725,486.65

ALABAMA.

Liabilities.	DECEMBER 7.	FEBRUARY 14.	APRIL 30.	JUNE 30.	OCTOBER 4.
	20 banks.	20 banks.	20 banks.	21 banks.	21 banks.
Capital stock	$3,494,000.00	$3,494,000.00	$3,494,000.00	$3,544,000.00	$3,544,000.00
Surplus fund	639,903.66	665,709.36	666,586.54	678,122.42	724,414.48
Undivided profits	571,535.79	414,197.36	550,368.39	569,585.87	495,214.88
Nat'l-bank circulation	783,050.00	779,170.00	773,030.00	765,230.00	748,580.00
State-bank circulation	....	....	....	....	....
Dividends unpaid	6,525.00	4,790.20	2,174.00	32,153.00	4,779.99
Individual deposits	5,689,818.85	5,867,040.38	5,306,489.89	4,881,579.28	4,785,060.18
U. S. deposits	79,296.45	249,350.58	288,840.26	293,360.86	295,743.18
Dep'ts U.S. dis. officers	851.46	387.52	11,159.74	4,637.71	2,256.82
Due to national banks	344,944.22	247,081.10	171,647.41	162,322.28	270,710.26
Due to State banks	109,743.70	127,833.12	107,165.52	107,895.78	72,367.30
Notes re-discounted	685,490.03	398,595.26	519,432.59	786,520.62	1,250,167.23
Bills payable	150,000.00	57,000.00	97,007.45	64,178.18	68,000.00
Total	12,555,159.16	12,299,654.88	12,047,901.79	11,889,586.00	12,261,294.41

MISSISSIPPI.

Liabilities.	DECEMBER 7.	FEBRUARY 14.	APRIL 30.	JUNE 30.	OCTOBER 4.
	12 banks.	12 banks.	12 banks.	12 banks.	12 banks.
Capital stock	$1,055,000.00	$1,055,000.00	$1,055,000.00	$1,055,000.00	$1,105,000.00
Surplus fund	128,868.27	190,213.12	190,213.12	210,513.12	242,289.50
Undivided profits	141,835.33	68,487.54	142,360.34	108,932.84	92,863.05
Nat'l-bank circulation	283,820.00	270,230.00	275,110.00	278,970.00	292,860.00
State-bank circulation	....	....	....	....	....
Dividends unpaid	....	728.00	20.00	18,875.00	382.00
Individual deposits	1,857,800.45	2,220,945.10	1,983,280.17	1,674,630.59	1,379,274.07
U. S. deposits	....	....	....	....	....
Dep'ts U.S. dis. officers	....	....	....	....	....
Due to national banks	82,780.75	56,204.37	51,940.58	24,959.74	111,275.89
Due to State banks	23,167.48	19,023.69	34,701.65	48,415.05	13,287.00
Notes re-discounted	224,603.35	34,150.75	16,171.00	71,910.17	492,008.85
Bills payable	15,000.00	....	....	....	85,000.00
Total	3,812,881.63	3,924,072.66	3,748,706.86	3,491,715.51	3,814,242.04

Abstract of reports since October 5, 1887, arranged

LOUISIANA.

Resources.	DECEMBER 7.	FEBRUARY 14.	APRIL 30.	JUNE 30.	OCTOBER 4.
	5 banks.	5 banks.	5 banks.	5 banks.	5 banks.
Loans and discounts.	$1,274,881.63	$959,500.12	$1,000,191.57	$935,436.78	$1,309,024.09
Bonds for circulation	125,000.00	125,000.00	125,000.00	125,000.00	125,000.00
Bonds for deposits ..		100,000.00	100,000.00	100,000.00	100,000.00
U.S. bonds on hand..	75,000.00		15,000.00	20,000.00	20,000.00
Other stock and b'ds	44,698.87	41,197.94	37,056.96	40,814.93	46,187.41
Due from res've ag'ts	100,397.47	231,013.41	157,041.50	215,583.20	48,541.12
Due from nat'l banks	7,635.73	45,315.80	97,033.50	59,720.13	10,559.24
Due from State banks	3,475.27	12,721.71	11,556.12	28,130.88	26,805.39
Real estate, etc......	9,218.29	9,338.19	9,354.34	9,354.34	9,354.34
Current expenses....	14,444.85	3,429.55	11,315.48	10,590.64	8,266.97
Premiums paid......	32,888.13	39,800.63	43,284.88	26,450.00	27,372.48
Cash items..........	19,843.96	5,032.65	2,035.98	5,558.44	7,330.46
Clear'g-house exch'gs					
Bills of other banks.	27,365.00	26,605.00	17,600.00	15,070.00	12,800.00
Fractional currency.	368.17	200.49	108.37	93.20	1,507.02
Trade dollars........					
Specie..............	117,745.65	107,281.35	142,762.30	138,164.10	130,949.05
Legal-tender notes ..	57,001.00	93,652.00	60,862.00	51,659.00	63,247.00
U.S. cert's of deposit					
5 % fund with Treas.	5,624.00	5,624.00	5,624.00	5,624.00	5,624.50
Due from U.S. Treas		10,000.00		15,000.00	
Total..........	1,915,478.02	1,876,768.84	1,851,807.00	1,802,249.74	2,049,229.07

CITY OF NEW ORLEANS.

Resources.	DECEMBER 7.	FEBRUARY 14.	APRIL 30.	JUNE 30.	OCTOBER 4.
	8 banks.	8 banks.	8 banks.	8 banks.	8 banks.
Loans and discounts	$10,853,741.15	$9,478,081.51	$9,463,871.70	$9,362,253.70	$11,010,516.97
Bonds for circulation.	1,375,000.00	1,375,000.00	1,375,000.00	1,375,000.00	1,375,000.00
Bonds for deposits ..	400,000.00	600,000.00	600,000.00	600,000.00	600,000.00
U.S. bonds on hand..	210,450.00	200,650.00	9,700.00	5,900.00	14,100.00
Other stocks and b'ds	1,612,830.28	1,030,681.05	2,326,554.20	2,120,072.56	2,038,075.66
Due from res've ag'ts	970,129.71	1,527,943.40	1,226,012.40	1,590,505.72	818,011.40
Due from nat'l banks	401,912.65	525,243.23	325,297.13	602,456.44	218,502.56
Due from State banks	492,537.63	600,921.28	403,756.20	2 9,174.03	247,541.59
Real estate, etc	477,726.32	407,401.27	404,181.05	390,256.51	304,174.39
Current expenses....	164,590.10	43,082.00	121,526.49		93,062.28
Premiums paid......	236,540.87	270,048.44	258,200.79	250,710.83	253,330.41
Cash items..........	5,402.28	5,898.39	2,716.24	8,346.25	4,728.04
Clear'g-house exch'gs	1,412,198.57	1,662,901.85	1,096,753.00	961,250.19	1,168,357.48
Bills of other banks..	95,208.00	167,643.00	176,947.00	110,840.00	109,602.00
Fractional currency.	4,215.91	4,844.01	7,441.40	9,548.64	8,944.17
Trade dollars........					
Specie..............	1,236,833.60	1,992,480.75	1,843,886.00	1,536,757.35	933,120.85
Legal-tender notes ..	951,776.00	1,792,593.00	1,464,112.00	1,415,076.00	1,211,014.00
U.S. cert's of deposit.					
5 % fund with Treas.	61,875.00	61,875.00	61,875.00	61,875.00	61,875.00
Due from U.S. Treas.	5,600.00	1,000.00		1,850.00	5,000.00
Total...........	20,968,597.36	22,679,371.78	21,167,839.00	20,602,882.22	20,594,046.80

TEXAS.

Resources.	DECEMBER 7.	FEBRUARY 14.	APRIL 30.	JUNE 30.	OCTOBER 4.
	91 banks.	94 banks.	96 banks.	98 banks.	100 banks.
Loans and discounts	$19,728,582.83	$20,212,080.26	$21,306,143.28	$21,793,400.44	$24,688,800.15
Bonds for circulation	2,415,300.00	2,515,500.00	2,552,500.00	2,615,500.00	2,634,000.00
Bonds for deposits...	400,000.00	400,000.00	400,000.00	400,000.00	400,000.00
U.S. bonds on hand..			1,500.00	1,500.00	
Other stocks and b'ds	401,544.04	380,953.47	385,622.07	387,347.62	467,410.22
Due from res've ag'ts	2,277,283.13	2,362,183.16	1,879,975.18	2,287,553.12	1,859,806.42
Due from nat'l banks	1,401,800.24	1,267,680.32	1,286,698.31	1,432,6.9.36	1,531,603.01
Due from State banks	890,144.42	752,905.34	761,152.28	891,432.01	820,839.27
Real estate, etc	1,138,241.30	1,214,411.37	1,255,223.90	1,277,529.67	1,443,619.20
Current expenses....	310,330.06	133,737.49	281,026.71	108,522.82	244,948.08
Premiums paid......	357,127.71	353,631.49	350,927.40	344,353.41	347,771.60
Cash items..........	199,391.72	199,671.14	163,007.04	258,670.34	200,523.39
Clear'g-house exch'gs					
Bills of other banks..	911,923.00	991,494.00	701,547.00	523,405.00	510,669.00
Fractional currency.	11,306.05	12,126.24	10,948.03	17,365.95	19,505.42
Trade dollars.......	11.00	12.00	12.00		
Specie..............	1,571,470.66	1,452,393.85	1,303,024.85	1,305,725.11	1,305,386.15
Legal-tender notes ..	2,130,613.00	2,145,971.00	1,581,313.00	1,600,410.00	1,817,165.00
U.S. cert's of deposit					
5 % fund with Treas.	107,087.55	108,513.00	109,389.50	112,488.75	115,188.75
Due from U.S. Treas.	4,926.62	4,987.12	10,754.62	9,030.62	4,159.84
Total...........	34,200,083.42	34,508,857.85	34,407,515.77	35,006,869.22	38,471,456.50

by States and reserve cities—Continued.

LOUISIANA.

Liabilities.	DECEMBER 7.	FEBRUARY 14.	APRIL 30.	JUNE 30.	OCTOBER 4.
	5 banks.	5 banks.	5 banks.	5 banks.	5 banks.
Capital stock	$500,000.00	$500,000.00	$500,000.00	$500,000.00	$500,000.00
Surplus fund	30,308.44	60,280.02	60,280.02	73,865.37	84,214.06
Undivided profits	60,607.93	23,842.24	56,534.71	38,151.20	45,067.21
Nat'l-bank circulation	101,490.00	101,070.00	101,980.00	105,665.00	110,415.00
State-bank circulation	....	....	....	....	....
Dividends unpaid	8.00	88.00	36.00	6,036.00	76.00
Individual deposits	868,092.80	1,065,219.26	1,014,616.29	965,714.61	788,735.80
U. S. deposits	....	110,000.00	110,000.00	110,000.00	110,000.00
Dep'ts U.S.dis.officers	....	....	....	....	....
Due to national banks	174,209.92	7,319.32	8,315.11	2,817.56	94,697.57
Due to State banks	218.80	....	44.87	....	12,396.28
Notes re-discounted	160,468.80	8,950.00	....	....	273,627.06
Bills payable	20,073.33	....	....	....	30,000.00
Total	1,915,478.02	1,870,768.84	1,851,807.00	1,802,249.74	2,049,229.07

CITY OF NEW ORLEANS.

Liabilities.	DECEMBER 7.	FEBRUARY 14.	APRIL 30.	JUNE 30.	OCTOBER 4.
	8 banks.	8 banks.	8 banks.	8 banks.	8 banks.
Capital stock	$2,925,000.00	$2,925,000.00	$2,925,000.00	$2,925,000.00	$2,925,000.00
Surplus fund	1,199,000.00	1,346,000.00	1,346,000.00	1,424,000.00	1,424,000.00
Undivided profits	738,976.51	368,320.62	554,007.83	151,913.88	349,849.53
Nat'l-bank circulation	1,235,775.00	1,229,835.00	1,225,615.00	1,207,765.00	1,216,595.00
State-bank circulation	492.00	....	....	....	....
Dividends unpaid	11,019.50	25,376.81	11,075.81	118,589.81	14,487.57
Individual deposits	11,046,301.91	14,012,506.64	12,926,349.81	12,707,884.11	11,123,200.02
U. S. deposits	402,353.70	641,086.75	635,921.07	641,030.90	641,791.25
Dep'ts U.S.dis.officers	....	....	....	....	....
Due to national banks	1,123,747.20	1,219,862.24	965,255.27	709,466.80	979,447.77
Due to State banks	1,327,581.24	910,763.72	558,614.81	717,231.63	1,036,806.55
Notes re-discounted	158,350.21	....	....	....	352,869.11
Bills payable	200,000.00	....	....	....	530,000.00
Total	20,968,597.36	22,679,371.78	21,167,830.60	20,602,882.22	20,594,046.80

TEXAS.

Liabilities.	DECEMBER 7.	FEBRUARY 14.	APRIL 30.	JUNE 30.	OCTOBER 4.
	91 banks.	94 banks.	96 banks.	98 banks.	100 banks.
Capital stock	$10,047,000.00	$10,743,700.00	$10,970,400.00	$11,327,358.26	$11,805,700.00
Surplus fund	2,457,987.96	2,490,480.54	2,530,920.54	2,564,207.66	2,776,767.43
Undivided profits	1,511,036.60	879,648.54	1,262,383.35	1,193,458.25	1,128,945.91
Nat'l-bank circulation	2,140,415.00	2,180,930.00	2,215,565.00	2,233,075.00	2,312,615.00
State-bank circulation	....	....	....	....	....
Dividends unpaid	5,380.00	23,864.52	4,280.55	150,283.05	11,545.06
Individual deposits	15,381,227.88	15,523,230.41	14,623,345.00	15,140,714.35	15,784,698.56
U. S. deposits	274,303.40	264,178.97	264,544.17	281,780.87	256,590.68
Dep'ts U.S.dis.officers	127,790.17	142,132.45	144,738.87	113,468.73	143,319.17
Due to national banks	984,052.57	1,093,685.84	822,371.06	843,846.98	1,185,243.31
Due to State banks	615,029.41	628,854.99	590,708.92	564,598.63	688,472.09
Notes re-discounted	670,860.43	517,131.59	956,752.31	1,133,077.45	2,038,626.00
Bills payable	45,000.00	10,000.00	21,500.00	61,000.00	338,033.35
Total	34,260,083.42	34,508,857.85	34,407,515.77	35,606,869.22	38,471,456.50

Abstract of reports since October 5, 1887, arranged

ARKANSAS.

Resources.	DECEMBER 7.	FEBRUARY 14.	APRIL 30.	JUNE 30.	OCTOBER 4.
	7 banks.	7 banks.	7 banks.	7 banks.	7 banks.
Loans and discounts.	$3, 018, 971. 45	$2, 815, 377. 26	$2, 769, 382. 24	$2, 559, 275. 99	$2, 768 208. 30
Bonds for circulation	410, 000. 00	410, 000. 00	410, 000. 00	410, 000. 00	410, 000. 00
Bonds for deposits...	150, 000. 00	150, 000. 00	150, 000. 00	150, 000. 00	150, 000. 00
U. S. bonds on hand..	51, 400. 00	51, 600. 00	66, 600. 00	55, 700. 00	55, 700. 00
Other stocks and b'ds	34, 803. 24	48, 589. 07	46, 776. 37	52, 635. 51	47, 091. 17
Due from res've ag'ts	167, 925. 51	352, 330. 75	365, 286. 07	338, 672. 95	283, 473. 04
Due from nat'l banks	87, 171. 91	56, 596. 12	127, 265. 62	98, 422. 93	40, 677. 27
Due from State banks	96, 804. 58	61, 555. 25	109, 616. 22	85, 401. 99	82, 005. 65
Real estate, etc......	33, 703. 20	32, 238. 98	32, 769. 93	32, 261. 98	32, 711. 93
Current expenses....	11, 936. 91	6, 928. 00	6, 746. 77	10, 767. 91	4, 160. 59
Premiums paid......	95, 065. 00	92, 309. 00	93, 246. 50	92, 271. 25	84, 958. 75
Cash items	8, 368. 67	10, 895. 08	15, 802. 06	9, 145. 69	8, 936. 07
Clear'g-house exch'gs	...	...	...	...	...
Bills of other banks..	54, 773. 00	33, 847. 00	39, 100. 00	39, 402. 00	35, 193. 00
Fractional currency.	768. 18	837. 47	870. 44	724. 21	968. 00
Trade dollars........	...	...	...	...	...
Specie..............	175, 733. 45	176, 155. 25	204, 025. 10	128, 330. 70	120, 750. 10
Legal-tender notes...	161, 856. 00	128, 195. 00	133, 303. 00	106, 007. 00	140, 834. 00
U. S. cert's of deposit	...	...	...	...	...
5 % fund with Treas.	18, 450. 00	18, 450. 00	18, 450. 00	17, 400. 00	18, 450. 00
Due from U. S. Treas.	1, 618. 30	...	500. 00	1, 224. 15	198. 30
Total............	4, 574, 499. 40	4, 445, 809. 18	4, 589, 740. 32	4, 187, 644. 21	4, 286, 327. 86

KENTUCKY.

	59 banks.	59 banks.	60 banks.	60 banks.	60 banks.
Loans and discounts.	$17, 569, 511. 27	$17, 879, 062. 96	$18. 334, 770. 68	$18, 423, 748. 32	$18, 600 858. 56
Bonds for circulation.	3, 311, 000. 00	3, 286, 000. 00	3, 302, 000 00	3, 190, 000. 00	2, 937, 000. 00
Bonds for deposits...	1, 370, 000. 00	1, 420, 000. 00	1, 445, 000. 00	1, 445, 000. 00	1, 445, 000 00
U. S. bonds on hand..	104, 150. 00	104, 050. 00	102, 400. 00	101, 300. 00	104, 300. 00
Other stocks and b'ds	741, 377. 72	783, 698. 09	713, 930. 58	710 490. 71	708, 868. 41
Due from res've ag'ts.	1, 780, 399. 11	1, 670, 905. 01	1, 337, 799. 83	1, 488, 346. 94	1, 756 776. 63
Due from nat'l banks.	937, 504. 50	1, 136, 278. 22	776, 712. 53	755, 601. 80	729, 063. 14
Due from State banks	232, 975. 34	351, 231. 40	276, 492. 61	240, 222. 66	235, 086. 06
Real estate, etc	532, 672. 89	531, 604. 01	524, 101. 44	533, 699. 72	530, 218. 09
Current expenses....	149, 221. 65	68, 813. 14	115, 213. 25	54, 578. 87	133, 499. 80
Premiums paid	398, 117. 95	388, 620. 13	388, 272. 45	366, 9.8. 64	365, 075. 30
Cash items	161, 524. 69	51, 433. 11	52, 365. 37	81, 501. 94	77, 179. 00
Clear'g-house exch'gs	...	...	...	...	...
Bills of other banks..	251, 810. 00	232, 735. 00	246, 986. 00	228, 723. 00	202, 465. 00
Fractional currency.	3, 131. 70	4, 068. 30	3, 318. 83	4, 031. 24	3, 413. 20
Trade dollars........	...	38. 00	55. 00	50. 00	23. 00
Specie	548, 929. 92	610, 658. 49	581, 878. 79	537, 912. 48	550, 901. 69
Legal-tender notes ..	544, 104. 00	564, 422. 00	566, 095. 00	607, 613. 00	567, 535. 00
U. S. cert's of deposit.	...	...	...	...	...
5 % fund with Treas.	145, 237. 94	141, 377. 94	140, 757. 94	136, 797. 94	129, 620. 40
Due from U. S. Treas.	951. 25	2, 002. 56	3, 000. 00	2, 850. 00	11, 301. 33
Total...........	28, 782, 709. 03	29, 216, 998. 36	28, 911, 150. 30	28, 910, 487. 26	29, 178, 194. 20

CITY OF LOUISVILLE.

	9 banks.	9 banks.	9 banks.	9 banks.	9 banks.
Loans and discounts.	$9, 454, 909. 73	$9, 327, 046. 69	$9, 488, 854. 87	$9, 172, 346. 60	$9, 197, 272. 62
Bonds for circulation.	694, 000. 09	600, 000. 00	600, 000. 00	600, 000. 00	500, 000. 00
Bonds for deposits ..	900, 000. 00	900, 000. 00	900, 000. 00	800, 000. 00	900, 000. 00
U. S. bonds on hand..	...	...	...	...	...
Other stocks and b'ds	225, 822. 02	216, 116. 58	222, 851. 30	188, 184. 72	154, 020. 93
Due from res've ag'ts.	653, 306. 14	789, 528. 09	894, 462. 51	875, 409. 62	847, 802. 35
Due from nat'l banks	359, 592. 24	336, 927. 97	271, 026. 63	424, 455. 09	368, 172. 65
Due from State banks	156, 805. 00	232, 882. 88	20?, 441. 50	205, 800. 10	194, 058. 60
Real estate, etc	155, 300. 52	158, 227. 14	153, 401. 83	154, 202. 79	193, 905. 38
Current expenses....	39, 574. 63	43, 788. 94	53, 938. 84	20, 688. 56	94, 423. 52
Premiums paid	91, 245. 74	85, 418. 75	80, 787. 50	71, 287. 50	80, 618. 75
Cash items	34, 173. 20	16, 072. 42	41, 670. 75	57, 448. 85	35, 500. 77
Clear'g-house exch'gs	87, 519. 18	120, 104. 32	91, 822. 57	105, 460. 19	34, 896. 66
Bills of other banks..	56, 674. 00	88, 948. 00	92, 865. 00	51, 096. 00	42, 780. 00
Fractional currency.	1, 641. 96	2, 093. 37	1, 639. 89	745. 88	505. 79
Trade dollars........	4. 00	...	...	...	...
Specie	239, 827. 45	304, 116. 60	381, 209. 69	399, 295. 70	342, 300. 75
Legal-tender notes ..	701, 643. 00	1, 021, 475. 00	986, 197. 00	679, 043. 00	582, 436. 00
U. S. cert's of deposit	...	...	...	...	...
5 % fund with Treas	31, 227. 50	26, 997. 50	26, 997. 50	26, 997. 50	22, 497. 50
Due from U. S. Treas	2, 000. 00	5, 500. 00	3, 000. 00	2, 000. 00	3, 000. 00
Total...........	13, 884, 236. 81	14, 374, 244. 25	14, 496, 220. 38	13, 834, 540. 19	13, 589, 342. 20

by States and reserve cities—Continued.

ARKANSAS.

Liabilities.	DECEMBER 7.	FEBRUARY 14.	APRIL 30.	JUNE 30.	OCTOBER 4.
	7 banks.	7 banks.	7 banks.	7 banks.	7 banks.
Capital stock	$950,000.00	$950,000.00	$950,000.00	$950,000.00	$950,000.00
Surplus fund	111,500.00	169,300.00	169,300.00	180,300.00	191,000.00
Undivided profits	137,441.50	68,095.02	100,661.08	99,332.34	104,748.14
Nat'l-bank circulation	365,000.00	363,050.00	359,910.00	362,240.00	368,940.00
State-bank circulation	....	....	....	....	....
Dividends unpaid	2,002.00	2,146.00	1,218.00	23,418.00	1,783.00
Individual deposits	2,569,259.72	2,502,578.11	2,061,081.42	2,304,841.60	2,180,190.12
U. S. deposits	116,162.88	116,554.74	110,523.41	128,782.51	129,627.28
Dep'ts U.S.dis.officers	43,831.12	41,320.78	40,476.50	31,217.49	30,372.72
Due to national banks	92,699.59	6,987.20	19,480.92	14,449.61	36,612.21
Due to State banks	61,349.97	76,245.00	146,603.49	93,062.66	71,340.58
Notes re-discounted	104,252.56	38,622.33	6,485.41	....	211,718.81
Bills payable	21,000.00	21,000.00	15,000.00	....	10,000.00
Total	4,574,499.40	4,445,899.18	4,589,740.32	4,187,644.21	4,286,327.86

KENTUCKY.

Liabilities.	DECEMBER 7.	FEBRUARY 14.	APRIL 30.	JUNE 30.	OCTOBER 4.
	59 banks.	59 banks.	60 banks.	60 banks.	60 banks.
Capital stock	$9,758,900.00	$9,938,900.00	$10,072,423.66	$10,099,300.00	$10,102,900.00
Surplus fund	2,340,618.35	2,318,360.71	2,323,527.14	2,395,037.00	2,386,927.24
Undivided profits	848,193.42	566,170.86	814,692.64	518,526.54	815,675.71
Nat'l-bank circulation	2,966,840.00	2,939,550.00	2,936,070.00	2,854,570.00	2,630,030.00
State-bank circulation	....	....	....	....	....
Dividends unpaid	19,981.50	33,755.00	26,666.00	130,890.50	35,187.00
Individual deposits	10,057,834.49	10,435,464.61	9,901,056.58	10,128,623.88	10,408,093.72
U. S. deposits	1,360,170.77	1,456,340.40	1,487,208.06	1,500,697.84	1,532,826.97
Dep'ts U.S.dis.officers	69,575.51	50,988.05	67,457.68	53,250.54	20,560.09
Due to national banks	574,172.47	506,535.13	528,832.03	453,780.91	548,285.58
Due to State banks	458,332.84	537,809.94	336,399.49	323,321.12	349,636.74
Notes re-discounted	293,090.58	368,117.66	416,217.02	442,488.93	290,071.10
Bills payable	35,000.00	5,000.00	....	10,000.00	58,000.00
Total	28,782,709.93	29,216,998.36	28,911,150.30	28,910,487.26	29,178,194.20

CITY OF LOUISVILLE.

Liabilities.	DECEMBER 7.	FEBRUARY 14.	APRIL 30.	JUNE 30.	OCTOBER 4.
	9 banks.	9 banks.	9 banks.	9 banks.	9 banks.
Capital stock	$3,551,500.00	$3,551,500.00	$3,551,500.00	$3,551,500.00	$3,051,500.00
Surplus fund	951,175.36	953,175.36	953,175.36	958,514.96	992,514.96
Undivided profits	220,200.29	230,066.75	200,866.49	145,261.02	287,540.04
Nat'l-bank circulation	624,490.00	539,890.00	539,890.00	539,890.00	449,800.00
State-bank circulation	....	....	....	....	....
Dividends unpaid	7,909.50	7,394.00	14,620.00	44,386.00	5,461.50
Individual deposits	3,889,851.30	3,944,022.42	4,288,213.32	4,006,706.65	3,890,913.33
U. S deposits	557,563.39	619,089.90	682,973.46	681,877.44	660,931.78
Dep'ts U.S.dis.officers	354,051.36	252,513.36	207,022.66	168,117.08	199,734.66
Due to national banks	1,419,310.96	1,917,914.97	1,985,144.54	1,732,013.69	1,577,213.68
Due to State banks	1,581,953.23	1,742,579.21	1,001,064.68	1,461,243.62	1,296,645.51
Notes re-discounted	676,170.92	565,498.28	411,758.67	404,939.73	440,996.23
Bills payable	50,000.00	50,000.00	....	140,000.00	130,000.00
Total	13,884,266.31	14,374,244.25	14,496,229.38	13,834,540.19	13,580,342.29

Abstract of reports since October 5, 1887, *arranged*

TENNESSEE.

Resources.	DECEMBER 7.	FEBRUARY 14.	APRIL 30.	JUNE 30.	OCTOBER 4.
	40 banks.	41 banks.	41 banks.	41 banks.	42 banks.
Loans and discounts.	$19,011,797.50	$18,518,909.48	$18,423,280.17	$18,206,079.29	$19,849,784.71
Bonds for circulation.	1,483,750.00	1,520,000.00	1,526,500.00	1,484,000.00	1,421,500.00
Bonds for deposits ..	450,000.00	450,000.00	450,000.00	450,000.00	450,000.00
U. S. bonds on hand .	2,100.00	1,200.00	100.00	....	1,050.00
Other stocks and b'ds	411,975.13	50[illegible],217.03	347,627.11	337,600.71	320,145.66
Due from res've ag'ts	1,122,803.76	1,148,817.58	1,127,318.84	1,100,377.52	815,851.75
Due from nat'l banks	903,534.85	1,063,908.27	966,736.59	781,240.24	704,606.08
Due from State banks	227,330.61	214,142.67	170,325.61	196,328.71	190,452.81
Real estate, etc	515,529.91	593,710.18	531,498.40	541,217.86	549,528.98
Current expenses....	148,028.96	158,645.49	155,423.57	90,590.59	128,333.07
Premiums paid......	234,448.17	232,587.66	228,903.91	222,528.26	211,011.51
Cash items	242,988.41	263,536.73	250,428.75	207,949.68	349,741.50
Clear'g house exch'gs	141,069.43	111,596.26	151,180.24	55,006.60	103,471.74
Bills of other banks .	371,123.00	428,456.00	364,102.00	245,909.00	283,918.00
Fractional currency.	6,780.91	8,521.21	9,981.22	10,047.73	10,391.50
Trade dollars	....	.85	1.00	....	1.00
Specie	830,371.94	963,485.53	882,314.10	920,886.84	836,713.85
Legal-tender notes ..	732,709.00	853,943.00	814,744.00	696,808.00	764,625.00
U. S. cert's of deposit	....	....	....	....	....
5% fund with Treas.	65,617.75	65,617.75	67,237.50	66,079.00	57,753.84
Due from U. S. Treas	23,747.52	83,635.92	19,913.32	19,699.07	11,941.75
Total	26,925,874.85	27,028,931.59	26,510,676.33	25,924,275.50	27,074,832.87

OHIO.

Resources.	DECEMBER 7.	FEBRUARY 14.	APRIL 30.	JUNE 30.	OCTOBER 4.
	192 banks.	195 banks.	195 banks.	197 banks.	197 banks.
Loans and discounts.	$51,494,140.11	$51,705,522.11	$52,744,614.34	$53,685,121.33	$53,872,028.28
Bonds for circulation.	10,112,050.00	9,752,630.00	9,763,150.00	9,801,650.00	9,476,300.00
Bonds for deposits ..	1,095,000.00	1,470,000.00	1,470,000.00	1,370,000.00	1,370,000.00
U. S. bonds on hand ..	231,400.00	247,600.00	230,000.00	133,850.00	134,000.00
Other stocks and b'ds	2,879,088.45	2,935,449.95	2,923,682.77	2,997,093.26	3,122,641.93
Due from res've ag'ts.	4,906,905.40	5,145,786.87	4,405,192.10	4,418,301.14	6,2[illegible]8,4[illegible]8.25
Due from nat'l banks.	1,817,221.09	1,732,932.87	1,481,713.89	1,537,135.61	1,672,686.78
Due from State banks	513,653.26	430,152.74	380,157.65	492,998.08	451,910.19
Real estate, etc	1,885,312.05	1,938,383.00	1,947,308.91	1,913,796.63	1,9[illegible]0,430.55
Current expenses....	261,680.37	323,416.23	508,228.49	295,074.41	440,822.47
Premiums paid......	727,445.41	738,980.54	731,757.39	664,149.11	648,709.63
Cash items	453,701.09	487,435.49	435,547.64	534,755.33	553,575.15
Clear'g-house exch'gs	17,633.26	57,289.46	49,258.07	37,579.49	78,905.33
Bills of other banks..	1,104,232.00	1,161,619.00	1,397,917.00	1,016,129.00	1,533,508.00
Fractional currency.	25,938.92	31,251.64	30,669.00	25,266.36	27,708.53
Trade dollars........	5.00	5.00	9.00	6.00	....
Specie	2,909,773.15	2,990,706.19	2,878,414.17	2,752,518.48	3,078,827.66
Legal-tender notes ..	2,731,698.00	2,719,450.00	3,110,985.00	2,704,438.00	3,238,154.00
U. S. cert's of deposit.	....	....	....	....	30,000.00
5% fund with Treas.	438,368.50	415,389.94	405,881.45	406,171.20	406,795.57
Due from U. S. Treas	29,087.70	43,646.49	27,218.35	14,908.55	42,317.73
Total..........	83,695,030.70	84,392,870.52	84,905,795.22	84,841,580.98	88,293,396.05

CITY OF CINCINNATI.

Resources.	DECEMBER 7.	FEBRUARY 14.	APRIL 30.	JUNE 30.	OCTOBER 4.
	15 banks.	14 banks.	14 banks.	14 banks.	13 banks.
Loans and discounts	$23,702,138.87	$22,190,400.73	$21,649,850.34	$21,739,798.99	$21,356,576.57
Bonds for circulation	2,740,000.00	2,297,000.00	2,277,000.00	2,027,000.00	1,977,000.00
Bonds for deposits ..	3,975,000.00	4,485,000.00	4,485,000.00	4,485,000.00	4,485,000.00
U. S. bonds on hand..	424,400.00	256,750.00	204,550.00	158,800.00	300,150.00
Other stocks and b'ds	2,437,574.09	2,099,053.43	2,283,246.85	2,505,255.15	2,349,612.63
Due from res've ag'ts	3,566,968.64	3,034,102.53	2,665,994.65	3,073,973.07	3,932,393.84
Due from nat'l banks.	1,839,316.59	1,301,998.99	1,276,347.51	1,267,248.24	1,740,193.94
Due from State banks	840,748.67	709,812.53	829,053.36	710,791.67	940,157.48
Real estate, etc	422,338.68	419,948.20	475,302.48	559,008.91	637,9[illegible]0.93
Current expenses....	153,396.77	148,711.29	139,259.88	60,972.01	197,685.61
Premiums paid......	856,800.04	878,570.94	831,143.38	862,636.32	791,340.83
Cash items	81,153.91	97,333.63	68,475.30	78,135.13	111,899.67
Clear'g-house exch'gs	242,840.89	205,051.44	319,586.45	293,499.59	258,002.40
Bills of other banks .	341,097.00	215,046.00	272,494.00	109,000.00	348,205.00
Fractional currency.	3,272.33	3,683.11	3,107.97	2,198.49	3,322.09
Trade dollars........	....	....	....	....	....
Specie	741,736.26	731,153.04	755,236.50	600,004.00	809,721.25
Legal-tender notes ..	1,838,658.00	1,575,113.00	2,213,381.00	1,519,858.00	2,616,647.00
U. S. cert's of deposit	1,190,000.00	1,260,000.00	1,180,000.00	1,200,000.00	1,400,000.00
5% fund with Treas.	123,570.00	103,365.00	97,285.00	91,215.00	88,965.00
Due from U. S. Treas.	3,000.00	....	....	....	520.00
Total..........	45,530,370.74	42,072,093.88	42,326,385.17	41,506,403.57	44,494,320.26

by States and reserve cities—Continued.

TENNESSEE.

Liabilities.	DECEMBER 7.	FEBRUARY 14.	APRIL 30.	JUNE 30.	OCTOBER 4.
	40 banks.	41 banks.	41 banks.	41 banks.	42 banks.
Capital stock	$7,485,000.00	$7,635,000.00	$7,680,400.00	$7,680,000.00	$7,715,000.00
Surplus fund	1,465,307.80	1,537,809.88	1,531,834.88	1,516,734.88	1,616,154.88
Undivided profits	804,846.76	602,132.83	777,074.06	806,648.82	874,322.31
Nat'l-bank circulation	1,322,235.00	1,314,865.00	1,343,900.00	1,322,100.00	1,253,520.00
State-bank circulation	....	....	....	....	....
Dividends unpaid	2,031.00	4,115.00	1,855.00	37,747.00	3,319.00
Individual deposits	11,580,737.78	12,570,608.63	12,331,424.91	11,636,337.87	11,240,740.07
U. S. deposits	357,778.66	369,113.69	375,822.81	387,258.11	358,679.64
Dep'ts U.S.dis.officers	100,485.94	77,346.78	71,880.40	60,467.50	71,518.83
Due to national banks	1,365,712.85	1,229,007.21	957,259.03	989,471.93	1,427,769.87
Due to State banks	639,500.84	900,111.55	711,354.46	589,903.90	454,272.27
Notes re-discounted	1,028,848.22	758,701.02	613,201.78	707,705.43	1,836,437.45
Bills payable	175,300.00	70,000.00	120,000.00	160,000.00	225,098.52
Total	26,925,874.85	27,028,931.59	26,516,676.33	25,924,375.50	27,074,832.87

OHIO.

Liabilities.	192 banks.	195 banks.	195 banks.	197 banks.	197 banks.
Capital stock	$23,030,000.00	$23,661,940.00	$24,116,690.00	$24,399,000.00	$24,399,000.00
Surplus fund	5,219,688.14	5,275,725.30	5,328,266.54	5,422,762.91	5,556,890.66
Undivided profits	1,895,505.84	1,887,667.99	2,548,157.14	2,020,353.44	2,464,847.16
Nat'l-bank circulation	9,039,566.00	8,672,016.00	8,707,376.00	8,712,581.00	8,430,451.00
State-bank circulation	3,899.00	3,859.00	3,899.00	3,899.00	3,899.00
Dividends unpaid	32,284.90	31,828.40	34,445.81	99,437.30	43,533.80
Individual deposits	40,468,317.51	40,556,015.62	39,738,126.57	40,163,480.67	43,261,260.17
U. S. deposits	959,585.08	1,427,399.77	1,372,941.82	1,313,993.94	1,326,213.42
Dep'ts U.S.dis.officers	123,385.45	114,272.97	175,435.17	134,966.66	115,392.09
Due to national banks	1,621,994.53	1,241,273.22	1,442,762.47	1,263,294.97	1,532,278.30
Due to State banks	560,121.39	664,688.88	646,503.30	571,405.63	630,393.88
Notes re-discounted	583,076.67	673,483.62	700,191.40	560,880.83	367,643.94
Bills payable	157,056.25	182,636.25	91,000.00	164,521.03	161,597.63
Total	83,695,030.76	84,392,876.52	84,905,795.22	84,841,586.98	88,293,296.05

CITY OF CINCINNATI.

Liabilities.	15 banks.	14 banks.	14 banks.	14 banks.	13 banks.
Capital stock	$10,180,000.00	$9,180,000.00	$9,180,000.00	$9,180,000.00	$8,900,000.00
Surplus fund	1,800,000.00	1,680,500.00	1,690,300.00	1,720,500.00	1,721,000.00
Undivided profits	1,009,667.85	686,562.38	800,239.77	581,627.27	879,132.69
Nat'l-bank circulation	2,457,100.00	2,043,700.00	2,020,120.00	1,795,200.00	1,750,700.00
State-bank circulation	....	....	....	....	....
Dividends unpaid	7,427.00	6,928.75	65,319.50	161,921.50	8,554.50
Individual deposits	17,249,350.96	15,017,884.65	15,402,264.63	15,635,804.89	18,091,014.57
U. S. deposits	4,239,468.31	4,872,110.16	4,873,951.08	4,836,581.44	4,832,871.85
Dep'ts U.S.dis.officers	....	....	....	....	....
Due to national banks	5,041,747.36	5,243,432.20	5,203,020.85	4,713,175.87	5,429,238.24
Due to State banks	2,747,066.62	2,603,720.52	2,384,498.21	2,083,584.12	2,231,008.41
Notes re-discounted	30,048.64	49,240.22	21,071.13	20,068.48	....
Bills payable	708,500.00	689,000.00	684,800.00	778,000.00	630,800.00
Total	45,530,370.74	42,072,093.88	42,326,385.17	41,506,463.57	44,494,320.26

Abstract of reports since October 5, 1887, arranged

CITY OF CLEVELAND.

Resources.	DECEMBER 7.	FEBRUARY 14.	APRIL 30.	JUNE 30.	OCTOBER 4.
	9 banks.	9 banks.	9 banks.	9 banks.	9 banks.
Loans and discounts	$16,862,780.83	$16,199,354.21	$16,071,572.73	$16,100,779.71	$16,890,437.16
Bonds for circulation	605,000.00	605,000.00	606,000.00	606,000.00	608,000.00
Bonds for deposits	340,000.00	340,000.00	340,000.00	340,000.00	340,000.00
U.S. bonds on hand	....	....	....	....	....
Other stocks and b'ds	102,493.50	165,200.50	202,746.50	197,740.50	188,740.70
Due from res've ag'ts	912,474.32	1,551,011.05	908,034.39	1,306,547.70	1,870,072.59
Due from nat'l banks	1,176,234.90	1,059,741.98	1,166,874.84	1,347,528.62	1,208,483.61
Due from State banks	503,604.29	420,890.25	425,906.85	508,058.40	466,209.25
Real estate, etc	643,616.63	719,207.19	711,551.25	711,747.56	708,821.43
Current expenses	20,698.35	110,596.42	167,860.51	92,280.18	171,670.58
Premiums paid	33,000.00	83,000.00	20,250.00	19,250.00	19,250.00
Cash items	63,692.15	84,415.46	81,280.01	118,142.08	86,493.58
Clear'g-house exch'gs	148,528.38	144,054.19	128,799.97	173,933.66	173,416.69
Bills of other banks	194,158.00	148,887.00	105,771.00	141,173.00	210,921.00
Fractional currenc.	4,006.84	3,273.71	6,095.80	3,697.53	3,836.71
Trade dollars	....	....	....	....	....
Specie	932,868.60	933,637.71	1,083,207.03	1,170,957.60	988,820.41
Legal-tender notes	1,053,000.00	604,500.00	1,059,000.00	732,000.00	1,018,000.00
U.S. cert's of deposit	15,000.00	15,000.00	15,000.00	15,000.00	15,000.00
5% fund with Treas.	25,525.00	27,225.00	26,469.75	27,179.00	27,270.00
Due from U.S. Treas	40.00	2,040.00	7,189.62	9,440.00	370.00
Total	23,636,615.88	23,177,033.67	23,223,700.25	23,627,456.54	25,038,041.51

INDIANA.

	93 banks.	92 banks.	94 banks.	94 banks.	94 banks.
Loans and discounts	$28,596,886.40	$28,234,236.73	$28,412,072.22	$28,252,014.04	$27,938,201.03
Bonds for circulation	4,873,800.00	4,818,800.00	4,738,800.00	4,713,800.00	4,573,800.00
Bonds for deposits	1,190,000.00	1,400,000.00	1,400,000.00	1,400,000.00	1,400,000.00
U.S. bonds on hand	821,700.00	591,700.00	555,450.00	518,700.00	411,950.00
Other stocks and b'ds	1,159,503.37	1,284,180.00	1,300,057.55	1,351,647.44	1,339,474.08
Due from res've ag'ts	3,515,637.92	3,502,736.00	3,206,587.73	3,132,788.70	3,700,173.05
Due from nat'l banks	2,082,905.13	1,924,080.07	1,604,807.32	1,542,344.57	1,702,807.43
Due from State banks	387,200.44	444,397.10	301,881.86	337,261.33	364,708.10
Real estate, etc	1,231,701.03	1,200,400.58	1,218,613.86	1,240,058.78	1,271,055.50
Current expenses	271,381.08	85,418.09	249,122.18	164,980.11	108,183.20
Premiums paid	539,107.72	488,608.87	478,045.26	450,388.50	396,157.38
Cash items	269,068.29	244,821.05	262,243.07	313,311.61	315,458.20
Clear'g-house exch'gs	84,657.30	111,814.35	150,625.03	126,315.80	119,723.90
Bills of other banks	987,077.00	924,304.00	1,111,461.00	844,762.00	957,413.00
Fractional currency	17,395.61	21,452.07	22,710.75	23,802.28	24,470.80
Trade dollars	4.00	11.40	8.40	7.00	7.00
Specie	2,470,324.45	2,378,697.25	2,394,062.08	2,223,175.70	2,150,521.51
Legal-tender notes	1,794,370.00	1,891,606.00	1,987,308.00	1,713,226.00	1,839,746.00
U.S. cert's of deposit	....	....	....	....	....
5% fund with Treas.	214,940.99	212,077.40	204,817.39	207,822.30	203,230.00
Due from U.S. Treas.	25,973.03	16,892.83	7,998.54	8,718.04	13,803.85
Total	50,432,839.76	49,806,937.44	49,706,633.14	48,577,124.50	49,100,892.49

ILLINOIS.

	160 banks.	161 banks.	162 banks.	162 banks.	163 banks.
Loans and discounts	$36,990,852.07	$37,179,943.22	$38,081,318.48	$38,165,457.78	$39,193,148.84
Bonds for circulation	4,759,000.00	4,697,000.00	4,672,000.00	4,619,500.00	4,574,500.00
Bonds for deposits	1,205,000.00	1,395,000.00	1,545,000.00	1,545,000.00	1,545,000.00
U.S. bonds on hand	365,200.00	360,250.00	362,000.00	347,000.00	292,800.00
Other stocks and b'ds	2,550,444.48	2,660,360.87	2,680,704.60	2,708,231.80	2,892,470.48
Due from res've ag'ts	6,817,225.07	7,323,320.48	6,874,956.15	8,612,244.04	7,382,818.57
Due from nat'l banks	1,496,198.19	1,500,580.02	1,600,745.67	1,613,862.75	1,873,873.21
Due from State banks	292,082.20	336,349.26	296,069.10	298,070.57	314,046.20
Real estate, etc	1,482,025.53	1,498,702.76	1,570,080.41	1,587,083.03	1,638,750.44
Current expenses	279,904.58	144,203.82	350,425.85	263,217.42	210,770.55
Premiums paid	589,224.81	619,484.72	617,658.08	598,008.43	570,080.07
Cash items	425,011.70	358,722.08	449,840.88	400,184.15	437,865.84
Clear'g-house exch'gs	69,560.58	80,807.17	112,120.83	97,527.79	93,781.23
Bills of other banks	855,472.00	806,554.00	951,785.00	961,000.00	919,017.00
Fractional currency	23,112.26	23,922.82	24,775.07	25,520.95	21,910.06
Trade dollars	16.00	1.00	6.00	8.00	10.00
Specie	2,673,625.83	2,475,005.97	2,571,254.17	2,773,251.21	2,621,931.42
Legal-tender notes	1,706,380.00	1,926,922.00	1,936,257.00	1,960,350.00	1,820,821.00
U.S. cert's of deposit	10,000.00	10,000.00	10,000.00	10,000.00	10,000.00
5% fund with Treas.	212,580.03	209,270.70	206,405.15	205,604.15	199,451.25
Due from U.S. Treas.	11,808.80	17,081.40	32,011.09	20,410.79	17,026.01
Total	62,404,724.82	63,800,710.38	65,657,810.33	66,844,670.86	66,636,620.79

by States and reserve cities—Continued.

CITY OF CLEVELAND.

Liabilities.	DECEMBER 7.	FEBRUARY 14.	APRIL 30.	JUNE 30.	OCTOBER 4.
	9 banks.	9 banks.	0 banks.	9 banks.	9 banks.
Capital stock	$6,750,000.00	$6,750,000.00	$6,650,000.00	$6,650,000.00	$6,650,000.00
Surplus fund	959,000.00	950,000.00	965,000.00	1,035,000.00	1,035,000.00
Undivided profits	331,305.04	465,725.51	685,782.84	440,100.55	668,358.70
Nat'l-bank circulation	514,500.00	544,500.00	545,380.00	544,980.00	543,380.00
State-bank circulation	....	....	....	....	....
Dividends unpaid	2,381.00	1,286.00	5,040.00	2,355.00	1,532.00
Individual deposits	9,087,433.40	10,598,553.13	10,742,141.30	11,080,912.06	12,357,401.69
U. S. deposits	351,351.05	358,903.33	355,301.00	356,507.38	350,758.24
Dep'ts U.S.dis.officers	19,719.45	5,447.27	9,699.00	1,700.10	11,270.72
Due to national banks	1,012,302.54	966,864.34	853,931.03	1,034,021.07	1,181,073.71
Due to State banks	1,043,692.27	858,849.17	685,685.53	771,103.57	1,176,578.82
Notes re-discounted	615,430.31	333,904.02	116,848.55	39,716.81	13,597.54
Bills payable	2,019,433.82	1,314,000.00	1,608,000.00	1,662,000.00	1,029,000.00
Total	23,636,615.88	23,177,033.67	23,223,709.25	23,627,456.54	25,038,041.51

INDIANA.

	93 banks.	92 banks.	94 banks.	94 banks.	94 banks.
Capital stock	$11,894,500.00	$11,914,500.00	$11,877,100.00	$11,906,450.00	$11,964,500.00
Surplus fund	3,534,421.12	3,561,687.34	3,566,454.30	3,578,593.55	3,591,277.70
Undivided profits	1,742,115.54	1,261,040.66	1,649,544.03	1,623,504.19	1,631,098.71
Nat'l-bank circulation	4,362,065.00	4,289,790.00	4,207,500.00	4,106,275.00	4,084,375.00
State-bank circulation	....	....	....	....	....
Dividends unpaid	19,256.81	24,805.91	11,377.80	79,918.05	19,654.54
Individual deposits	25,087,456.17	24,968,545.27	24,908,444.05	23,761,075.00	24,503,013.41
U. S. deposits	858,070.05	1,217,240.03	1,178,187.57	1,300,990.80	1,225,730.89
Dep'ts U.S.dis.officers	252,785.49	224,124.06	261,961.42	138,852.59	213,223.40
Due to national banks	1,490,799.49	1,244,957.93	1,048,262.33	993,532.48	1,028,372.22
Due to State banks	1,062,776.04	983,111.74	868,229.06	886,031.92	816,518.44
Notes re-discounted	125,504.05	177,125.50	108,072.58	93,900.92	18,128.00
Bills payable	3,000.00	....	21,500.00	18,000.00	5,000.00
Total	50,432,839.76	49,866,937.44	49,706,633.14	48,577,124.50	49,100,892.40

ILLINOIS.

	160 banks.	161 banks.	162 banks.	162 banks.	163 banks.
Capital stock	$14,381,500.00	$14,414,000.00	$14,449,000.00	$14,574,000.00	$14,824,000.00
Surplus fund	4,662,504.55	4,795,509.96	4,497,049.40	4,692,510.37	4,605,916.44
Undivided profits	2,308,277.11	1,835,046.23	2,195,235.81	2,215,166.92	2,236,223.00
Nat'l-bank circulation	4,245,715.00	4,152,435.00	4,095,060.00	4,017,885.00	3,965,075.00
State-bank circulation	....	....	....	....	....
Dividends unpaid	20,121.25	34,610.36	39,772.61	92,495.61	22,895.50
Individual deposits	33,967,145.77	35,508,064.18	37,106,585.07	38,030,860.69	37,437,793.54
U. S. deposits	1,115,245.61	1,301,875.03	1,428,682.79	1,346,830.63	1,447,309.65
Dep'ts U.S.dis.officers	27,991.50	111,537.16	137,773.12	214,102.83	112,517.95
Due to national banks	644,167.27	580,730.05	716,642.55	618,628.39	509,830.18
Due to State banks	763,244.18	956,941.74	835,534.56	1,063,477.00	1,089,208.66
Notes re-discounted	209,812.58	115,867.67	95,531.43	50,713.33	229,741.81
Bills payable	59,000.00	3,000.00	60,000.00	12,000.00	45,500.00
Total	62,404,724.82	63,899,716.38	65,657,810.33	66,844,670.86	66,636,620.79

Abstract of reports since October 5, 1887, arranged

CITY OF CHICAGO.

Resources.	DECEMBER 7.	FEBRUARY 14.	APRIL 30.	JUNE 30.	OCTOBER 4.
	18 banks.	18 banks.	18 banks.	19 banks.	19 banks.
Loans and discounts.	$60, 842, 435. 12	$60, 292, 562. 17	$66, 510, 531. 13	$65, 521, 416. 27	$65, 336, 358. 22
Bonds for circulation.	1, 050, 000. 00	1, 050, 000. 00	1, 050, 000. 00	1, 100, 000. 00	1, 100, 000. 00
Bonds for deposits ..	700, 000. 00	1, 000, 000. 00	1, 000, 000. 00	1, 000, 000. 00	1, 000, 000. 00
U. S. bonds on hand..	407, 350. 00	658, 500. 00	448, 650. 00	570, 150. 00	651, 250. 00
Other stocks and b'ds	2, 319, 617. 68	2, 302, 636. 43	2, 755, 991. 07	2, 811, 299. 28	2, 473, 755. 98
Due from res've ag'ts	......	......	......	......	......
Due from nat'l banks	8, 275, 991. 56	10, 287, 434. 04	7, 591, 377. 85	8, 947, 171. 65	11, 013, 619. 71
Due from State banks	2, 582, 120. 55	2, 2-9, 902. 77	2, 083, 580. 71	2, 503, 399. 20	2, 802, 4[illegible]0. 50
Real estate, etc......	724, 196. 57	724, 945. 00	705, 498. 39	773, 932. 85	793, 690. 16
Current expenses....	127, 663. 86	80, 976. 61	147, 732. 48	10, 937. 70	46, 961. 84
Premiums paid......	171, 846. 98	173, 603. 85	171, 539. 15	157, 002. 49	151, 454. 94
Cash items..........	53, 489. 89	28, 333. 66	30, 052. 39	40, 098. 66	22, 318. 09
Clear'g-house exch'gs	4, 131, 984. 70	2, 985, 407. 85	4. 410, 811. 58	4, 673, 553. 87	6, 289, 976. 31
Bills of other banks..	1, 009, 085. 00	1, 003, 539. 00	1, 286, 564. 00	1, 337, 068. 00	810, 171. 00
Fractional currency	16, 072. 49	30, 030. 01	24, 840. 26	23, 794. 36	30, 563. 26
Trade dollars	......	......	......	......	......
Specie	12, 430, 727. 40	12, 731, 858. 91	13, 373, 556. 75	14, 128, 319. 40	13, 071, 241. 60
Legal-tender notes ..	5, 369, 947. 00	7, 651, 805. 00	7, 495, 067. 00	8, 109, 737. 00	7, 792, 199. 00
U. S. cert's of deposit	50, 000. 00	60, 000. 00	290, 000. 00	250, 000. 00	50, 0[illegible]0. 00
5 % fund with Treas	47, 250. 00	47, 250. 00	47, 250. 00	49, 500. 00	48, 980. 00
Due from U. S. Treas	45, 000. 00	100, 500. 00	64, 100. 00	81, 000. 00	80, 160. 00
Total..........	100, 355, 678. 80	104, 490, 436. 10	110, 087, 131. 76	112, 068, 410. 23	113, 565, 131. 60

MICHIGAN.

	101 banks.	101 banks.	101 banks.	101 banks.	101 banks.
Loans and discounts	$29, 067, 261. 83	$29, 301, 743. 38	$29, 843, 445. 07	$28, 762, 791. 05	$28, 890, 400. 76
Bonds for circulation.	3, 000, 250. 00	2, 992, 750. 00	2, 972, 750. 00	2, 800, 000. 00	2, 784, 000. 00
Bonds for deposits ..	50, 000. 00	50, 000. 00	50, 000. 00	50, 000. 00	50, 000. 00
U. S. bonds on hand..	43, 550. 00	20, 150. 00	20, 700. 00	27, 700. 00	27, 500. 00
Other stocks and b'ds	693, 510. 05	674, 079. 57	611, 218. 32	635, 863. 18	734, 050. 58
Due from res've ag'ts	2, 790, 422. 20	3, 165, 852. 40	2, 742, 604. 75	2, 852, 219. 10	3, 621, 869. 18
Due from nat'l banks	585, 004. 62	598, 250. 65	551, 863. 12	483, 591. 49	524, 830. 03
Due from State banks	144, 461. 10	99, 214. 04	120, 955. 70	146, 797. 13	166, 269. 73
Real estate, etc......	1, 134, 806. 41	1, 167, 777. 56	1, 186, 145. 20	1, 172, 222. 34	1, 229, 276. 43
Current expenses....	228, 627. 69	88, 291. 06	191, 636. 69	92, 932. 71	159, 806. 99
Premiums paid......	263, 504. 21	249, 226. 03	242, 977. 27	240, 285. 63	239, 466. 70
Cash items..........	171, 511. 36	141, 622. 12	145, 003. 99	194, 533. 54	104, 335. 56
Clear'g-house exch'gs	94, 657. 88	60, 668. 72	59, 540. 82	64, 734. 58	50, 309. 74
Bills of other banks..	461, 952. 00	382, 625. 00	455, 195. 00	348, 774. 00	412, 556. 00
Fractional currency.	12, 514. 59	10, 199. 44	18, 051. 09	15, 266. 24	13, 786. 93
Trade dollars........	7. 00	7. 00	8. 00	2. 00	2. 00
Specie	1, 713, 104. 54	1, 718, 540. 02	1, 549, 377. 80	1, 425, 066. 91	1, 385, 425. 60
Legal-tender notes ..	849, 226. 00	743, 951. 00	896, 648. 00	823, 925. 00	905, 523. 00
U. S. cert's of deposit.	......	......	......	......	......
5 % fund with Treas.	132, 735. 50	132, 180. 00	131, 772. 50	124, 336. 50	123, 007. 50
Due from U. S. Treas.	14, 627. 85	17, 371. 05	9, 217. 10	27, 600. 35	23, 238. 85
Total..........	41, 451, 824. 83	41, 634, 499. 04	41, 809, 305. 42	40, 297, 441. 75	41, 536, 256. 48

CITY OF DETROIT.

	8 banks.	8 banks.	8 banks.	8 banks.	8 banks.
Loans and discounts	$13, 190, 183. 80	$12, 964, 471. 12	$12, 806, 554. 47	$12, 493, 486. 79	$13, 734, 519. 72
Bonds for circulation	400, 000. 00	400, 000. 00	400, 000. 00	400, 000. 00	400, 000. 00
Bonds for deposits...	700, 000. 00	700, 000. 00	700, 000. 00	700, 000. 00	700, 000. 00
U. S. bonds on hand..	......	500. 00	......	......	......
Other stocks and b'ds	3, 630. 75	3, 384. 00	2, 884. 00	2, 884. 00	6, 164. 00
Due from res've ag'ts	1, 756, 937. 01	1, 937, 665. 20	1, 444, 712. 84	2, 125, 387. 58	2, 511, 708. 84
Due from nat'l banks.	822, 060. 41	672, 871. 53	703, 865. 51	666, 380. 44	1, 316, 590. 05
Due from State banks	218, 697. 12	221, 041. 37	205, 442. 84	181, 171. 56	308, 939. 99
Real estate, etc......	128, 162. 96	150, 016. 06	150, 016. 06	151, 016. 06	158, 840. 66
Current expenses....	58, 436. 13	14, 605. 01	32, 890. 03	45, 587. 92	29, 421. 98
Premiums paid......	244, 750. 97	233, 752. 50	233, 625. 00	233, 625. 00	233, 625. 00
Cash items..........	44, 272. 81	24, 207. 31	31, 407. 23	34, 276. 70	27, 180. 65
Clear'g-house exch'gs	208, 637. 70	255, 272. 05	265, 944. 78	349, 159. 43	374, 834. 39
Bills of other banks..	154, 630. 00	126, 162. 00	164, 303. 00	168, 495. 00	194, 031. 00
Fractional currency	7, 267. 00	8, 202. 53	7, 460. 47	8, 305. 90	8, 092. 90
Trade dollars........	......	......	......	......	......
Specie	1, 142, 217. 38	1, 219, 595. 31	1, 223, 998. 83	1, 226, 738. 05	1, 089, 554. 86
Legal-tender notes ..	745, 720. 00	641, 381. 00	669, 673. 00	532, 600. 00	808, 002. 00
U. S. cert's of deposit	......	......	......	......	......
5 % fund with Treas.	18, 000. 00	18, 000. 00	18, 000. 00	18, 000. 00	18, 000. 00
Due from U. S. Treas.	30, 459. 26	14, 719. 26	2 , 417. 11	22, 356. 51	7, 345. 46
Total..........	19, 943, 072. 30	19, 605, 909. 25	19, 081, 285. 17	19, 350, 470. 94	21, 926, 897. 50

by States and reserve cities—Continued.

CITY OF CHICAGO.

Liabilities.	DECEMBER 7.	FEBRUARY 14.	APRIL 30.	JUNE 30.	OCTOBER 4.
	18 banks.	18 banks.	18 banks.	19 banks.	19 banks.
Capital stock	$15,050,000.00	$15,050,000.00	$15,050,000.00	$15,250,000.00	$15,250,000.00
Surplus fund	4,187,000.00	4,870,000.00	4,901,000.00	5,233,788.78	5,330,788.78
Undivided profits	2,150,746.50	1,403,705.01	1,702,200.37	1,502,321.23	1,741,086.84
Nat'l-bank circulation	803,705.00	792,600.00	758,570.00	728,260.00	744,420.00
State-bank circulation	....	....	....	....	....
Dividends unpaid	3,502.00	4,505.50	6,800.00	337,266.00	34,742.00
Individual deposits	44,833,490.02	44,386,895.02	50,716,987.90	48,800,573.17	52,731,931.60
U. S. deposits	709,012.64	873,220.88	1,014,160.68	934,703.20	931,341.93
Dep'ts U.S.dis.officers	....	20,140.08	20,842.10	16,261.77	19,996.16
Due to national banks	19,157,228.25	21,003,327.15	20,081,654.37	23,645,066.72	22,057,473.35
Due to State banks	13,385,935.19	15,251,452.08	14,521,798.45	15,573,375.58	14,471,736.23
Notes re-discounted	....	211,410.38	338,017.83	186,703.68	211,614.71
Bills payable	15,000.00	15,000.00	15,000.00	....	40,000.00
Total	100,355,678.80	104,490,436.10	110,087,131.76	112,088,410.23	113,565,131.60

MICHIGAN.

	101 banks.	101 banks.	101 banks.	101 banks.	101 banks.
Capital stock	$10,800,850.00	$10,880,040.00	$10,889,000.00	$10,804,500.00	$10,974,000.00
Surplus fund	2,212,616.80	2,300,934.37	2,302,934.37	2,350,112.50	2,423,195.00
Undivided profits	1,780,166.29	1,199,096.77	1,506,460.76	1,305,363.04	1,529,564.57
Nat'l-bank circulation	2,666,605.00	2,640,240.00	2,643,670.00	2,435,880.00	2,485,900.00
State-bank circulation	....	....	....	....	....
Dividends unpaid	22,693.26	18,514.64	8,555.00	107,528.31	13,946.71
Individual deposits	22,536,347.33	23,051,175.37	22,468,730.05	21,357,450.12	22,755,584.65
U. S. deposits	45,115.71	47,533.60	48,330.03	47,831.05	41,131.55
Dep'ts U.S.dis.officers	2,556.56	2,095.34	377.51	2,104.65	6,707.82
Due to national banks	206,132.32	234,853.88	245,487.68	213,706.70	234,581.03
Due to State banks	334,812.46	470,029.61	382,352.15	368,373.00	387,621.15
Notes re-discounted	697,920.10	708,485.46	1,187,788.97	1,070,400.30	658,302.71
Bills payable	....	5,000.00	5,000.00	15,000.00	5,000.00
Total	41,451,824.83	41,634,499.04	41,809,305.42	40,297,441.75	41,536,256.48

CITY OF DETROIT.

	8 banks.	8 banks.	8 banks.	8 banks.	8 banks.
Capital stock	$4,000,000.00	$4,000,000.00	$4,000,000.00	$4,000,000.00	$4,000,000.00
Surplus fund	454,000.00	487,000.00	492,000.00	500,000.00	504,000.00
Undivided profits	501,373.39	348,003.50	415,756.62	392,124.48	423,157.16
Nat'l-bank circulation	330,920.00	334,390.00	345,530.00	340,920.00	343,280.00
State-bank circulation	....	....	....	....	....
Dividends unpaid	240.00	828.44	427.50	88,102.50	12,492.50
Individual deposits	9,630,920.11	9,178,609.21	8,587,200.26	8,802,061.21	10,866,030.87
U. S. deposits	442,666.30	638,217.19	652,241.13	634,134.05	557,669.55
Dep'ts U.S.dis.officers	277,805.19	112,905.55	101,205.94	115,773.14	180,491.88
Due to national banks	1,544,510.13	1,523,802.45	1,600,051.64	1,380,108.03	1,647,144.77
Due to State banks	2,538,024.10	2,886,244.38	2,624,044.25	2,800,357.02	3,200,104.40
Notes re-discounted	216,607.08	95,308.53	202,731.83	146,820.61	51,533.42
Bills payable	....	....	....	....	140,000.00
Total	19,943,072.30	19,605,090.25	19,081,285.17	19,359,470.94	21,926,807.50

Abstract of reports since October 5, 1887, arranged

WISCONSIN.

Resources.	DECEMBER 7.	FEBRUARY 14.	APRIL 30.	JUNE 30.	OCTOBER 4.
	54 banks.	54 banks.	54 banks.	55 banks.	56 banks.
Loans and discounts	$13, 552, 143. 14	$13, 879, 261. 36	$14, 533, 232. 71	$14, 677, 159. 76	$14, 965, 378. 24
Bonds for circulation	1, 397, 000. 00	1, 398, 000. 00	1, 404, 000. 00	1, 429, 000. 00	1, 391, 500. 00
Bonds for deposits	150, 000. 00	150, 000. 00	150, 000. 00	150, 000. 00	150, 000. 00
U. S. bonds on hand	12, 850. 00	12, 750. 00	5, 950. 00	1, 050. 00	1, 000. 00
Other stocks and b'ds	636, 882. 49	634, 750. 00	642, 216. 00	614, 910. 88	577, 126. 86
Due from res've ag'ts	2, 099, 498. 18	2, 372, 965. 50	2, 069, 315. 21	1, 999, 498. 23	1, 780, 092. 61
Due from nat'l banks	431, 619. 17	458, 190. 81	362, 576. 69	357, 315. 67	355, 374. 59
Due from State banks	132, 670. 73	123, 905. 49	104, 757. 08	116, 397. 90	133, 913. 69
Real estate, etc	436, 047. 51	458, 670. 11	467, 735. 14	481, 538. 40	505, 819. 51
Current expenses	94, 801. 41	38, 184. 97	89, 098. 28	41, 934. 74	70, 946. 36
Premiums paid	131, 390. 24	113, 138. 12	111, 172. 13	114, 165. 53	112, 804. 35
Cash items	91, 104. 18	86, 782. 56	86, 931. 41	92, 021. 47	140, 038. 75
Clear'g-house exch'gs	....	....	....	....	....
Bills of other banks	281, 335. 00	264, 703. 00	276, 232. 00	226, 690. 00	225, 154. 00
Fractional currency	9, 651. 54	10, 220. 93	10, 174. 91	9, 050. 35	9, 849. 75
Trade dollars	....	....	....	....	....
Specie	977, 312. 17	935, 720. 76	1, 032, 626. 98	939, 153. 50	949, 014. 41
Legal-tender notes	520, 708. 00	473, 442. 00	502, 714. 00	429, 344. 00	401, 545. 00
U. S. cert's of deposit	....	....	....	....	....
5 % fund with Treas.	62, 257. 25	61, 526. 05	58, 087. 25	62, 702. 00	61, 915. 25
Due from U. S. Treas.	4, 508. 00	10, 730. 05	4, 409. 70	3, 441. 40	2, 500. 00
Total	21, 022, 919. 01	21, 503, 033. 30	21, 911, 229. 55	21, 745, 322. 92	21, 924, 073. 37

CITY OF MILWAUKEE.

	3 banks.	3 banks.	3 banks.	3 banks.	3 banks.
Loans and discounts	$3, 807, 740. 00	$3, 923, 568. 98	$4, 238, 755. 97	$4, 457, 344. 45	$4, 109, 909. 05
Bonds for circulation	300, 000. 00	300, 000. 00	300, 000. 00	300, 000. 00	300, 000. 00
Bonds for deposits	580, 000. 00	580, 000. 00	580, 000. 00	580, 000. 00	580, 000. 00
U. S. bonds on hand	1, 200. 00	1, 300. 00	52, 000. 00	....	550. 00
Other stocks and b'ds	428, 862. 03	394, 486. 25	424, 706. 43	425, 081. 13	424, 368. 70
Due from res've ag'ts	649, 232. 16	1, 070, 187. 68	866, 880. 84	848, 657. 48	1, 093, 275. 69
Due from nat'l banks	65, 305. 39	115, 889. 57	77, 328. 54	110, 322. 11	180, 910. 65
Due from State banks	26, 178. 99	21, 862. 68	22, 572. 66	24, 309. 37	31, 151. 30
Real estate, etc	90, 000. 00	90, 000. 00	90, 000. 00	90, 000. 00	110, 000. 00
Current expenses	10, 830. 09	2, 815. 32	9, 848. 90	....	6, 044. 89
Premiums paid	26, 174. 96	21, 141. 79	33, 149. 16	28, 522. 91	28, 040. 86
Cash items	5, 053. 89	5, 105. 03	3, 303. 07	12, 440. 83	8, 433. 49
Clear'g-house exch'gs	135, 981. 88	123, 838. 61	175, 307. 06	129, 995. 20	193, 106. 34
Bills of other banks	17, 277. 00	13, 026. 00	16, 416. 00	21, 708. 00	17, 400. 00
Fractional currency	2, 299. 38	5, 378. 19	5, 058. 85	4, 078. 97	4, 625. 74
Trade dollars	....	....	....	....	....
Specie	566, 380. 00	834, 881. 00	686, 324. 00	828, 722. 00	593, 184. 00
Legal-tender notes	440, 336. 00	430, 267. 00	585, 604. 00	265, 515. 00	374, 586. 00
U. S. cert's of deposit	....	....	....	....	....
5 % fund with Treas.	13, 500. 00	13, 500. 00	13, 500. 00	13, 500. 00	13, 500. 00
Due from U. S. Treas	900. 00	....	8, 000. 00	....	12, 000. 00
Total	7, 193, 801. 97	7, 953, 338. 10	8, 189, 455. 18	8, 140, 702. 45	8, 171, 995. 51

IOWA.

	129 banks.	127 banks.	128 banks.	129 banks.	129 banks.
Loans and discounts	$24, 760, 426. 73	$24, 105, 703. 07	$24, 501, 146. 58	$24, 629, 303. 01	$20, 322, 438. 59
Bonds for circulation	3, 078, 000. 00	3, 093, 000. 00	3, 093, 000. 00	3, 082, 500. 00	3, 082, 500. 00
Bonds for deposits	150, 000. 00	200, 000. 00	200, 000. 00	200, 000. 00	200, 000. 00
U. S. bonds on hand	450. 00	550. 00	550. 00	550. 00	150. 00
Other stocks and b'ds	900, 378. 64	1, 058, 027. 07	930, 588. 01	990, 540. 39	1, 000, 582. 27
Due from res've ag'ts	2, 807, 120. 02	4, 359, 806. 48	4, 528, 178. 82	4, 344, 123. 75	3, 078, 305. 96
Due from nat'l banks	1, 588, 704. 90	2, 216, 570. 24	2, 638, 641. 68	2, 778, 552. 13	1, 700, 864. 90
Due from State banks	278, 096. 54	327, 001. 60	300, 136. 38	257, 220. 53	360, 672. 10
Real estate, etc	1, 684, 726. 00	1, 701, 076. 82	1, 690, 470. 59	1, 700, 993. 22	1, 725, 355. 78
Current expenses	323, 287. 66	112, 147. 85	284, 557. 27	161, 712. 24	216, 714. 28
Premiums paid	247, 256. 50	239, 872. 59	231, 625. 47	217, 941. 30	208, 348. 26
Cash items	334, 606. 43	272, 032. 95	367, 275. 36	351, 252. 93	377, 065. 68
Clear'g-house exch'gs	....	....	....	....	....
Bills of other banks	548, 453. 00	596, 706. 00	713, 118. 00	635, 487. 00	628, 914. 00
Fractional currency	13, 772. 17	16, 572. 35	18, 390. 81	17, 352. 10	15, 337. 73
Trade dollars	1. 00	....	....	....	....
Specie	1, 408, 938. 70	1, 480, 998. 12	1, 725, 880. 53	1, 500, 743. 50	1, 626, 264. 65
Legal-tender notes	1, 095, 428. 00	1, 126, 561. 00	1, 218, 948. 00	1, 090, 990. 00	1, 090, 878. 00
U. S. cert's of deposit	....	....	....	....	....
5 % fund with Treas.	135, 192. 62	135, 330. 12	132, 785. 22	136, 318. 46	133, 396. 42
Due from U. S. Treas	9, 851. 30	16, 475. 00	12, 130. 50	15, 533. 06	12, 948. 76
Total	39, 454, 696. 36	41, 149, 121. 26	42, 596, 436. 22	42, 120, 122. 62	41, 810, 707. 38

by States and reserve cities—Continued.

WISCONSIN.

Liabilities.	DECEMBER 7.	FEBRUARY 14.	APRIL 30.	JUNE 30.	OCTOBER 4.
	54 banks.	54 banks.	54 banks.	55 banks.	56 banks.
Capital stock	$4,530,000.00	$4,550,000.00	$4,550,000.00	$4,610,000.00	$4,680,000.00
Surplus fund	1,195,585.76	1,248,850.81	1,257,411.38	1,283,261.14	1,310,345.30
Undivided profits	625,737.75	385,393.10	546,093.35	538,630.59	608,008.34
Nat'l-bank circulation	1,248,853.00	1,243,900.00	1,250,750.00	1,270,765.00	1,241,925.00
State-bank circulation	....	....	....	....	....
Dividends unpaid	475.00	4,461.00	9,203.12	25,923.12	2,152.28
Individual deposits	13,077,477.21	13,748,238.77	13,904,192.18	13,642,327.22	13,645,711.18
U. S. deposits	121,457.91	130,408.26	129,087.40	135,953.89	126,473.12
Dep'ts U.S.dis.officers	15,176.07	8,994.75	13,214.61	8,822.15	14,598.53
Due to national banks	69,550.68	62,501.85	43,927.72	45,042.73	46,208.30
Due to State banks	85,140.67	109,387.51	116,234.64	94,416.98	57,518.73
Notes re-discounted	53,464.96	10,717.25	90,125.15	89,280.10	101,132.20
Bills payable	....	....	....	....	81,000.00
Total	21,022,919.01	21,508,038.30	21,911,220.55	21,745,322.92	21,924,073.37

CITY OF MILWAUKEE.

	3 banks.	3 banks.	3 banks.	3 banks.	3 banks.
Capital stock	$650,000.00	$650,000.00	$650,000.00	$850,000.00	$850,000.00
Surplus fund	390,000.00	390,000.00	390,000.00	370,000.00	370,000.00
Undivided profits	195,957.52	170,910.58	211,079.92	122,825.85	182,255.53
Nat'l-bank circulation	270,000.00	270,000.00	270,000.00	270,000.00	270,000.00
State-bank circulation	....	....	....	....	....
Dividends unpaid	....	....	....	....	....
Individual deposits	3,741,488.48	4,151,205.04	4,604,198.83	4,398,969.91	4,228,090.20
U. S. deposits	393,463.66	534,134.71	537,194.50	506,341.63	424,235.35
Dep'ts U.S.dis.officers	213,768.73	86,559.68	64,408.06	91,364.04	173,101.78
Due to national banks	1,004,110.51	1,239,378.06	1,090,480.71	1,078,995.31	960,234.58
Due to State banks	335,073.07	461,060.08	351,193.16	457,295.71	480,085.30
Notes re-discounted	....	....	....	....	220,752.08
Bills payable	....	....	....	....	....
Total	7,193,861.97	7,953,338.10	8,189,455.18	8,140,792.45	8,171,995.51

IOWA.

	129 banks.	127 banks.	128 banks.	129 banks.	129 banks.
Capital stock	$10,222,300.00	$10,041,500.00	$10,075,000.00	$10,115,000.00	$10,148,000.00
Surplus fund	2,578,182.35	2,606,901.00	2,603,379.68	2,654,285.37	2,707,926.93
Undivided profits	1,430,223.62	986,878.24	1,329,465.77	1,227,009.50	1,258,005.85
Nat'l-bank circulation	2,732,218.00	2,746,513.00	2,725,913.00	2,714,603.00	2,732,583.00
State-bank circulation	....	....	....	....	....
Dividends unpaid	26,146.34	33,546.40	31,938.00	97,212.25	23,504.16
Individual deposits	19,083,230.18	20,596,448.19	21,235,500.34	20,688,712.98	21,278,399.67
U. S. deposits	56,536.73	146,920.48	151,182.33	149,000.17	139,214.91
Dep'ts U.S.dis.officers	68,573.69	52,008.71	48,271.63	53,382.05	52,600.94
Due to national banks	1,036,483.90	1,381,340.88	1,708,561.84	1,732,889.88	1,145,439.23
Due to State banks	1,740,369.27	2,158,098.36	2,402,845.36	2,587,708.54	1,896,700.39
Notes re-discounted	455,417.28	368,965.00	189,323.27	130,058.28	385,912.30
Bills payable	25,600.00	40,000.00	5,000.00	10,000.00	52,500.00
Total	39,454,696.36	41,149,121.26	42,596,436.22	42,120,122.62	41,840,797.38

Abstract of reports since October 5, 1887, arranged

MINNESOTA.

Resources.	DECEMBER 7.	FEBRUARY 14.	APRIL 30.	JUNE 30.	OCTOBER 4.
	57 banks.	57 banks.	56 banks.	56 banks.	56 banks.
Loans and discounts	$37, 187, 480. 84	$35, 820, 947. 72	$36, 763, 356. 69	$37, 238, 045. 54	$36, 750, 456. 54
Bonds for circulation	1, 813, 550. 00	1, 821, 050. 00	1, 778, 550. 00	1, 791, 050. 00	1, 784, 800. 00
Bonds for deposits	750, 000. 00	950, 000. 00	950, 000. 00	950, 000. 00	950, 000. 00
U. S. bonds on hand	600. 00	600. 00	200. 00	200. 00	200. 00
Other stocks and b'ds	688, 647. 51	688, 205. 15	665, 874. 11	631, 772. 01	601, 887. 40
Due from res've ag'ts	2, 588, 678. 40	3, 637, 910. 82	2, 580, 302. 02	3, 502, 141. 08	4, 272, 909. 52
Due from nat'l banks	1, 740, 455. 21	1, 724, 073. 34	1, 522, 670. 25	1, 470, 950. 42	1, 788, 774. 49
Due from State banks	764, 612. 68	670, 887. 01	508, 850. 84	457, 284. 07	780, 409. 82
Real estate, etc	1, 715, 800. 56	1, 701, 572. 00	1, 850, 280. 82	1, 883, 217. 22	1, 085, 933. 01
Current expenses	233, 075. 40	73, 121. 35	306, 076. 41	103, 374. 43	105, 227. 82
Premiums paid	265, 103. 31	279, 028. 40	252, 042. 72	244, 157. 40	235, 643. 00
Cash items	172, 928. 55	91, 104. 12	184, 170. 77	134, 209. 29	200, 570. 45
Clear'g-house exch'gs	700, 481. 81	488, 523. 10	486, 518. 33	638, 050. 07	858, 809. 12
Bills of other banks	526, 378. 00	463, 431. 00	502, 512. 00	303, 821. 00	514, 272. 00
Fractional currency	9, 120. 01	8, 172. 21	14, 121. 08	10, 709. 07	14, 596. 54
Trade dollars	12. 00	11. 00	13. 00	13. 00	7. 00
Specie	2, 298, 171. 48	2, 933, 748. 23	2, 788, 202. 08	2, 734, 275. 45	2, 169, 216. 04
Legal-tender notes	930, 645. 00	847, 113. 00	875, 785. 00	912, 122. 00	932, 105. 00
U. S. cert's of deposit	....	....	....	....	....
5% fund with Treas.	77, 350. 94	77, 285. 51	78, 010. 21	78, 132. 31	76, 353. 01
Due from U. S. Treas.	30, 404. 00	32, 540. 65	14, 000. 65	14, 530. 65	27, 766. 65
Total	52, 498, 973. 21	52, 701, 008. 01	52, 127, 984. 58	53, 545, 103. 01	54, 110, 111. 47

MISSOURI.

	35 banks.	33 banks.	34 banks.	34 banks.	34 banks.
Loans and discounts	$5, 290, 064. 37	$4, 792, 400. 83	$4, 845, 508. 60	$4, 768, 870. 00	$5, 218, 112. 74
Bonds for circulation	782, 750. 00	732, 750. 00	757, 750. 00	757, 750. 00	782, 750. 00
Bonds for deposits	....	....	....	....	....
U. S. bonds on hand	4, 300. 00	4, 500. 00	26, 700. 00	26, 700. 00	26, 800. 00
Other stocks and b'ds	491, 804. 52	509, 015. 75	534, 861. 15	546, 988. 13	508, 029. 96
Due from res've ag'ts	724, 240. 19	1, 138, 202. 00	1, 001, 315. 08	1, 038, 070. 69	827, 003. 07
Due from nat'l banks	119, 008. 13	114, 092. 37	152, 708. 85	187, 373. 24	103, 576. 73
Due from State banks	98, 352. 37	115, 216. 67	87, 332. 53	104, 477. 23	86, 083. 56
Real estate, etc	292, 705. 65	285, 301. 58	299, 712. 98	310, 185. 88	320, 549. 22
Current expenses	71, 874. 07	89, 157. 31	68, 131. 93	46, 858. 17	46, 038. 11
Premiums paid	70, 597. 13	61, 073. 82	67, 104. 55	65, 186. 33	61, 097. 10
Cash items	35, 081. 73	61, 763. 09	56, 240. 48	49, 797. 54	56, 256. 30
Clear'g-house exch'gs	....	....	....	....	....
Bills of other banks	179, 447. 00	104, 510. 00	189, 501. 00	176, 634. 00	154, 797. 00
Fractional currency	1, 958. 99	1, 728. 80	1, 778. 06	1, 873. 07	1, 878. 86
Trade dollars	....	....	....	....	....
Specie	312, 269. 55	299, 140. 45	325, 766. 64	320, 900. 00	281, 414. 51
Legal-tender notes	278, 281. 00	260, 404. 00	270, 186. 00	262, 636. 00	262, 222. 00
U. S. cert's of deposit	....	....	....	....	....
5 % fund with Treas	34, 658. 25	32, 412. 75	33, 587. 75	34, 097. 75	32, 972. 75
Due from U. S. Treas	1, 028. 64	1, 518. 64	. 70	4, 220. 50	750. 50
Total	8, 793, 906. 59	8, 614, 550. 75	8, 717, 837. 45	8, 781, 610. 98	8, 812, 592. 50

CITY OF SAINT LOUIS.

	4 banks.	4 banks.	4 banks.	4 banks.	4 banks.
Loans and discounts	$7, 991, 386. 10	$8, 050, 806. 77	$7, 409, 078. 20	$7, 259, 920. 32	$8, 207, 631. 01
Bonds for circulation	600, 000. 00	600, 000. 00	600, 000. 00	600, 000. 00	300, 000. 00
Bonds for deposits	450, 000. 00	450, 000. 00	450, 000. 00	450, 000. 00	450, 000. 00
U. S. bonds on hand	500. 00	750. 00	....	2, 000. 00	8, 400. 00
Other stocks and b'ds	934, 053. 00	935, 853. 00	946, 053. 00	931, 003. 00	897, 703. 00
Due from res've ag'ts	....	....	....	....	....
Due from nat'l banks	1, 527, 063. 18	1, 192, 040. 50	1, 242, 833. 67	1, 805, 600. 57	1, 589, 935. 36
Due from State banks	166, 120. 89	148, 832. 34	89, 084. 37	117, 991. 39	151, 238. 07
Real estate, etc	279, 036. 96	270, 714. 46	270, 795. 66	277, 870. 85	278, 531. 85
Current expenses	54, 737. 58	40, 711. 81	63, 807. 53	16, 833. 42	133, 362. 07
Premiums paid	102, 074. 75	94, 518. 50	93, 018. 50	91, 518. 50	89, 718. 50
Cash items	18, 645. 22	35, 425. 53	47, 614. 29	52, 074. 08	36, 335. 16
Clear'g-house exch'gs	499, 114. 80	781, 870. 88	753, 126. 54	603, 807. 33	815, 264. 77
Bills of other banks	123, 582. 00	248, 838. 00	240, 208. 00	415, 887. 00	127, 052. 00
Fractional currency	1, 977. 56	3, 101. 67	1, 730. 52	1, 328. 84	4, 320. 35
Trade dollars	....	....	....	....	....
Specie	1, 222, 712. 00	1, 512, 480. 00	1, 620, 189. 50	1, 765, 403. 50	962, 497. 00
Legal-tender notes	900, 407. 00	1, 318, 225. 00	1, 633, 317. 00	1, 740, 628. 00	964, 070. 00
U. S. cert's of deposit	140, 000. 00	140, 000. 00	190, 000. 00	100, 000. 00	100, 000. 00
5 % fund with Treas	29, 095. 00	29, 095. 00	29, 095. 00	29, 095. 00	16, 200. 00
Due from U. S. Treas	....	5, 000. 00	7, 000. 00	3, 000. 00	5, 500. 00
Total	15, 193, 226. 13	15, 936, 087. 46	15, 783, 147. 78	16, 423, 747. 30	15, 348, 360. 24

by States and reserve cities—Continued.

MINNESOTA.

Liabilities.	DECEMBER 7.	FEBRUARY 14.	APRIL 30.	JUNE 30.	OCTOBER 4.
	57 banks.	57 banks.	56 banks.	56 banks.	56 banks.
Capital stock	$13, 693, 537. 00	$14, 215, 000. 00	$13, 920, 000. 00	$13, 970, 000. 00	$13, 961, 500. 00
Surplus fund	2, 366, 052. 39	2, 557, 262. 39	2, 400, 862. 39	2, 511, 562. 39	2, 536, 362. 39
Undivided profits	2, 076, 824. 85	1, 428, 493. 07	1, 835, 730. 71	1, 645, 998. 86	1, 696, 722. 26
Nat'l-bank circulation	1, 615, 505. 00	1, 609, 195. 00	1, 580, 465. 00	1, 588, 205. 00	1, 585, 360. 00
State-bank circulation	....	....	....	....	....
Dividends unpaid	11, 650. 50	14, 260. 33	3, 740. 00	226, 516. 00	11, 440. 00
Individual deposits	25, 047, 608. 42	25, 073, 226. 58	25, 336, 925. 34	25, 731, 175. 33	26, 701, 823. 91
U. S. deposits	481, 281. 70	670, 876. 45	678, 282. 84	665, 677. 45	668, 313. 62
Dep'ts U.S.dis.officers	206, 571. 46	265, 447. 75	241, 294. 53	257, 896. 01	244, 137. 68
Due to national banks	2, 663, 386. 01	2, 806, 457. 41	2, 450, 865. 99	2, 066, 304. 56	2, 362, 318. 94
Due to State banks	2, 793, 838. 58	2, 835, 543. 82	2, 561, 550. 07	3, 334, 320. 77	3, 511, 350. 65
Notes re-discounted	1, 516, 342. 30	1, 202, 070. 81	977, 767. 71	1, 537, 506. 04	773, 352. 66
Bills payable	18, 175. 00	23, 175. 00	50, 500. 00	10, 000. 00	54, 420. 36
Total	52, 493, 973. 21	52, 701, 608. 61	52, 127, 984. 58	53, 545, 163. 01	54, 110, 111. 47

MISSOURI.

Liabilities.	DECEMBER 7.	FEBRUARY 14.	APRIL 30.	JUNE 30.	OCTOBER 4.
	35 banks.	33 banks.	34 banks.	34 banks.	34 banks.
Capital stock	$2, 531, 000. 00	$2, 331, 000. 00	$2, 401, 000. 00	$2, 421, 000. 00	$2, 431, 000. 00
Surplus fund	558, 992. 48	520, 268. 40	520, 808. 40	538, 956. 03	578, 530. 77
Undivided profits	365, 185. 07	184, 446. 57	250, 447. 03	230, 351. 07	228, 231. 75
Nat'l-bank circulation	696, 125. 00	655, 515. 00	678, 895. 00	677, 035. 00	656, 195. 00
State-bank circulation	....	....	....	....	....
Dividends unpaid	2, 526. 00	1, 968. 00	474. 00	12, 859. 00	1, 265. 00
Individual deposits	4, 388, 834. 22	4, 733, 419. 64	4, 690, 096. 43	4, 687, 910. 19	4, 663, 652. 11
U. S. deposits	....	....	....	....	....
Dep'ts U.S.dis.officers	....	....	....	....	....
Due to national banks	21, 251. 89	33, 973. 92	36, 922. 98	45, 335. 36	54, 877. 68
Due to State banks	56, 620. 48	43, 394. 03	32, 407. 20	39, 085. 10	63, 391. 09
Notes re-discounted	137, 371. 45	96, 565. 10	88, 726. 32	70, 078. 24	132, 429. 10
Bills payable	36, 000. 00	5, 000. 00	....	....	3, 000. 00
Total	8, 793, 906. 50	8, 614, 530. 75	8, 717, 837. 45	8, 731, 619. 98	8, 812, 592. 50

CITY OF SAINT LOUIS.

Liabilities.	DECEMBER 7.	FEBRUARY 14.	APRIL 30.	JUNE 30.	OCTOBER 4.
	4 banks.	4 banks.	4 banks.	4 banks.	4 banks.
Capital stock	$2, 700, 000. 00	$2, 700, 000. 00	$3, 200, 000. 00	$3, 200, 000. 00	$3, 200, 000. 00
Surplus fund	1, 040, 000. 00	1, 040, 000. 00	640, 000. 00	640, 000. 00	640, 000. 00
Undivided profits	329, 006. 78	324, 282. 44	316, 116. 85	219, 903. 21	465, 252. 88
Nat'l-bank circulation	590, 090. 00	587, 600. 00	586, 300. 00	549, 090. 00	324, 000. 00
State-bank circulation	....	....	....	....	....
Dividends unpaid	11, 860. 18	9, 034. 18	7, 676. 18	58, 300. 18	7, 996. 68
Individual deposits	5, 693, 555. 27	5, 624, 214. 69	5, 520, 109. 97	5, 644, 449. 90	5, 332, 210. 15
U. S. deposits	425, 749. 15	426, 289. 94	426, 289. 94	428, 350. 77	428, 350. 77
Dep'ts U.S.dis.officers	....	....	....	....	....
Due to national banks	2, 061, 464. 99	2, 505, 656. 74	2, 346, 407. 40	2, 842, 671. 06	2, 373, 765. 75
Due to State banks	2, 121, 652. 81	2, 530, 709. 47	2, 539, 077. 44	2, 840, 976. 18	2, 452, 362. 93
Notes re-discounted	69, 846. 95	99, 200. 00	....	....	124, 415. 09
Bills payable	150, 000. 00	....	....	....	....
Total	15, 193, 226. 13	15, 936, 067. 46	15, 783, 147. 78	16, 423, 747. 30	15, 348, 360. 24

Abstract of reports since October 5, 1887, arranged

KANSAS CITY.

Resources.	DECEMBER 7.	FEBRUARY 14.	APRIL 30.	JUNE 30.	OCTOBER 4.
	8 banks.	8 banks.	8 banks.	9 banks.	10 banks.
Loans and discounts.	$13, 524, 585. 43	$12, 623, 822. 48	$13, 487, 386. 78	$14, 139, 968. 65	$14, 765, 204. 97
Bonds for circulation.	400, 000. 00	400, 000. 00	400, 000. 00	450, 000. 00	500, 000. 00
Bonds for deposits...	300, 000. 00	1, 000, 000. 00	1, 000, 000. 00	1, 000, 000. 00	1, 000, 000. 00
U. S. bonds on hand..	3, 650. 00	3, 850. 00	300. 00	600. 00	3, 000. 00
Other stocks and b'ds	311, 768. 07	507, 707. 96	480, 740. 88	498, 998. 38	683, 564. 46
Due from res've ag'ts.	1, 754, 772. 45	2, 206, 210. 73	2, 338, 658. 18	2, 095, 825. 54	2, 265, 546. 95
Due from nat'l banks.	528, 882. 16	433, 691. 75	300, 665. 01	532, 136. 56	660, 376. 93
Due from State banks	805, 034. 21	1, 019, 965. 37	933, 657. 61	1, 012, 906. 96	1, 345, 829. 50
Real estate, etc......	361, 946. 08	367, 836. 63	403, 023. 47	443, 131. 37	458, 540. 31
Current expenses....	52, 135. 08	59, 758. 20	46, 660. 90	77, 785. 67	28, 261. 52
Premiums paid......	130, 769. 40	220, 127. 15	208, 094. 78	210, 105. 28	206, 500. 28
Cash items..........	19, 072. 98	11, 298. 43	23, 205. 00	25, 005. 59	41, 271. 25
Clear'g-house exch'gs	464, 154. 75	365, 891. 60	702, 284. 93	512, 241. 46	580, 807. 74
Bills of other banks..	550, 108. 00	528, 844. 00	694, 270. 00	489, 977. 00	526, 895. 00
Fractional currency.	3, 343. 53	6, 428. 02	6, 168. 35	5, 028. 68	5, 092. 68
Trade dollars........	....	....	....	....	....
Specie..............	1, 319, 879. 75	1, 610, 408. 24	1, 912, 748. 75	1, 823, 154. 85	1, 504, 628. 47
Legal-tender notes..	1, 403, 666. 00	1, 137, 079. 00	1, 274, 136. 00	1, 063, 003. 00	1, 495, 785. 00
U. S. cert's of deposit.	....	....	....	....	....
5 % fund with Treas.	18, 000. 00	18, 000. 00	18, 000. 00	20, 250. 00	22, 500. 00
Due from U. S. Treas.	....	750. 00	2, 500. 00	1, 530. 00	20, 000. 00
Total..........	22, 132, 667. 84	22, 521, 069. 56	24, 241, 481. 54	25, 002, 548. 99	26, 113, 805. 06

CITY OF SAINT JOSEPH.

	2 banks.	2 banks.	2 banks.	2 banks.	2 banks.
Loans and discounts.	$1, 044, 715. 50	$1, 962, 675. 25	$1, 928, 114. 88	$1, 877, 458. 14	$1, 754, 551. 58
Bonds for circulation.	160, 550. 00	160, 550. 00	160, 550. 00	160, 750. 00	100, 000. 00
Bonds for deposits..	350, 000. 00	450, 000. 00	450, 000. 00	450, 000. 00	400, 000. 00
U. S. bonds on hand..	....	....	....	....	....
Other stocks and b'ds	7, 954. 88	7, 954. 88	7, 054. 88	8, 809. 21	12, 250. 00
Due from res've ag'ts.	278, 846. 05	282, 874. 31	302, 338. 06	460, 802. 22	503, 590. 46
Due from nat'l banks.	56, 051. 33	45, 990. 70	114, 191. 50	164, 403. 48	153, 115. 63
Due from State banks	40, 073. 02	39, 884. 00	89, 042. 86	157, 258. 69	96, 936. 16
Real estate, etc......	26, 029. 20	28, 029. 20	37, 341. 59	37, 380. 59	37, 380. 59
Current expenses....	13, 086. 31	4, 071. 55	7, 478. 61	8, 891. 93	3, 807. 04
Premiums paid......	45, 278. 12	69, 840. 83	65, 000. 00	65, 052. 00	55, 000. 00
Cash items..........	12, 890. 86	11, 640. 35	7, 750. 66	11, 488. 76	18, 982. 37
Clear'g-house exch'gs	23, 800. 64	13, 338. 50	27, 086. 49	17, 090. 68	25, 507. 75
Bills of other banks..	12, 629. 00	9, 327. 00	20, 388. 00	16, 633. 00	12, 443. 00
Fractional currency.	267. 20	522. 83	386. 79	230. 71	479. 38
Trade dollars........	....	....	....	....	....
Specie..............	217, 830. 10	166, 480. 40	178, 675. 75	166, 074. 30	174, 373. 70
Legal-tender notes..	141, 675. 00	192, 815. 00	192, 126. 00	146, 251. 00	166, 170. 00
U. S. cert's of deposit.	....	....	....	....	....
5 % fund with Treas.	7, 222. 50	7, 222. 50	7, 222. 50	7, 232. 50	4, 490. 00
Due from U. S. Treas.	2, 000. 00	....	....	3, 000. 00	....
Total..........	3, 341, 826. 71	3, 453, 227. 29	3, 685, 340. 47	3, 759, 716. 21	3, 514, 086. 61

KANSAS.

	146 banks.	149 banks.	155 banks.	156 banks.	160 banks.
Loans and discounts	$21, 527, 770. 33	$21, 439, 895. 63	$21, 722, 559. 23	$22, 087, 333. 80	$23, 019, 671. 91
Bonds for circulation.	2, 857, 000. 00	2, 907, 000. 00	3, 025, 750. 00	3, 032, 000. 00	3, 138, 250. 00
Bonds for deposits...	525, 000. 00	675, 000. 00	725, 000. 00	750, 000. 00	750, 000. 00
U. S. bonds on hand..	13, 450. 00	8, 450. 00	20, 450. 00	27, 150. 00	9, 150. 00
Other stocks and b'ds	503, 412. 49	503, 705. 75	525, 312. 53	469, 271. 96	452, 137. 67
Due from res've ag'ts.	2, 352, 357. 41	2, 651, 318. 62	3, 107, 900. 89	3, 477, 643. 35	3, 520, 669. 86
Due from nat'l banks	872, 173. 66	694, 111. 43	745, 397. 00	901, 236. 55	790, 458. 78
Due from State banks	481, 635. 73	350, 887. 18	451, 432. 95	481, 275. 68	487, 058. 53
Real estate, etc......	1, 507, 616. 19	1, 623, 797. 03	1, 743, 089. 54	1, 755, 963. 75	1, 845, 612. 18
Current expenses....	313, 826. 80	168, 941. 98	300, 022. 86	243, 397. 43	239, 065. 65
Premiums paid......	397, 500. 90	415, 086. 48	429, 102. 20	432, 722. 97	432, 480. 12
Cash items..........	233, 279. 31	184, 761. 61	173, 511. 10	225, 720. 01	242, 588. 61
Clear'g-house exch'gs	15, 650. 87	7, 912. 95	11, 377. 43	13, 764. 03	13, 839. 17
Bills of other banks..	710, 965. 00	532, 827. 00	720, 609. 00	641, 057. 00	656, 681. 00
Fractional currency.	9, 927. 73	12, 593. 84	13, 028. 17	12, 112. 98	12, 213. 32
Trade dollars........	....	....	....	....	....
Specie..............	1, 345, 532. 16	1, 340, 500. 34	1, 317, 431. 06	1, 328, 749. 62	1, 238, 505. 90
Legal-tender notes..	1, 144, 304. 00	1, 100, 806. 00	1, 250, 027. 00	1, 270, 592. 00	1, 283, 579. 00
U. S. cert's of deposit.	....	....	....	....	....
5 % fund with Treas.	123, 477. 42	127, 309. 24	129, 050. 41	133, 845. 50	138, 635. 24
Due from U. S. Treas.	4, 232. 01	5, 223. 99	5, 965. 34	6, 557. 24	6, 718. 30
Total..........	34, 930, 282. 10	34, 750, 210. 07	36, 426, 106. 71	37, 296, 303. 87	38, 276, 715. 24

by States and reserve cities—Continued.

KANSAS CITY.

Liabilities.	DECEMBER 7. 8 banks.	FEBRUARY 14. 8 banks.	APRIL 30. 8 banks.	JUNE 30. 9 banks.	OCTOBER 4. 10 banks.
Capital stock	$5,975,000.00	$6,025,000.00	$6,050,000.00	$6,225,000.00	$6,600,000.00
Surplus fund	437,000.00	512,000.00	535,000.00	540,000.00	623,000.00
Undivided profits	396,050.89	279,027.64	336,091.43	384,238.53	347,594.06
Nat'l-bank circulation	360,000.00	300,000.00	300,000.00	405,000.00	450,000.00
State-bank circulation	....	....	....	....	....
Dividends unpaid	....	932.00	....	100,000.00	110.00
Individual deposits	9,543,734.67	8,834,352.52	9,490,591.42	9,432,690.13	10,101,424.71
U. S. deposits	168,178.61	1,003,646.54	1,006,205.13	1,003,660.13	1,006,127.09
Dep'ts U.S.dis.officers	10,954.42	4,158.89	5,072.92	4,201.98	7,709.54
Due to national banks	2,270,000.04	2,582,426.82	2,866,000.55	3,011,170.25	3,539,770.55
Due to State banks	2,684,505.88	2,918,123.15	3,575,895.50	3,896,578.97	3,448,009.11
Notes re-discounted	267,243.33	....	16,564.50	....	....
Bills payable	....	....	....	....	....
Total	22,132,667.84	22,521,669.50	24,241,481.54	25,002,548.90	26,113,805.06

CITY OF SAINT JOSEPH.

	2 banks.	2 banks.	2 banks.	2 banks.	2 banks.
Capital stock	$300,000.00	$300,000.00	$300,000.00	$300,000.00	$300,000.00
Surplus fund	106,000.00	110,000.00	110,000.00	110,000.00	110,000.00
Undivided profits	54,809.87	20,570.42	18,359.45	19,300.62	39,246.30
Nat'l-bank circulation	144,450.00	144,450.00	144,450.00	144,650.00	89,990.00
State-bank circulation	....	....	....	....	....
Dividends unpaid	....	....	....	....	....
Individual deposits	1,773,474.35	1,815,614.08	2,051,306.42	1,966,966.41	1,820,080.61
U. S. deposits	376,611.98	484,729.75	489,202.61	477,183.47	410,328.50
Dep'ts U.S.dis.officers	4,414.35	4,581.22	386.27	8,865.23	19,721.43
Due to national banks	128,654.48	143,816.08	130,287.35	209,179.01	194,376.50
Due to State banks	305,742.91	376,465.74	391,357.37	523,571.47	511,248.21
Notes re-discounted	147,578.77	5,000.00	....	....	....
Bills payable	....	50,000.00	50,000.00	....	....
Total	3,341,826.71	3,453,227.29	3,085,340.47	3,750,716.21	3,514,080.61

KANSAS.

	146 banks.	140 banks.	155 banks.	156 banks.	160 banks.
Capital stock	$11,234,280.00	$11,074,100.00	$12,236,000.00	$12,355,400.00	$12,854,700.00
Surplus fund	1,448,377.84	1,647,065.44	1,683,854.03	1,740,939.49	1,842,280.56
Undivided profits	1,383,474.69	776,640.54	1,190,018.58	1,146,504.25	1,049,547.46
Nat'l-bank circulation	2,498,065.00	2,565,285.00	2,628,855.00	2,692,305.00	2,818,570.00
State-bank circulation	....	....	....	....	....
Dividends unpaid	2,126.63	16,623.00	11,449.50	135,582.50	13,049.00
Individual deposits	16,017,008.48	15,490,268.65	16,242,994.78	16,838,622.10	17,405,465.99
U. S. deposits	293,188.59	430,606.60	460,704.20	542,614.35	575,704.33
Dep'ts U.S.dis.officers	231,756.45	224,400.91	212,410.62	186,204.41	135,806.66
Due to national banks	233,754.75	258,787.06	327,402.07	433,510.50	393,704.07
Due to State banks	383,330.21	408,504.81	474,971.07	417,075.35	404,421.01
Notes re-discounted	1,079,250.47	1,005,871.06	668,715.26	610,635.83	529,709.56
Bills payable	132,000.00	213,000.00	288,011.00	188,000.00	193,000.00
Total	34,939,282.10	34,750,219.07	36,426,106.71	37,296,393.87	38,270,715.24

Abstract of reports since October 5, 1887, arranged

NEBRASKA.

Resources.	DECEMBER 7.	FEBRUARY 14.	APRIL 30.	JUNE 30.	OCTOBER 4.
	96 banks.	95 banks.	95 banks.	96 banks.	97 banks.
Loans and discounts.	$14,002,015.06	$13,950,378.35	$14,009,468.34	$13,864,639.42	$15,030,632.53
Bonds for circulation.	1,503,500.00	1,503,500.00	1,503,500.00	1,528,500.00	1,541,000.00
Bonds for deposits ..					
U. S. bonds on hand ..		12,500.00			
Other stocks and b'ds	205,887.30	188,680.65	185,702.05	158,539.56	184,551.80
Due from res've ag'ts.	1,191,559.13	1,531,492.12	1,697,593.53	2,005,377.58	1,737,320.03
Due from nat'l banks.	384,406.90	451,490.61	465,650.12	684,865.26	510,228.96
Due from State banks	101,283.90	129,881.50	111,998.02	125,172.52	115,205.53
Real estate, etc......	992,881.16	1,018,311.69	1,030,541.99	1,027,789.00	1,069,726.36
Current expenses....	216,559.73	166,528.36	228,380.72	179,653.66	163,217.14
Premiums paid......	165,059.81	156,613.65	151,861.39	152,937.44	147,840.01
Cash items..........	189,426.92	216,742.28	221,633.84	201,828.98	241,547.93
Clear'g-house exch'gs					
Bills of other banks..	118,542.00	123,346.00	120,065.00	130,694.00	147,802.00
Fractional currency.	5,488.94	7,280.54	6,825.14	5,467.45	6,163.78
Trade dollars.......			2.00	2.00	
Specie	708,012.76	728,709.95	720,962.71	733,000.26	736,408.30
Legal-tender notes ..	309,449.00	300,620.00	363,713.00	378,022.00	390,923.00
U. S. cert's of deposit.					
5 % fund with Treas.	67,642.75	67,642.75	67,043.75	67,143.75	69,330.75
Due from U. S. Treas.	2,620.57	4,880.00	4,215.00	1,530.00	3,693.00
Total..........	20,165,235.93	20,548,688.45	20,898,704.60	21,245,262.88	22,095,183.80

CITY OF OMAHA.

Resources.	DECEMBER 7.	FEBRUARY 14.	APRIL 30.	JUNE 30.	OCTOBER 4.
	8 banks.	8 banks.	7 banks.	8 banks.	7 banks.
Loans and discounts.	$8,466,949.19	$8,356,013.18	$8,043,073.50	$8,815,029.10	$8,532,659.14
Bonds for circulation	350,000.00	350,000.00	325,000.00	350,000.00	325,000.00
Bonds for deposits...	650,000.00	725,000.00	855,000.00	855,000.00	855,000.00
U. S. bonds on hand..					
Other stocks and b'ds	180,423.36	141,909.95	134,968.73	53,603.91	72,929.78
Due from res've ag'ts	1,409,214.05	1,565,023.18	917,287.93	2,117,096.84	1,800,538.12
Due from nat'l banks	715,061.28	538,395.67	620,121.60	711,070.63	674,392.93
Due from State banks	512,888.22	542,524.96	484,199.83	690,010.01	557,140.91
Real estate, etc......	431,080.13	469,396.91	493,250.88	542,599.02	706,711.04
Current expenses....	62,879.61	72,043.08	71,706.93	51,087.06	47,812.47
Premiums paid......	96,180.51	126,549.26	148,543.01	152,386.76	141,468.01
Cash items..........	95,647.14	99,000.20	94,964.46	143,568.40	191,526.29
Clear'g-house exch'gs	278,356.18	214,175.43	235,975.08	212,238.95	343,863.55
Bills of other banks..	210,968.00	155,830.00	192,806.00	213,556.00	264,824.00
Fractional currency.	3,491.93	5,449.41	6,360.52	3,527.52	4,203.28
Trade dollars.......					
Specie	951,957.59	1,014,184.75	1,158,443.31	1,127,432.15	1,022,208.22
Legal-tender notes ..	665,968.00	934,391.00	965,140.00	826,742.00	1,018,176.00
U. S. cert's of deposit.					
5 % fund with Treas.	15,750.00	15,750.00	13,575.00	15,750.00	14,625.00
Due from U. S. Treas.	100.00	800.00		2,550.00	800.00
Total..........	15,112,515.78	15,318,136.58	15,660,566.89	16,684,394.35	17,663,900.76

COLORADO.

Resources.	DECEMBER 7.	FEBRUARY 14.	APRIL 30.	JUNE 30.	OCTOBER 4.
	31 banks.	31 banks.	32 banks.	33 banks.	34 banks.
Loans and discounts.	$12,697,993.26	$12,440,291.15	$13,635,051.42	$13,838,765.46	$14,072,835.04
Bonds for circulation.	989,000.00	1,014,000.00	1,026,500.00	1,038,000.00	1,071,500.00
Bonds for deposits...	950,000.00	1,050,000.00	1,050,000.00	1,100,000.00	1,100,000.00
U. S. bonds on hand..	16,000.00	8,000.00	8,000.00	8,000.00	1,000.00
Other stocks and b'ds	929,004.90	791,264.82	784,108.53	801,327.64	901,781.93
Due from res've ag'ts.	2,306,734.37	2,786,254.25	2,533,519.49	2,859,940.04	3,084,817.75
Due from nat'l banks.	1,363,063.17	1,528,650.61	1,349,739.57	1,483,473.47	1,903,089.27
Due from State banks	581,678.17	629,316.84	516,238.86	636,270.68	734,903.97
Real estate, etc......	380,634.54	392,452.05	402,613.60	481,521.28	451,668.77
Current expenses....	121,005.18	67,481.29	107,988.98	31,127.20	64,443.91
Premiums paid......	190,478.09	217,806.49	198,000.50	191,800.76	170,033.57
Cash items..........	97,906.65	63,777.89	111,049.58	94,531.70	111,857.12
Clear'g-house exch'gs	223,006.33	253,490.77	390,730.21	245,227.30	331,569.37
Bills of other banks..	468,810.00	461,074.00	394,723.00	456,686.00	320,108.00
Fractional currency.	4,248.98	6,020.33	6,465.10	5,038.34	9,254.59
Trade dollars.......					
Specie...............	1,449,120.11	1,387,705.35	1,224,870.03	1,360,664.37	1,455,536.21
Legal-tender notes ..	964,296.00	947,065.00	980,802.00	1,096,894.00	936,000.00
U. S. cert's of deposit					
5 % fund with Treas.	43,284.00	46,754.00	46,191.50	46,133.50	48,216.50
Due from U. S. Treas.	13,863.03	11,153.20	9,277.40	6,988.05	9,101.88
Total..........	23,796,706.68	24,103,557.04	24,746,534.77	25,715,393.79	27,706,726.83

by States and reserve cities—Continued.

NEBRASKA.

Liabilities.	DECEMBER 7.	FEBRUARY 14.	APRIL 30.	JUNE 30.	OCTOBER 4.
	96 banks.	95 banks.	95 banks.	96 banks.	97 banks.
Capital stock	$6,030,000.00	$6,020,000.00	$6,065,000.00	$6,140,000.00	$6,235,000.00
Surplus fund	917,273.37	992,720.58	1,004,888.61	1,012,455.81	1,093,450.70
Undivided profits	714,764.58	482,940.93	653,712.73	656,967.55	627,618.16
Nat'l-bank circulation	1,350,930.00	1,350,500.00	1,348,550.00	1,350,480.00	1,384,710.00
State-bank circulation	.....	.....	.....	.....	.....
Dividends unpaid	630.00	7,486.78	666.00	36,755.00	5,038.77
Individual deposits	9,175,706.45	9,698,068.44	10,190,430.69	10,421,298.58	10,706,291.45
U. S. deposits	.....	.....	.....	.....	.....
Dep'ts U.S.dis.officers	.....	.....	.....	.....	.....
Due to national banks	305,494.21	249,168.95	280,347.15	492,528.39	289,721.20
Due to State banks	292,959.10	444,298.71	544,580.94	600,638.91	544,941.61
Notes re-discounted	1,360,359.22	1,278,427.50	741,172.82	459,379.75	1,079,411.82
Bills payable	17,000.00	45,050.56	49,400.66	35,848.89	40,000.00
Total	20,165,235.93	20,548,068.45	20,808,764.60	21,243,262.88	22,005,183.80

CITY OF OMAHA.

	8 banks.	8 banks.	7 banks.	8 banks.	7 banks.
Capital stock	$2,400,000.00	$2,400,000.00	$2,400,000.00	$2,500,000.00	$3,050,000.00
Surplus fund	579,000.00	583,500.00	633,000.00	656,000.00	413,000.00
Undivided profits	207,150.71	180,713.24	160,563.08	120,553.73	116,621.80
Nat'l-bank circulation	314,450.00	314,200.00	292,000.00	314,250.00	291,900.00
State-bank circulation	.....	.....	.....	.....	.....
Dividends unpaid	480.00	1,540.00	1,640.00	19,120.00	4,840.00
Individual deposits	7,622,840.70	7,141,737.17	7,081,718.22	7,673,898.89	8,323,281.47
U. S. deposits	284,961.78	401,376.08	577,983.00	658,403.54	651,078.04
Dep'ts U.S.dis.officers	215,015.81	320,923.31	296,179.23	190,565.25	213,553.22
Due to national banks	1,623,984.59	1,950,050.65	2,295,773.53	2,527,768.61	2,554,176.61
Due to State banks	1,311,943.26	1,707,755.28	1,708,646.91	2,195,234.33	1,972,447.02
Notes re-discounted	552,688.93	306,431.85	123,000.00	28,000.00	73,000.00
Bills payable	.....	.....	.....	.....	.....
Total	15,112,515.78	15,318,136.58	15,660,506.80	16,884,394.35	17,663,900.76

COLORADO.

	31 banks.	31 banks.	32 banks.	33 banks.	34 banks.
Capital stock	$2,780,200.00	$2,885,000.00	$2,915,000.00	$3,075,000.00	$3,437,800.00
Surplus fund	930,000.00	992,650.00	1,033,150.00	1,124,255.00	1,159,490.42
Undivided profits	995,844.80	711,671.62	884,004.95	636,977.95	779,449.61
Nat'l-bank circulation	870,800.00	906,650.00	901,890.00	930,710.00	958,670.00
State-bank circulation	.....	.....	.....	.....	.....
Dividends unpaid	1,055.00	1,705.00	315.00	38,575.00	571.00
Individual deposits	15,187,717.54	15,276,989.54	15,829,407.60	16,744,066.12	17,538,726.85
U. S. deposits	746,240.27	891,733.55	903,023.98	970,253.23	931,733.72
Dep'ts U.S.dis.officers	105,041.15	139,058.66	171,800.30	114,009.20	188,641.50
Due to national banks	1,089,113.79	1,302,585.40	1,141,604.22	1,258,133.57	1,567,091.65
Due to State banks	965,504.13	956,888.93	924,254.43	781,846.54	1,167,551.90
Notes re-discounted	20,320.00	45,748.56	41,348.56	21,000.00	17,000.00
Bills payable	5,000.00	2,785.60	645.64	500.00	.....
Total	23,706,796.68	24,103,557.04	24,746,534.77	25,715,395.79	27,706,726.83

Abstract of reports since October 5, 1887, arranged

NEVADA.

Resources.	DECEMBER 7.	FEBRUARY 14.	APRIL 30.	JUNE 30.	OCTOBER 4.
	2 banks.	2 banks.	2 banks.	2 banks.	2 banks.
Loans and discounts	$551,283.15	$483,014.57	$552,811.36	$578,867.11	$597,707.00
Bonds for circulation	37,500.00	37,500.00	62,500.00	62,500.00	70,500.00
Bonds for deposits	....	....	....	....	....
U. S. bonds on hand	....	....	....	....	....
Other stocks and b'ds	28,075.29	20,708.40	20,948.49	29,394.51	37,580.88
Due from res've ag'ts	7,208.19	5,210.67	1,958.30	10,227.30	19,602.23
Due from nat'l banks	198.24	200.01	2,172.62	318.85	852.30
Due from State banks	2,237.00	7,457.81	6,707.27	1,476.77	6,533.50
Real estate, etc	36,180.55	38,340.55	38,020.00	38,020.00	38,020.00
Current expenses	9,103.44	1,947.78	5,775.75	2,397.31	4,269.43
Premiums paid	5,407.62	5,025.00	6,850.00	6,860.00	9,140.00
Cash items	1,984.10	1,256.10	1,356.40	1,102.06	9,086.56
Clear'g-house exch'gs	....	....	....	....	....
Bills of other banks	70.00	145.00	1,060.00	710.00	455.00
Fractional currency	8.86	11.20	31.03	15.60	42.82
Trade dollars	....	....	....	....	....
Specie	55,752.25	60,254.45	69,115.00	47,543.80	55,540.59
Legal-tender notes	865.00	295.00	690.00	278.00	4,553.00
U. S. cert's of deposit	....	....	....	....	....
5% fund with Treas.	1,687.50	1,687.50	1,687.50	2,812.50	3,172.50
Due from U. S. Treas.	....	....	372.00	....	500.00
Total	737,711.85	669,817.09	772,101.14	782,590.93	857,070.81

CALIFORNIA.

Resources.	DECEMBER 7.	FEBRUARY 14.	APRIL 30.	JUNE 30.	OCTOBER 4.
	30 banks.	31 banks.	34 banks.	36 banks.	35 banks.
Loans and discounts	$15,256,083.02	$15,038,580.80	$15,159,038.43	$14,812,347.10	$14,026,044.21
Bonds for circulation	1,088,750.00	1,188,750.00	1,288,750.00	1,276,250.00	1,276,250.00
Bonds for deposits	200,000.00	500,000.00	500,000.00	506,000.00	500,000.00
U. S. bonds on hand	229,000.00	106,850.00	106,500.00	73,000.00	31,000.00
Other stocks and b'ds	704,738.97	605,218.00	588,093.81	603,188.76	601,568.16
Due from res've ag'ts	2,711,723.18	1,058,474.18	1,897,203.10	1,901,223.62	1,702,731.94
Due from nat'l banks	780,702.63	640,421.52	542,908.95	335,210.01	354,881.29
Due from State banks	888,905.94	647,838.14	707,055.10	650,870.33	407,897.09
Real estate, etc	719,324.17	732,170.82	790,831.25	894,901.05	936,472.42
Current expenses	133,588.84	63,715.17	131,523.20	80,161.47	106,083.48
Premiums paid	256,425.84	319,572.23	330,313.10	297,981.43	283,551.54
Cash items	177,063.12	182,043.73	181,012.08	175,171.26	177,268.15
Clear'g-house exch'gs	21,938.56	20,036.00	11,642.34	16,938.80	17,025.65
Bills of other banks	182,697.00	158,271.00	69,814.00	94,080.00	95,147.00
Fractional currency	1,311.74	2,920.86	4,103.00	2,777.01	2,706.94
Trade dollars	....	....	....	....	1.00
Specie	3,759,345.34	3,448,132.41	2,981,711.53	2,628,050.53	2,610,700.98
Legal-tender notes	299,020.00	589,502.00	313,725.00	228,811.00	182,492.00
U. S. cert's of deposit	....	....	....	....	....
5% fund with Treas.	48,092.00	50,844.50	53,913.00	55,538.00	57,431.00
Due from U. S. Treas	4,150.00	12,910.00	2,909.00	5,791.25	7,645.00
Total	27,404,451.25	26,906,201.45	25,782,306.05	24,632,900.68	24,074,571.85

SAN FRANCISCO.

Resources.	DECEMBER 7.	FEBRUARY 14.	APRIL 30.	JUNE 30.	OCTOBER 4.
	3 banks.	3 banks.	3 banks.	3 banks.	3 banks.
Loans and discounts	$4,531,980.43	$4,615,163.35	$5,017,067.19	$4,779,054.98	$5,244,417.43
Bonds for circulation	750,000.00	750,000.00	750,000.00	750,000.00	650,000.00
Bonds for deposits	....	....	....	....	100,000.00
U. S. bonds on hand	....	....	....	....	....
Other stocks and b'ds	375,000.00	375,000.00	375,000.00	375,000.00	375,000.00
Due from res've ag'ts	107,568.50	115,281.02	108,040.43	153,661.33	198,436.30
Due from nat'l banks	152,247.28	140,472.80	181,695.16	185,157.04	108,002.05
Due from State banks	272,115.80	298,813.02	301,084.48	317,243.09	320,784.23
Real estate, etc	50,016.94	48,407.01	47,477.04	179,902.39	107,547.98
Current expenses	6,708.71	7,592.04	5,225.54	5,025.54	5,054.30
Premiums paid	73,014.25	71,970.50	75,445.50	75,783.00	70,008.00
Cash items	4,911.43	3,950.23	2,244.17	2,606.50	2,210.87
Clear'g-house exch'gs	146,774.53	102,057.04	804,294.77	152,889.36	186,818.88
Bills of other banks	6,400.00	7,280.00	10,070.00	1,585.00	800.00
Fractional currency	108.36	326.00	517.09	105.48	80.78
Trade dollars	....	....	....	....	....
Specie	1,251,400.85	919,540.78	1,020,742.25	1,004,383.08	1,142,170.82
Legal-tender notes	7,486.00	33,040.00	7,810.00	2,307.00	12,282.00
U. S. cert's of deposit	....	....	....	....	....
5 % fund with Treas	33,750.00	33,750.00	33,750.00	33,750.00	20,250.00
Due from U. S. Treas	807.22	5,875.00	4,666.67	2,850.00	2,850.00
Total	7,771,109.30	7,020,324.79	8,306,031.19	8,021,304.09	8,710,003.64

by States and reserve cities—Continued.

NEVADA.

Liabilities.	DECEMBER 7.	FEBRUARY 14.	APRIL 30.	JUNE 30.	OCTOBER 4.
	2 banks.	2 banks.	2 banks.	2 banks.	2 banks.
Capital stock	$150, 000. 00	$150, 000. 00	$250, 000. 00	$250, 000. 00	$282, 000. 00
Surplus fund	40, 000. 00	60, 000. 00	85, 000. 00	85, 000. 00	98, 000. 00
Undivided profits	17, 780. 72	3, 167. 25	9, 850. 76	17, 193. 77	10, 119. 23
Nat'l-bank circulation	33, 730. 00	33, 730. 00	33, 010. 00	46, 410. 00	63, 410. 00
State-bank circulation					
Dividends unpaid					
Individual deposits	311, 797. 20	272, 201. 20	331, 554. 90	280, 221. 40	271, 142. 21
U. S. deposits					
Dep'ts U. S. dis. officers					
Due to national banks	100, 843. 87	62, 782. 33	47, 734. 76	60, 501. 72	70, 710. 02
Due to State banks	83, 550. 97	23, 346. 31	15, 010. 72	37, 273. 04	61, 605. 35
Notes re-discounted		14, 500. 00			
Bills payable		50, 000. 00			
Total	737, 711. 85	669, 817. 09	772, 101. 14	782, 599. 93	857, 076. 81

CALIFORNIA.

	30 banks.	31 banks.	34 banks.	36 banks.	35 banks.
Capital stock	$4, 225, 000. 00	$4, 465, 000. 00	$5, 043, 580. 00	$5, 335, 000. 00	$5, 475, 000. 00
Surplus fund	781, 550. 05	879, 904. 34	903, 848. 07	963, 905. 31	1, 018, 528. 74
Undivided profits	778, 563. 99	587, 150. 13	804, 752. 43	753, 687. 64	838, 542. 24
Nat'l-bank circulation	956, 720. 00	980, 520. 00	1, 065, 260. 00	1, 081, 790. 00	1, 103, 570. 00
State-bank circulation					
Dividends unpaid	1, 765. 25	20, 279. 25	10, 433. 14	30, 955. 75	6, 387. 00
Individual deposits	20, 213, 405. 53	19, 066, 386. 27	16, 769, 842. 63	15, 300, 066. 09	14, 389, 112. 35
U. S. deposits	34, 687. 54	432, 623. 60	451, 062. 34	439, 706. 80	510, 599. 80
Dep'ts U. S. dis. officers	113, 572. 74	93, 615. 47	92, 607. 38	96, 136. 86	27, 208. 50
Due to national banks	90, 848. 40	123, 662. 70	200, 024. 55	119, 058. 59	182, 863. 51
Due to State banks	262, 837. 75	249, 119. 00	340, 799. 04	294, 597. 49	163, 721. 90
Notes re-discounted			91, 036. 77	157, 995. 22	319, 037. 72
Bills payable	5, 500. 00				40, 000. 00
Total	27, 464, 451. 25	26, 906, 261. 45	25, 782, 306. 95	24, 632, 900. 68	24, 074, 571. 85

SAN FRANCISCO.

	3 banks.	3 banks.	3 banks.	3 banks.	3 banks.
Capital stock	$2, 700, 000. 00	$2, 700, 000. 00	$2, 700, 000. 00	$2, 700, 000. 00	$2, 700, 000. 00
Surplus fund	262, 744. 16	276, 871. 44	280, 361. 28	310, 000. 00	435, 000. 00
Undivided profits	261, 411. 23	271, 230. 75	311, 267. 45	346, 051. 05	235, 125. 20
Nat'l-bank circulation	668, 740. 00	663, 060. 00	665, 290. 00	654, 820. 00	575, 650. 00
State-bank circulation					
Dividends unpaid	2, 653. 75	2, 080. 50	8, 361. 00	5, 111. 75	2, 838. 50
Individual deposits	2, 660, 027. 78	2, 892, 664. 24	3, 342, 812. 18	3, 105, 742. 71	3, 685, 065. 61
U. S. deposits					89, 041. 02
Dep'ts U. S. dis. officers					
Due to national banks	787, 072. 16	517, 290. 10	697, 470. 44	655, 263. 85	653, 587. 16
Due to State banks	418, 560. 22	295, 027. 76	300, 438. 84	243, 772. 33	340, 296. 15
Notes re-discounted					
Bills payable					
Total	7, 771, 100. 30	7, 620, 324. 79	8, 306, 031. 19	8, 021, 364. 69	8, 710, 603. 64

Abstract of reports since October 5, 1887, arranged

OREGON.

Resources.	DECEMBER 7.	FEBRUARY 14.	APRIL 30.	JUNE 30.	OCTOBER 4.
	23 banks.	23 banks.	25 banks.	25 banks.	27 banks.
Loans and discounts	$5, 652, 858. 07	$5, 613, 158. 85	$6, 234, 573. 10	$6, 273, 981. 56	$6, 816, 109. 59
Bonds for circulation.	644, 800. 00	644, 800. 00	669, 800. 00	494, 800. 00	519, 800. 00
Bonds for deposits ..	600, 000. 00	600, 000. 00	600, 000. 00	600, 000. 00	600, 000. 00
U. S. bonds on hand..					
Other stocks and b'ds	713, 417. 33	726, 586. 02	765, 267. 39	718, 312. 27	747, 493. 56
Due from res've ag'ts.	193, 112. 02	111, 640. 02	275, 335. 69	390, 746. 37	327, 658. 99
Due from nat'l banks	417, 514. 67	274, 991. 23	334, 804. 53	414, 075. 81	537, 665. 50
Due from State banks	263, 306. 87	224, 851. 06	239, 833. 50	280, 270. 67	383, 206. 47
Real estate, etc	288, 710. 49	294, 028. 18	301, 051. 51	295, 267. 51	311, 790. 47
Current expenses....	67, 337. 88	25, 272. 48	63, 762. 05	57, 948. 72	53, 395. 84
Premiums paid	87, 829. 09	84, 438. 44	90, 649. 22	91, 213. 79	93, 335. 73
Cash items	55, 515. 33	45, 877. 99	78, 256. 04	45, 719. 55	82, 103. 89
Clear'g-house exch'gs					
Bills of other banks..	18, 493. 00	9, 667. 00	15, 750. 00	15, 710. 00	36, 080. 00
Fractional currency .	1, 691. 16	1, 648. 37	1, 732. 43	1, 150. 90	1, 218. 60
Trade dollars........					
Specie	964, 318. 35	971, 793. 00	912, 258. 75	938, 591. 55	940, 619. 30
Legal-tender notes ..	47, 754. 00	51, 277. 00	44, 631. 00	36, 749. 00	86, 502. 00
U. S. cert's of deposit					
5 % fund with Treas.	29, 010. 50	29, 010. 50	29, 010. 00	21, 135. 50	22, 265. 50
Due from U. S. Treas	3, 030. 00	500. 00	1, 024. 00	4, 414. 00	5, 314. 50
Total	10, 049, 709. 06	9, 709, 550. 64	10, 687, 830. 11	10, 680, 695. 20	11, 564, 559. 94

ARIZONA.

	1 bank.	1 bank.	1 bank.	1 bank.	1 bank.
Loans and discounts.	$144, 326. 18	$122, 164. 41	$119, 922. 81	$136, 178. 70	$154, 222. 37
Bonds for circulation.	25, 000. 00	25, 000. 00	25, 000. 00	25, 000. 00	25, 000. 00
Bonds for deposits...					
U. S. bonds on hand .					
Other stocks and b'ds	58, 268. 68	54, 600. 00	53, 106. 66	53, 506. 67	55, 330. 18
Due from res've ag'ts.					
Due from nat'l banks.					
Due from State banks	716. 60	11, 852. 00	15, 080. 43	5, 228. 65	2, 060. 33
Real estate, etc......	12, 954. 50	12, 954. 50	9, 454. 50	9, 454. 50	9, 454. 50
Current expenses ...	3, 505. 94	920. 35	3, 207. 63		2, 513. 23
Premiums paid	2, 500. 00	1, 875. 00	1, 875. 00	1, 875. 00	1, 875. 00
Cash items	60. 00	22. 50		190. 00	92. 70
Clear'g-house exch'gs					
Bills of other banks..	2, 887. 00	5, 552. 00	6, 640. 00	5, 179. 00	612. 00
Fractional currency					
Trade dollars					
Specie..............	23, 614. 65	20, 476. 00	27, 623. 85	14, 899. 79	15, 947. 10
Legal-tender notes ..	13, 815. 00	15, 660. 00	12, 000. 00	10, 000. 00	9, 000. 00
U. S. cert's of deposit.					
5 % fund with Treas.	1, 125. 00	1, 125. 00	1, 125. 00	1, 125. 00	1, 125. 00
Due from U. S. Treas.					
Total	288, 773. 55	272, 293. 41	275, 125. 87	262, 716. 40	277, 238. 41

DAKOTA.

	62 banks.	62 banks.	60 banks.	58 banks.	58 banks.
Loans and discounts.	$6, 877, 896. 01	$6, 963, 878. 06	$7, 189, 044. 18	$7, 262, 171. 17	$7, 414, 590. 68
Bonds for circulation.	962, 500. 00	962, 500. 00	937, 500. 00	925, 000. 00	937, 500. 00
Bonds for deposits ..	275, 000. 00	275, 000. 00	325, 000. 00	325, 000. 00	325, 000. 00
U. S. bonds on hand..					
Other stocks and b'ds	526, 404. 35	517, 230. 06	481, 498. 81	491, 872. 30	530, 033. 99
Due from res've ag'ts	485, 149. 34	615, 322. 19	561, 303. 49	499, 423. 44	596, 721. 25
Due from nat'l banks	828, 475. 00	905, 602. 88	597, 723. 36	506, 324. 33	914, 100. 73
Due from State banks	121, 771. 62	162, 693. 67	104, 574. 93	81, 754. 42	145, 125. 94
Real estate, etc	797, 753. 74	810, 323. 42	802, 347. 44	779, 606. 01	802, 647. 75
Current expenses....	158, 754. 22	69, 602. 54	147, 871. 62	96, 418. 35	102, 113. 62
Premiums paid	137, 516. 86	127, 000. 48	135, 706. 54	132, 393. 32	127, 172. 56
Cash items	165, 912. 54	115, 300. 94	119, 078. 07	111, 319. 49	160, 100. 83
Clear'g-house exch'gs					
Bills of other banks..	104, 420. 00	125, 346. 00	123, 473. 00	102, 853. 00	147, 632. 00
Fractional currency .	2, 327. 78	3, 482. 82	3, 414. 42	3, 235. 17	2, 855. 53
Trade dollars				1. 00	
Specie	581, 208. 34	419, 087. 25	415, 738. 86	360, 971. 03	470, 615. 00
Legal-tender notes ..	382, 843. 00	357, 490. 00	312, 876. 00	320, 660. 00	368, 523. 00
U. S. cert's of deposit					
5 % fund with Treas	42, 307. 75	43, 308. 25	41, 633. 75	41, 091. 25	42, 172. 75
Due from U. S. Treas	351. 50	4, 012. 00	1, 040. 00	1, 150. 00	2, 815. 00
Total	12, 540, 601. 11	12, 486, 183. 16	12, 300, 725. 07	12, 041, 153. 28	13, 089, 721. 63

by States and reserve cities—Continued.

OREGON.

Liabilities.	DECEMBER 7.	FEBRUARY 14.	APRIL 30.	JUNE 30.	OCTOBER 4.
	23 banks.	23 banks.	25 banks.	25 banks.	27 banks.
Capital stock	$1,615,000.00	$2,000,000.00	$2,165,000.00	$2,290,000.00	$2,300,000.00
Surplus fund	158,850.00	246,550.00	248,550.00	251,530.00	287,930.00
Undivided profits	1,041,438.22	716,186.13	708,225.70	881,565.85	900,037.04
Nat'l-bank circulation	578,750.00	505,470.00	562,520.00	402,960.00	447,600.00
State-bank circulation	....	....	....	....	....
Dividends unpaid	1,380.00	4,872.00	3,072.00	37,272.00	3,007.00
Individual deposits	5,100,657.88	4,755,330.81	5,079,100.55	5,445,710.53	6,017,643.47
U. S. deposits	240,143.23	279,339.76	219,836.43	305,106.23	303,140.38
Dep'ts U.S.dis.officers	333,501.21	357,951.51	371,272.56	329,371.48	252,575.03
Due to national banks	448,140.90	374,895.41	410,582.54	533,647.15	547,680.27
Due to State banks	307,848.22	293,069.27	174,980.22	176,967.50	422,706.33
Notes re-discounted	15,000.00	25,000.00	25,000.00	15,000.00	21,500.00
Bills payable	....	282.75	700.00	544.40	409.02
Total	10,049,709.66	9,700,550.64	10,637,830.11	10,689,095.20	11,564,350.94

ARIZONA.

	1 bank.	1 bank.	1 bank.	1 bank.	1 bank.
Capital stock	$100,000.00	$100,000.00	$100,000.00	$100,000.00	$100,000.00
Surplus fund	....	5,000.00	5,000.00	5,000.00	9,000.00
Undivided profits	11,002.10	5,073.47	13,393.31	13,122.22	10,892.27
Nat'l-bank circulation	22,500.00	22,500.00	22,500.00	22,490.00	22,500.00
State-bank circulation	....	....	....	....	....
Dividends unpaid	....	....	....	....	....
Individual deposits	131,115.56	138,783.56	130,605.33	121,839.28	115,419.39
U.S. deposits	....	....	....	....	....
Dep'ts U.S.dis.officers	....	....	....	....	....
Due to national banks	....	....	....	....	....
Due to State banks	23,255.89	336.38	3,627.23	204.90	19,426.75
Notes re-discounted	....	....	....	....	....
Bills payable	....	....	....	....	....
Total	288,773.55	272,203.41	275,125.87	262,710.40	277,238.41

DAKOTA.

	62 banks.	62 banks.	60 banks.	58 banks.	58 banks.
Capital stock	$3,725,000.00	$3,725,000.00	$3,625,000.00	$3,575,000.00	$3,625,000.00
Surplus fund	667,331.15	701,892.03	712,302.03	778,442.03	783,303.32
Undivided profits	556,597.37	275,016.45	419,028.04	376,426.30	373,205.66
Nat'l-bank circulation	860,900.00	861,770.00	838,555.00	825,780.00	839,100.00
State-bank circulation	....	....	....	....	....
Dividends unpaid	900.00	1,903.00	8,120.58	32,461.14	1,042.16
Individual deposits	5,856,720.99	5,944,549.07	5,740,025.54	5,515,144.43	6,126,150.28
U. S. deposits	255,515.02	241,318.24	316,279.01	310,574.37	295,983.60
Dep'ts U.S.dis.officers	17,932.05	20,865.02	17,2[illegible]0.99	12,582.43	33,680.85
Due to national banks	131,010.45	98,514.87	85,621.77	66,481.22	135,152.37
Due to State banks	287,092.77	297,323.78	207,836.32	210,614.31	207,001.10
Notes re-discounted	158,502.31	211,936.66	108,145.70	310,646.99	427,884.29
Bills payable	23,000.00	37,003.44	37,500.00	18,006.00	70,000.00
Total	12,540,601.11	12,486,183.16	12,300,725.07	12,041,153.28	13,089,721.63

Abstract of reports since October 5, 1887, arranged

IDAHO.

Resources.	DECEMBER 7.	FEBRUARY 14.	APRIL 30.	JUNE 30.	OCTOBER 4.
	6 banks.	6 banks.	6 banks.	7 banks.	7 banks.
Loans and discounts	$595, 636. 73	$611, 101. 29	$639, 547. 03	$714, 434. 61	$675, 988. 37
Bonds for circulation	92, 800. 00	92, 800. 00	92, 800. 00	105, 300. 00	112, 800. 00
Bonds for deposits	60, 000. 00	70, 000. 00	70, 000. 00	70, 000. 00	70, 000. 00
U. S. bonds on hand	....	....	....	....	....
Other stocks and b'ds	180, 314. 48	123, 967. 64	130, 130. 49	138, 888. 08	142, 481. 51
Due from res've ag'ts	12, 983. 41	8, 061. 35	4, 712. 88	19, 203. 74	47, 091. 18
Due from nat'l banks	37, 022. 69	11, 620. 98	21, 773. 68	49, 191. 57	151, 049. 26
Due from State banks	25, 730. 51	42, 866. 36	25, 382. 37	61, 158. 54	76, 267. 85
Real estate, etc	44, 704. 82	47, 200. 38	55, 225. 85	65, 969. 16	72, 525. 15
Current expenses	19, 778. 89	7, 805. 64	11, 377. 68	9, 245. 82	7, 414. 17
Premiums paid	15, 716. 69	10, 560. 44	15, 169. 82	14, 810. 25	14, 218. 37
Cash items	6, 528. 56	5, 473. 88	5, 171. 32	7, 708. 16	11, 213. 70
Clear'g-house exch'gs	....	....	....	....	....
Bills of other banks	31, 615. 00	26, 880. 00	19, 122. 00	23, 221. 00	18, 279. 00
Fractional currency	48. 06	35. 72	18. 68	67. 83	80. 62
Trade dollars	....	....	....	....	....
Specie	58, 443. 75	85, 558. 51	71, 717. 30	94, 037. 98	117, 510. 85
Legal-tender notes	50, 023. 00	51, 361. 00	44, 747. 00	75, 619. 00	90, 248. 00
U. S. cert's of deposit	....	....	....	....	....
5 % fund with Treas.	2, 825. 00	4, 175. 00	3, 625. 00	4, 175. 00	5, 075. 00
Due from U. S. Treas.	2, 470. 00	....	....	....	155. 00
Total	1, 245, 636. 50	1, 205, 568. 19	1, 210, 521. 10	1, 453, 030. 74	1, 613, 001. 03

MONTANA.

	17 banks.	17 banks.	17 banks.	17 banks.	17 banks.
Loans and discounts	$8, 584, 520. 44	$8, 542, 334. 69	$8, 557, 400. 98	$8, 646, 347. 75	$8, 777, 362. 16
Bonds for circulation	480, 600. 00	480, 600. 00	480, 600. 00	480, 600. 00	480, 600. 00
Bonds for deposits	200, 000. 00	200, 000. 00	200, 000. 00	200, 000. 00	200, 000. 00
U. S. bonds on hand	10, 150. 00	10, 150. 00	10, 150. 00	10, 150. 00	10, 150. 00
Other stocks and b'ds	554, 111. 76	456, 491. 93	460, 285. 33	506, 442. 79	559, 708. 63
Due from res've ag'ts	660, 794. 34	512, 247. 40	480, 400. 66	605, 514. 45	905, 191. 31
Due from nat'l banks	554, 624. 94	619, 261. 91	307, 481. 90	486, 576. 34	865, 084. 37
Due from State banks	327, 221. 59	285, 405. 23	355, 162. 39	322, 556. 17	350, 660. 30
Real estate, etc	417, 583. 00	417, 115. 87	421, 275. 35	428, 575. 42	451, 454. 06
Current expenses	95, 713. 98	28, 712. 14	56, 540. 41	17, 621. 98	53, 769. 62
Premiums paid	57, 541. 38	58, 447. 66	51, 307. 04	48, 307. 04	46, 723. 85
Cash items	64, 600. 55	112, 488. 25	75, 608. 65	51, 685. 18	62, 942. 54
Clear'g-house exch'gs	....	....	....	....	....
Bills of other banks	114, 838. 00	106, 355. 00	111, 004. 00	67, 386. 00	117, 600. 00
Fractional currency	2, 548. 42	1, 754. 78	1, 104. 41	2, 771. 70	1, 946. 32
Trade dollars	....	....	....	....	....
Specie	937, 983. 45	830, 309. 20	827, 894. 90	963, 241. 35	870, 407. 00
Legal-tender notes	506, 244. 00	441, 342. 00	504, 325. 00	489, 697. 00	542, 922. 00
U. S. cert's of deposit	....	....	....	....	....
5 % fund with Treas.	21, 624. 50	21, 624. 50	21, 624. 50	21, 624. 50	21, 625. 00
Due from U. S. Treas.	9, 713. 76	3, 905. 44	2, 961. 94	4, 474. 19	11, 626. 09
Total	13, 690, 504. 20	13, 118, 636. 00	12, 985, 133. 46	13, 353, 571. 86	14, 329, 173. 25

NEW MEXICO.

	9 banks.	9 banks.	9 banks.	9 banks.	9 banks.
Loans and discounts	$1, 814, 553. 09	$1, 732, 466. 59	$1, 792, 219. 01	$1, 812, 465. 00	$1, 790, 752. 93
Bonds for circulation	240, 000. 00	240, 000. 00	240, 000. 00	240, 000. 00	252, 500. 00
Bonds for deposits	125, 000. 00	125, 000. 00	150, 000. 00	150, 000. 00	150, 000. 00
U. S. bonds on hand	....	....	....	....	....
Other stocks and bd's	42, 334. 47	25, 241. 43	23, 984. 23	29, 052. 69	40, 273. 71
Due from res've ag'ts	172, 460. 62	186, 816. 90	176, 178. 46	288, 568. 18	323, 317. 05
Due from nat'l banks	291, 401. 88	390, 208. 71	252, 084. 47	403, 922. 55	389, 926. 42
Due from State banks	56, 436. 31	106, 728. 74	60, 816. 94	57, 032. 84	57, 835. 75
Real estate, etc	175, 934. 02	165, 429. 02	170, 537. 48	170, 440. 38	174, 420. 62
Current expenses	45, 883. 90	14, 855. 12	26, 085. 98	10, 807. 53	19, 115. 47
Premiums paid	21, 357. 81	20, 887. 10	21, 474. 60	17, 862. 10	18, 648. 35
Cash items	13, 066. 29	25, 274. 15	21, 881. 69	16, 940. 16	7, 758. 01
Clear'g-house exch'gs	....	....	....	....	....
Bills of other banks	25, 063. 00	22, 746. 00	25, 651. 00	14, 736. 00	24, 248. 00
Fractional currency	1, 160. 00	1, 544. 16	1, 435. 13	1, 001. 67	512. 18
Trade dollars	....	....	....	....	....
Specie	105, 451. 60	138, 497. 10	138, 544. 50	130, 249. 75	124, 448. 85
Legal-tender notes	82, 968. 00	81, 814. 00	76, 682. 00	84, 077. 00	84, 409. 00
U. S. cert's of deposit	....	....	....	....	....
5 % fund with Treas.	10, 799. 50	10, 799. 50	10, 799. 50	10, 800. 00	10, 932. 00
Due from U. S. Treas.	837. 12	388. 12	900. 12	1, 217. 62	17. 12
Total	3, 225, 607. 01	3, 288, 757. 54	3, 189, 936. 01	3, 439, 202. 47	3, 469, 145. 06

by States and reserve cities—Continued.

IDAHO.

Liabilities.	DECEMBER 7.	FEBRUARY 14.	APRIL 30.	JUNE 30.	OCTOBER 4.
	6 banks.	6 banks.	6 banks.	7 banks.	7 banks.
Capital stock	$350,000.00	$350,000.00	$350,000.00	$400,000.00	$430,000.00
Surplus fund	28,981.13	58,000.00	58,000.00	60,000.00	85,000.00
Undivided profits	101,456.13	77,002.21	87,854.70	92,177.75	57,338.69
Nat'l-bank circulation	82,525.00	82,080.00	82,775.00	82,490.00	99,045.00
State-bank circulation	....	....	....	....	....
Dividends unpaid	....	....	....	40.00	....
Individual deposits	577,169.07	540,417.02	624,710.30	678,959.55	845,144.86
U. S. deposits	56,247.78	66,305.08	68,373.52	66,015.00	65,978.09
Dep'ts U.S. dis. officers	689.85	1,469.07	920.34	3,597.44	3,600.16
Due to national banks	8,528.52	14,743.43	6,856.33	9,923.08	8,002.21
Due to State banks	40,039.11	15,550.48	31,521.01	50,827.23	17,841.52
Notes re-discounted	....	....	....	....	....
Bills payable	....	....	....	....	....
Total	1,245,636.59	1,205,568.19	1,210,521.10	1,453,030.74	1,613,001.03

MONTANA.

	17 banks.	17 banks.	17 banks.	17 banks.	17 banks.
Capital stock	$1,975,000.00	$1,975,000.00	$1,950,000.00	$1,950,000.00	$1,950,000.00
Surplus fund	420,450.00	501,250.00	501,250.00	497,250.00	506,000.00
Undivided profits	1,178,208.32	1,035,692.20	1,153,064.60	1,177,651.80	1,271,282.93
Nat'l-bank circulation	428,811.00	429,300.00	426,160.00	423,320.00	421,450.00
State-bank circulation	....	....	....	....	....
Dividends unpaid	4,885.00	7,030.00	7,930.00	5,000.00	1,450.00
Individual deposits	8,790,205.37	8,247,107.10	8,090,107.16	8,451,326.63	9,068,342.41
U. S. deposits	126,345.34	150,042.91	117,100.30	108,324.45	77,276.15
Dep'ts U.S. dis. officers	54,194.10	38,012.36	76,236.43	86,662.78	105,312.00
Due to national banks	454,438.78	415,596.76	327,221.47	331,246.92	565,180.11
Due to State banks	191,210.85	196,922.23	186,205.59	177,243.99	271,140.89
Notes re-discounted	66,746.44	111,692.35	104,857.91	135,545.29	71,788.76
Bills payable	....	10,000.00	45,000.00	10,000.00	....
Total	13,690,504.20	13,118,636.00	12,985,133.46	13,353,571.86	14,329,173.25

NEW MEXICO.

	9 banks.	9 banks.	9 banks.	9 banks.	9 banks.
Capital stock	$850,000.00	$850,000.00	$850,000.00	$850,000.00	$900,000.00
Surplus fund	174,935.86	175,275.93	176,975.93	190,225.93	185,725.93
Undivided profits	74,093.13	22,107.05	54,253.31	41,818.04	48,60[illegible].74
Nat'l-bank circulation	211,500.00	216,000.00	215,500.00	211,500.00	226,410.00
State-bank circulation	....	....	....	....	....
Dividends unpaid	68.00	450.00	146.00	16,106.00	119.00
Individual deposits	1,561,730.33	1,657,499.06	1,537,629.16	1,675,434.98	1,754,851.18
U. S. deposits	27,783.80	10,848.38	14,220.66	45,348.67	70,506.82
Dep'ts U.S. dis. officers	80,114.14	115,840.46	135,843.03	101,763.14	61,737.08
Due to national banks	126,078.84	128,540.64	156,092.45	229,341.46	163,480.75
Due to State banks	76,002.62	77,460.87	12,827.78	33,735.76	29,871.37
Notes re-discounted	27,977.20	34,735.15	36,447.69	43,928.49	27,834.50
Bills payable	14,723.69	....	....	....	....
Total	3,225,607.61	3,288,757.54	3,180,986.01	3,439,302.47	3,469,145.06

Abstract of reports since October 5, 1887, arranged

UTAH.

Resources.	DECEMBER 7.	FEBRUARY 14.	APRIL 30.	JUNE 30.	OCTOBER 4.
	7 banks.	7 banks.	7 banks.	7 banks.	7 banks.
Loans and discounts	$2,288,498.58	$2,295,910.75	$2,505,686.87	$2,395,523.09	$2,458,930.82
Bonds for circulation	300,000.00	300,000.00	300,000.00	300,000.00	300,000.00
Bonds for deposits	200,000.00	200,000.00	200,000.00	200,000.00	200,000.00
U. S. bonds on hand	126,000.00	126,000.00	76,000.00	26,900.00	26,900.00
Other stocks and b'ds	108,711.57	380,200.32	331,100.32	332,288.02	331,243.62
Due from res've ag'ts	230,631.55	242,457.57	202,370.32	255,206.85	433,820.53
Due from nat'l banks	116,770.04	130,758.02	183,704.11	143,992.33	140,704.55
Due from State banks	69,085.17	140,200.04	70,884.07	85,201.84	89,003.88
Real estate, etc	125,825.11	123,064.01	155,751.23	153,757.71	153,651.60
Current expenses	27,119.00	13,127.52	16,234.57	4,887.11	25,034.07
Premiums paid	90,060.03	94,470.38	81,540.88	60,549.88	66,049.88
Cash items	16,101.45	7,243.13	18,853.25	16,420.05	10,225.18
Clear'g house exch'gs	......	......	......	......	......
Bills of other banks	60,824.00	53,548.00	60,345.00	61,415.00	38,536.00
Fractional currency	236.78	571.76	273.77	783.22	432.88
Trade dollars	......	......	......	12.00	12.00
Specie	390,971.35	318,002.70	348,037.30	335,644.60	306,127.75
Legal-tender notes	70,884.00	71,143.00	60,873.00	60,071.00	55,523.00
U. S. cert's of deposit	......	......	......	......	......
5 % fund with Treas	17,050.00	17,550.00	17,050.00	17,550.00	17,550.00
Due from U. S. Treas	......	......	......	......	......
Total	4,425,758.92	4,624,444.00	4,808,575.71	4,550,054.20	4,841,328.42

WASHINGTON.

	20 banks.	21 banks.	22 banks.	23 banks.	24 banks.
Loans and discounts	$4,144,735.27	$4,541,843.30	$4,974,270.47	$5,483,504.76	$6,232,112.07
Bonds for circulation	480,000.00	405,000.00	507,500.00	521,250.00	471,250.00
Bonds for deposits	......	......	50,000.00	50,100.00	100,000.00
U. S. bonds on hand	500.00	500.00	500.00	500.00	500.00
Other stocks and b'ds	405,305.60	437,588.00	358,000.40	388,037.78	487,702.82
Due from res've ag'ts	177,401.35	144,480.84	366,475.03	402,533.92	723,148.03
Due from nat'l banks	324,547.04	357,253.42	412,022.84	617,257.52	576,188.32
Due from State banks	102,721.14	124,102.43	232,881.38	234,141.43	241,809.17
Real estate, etc	239,602.25	243,046.74	250,913.80	270,746.26	311,126.73
Current expenses	46,330.85	29,500.10	54,540.83	50,131.30	54,119.79
Premiums paid	77,000.88	80,796.71	93,712.97	98,533.04	92,132.53
Cash items	54,756.57	45,810.86	72,100.14	68,816.84	111,544.27
Clear'g-house exch'gs	......	......	......	......	......
Bills of other banks	48,440.00	32,065.00	42,003.00	46,008.00	53,854.00
Fractional currency	303.02	793.70	1,315.00	801.65	1,701.03
Trade dollars	......	......	......	......	......
Specie	619,647.65	608,041.38	712,050.20	662,278.62	740,740.00
Legal-tender notes	68,678.00	73,220.00	94,245.00	60,970.00	102,565.00
U. S. cert's of deposit	......	......	......	......	......
5 % fund with Treas	21,080.00	20,080.00	21,725.00	21,025.50	20,305.00
Due from U. S. Treas	490.00	140.00	800.00	1,200.00	800.00
Total	6,872,730.01	7,318,325.47	8,255,016.57	9,075,406.62	10,340,669.75

WYOMING.

	8 banks.	8 banks.	8 banks.	8 banks.	9 banks.
Loans and discounts	$2,401,259.76	$2,378,257.07	$2,342,081.22	$2,356,814.40	$2,418,833.91
Bonds for circulation	223,750.00	223,750.00	223,750.00	223,750.00	248,750.00
Bonds for deposits	......	......	......	......	......
U. S. bonds on hand	......	......	......	......	......
Other stocks and b'ds	80,456.42	52,887.00	63,840.83	77,330.10	58,453.10
Due from res've ag'ts	108,812.26	77,203.53	128,342.55	129,066.58	340,365.55
Due from nat'l banks	61,833.00	75,789.00	54,064.62	48,281.02	109,193.90
Due from State banks	5,477.60	1,802.50	5,323.37	9,187.50	11,554.25
Real estate, etc	87,600.18	67,801.21	93,244.42	93,701.47	101,081.31
Current expenses	40,930.23	16,094.51	33,524.04	17,171.71	35,959.23
Premiums paid	23,092.90	21,284.78	21,584.78	20,709.78	23,190.94
Cash items	17,080.97	14,907.57	17,090.78	16,022.72	14,561.43
Clear'g-house exch'gs	......	......	......	......	......
Bills of other banks	22,281.00	20,831.00	17,001.00	14,025.00	27,241.00
Fractional currency	508.00	476.73	573.56	660.04	934.47
Trade dollars	......	......	......	......	......
Specie	233,664.10	237,597.50	199,615.85	184,726.50	210,176.00
Legal-tender notes	30,102.00	33,000.00	30,461.00	20,000.00	33,783.00
U. S. cert's of deposit	......	......	......	......	......
5 % fund with Treas	10,068.75	10,068.75	10,068.75	10,068.75	11,193.75
Due from U. S. Treas	......	......	......	......	......
Total	3,407,075.06	3,261,002.23	3,242,073.37	3,228,133.67	3,654,273.93

by States and reserve cities—Continued.

UTAH.

Liabilities.	DECEMBER 7.	FEBRUARY 14.	APRIL 30.	JUNE 30.	OCTOBER 4.
	7 banks.	7 banks.	7 banks.	7 banks.	7 banks.
Capital stock	$850,000.00	$850,000.00	$850,000.00	$850,000.00	$850,000.00
Surplus fund	373,278.00	387,278.00	387,276.00	400,650.00	422,150.00
Undivided profits	120,417.09	104,332.58	148,611.06	138,923.91	159,431.92
Nat'l-bank circulation	285,100.00	276,050.00	279,960.00	274,100.00	269,690.00
State-bank circulation	....	....	....	....	....
Dividends unpaid	1,201.00	2,269.00	1,708.00	1,792.00	1,423.00
Individual deposits	2,480,139.07	2,673,559.46	2,664,043.29	2,512,578.95	2,863,157.52
U.S. deposits	144,611.87	110,771.33	12[illegible],083.56	166,179.62	136,430.25
Dept's U.S. dis. officers	50,401.59	70,752.64	72,434.11	19,913.06	62,294.72
Due to national banks	54,674.04	69,092.90	138,398.25	98,503.88	34,658.41
Due to State banks	26,955.34	22,323.79	100,779.32	40,552.78	37,092.60
Notes re-discounted	20,890.92	40,014.30	31,260.12	13,770.00	5,000.00
Bills payable	....	....	....	15,000.00	....
Total	4,425,758.92	4,024,444.00	4,808,575.71	4,550,034.20	4,841,328.42

WASHINGTON.

	20 banks.	21 banks.	22 banks.	23 banks.	24 banks.
Capital stock	$1,520,000.00	$1,620,000.00	$1,688,000.00	$1,800,000.00	$1,855,000.00
Surplus fund	243,456.93	274,316.53	274,316.53	294,066.53	322,750.00
Undivided profits	596,745.79	550,033.77	649,798.32	691,612.50	755,726.07
Nat'l-bank circulation	431,500.00	426,480.00	434,880.00	450,740.00	420,520.00
State-bank circulation	....	....	....	....	....
Dividends unpaid	260.00	10,260.00	1,040.00	27,480.00	1,102.00
Individual deposits	3,858,845.08	4,171,710.58	4,802,128.67	5,499,089.52	6,628,880.49
U.S. deposits	....	....	51,955.81	54,127.13	98,901.60
Dep'ts U.S. dis. officers	....	....	....	50.92	1,004.02
Due to national banks	136,710.73	102,024.24	135,550.31	154,340.54	94,552.83
Due to State banks	85,211.48	163,494.35	127,337.03	100,696.48	162,231.84
Notes re-discounted	....	....	....	3,200.00	....
Bills payable	....	....	....	....	....
Total	6,872,730.01	7,318,325.47	8,265,016.57	9,075,406.62	10,340,069.75

WYOMING.

	8 banks.	8 banks.	8 banks.	8 banks.	9 banks.
Capital stock	$1,075,000.00	$1,075,000.00	$1,075,000.00	$1,075,000.00	$1,175,000.00
Surplus fund	213,367.80	223,030.78	228,530.78	230,000.00	212,500.00
Undivided profits	202,045.43	138,174.67	169,604.44	162,626.06	114,885.45
Nat'l bank circulation	201,375.00	200,825.00	200,145.00	199,375.00	220,515.00
State-bank circulation	....	....	....	....	....
Dividends unpaid	....	300.00	....	3,000.00	....
Individual deposits	1,651,380.68	1,351,610.86	1,312,494.37	1,302,252.23	1,730,927.16
U.S. deposits	....	....	....	....	....
Dep'ts U.S. dis. officers	....	....	....	....	....
Due to national banks	28,332.87	36,718.44	17,717.61	17,416.01	36,132.23
Due to State banks	15,770.27	6,895.65	7,209.22	15,914.23	38,004.59
Notes re-discounted	95,394.01	211,127.83	220,771.95	220,040.24	99,806.50
Bills payable	15,000.00	18,000.00	2,500.00	2,500.00	26,500.00
Total	3,497,675.06	3,261,692.23	3,242,073.37	3,228,133.67	3,654,273.93

A SUMMARY

OF THE

STATE AND CONDITION

OF

THE NATIONAL BANKS,

BY STATES,

FROM 1863 TO 1888.

11028—CUR 88——20

SUMMARY, BY STATES, OF THE NUMBER OF NATIONAL BANKS, THE IMPORTANT ITEMS OF RESOURCES AND LIABILITIES, AND THE TOTALS, IN THOUSANDS, AS SHOWN BY LATEST RETURNS IN EACH ANNUAL REPORT TO CONGRESS, FROM 1863 TO 1888, INCLUSIVE.

MAINE.

Date.	No. of banks.	Loans and discounts.	U. S. bonds.	Cash and cash items.	Capital.	Surplus.	Undivided profits.	Outstanding circulation.	Individual deposits.	Total.
		Thousands.	*Thousands.*	*Thousands.*	*Thousands.*	*Thousands.*	*Thousands.*	*Thousands.*	*Thousands.*	*Thousands.*
1863	1	$5	$51	$11	$50	....	....	....	$19	$69
1864	16	2,808	2,858	702	2,540	$7	$150	$1,240	1,213	7,433
1865	58	8,750	8,831	1,921	8,341	103	715	4,399	5,126	22,653
1866	61	10,396	8,883	2,095	9,085	572	685	7,243	6,542	24,997
1867	61	9,870	8,791	1,773	9,085	758	734	7,475	4,802	23,640
1868	61	10,169	9,015	1,604	9,085	1,107	637	7,470	5,076	24,236
1869	61	11,113	8,558	1,541	9,125	1,308	810	7,401	4,503	24,005
1870	61	11,377	8,206	1,688	9,125	1,531	929	7,400	4,855	24,609
1871	61	12,131	8,078	1,701	9,125	1,665	1,110	7,381	5,588	25,736
1872	61	12,567	9,076	1,938	9,125	1,779	1,293	7,498	5,492	26,070
1873	63	13,523	9,449	1,930	9,440	1,802	1,408	7,783	6,494	26,012
1874	64	13,789	9,458	1,984	9,740	2,149	1,396	7,802	6,325	28,052
1875	69	14,047	9,800	1,918	10,310	2,103	1,558	8,103	6,431	29,146
1876	71	14,608	8,657	1,496	10,610	2,302	1,362	7,806	6,688	29,735
1877	71	14,644	9,751	1,711	10,660	2,305	1,303	7,885	6,126	28,904
1878	72	13,560	10,192	1,684	10,700	2,389	1,235	8,313	5,956	29,112
1879	69	13,871	10,050	1,530	10,435	2,391	1,177	8,229	6,189	29,104
1880	69	14,915	9,816	1,803	10,435	2,437	1,243	8,345	8,194	31,459
1881	69	17,324	9,594	1,672	10,385	2,587	1,340	8,211	8,325	32,618
1882	71	18,038	9,530	2,121	10,335	2,595	1,432	8,090	10,434	35,986
1883	72	18,778	9,290	2,074	10,483	2,575	1,410	8,080	10,032	33,470
1884	71	17,440	9,097	1,801	10,800	2,433	1,236	7,862	9,522	32,216
1885	71	16,604	8,904	2,107	10,360	2,486	1,142	7,083	10,095	32,561
1886	71	18,041	7,841	1,899	10,360	2,343	1,198	6,833	10,250	31,992
1887	72	19,174	5,064	1,757	10,441	2,401	1,344	4,870	10,116	30,440
1888	75	20,192	5,131	1,888	10,660	2,550	1,394	4,403	11,065	31,720

NEW HAMPSHIRE.

Date.	No. of banks.	Loans and discounts.	U. S. bonds.	Cash and cash items.	Capital.	Surplus.	Undivided profits.	Outstanding circulation.	Individual deposits.	Total.
1863	1	37	63	....	100	....	....	....	....	101
1864	5	391	989	137	660	....	41	418	365	1,935
1865	38	3,113	5,691	823	4,635	152	319	2,394	1,390	10,814
1866	39	3,831	5,916	945	4,735	306	300	4,026	2,228	12,104
1867	39	3,972	5,789	900	4,735	416	334	4,190	1,942	12,159
1868	40	4,264	5,932	830	4,785	501	420	4,255	2,003	12,443
1869	41	4,054	5,683	810	4,835	612	456	4,256	1,895	12,405
1870	41	4,999	5,503	745	4,835	726	479	4,267	2,318	12,844
1871	41	5,304	5,550	815	4,835	814	472	4,291	2,678	13,402
1872	42	5,974	5,596	839	5,098	870	541	4,487	2,732	13,984
1873	42	6,535	5,521	800	5,135	910	582	4,556	2,890	14,321
1874	43	6,676	5,695	822	5,315	1,018	536	4,660	3,005	14,856
1875	44	6,890	5,865	780	5,465	1,035	540	4,778	3,049	15,174
1876	45	6,622	5,975	789	5,615	903	528	4,935	2,738	15,173
1877	46	6,662	6,180	821	5,740	1,006	504	4,985	3,048	15,721
1878	46	6,547	6,501	867	5,740	1,031	589	5,048	3,166	16,007
1879	45	6,355	6,366	863	5,630	1,046	527	5,008	3,350	15,944
1880	47	7,188	6,205	975	5,830	1,081	504	5,160	3,944	17,105
1881	47	7,547	6,358	801	5,830	1,110	559	5,158	4,293	17,720
1882	49	8,137	6,323	1,011	6,080	1,103	583	5,147	4,560	18,338
1883	49	8,537	6,351	1,020	6,155	1,198	560	5,278	4,983	19,102
1884	48	8,454	6,206	907	6,105	1,105	589	5,174	4,961	18,938
1885	48	8,371	6,187	1,002	6,105	1,220	582	5,149	5,425	19,520
1886	49	9,083	5,055	1,083	6,155	1,328	608	4,170	5,706	18,992
1887	49	9,695	4,371	1,150	6,205	1,454	639	3,588	6,123	19,250
1888	49	10,150	4,127	1,194	6,205	1,497	735	3,277	6,362	18,507

SUMMARY, BY STATES, OF THE NUMBER OF NATIONAL BANKS, THE IMPORTANT ITEMS OF RESOURCES AND LIABILITIES, AND THE TOTALS, ETC.—Continued.

VERMONT.

Date.	No. of banks.	Loans and discounts.	U. S. bonds.	Cash and cash items.	Capital.	Surplus.	Undivided profits.	Outstanding circulation.	Individual deposits.	Total.
		Thousands.	*Thousands.*	*Thousands.*	*Thousands.*	*Thousands.*	*Thousands.*	*Thousands.*	*Thousands.*	*Thousands.*
1863	0	....	....	....	....	....	....	....	....	....
1864	10	$804	$1,852	$311	$1,400	$2	$69	$1,083	$309	$3,480
1865	27	2,566	6,008	753	4,863	60	109	3,017	1,019	10,384
1866	39	4,726	7,044	1,104	6,310	211	411	5,496	2,031	15,133
1867	40	5,206	7,820	1,153	6,510	415	411	5,688	1,968	15,480
1868	40	5,781	7,810	1,080	6,560	586	438	5,711	2,434	16,090
1869	40	6,524	7,407	932	6,810	870	431	5,901	1,901	16,236
1870	42	7,706	7,618	1,090	7,460	1,031	401	5,994	2,664	18,031
1871	41	8,064	8,022	1,046	7,610	1,128	421	6,554	3,052	19,188
1872	41	8,928	8,062	986	7,000	1,258	493	6,654	3,499	19,928
1873	42	9,991	8,171	989	7,810	1,481	468	6,789	4,385	21,292
1874	42	10,421	8,239	1,011	7,863	1,671	537	6,840	4,051	21,324
1875	45	11,225	8,472	1,102	8,397	1,911	530	6,979	4,490	22,661
1876	46	11,444	8,412	983	8,704	2,004	593	6,972	4,037	22,767
1877	46	11,212	8,337	939	8,509	2,126	624	6,995	3,769	22,440
1878	46	10,320	8,439	934	8,466	2,070	535	6,939	3,589	21,840
1879	47	10,048	8,078	1,011	8,490	2,058	542	6,999	3,806	22,154
1880	47	10,080	8,408	1,093	8,301	1,945	558	6,992	5,038	22,992
1881	47	11,012	7,703	1,012	8,151	1,770	608	6,443	5,191	22,364
1882	46	12,187	7,404	1,012	7,786	1,707	623	6,487	5,955	22,989
1883	47	12,054	7,381	036	7,980	1,796	600	6,518	5,455	22,822
1884	49	11,554	6,590	861	8,011	1,620	626	5,776	4,922	21,383
1885	47	10,589	6,300	963	7,541	1,474	501	5,356	5,154	20,380
1886	49	11,818	5,408	904	7,691	1,501	576	4,569	5,915	20,735
1887	49	12,880	4,170	022	7,506	1,572	668	3,478	6,627	20,435
1888	49	12,800	4,180	032	7,566	1,690	732	3,228	6,697	20,848

MASSACHUSETTS.

Date.	No. of banks.	Loans and discounts.	U. S. bonds.	Cash and cash items.	Capital.	Surplus.	Undivided profits.	Outstanding circulation.	Individual deposits.	Total.
1863	1	104	50	25	150	....	1	....	92	243
1864	51	17,532	19,800	8,300	18,014	1,231	1,010	5,800	12,695	51,826
1865	207	88,432	80,217	35,865	79,582	8,715	2,764	41,116	54,334	221,035
1866	207	99,464	77,013	37,405	79,832	11,125	2,568	55,573	66,326	236,474
1867	206	102,128	75,608	29,154	79,682	13,054	3,133	56,442	57,262	229,122
1868	207	100,128	76,500	29,830	79,882	16,030	3,808	56,756	62,708	237,402
1869	206	120,417	73,482	27,175	85,822	18,290	4,479	56,044	58,152	240,305
1870	206	127,100	71,795	25,849	87,022	19,925	4,358	56,232	64,133	250,085
1871	208	141,172	71,957	30,004	87,872	21,443	4,007	56,777	74,952	271,220
1872	211	141,950	69,927	24,009	88,072	22,759	5,510	57,873	65,849	260,910
1873	217	156,110	69,978	25,083	90,852	23,025	11,451	58,453	72,469	278,485
1874	220	168,278	69,885	20,021	92,014	20,217	6,383	57,909	82,012	293,069
1875	232	172,105	72,290	31,240	95,587	26,719	6,408	59,696	87,702	300,708
1876	236	165,200	71,305	26,708	96,490	25,875	5,634	55,950	84,986	300,061
1877	237	162,870	73,319	24,340	96,447	24,958	4,875	58,484	79,330	292,119
1878	236	150,356	87,112	25,571	95,215	22,820	4,511	61,070	80,614	298,780
1879	241	152,353	84,355	24,962	94,057	22,380	4,574	65,537	84,974	301,037
1880	242	180,490	80,468	32,648	95,005	23,230	5,471	69,457	110,042	346,207
1881	244	205,353	82,081	37,396	96,177	24,580	6,380	71,207	125,108	368,285
1882	244	195,126	78,306	32,005	93,852	24,051	6,853	68,573	114,307	340,214
1883	246	194,175	74,202	29,117	96,602	25,303	7,273	65,490	116,026	344,218
1884	249	195,882	68,406	30,589	96,077	25,149	7,345	59,933	110,602	335,373
1885	249	211,504	64,042	35,501	96,046	24,032	5,029	55,017	132,042	359,080
1886	250	211,061	52,508	31,824	96,140	25,452	6,803	46,246	128,517	343,291
1887	252	215,719	35,006	30,504	95,740	26,810	7,720	30,314	128,128	330,042
1888	253	230,988	34,455	34,091	96,141	27,655	8,325	25,158	144,302	355,596

SUMMARY, BY STATES, OF THE NUMBER OF NATIONAL BANKS, THE IMPORTANT ITEMS OF RESOURCES AND LIABILITIES, AND THE TOTALS, ETC.—Continued.

RHODE ISLAND.

Date.	No. of banks.	Loans and discounts.	U. S. bonds.	Cash and cash items.	Capital.	Surplus.	Undivided profits.	Outstanding circulation.	Individual deposits.	Total.
		Thousands.	Thousands.	Thousands.	Thousands.	Thousands.	Thousands.	Thousands.	Thousands.	Thousands.
1863	0	....	....	....	....	....	....	....	....	....
1864	1	$534	$331	$200	$500	....	....	$363	$231	$1,461
1865	55	19,230	11,436	2,730	19,106	$689	$660	4,250	5,378	36,251
1866	62	21,737	14,771	3,524	20,365	895	731	12,208	6,607	43,481
1867	62	21,102	14,870	2,086	20,365	1,063	977	12,419	6,021	42,754
1868	62	21,358	14,864	2,514	20,365	1,302	1,030	12,429	6,235	42,503
1869	62	22,485	14,710	2,381	20,365	1,672	1,237	12,400	5,789	42,941
1870	62	22,865	14,068	2,257	20,365	1,908	1,237	12,378	5,941	43,596
1871	62	24,321	15,154	2,522	20,365	2,320	1,207	13,095	7,308	46,271
1872	62	25,023	15,223	2,016	20,405	3,005	1,298	13,275	6,902	46,637
1873	62	26,362	15,222	2,459	20,505	3,511	1,029	13,273	7,283	48,043
1874	62	28,160	14,932	2,171	20,505	4,082	1,642	12,991	7,931	49,009
1875	62	28,217	14,990	2,365	20,580	4,290	1,580	12,910	7,306	48,884
1876	62	27,413	14,989	2,410	20,580	4,336	1,420	12,403	8,073	48,591
1877	62	25,531	14,792	2,325	20,080	3,628	1,293	12,203	7,184	46,217
1878	61	24,144	15,655	2,008	20,010	3,510	1,202	12,060	6,794	46,002
1879	61	24,320	16,603	1,918	20,010	3,527	1,066	13,277	7,646	47,401
1880	61	26,132	16,121	2,597	20,010	3,604	1,087	13,901	8,900	49,556
1881	62	28,519	17,215	2,477	20,065	3,763	1,211	14,719	11,317	53,521
1882	62	30,079	16,297	2,340	20,315	3,961	1,327	14,143	11,461	53,744
1883	63	30,812	16,237	2,258	20,540	4,071	1,348	14,187	11,719	54,565
1884	63	30,178	15,627	2,464	20,540	4,001	1,483	13,086	11,562	53,779
1885	61	31,003	13,997	2,507	20,340	3,955	1,268	12,057	13,096	53,291
1886	61	33,111	10,644	2,414	20,340	4,082	1,636	9,193	13,749	51,928
1887	61	34,521	5,471	2,253	20,340	4,244	1,887	4,643	13,918	47,923
1888	60	35,560	5,339	2,379	20,284	4,304	1,942	4,589	14,999	49,621

CONNECTICUT.

Date.	No. of banks.	Loans and discounts.	U. S. bonds.	Cash and cash items.	Capital.	Surplus.	Undivided profits.	Outstanding circulation.	Individual deposits.	Total.
1863	2	308	179	45	314	....	7	....	378	724
1864	20	4,561	6,023	944	5,074	186	338	3,009	2,447	13,615
1865	81	23,625	22,188	4,210	23,900	2,390	1,433	9,816	11,060	58,706
1866	82	26,236	22,670	4,503	24,584	2,897	1,541	16,896	12,257	62,533
1867	82	27,453	22,844	4,204	24,584	3,476	1,619	17,352	11,327	61,105
1868	81	28,250	22,934	3,812	24,624	3,858	1,633	17,347	12,420	62,103
1869	81	29,068	21,774	3,659	24,607	4,484	1,708	17,363	11,554	63,013
1870	81	31,530	21,203	3,772	25,037	5,080	1,576	17,280	11,982	64,674
1871	81	34,111	21,567	3,754	25,057	5,583	1,727	17,653	14,142	67,525
1872	81	35,611	20,791	4,090	25,292	6,214	1,744	17,846	14,332	67,784
1873	80	35,809	20,724	3,661	25,325	6,782	1,823	17,854	13,706	69,306
1874	80	35,395	20,731	4,081	25,425	7,253	1,748	17,582	13,820	67,673
1875	81	36,380	20,809	4,250	25,796	7,544	1,732	17,292	15,649	70,383
1876	82	34,424	20,597	3,993	26,040	7,461	1,675	16,732	14,602	68,507
1877	81	33,003	21,206	3,871	25,548	6,403	1,409	16,606	14,764	66,392
1878	82	30,809	22,711	4,167	25,505	6,215	1,311	17,471	15,741	67,955
1879	84	34,012	22,717	3,843	25,505	6,261	1,269	18,039	17,133	69,794
1880	84	39,853	20,885	4,245	25,405	6,008	1,461	17,604	21,147	74,531
1881	85	43,623	21,326	4,426	25,540	6,701	1,747	17,906	25,761	80,113
1882	86	43,460	20,220	4,482	25,857	6,789	1,948	17,218	24,933	78,567
1883	88	42,183	19,879	4,430	25,927	6,870	1,940	17,111	22,542	76,632
1884	88	40,557	19,152	4,444	25,957	6,894	1,806	16,482	21,147	77,436
1885	84	40,601	18,901	4,702	24,922	6,718	1,739	15,933	24,483	77,041
1886	84	42,845	15,943	4,862	24,672	6,855	2,057	13,654	25,847	77,071
1887	83	43,114	10,438	4,200	24,505	6,908	1,937	8,690	24,479	70,296
1888	84	43,818	12,026	4,426	24,194	6,925	1,903	7,871	27,505	74,763

SUMMARY, BY STATES, OF THE NUMBER OF NATIONAL BANKS, THE IMPORTANT ITEMS OF RESOURCES AND LIABILITIES, AND THE TOTALS, ETC.—Continued.

NEW YORK.*

Date.	No. of banks.	Loans and discounts.	U. S. bonds.	Cash and cash items.	Capital.	Surplus.	Undivided profits.	Outstanding circulation.	Individual deposits.	Total.
		Thousands.	Thousands.	Thousands.	Thousands.	Thousands.	Thousands.	Thousands.	Thousands.	Thousands.
1863	5	$170	$318	$77	$483	....	$4	....	$130	$767
1864	81	9,193	10,343	2,[illegible]	8,[illegible]	[illegible]	622	3,836	7,983	26,845
1865	244	53,933	39,635	13,244	50,732	2,913	3,623	10,419	43,168	155,[illegible]
1866	250	62,572	42,012	15,972	49,733	4,253	4,034	30,196	52,635	147,451
1867	248	63,856	42,963	14,693	48,313	5,183	4,406	31,911	50,528	143,141
1868	243	68,300	42,774	13,088	40,097	6,152	4,923	32,018	54,181	147,386
1869	240	68,287	39,037	11,876	38,472	6,879	5,316	31,036	47,117	140,464
1870	238	68,834	38,724	12,100	39,013	7,603	5,[illegible]	30,639	47,383	143,720
1871	237	77,397	38,843	11,268	39,236	8,160	5,012	30,302	55,903	150,121
1872	236	79,238	37,789	10,303	38,939	8,784	5,461	30,796	53,734	147,573
1873	229	80,610	35,367	10,847	38,173	9,210	5,080	30,204	56,364	150,209
1874	228	77,097	36,183	10,673	37,553	9,323	5,636	29,685	57,027	148,034
1875	238	75,062	33,471	12,890	37,463	9,357	5,811	28,911	56,909	147,767
1876	234	74,839	33,028	9,238	37,197	9,623	5,421	27,423	53,112	141,312
1877	234	69,063	36,704	9,607	35,710	9,367	5,078	27,389	52,386	137,739
1878	233	65,876	38,367	9,[illegible]	35,294	9,106	4,[illegible]	27,700	50,558	135,085
1879	238	64,300	30,924	9,770	34,472	8,777	4,492	27,960	56,722	140,190
1880	240	74,386	36,042	10,972	34,697	9,1[illegible]	4,670	28,149	63,450	152,205
1881	240	83,098	38,614	11,767	34,630	9,476	5,126	27,844	77,162	162,394
1882	256	88,278	35,836	12,229	35,931	9,732	5,776	26,326	84,066	172,978
1883	267	95,743	34,336	12,383	36,344	10,239	6,013	27,733	88,467	175,918
1884	274	93,936	32,361	12,957	37,023	10,362	6,265	26,656	90,874	171,156
1885	273	91,120	31,264	14,988	36,370	10,194	5,820	25,219	84,952	177,186
1886	271	101,317	27,710	14,736	36,093	10,733	6,471	22,827	93,084	178,662
1887	275	107,989	22,774	13,994	36,474	11,368	6,739	18,423	93,282	178,088
1888	276	110,170	22,339	14,833	36,793	12,099	7,033	16,092	99,451	184,083

* Exclusive of New York City.

NEW YORK CITY.

Date.	No. of banks.	Loans and discounts.	U. S. bonds.	Cash and cash items.	Capital.	Surplus.	Undivided profits.	Outstanding circulation.	Individual deposits.	Total.
1863	2	282	400	[illegible]	500	....	2	....	202	873
1864	12	17,[illegible]	12,963	12,135	11,185	36	611	3,728	13,517	46,430
1865	57	121,928	67,744	132,363	74,[illegible]	16,758	8,[illegible]	17,618	176,891	383,[illegible]
1866	58	167,243	83,493	165,[illegible]	73,000	13,[illegible]	8,247	30,487	211,273	422,[illegible]
1867	57	180,368	61,382	172,473	74,810	18,049	7,[illegible]	34,050	212,076	411,049
1868	54	183,883	58,[illegible]	182,096	74,358	18,871	8,[illegible]	35,031	224,171	432,318
1869	54	158,744	48,248	151,818	73,218	17,709	13,[illegible]	34,063	190,328	[illegible],363
1870	54	165,082	48,126	128,[illegible]	73,435	18,[illegible]	[illegible]	32,943	167,010	373,132
1871	54	168,[illegible]	48,731	130,[illegible]	73,235	19,[illegible]	[illegible]	30,633	157,062	422,746
1872	50	183,411	39,663	142,024	71,[illegible]	20,[illegible]	[illegible]	25,671	188,327	[illegible],977
1873	48	193,343	37,832	118,778	[illegible]	21,923	14,[illegible]	27,482	167,313	399,456
1874	48	202,[illegible]	30,183	130,142	[illegible]	[illegible]	12,[illegible]	23,292	201,323	421,734
1875	48	202,442	33,313	115,[illegible]	68,[illegible]	22,[illegible]	11,943	18,309	173,404	369,736
1876	47	181,314	33,147	128,[illegible]	[illegible]	18,[illegible]	8,897	14,853	184,083	384,224
1877	47	169,271	41,227	103,583	57,[illegible]	16,[illegible]	9,247	13,335	162,400	344,782
1878	47	160,717	62,374	116,918	53,[illegible]	15,920	8,[illegible]	20,028	172,442	364,779
1879	47	185,177	41,336	130,363	51,[illegible]	15,[illegible]	9,097	22,329	218,334	429,810
1880	47	228,403	28,002	173,722	50,650	18,183	10,396	18,583	292,045	477,084
1881	48	248,[illegible]	31,668	214,364	51,150	19,047	12,832	20,113	295,[illegible]	542,631
1882	50	179,[illegible]	26,471	244,432	51,[illegible]	21,314	13,971	19,270	323,269	537,342
1883	48	245,470	22,394	144,[illegible]	50,[illegible]	23,873	11,282	13,384	221,672	457,218
1884	44	236,[illegible]	[illegible]	143,740	44,250	22,683	11,031	13,203	184,556	415,701
1885	44	236,390	17,632	176,907	45,[illegible]	22,176	10,467	9,017	226,928	479,249
1886	45	233,843	13,344	130,816	45,130	27,731	10,834	8,130	194,916	463,032
1887	46	306,[illegible]	13,040	144,132	49,150	30,580	10,091	8,206	225,282	460,421
1888	46	302,772	17,744	166,362	49,160	31,061	12,415	6,096	261,466	567,062

SUMMARY, BY STATES, OF THE NUMBER OF NATIONAL BANKS, THE IMPORTANT ITEMS OF RESOURCES AND LIABILITIES, AND THE TOTALS, ETC.—Continued.

NEW JERSEY.

Date.	No. of banks.	Loans and discounts.	U. S. bonds.	Cash and cash items.	Capital.	Surplus.	Undivided profits.	Outstanding circulation.	Individual deposits.	Total.
		Thousands.	*Thousands*	*Thousands.*	*Thousands.*	*Thousands.*	*Thousands.*	*Thousands.*	*Thousands*	*Thousands.*
1863	1	$35	$60	$31	$84	....	$2	....	$108	$2 8
1864	15	1,223	2,530	508	1,068	....	127	$1,298	1,249	5,109
1865	54	14,641	12,052	3,664	10,933	$1,166	862	3,987	11,729	35,911
1866	54	16,831	12,086	4,009	11,233	1,607	914	8,061	14,076	39,915
1867	54	17,931	11,813	3,531	11,333	1,938	1,010	9,056	12,710	38,571
1868	55	19,195	11,930	3,510	11,483	2,245	1,196	9,318	14,165	40,684
1869	54	20,324	11,545	3,305	11,465	2,451	1,271	9,238	13,810	41,069
1870	54	21,216	11,268	3,436	11,803	2,619	1,350	9,237	14,727	42,557
1871	57	24,522	12,131	3,771	12,480	2,900	1,456	9,854	18,706	48,502
1872	59	25,401	12,288	3,679	13,184	3,205	1,574	10,391	17,439	48,760
1873	62	26,058	12,700	3,777	13,858	3,517	1,654	10,920	17,396	50,920
1874	62	25,053	12,963	4,156	13,808	3,087	1,513	11,094	17,000	50,488
1875	66	26,000	12,801	4,116	14,245	3,825	1,507	11,014	18,730	52,272
1876	69	24,312	13,010	3,061	14,294	3,804	1,591	10,787	18,106	51,131
1877	69	24,154	13,252	3,923	14,203	3,876	1,593	11,065	17,797	50,604
1878	68	22,572	14,248	4,001	14,033	3,703	1,375	11,279	18,584	51,001
1879	68	23,732	14,832	3,800	13,445	3,680	1,380	11,044	19,737	51,529
1880	66	26,496	13,266	4,412	12,995	3,714	1,390	10,664	24,525	55,832
1881	67	29,267	13,020	4,240	12,900	3,844	1,651	10,387	28,251	59,504
1882	66	31,482	12,131	4,021	12,375	3,623	1,583	9,770	28,606	58,546
1883	69	33,349	11,214	4,023	12,263	3,824	1,703	9,351	29,700	59,761
1884	71	30,182	10,406	5,179	12,253	3,886	1,702	8,437	28,743	57,980
1885	72	29,365	10,480	5,018	12,208	3,800	1,821	8,007	32,501	60,734
1886	74	35,564	9,140	5,793	12,298	4,082	2,008	7,258	35,737	64,849
1887	81	40,408	7,557	5,238	13,024	4,501	2,137	6,001	38,644	67,715
1888	85	42,062	8,681	5,906	13,318	5,155	2,158	5,903	42,138	74,843

PENNSYLVANIA.

Date.	No. of banks.	Loans and discounts.	U. S. bonds.	Cash and cash items.	Capital.	Surplus.	Undivided profits.	Outstanding circulation.	Individual deposits.	Total.
1863	15	855	1,630	453	1,080	....	25	....	2,004	3,927
1864	80	11,938	15,375	7,059	10,508	44	803	7,208	16,708	41,410
1865	195	64,012	66,080	36,698	46,502	7,733	6,326	28,572	68,770	187,243
1866	201	69,001	58,523	44,742	48,501	8,712	4,505	36,595	78,026	188,063
1867	199	78,028	55,375	34,128	49,262	10,543	4,791	37,975	71,991	187,981
1868	198	82,903	54,805	35,166	49,307	12,074	4,680	38,234	75,064	192,444
1869	197	85,292	50,018	29,863	49,610	13,342	4,808	38,227	68,982	186,624
1870	196	87,589	48,702	28,227	49,400	14,220	4,487	38,170	68,553	185,944
1871	197	97,656	54,402	33,021	50,810	14,907	4,880	39,813	81,937	211,710
1872	201	102,580	49,444	27,860	51,820	15,924	4,903	40,737	80,760	206,350
1873	202	109,404	49,594	27,823	52,710	17,123	4,701	41,525	86,846	218,544
1874	204	112,779	49,967	30,640	53,010	17,665	5,158	41,504	89,152	220,668
1875	228	118,115	50,990	32,173	56,048	17,985	5,108	42,100	96,373	234,458
1876	237	115,788	49,354	37,389	57,209	18,170	4,980	39,425	97,571	235,857
1877	232	112,464	49,184	36,438	55,927	18,100	4,757	39,320	90,504	223,077
1878	234	102,338	53,180	29,327	55,603	17,823	4,197	40,496	84,307	216,089
1879	235	106,560	55,722	32,813	55,117	17,620	4,422	42,028	96,637	233,211
1880	240	121,814	53,730	38,506	56,153	17,800	4,902	42,890	110,501	264,175
1881	245	139,206	56,407	38,024	56,518	19,061	6,129	42,420	138,046	287,581
1882	253	154,440	56,378	41,870	57,452	19,733	6,325	40,619	148,490	297,030
1883	271	160,014	49,604	39,815	59,203	21,139	6,043	41,170	151,621	302,611
1884	281	155,501	46,856	41,191	60,422	22,091	6,816	39,052	143,543	295,802
1885	285	157,723	45,841	40,306	61,001	23,007	6,738	37,480	156,634	306,066
1886	294	180,196	37,357	44,449	63,703	24,091	7,575	30,802	166,207	319,389
1887	303	195,902	21,329	43,021	66,389	26,367	7,931	17,350	175,239	321,071
1888	313	206,733	22,438	46,394	67,030	28,218	8,338	16,566	190,494	344,849

SUMMARY, BY STATES, OF THE NUMBER OF NATIONAL BANKS, THE IMPORTANT ITEMS OF RESOURCES AND LIABILITIES, AND THE TOTALS, ETC.—Continued.

DELAWARE.

Date.	No. of banks.	Loans and discounts.	U. S. bonds.	Cash and cash items.	Capital.	Surplus.	Undivided profits.	Outstanding circulation.	Individual deposits.	Total.
		Thousands.	*Thousands.*	*Thousands.*	*Thousands.*	*Thousands.*	*Thousands.*	*Thousands.*	*Thousands.*	*Thousands.*
1863	0	....	....	....	....	....	....	....	....	....
1864	1	$255	$281	$96	$300	....	$6	$124	$150	$716
1865	11	1,752	1,376	367	1,328	$242	62	413	1,555	4,470
1866	11	2,205	1,485	408	1,428	259	71	1,161	1,532	4,930
1867	11	2,144	1,421	398	1,428	288	68	1,196	1,483	4,753
1868	11	2,235	1,447	377	1,428	309	79	1,191	1,370	4,727
1869	11	2,183	1,409	408	1,428	318	81	1,186	1,436	4,841
1870	11	2,224	1,417	383	1,428	314	77	1,186	1,320	4,727
1871	11	2,419	1,504	425	1,528	360	77	1,278	1,052	5,256
1872	11	2,616	1,514	390	1,528	387	87	1,284	1,730	5,309
1873	11	2,480	1,514	418	1,523	422	72	1,286	1,530	5,26[illegible]
1874	11	2,510	1,514	460	1,523	429	89	1,280	1,642	5,245
1875	11	2,637	1,513	469	1,523	438	91	1,283	2,011	5,672
1876	13	2,684	1,601	520	1,621	449	99	1,385	1,918	5,727
1877	13	2,808	1,608	415	1,664	450	111	1,389	2,171	6,028
1878	14	3,028	1,602	506	1,764	454	105	1,408	2,199	6,240
1879	14	2,847	1,845	496	1,764	463	108	1,437	2,401	6,437
1880	14	3,318	1,998	552	1,764	476	138	1,482	3,057	7,208
1881	14	3,497	2,106	622	1,744	509	143	1,438	3,754	7,998
1882	14	4,003	1,931	570	1,744	543	187	1,451	4,122	8,413
1883	15	4,011	1,806	633	1,784	616	186	1,466	4,539	8,989
1884	15	4,337	1,826	654	1,824	645	194	1,576	3,871	8,631
1885	15	3,007	1,831	706	1,824	684	208	1,551	3,987	8,516
1886	16	4,662	1,675	789	2,034	724	226	1,442	4,158	8,951
1887	17	5,004	1,646	655	2,084	790	238	1,416	4,050	8,914
1888	18	5,415	1,649	758	2,130	831	271	1,407	4,978	9,909

MARYLAND.

Date.	No. of banks.	Loans and discounts.	U. S. bonds.	Cash and cash items.	Capital.	Surplus.	Undivided profits.	Outstanding circulation.	Individual deposits.	Total.
1863	0	....	....	....	....	....	....	....	....	....
1864	3	1,172	2,778	1,066	1,560	20	160	1,106	1,900	5,460
1865	27	16,108	11,732	8,077	11,910	1,170	855	2,247	15,212	38,923
1866	32	17,472	11,960	7,725	12,590	1,292	878	8,246	14,130	40,872
1867	32	17,204	11,567	6,752	12,590	1,475	1,032	8,765	13,358	40,130
1868	32	18,190	11,639	6,804	12,790	1,775	959	8,848	13,313	40,977
1869	31	18,210	10,945	5,554	12,740	2,045	1,088	8,807	11,798	39,332
1870	31	20,173	10,787	5,714	13,240	2,280	1,015	8,830	12,878	41,473
1871	32	22,279	10,868	5,917	13,590	2,377	1,239	9,090	14,410	44,713
1872	33	22,840	11,074	5,516	13,640	2,548	1,338	9,183	15,252	45,643
1873	33	23,704	11,207	5,237	13,640	2,835	1,303	9,161	15,272	46,604
1874	31	23,882	10,604	6,033	13,650	2,966	1,418	8,845	15,747	45,920
1875	31	24,733	10,340	5,823	13,774	3,035	1,433	8,685	17,204	47,220
1876	31	22,041	10,028	6,092	13,774	3,055	1,012	7,222	16,480	44,506
1877	32	23,807	9,936	7,445	13,290	3,204	901	7,194	17,648	45,081
1878	32	21,598	10,242	5,715	12,865	3,031	917	7,144	16,026	42,813
1879	33	22,509	10,503	6,856	12,795	2,989	1,009	7,360	17,936	45,765
1880	35	27,705	10,506	6,323	13,222	3,121	1,104	8,068	21,432	50,850
1881	38	30,255	11,178	8,523	13,603	3,260	1,439	8,605	20,117	57,083
1882	39	31,576	10,650	6,805	13,922	3,344	1,644	8,794	23,996	55,600
1883	41	33,089	10,290	6,988	14,208	3,626	1,610	8,628	25,571	58,228
1884	44	32,737	9,087	6,841	14,392	3,793	1,710	7,498	23,304	54,784
1885	44	31,543	9,036	9,576	14,430	3,979	1,559	6,900	26,630	57,501
1886	45	33,658	7,448	6,561	14,430	4,048	1,739	6,166	24,603	55,095
1887	48	33,152	4,166	6,420	14,510	4,446	1,470	3,155	24,830	52,088
1888	48	35,888	3,080	7,122	14,580	4,812	1,535	1,930	20,985	55,537

SUMMARY, BY STATES, OF THE NUMBER OF NATIONAL BANKS, THE IMPORTANT ITEMS OF RESOURCES AND LIABILITIES, AND THE TOTALS, ETC.—Continued.

DISTRICT OF COLUMBIA.

Date.	No. of banks.	Loans and discounts.	U. S. bonds.	Cash and cash items.	Capital.	Surplus.	Undivided profits.	Outstanding circulation.	Individual deposits.	Total.
		Thousands.	*Thousands.*	*Thousands.*	*Thousands.*	*Thousands.*	*Thousands.*	*Thousands.*	*Thousands.*	*Thousands.*
1863	1	$99	$175	$54	$300	....	....	....	$31	$531
1864	1	775	1,088	1,201	500	$8	$55	$440	3,778	4,847
1865	6	2,093	8,293	3,403	1,550	67	265	1,044	5,483	18,396
1866	5	1,438	3,755	1,145	1,350	171	88	1,067	1,448	7,131
1867	5	1,424	2,892	1,248	1,350	205	153	1,033	1,855	6,547
1868	5	1,527	2,024	1,312	1,350	235	260	1,034	2,121	6,290
1869	3	1,476	1,560	760	1,050	241	97	810	1,497	4,315
1870	3	1,419	1,438	777	1,050	251	57	810	1,363	4,244
1871	3	1,483	1,332	846	1,030	250	63	826	1,481	4,612
1872	5	2,393	1,820	1,145	1,563	326	108	1,327	2,870	6,522
1873	4	1,808	1,291	495	1,152	284	73	976	1,765	4,473
1874	5	1,883	1,301	451	1,352	301	128	1,059	1,761	4,792
1875	5	2,138	1,470	482	1,532	311	154	1,187	1,716	5,192
1876	5	2,049	1,089	536	1,532	325	101	832	1,611	4,788
1877	6	1,808	1,109	511	1,433	348	108	860	1,788	4,732
1878	7	1,913	1,497	606	1,507	342	115	1,014	2,104	5,260
1879	6	1,480	1,570	847	1,377	343	102	948	1,924	4,861
1880	6	1,736	1,445	710	1,377	330	117	917	2,155	5,092
1881	6	2,090	1,515	636	1,377	309	117	844	2,527	5,372
1882	6	2,201	1,419	652	1,377	291	137	810	3,102	5,881
1883	6	2,531	1,513	802	1,377	339	141	848	3,367	6,272
1884	6	2,356	1,510	1,013	1,377	362	152	847	3,211	6,150
1885	6	2,519	1,632	1,373	1,377	367	173	815	4,212	7,135
1886	7	3,417	2,103	2,113	1,577	443	254	679	6,879	10,132
1887	8	4,375	2,035	2,112	1,827	541	246	729	7,272	10,944
1888	8	4,593	1,946	2,255	1,827	627	274	637	8,056	11,836

VIRGINIA.

Date.	No. of banks.	Loans and discounts.	U. S. bonds.	Cash and cash items.	Capital.	Surplus.	Undivided profits.	Outstanding circulation.	Individual deposits.	Total.
1863	0	....	....	....	....	....	....	....	....	....
1864	1	250	175	53	100	....	16	80	388	507
1865	10	1,809	1,877	1,077	1,089	34	121	612	3,910	7,246
1866	20	3,410	2,812	1,464	2,500	67	184	2,041	3,558	8,944
1867	19	3,499	2,654	1,252	2,400	148	182	2,030	3,310	8,660
1868	19	3,889	2,585	1,143	2,400	166	184	2,050	3,478	9,050
1869	16	4,044	2,583	688	2,223	169	162	2,060	2,936	8,530
1870	17	4,703	2,736	864	2,375	225	180	2,128	3,593	9,522
1871	23	7,155	4,051	1,272	3,570	322	209	3,160	5,079	14,601
1872	24	8,527	4,318	1,203	3,835	428	349	3,403	6,459	15,978
1873	23	7,758	3,684	1,102	3,585	540	368	2,880	6,068	14,766
1874	20	7,046	3,744	1,149	3,536	640	360	2,800	5,035	13,775
1875	20	7,456	3,412	1,201	3,587	730	421	2,541	5,064	13,756
1876	19	6,958	3,174	1,172	3,385	781	375	2,265	5,186	13,178
1877	19	6,601	3,202	1,297	3,285	830	321	2,108	5,283	12,855
1878	18	6,380	3,225	1,172	3,185	810	232	2,176	4,975	12,402
1879	17	6,582	3,187	1,126	2,806	793	243	2,280	5,020	12,735
1880	17	7,447	3,306	1,209	2,806	823	310	2,303	6,600	14,348
1881	18	9,227	3,608	1,375	2,906	943	415	2,445	9,089	17,413
1882	21	10,444	3,848	2,056	3,203	1,070	493	2,647	10,293	19,371
1883	23	12,039	3,840	1,945	3,496	1,060	623	2,615	12,386	22,022
1884	24	11,738	3,191	2,168	3,537	1,263	503	2,281	10,706	19,976
1885	24	9,400	2,644	2,007	3,576	1,143	475	2,008	8,377	17,076
1886	24	10,552	2,788	2,039	3,732	1,228	506	1,915	9,532	18,336
1887	25	10,825	2,612	1,800	3,796	1,415	488	1,204	9,786	18,802
1888	26	11,109	2,855	2,027	3,846	1,516	513	1,026	10,177	20 115

SUMMARY, BY STATES, OF THE NUMBER OF NATIONAL BANKS, THE IMPORTANT ITEMS OF RESOURCES AND LIABILITIES, AND THE TOTALS, ETC.—Continued.

WEST VIRGINIA.

Date.	No. of banks.	Loans and discounts.	U. S. bonds.	Cash and cash items.	Capital.	Surplus.	Undivided profits.	Outstanding circulation.	Individual deposits.	Total.
		Thousands.	*Thousands.*	*Thousands.*	*Thousands.*	*Thousands.*	*Thousands.*	*Thousands.*	*Thousands.*	*Thousands.*
1863	0	....	....	....	....	....	....	....	....	....
1864	2	$265	$326	$204	$180	....	$28	$134	$592	$1,060
1865	13	1,368	2,280	738	1,652	$48	73	414	2,825	4,807
1866	15	2,632	2,072	1,076	2,216	107	110	1,064	2,770	7,576
1867	15	2,333	2,084	853	2,216	171	102	1,075	2,457	7,214
1868	15	2,510	2,074	705	2,216	220	97	1,071	2,514	7,364
1869	14	2,881	2,575	542	2,110	287	95	1,887	2,112	6,848
1870	14	2,890	2,400	608	2,116	302	104	1,888	2,060	6,090
1871	14	3,478	2,531	514	2,201	272	118	2,062	2,296	7,096
1872	17	4,243	2,704	585	2,506	320	142	2,280	2,060	8,675
1873	17	4,340	2,733	620	2,506	357	151	2,272	2,843	8,860
1874	17	3,382	2,290	576	2,137	391	120	1,880	2,128	7,056
1875	16	2,797	1,702	434	1,840	380	132	1,504	1,555	5,601
1876	15	2,524	1,597	354	1,740	442	107	1,303	1,240	5,054
1877	15	2,520	1,608	375	1,746	410	114	1,407	1,297	5,100
1878	15	2,390	1,540	455	1,656	406	109	1,326	1,381	5,050
1879	15	2,382	1,558	404	1,656	400	98	1,347	1,553	5,213
1880	17	2,946	1,651	527	1,761	436	110	1,429	2,040	5,930
1881	17	3,170	1,603	614	1,736	454	118	1,387	2,349	6,281
1882	18	3,480	1,644	603	1,836	408	136	1,431	2,584	6,733
1883	19	3,522	1,591	688	1,867	400	139	1,382	2,808	6,865
1884	21	3,636	1,553	653	2,001	514	141	1,356	2,695	6,990
1885	21	3,602	1,479	628	2,011	512	136	1,202	2,520	6,693
1886	20	3,565	1,143	644	1,980	485	138	880	2,685	6,439
1887	20	4,019	856	648	1,961	409	122	656	3,080	6,601
1888	20	4,144	817	685	1,966	458	157	626	3,371	6,908

NORTH CAROLINA.

Date.	No. of banks.	Loans and discounts.	U. S. bonds.	Cash and cash items.	Capital.	Surplus.	Undivided profits.	Outstanding circulation.	Individual deposits.	Total.
1863	0	....	....	....	....	....	....	....	....	....
1864	0	....	....	....	....	....	....	....	....	....
1865	2	24	61	54	68	....	3	....	52	141
1866	5	415	415	170	378	8	41	108	318	1,182
1867	5	617	546	108	585	26	44	280	348	1,582
1868	6	873	635	441	663	41	56	316	820	2,247
1869	6	1,420	730	378	847	53	102	370	1,402	3,020
1870	6	1,512	923	300	850	70	120	520	1,562	3,519
1871	9	2,449	1,685	460	1,610	87	196	1,338	2,081	5,645
1872	10	3,063	1,900	458	1,953	103	102	1,549	2,438	6,768
1873	10	3,480	1,970	602	2,100	140	186	1,608	2,540	7,142
1874	11	3,109	2,180	502	2,200	181	209	1,818	2,252	7,128
1875	11	3,373	1,931	524	2,200	210	269	1,603	2,270	6,942
1876	15	3,716	1,700	407	2,556	257	304	1,440	2,284	7,213
1877	15	3,873	1,608	402	2,601	287	310	1,272	2,253	7,106
1878	15	4,050	1,924	530	2,551	207	237	1,526	2,442	7,630
1879	15	3,836	2,254	577	2,501	203	225	1,753	2,341	7,727
1880	15	4,187	2,200	570	2,501	320	214	1,815	2,883	8,420
1881	15	4,877	2,143	705	2,501	348	274	1,077	3,041	8,838
1882	15	4,738	1,768	700	2,501	475	256	1,344	2,800	8,375
1883	15	4,832	1,568	655	2,401	473	308	1,152	3,215	8,354
1884	15	5,134	1,409	706	2,401	533	201	1,130	3,206	8,657
1885	15	4,672	1,417	720	2,004	472	236	998	3,238	8,150
1886	17	5,080	1,275	700	2,376	510	235	861	3,302	8,350
1887	18	5,323	1,020	648	2,412	544	271	706	3,537	8,507
1888	18	5,245	916	631	2,266	562	270	648	3,320	8,083

SUMMARY, BY STATES, OF THE NUMBER OF NATIONAL BANKS, THE IMPORTANT ITEMS OF RESOURCES AND LIABILITIES, AND THE TOTALS, ETC.—Continued.

SOUTH CAROLINA.

Date.	No. of banks.	Loans and discounts.	U. S. bonds.	Cash and cash items.	Capital.	Surplus.	Undivided profits.	Outstanding circulation.	Individual deposits.	Total.
		Thousands.	*Thousands.*	*Thousands.*	*Thousands.*	*Thousands.*	*Thousands.*	*Thousands.*	*Thousands.*	*Thousands.*
1863	0	....	....	....	....	....	....	....	....	....
1864	0	....	....	....	....	....	....	....	....	....
1865	0	....	....	....	....	....	....	....	....	....
1866	2	$732	$144	$390	$500	$2	$82	$63	$823	$1,502
1867	2	827	171	326	585	14	92	148	586	1,531
1868	3	1,204	204	381	685	51	70	140	1,206	2,237
1869	3	1,484	278	415	824	74	94	181	1,028	2,400
1870	3	1,829	375	437	1,081	121	70	360	961	2,860
1871	7	2,818	1,380	559	1,900	151	116	1,224	1,656	5,330
1872	8	3,274	1,853	530	2,400	189	180	1,650	1,691	6,302
1873	12	4,044	2,425	372	3,168	339	208	2,181	1,499	7,938
1874	12	4,034	2,010	409	3,135	362	313	1,706	1,605	7,799
1875	12	4,500	1,760	654	3,135	407	234	1,566	1,920	8,204
1876	12	4,103	1,585	674	3,185	462	229	1,271	1,620	7,722
1877	12	3,880	1,620	410	2,871	450	242	1,224	1,623	7,148
1878	12	3,766	1,620	575	2,851	433	203	1,200	1,640	7,222
1879	12	3,468	1,700	757	2,450	354	254	1,301	2,101	7,101
1880	12	4,115	1,690	690	2,450	368	307	1,331	2,586	7,828
1881	13	4,483	1,685	676	1,885	418	305	1,187	2,970	7,978
1882	13	4,306	1,610	517	1,885	608	358	1,170	2,505	7,701
1883	13	4,530	1,505	640	1,885	754	443	1,118	2,584	7,791
1884	14	4,646	1,501	759	1,935	773	588	1,096	2,418	7,931
1885	14	4,500	1,414	840	1,935	802	500	1,002	2,723	8,166
1886	16	4,764	1,250	808	1,779	814	580	874	3,600	8,463
1887	15	4,944	1,023	1,001	1,698	779	709	560	3,545	8,633
1888	16	5,970	1,172	646	1,773	788	798	420	3,096	9,361

GEORGIA.

Date.	No. of banks.	Loans and discounts.	U. S. bonds.	Cash and cash items.	Capital.	Surplus.	Undivided profits.	Outstanding circulation.	Individual deposits.	Total.
1863	0	....	....	....	....	....	....	....	....	....
1864	0	....	....	....	....	....	....	....	....	....
1865	1	97	40	219	100	....	15	....	350	466
1866	9	1,441	1,775	1,060	1,600	30	102	1,070	1,916	5,226
1867	8	1,786	1,784	812	1,600	105	199	1,224	1,207	4,862
1868	8	2,092	1,684	1,221	1,600	134	233	1,232	2,074	5,757
1869	7	2,275	1,384	836	1,500	187	232	1,147	1,631	5,001
1870	8	2,504	1,646	1,057	1,815	230	295	1,148	1,682	5,777
1871	10	3,167	2,306	926	2,364	260	282	1,804	1,793	7,031
1872	11	3,169	2,506	1,083	2,615	367	298	2,115	1,932	7,057
1873	13	3,906	2,637	706	2,785	419	423	2,215	1,821	8,092
1874	13	3,445	2,076	755	2,785	456	374	2,223	1,578	7,773
1875	12	3,108	2,151	1,071	2,663	450	251	1,735	1,557	7,053
1876	12	2,719	2,100	803	2,335	401	192	1,804	1,653	6,638
1877	12	2,775	2,102	783	2,141	353	164	1,624	1,604	6,369
1878	12	2,580	2,157	989	2,041	367	170	1,772	1,625	6,508
1879	13	3,045	2,204	878	2,166	381	177	1,800	1,708	7,249
1880	13	3,602	2,323	862	2,221	432	180	1,940	2,012	7,850
1881	12	4,468	2,273	1,107	2,281	481	252	1,807	2,766	8,818
1882	12	4,711	2,104	944	2,281	545	303	1,825	2,752	8,965
1883	13	5,252	1,962	845	2,331	635	323	1,659	2,813	9,199
1884	15	4,931	1,975	1,046	2,436	815	282	1,638	2,541	9,135
1885	16	5,383	1,902	1,226	2,472	813	337	1,571	3,335	9,667
1886	17	6,306	1,224	1,203	2,686	898	433	979	4,010	10,215
1887	21	7,789	1,139	1,401	3,051	952	513	878	5,003	12,156
1888	24	8,662	1,120	1,340	3,361	1,055	617	860	4,813	12,988

SUMMARY, BY STATES, OF THE NUMBER OF NATIONAL BANKS, THE IMPORTANT ITEMS OF RESOURCES AND LIABILITIES, AND THE TOTALS, ETC.—Continued.

FLORIDA.

Date.	No. of banks.	Loans and discounts.	U. S. bonds.	Cash and cash items.	Capital.	Surplus.	Undivided profits.	Outstanding circulation.	Individual deposits.	Total.
		Thousands.	*Thousands.*	*Thousands.*	*Thousands.*	*Thousands.*	*Thousands.*	*Thousands.*	*Thousands.*	*Thousands.*
1863	0									
1864	0									
1865	0									
1866	0									
1867	0									
1868	0									
1869	0									
1870	0									
1871	0									
1872	0									
1873	0									
1874	1	$3	$30	$30	$38			$27	$11	$76
1875	1	56	50	33	50		$5	41	71	167
1876	1	59	53	34	50	$1	4	44	66	166
1877	1	77	50	16	50	2	2	45	48	167
1878	1	82	68	15	50	2	8	45	51	185
1879	1	73	90	26	50	2	6	45	100	206
1880	2	129	81	31	100	2	4	45	157	312
1881	2	200	81	69	100	8	8	67	319	502
1882	2	292	80	90	100	11	15	55	401	582
1883	2	371	80	97	100	15	13	58	401	600
1884	3	432	93	109	150	16	11	82	496	787
1885	5	645	203	207	300	20	36	120	782	1,334
1886	9	1,298	301	298	550	33	60	105	1,437	2,462
1887	8	1,442	282	318	500	66	52	147	1,516	2,508
1888	13	1,980	480	402	897	99	79	195	2,049	3,725

ALABAMA.

Date.	No. of banks.	Loans and discounts.	U. S. bonds.	Cash and cash items.	Capital.	Surplus.	Undivided profits.	Outstanding circulation.	Individual deposits.	Total.
1863	0									
1864	0									
1865	*a* 2									
1866	3	458	459	1,066	500	8	75	262	1,033	2,208
1867	2	428	311	171	400	14	40	268	294	1,091
1868	2	380	311	263	400	14	54	267	322	1,114
1869	2	325	311	175	400	14	72	261	286	1,039
1870	2	526	311	108	400	15	74	265	312	1,074
1871	7	1,011	842	214	948	38	45	693	536	2,334
1872	8	1,580	1,184	370	1,287	75	72	1,013	1,001	3,581
1873	9	1,743	1,430	302	1,579	127	93	1,269	872	4,075
1874	9	1,006	1,571	434	1,635	163	69	1,383	977	4,410
1875	9	1,455	1,612	463	1,635	182	80	1,401	957	4,353
1876	10	1,700	1,643	449	1,603	168	65	1,430	850	4,468
1877	10	1,760	1,521	353	1,668	186	77	1,349	768	4,231
1878	10	2,133	1,691	453	1,668	161	86	1,439	1,188	5,083
1879	10	1,923	1,711	644	1,668	193	101	1,463	1,407	5,156
1880	9	2,236	1,556	421	1,518	221	144	1,320	1,810	5,037
1881	9	2,244	1,497	526	1,518	250	197	1,280	1,719	5,326
1882	9	2,532	1,277	488	1,408	283	187	1,009	1,647	5,196
1883	10	2,380	1,288	463	1,403	277	191	1,069	1,568	4,996
1884	10	2,099	1,134	584	1,735	256	188	929	1,828	5,777
1885	10	3,266	1,217	580	1,835	291	213	900	2,143	6,248
1886	12	4,316	1,073	637	1,935	357	324	872	3,350	7,669
1887	20	8,503	951	1,062	3,485	640	451	782	5,925	13,016
1888	21	7,450	1,163	1,124	3,544	724	495	749	4,785	12,261

a No report.

SUMMARY, BY STATES, OF THE NUMBER OF NATIONAL BANKS, THE IMPORTANT ITEMS OF RESOURCES AND LIABILITIES, AND THE TOTALS, ETC.—Continued.

MISSISSIPPI.

Date.	No. of banks.	Loans and discounts.	U. S. bonds.	Cash and cash items.	Capital.	Surplus.	Undivided profits.	Outstanding circulation.	Individual deposits.	Total.
		Thousands.	*Thousands.*	*Thousands.*	*Thousands.*	*Thousands.*	*Thousands.*	*Thousands.*	*Thousands.*	*Thousands.*
1863	0	....	....	....	....	....	....	....	....	....
1864	0	....	....	....	....	....	....	....	....	....
1865	1	$16	$57	$70	$30	....	$6	....	$80	$163
1866	2	182	126	102	150	$25	21	$41	188	464
1867	2	180	77	85	150	7	17	66	152	403
1868	1	63	45	17	100	2	6	41	....	148
1869	0	....	....	....	....	....	....	....	....	....
1870	0	....	....	....	....	....	....	....	....	....
1871	0	....	....	....	....	....	....	....	....	....
1872	0	....	....	....	....	....	....	....	....	....
1873	0	....	....	....	....	....	....	....	....	....
1874	0	....	....	....	....	....	....	....	....	....
1875	0	....	....	....	....	....	....	....	....	....
1876	0	....	....	....	....	....	....	....	....	....
1877	0	....	....	....	....	....	....	....	....	....
1878	0	....	....	....	....	....	....	....	....	....
1879	0	....	....	....	....	....	....	....	....	....
1880	0	....	....	....	....	....	....	....	....	....
1881	0	....	....	....	....	....	....	....	....	....
1882	1	132	75	52	75	....	9	68	108	284
1883	3	326	150	124	175	3	23	138	310	704
1884	4	406	182	107	305	11	25	158	307	903
1885	6	1,075	177	166	475	39	38	151	507	1,029
1886	7	1,626	215	213	625	69	61	181	942	2,287
1887	12	2,293	320	354	1,055	127	102	277	1,264	3,392
1888	12	2,647	393	400	1,105	242	93	293	1,370	3,814

LOUISIANA.

Date.	No. of banks.	Loans and discounts.	U. S. bonds.	Cash and cash items.	Capital.	Surplus.	Undivided profits.	Outstanding circulation.	Individual deposits.	Total.
1863	0	....	....	....	....	....	....	....	....	....
1864	1	168	300	2,343	500	....	76	166	2,210	3,121
1865	1	294	721	3,777	500	17	183	180	5,069	6,572
1866	3	1,883	1,320	2,027	1,800	35	340	710	3,637	7,339
1867	2	1,407	1,218	540	1,300	59	110	1,064	684	3,651
1868	2	1,004	1,208	993	1,300	62	105	1,059	1,124	3,781
1869	2	1,432	1,208	680	1,300	70	93	1,052	1,483	4,089
1870	2	1,816	1,208	541	1,300	107	102	1,048	1,446	4,257
1871	7	5,851	2,058	1,714	3,500	145	247	2,400	4,070	12,054
1872	9	7,770	4,114	2,370	4,850	220	311	3,540	6,425	17,427
1873	9	9,108	3,900	2,490	4,750	297	300	3,335	7,512	18,710
1874	7	5,877	2,784	2,053	3,850	272	358	2,300	4,901	12,732
1875	7	6,833	2,564	2,107	3,650	483	353	2,273	5,073	13,751
1876	7	6,422	984	2,514	3,300	539	284	883	5,922	11,783
1877	7	6,507	800	2,256	3,300	516	269	713	5,237	11,358
1878	7	5,341	1,781	2,139	2,875	573	340	1,385	4,830	10,640
1879	7	5,670	2,258	2,196	2,875	448	299	1,697	5,207	11,574
1880	7	7,107	2,153	2,348	2,875	570	320	1,874	6,013	13,256
1881	7	8,076	2,518	3,723	2,875	815	330	2,157	8,478	16,264
1882	8	8,829	2,578	2,758	2,975	985	302	2,240	8,058	16,008
1883	8	9,467	2,577	2,378	3,225	1,102	414	2,240	8,136	16,310
1884	9	8,677	2,429	2,727	3,625	1,201	555	2,158	7,122	16,037
1885	9	9,800	2,232	2,974	3,625	1,300	506	1,970	8,904	17,033
1886	9	9,771	1,811	3,550	3,525	1,154	452	1,540	9,559	18,153
1887	13	11,133	1,758	3,397	3,425	1,229	505	1,317	10,402	19,900
1888	13	12,419	2,234	3,730	3,425	1,508	395	1,327	11,912	22,618

SUMMARY, BY STATES, OF THE NUMBER OF NATIONAL BANKS, THE IMPORTANT ITEMS OF RESOURCES AND LIABILITIES, AND THE TOTALS, ETC.—Continued.

TEXAS.

Date.	No. of banks.	Loans and discounts.	U. S. bonds.	Cash and cash items.	Capital.	Surplus.	Undivided profits.	Outstanding circulation.	Individual deposits.	Total.
		Thousands.	*Thousands.*	*Thousands.*	*Thousands.*	*Thousands.*	*Thousands.*	*Thousands.*	*Thousands.*	*Thousands.*
1863	0	......	......	......	......	......	......	......	......	......
1864	0	......	......	......	......	......	......	......	......	......
1865	0	......	......	......	......	......	......	......	......	......
1866	4	$200	$430	$439	$428	$4	$30	$170	$620	$1,369
1867	4	331	674	567	576	12	89	405	495	2,018
1868	4	509	673	401	525	37	73	396	634	1,922
1869	4	475	703	426	525	42	84	386	562	1,780
1870	4	532	681	480	525	50	58	386	617	1,891
1871	5	854	801	573	625	58	78	507	1,006	2,656
1872	5	1,094	900	498	725	88	70	592	808	2,782
1873	7	1,180	1,025	609	925	180	79	670	1,044	3,334
1874	9	1,375	1,054	635	1,095	221	88	772	1,038	3,537
1875	10	1,367	964	518	1,200	260	84	673	1,081	3,618
1876	10	1,522	849	550	1,025	297	67	587	1,174	3,622
1877	12	1,706	830	665	1,123	294	127	592	1,413	4,003
1878	11	1,508	825	687	1,050	296	76	533	1,516	3,809
1879	11	1,512	935	870	1,050	296	80	507	1,604	4,120
1880	13	2,044	1,030	784	1,300	279	106	732	2,081	5,021
1881	15	3,257	1,236	1,159	1,475	316	228	905	3,691	7,484
1882	21	5,602	1,421	1,402	1,950	472	323	1,057	5,487	10,573
1883	43	10,099	1,927	2,200	3,652	1,049	683	1,462	8,003	16,789
1884	59	11,945	2,016	2,428	5,970	1,683	765	1,647	7,928	19,940
1885	68	13,777	2,076	2,714	6,880	2,002	844	1,730	9,184	22,733
1886	74	16,657	2,308	3,158	7,685	2,106	1,102	1,737	11,647	26,842
1887	91	20,762	2,765	4,063	9,920	2,431	1,119	2,108	13,710	32,969
1888	100	24,689	3,034	4,033	11,806	2,777	1,129	2,318	15,785	38,471

ARKANSAS.

Date.	No. of banks.	Loans and discounts.	U. S. bonds.	Cash and cash items.	Capital.	Surplus.	Undivided profits.	Outstanding circulation.	Individual deposits.	Total.
1863	0	......	......	......	......	......	......	......	......	......
1864	0	......	......	......	......	......	......	......	......	......
1865	0	......	......	......	......	......	......	......	......	......
1866	2	244	252	118	200	......	24	130	172	738
1867	2	361	384	195	200	20	27	170	384	1,012
1868	2	418	307	108	200	32	16	179	375	1,029
1869	2	171	271	80	200	37	1	170	73	507
1870	2	188	256	41	200	36	3	179	104	620
1871	2	185	254	40	200	31	7	179	108	613
1872	2	170	233	37	205	20	13	161	115	582
1873	2	220	255	63	205	21	19	183	120	618
1874	2	227	255	43	205	24	18	181	138	617
1875	2	174	155	43	205	26	16	94	79	481
1876	2	263	155	48	205	29	8	95	179	581
1877	2	239	206	46	205	30	9	185	186	608
1878	2	274	320	75	205	32	8	184	250	750
1879	2	264	305	93	205	36	9	184	255	784
1880	2	248	308	63	205	40	10	184	265	770
1881	2	381	325	74	205	42	21	184	412	952
1882	2	578	300	113	305	64	25	184	473	1,137
1883	5	1,103	457	218	455	70	58	207	1,007	2,076
1884	4	1,043	378	251	405	148	23	249	951	1,968
1885	6	1,801	500	260	705	166	48	323	1,514	2,938
1886	6	2,104	523	339	755	205	55	298	1,908	3,577
1887	7	2,794	611	341	950	112	102	349	2,313	4,301
1888	7	2,768	616	325	950	191	105	309	2,180	4,286

SUMMARY, BY STATES, OF THE NUMBER OF NATIONAL BANKS, THE IMPORTANT ITEMS OF RESOURCES AND LIABILITIES, AND THE TOTALS, ETC.—Continued.

KENTUCKY.

Date.	No. of banks.	Loans and discounts.	U.S. bonds.	Cash and cash items.	Capital.	Surplus.	Undivided profits.	Outstanding circulation.	Individual deposits.	Total.
		Thousands.	*Thousands.*	*Thousands.*	*Thousands.*	*Thousands.*	*Thousands.*	*Thousands.*	*Thousands.*	*Thousands.*
1863	0	....	....	....	....	....	....	....	....	....
1864	1	$83	$352	$142	$200	$4	$20	$90	$130	$550
1865	11	2,284	2,465	1,275	2,272	28	101	1,231	2,120	6,841
1866	15	2,903	3,074	885	2,840	198	107	2,300	1,700	7,827
1867	15	3,155	3,084	787	2,885	107	177	2,384	1,583	7,861
1868	15	3,107	3,022	8.9	2,885	264	207	2,330	1,416	7,088
1869	16	3,380	2,970	649	2,885	331	236	2,349	1,732	7,923
1870	17	3,762	3,003	689	3,110	396	221	2,414	1,859	8,419
1871	29	6,437	5,765	986	6,234	402	350	4,822	2,839	15,501
1872	33	8,412	7,197	1,110	7,075	570	498	6,380	3,163	18,984
1873	36	0,500	7,655	1,297	8,221	751	565	6,783	4,040	21,452
1874	43	12,580	9,430	1,935	9,900	970	750	7,980	5,449	27,333
1875	50	13,623	9,712	1,794	10,395	1,263	839	8,157	5,643	28,745
1876	48	13,488	9,470	1,647	10,097	1,509	604	7,856	5,200	28,362
1877	46	13,705	9,264	1,629	10,037	1,566	677	7,695	5,257	27,821
1878	48	12,428	9,805	1,926	9,957	1,444	627	7,784	5,836	28,187
1879	48	12,618	10,844	1,997	9,987	1,410	587	8,611	6,649	30,488
1880	49	15,847	10,906	2,021	10,197	1,518	586	8,858	8,510	33,383
1881	50	17,986	11,358	2,074	10,435	1,842	686	8,885	10,675	37,028
1882	57	19,504	11,308	2,416	11,421	2,002	914	9,190	11,506	38,936
1883	65	22,456	11,902	2,735	12,568	2,362	834	9,434	13,570	43,443
1884	67	22,873	11,712	2,641	13,010	2,666	878	9,182	11,900	42,380
1885	68	22,731	10,634	2,859	13,200	2,732	1,008	8,265	11,636	41,642
1886	68	25,243	7,703	2,532	13,310	3,104	1,054	5,449	13,097	41,636
1887	68	27,136	6,144	2,809	13,310	3,242	1,010	3,080	14,509	42,477
1888	69	27,798	5,886	2,606	13,754	3,379	1,103	3,080	14,299	42,768

TENNESSEE.

Date.	No. of banks.	Loans and discounts.	U.S. bonds.	Cash and cash items.	Capital.	Surplus.	Undivided profits.	Outstanding circulation.	Individual deposits.	Total.
1863	0	....	....	....	....	....	....	....	....	....
1864	8	87	485	554	840	....	100	127	939	1,850
1865	7	1,012	3,228	2,246	1,025	37	146	459	3,821	7,451
1866	10	2,195	2,298	1,811	1,700	183	210	1,030	4,480	8,177
1867	12	2,520	2,132	1,163	1,930	167	150	1,112	2,867	6,961
1868	12	2,240	2,481	1,020	1,925	165	141	1,143	3,087	6,969
1869	13	3,321	1,900	853	2,017	193	230	1,145	3,300	7,450
1870	13	3,207	2,175	886	1,950	222	195	1,309	2,831	7,604
1871	19	4,505	3,084	1,076	2,817	260	204	2,380	3,604	10,130
1872	22	5,224	3,407	1,132	3,140	335	275	2,726	3,914	11,340
1873	23	5,154	3,450	1,102	3,101	433	252	2,606	4,250	11,363
1874	24	4,751	3,307	1,372	3,255	447	246	2,618	3,836	10,932
1875	27	4,816	3,189	1,203	3,455	515	250	2,474	3,506	10,702
1876	25	5,019	3,051	1,200	3,350	564	230	2,308	4,343	11,400
1877	25	5,060	3,277	1,438	3,080	571	207	2,302	4,675	11,491
1878	25	4,735	3,507	1,855	3,080	479	211	2,427	5,273	12,320
1879	24	4,967	3,234	1,365	2,955	450	206	2,370	4,684	11,247
1880	23	6,341	3,234	1,711	3,005	556	207	2,477	6,586	13,391
1881	25	7,937	3,303	2,002	3,430	645	205	2,627	8,322	16,132
1882	29	8,435	3,492	1,812	3,715	695	331	2,781	7,500	15,822
1883	30	10,475	3,264	1,915	4,315	810	384	2,508	8,410	18,069
1884	33	11,458	2,925	1,776	5,005	1,066	431	2,207	8,258	18,567
1885	32	11,554	2,726	1,778	5,008	998	473	2,114	7,784	18,398
1886	33	13,608	1,930	1,783	5,418	885	671	1,328	9,224	20,260
1887	40	19,233	1,941	2,475	7,400	1,461	611	1,327	11,750	27,104
1888	42	19,850	1,873	2,418	7,715	1,616	872	1,254	11,241	27,075

SUMMARY, BY STATES, OF THE NUMBER OF NATIONAL BANKS, THE IMPORTANT ITEMS OF RESOURCES AND LIABILITIES, AND THE TOTALS, ETC.—Continued.

OHIO.

Date.	No. of banks.	Loans and discounts.	U. S. bonds.	Cash and cash items.	Capital.	Surplus.	Undivided profits.	Outstanding circulation.	Individual deposits.	Total.
		Thousands.	*Thousands.*	*Thousands.*	*Thousands.*	*Thousands.*	*Thousands.*	*Thousands.*	*Thousands.*	*Thousands.*
1863	20	$2,516	$1,403	$1,126	$2,303	....	$69	....	$2,806	$5,810
1864	82	10,367	12,402	7,332	9,772	$61	831	$5,750	14,867	34,979
1865	134	22,104	29,611	13,994	21,116	730	1,829	14,731	26,040	73,389
1866	135	28,333	28,523	11,151	21,805	1,834	2,099	18,121	23,274	75,310
1867	135	29,069	27,771	9,285	21,905	2,715	1,796	18,303	23,896	74,511
1868	135	30,924	27,521	8,524	21,556	3,402	1,916	18,272	23,002	75,078
1869	132	33,589	24,520	7,134	22,180	4,021	1,949	17,076	21,018	73,030
1870	130	33,865	23,300	7,017	22,105	4,121	1,797	17,541	21,046	72,068
1871	130	39,227	24,273	8,069	23,050	4,503	1,964	18,607	28,512	84,520
1872	158	47,999	26,796	8,374	26,701	5,119	2,355	21,706	30,018	94,464
1873	168	54,407	27,013	8,866	28,843	5,659	2,635	22,848	33,914	103,827
1874	169	52,007	27,954	9,139	29,173	6,122	2,045	22,870	32,029	101,125
1875	173	56,186	28,397	9,384	29,044	6,347	3,156	22,835	34,440	106,133
1876	170	50,264	26,847	8,704	29,033	6,237	2,932	21,435	30,025	97,724
1877	165	48,914	26,243	8,704	28,372	5,584	2,714	20,470	30,213	95,503
1878	163	44,172	26,002	10,178	27,287	5,816	2,477	19,952	30,266	93,323
1879	162	46,821	27,197	12,182	26,222	4,946	2,270	20,366	40,593	104,252
1880	170	54,402	26,801	13,193	26,502	5,107	2,554	20,045	46,773	113,863
1881	177	66,960	29,167	15,104	29,380	5,421	3,348	21,468	60,060	135,420
1882	186	74,443	27,824	14,636	32,004	5,578	3,350	20,840	60,785	136,115
1883	200	76,824	20,008	15,108	35,183	6,033	3,487	23,148	59,615	130,920
1884	204	70,664	26,673	14,716	36,308	6,202	3,212	21,164	51,684	130,317
1885	203	71,137	24,337	16,217	36,710	6,400	3,095	19,011	54,654	132,369
1886	209	85,374	22,606	17,188	38,204	6,805	3,558	16,208	67,075	150,043
1887	216	93,388	18,479	16,532	39,806	7,918	3,720	12,780	69,959	153,732
1888	219	92,125	18,808	17,187	39,949	8,313	4,032	10,725	73,710	157,820

INDIANA.

Date.	No. of banks.	Loans and discounts.	U. S. bonds.	Cash and cash items.	Capital.	Surplus.	Undivided profits.	Outstanding circulation.	Individual deposits.	Total.
1863	9	478	700	274	865	....	6	....	784	1,732
1864	31	3,277	4,315	2,058	3,550	35	258	2,828	3,734	10,853
1865	70	9,237	14,074	5,031	12,260	321	740	8,275	10,526	33,259
1866	71	13,220	14,278	4,087	12,769	917	734	10,872	7,708	34,288
1867	70	13,210	14,211	3,085	12,767	1,557	748	10,905	7,148	34,002
1868	70	14,609	14,056	3,322	12,767	2,184	802	10,990	8,007	35,487
1869	69	16,832	14,072	2,951	13,187	2,815	836	11,306	8,456	37,408
1870	69	17,055	13,029	2,790	13,277	3,207	712	10,923	7,965	37,159
1871	72	18,866	15,183	3,278	14,762	3,471	840	12,356	10,598	43,031
1872	87	23,523	16,651	3,364	16,563	3,846	1,043	14,073	12,097	49,427
1873	92	27,147	16,920	3,300	17,032	4,248	1,110	14,472	14,023	53,146
1874	93	25,728	16,066	4,034	17,064	4,500	1,345	14,555	12,538	52,350
1875	103	28,049	16,255	4,214	18,563	4,672	1,512	13,881	14,467	54,931
1876	99	25,697	14,052	3,640	17,258	4,808	1,409	11,967	12,867	49,807
1877	99	24,632	13,877	4,031	16,404	4,504	1,405	11,721	13,305	49,105
1878	94	20,498	14,209	4,802	15,035	4,110	1,295	11,430	13,840	47,759
1879	91	19,873	13,155	4,768	13,278	3,913	1,216	10,350	17,181	48,919
1880	92	23,193	12,349	5,160	13,203	3,977	1,216	9,850	19,871	51,812
1881	93	25,162	12,276	5,350	13,004	3,854	1,401	8,708	24,206	51,169
1882	94	27,585	10,930	5,753	13,324	3,208	1,501	8,117	24,943	55,372
1883	98	28,745	11,020	5,085	14,029	3,717	1,519	8,595	23,512	54,909
1884	95	25,760	9,006	5,402	13,829	3,727	1,502	7,616	19,255	48,771
1885	90	23,358	8,012	5,362	12,190	3,032	1,479	6,734	19,845	49,192
1886	92	25,060	8,043	5,912	12,945	3,412	1,322	5,078	23,305	49,705
1887	93	28,030	6,789	6,105	11,805	3,532	1,505	4,218	25,254	50,084
1888	94	27,938	6,446	5,624	11,965	3,501	1,631	4,084	24,503	49,101

SUMMARY, BY STATES, OF THE NUMBER OF NATIONAL BANKS, THE IMPORTANT ITEMS OF RESOURCES AND LIABILITIES, AND THE TOTALS, ETC.—Continued.

ILLINOIS.

Date.	No. of banks.	Loans and discounts.	U. S. bonds.	Cash and cash items.	Capital.	Surplus.	Undivided profits.	Outstanding circulation.	Individual deposits.	Total.
		Thousands.	*Thousands.*	*Thousands.*	*Thousands.*	*Thousands.*	*Thousands.*	*Thousands.*	*Thousands.*	*Thousands.*
1863	3	$186	$109	$101	$275	....	$5	....	$313	$655
1864	36	4,527	4,473	3,270	3,916	$18	358	$2,140	5,559	14,510
1865	76	12,228	12,624	9,218	10,715	310	832	7,495	15,783	39,812
1866	82	17,202	13,035	8,530	11,570	865	1,023	9,383	16,446	44,112
1867	82	18,320	13,071	9,563	11,620	1,600	1,110	9,482	18,063	47,167
1868	83	23,313	12,061	10,683	12,070	2,804	1,071	9,597	22,884	54,411
1869	83	32,924	12,329	8,238	12,470	3,450	1,220	9,819	18,023	51,973
1870	81	27,821	12,661	8,779	12,770	3,928	1,365	10,132	21,608	56,482
1871	110	36,223	10,959	12,487	17,317	4,430	1,588	13,644	28,720	77,250
1872	132	43,069	18,833	11,581	19,558	4,365	1,818	15,600	32,595	84,175
1873	134	44,708	18,427	11,412	20,267	5,507	1,880	15,202	32,504	87,900
1874	143	45,554	18,131	14,796	20,564	6,342	1,796	14,704	38,051	95,579
1875	146	49,537	14,602	12,500	19,466	7,098	1,930	11,414	38,287	90,830
1876	146	45,308	12,206	10,878	18,546	6,044	1,707	9,384	32,486	83,041
1877	144	40,999	11,878	12,725	18,046	6,398	1,659	9,038	32,835	78,160
1878	139	34,808	13,315	12,484	15,730	5,870	1,438	8,003	31,545	73,296
1879	136	38,403	13,810	12,788	14,835	5,539	1,738	8,314	35,850	80,918
1880	136	45,662	13,484	18,010	14,965	5,823	1,874	8,567	49,392	102,025
1881	139	62,061	15,360	28,439	15,200	6,360	2,032	8,165	72,972	133,384
1882	148	73,118	14,723	20,022	18,990	5,846	2,650	8,709	69,763	129,583
1883	162	75,257	13,109	23,408	23,004	6,604	2,086	8,592	67,821	133,878
1884	167	71,680	11,700	24,103	24,100	7,300	3,491	7,757	62,620	127,772
1885	165	76,906	10,913	26,991	25,424	6,887	2,481	6,877	68,664	140,710
1886	168	88,126	9,263	24,719	27,887	7,633	2,975	6,038	73,175	149,169
1887	178	97,204	8,252	31,508	29,391	8,521	3,836	5,036	81,809	166,888
1888	182	104,530	9,124	34,338	30,074	9,937	3,077	4,730	90,170	180,202

MICHIGAN.

Date.	No. of banks.	Loans and discounts.	U. S. bonds.	Cash and cash items.	Capital.	Surplus.	Undivided profits.	Outstanding circulation.	Individual deposits.	Total.
1863	1	32	43	30	75	....	1	....	52	128
1864	14	1,002	1,161	1,286	1,217	17	117	700	2,215	4,708
1865	35	3,681	3,786	2,340	4,148	160	241	1,600	4,307	11,605
1866	42	6,361	5,152	2,605	4,985	384	350	3,705	6,849	17,068
1867	42	6,988	5,085	2,209	5,070	684	392	3,811	6,388	17,131
1868	42	8,221	4,979	2,425	5,210	1,066	424	3,809	7,653	19,131
1869	41	9,518	4,794	1,929	5,585	1,201	427	3,804	6,030	18,973
1870	41	9,655	4,940	1,877	5,585	1,520	502	3,897	6,283	19,019
1871	60	12,700	6,207	2,449	7,264	1,029	733	5,146	9,555	26,151
1872	71	16,350	7,573	2,730	8,695	2,030	814	6,293	11,152	30,801
1873	77	18,890	8,227	2,946	9,762	2,327	980	6,940	11,876	34,200
1874	79	17,905	8,207	3,067	10,202	2,556	1,117	7,049	11,450	34,112
1875	81	19,101	7,844	2,714	10,447	2,815	1,282	6,615	11,381	34,565
1876	79	17,728	6,969	2,631	9,972	3,005	1,146	5,556	11,128	32,517
1877	80	17,202	6,881	2,967	9,857	2,065	1,227	5,606	10,473	31,911
1878	79	15,996	7,137	3,380	9,628	2,710	1,086	5,380	11,660	32,394
1879	79	16,902	8,023	3,519	9,337	2,586	1,164	6,101	14,265	35,657
1880	79	19,938	7,887	3,929	9,335	2,501	1,358	6,108	18,295	39,563
1881	80	24,530	7,158	4,841	9,435	2,787	1,651	5,615	23,127	44,871
1882	85	29,825	7,504	5,096	10,855	2,507	1,810	5,703	26,230	50,620
1883	88	32,078	6,287	4,808	11,063	2,150	1,678	4,973	26,804	50,804
1884	98	29,716	5,721	4,503	12,445	2,420	1,502	4,474	23,043	47,571
1885	102	29,970	5,461	5,302	13,095	2,194	1,319	3,851	25,880	51,051
1886	108	36,249	4,920	5,772	13,905	2,453	1,641	3,750	28,806	55,177
1887	108	42,482	4,008	5,791	14,558	2,044	1,848	3,002	33,000	61,309
1888	109	42,625	3,962	5,635	14,975	2,927	1,953	2,820	33,623	63,463

SUMMARY, BY STATES, OF THE NUMBER OF NATIONAL BANKS, THE IMPORTANT ITEMS OF RESOURCES AND LIABILITIES, AND THE TOTALS, ETC.—Continued.

WISCONSIN.

Date.	No. of banks.	Loans and discounts.	U. S. bonds.	Cash and cash items.	Capital.	Surplus.	Undivided profits.	Outstanding circulation.	Individual deposits.	Total.
		Thousands.	*Thousands.*	*Thousands.*	*Thousands.*	*Thousands.*	*Thousands.*	*Thousands.*	*Thousands.*	*Thousands.*
1863	1	$102	$67	$146	$200	....	$1	....	$262	$463
1864	14	1,105	1,314	1,123	961	$19	61	$642	1,931	4,164
1865	34	3,108	3,137	2,305	2,707	64	175	1,931	4,446	10,166
1866	37	3,785	3,721	1,988	2,935	228	245	2,502	4,661	11,375
1867	37	3,953	3,706	2,067	2,935	403	282	2,553	4,532	11,533
1868	36	4,637	3,550	1,975	2,860	550	271	2,442	4,778	11,778
1869	34	4,712	3,275	1,203	2,710	504	338	2,321	3,808	10,656
1870	32	4,562	3,123	1,229	2,535	617	304	2,225	3,865	10,480
1871	41	6,160	3,823	1,621	3,300	686	315	2,852	5,300	13,902
1872	42	7,323	3,774	1,518	3,300	749	309	2,863	6,395	15,212
1873	45	8,232	3,879	1,931	3,565	944	321	3,007	7,265	17,100
1874	47	8,074	4,028	1,854	3,765	1,034	337	3,052	7,072	16,705
1875	42	8,061	2,988	1,761	3,500	1,080	361	2,216	7,046	15,683
1876	40	7,408	2,939	1,539	3,400	1,012	347	2,073	6,120	14,133
1877	41	7,634	2,978	2,006	3,450	989	365	2,138	6,775	15,078
1878	38	7,286	2,987	1,660	3,265	955	360	1,959	6,207	14,162
1879	36	7,355	3,216	1,754	3,100	910	405	2,182	7,172	15,342
1880	36	8,910	3,118	2,023	3,050	908	507	2,183	9,759	18,475
1881	34	10,822	3,432	2,395	3,025	931	668	2,331	12,335	21,208
1882	41	13,184	3,400	2,491	3,585	926	705	2,380	13,724	23,556
1883	45	13,842	3,167	2,641	4,035	1,021	637	2,183	14,409	24,402
1884	50	13,308	3,185	2,813	4,400	1,205	532	2,221	12,814	23,123
1885	50	13,619	3,033	3,216	4,435	1,262	550	1,965	15,273	25,582
1886	50	15,938	2,857	3,078	4,635	1,366	643	1,863	16,608	27,165
1887	56	17,777	2,419	3,121	5,002	1,514	660	1,496	17,263	28,852
1888	59	19,165	2,424	3,097	5,530	1,689	790	1,512	17,874	30,096

IOWA.

Date.	No. of banks.	Loans and discounts.	U. S. bonds.	Cash and cash items.	Capital.	Surplus.	Undivided profits.	Outstanding circulation.	Individual deposits.	Total.
1863	3	92	131	100	97	....	4	....	245	390
1864	20	936	1,267	1,097	1,145	4	62	555	1,693	4,004
1865	36	2,884	3,870	2,800	3,106	37	230	1,804	5,110	11,128
1866	45	4,040	4,613	2,225	3,722	176	378	3,160	4,890	13,079
1867	45	5,249	4,442	2,015	3,842	351	396	3,205	5,234	13,523
1868	44	6,107	4,350	2,040	3,602	554	419	3,153	6,444	14,800
1869	43	6,470	4,120	1,680	3,742	813	417	3,085	5,252	13,891
1870	43	6,670	4,123	1,530	3,802	809	450	3,214	5,248	14,306
1871	57	8,063	5,154	1,917	4,780	937	481	4,143	7,014	18,097
1872	70	10,203	5,961	2,058	5,632	1,041	599	4,802	7,853	20,926
1873	75	10,787	6,180	1,972	5,812	1,252	613	4,986	9,880	22,902
1874	75	11,309	6,357	2,343	6,017	1,337	710	5,220	9,232	23,206
1875	81	12,770	5,406	2,618	6,352	1,478	830	4,420	10,851	24,032
1876	78	11,647	4,746	2,016	6,287	1,569	730	3,881	8,004	21,198
1877	78	10,614	4,847	2,200	6,057	1,508	724	3,882	7,842	20,808
1878	70	9,635	4,808	2,110	5,057	1,414	574	3,906	7,120	19,619
1879	73	9,604	5,068	2,476	5,707	1,380	544	4,036	8,752	21,125
1880	75	11,373	5,265	2,897	5,867	1,419	633	4,234	11,608	24,812
1881	76	13,725	5,824	3,374	5,950	1,542	748	4,414	15,770	29,997
1882	88	17,709	5,814	3,506	7,135	1,642	858	4,683	16,160	32,305
1883	110	20,124	5,600	3,318	9,055	1,950	1,000	4,596	16,648	35,265
1884	123	21,238	5,060	3,313	10,146	2,194	1,067	4,164	16,124	35,609
1885	125	21,824	4,634	3,474	10,155	2,291	1,145	3,814	17,054	36,845
1886	128	22,518	4,283	3,487	10,295	2,433	1,186	3,422	17,814	37,962
1887	128	24,155	3,211	3,560	10,150	2,573	1,186	2,714	19,283	38,810
1888	129	26,322	3,283	3,885	10,148	2,708	1,258	2,753	21,278	41,841

SUMMARY, BY STATES, OF THE NUMBER OF NATIONAL BANKS, THE IMPORTANT ITEMS OF RESOURCES AND LIABILITIES, AND THE TOTALS, ETC.—Continued.

MINNESOTA.

Date.	No. of banks.	Loans and discounts.	U. S. bonds.	Cash and cash items.	Capital.	Surplus.	Undivided profits.	Outstanding circulation.	Individual deposits.	Total.
		Thousands.	*Thousands.*	*Thousands.*	*Thousands.*	*Thousands.*	*Thousands.*	*Thousands.*	*Thousands.*	*Thousands.*
1863	0	....	....	....	....	....	....	....	....	....
1864	1	$390	$781	$414	$500	....	$23	$197	$808	$1,904
1865	11	1,107	2,158	680	1,345	$24	74	1,028	1,894	4,582
1866	15	2,124	1,941	680	1,600	49	141	1,475	1,746	5,391
1867	15	2,080	1,873	788	1,660	147	205	1,431	1,811	5,466
1868	15	2,502	1,809	725	1,650	183	203	1,420	2,258	6,039
1869	17	2,981	2,041	601	1,780	286	202	1,495	2,157	6,441
1870	17	3,219	2,119	820	1,780	331	201	1,516	2,985	7,296
1871	23	4,568	2,790	912	2,308	357	272	2,030	4,360	10,191
1872	29	5,980	3,297	1,049	3,100	407	338	2,508	4,986	12,276
1873	32	7,558	3,933	1,465	4,150	604	302	3,032	6,812	15,943
1874	32	8,349	4,343	1,323	4,350	740	341	3,359	6,297	16,031
1875	33	8,600	3,645	1,278	4,420	831	387	2,752	5,908	15,719
1876	33	8,756	3,114	1,204	4,430	805	401	2,286	5,962	15,106
1877	31	8,932	3,062	1,255	4,430	818	404	2,299	6,130	15,278
1878	31	9,083	3,004	1,112	4,770	770	417	2,345	6,191	15,766
1879	30	10,005	3,837	1,430	4,060	786	387	2,494	7,104	16,730
1880	30	12,201	2,755	1,631	5,150	937	452	2,061	8,918	18,700
1881	27	15,038	2,025	2,255	4,900	982	588	1,845	12,650	24,000
1882	33	17,008	2,707	2,303	5,920	1,172	731	1,987	14,046	26,560
1883	43	24,085	2,918	2,948	9,152	1,429	891	2,127	17,030	34,127
1884	50	25,320	2,737	2,977	11,358	1,718	1,046	1,996	15,971	36,230
1885	49	28,172	2,618	3,837	11,390	1,852	1,201	1,885	19,651	40,980
1886	53	31,911	2,559	4,235	12,290	2,192	1,327	1,798	22,089	45,801
1887	58	38,057	2,632	4,835	13,740	2,380	1,756	1,676	27,038	54,395
1888	56	36,750	2,735	4,794	13,965	2,536	1,697	1,585	26,702	54,110

MISSOURI.

Date.	No. of banks.	Loans and discounts.	U. S. bonds.	Cash and cash items.	Capital.	Surplus.	Undivided profits.	Outstanding circulation.	Individual deposits.	Total.
1863	1	47	105	87	100	....	1	....	75	241
1864	7	1,968	2,250	1,209	1,631	194	161	585	2,533	6,118
1865	11	4,046	4,047	3,934	3,574	586	216	1,028	5,022	14,144
1866	15	6,441	4,212	3,053	4,070	710	279	2,409	5,798	15,620
1867	17	9,463	5,343	3,250	7,559	667	550	3,373	6,444	21,739
1868	18	11,722	5,557	3,410	7,810	735	646	4,082	8,250	23,729
1869	18	10,817	5,356	2,753	7,810	835	719	4,130	5,919	22,603
1870	18	11,242	5,233	3,001	7,700	900	523	4,157	5,826	23,031
1871	20	12,460	6,601	3,020	8,885	1,020	605	5,470	6,720	27,135
1872	30	15,038	7,083	2,534	9,425	1,271	806	6,012	6,338	29,339
1873	37	16,151	7,254	2,685	9,545	1,434	925	6,131	8,158	31,633
1874	35	14,006	4,894	2,655	9,193	1,425	831	4,010	7,350	26,984
1875	35	14,353	3,637	2,981	9,095	1,414	770	2,957	8,746	27,086
1876	32	14,688	2,914	2,779	7,985	1,410	739	2,343	8,827	25,900
1877	30	10,830	2,516	2,741	5,285	1,049	603	1,914	6,846	19,947
1878	22	8,032	2,332	2,282	4,125	902	541	1,482	5,728	16,393
1879	20	8,961	2,476	2,487	3,850	942	517	1,077	5,853	17,039
1880	21	10,839	2,401	3,918	4,050	1,079	488	1,735	8,391	22,620
1881	22	13,913	3,555	4,200	4,653	921	567	2,318	10,255	26,408
1882	23	12,801	2,589	3,768	4,960	1,007	832	1,863	9,008	23,988
1883	34	16,808	3,000	3,964	5,850	1,210	590	2,118	11,623	29,437
1884	40	15,915	2,548	3,036	6,315	1,449	716	1,889	10,708	27,014
1885	42	16,472	2,927	3,854	6,561	1,480	759	2,018	11,607	28,706
1886	44	22,245	3,136	5,710	8,841	1,735	812	2,091	10,003	38,351
1887	50	31,899	3,009	8,629	11,757	2,167	1,043	1,767	23,462	53,677
1888	50	29,970	3,581	8,537	12,531	1,952	1,070	1,520	21,927	53,789

SUMMARY, BY STATES, OF THE NUMBER OF NATIONAL BANKS, THE IMPORTANT ITEMS OF RESOURCES AND LIABILITIES, AND THE TOTALS, ETC.—Continued.

KANSAS.

Date.	No. of banks.	Loans and discounts.	U. S. bonds.	Cash and cash items.	Capital.	Surplus.	Undivided profits.	Outstanding circulation.	Individual deposits.	Total.
		Thousands.	*Thousands.*	*Thousands.*	*Thousands.*	*Thousands.*	*Thousands.*	*Thousands.*	*Thousands.*	*Thousands.*
1863	0	....	....	....	....	....	....	....	....	....
1864	1	$113	$85	$63	$100	....	$11	$30	$96	$279
1865	2	203	527	209	200	$4	20	76	2,479	2,910
1866	4	325	559	314	330	39	21	262	442	1,470
1867	5	400	709	208	400	89	35	311	533	1,948
1868	5	447	835	243	400	60	29	338	790	2,149
1869	5	476	812	270	400	63	46	338	667	2,102
1870	5	691	737	342	410	83	50	366	748	2,257
1871	11	1,279	1,095	384	802	114	71	606	1,288	3,632
1872	24	2,335	1,960	654	1,620	153	147	1,341	2,458	6,546
1873	26	2,806	2,223	584	1,965	261	170	1,490	2,589	7,304
1874	24	2,338	1,907	582	1,730	285	112	1,351	2,215	6,304
1875	19	2,147	1,585	438	1,420	283	110	1,036	2,039	5,412
1876	17	1,984	1,390	376	1,260	255	126	909	1,994	5,048
1877	15	2,071	1,230	409	1,065	253	106	792	2,111	4,728
1878	11	1,332	1,035	443	800	179	61	564	1,579	3,654
1879	12	1,562	1,244	557	838	185	80	673	2,138	4,439
1880	12	1,794	1,147	763	875	193	101	683	2,548	4,990
1881	13	2,509	1,170	787	925	245	142	679	3,239	5,872
1882	20	3,480	1,307	986	1,335	281	196	793	4,211	7,405
1883	36	5,995	1,509	1,717	2,250	365	296	1,031	6,904	11,865
1884	59	8,508	1,842	2,233	3,845	431	462	1,297	8,362	15,491
1885	74	10,731	2,055	2,301	4,906	609	573	1,436	10,090	18,818
1886	98	14,662	2,501	2,890	6,732	1,087	705	1,687	12,591	24,303
1887	139	21,307	3,285	3,863	10,531	1,435	970	2,295	17,741	34,948
1888	160	23,020	3,897	3,592	12,855	1,842	1,050	2,819	17,465	38,277

NEBRASKA.

Date.	No. of banks.	Loans and discounts.	U. S. bonds.	Cash and cash items.	Capital.	Surplus.	Undivided profits.	Outstanding circulation.	Individual deposits.	Total.
1863	0	....	....	....	....	....	....	....	....	....
1864	1	11	30	9	35	....	1	12	17	74
1865	2	138	144	92	115	....	31	27	837	525
1866	3	201	327	226	200	5	58	148	645	1,242
1867	3	509	743	449	283	6	117	166	1,207	2,327
1868	4	703	697	504	400	16	137	169	1,415	3,216
1869	4	1,012	904	292	500	54	95	168	1,342	2,743
1870	4	1,122	717	250	500	61	87	167	1,192	2,900
1871	6	1,140	1,044	280	650	68	121	532	1,613	3,502
1872	9	1,724	1,250	425	850	114	88	756	2,142	4,487
1873	10	2,019	1,281	433	905	160	108	709	2,378	5,018
1874	10	2,196	1,400	612	1,025	129	96	865	2,518	5,321
1875	10	2,207	1,251	480	1,000	159	110	847	2,570	5,415
1876	9	2,263	1,184	451	950	172	74	795	2,660	5,270
1877	10	2,454	1,189	479	950	174	160	686	2,509	5,281
1878	10	2,483	1,188	665	950	223	155	704	2,719	5,616
1879	10	2,897	1,320	670	925	210	132	727	2,968	6,345
1880	10	3,193	1,112	809	850	230	164	681	3,724	6,940
1881	12	4,272	1,465	1,150	910	294	190	665	5,242	9,128
1882	23	6,775	1,843	1,300	1,715	323	374	1,099	6,113	12,140
1883	40	9,732	2,182	1,598	2,800	455	557	1,547	9,419	17,921
1884	63	12,508	2,406	2,006	4,735	637	677	1,705	9,996	21,057
1885	75	15,433	2,465	2,377	5,949	945	568	1,774	11,317	25,458
1886	88	18,967	2,402	2,914	7,184	1,197	631	1,603	14,214	29,675
1887	103	22,942	2,404	3,823	8,400	1,484	675	1,660	17,858	35,778
1888	104	24,563	2,721	4,456	9,285	1,506	744	1,676	19,120	39,750

SUMMARY, BY STATES, OF THE NUMBER OF NATIONAL BANKS, THE IMPORTANT ITEMS OF RESOURCES AND LIABILITIES, AND THE TOTALS, ETC.—Continued.

COLORADO.

Date.	No. of banks.	Loans and discounts.	U. S. bonds.	Cash and cash items.	Capital.	Surplus.	Undivided profits.	Outstanding circulation.	Individual deposits.	Total.
		Thousands.	*Thousands.*	*Thousands.*	*Thousands.*	*Thousands.*	*Thousands.*	*Thousands.*	*Thousands.*	*Thousands.*
1863	0	....	....	....	....	....	....	....	....	....
1864	0	....	....	....	....	....	....	....	....	....
1865	1	$179	$70	$31	$200	....	$20	$45	$102	$427
1866	3	417	188	173	350	$20	58	60	530	1,100
1867	3	445	498	240	350	58	117	254	663	1,647
1868	3	424	503	204	350	58	140	254	781	1,757
1869	3	552	453	263	350	78	77	254	773	1,708
1870	3	532	578	306	350	73	63	254	1,553	2,483
1871	4	873	676	319	400	73	76	300	1,458	2,561
1872	6	1,501	730	461	575	83	146	476	2,019	3,513
1873	6	1,793	765	526	575	166	208	475	2,376	4,110
1874	9	1,991	760	675	725	243	172	501	2,330	4,348
1875	9	2,362	783	717	875	284	206	601	2,513	4,826
1876	10	2,403	644	566	825	274	121	484	2,473	4,438
1877	13	2,411	709	609	1,010	158	121	545	2,933	5,208
1878	13	2,763	847	744	1,010	166	89	635	3,635	6,036
1879	14	3,805	1,416	1,203	1,070	207	141	727	6,170	9,406
1880	14	5,060	1,318	1,394	1,070	200	267	837	8,288	11,927
1881	17	6,511	1,382	1,810	1,277	468	325	985	10,252	14,675
1882	19	6,888	1,501	1,967	1,440	564	440	1,028	10,338	15,546
1883	22	7,671	1,720	2,138	1,640	776	868	1,094	10,838	16,704
1884	23	6,685	1,408	2,138	1,807	916	573	985	9,106	14,883
1885	25	7,609	1,433	2,255	2,025	1,003	454	927	10,282	17,061
1886	27	9,934	1,821	2,482	2,405	865	556	914	12,997	20,093
1887	31	12,402	1,905	3,133	2,752	929	812	880	15,820	24,713
1888	34	14,073	2,173	3,302	3,458	1,159	770	950	17,539	27,767

NEVADA.

Date.	No. of banks.	Loans and discounts.	U. S. bonds.	Cash and cash items.	Capital.	Surplus.	Undivided profits.	Outstanding circulation.	Individual deposits.	Total.
1863	0	....	....	....	....	....	....	....	....	....
1864	0	....	....	....	....	....	....	....	....	....
1865	0	....	....	....	....	....	....	....	....	....
1866	1	114	155	80	155	2	7	120	65	370
1867	1	166	155	66	155	4	22	132	100	428
1868	1	177	153	70	155	6	28	131	123	442
1869	0	....	....	....	....	....	....	....	....	....
1870	0	....	....	....	....	....	....	....	....	....
1871	0	....	....	....	....	....	....	....	....	....
1872	0	....	....	....	....	....	....	....	....	....
1873	0	....	....	....	....	....	....	....	....	....
1874	0	....	....	....	....	....	....	....	....	....
1875	0	....	....	....	....	....	....	....	....	....
1876	0	....	....	....	....	....	....	....	....	....
1877	0	....	....	....	....	....	....	....	....	....
1878	0	....	....	....	....	....	....	....	....	....
1879	0	....	....	....	....	....	....	....	....	....
1880	1	112	40	23	50	....	4	36	65	186
1881	1	181	40	47	75	9	6	36	114	280
1882	1	205	40	42	75	14	6	34	163	319
1883	1	217	40	31	75	20	6	35	167	321
1884	1	245	40	48	75	25	10	35	189	367
1885	1	248	45	56	75	25	11	35	215	383
1886	1	260	25	66	100	30	10	22	220	433
1887	2	514	38	60	150	40	12	34	351	700
1888	2	597	71	73	282	98	10	63	271	857

SUMMARY, BY STATES, OF THE NUMBER OF NATIONAL BANKS, THE IMPORTANT ITEMS OF RESOURCES AND LIABILITIES, AND THE TOTALS, ETC.—Continued.

CALIFORNIA.

Date.	No. of banks.	Loans and discounts.	U. S. bonds.	Cash and cash items.	Capital.	Surplus.	Undivided profits.	Outstanding circulation.	Individual deposits.	Total.
		Thousands.	*Thousands.*	*Thousands.*	*Thousands.*	*Thousands.*	*Thousands.*	*Thousands.*	*Thousands.*	*Thousands.*
1863	0	....	....	....	....	....	....	....	....	....
1864	0	....	....	....	....	....	....	....	....	....
1865	0	....	....	....	....	....	....	....	....	....
1866	0	....	....	....	....	....	....	....	....	....
1867	0	....	....	....	....	....	....	....	....	....
1868	0	....	....	....	....	....	....	....	....	....
1869	0	....	....	....	....	....	....	....	....	....
1870	0	....	....	....	....	....	....	....	....	....
1871	1	$852	$500	$118	$1,000	....	$41	$277	$100	$1,517
1872	3	4,903	1,757	833	2,800	$241	123	1,366	3,144	8,068
1873	5	4,443	2,542	1,460	3,200	150	141	1,088	3,103	9,591
1874	6	6,708	2,641	1,924	3,550	244	160	2,108	5,406	12,293
1875	9	5,655	2,800	1,343	4,680	391	240	2,172	3,654	11,648
1876	9	5,402	1,791	1,142	4,700	347	167	1,414	2,499	9,403
1877	9	5,254	1,818	1,282	4,300	225	201	1,300	2,085	9,452
1878	9	5,390	1,875	1,035	4,300	285	172	1,437	3,403	10,070
1879	8	4,568	1,836	1,380	3,550	317	122	1,451	2,870	8,721
1880	10	5,058	1,964	1,521	3,150	347	178	1,502	3,873	9,081
1881	11	6,476	1,970	2,312	3,300	444	314	1,334	6,105	12,794
1882	11	7,690	2,140	2,015	3,300	510	382	1,204	7,434	13,992
1883	15	8,175	2,105	2,245	3,550	504	402	1,477	8,124	14,782
1884	15	7,519	1,503	2,006	3,550	686	420	1,347	6,531	12,840
1885	17	8,108	1,583	1,740	3,815	783	438	1,305	6,710	13,039
1886	21	12,101	1,780	3,044	5,385	908	563	1,393	11,215	20,465
1887	33	19,300	2,200	5,604	6,870	1,027	864	1,600	22,136	34,600
1888	38	16,870	2,557	4,534	8,175	1,454	1,074	1,679	18,074	32,791

OREGON.

Date.	No. of banks.	Loans and discounts.	U. S. bonds.	Cash and cash items.	Capital.	Surplus.	Undivided profits.	Outstanding circulation.	Individual deposits.	Total.
1863	0	....	....	....	....	....	....	....	....	....
1864	0	....	....	....	....	....	....	....	....	....
1865	0	....	....	....	....	....	....	....	....	....
1866	1	39	101	20	100	....	7	88	23	218
1867	1	67	102	108	100	....	7	83	51	375
1868	1	54	159	100	100	....	28	88	36	390
1869	1	137	210	185	100	5	11	88	115	588
1870	1	323	315	184	200	5	47	06	266	1,006
1871	1	600	475	160	250	6	95	223	495	1,636
1872	1	725	331	183	250	9	157	221	565	1,621
1873	1	732	353	121	250	50	177	223	447	1,538
1874	1	710	458	164	250	50	220	221	556	1,581
1875	1	755	465	171	250	50	259	200	562	1,659
1876	1	788	468	141	250	50	302	223	627	1,723
1877	1	896	503	285	250	50	240	221	845	1,906
1878	1	883	540	128	250	50	284	202	708	1,935
1879	1	767	751	108	250	50	287	213	711	1,891
1880	1	954	759	210	250	50	341	223	981	2,204
1881	1	1,022	903	381	250	50	321	223	1,583	3,004
1882	2	1,724	921	481	300	52	303	257	2,104	4,044
1883	6	2,599	901	610	505	60	441	324	2,290	4,708
1884	8	2,181	957	524	605	68	562	359	2,074	4,450
1885	9	2,202	961	505	710	82	619	347	2,550	5,032
1886	18	3,504	1,232	783	1,320	92	740	525	3,092	7,580
1887	23	5,780	1,245	1,108	1,705	153	659	566	5,325	10,036
1888	27	6,810	1,120	1,174	2,300	288	600	448	6,018	11,565

SUMMARY, BY STATES, OF THE NUMBER OF NATIONAL BANKS, THE IMPORTANT ITEMS OF RESOURCES AND LIABILITIES, AND THE TOTALS, ETC.—Continued.

ARIZONA.

Date.	No. of banks.	Loans and discounts.	U. S. bonds.	Cash and cash items.	Capital.	Surplus.	Undivided profits.	Outstanding circulation.	Individual deposits.	Total.
		Thousands.	*Thousands.*	*Thousands.*	*Thousands.*	*Thousands.*	*Thousands.*	*Thousands.*	*Thousands.*	*Thousands.*
1863	0									
1864	0									
1865	0									
1866	0									
1867	0									
1868	0									
1869	0									
1870	0									
1871	0									
1872	0									
1873	0									
1874	0									
1875	0									
1876	0									
1877	0									
1878	0									
1879	0									
1880	0									
1881	0									
1882	1	$114	$109	$97	$100		$10	$19	$211	$380
1883	1	57	100	71	100	$1	15	81	107	214
1884	2	135	47	71	150	3	7	40	143	351
1885	0									
1886	0									
1887	1	174	25	35	100		6	22	133	335
1888	1	154	25	27	100	9	11	22	115	277

DAKOTA.

Date.	No. of banks.	Loans and discounts.	U. S. bonds.	Cash and cash items.	Capital.	Surplus.	Undivided profits.	Outstanding circulation.	Individual deposits.	Total.
1863	0									
1864	0									
1865	0									
1866	0									
1867	0									
1868	0									
1869	0									
1870	0									
1871	0									
1872	0									
1873	1	37	80	20	50	1	2	45	41	184
1874	1	43	80	10	50	2	3	45	22	151
1875	1	64	80	12	50	9	4	44	65	202
1876	1	71	100	17	50	10	4	43	128	280
1877	1	98	100	20	50	10	7	45	132	294
1878	3	233	173	132	175	10	18	98	578	931
1879	4	354	210	146	205	21	40	117	782	1,190
1880	6	882	207	316	425	56	74	219	1,191	2,071
1881	8	1,174	393	356	575	83	160	304	1,741	2,435
1882	17	2,517	681	637	1,005	139	240	585	2,945	5,111
1883	30	3,649	900	856	1,767	358	330	602	4,060	7,752
1884	36	3,536	578	665	2,258	443	297	628	3,048	7,117
1885	41	4,000	912	923	2,402	501	279	647	3,720	8,676
1886	52	5,210	1,122	979	3,016	521	311	770	4,586	9,907
1887	62	6,834	1,238	1,211	3,720	664	383	862	5,849	12,472
1888	58	7,415	1,263	1,195	3,625	793	373	839	6,128	13,090

SUMMARY, BY STATES, OF THE NUMBER OF NATIONAL BANKS, THE IMPORTANT ITEMS OF RESOURCES AND LIABILITIES, AND THE TOTALS, ETC.—Continued.

IDAHO.

Date.	No. of banks.	Loans and discounts.	U. S. bonds.	Cash and cash items.	Capital.	Surplus.	Undivided profits.	Outstanding circulation.	Individual deposits.	Total.
		Thousands.	*Thousands.*	*Thousands.*	*Thousands.*	*Thousands.*	*Thousands.*	*Thousands.*	*Thousands.*	*Thousands.*
1863	0									
1864	0									
1865	0									
1866	0									
1867	1	$72	$52	$26	$100		$8	$29	$27	$184
1868	1	66	75	22	100	$11	8	64	19	201
1869	1	84	75	39	100	5		63	67	253
1870	1	69	75	32	100	7	2	63	69	258
1871	1	106	100	37	100	10	1	89	124	338
1872	1	87	100	33	100	12	10	89	95	325
1873	1	81	100	30	100	15	9	88	79	309
1874	1	95	100	49	100	19	10	89	157	377
1875	1	124	100	41	100	28	9	86	152	384
1876	1	70	100	40	100	20	9	87	131	363
1877	1	90	100	41	100	21	3	85	127	346
1878	1	103	100	24	100	20	11	84	136	359
1879	1	120	100	34	100	20	5	86	131	355
1880	1	108	100	56	100	20	7	81	128	349
1881	1	101	200	75	100	20	10	83	320	534
1882	1	132	100	81	100	20	9	81	274	485
1883	3	241	125	84	200	20	22	99	392	757
1884	4	302	118	114	250	20	42	58	438	824
1885	4	351	68	138	250	20	63	60	417	854
1886	6	486	105	156	350	21	83	93	466	1,016
1887	6	578	143	149	350	29	89	82	577	1,234
1888	7	676	183	243	430	85	57	99	845	1,613

MONTANA.

Date.	No. of banks.	Loans and discounts.	U. S. bonds.	Cash and cash items.	Capital.	Surplus.	Undivided profits.	Outstanding circulation.	Individual deposits.	Total.
1863	0									
1864	0									
1865	0									
1866	0									
1867	1	75	60	36	100		20	36	49	218
1868	1	93	60	59	100	10	8	30	67	255
1869	1	127	60	57	100	10	20	36	76	359
1870	1	133	60	99	100	10	2	36	118	342
1871	1	219	120	110	100	10	16	71	201	522
1872	4	458	276	351	300	10	54	146	446	1,354
1873	5	612	315	335	350	47	101	217	630	1,509
1874	5	728	436	341	350	70	63	256	786	1,713
1875	5	791	406	290	350	76	79	229	880	1,784
1876	5	751	386	273	350	77	67	211	770	1,653
1877	5	811	387	284	350	87	70	203	832	1,730
1878	3	868	280	181	200	75	108	110	747	1,528
1879	2	633	230	191	150	80	101	88	684	1,184
1880	3	978	380	168	200	30	153	156	1,102	1,824
1881	3	1,301	380	186	200	40	229	158	1,240	2,229
1882	7	2,791	646	540	655	74	354	380	3,040	4,837
1883	10	4,730	713	639	1,210	170	429	309	4,550	7,398
1884	13	5,191	674	856	1,650	266	542	426	4,741	8,190
1885	15	5,515	639	1,053	1,810	298	741	378	5,380	9,288
1886	16	6,418	656	1,499	1,864	333	893	400	6,979	11,276
1887	17	8,287	691	1,554	1,975	420	1,091	423	8,120	13,139
1888	17	8,777	691	1,029	1,950	506	1,271	421	9,068	14,329

SUMMARY, BY STATES, OF THE NUMBER OF NATIONAL BANKS, THE IMPORTANT ITEMS OF RESOURCES AND LIABILITIES, AND THE TOTALS, ETC.—Continued.

NEW MEXICO.

Date.	No. of banks.	Loans and discounts.	U. S. bonds.	Cash and cash items.	Capital.	Surplus.	Undivided profits.	Outstanding circulation.	Individual deposits.	Total.
		Thousands.	*Thousands.*	*Thousands.*	*Thousands.*	*Thousands.*	*Thousands.*	*Thousands.*	*Thousands.*	*Thousands.*
1863	0	....	....	....	....	....	....	....	....	....
1864	0	....	....	....	....	....	....	....	....	....
1865	0	....	....	....	....	....	....	....	....	....
1866	0	....	....	....	....	....	....	....	....	....
1867	0	....	....	....	....	....	....	....	....	....
1868	0	....	....	....	....	....	....	....	....	....
1869	0	....	....	....	....	....	....	....	....	....
1870	0	....	....	....	....	....	....	....	....	....
1871	1	$88	$150	$30	$150	$1	$4	$135	$46	$337
1872	1	179	150	22	150	5	7	135	91	389
1873	2	321	300	59	300	13	15	270	160	703
1874	2	353	300	54	300	24	5	270	183	78[illegible]
1875	2	408	300	63	300	35	7	206	339	947
1876	2	379	300	56	300	40	25	209	224	859
1877	2	357	460	104	300	31	28	268	280	1,105
1878	2	331	400	91	300	38	35	206	281	1,068
1879	2	275	400	114	300	31	13	206	258	1,005
1880	4	542	560	127	400	55	33	351	591	1,627
1881	4	722	560	197	400	101	50	352	990	2,214
1882	6	1,044	620	235	500	138	70	407	1,182	2,803
1883	6	1,125	670	248	550	144	73	409	1,109	2,758
1884	8	1,143	678	291	630	163	69	410	1,128	2,729
1885	8	1,424	623	266	650	153	50	370	1,750	3,270
1886	9	1,504	510	346	825	164	53	253	1,539	3,271
1887	9	1,751	305	237	850	177	41	210	1,497	3,135
1888	9	1,791	403	252	900	186	49	226	1,755	3,409

UTAH.

Date.	No. of banks.	Loans and discounts.	U. S. bonds.	Cash and cash items.	Capital.	Surplus.	Undivided profits.	Outstanding circulation.	Individual deposits.	Total.
1863	0	....	....	....	....	....	....	....	....	....
1864	0	....	....	....	....	....	....	....	....	....
1865	0	....	....	....	....	....	....	....	....	....
1866	1	142	50	16	150	....	14	45	77	291
1867	1	174	150	17	150	4	10	135	50	384
1868	1	159	165	37	150	13	7	135	73	381
1869	0	....	....	....	....	....	....	....	....	....
1870	1	96	145	7	100	22	....	124	148	414
1871	1	256	150	57	100	25	....	133	303	582
1872	2	506	300	68	250	77	7	225	400	1,185
1873	3	734	525	176	450	51	51	404	509	1,783
1874	2	446	150	98	300	65	80	135	249	804
1875	2	407	100	144	300	100	36	90	301	843
1876	1	201	75	122	200	35	30	45	258	565
1877	1	208	50	200	200	40	30	39	360	672
1878	1	218	50	150	200	40	34	40	320	640
1879	1	285	251	170	200	50	27	78	573	1,004
1880	1	289	300	157	200	65	33	179	569	1,093
1881	1	359	450	209	200	100	54	153	944	1,527
1882	3	949	410	307	350	125	68	209	1,088	2,032
1883	4	1,010	510	261	450	170	78	308	1,480	2,650
1884	5	1,216	563	240	600	244	65	400	1,401	2,812
1885	6	1,365	538	307	800	275	67	325	1,627	3,209
1886	7	1,821	500	400	837	308	137	308	2,048	3,702
1887	7	2,110	691	462	850	373	115	202	2,335	4,262
1888	7	2,450	617	524	850	422	159	270	2,863	4,841

SUMMARY, BY STATES, OF THE NUMBER OF NATIONAL BANKS, THE IMPORTANT ITEMS OF RESOURCES AND LIABILITIES, AND THE TOTALS, ETC.—Continued.

WASHINGTON TERRITORY.

Date.	No. of banks.	Loans and discounts.	U. S. bonds.	Cash and cash items.	Capital.	Surplus.	Undivided profits.	Outstanding circulation.	Individual deposits.	Total.
		Thousands.	*Thousands.*	*Thousands.*	*Thousands.*	*Thousands.*	*Thousands.*	*Thousands.*	*Thousands.*	*Thousands.*
1863	0									
1864	0									
1865	0									
1866	0									
1867	0									
1868	0									
1869	0									
1870	0									
1871	0									
1872	0									
1873	0									
1874	0									
1875	0									
1876	0									
1877	0									
1878	1	$126	$100	$88	$150		$8	$45	$92	$353
1879	1	202	160	24	150	$3	22	90	160	434
1880	1	301	150	53	150	30	24	135	292	639
1881	2	510	130	50	200	30	89	117	456	892
1882	2	756	184	85	200	32	140	162	581	1,179
1883	12	1,851	328	329	700	44	230	253	1,623	3,069
1884	15	2,088	326	280	955	90	308	292	1,242	3,098
1885	15	2,035	380	347	1,005	140	375	323	1,450	3,410
1886	18	2,436	453	475	1,115	155	406	348	2,287	4,458
1887	18	3,832	406	608	1,280	233	476	357	3,038	6,254
1888	24	6,232	572	1,044	1,855	323	756	421	6,620	10,341

WYOMING.

Date.	No. of banks.	Loans and discounts.	U. S. bonds.	Cash and cash items.	Capital.	Surplus.	Undivided profits.	Outstanding circulation.	Individual deposits.	Total.
1863	0									
1864	0									
1865	0									
1866	0									
1867	0									
1868	0									
1869	0									
1870	0									
1871	1	77	30	15	75		3	27	55	161
1872	1	99	30	26	75		5	27	81	188
1873	2	203	60	34	125		23	51	162	363
1874	2	199	60	58	125	10	26	54	190	412
1875	2	246	60	62	125	10	49	40	297	539
1876	2	198	60	96	125	21	29	50	265	498
1877	2	303	60	89	125	25	62	52	311	580
1878	2	285	60	120	125	25	80	42	309	657
1879	2	385	60	79	125	50	58	53	444	753
1880	2	402	64	109	150	50	30	52	535	841
1881	3	730	94	201	225	50	48	83	850	1,806
1882	4	991	194	219	425	78	71	127	1,185	1,9[illegible]8
1883	4	1,313	219	242	425	108	95	123	1,604	2,436
1884	4	1,604	235	200	525	78	107	138	1,418	2,509
1885	5	1,861	155	300	800	140	152	140	1,744	3,067
1886	6	2,335	180	401	900	167	193	160	1,708	3,398
1887	8	2,527	224	305	1,075	210	180	201	1,697	3,568
1888	9	2,419	249	298	1,175	213	115	221	1,731	3,654

INDEX.

Page.

TABLES CONTAINED IN THE APPENDIX.

www.ingramcontent.com/pod-product-compliance
Lightning Source LLC
Chambersburg PA
CBHW031129120726
47905CB00006B/1619
9783741190452